AESTHETICS TODAY

AESTHETICS TODAY

Readings selected, edited, and introduced by

MORRIS PHILIPSON

Meridian Books
THE WORLD PUBLISHING COMPANY
Cleveland and New York

MORRIS PHILIPSON

Morris Philipson was born in New Haven, Connecticut, in 1926. After spending a year at the Université de Paris, he did his undergraduate and master's work at the University of Chicago, and received his doctorate from Columbia University. In 1952 he was a teaching fellow in the humanities program at the College of the University of Chicago. He has taught English literature, cultural history, and philosophy at Hofstra College, the Juilliard School of Music, and Hunter College. For 1956–1957 he was awarded a Fulbright fellowship to study at the University of Munich. Dr. Philipson edited the Meridian volume of Aldous Huxley, *On Art and Artists* (1960), and has published articles and stories in, among other publications, *The Reporter, Esquire, The Journal of Philosophy, Commonweal, Saturday Review,* and *New Directions 16.* He is presently editor of Vintage Books, and a member of the editorial staff of Random House, Inc.

AN ORIGINAL MERIDIAN BOOK

Published by The World Publishing Company
2231 West 110 Street, Cleveland 2, Ohio
First printing April 1961

CONTENTS

V

PSYCHOLOGY AND AESTHETICS

VI

AESTHETICS AS A PHILOSOPHIC DISCIPLINE

PREFACE

All collections such as this one are *incomplete*, otherwise they would have to be encyclopedic series of books; and they are *biased*, otherwise they would be without any particular principle of organization or they would constitute a smörgåsbord sampling of every "going" position. The limitation of this anthology is evident in the absence of "definitive" positions. There is a minimum number of essays here in which questions of the form "What *is* so-and-so?" are asked and then categorically answered. Most of the material demonstrates the hypothetical nature of its propositions and tries only to work out some of the implications that may be tested. This characteristic is surely related to the bias of the collection, namely, a pragmatic attitude more concerned with the formulation of problems, and examination of conditions for future solutions, than with the construction of mausoleums for past achievements. If this volume is to be satisfactory as a representation of aesthetics *today*, it must consist primarily of such arguments as express the issues *currently* stimulating the minds of philosophers, historians, and critics interested in achieving a better understanding of art.

One consequence of this partiality is that instead of bits and pieces by a vast number of writers, only twenty selections are included here, and each of them, whether originally an independent essay, or a book chapter, is presented in its entirety. Another consequence is that this book of aesthetics is not a collection of writings by philosophers alone but by historians, critics of music, literature, and painting, and social scientists as well. Although aesthetics, strictly speaking, is a philosophic discipline, in practice, significant contributions to the theory of art are often made by non-professional philosophers. This is obviously as much a consequence of the haphazard training of most philosophers as it is evidence of the general nature of questions with which practitioners in other "fields" must also concern themselves.

The collection is organized to deal with the following topics: relations between the arts and general cultural purposes; relations between form and content with respect to the concept of style; problems involved in applying ideas of expression and communication to interpreting works of art; relations between art and the nature of knowledge; problems involved in the application of psychological and psychoanalytic hypotheses to the study of art; and lastly, issues currently under active consideration within aesthetics as a philosophic discipline. The editor's comments and notes are found in the introductions to the separate sections.

Every effort has been made to avoid duplication of materials readily available in other collections. The best complementary readings are to be found in the following anthologies: *The Problems of Aesthetics*, edited by Eliseo Vivas and Murray Krieger (New York: Rinehart & Company, 1953), *A Modern Book of Esthetics*, edited by Melvin Rader (New York: Henry Holt and Company, 1952), and *Problems in Aesthetics*, edited by Morris Weitz (New York, The Macmillan Co., 1959). Recommended for better understanding of the more general philosophical issues involved are: *Philosophical Problems*, edited by Maurice Mandelbaum, Francis W. Gramlich, and Alan Ross Anderson (New York: The Macmillan Company, 1957), and *Contemporary Philosophic Problems*, edited by Yervant H. Krikorian and Abraham Edel (New York: The Macmillan Company, 1959). The best general historical treatment of the subject is *A History of Esthetics* by Katharine Gilbert and Helmut Kuhn (Bloomington: Indiana University Press, 1953).

MORRIS PHILIPSON

I
ART AND CULTURAL PURPOSES
INTRODUCTION

A philosophic sociology of art would be the all-embracing approach to the theory of art, since the culture of a particular place and time "encompasses" the artist and his work, as well as his immediate audience. A number of criteria—sociological, historical, psychological, etc.—may be used to make such analyses. Depending on one's principles of interpretation, a great variety of meanings will be derived from the study of the same subject matter. The four selections that follow exemplify such differences. Each is written by a serious critic who appears to have considerable respect for and to take pleasure in works of art. In these selections, the authors are primarily concerned with the relations between the arts and other cultural values, either individual or collective.

The most general treatment of the subject, and the best presentation to lay as cornerstone to this anthology, is from Jacques Barzun's book *Of Human Freedom*, the chapter entitled "The Arts, the Snobs, and the Democrat." With his large view of the relations that have subsisted historically between art and society, Dean Barzun asks the question, What kind of art can a *democratic* society expect? His answer is the pragmatic one that genuinely accepts the *fact* of differences of taste. He concentrates on what a work of art *does* for the person who enjoys it, rather than on the abstract question of what a work of art *is*. Barzun's no-nonsense approach clears the air of the snobbery that befogs much that has been written about the function of art in culture.

The three fallacies he argues against, as standing in the way of a fitting democratic attitude toward art, are the "absolutes": (1) that art should appeal to the simplest minds as well as the most cultivated; (2) that there is a socially approved list of The Best Works of Art; and (3) that everyone should become an enthusiastic enjoyer of the arts. No one will deny that there are differences of taste. But that, in a democratic society, such differences "ought" to be eliminated seems to him a chimera, for the simple and incontrovertible reason that no one knows what makes the enjoyment of art possible. His statement, "The appreciation of art does not coincide with intelligence. . . . What it correlates with no one knows," cannot be taken too seriously. The enjoyment of art may remain impossible to measure in any sense, and that it has been in any scientific way correlated with economic, educational, social, or ethnic "advantage" is a naive delusion. The only attitude that can be maintained as consistent with the principles of a democratic society is that which enables each one to find "his own proper diet."

Barzun's position might be misunderstood to make criticism impossible. But, the only significant art criticism, he would propose, is the help that a critic offers to enable one to find his own diet. This is the pragmatic usefulness of criticism; anything else is dogmatic, in a realm of experience where no "ultimate authority" matters (except for the purposes of snobbism). This is not to say that there are no standards; there will always be the distinction between popular art and art for the connoisseur. But Barzun underlines the historical fact that such standards as make criticism useful are in no sense absolute, eternal, or universal. Barzun's position is a clear-cut attack on the essentially antidemocratic cant that passes for the "aesthetes'" love of art in their social struggle against the Philistines. It should not be forgotten that this selection is taken from Barzun's book on human *freedom*.

The essay by Nikolai Shamota, "On Tastes in Art," appeared in *Soviet Literature*. Published by the Union of Soviet Writers, the magazine is translated into English, French, German, Polish, and Spanish for the widest possible distribution outside of the U.S.S.R. In direct contrast to Barzun's pragmatism, Shamota presents a theory of art that assumes all three of the "absolutes" Barzun considers fallacious. Essential to his position is the idea that differences of taste are reducible to particular social causes. While in the West it appears that the most current causally-reductive hypotheses for explaining differences of taste are psychoanalytic, in the Soviet Union such differences are interpreted simply as functions of socio-economic differences. This assumes a psychology of conditioned reflexes in which the most important elements are social class distinctions. Moreover, art, like every other human activity, is taken to be a tool in the political "war" for social betterment. It has its function to perform in the ideological struggle. In other words, all art is only propaganda. The result is the dogmatism of the only officially acceptable kind of art—socialist realism,* which offers a political standard for all of the arts. Shamota's article states the tenets of this position succinctly. This communist aesthetics, however, is not to be mistaken for an exact standard of criticism; Shamota grants that different artists have "different ways of passing an artistic 'judgment,'" although he does not go on to elaborate such,

---

* For a Soviet writer's own criticism of this aesthetics, see "Socialist Realism," in *Dissent*, Winter 1960, and Lionel Abel's analysis of it, "Art While Being Ruled," in *Commentary*, May 1960.

formal, considerations. It goes without saying that works of propaganda might be artistically satisfying. Surely the works of Sholokhov, to whom Shamota refers, and those of such Soviet writers as Fedin and Leonov, whom he does not mention, which can qualify as works of "socialist realism" are art works of stature in any estimation of world literature.

We Americans can compare the communist-propaganda theory of art only to our experience of advertising, which is commercial propaganda. What we have seen in the U.S. during the past twenty years is the change from the "hard sell" to the "soft sell." Advertising has become a form of entertainment. For the cultivated, the "soft sell" seems to be the death wish of advertising; it appears suicidal because one can be amused by the *forms* it takes, and disregard the subject matter. Should Soviet propaganda-art gradually become more entertaining, its argument will become indifferent to its audience. Indeed, Mr. George Steiner has remarked, to the British audience of *The Listener*, that the ideology of the Communist Party is the Soviet equivalent of the theology of the Church of England; everyone "respectable" professes to believe in it, but nobody bothers to think much about it.

Still, the Shamota essay states clearly a theory of art in the service of information and inspiration of a specific content. Fundamentally, it is a classic expression of the theory that art is a tool in making a unified culture, only one of the means to an end independent of the means. The most extreme contrast to Barzun's pragmatism, this Soviet orthodoxy makes a mockery of the appearance that its appeal is to the ideal of "democracy."

The third selection in this section, Coomaraswamy's "Theory of Art in Asia," is a scholarly interpretation that might have been classified among the papers on "Aesthetics as a Philosophic Discipline." But here it better serves the purpose of presenting a comparative study in theories of art, relating Indian and Chinese aesthetics to their origins in prior religious and metaphysical principles. As an interpretation of the arts in the Orient, Coomaraswamy's essay draws upon the historically developed cultures that support and use the arts for so transcending a purpose that creation and appreciation can be spoken of "in the order of personal devotion." The author draws a parallel between this conception of Oriental art and the aesthetics of Christian scholasticism and concludes that Asiatic and Christian art endeavor "to represent things more nearly as they are in God, or nearer to their source." In effect, this aesthetics, too, is an apology for propagandistic art, being a justification for art as a conditioning means that leads one toward living a certain kind of life. Sanctioned by long tradition, and directed toward individual rather than collective salvation, it is no less a tool than "socialist realism" for the "perfecting of character." It conceives of art as a heuristic and training device for the expression and communication of a certain vision of reality, ultimately "true" for all, and such that its criteria will enable one to judge the most beautiful by the degree to which it represents the most true.

Unlike the three preceding pieces, Louis Kronenberger's popular essay called "America and Art" is, strictly speaking, a work of criticism rather than aesthetics. Concerned with art in American culture, it is an astringent statement of what Kronenberger believes to be the drawbacks to America's achievement of what is best in the arts, at least at the present time. Implicit throughout the essay are the author's assumptions concerning the values of civilization both within and beyond the functions of the arts. Kronenberger's attitude may appear to be directly opposite to that of the Soviet and Oriental writers because he is pointing out that art in America does not function as exhortation or exercise for the cultivation of a particular cultural pattern, but rather, as a "compensation" for the lack of agreement concerning such models. But implicit in Kronenberger's position is his commitment to the "humanist tradition" with *its* standards and *its* purposes. To come full circle, it may be that Barzun's criterion of freedom is a principle that makes sense only in what Kronenberger takes to be the humanist tradition.

THE ARTS, THE SNOBS,
AND THE DEMOCRAT *

Jacques Barzun

If a democratic society is left to its own devices, what kind of art can it expect? Henry Adams, almost fifty years ago, was already concerned over the frittering away of cultural energy that might result from free democracy. His assumption was that in the past, notably in the Middle Ages, there was an imposed standard to give coherence to individual effort, a central authority to pay for great works of art, and a consequent richness of production. Moreover, having an absolute standard, the artist could warn, instruct, and glorify what was socially sound. He could criticize life and mold it to a common morality.

This is an historical appeal which must be met at the outset with two denials. The absolute unity of the medieval scene is imaginary rather than real, and the criticism-of-life theory is recent. It is in fact contemporary with democracy as we know it. If we pick up the critical works of Aristotle, Pope, or Lessing, we are at once struck by the fact that they were hardly concerned about the poet's rapport with his environment. He was said to write well or ill according as he possessed skill and inventiveness, judgment and power. Those were the variables, while Nature was One. The spirit or breath that made the artistic mill go round was supposed to originate in the bosoms of nine barefoot ladies, as old as the hills on which they lived, and who therefore no longer bothered to suit their attire to changes in fashion.

Since about 1800, owing chiefly to the historical-minded Romanticists, criticism has changed. Nature means a particular clime and time. Art is a particular, personal gift. We expect individual forms from individual talents. We clamor for an American literature, native music, and circumstantial landscapes. We put the artist on the spot and expect him to stay there. The products of art must smell of the soil, or at least of the asphalt of a particular city. Woe to the poet whose free verse is too free of vital statistics, or to the novelist who does not "formulate" properly! We demand, but how do we provide?

The usual reply is that great art flourishes whenever the

* [From *Of Human Freedom* (Boston and New York: Little, Brown and Company, 1939). The text of this chapter has been slightly revised by the author. Reprinted by permission of the author.]

civilization as a whole is great and wherever there is a people with high artistic ideals. The mind leaps back to the Greeks (a people entirely composed of artists), then to the age that built the cathedrals (an age entirely peopled with mystics) —and stops there. The argument runs in a circle: a civilization is great because of its art, and conversely.

The commonplaces about the Greeks and the cathedrals furnish only one useful clue to the relation between art and society. They suggest that art has to be paid for, if only to keep the artists alive. Now people will pay for something only if they think it worth having; if they can, as the phrase goes, appreciate it. Art can flourish only in a civilization that enjoys a little superfluity of goods and whose population has some little respect for art. So far the account is familiar enough. When it is applied to our own society it seems to break down. We certainly possess as large a material surplus as any previous civilization, and we have high ideals, enshrined in familiar platitudes. But ask any social-minded critic what the present relation of the artist to society is and he answers: Divorce. The artist is divorced from society. Society does not support him adequately; his social status is uncertain, and his productions are either soliloquies or else syntheses of the world spirit that the world spirit refuses to recognize. We blame democracy or capitalism or the shortage of genius, but we do not deem ourselves as culturally well off as the Greeks of Pericles's time or the medieval inhabitants of Chartres.

Generalities about a "whole people" are likely to be wrong, and if we take a look at the Greeks of Pericles's time we are sure of it. The Greeks, to begin with, were only the Athenians with a sprinkling of resident foreigners; they were a cityful not of aesthetes but of politicians, businessmen, idlers, and slaves. The passion for the arts was limited to a few contemplative souls, the same who cultivated philosophy, science, and the making of utopias. We always quote Pericles's boast about cultivating art without effeminacy, but we conveniently forget that he also said the deeds of the Greek soldiers were the best proof of Athens' greatness, and that "far from needing a Homer for our panegyrist, or other of his craft whose verses might charm for the moment . . . we have forced every sea and land to be the highway of our daring, and everywhere, whether for evil or for good, have left imperishable monuments behind us."

The Greeks who did not need Homer are of course the same Greeks who built the Acropolis, carved the frieze of the Parthenon, and wrote immortal books; but they are the "same" only in the usual sense in which artists and their society are identified. Artists and philosophers then as now met with disapproval or encouragement, were rewarded, exiled, or put to death according to the usual chances of life. They left artistic monuments behind them because they individually struck a balance of conditions in their favor, not because Greek society as a whole was purposely designed to foster art. Except for the artists themselves, art was but an adjunct to religion and civic pride.

The Romans similarly valued works of art; a few for the sake of art itself, and the rest for the sake of conspicuous consumption. After the disintegration of Rome, the Christian faith used art largely as propaganda and it was only after the lapse of a few centuries that this faith became so taken for granted as to permit free expression for the artist. He could then work with naïveté or sophistication and remain free on the doctrinal side, sure of his audience and supported financially by the church. This financing, however, was anything but the spontaneous offering of a "whole people" that some modern collectivists like to dwell on. Like the Pyramids, the cathedrals were put up with the aid of forced labor and forced contributions, which does not, of course, exclude true religious emotion or civic pride.

The Western tradition about art seems fairly uniform: art is tolerated and financed as an aid to patriotism and religion, but even then only when the religion is so well established and the patriotism so circumscribed that they seem, not the fruits of indoctrination, but rather an obvious truth and a universal feeling. Athenian patriotism was of that kind, for the city was the only source of protection for the individual, and was also an object of religious worship. On a broader intellectual and geographical basis, the church of the Middle Ages produced the stained glass and architecture of the cathedrals and the illuminations of the monastery, but church and monastery were maintained at public and private expense for other, more immediate reasons than the pure love of art.

2

The modern period has seen a rapid succession of methods for financing art and artists. The Italian despots and popes were "patrons" like the kings of France and England, partly for show and partly from genuine love of art. Richelieu and Colbert's system of pensions brought with it a kind of journalistic obligation. They were the first to pay regularly for propaganda. Music was supported in the same practical way. It was a commodity for use with meals, at weddings, and so forth.

In literature, the change from patronage to public subscription came in the eighteenth century, traditionally with Pope's translation of Homer, which netted him a fortune before its completion. Since then, with some exceptional throwbacks to the system of state sinecures, literature has depended in one form or another upon public favor, while the more expensive arts of architecture, painting, drama, and music have been paid for partly by the public, partly by the state.

It is within the most recent period, say the last seventy-five years, that there has been increasing talk of the divorce between the artist and society. National patriotism and the Protestant sects have neither of them been productive in the same sense as ancient patriotism and medieval religion. These older emotions have been replaced by others equally strong but not nearly so unanimous within the given society. It is this unanimity that totalitarians of all kinds seek to restore and it is the diversity that democracy supposedly values, though it neglects to pay for it.

The result is that unless his temperament permits him to have a wide appeal, the modern artist must live on some form of charity. A great painter like Daumier cannot sell his pictures and dies in a house given him by a friend. A great architect like Louis Sullivan dies with plans for buildings never built because fame was too slow in coming. Or a great poet like Walt Whitman ends his days in obscurity and misery as if his life had been idle and profligate.

At the same time, "going concerns" like orchestral societies, museums, and opera houses must continually beg from their patrons and trustees; they amalgamate or stop activities for lack of funds. Literature somehow pays its own way, although poetry and works of a philosophical cast are generally "carried" by cultured publishers out of the proceeds of best sellers. Scholarship and pure science are almost exclusively supported by foundations and universities, both of them endowed by charitable gifts. There is a gap between what we pretend to want as a civilization and what we are willing to pay for as a people.

The spread of literacy has added confusion to natural avarice. A vastly increased public now demands and gets a vast amount of literature, painting, and music. But this culture is designed for an audience whose tastes never stray from the comfortable love story, the pretty picture, or the catchy tune.[1] Banality, a simple moral, and a soothing effect constitute that public the artistic experience; and the same education which has created the public has enabled a great many industrious workers to supply the demand.

Discussions about art are consequently vitiated by a confusion between art of this easygoing kind, intended for daily consumption, and art of a different kind, designed for connoisseurs. Of the former kind our society probably has more, and pays better for it in the shape of movies, novels, and magazines, than any previous civilization. And contrary to current belief, the making of "consumer" art is by no means easy and by no means reprehensible. Indignation is as out of place in speaking of jazz or a Sousa march as it is in front of a dish of boiled potatoes; and the refusal to call the march music is as critically unsound as to refuse to call the potatoes food.

The distinction between the two types of art is a difference of density rather than of species. In the same number of bars of Beethoven and Sousa, there is, in Beethoven, *more* of the essence of music, giving a thicker, more intense effect likely to alienate the unfamiliar listener by "boring" him, just as the palate accustomed to that richer food is bored by the thinness of the popular tune.[2] The feeling that this is not the only difference is due to the fact that as an art grows more and more complex and dense, the number of relations among simple elements increases until those relations look like extraordinarily refined experiences denied to the common herd. Yet there is no real barrier to be leaped over by an effort of genius between understanding a "vulgar" dance tune and a Beethoven symphony.

To have a fitting art, therefore, democracy must steer clear of three fallacious absolutes: One, Tolstoy's demand that art should appeal to the simplest minds as well as the most cultivated. Two, the belief that there is a socially approved list of books, pictures, and symphonies called The Best—an island for the elect in a Sargasso Sea of vulgarity. Three, the utopian's desire that everyone become an enthusiastic enjoyer of the arts. At one point these three absolutes converge: the habit of drawing moral distinctions between good and bad, high and low, in art, which hinders everybody from finding his own proper diet. Democratic art *can* mean the same art for everybody, but it must mean also *equivalent* art for different tastes. A deplorable yearning for sameness still seems to haunt the proponents of the good life, although they never explain why everybody should go to the opera rather than to a chess tournament. Nor has it ever been made clear why makers of utopias invariably promise us a leisure full of "pop" concerts and first editions. Why not mathematical congresses and horse races?

As it is, there is already too much social snobbery about art. No predestination of birth or brains selects those for whom the arts are a habitual need. Yet if anything ought to be, and easily can be, open to free choice, it is the realm of art. Presumably the readers of pulp magazines choose the one they like—detective or erotic—but in the so-called upper reaches of culture many who ought to know better sit through concerts that bore them, feel ashamed of the things they truly enjoy, and think that the pain of tramping through museums is credit to their account in the spiritual bank. Too many artists likewise are warped or thrown into false competition by the snobbery of critics and patrons who would honestly prefer pushpin to poetry, and who pretend at the same time that nothing is good enough for them.

This misguided reverence for the "spiritual value" of art, this pseudodemocratic desire to give the best of it to everybody, is touching but chimerical. The language of art is a special language, the understanding of which is not limited to any class, race, or nation, and which is completely unteachable by the usual methods. This is obvious enough from the forced feeding of Shakespeare and Scott in the schools. As Hazlitt pointed out long ago, there is no primer to Parnassus. The appreciation of art does not coincide with intelligence, nor even with the abilities of the art dealer or musical performer. What it correlates with no one knows, for a *Varieties of Artistic Experience* has not yet been written.

The fact remains that art is something for the few, and who those few are is unpredictable. They are not superior for being the few, and no proof exists that they are happier. The many, including representatives of the rich, the wellborn, and the able, are made acutely unhappy by repeated attempts to kindle art in their soul under forced draft, and the minority is too often badgered by the snobs striving to impose their fashionable favorite on everybody else. Either form of compulsion leaves the great majority indifferent or hostile to art, and Philistinism—if we must call it that—had better be accepted as inevitable than fought by the undemocratic methods now in use. Its chief danger is not that it interferes with a businesslike financing of art, but rather that it tempts the genuine artist or connoisseur to a universal crusade which neither history nor true democracy justifies.

3

Our predecessors in Philistinism, however, left a "characteristic art" to posterity. Whether the profiteers of the Peloponnesian War liked it or not, there stood the Parthenon and there it stands now. How can we be sure that without fascist or communist or snobbish absolutes, a free democracy will endow posterity with forms equally impressive, and expressive too of our feelings and capacities? The question, as we have seen, cannot be resolved out of hand by saying, "Let there be a dictator who is also a great critic," or "Let us set up a board to reward the worthy artist." These devices always rely on political means, and are based on political ideas, the mischief of which is that, being applied from without like a coat of paint, they give to art a uniform flat appearance which is the reverse of expressiveness.

The more practical point of attack is the interested customers themselves—the people who want art more than entertainment or luxury. They are few, but they can exploit the wants of the greater number who use art for other purposes than contemplation: those who want, and are willing to pay for, skyscrapers, private houses, packaged goods, decorated walls in public buildings, open-air statuary, tombstones, national pageants, and patriotic poetry. With all these habitual (if not normal) desires functioning and fulfilled, we ought to make a pretty good showing in history. They correspond to the patriotic and religious motives of earlier civilizations. The only danger is that these magnificent opportunities will be wasted by repeated concessions to the popular liking for a tame, undisturbing sort of art as nearly like pushpin as possible.

That popular liking is in fact seldom consulted, and what it objects to is not art itself but novelty, which offends visual and other habits. If the offending object outstays the old habit, a new one is formed. That is how national styles change. The responsibility for great and expressive art therefore falls on the so-called connoisseurs and arbiters of art—the critics, curators, teachers, and historians—who are in positions of authority, who shape the tastes and make the decisions, and who either yield to the fear of popular outcry or brave it in the knowledge that it will die and the work of art remain.

Critical lag or backwardness is thus harmless in the Philistines and fatal among the elite. It is inexcusable in the few who actually have it in their power to choose between the new creation and the hackneyed copy. The ability to make that choice depends on being a connoisseur not only of past, but of living contemporary art. The whole matter of divorcing or remarrying the artist and society comes down to this: If it was possible for a relatively small group of fanciers to "accept" Cézanne and Van Gogh in 1930, there seems to be no reason in the conformation of the human brain why these artists should not have been accepted thirty years before. Nor is there any reason in economics why a canvas by Daumier which could not have been given away in 1875 should now fetch half a million. We imagine that we need time; the fact that critics and public "come around" and are willing at last to like what has been shown them for fifty years when something still newer is brought forth has led to a belief in a dignified critical progress following the artistic evolution at a respectful distance. It is nothing of the kind: it is fatigue.

This lesson of art history is never learned, we never catch up with contemporary art, because we are a quarter of a century behindhand with a pile of past art to absorb, a fact which we express with unconscious smugness by saying of the great artist that he was "ahead of his time." The artist, if he is creative at all, is with his time, even when he works against it. He is organizing (pro or con) the perceptions that he acquires from the process of living and not from the contemplation of past art. The public, however, is apparently receptive only to art that looks, not like organized life, but like other art. And the fault—since there is no personal conspiracy or malignity in this vicious circle—lies in our methods of criticism and education.

Complaints against critics are as old as art itself. Swift compared the fraternity to two other ancient and disreputable professions because, like them, critics never change their character or their trade. Many people, feeling the inadequacy of critics, make a point of disregarding them all, together with their academic counterparts, the historians of art. Yet, rightly understood, criticism is the quickest way to discover the relation that obtains between an age and its artists, and once we grasp that relation there is a chance that we can understand and accept living art without the usual fits and tantrums of denunciation. What we need is a knowledge of what good art does, not a knowledge of what art is good. The two things are quite different, though conservative objection to new art always confuses the two. Even the word "connoisseur," which I have been using for want of a better, is misleading. It suggests "the best that has been said and thought in the world," than which there is, by now, no more prissy, inartistic, anticultural principle.

But how can the baneful tradition be overcome? Let anyone interested in an artist or work of art turn to the available criticism on the subject, reading not one book but five or six indiscriminately, and the trick is done: the discovery is made that upon the oldest and best-known works of art there is no fundamental agreement. There is no consensus of opinion but a *dis*sensus; no such thing as the judgment of Posterity, but a chaos of contradictory views. The Past, culturally speaking, is not a fixed but a changing thing, different with every new generation. Criticism is not the field of Armageddon, where one battles for the Lord, but Dover Beach, where ignorant armies clash by night.

Art lives in its own day as well as later by virtue of its appeal to some, and not to all, of the connoisseurs of art. There may be an unconscious logrolling among them to accept one another's favorites, but the conflict is real and it is both dishonest and dangerous to gloss it over. To throw out the testimony of a competent critic when he registers his dislike of a great name, say Milton or Brahms, is to treat both art and the critic politically instead of culturally. The chances are that he is all along an honest observer of his own feelings and of the particular work of art. His failure to admire is due to a personal limitation, of course, but that limitation is true of every individual. And this failure of perception is a more universal truth about culture than is the alleged universal appeal of any great artist.

We speak confidently of world poets; we affirm the universal appeal of music; we term classics those works which, we like to think, everyone would agree to regard as first-rate. These generalizations are figments of our conceit, repeated by each little clique or national group in its own circle. Such cliques are like the small country dairy that advertises, "Cream sent to all parts of the world." Go from clique to clique and you will awaken to the differences that exist about the merits of the best-established names. Travel from country to country and the elite of each will give you a very different list of world poets; and as for music and painting, no two "lovers" of either art will consent to admit the same dozen names to their private pantheon.

The motives for humility are not exhausted yet. For one thing, in speaking of universal art we almost always forget the civilizations of China, India, and Japan, comprising far more than half the population of the world, and for whom the "world fame" of a Beethoven or a Shakespeare is a very dim effulgence indeed. For another, even in our restricted circles, the accident of agreement upon certain authors does not mean anything like agreement about their qualities, their best works, or their significance in the history of art. At the risk of tediousness it must be repeated that this diversity does not obtain concerning only recent or second-rate artists, or about inherently controversial figures like Michelangelo, Spinoza, or Berlioz; it obtains about the supposedly solid and accepted ones like Milton, Dante, and Beethoven, as an overwhelming number of references could show. The supposed "consensus" is merely a temporary fashion which prohibits the voicing of doubts but does not abolish their existence. It is the fashion now to pay lip service to Shakespeare and Bach and Dante, but it has not always been so. And even today the number of times that a sincere communion takes place between the works of these artists and the minds of their admirers is comparatively small.

When, therefore, an honorable citizen of the republic of letters tells us that such or such a Titan is overrated, or empty, or boring, the probability is that he has read him and made the discovery, while we merely repeat old tags of perfunctory admiration. We must in any case listen to his reasons, agree or disagree, but ever resist the temptation of throwing his vote into the wastebasket in order that our candidate may be unanimously elected. Once we make up our minds to accept this democratic diversity in criticism we can enjoy art with decency. Instead of hoping that some day the entire globe will worship at our shrines, or pretending all the while that it does, we discover that varied artistic experiences can be equally valid; we discover that a great work of art is not an absolute good in itself, but a means whereby individual experience is organized and extended; we see that it is our culture and our personal history that push us to Bach and to Dante, as well as an inherent, though not inescapable, good in them that pulls us. The medium of communication is art, but the medium of comprehension is life. As life wears a different aspect for each individual, the language of the artist is bound to carry diverse meanings to each beholder, and sometimes no meaning at all. The diversity of meanings does not cancel them out, nor is there some secret formula of decipherment, different for each artist, that must be painfully inculcated in the young lest they be eternally damned.

Considered in this light, works of art, instead of stringing themselves along an evolutionary line according to technique, regroup themselves within their historical period. They reveal to the observer what it is that the artists do in paint, words, or sound with the data of their epoch. That is the true, the only relation between art and society which dictators, critics, and prophets are fumbling for. If it could be grasped by any generation of teachers and critics, they would be enabled to leap over the cultural lag of twenty-five years and understand their own artists; they could select with less fear of being duped; and instead of seeing chaos or believing in decadence, they would find a few common tendencies under the surface variety of style, subject matter, and message.

This hope of a critically alert culture may be visionary, but it is at any rate worth following. All the other methods seem to have failed though we refuse to acknowledge the failure. We blame the artist, the government, the economic system—anybody and anything but ourselves—complaining century after century of "sterility" and "decadence" in arts and artists which our posterity finds alive and kicking.

4

I have said that the language of art is not teachable by an analysis of techniques, nor explained by an application to the ordinary histories of art. What is taught in schools and printed in textbooks—usually in despair of anything better —is not so much wrongheaded as overschematic and absolute-minded. Literature is scanned for references to contemporary events; "influences" are traced, which really means that similarities are found—a very different thing; lives of artists are consulted in the hope of linking the mood of a poem with the domestic joys and calamities of the author. All these attempts are illusory so far as "explanation" is concerned. The "factors" sought for are interesting and real but they act in more indirect and complex ways than anyone knows. Scholarship can lay the foundations but cannot supply the understanding: we have learned little about music when we know that Mozart wrote a gay symphony under conditions of sorrow; we are no closer to Courbet's painting when we find he was affiliated with the Paris Commune.

If not through bare historical pickings, nor through technical analysis, nor through systematic search for this and that, how can we get the "feel" for art which is prerequisite to understanding its individual and social function? Chiefly through multiplied contacts with art of all periods and all kinds. Then through a deliberate discarding of all irrelevant emotions save pleasure. Political partisanship, "improving oneself," or agreeing with the best people is anathema. When art is taken personally, as a conversation with the dead or distant, free from ulterior motives and from pride of knowledge, then the dates, life histories, and technical details find their proper place. Instead of barring the road, they fill out the landscape of art.

Discussing pure poetry or speculating whether Balzac's works have a right to be called novels—I have even heard it maintained that Beethoven's works were not "strictly" music —can only be the pastimes of people for whom art itself is too strong a dose of seriousness and fun, and who prefer logomachy to experience. Such a preference usually ends in a cult for a single artist: everything else becomes too rash, too imperfect, not pure enough for the delicate appetite fed only on the best.

The entire history of art condemns these confining dogmas. Technique, tradition, narrow disdains and dislikes, creeds of the pure and the absolute, national and provincial ideals, are the hobgoblins of the pseudocultured. Technique and traditions have been means to an end, and they will continue to be so with alterations and additions by creative minds. They are strong and real enough to need no coddling and codifying at the hands of people who, while they are the "intelligent posterity" of yesterday, are the "blind contemporaries" of today. The only rule of art and the only safe prediction regarding its course is that the unexpected always happens. Its corollary is that no sooner has a critic or an age demonstrated by *a* plus *b* that some artistic purpose or device is impossible than an artist is found somewhere successfully doing it. The utter futility of legislating for art, and the complete uselessness of copying former masterpieces, should be the first tenets of any practical plan of art teaching and art appreciation.

A democracy where the individual can freely choose his

cultural sustenance can safely leave to human genius the making of an art adequate to its greatness. The way is perhaps inefficient, but it is less harmful than the deadly efficiency of the political mentors or the state patronage of the older democratic countries. Even under artistic *laissez faire*, however, there are certain cultural duties. For the masses of the citizens they are negative: hands off. For those more immediately concerned with the arts, they are more strenuous. Granting freedom to the artist means relieving him from the necessity of justifying himself, showing a greater appetite for a variety of styles and individual manners, stifling critical suspiciousness and doctrinaire expectations, and taking what is offered for what it is worth instead of trying to make it fit into the set categories of what is American, or modern, or classical, or proletarian.

The desirable pragmatic attitudes toward art may be difficult to instill even in the small group directly interested in culture. But a beginning might be made through our schools where there has long been a distrust of fixity and the absolutism of the True, the Good, and the Beautiful. Any small gain in this direction would go far toward lessening the arbitrary cultural pressure on the whole nation and thus permit it to foster (and finance) more freely its own art in its own day, for its own pleasure and the incidental edification of posterity.

NOTES

1. There are supposed to be 15,000 copyrighted songs beginning "I love you." The meaning of the word "copyright" acquires from such statistics an ambiguous if not an ironic sense.

2. This density spoken of here should not be construed in a material sense as meaning more *notes* to the bar or more instruments playing them, but a greater condensation of experience or significance in the ordinary means employed—melody, rhythm, harmony, and so forth. The magic involved defies analysis, as one realizes on perceiving the effect produced by a common chord or other simple device in the hands of a great artist.

ON TASTES IN ART [THE SOVIET VIEW] *

Nikolai Shamota

There is a saying: Every man to his taste. And although sayings are usually considered to sum up popular experiences, this one must be approached with caution, for people do have tastes in common, after all. There are national similarities in tastes within very broad limits ranging from national music and dance to national costume. And there are tastes which whole classes have in common. It is sufficient to recall what Nikolai Chernyshevsky said about the different conceptions of feminine beauty among aristocrats and among the working people:

> An extremely fresh complexion and rosy cheeks are the first criteria of beauty as the common people conceive of it. . . . In short, in the descriptions of beautiful girls in our folk songs you will not find a single attribute of beauty which is not an expression of robust health and a balanced constitution. . . . How different is the conception of feminine beauty in fashionable society! For several generations the young lady's ancestors have not done any physical work, and with each new generation the muscles of the arms and legs weaken, the bones become thinner, with the inevitable result that the hands and feet become small and delicate.

The tastes of people are formed by their conditions and manner of life. They have their origin in social practices, unite people and, I would say, most despotically interfere in the fate of art, subordinating it to themselves. Tastes dictate artistic programs and platforms, bring to life new schools and trends and decide the fates of those that are already established. They also determine the basic features of the dominating artistic method of a given period.

True, far from all writers and artists are sufficiently modest to agree that their art is but the individual expression of social tastes and predilections. They are under the impression that it is they who determine tastes. There is no doubt, of course, that art does influence taste and the artistic views of the public. It helps or, sometimes, spoils them. It creates its own readership and its own audience, and teaches them to understand and appreciate its conventions. But art can exert its

* [From *Soviet Literature*, No. 12 (Moscow: 1957).]

influence only if it is based on the broader aesthetic likes of the people, which have resulted from all their social experiences.

It cannot be otherwise. Like a child who, when he first appears in the world, finds conditions of life ready and waiting and accepts them unconsciously, the artist, entering upon his career, finds ready-made tastes, habits, and conventions which have been formed before him and, at least in the beginning, he himself becomes the vehicle of these tastes, habits, and conventions. It is only natural for an individual person to be dependent on the society he lives in. Consequently it is not a question of whether his views and tastes do or do not depend on the views and tastes of other people, but a question of upon whom, upon what social forces they depend.

Artistic views and conceptions cannot exist apart from a person's general attitude to life. On the contrary, these aesthetic views are a vital part of that attitude. One sees this, first of all, in the social conceptions of the "beautiful" and the "ugly," conceptions which influence the quality and loftiness of the aesthetic ideal and form that angle from which judgment is passed on the phenomena of reality and social ideas.

The conception of what is beautiful, together with other social conceptions, also influences the choice of the hero in literature. In the early nineteenth century the mere passive rejection of reality, as that of Onegin or Pechorin [1] was sufficient for them to be regarded as progressive types. But as the period of popular unrest approached, the period of the 1860's, it demanded a more active, energetic hero. Oblomov swept the former heroes off their pedestal, clearing the way for Rakhmetov.[2] During the period of the proletarian liberation movement Pavel Vlasov [3] reflected the new, socialist conceptions of the ideal of man.

Thus, it is possible to see how, in the process of development of social consciousness, the artists' views on phenomena of life which were similar in their essence also changed gradually. And these views changed only because they were part of the social consciousness which also changes from period to period.

Society's views on art indicate to art what its place in the life of the people is and determine what its subject matter should be. Receding reactionary social forces demand of art "pure" beauty and abstract dreams. On the other hand, new, ascending social forces, in their development, regard art as a participant in the earthly struggle.

The victory of realism was, essentially, a considerable victory of the view originating in the heart of society, that the real life of people is the realm of art and life by no means indulges in "pure," "unearthly" beauty. In life one has to fight for the beautiful!

Nekrasov called his muse a muse of vengeance and sorrow. The writer Lesya Ukrainka likened the poetic word to the sword. The poet Bryusov said that the poetic dream was a draft animal. At the same time the champions of "pure" art indulged in charming the ear of the privileged classes with euphonious combinations of sounds; they invented "golden legends" and "lovely dreams" for their sophisticated readers.

Thus a struggle which is part of the ideological struggle has been and is being waged as regards artistic tastes. Every class strives to spread its aesthetic conceptions through all society, whether it be in philosophy, morals, law, or other fields.

During the height of the 1905 Revolution Lenin advanced the slogan: "Literature must become part of the general proletarian cause." And as part of the general proletarian cause it had to raise and did raise the banner of realism, for only the soberest realism, the most profound interest in revealing the truth of life, formed the basis of proletarian policy, morals, aesthetics. The proletariat expected from art a realism that was impregnated with socialist ideals, with revolutionary fervor, with a feeling of closeness to the people and faith in the beauty and intelligence of the man of labor.

That society which wrote on its banner, "Workers of the World, Unite!" was heart and soul interested in the development of those qualities in art, which made it a means of understanding the world, of passing high moral judgments, of achieving social contacts and conscious unity. For this very reason the sources of socialist realism must be sought in the consciousness of those who have taken upon themselves that difficult and noble mission of remaking the world on socialist principles. It is therefore not surprising that the method of socialist realism expresses the aesthetic tastes of Soviet society, a society advancing toward Communism.

Among the many untrue things said about socialist realism is the allegation that in 1934 socialist realism was "declared" the Party line in the field of art by people who were at the head of art but who did not create it. However, such things are possible only in ordinary life, as when parents decide upon names for their children before the infants are born. In history such things do not occur. The offspring of socialist culture received its name only when it had learned to speak "at the top of its voice," when it had already been working for the new culture a long time.

2

What are the distinguishing features of these new views on art, the basis of which can be called socialist realism?

In the first place, a new aesthetic ideal appeared, one which guided people in their judgments of the phenomena of life and their reflection in art. The viewpoint of the workers and peasants became the viewpoint of art. And this viewpoint dictates that art should take an active part in the transformation of the world.

The struggle for socialism inspired active public initiative and aroused the social activity of man, that noblest human quality. This, in turn, meant that art had to portray characters who were fighters. That accounted for Pavel Vlasov's appearance in Gorky's novel *Mother,* Klychkov and Chapayev in Furmanov's *Chapayev,* Davidov in Sholokhov's *Virgin Soil Upturned* and dozens of other characters in Soviet literature.

The art of socialist realism, which expresses the tastes of the people, fights for a peaceful life for creative labor and arouses revolutionary thoughts and feelings. Working along this line our literature has created the image of a new man, one who is true to the socialist idea and is capable of fighting for it. This character is a very real person for he steps straight from life. He is not an exceptional individual who has risen above the masses. There are millions like him. He is a collectivist and therein lies his charm and beauty. Literature's interest in and profound respect for him reflect an interest in and respect for the people.

It seems to me that a wholesome taste on the part of the people, the efficacy of their aesthetic judgments upon the good and bad phenomena of reality, in other words, their high revolutionary principles are among the chief features of socialist views on art, uniting the readers and our writers. Passivity is alien to our social life. That explains why objectivism and naturalism, despite their vitality, do not find fertile soil under our conditions.

It goes without saying that the efficacy of aesthetic tastes must not be interpreted as an expression of direct evaluations, direct answers as to what is good and what is bad. Different writers have different ways of passing an artistic "judgment," depending on their creative manner, their preferences in style, their personal temperament, and so on. What is clear is that the art of socialist realism makes lofty, truly ideal demands of people and of life and leaves no doubt as to what it believes in, what it loves, and what it is fighting for.

The romance of the tremendous socialist transformations, the striving for the future lend a romantic quality to our artistic tastes and views, a quality based on real life and on real social forces. That is why the absence of any perspective, the narrowness of one's views, or what is called "lack of imagination" are alien to socialist realism, unnatural as regards our spiritual life.

When people of labor were freed from oppression, a new attitude toward labor appeared, one which regards it as the source of all wealth. If it is true that labor created man, it is also true that free labor is shaping the person of a free, communist society.

In a country where a new form of society is being created by the labor of millions, a man's attitude toward labor is of decisive significance in evaluating his qualities. This evaluation extends into the spheres of aesthetics and morals, makes important corrections in our conceptions of beauty, honesty, nobility. It is therefore not surprising that the attitude of the characters of our books toward labor, their position in the conflict between the socialist and the petty bourgeois approach to labor serve as an important line of demarcation between the positive and the negative, between the moral and the immoral, between the beautiful and the ugly.

3

The historian of the spiritual life of Soviet society can note the unprecedented breadth of interests in ordinary Soviet people of today. The soldier at the front during the Civil War, who learned to read by studying the revolutionary posters and slogans in 1917 and 1918, was already able to think on a world scale. Men of his kind were fully able to understand Shvandya in Trenyov's play, *Lyubov Yarovaya,* and the communist Nagulnov in Sholokhov's novel, *Virgin Soil Upturned.* And they were able to comprehend the most difficult forms of spiritual struggle, as those experienced by Grigori Melekhov in *And Quiet Flows the Don.*

The spiritual interests of Soviet people became even richer during the years of the first Five-Year Plans when, as Boris Gorbatov put it, the entire country was raving about speed, expanses, roads, when the entire country was in motion, was "on its way." Under such conditions how could our literature fail to visit Komsomolsk-on-Amur which was being built, the Arctic Circle, the Fergana Canal, or the Don *stanitsas* (Cossack villages)?

As a result of the breadth of interests of the people in real life, their artistic interests became broader and made art a trail blazer, a traveler, explorer, and seeker of the new.

One of the most obvious qualities of socialist art is, of course, its democratic form. Millions of ordinary people have become readers, music lovers, and theatergoers. In life they refuse to put up with what is false or insincere, and so they value, more than anything else, clarity and honesty in art, and accessibility of its form. That by no means implies that a democratic form is synonymous with primitiveness. Such accusations of primitiveness originated among those people who considered the socialist revolution "the beginning of the end of civilization," and who pictured the revolutionary hero as a vandal trampling the flowers of civilization with his muzhik's boot. No, democratic forms do not indicate a retreat, a return to the initial stages of artistic culture, but such a perfection of all artistic means when the loftiest ideas of today gain in latitude, clarity, brilliance, become accessible to all the people, and their significance finds expression in all elements of art.

It would be absurd to assume that there are no differences in views among readers regarding one or another work, differences which are at times very substantial. Views on art are bound, perhaps more than any others, with the emotional life of individuals. And it is the duty of art which is based on the most progressive, the finest human qualities, to develop and improve their tastes in art. Literature must not lag behind the reader; it must move ahead of him, must be the noblest expression of all that the reader needs, even if he himself has not as yet become aware of it.

A basis for the aesthetic views of Soviet society has already been formed. That basis has found its artistic reflection in the method of socialist realism. People who do not believe in socialist realism—I am not referring to those who do not believe in socialism itself—should, at any rate, attempt to understand that in our books we like bold, strong, brave revolutionaries because we have known them in life and have come to love them in life. We like the optimism of our literature because we ourselves are optimists, for we know our goal in life and see how it is being achieved with our aid. And they should attempt to understand that we want art to be the severe and irreconcilable foe of all that is false because we are building and will build a life that is just and beautiful.

NOTES

1. Onegin and Pechorin—main characters in Pushkin's *Evgeni Onegin* and Lermontov's *Hero of Our Time*.
2. Oblomov—the main character in Goncharov's novel of the same name. Rakhmetov—one of the characters in Chernyshevsky's novel *What Is to Be Done?*
3. Pavel Vlasov—the main character in Gorky's novel *Mother*.

THE THEORY OF ART IN ASIA *

Ananda K. Coomaraswamy

Tadbhavatu krtârthatā vaidagdhyasya,
Mālatīmādhava, I, 32 f.

In the following pages there is presented a statement of
Oriental aesthetic theory based mainly on Indian and partly
on Chinese sources; at the same time, by means of notes and
occasional remarks, a basis is offered for a general theory of
art co-ordinating Eastern and Western points of view. Whenever European art is referred to by way of contrast or elucidation, it should be remembered that "European art" is of
two very different kinds, one Christian and scholastic, the
other post-Renaissance and personal. It will be evident enough
from our essay on Eckhart, and might have been made equally
clear from a study of St. Thomas and his sources, that there
was a time when Europe and Asia could and did actually
understand each other very well. Asia has remained herself;
but subsequent to the extroversion of the European consciousness and its preoccupation with surfaces, it has become
more and more difficult for European minds to think in terms
of unity, and therefore more difficult to understand the Asiatic
point of view. It is just possible that the mathematical development of modern science, and certain corresponding tendencies in modern European art on the one hand, and the
penetration of Asiatic thought and art into the Western environment on the other, may represent the possibility of a renewed *rapprochement*. The peace and happiness of the world
depend on this possibility. But for the present, Asiatic thought
has hardly been, can hardly be, presented in European
phraseology without distortion, and what is called the appreciation of Asiatic art is mainly based on categorical mis-
interpretations. Our purpose in the present volume is to place
the Asiatic and the valid European views side by side, not
as curiosities, but as representing actual and indispensable
truth; not endeavoring to prove by any argumentation what

* [Reprinted by permission of the publishers, from Ananda K.
Coomaraswamy, *The Transformation of Nature in Art* (Cambridge, Mass.: Harvard University Press, copyright 1934, by the
President and Fellows of Harvard College). Extensive notes have
not been included here. The reference numbers following Chinese
words are those of Giles's *Chinese-English Dictionary* (London:
Quaritch, Ltd.).]

should be apparent to the consciousness of the intelligent—
sacetasām anubhavaḥ pramāṇaṁ tatra kevalaṁ!

The scope of the discussion permits only a brief reference
to Muḥammadan art: Islāmic aesthetics could be presented
only by an author steeped in Arabic philosophy and familiar
with the literature on calligraphy, poetics, and the legitimacy
of music. But it must be pointed out in passing that this
Islāmic art, which in so many ways links East with West, and
yet by its aniconic character seems to stand in opposition to
both, really diverges not so much in fundamental principles
as in literal interpretation. For naturalism is antipathetic to
religious art of all kinds, to art of any kind, and the spirit
of the traditional Islāmic interdiction of the representation of
living forms is not really infringed by such ideal representations as are met with in Indian or Christian iconography, or
Chinese animal painting. The Muḥammadan interdiction refers
to such naturalistic representations as could theoretically,
at the Judgment Day, be required to function biologically;
but the Indian icon is not constructed as though to function
biologically, the Christian icon cannot be thought of as moved
by any other thing than its form, and each should, strictly
speaking, be regarded as a kind of diagram, expressing certain
ideas, and not as the likeness of anything on earth.

Let us now consider what is art and what are the values
of art from an Asiatic, that is, mainly Indian and Far Eastern,
point of view. It will be natural to lay most stress on India,
because the systematic discussion of aesthetic problems has
been far more developed there than in China, where we have
to deduce the theory from what has been said and done by
painters, rather than from any doctrine propounded by
philosophers or rhetoricians.

In the first place, then, we find it clearly recognized that
the formal element in art represents a purely mental activity,
citta-saññā. From this point of view, it will appear natural
enough that India should have developed a highly specialized
technique of vision. The maker of an icon, having by various
means proper to the practice of Yoga eliminated the dis-
tracting influences of fugitive emotions and creature images,
self-willing and self-thinking, proceeds to visualize the form
of the *devatā*, angel or aspect of God, described in a given
canonical prescription, *sādhana, mantram, dhyāna*. The mind
"pro-duces" or "draws" (*ākarṣati*) this form to itself, as
though from a great distance. Ultimately, that is, from
Heaven, where the types of art exist in formal operation;
immediately, from "the immanent space in the heart" (*antar-
hṛdaya-ākāśa*), the common focus (*saṁstāva*, "concord") of
seer and seen, at which place the only possible experience of
reality takes place. The true-knowledge-purity-aspect (*jñāna-*

sattva-rūpa) thus conceived and inwardly known (*antar-jñeya*) reveals itself against the ideal space (*ākāśa*) like a reflection (*pratibimbavat*), or as if seen in a dream (*svap-navat*). The imager must realize a complete self-identification with it (*ātmānaṁ . . . dhyāyāt*, or *bhāvayet*), whatever its peculiarities (*nānālakṣaṇâlaṁkṛtam*), even in the case of opposite sex or when the divinity is provided with terrible supernatural characteristics; the form thus known in an act of non-differentiation, being held in view as long as may be necessary (*evaṁ rūpaṁ yāvad icchati tāvad vibhāvayet*), is the model from which he proceeds to execution in stone, pigment, or other material.

The whole process, up to the point of manufacture, belongs to the established order of personal devotions, in which worship is paid to an image mentally conceived (*dhyātvā yajet*); in any case, the principle involved is that true knowledge of an object is not obtained by merely empirical observation or reflex registration (*pratyakṣa*), but only when the knower and known, seer and seen, meet in an act transcending distinction (*anayor advaita*). To worship any Angel in truth one must become the Angel: "whoever worships a divinity as other than the self, thinking 'He is one, and I another,' knows not," *Bṛhadāraṇyaka Upaniṣad*, I, 4, 10.

The procedure on the part of the imager, above outlined, implies a real understanding of the psychology of aesthetic intuition. To generalize, whatever object may be the artist's chosen or appointed theme becomes for the time being the single object of his attention and devotion; and only when the theme has thus become for him an immediate experience can it be stated authoritatively from knowledge. Accordingly, the language of Yoga may be employed even in the case of a portrait, for example *Mālavikâgnimitra*, II, 2, where, the painter having missed something of the beauty of the model, this is attributed to a relaxation of concentration, an imperfect absorption, *śithila-samādhi*, not to want of observation. Even when a horse is to be modeled from life we still find the language of Yoga employed: "having concentrated, he should set to work" (*dhyātvā kuryāt*), *Śukranītisāra*, IV, 7, 73.

Here indeed European and Asiatic art meet on absolutely common ground; according to Eckhart, the skilled painter shows his art, but it is not himself that it reveals to us, and in the words of Dante, "Who paints a figure, if he cannot be it, cannot draw it" (*Chi pinge figura, si non può esser lei, non la può porre*). It should be added that the idea of Yoga covers not merely the moment of intuition, but also execution: Yoga is dexterity in action, *karmasu kauśala*, *Bhagavad Gītā*, II, 50. So, for example, in Śaṅkarâcārya's metaphor of the arrow maker "who perceives nothing beyond his work when he is buried in it," and the saying, "I have learnt concentration from the maker of arrows." The words *yogyā*, application, study, practice, and *yukti*, accomplishment, skill, virtuosity, are often used in connection with the arts.

An ideal derivation of the types that are to be represented or made by the human artist is sometimes asserted in another way, all the arts being thought of as having a divine origin, and as having been revealed or otherwise brought down from Heaven to Earth: "our Śaiva Āgamas teach that the architecture of our temples is all Kailāsabhāvanā, that is of forms prevailing in Kailāsa." A very striking enunciation of this principle will be found in *Aitareya Brāhmaṇa*, VI, 27: "It is in imitation [*anukriti*] of the angelic [*deva*] works of art [*śilpāni*] that any work of art [*śilpa*] is accomplished [*adhigamyate*] here; for example, a clay elephant, a brazen object, a garment, a gold object, and a mule chariot are works of art. A work of art [*śilpa*], indeed [*ha*], is accomplished in him who comprehends this. For these [angelic] works of art [*śilpāni*, viz. the metrical Śilpa texts] are in integration of the Self [*ātma-saṁskṛti*]; and by them the sacrificer likewise integrates himself [*ātmānaṁ saṁskurute*] in the mode of rhythm [*chandomaya*]." Corresponding to this are many passages of the Ṛg *Veda* in which the artistry of the incantation (*mantra*) is compared to that of a weaver or carpenter. Sometimes the artist is thought of as visiting some heaven, and there seeing the form of the angel or architecture to be reproduced on earth; sometimes the architect is spoken of as controlled by Viśvakarma, originally an essential name of the Supreme Artificer, later simply of the master architect of the angels, and patron of human craftsmen; or Viśvakarma may be thought of as himself assuming the form of a human architect in order to produce a particular work; or the required form may be revealed in a dream.

Nor is any distinction of kind as between fine and decorative, free or servile, art to be made in this connection. Indian literature provides us with numerous lists of the eighteen or more professional arts (*śilpa*) and the sixty-four avocational arts (*kalā*); and these embrace every kind of skilled activity, from music, painting, and weaving to horsemanship, cookery, and the practice of magic, without distinction of rank, all being equally of angelic origin.

It is thus, and will become further, evident that all the forms of Indian art and its derivatives in the Far East are ideally determined. We must now give greater precision to this statement, discussing what is implied in Asia by likeness or imitation, and what is the nature of Asiatic types. Lastly we shall be in a position to consider the formal theory of aesthetic experience.

First of all with regard to representation (*ākṛti, sādṛśya,* Ch. *hsing-ssŭ,* 4617, 10289, and *wu-hsing,* 12777, 4617) and imitation (*anukāra, anukaraṇa, anukṛti*). We find it stated that "*sādṛśya* is essential to the very substance [*pradhāna*] of painting," *Viṣṇudharmottara,* XLII, 48; the word has usually been translated by "likeness," and may bear this sense, but it will be shown below that the meaning properly implied is something more like "correspondence of formal and representative elements in art." In drama we meet with such definitions as *lokavṛtta-anukaraṇa,* "following the movement (or operation) of the world," and *yo 'yaṁ svabhāvo lokasya . . . nāṭyam ity abhidhīyate,* "which designates the intrinsic nature of the world"; or again, what is to be exhibited on the stage is *avasthāna,* "conditions" or "emotional situations," or the hero, Rāma, or the like, is thought of as the model, *anukārya.* In China, in the third canon of Hsieh Ho, we have "According to nature [*wu,* 12777] make shape [*hsing,* 4617]"; and the common later phrase *hsing-ssŭ,* "shape-resemblance," in the same way seems to define art as an imitation of Nature. In Japan, Seami, the great author and critic of Nō, asserts that the arts of music and dancing consist entirely in imitation (*monomane*).

However, if we suppose that all this implies a conception of art as something seeking its perfection in the nearest possible approaches to illusion we shall be greatly mistaken. It will appear presently that we should err equally in supposing that Asiatic art represents an "ideal" world, a world "idealized" in the popular (sentimental, religious) sense of the words, that is, perfected or remodeled nearer to the heart's desire; which were it so might be described as a blasphemy against the witness of Perfect Experience, and a cynical depreciation of life itself. We shall find that Asiatic art is ideal in the mathematical sense: like Nature (*natura naturans*), not in appearance (viz. that of *ens naturata*), but in operation.

It should be realized that from the Indian (metaphysical) and scholastic points of view, subjective and objective are not irreconcilable categories, one of which must be regarded as real to the exclusion of the other. Reality (*satya*) subsists there where the intelligible and sensible meet in the common unity of being, and cannot be thought of as existing in itself outside and apart from, but rather *as,* knowledge or vision, that is, only in act. All this is also implied in the scholastic definition of truth as *adaequatio rei et intellectus,* Aristotle's identity of the soul with what it knows, or according to St. Thomas, "knowledge comes about in so far as the object known is within the knower" (*Sum. Theol.*, I, Q. 59, A. 2), in radical contradiction to the conception of knowledge and being as independent acts, which point of view is only logically, and not immediately, valid. Translating this from psychological to theological terms, we should say not that God has knowledge, but that Knowledge (Pure Intellect, *prajñā*) is one of the names of God (who is pure act); or metaphysically, by an identification of Being (*sat*) with Intelligence (*cit*), as in the well-known concatenation *sac-cit-ānanda* (where it is similarly implied that love subsists only in the act of love, not in the lover or beloved but in union).

Now as to *sādṛśya*: literal meanings are sym-visibility, consimilarity; secondary meanings, co-ordination, analogy. That aesthetic *sādṛśya* does not imply naturalism, versimilitude, illustration, or illusion in any superficial sense is sufficiently shown by the fact that in Indian lists of factors essential to painting it is almost always mentioned with *pramāṇa*, "criterion of truth," here "ideal proportion"; in the Indian theories of knowledge empirical observation (*pratyakṣa*) as supplying only a test, and not the material of theory, is regarded as the least valid among the various *pramāṇas*. *Pramāṇa* will be discussed more fully below; here it will suffice to point out that the constant association of *sādṛśya* and *pramāṇa* in lists of the essentials in painting, for example the Six Limbs, precludes our giving to either term a meaning flatly contradicting that of the other. Ideal form and natural shape, although distinct in principle, were not conceived as incommensurable, but rather as coincident in the common unity of the symbol.

In Rhetoric, *sādṛśya* is illustrated by the example "The young man is a lion" (Bhartṛmitra, *Abhidhā-vṛtti-mātrikā*, p. 17, and commonly quoted elsewhere); and this analogy very well demonstrates what is really meant by aesthetic "imitation." Vasubandhu, *Abhidharmakośa*, IX, Poussin, pp. 280, 281, explains the relation of knowledge (*vijñāna*) to its object by saying that knowledge arises only in the act of knowing, by an immediate assimilation (*tadākāratā*) to its object, neither knower nor known existing apart from the act of knowledge. The nature of the assimilation (*tadākāratā*) is illustrated by the *sādṛśya* of seed and fruit, which is one of reciprocal causality. The Nyāya-Vaiśeṣika definition of *sādṛśya* (quoted by Das Gupta, *History of Indian Philosophy*, I, 318) viz. *tadbhinnatve sati tadgata-bhūyodhar-mavattvam*, is literally "the condition of embracing in itself things of a manifold nature which are distinct from itself," or more briefly the condition of "identity in difference."

Sādṛśya is then "similitude," but rather such as is implied by "simile" than by "simulacrum." It is in fact obvious that the likeness between anything and any representation of it cannot be a likeness of nature, but must be analogical or exemplary, or both of these. What the representation imitates is the idea or species of the thing, by which it is known intellectually, rather than the substance of the thing as it is perceived by the senses.

Sādṛśya, "visual correspondence," has nevertheless been commonly misinterpreted as having to do with two appearances, that of the work of art and that of the model. It refers, actually, to a quality wholly self-contained within the work of art itself, a correspondence of mental and sensational factors in the work. This correspondence is indeed analogous to the correspondence of person and substance in the thing to be "imitated"; but the object and the work of art are independently determined, each to its own good, and physically incommensurable, being the same only as to type. *Sādṛśya* as the ground (*pradhāna*) of painting may be compared to *sāhitya* as the body (*śarīra*) of poetry, consistently defined as the "consent of sound and meaning" (*śabdârtha*), and to *sārūpya*, denoting the aspectual co-ordination of concept and percept essential to knowledge. Accordingly, the requirement of *sādṛśya* does not merely not exclude the formal element in art, but positively asserts the necessity of a concord of pictorial and formal elements. The whole point of view outlined above is already implied in the *Kauṣītaki Upaniṣad*, III, 8, where the sensational and intelligible (formal) elements of appearance are distinguished as *bhūta-mātrā* and *prajñā-mātrā*, and it is asserted that "truly, from either alone, no aspect [*rūpa*] whatsoever would be produced."

As to the Indian drama, the theme is exhibited by means of gestures, speech, costume, and natural adaptation of the actor for the part; and of these four, the first three are highly conventional in any case, while with regard to the fourth not only is the appearance of the actor formally modified by make-up or even a mask, but Indian treatises constantly emphasize that the actor should not be carried away by the emotions he represents, but should rather be the ever-conscious master of the puppet show performed by his own body on the stage. The exhibition of his own emotions would not be art.

As to Chinese *wu-hsing* and *hsing-ssŭ*, a multitude of passages could be adduced to show that it is not the outward appearance (*hsing*) as such, but rather the idea (*i*, 5367) in the mind of the artist, or the immanent divine spirit (*shên*, 9819), or the breath of life (*ch'i*, 1064), that is to be revealed by a right use of natural forms. We have not merely the first canon of Hsieh Ho, which asserts that the work of art must reveal "the operation [*yün*, 13817] of the spirit [*ch'i*] in life-movement," but also such sayings as "By means of natural shape [*hsing*] represent divine spirit [*shên*]," "The painters of old painted the idea [*i*] and not merely the shape [*hsing*]," "When Chao Tze Yün paints, though he makes few brush-strokes, he expresses the idea [*i*, 5367] already conceived; mere skill [*kung*, 6553] cannot accomplish [*nêng*] this" (*Ostasiatische Zeitschrift*, n.f. 8, p. 105, text 4), or with reference to a degenerate period, "Those painters who neglect natural shape [*hsing*] and secure the formative idea [*i chih*, 5367, 1783] are few," "What the age means by pictures is resemblance [*ssŭ*]," and "The form was like [*hsing-ssŭ*], but the expression [*yün*, 13843] weak."

The Japanese Nō, which "can move the heart when not only representation but song, dance, mimic, and rapid action are all eliminated, emotion as it were springing out of quiescence," is actually the most formal and least naturalistic of all kinds of drama in the world.

Thus none of the terms cited by any means implies a view of art as finding its perfection in illusion; for the East, as for St. Thomas, *ars imitatur naturam in sua operatione*.

The principle most emphasized in Indian treatises as essential to art is *pramāna*. The Indian theories of knowledge regard as the source of truth not empirical perception (*pratyakṣa*) but an inwardly known model (*antarjñeya-rūpa*) "which at the same time gives form to knowledge and is the cause of knowledge" (Dignāga, *kārikā* 6), it being only required that such knowledge shall not contradict experience. It will be realized that this is also the method of science, which similarly uses experiment as the test rather than as the source of theory. *Pramāna* as principle is the self-evident immediate (*svataḥ*) perception of what is correct under given conditions. As independent of memory, *pramāna* cannot be identified with authority, but it may embody elements derived from authority, when considered not as principle but as canon. As not contrary to experience, *pramāna* means what is "true" here and now, but might not be correct in the light of wider experience or under changed conditions; in other words, the "development" of a theory is not excluded, nor the development of a design while in the course of execution. The doctrine can also be made clearer by the analogy of conscience, Anglo-Saxon "inwit" still understood as an inward criterion which at the same time gives form to conduct and is the cause of conduct. But whereas the Occidental conscience operates only in the field of ethics, and as to art a man is not ashamed to say "I know what I like," the Oriental conscience, *pramāna*, cf. Chinese *chih*, 1753, *liang*, 7015, *chêng*, 720 (used by Hsüan Tsang), *i*, 5367, etc., governs all forms of activity, mental, aesthetic, and ethical (*speculabilium, facti-*

bilium, agibilium). Truth, Beauty, and Love as activities and therefore relative, are thus connected by analogy, and not by likeness, none deriving its sanction from any other, but each from a common principle of order inherent in the nature of God, or in Chinese terms of Heaven and Earth. To sum up, *pramāṇa* means in philosophy the norm of properly directed thought, in ethics the norm of properly directed action, in art the norm of properly conceived design, practically the *recta ratio factibilium* of St. Thomas.

Thus the idea of *pramāṇa* implies the existence of types or archetypes, which might at first thought be compared with those of Plato and the derived European tradition. But whereas Platonic types are types of being, external to the conditioned universe and thought of as absolutes reflected in phenomena, Indian types are those of sentient activity or functional utility conceivable only in a contingent world. Oriental types, Indian Śiva-Śakti, Chinese Yang and Yin, or Heaven and Earth, are not thought of as mechanically reflected in phenomena, but as representing to our mentality the operative principles by which we "explain" phenomena—just as, for example, the concept of the shortest distance between two points may be said to "explain" the existence of a perceptible straight line. Thus Indian types representing sentiences or powers are analogous to those of scholastic theology and the energies of science, but not comparable with Plato's types.

Just as conscience is externalized in rules of conduct, or the principles of thought in logic, so aesthetic *pramāṇa* finds expressions in rules (*vidhi, niyama*), or canons of proportion (*tāla, tālamāna, pramāṇāni*), proper to different types, and in the *lakṣaṇas* of iconography and cultivated taste, prescribed by authority and tradition; and only that art "which accords with canonical standards [*śāstra-māna*] is truly lovely, none other, forsooth!" (*Śukranītisāra*, IV, 4, 105–6). As to the necessity for such rules, contingent as they are by nature, and yet binding in a given environment, this follows from the imperfection of human nature as it is in itself. Man is indeed more than a merely instinctive and behavioristic animal, but he has not yet attained to such an identification of the inner and outer, contemplative and active, life as should enable him to act at the same time without discipline and altogether conveniently. On the one hand, the gamboling of lambs, however charming, is not yet dancing; on the other, the human artist, even the master whom Ching Hao calls "Profound" or "Mysterious" (*miao*, 7857) and who "works in a style appropriate to his subject," can hardly lay claim to the spontaneity of the "Divine" (*shên*, 9819) painter "who makes no effort of his own, his hand moves spontaneously."

There exists, in fact, dating from the T'ang period, a threefold Chinese classification (*San p'ing*, 9552, 9273) of painting as Divine (*shên*, 9819), Profound or Mysterious (*miao*, 7857), and Accomplished (*nêng*, 8184). The first of these implies an absolute perfection; representing rather the goal than the attainable in human art; the second is such mastery as approaches perfection, the third is mere dexterity. A fourth class, the Marvelous or Extraordinary (*i*, 5536), was added later, with Taoist implications, to denote a more personal kind of "philosophical" or "literary" painting, great in achievement, though not the work of professional artists, and not governed by traditional rules; *i* thus corresponds very nearly to what is meant by "genius," with all its virtues and limitations.

A striking Indian parallel to the *San p'ing* occurs in Rājaśekhara's *Kāvya-mīmāṁsā*, Ch. II, where the creative faculty (*kārayitrī pratibhā*) is considered as of three kinds, viz. Innate (*sahajā*), Gotten (*āhāryā*), and Learned (*aupadeśikā*), poets being correspondingly classed as *sārasvata* (from Sarasvatī, Sakti of Brahmā, and mother of learning and wisdom), *ābhyāsika* (trained, adept, vocational), and *aupadeśika* (taught, depending on rules or recipes). Here *sārasvata* and *sahaja* clearly correspond to *shên;* *āhāryā* and *ābhyāsika* to *miao,* involving the idea of mastery; and *aupadeśikā* to *nêng,* having a trick rather than a habit. The one thing most necessary to the human workman is *abhyāsa,* "practice," otherwise thought of as *anuśila,* "devoted application" or "obedience," the fruit of which is *śliṣṭatva,* "habitus," or second nature, skill, lit. "clingingness," "adherence"; and this finds expression in the performance as *mādhurya,* "grace" or "facility" (*Nāṭya Śāstra,* Benares ed., XXVI, 34; *Kāvyamālā* ed., XXII, 34).

The Six Canons of Hsieh Ho, referring to painting, were first published in the fifth century, and have remained authoritative to the present day. They have been discussed at great length by Far Eastern and European authors, the chief differences of opinion centering on the Taoist or Confucian interpretation of the first canon. The following version is based directly on the text:

(1) Operation or revolution (*yün*, 13817), or concord or reverberation (*yün*, 13843), of the spirit (*ch'i*, 1064) in life movement.

(2) Rendering of the "bones" (essential structure) by the brush.

(3) According to the object (natural species, *wu*, 12777) make shape (*hsing*, 4617).

(4) According to the kind, apply, or distribute, color.

(5) Right composition, lit. "design due-placing."

(6) Traditional (*ch'uan*, 2740) procedure, lit. "handed down model, or method, draw accordingly."

Of these canons, the first is of primary metaphysical importance, and may be said to control all the others, each of which taken by itself has a straightforward meaning. The second canon demands a rendering of character rather than of mere outward aspect; the third and fourth refer to mass and color as means of representation; the fifth refers to the proper and appropriate placing of things represented, according to their natural relationships, and must thus be distinguished from composition or design in the sense in which these words are now used; the last implies the copying of ancient masterpieces and adherence to wonted methods and ascertained rules. These Six Canons have close analogies in Indian theory, but there is no good reason to suppose that they are of Indian origin.

In connection with the last canon, it may be remarked that a condition of spontaneity (*shên, sahaja*) outside of and above ascertained rules, though not against them, can be imagined, as in the *Bhagavad Gītā*, II, 46, where the knower of Brahman is said to have no further use for the Vedas, or when St. Augustine says, "Love God, and do what you will." But if the liberated being (*jīvanmukta*) or saint in a state of grace is thus free to act without deliberation as to duty, it is because for him there no longer exists a separation of self and not-self; if for the true Yogin *pratyakṣa* must imply a presentation indistinguishable from that of the inwardly known form (*jñāna-sattva-rūpa*), this will be evidence, not of genius, but of a fully matured self (*kṛtâtman*), a perfected visual habit, such that the seer now sees not merely projected sensations, but as he ought to see, virtually without duality, loving all things alike.

All art thus tends towards a perfection in which pictorial and formal elements are not merely reconciled, but completely identified. At this distant but ever virtually present point, all necessity for art disappears, and the Islāmic doctors are justified in their assertion that the only true artist (*muṣavvir*) is God, in Indian terms *nirmāṇa-kāraka*.

The metaphor of God as the supreme artist appears also in the Christian scholastic tradition, for example St. Thomas (*Sum. Theol.*, Q. 74, A. 3), "as the giving form to a work of art is by means of the form of the art in the mind of the artist, which may be called his intelligible word, so the giving form to every creature is by the word of God; and for this reason in the works of distinction and adornment the Word is mentioned . . . the words, *God saw that it was good* . . . express a certain satisfaction taken by God in his works, as of an artist in his art." Eckhart makes constant use of the same idea. Needless to point out, the concept of "creation" (*nirmāṇa, karma*) is a religious (*bhaktivāda*) translation of what in metaphysics is spoken of as manifestation, procession, or expression (*sṛṣṭi*); or psychologically simply as a "coming to be" (*utpāda, bhava, yathā-bhūta*, etc.), dependent on second or mediate causes.

As the author of the *Chieh Tzŭ Yüan* expresses it, "When painting has reached divinity [*shên*] there is an end of the matter." A conception of this kind can be recognized in the Chinese story of the painter Wu Tao-tzŭ, who painted on a palace wall a glorious landscape, with mountains, forests, clouds, birds, men, and all things as in Nature, a veritable world-picture; while the Emperor his patron was admiring this painting, Wu Tao-tzŭ pointed to a doorway on the side of a mountain, inviting the Emperor to enter and behold the marvels within. Wu Tao-tzŭ himself entered first, beckoning the Emperor to follow; but the door closed, and the painter was never seen again. A corresponding disappearance of the work of art, when perfection has been attained, is mythically expressed in other legends, such as those of painted dragons that flew from the walls on which they were painted, first told of the artist Chang Sêng Yu in the Liang Dynasty.

Such is the perfection toward which art and artist tend, art becoming manifested life, and the artist passing beyond our ken. But to lay claim therefore to a state of liberty and superiority to discipline (*anācāra*) on behalf of the human artist, to idolize one who is still a man as something more than man, to glorify rebellion and independence, as in the modern deification of genius and tolerance of the vagaries of genius, is plainly preposterous, or as Muslims would say blasphemous, for who shall presume to say that he indeed knows Brahman, or truly and completely loves God? The ultimate liberty of spontaneity is indeed conceivable only as a workless manifestation in which art and artist are perfected; but what thus lies beyond contingency is no longer "art," and in the meantime the way to liberty has nothing whatever in common with any willful rebellion or calculated originality; least of all has it anything to do with functional self-expression. Ascertained rules should be thought of as the vehicle assumed by spontaneity, insofar as spontaneity is possible for us, rather than as any kind of bondage. Such rules are necessary to any being whose activity depends on will, as expressed in India with reference to the drama: "All the activities of the angels, whether at home in their own places, or abroad in the breaths of life, are intellectually emanated; those of men are put forth by conscious effort; therefore it is that the works to be done by men are defined in detail," *Nāṭya Śāstra*, II, 5. As expressed by St. Thomas (*Sum. Theol.*, I, Q. 59, A. 2), "there alone are essence and will identified where all good is contained within the essence of him who wills . . . this cannot be said of any creature." In tending toward an ultimate coincidence of discipline and will, the artist does indeed become ever less and less conscious of rules, and for the virtuoso intuition and performance are already apparently simultaneous; but at every stage the artist will delight in rules, as the master of language delights in grammar, though he may speak without constant reference to the treatises on syntax. It is of the essence of art to bring back into order the multiplicity of Nature, and it is in this sense that he "prepares all creatures to return to God."

It should be hardly necessary to point out that art is by definition essentially conventional (*saṁketita*); for it is only by convention that nature can be made intelligible, and only by signs and symbols, *rūpa, pratīka*, that communication is made possible. A good example of the way in which we take the conventionality of art for granted is afforded by the story of a famous master who was commissioned to paint a bamboo forest. With magnificent skill he painted entirely in red. The patron objected that this was unnatural. The painter inquired, "In what color should it have been painted?" and the patron replied, "In black, of course." "And who," said the artist, "ever saw a black-leaved bamboo?"

The whole problem of symbolism (*pratīka*, "symbol") is discussed by Śaṅkarâcārya, Commentary on the *Vedânta Sūtras*, I, 1, 20. Endorsing the statement that "all who sing here to the harp, sing Him," he points out that this Him refers to the highest Lord only, who is the ultimate theme even of worldly songs. And as to anthropomorphic expressions in scripture, "we reply that the highest Lord may, when he pleases, assume a bodily shape formed of Māyā, in order to gratify his devout worshippers"; but all this is merely analogical, as when we say that the Brahman abides here or there, which in reality abides only in its own glory (cf. ibid., I, 2, 29). The representation of the invisible by the visible is also discussed by Deussen, *Philosophy of the Upanishads*, pp. 99–101.

Conventionality has nothing to do with calculated simplification (as in modern designing), or with degeneration from representation (as often assumed by the historians of art). It is unfortunate indeed that the word conventional should have come to be used in a deprecatory sense with reference to decadent art. Decadent art is simply an art which is no longer felt or energized, but merely denotes, in which there exists no longer any real correspondence between the formal and pictorial elements, its meaning as it were negated by the weakness or incongruity of the pictorial element; but it is often, as for example in late Hellenistic art, actually *far less* conventional than are the primitive or classic stages of the same sequence. True art, pure art, never enters into competition with the unattainable perfection of the world, but relies exclusively on its own logic and its own criteria, which cannot be tested by standards of truth or goodness applicable in other fields of activity. If, for example, an icon is provided with numerous heads or arms, or combines anthropomorphic and theriomorphic elements, arithmetic and observation will assist us to determine whether or not the iconography is correct (*āgamârthâvisaṁvādi, śāstramāna*), but only our own response to its qualities of energy and characteristic order will enable us to judge it as a work of art. If Kṛṣṇa is depicted as the seducer of the milkmaids of Braja, it would be ridiculous to raise objections on moral grounds, as though a model on the plane of conduct had been presented; for here art, by a well-understood convention, deals with the natural relation of the soul to God ("all creation is female to God"), and if we cannot understand or will not accept the tradition, that is simply an announcement of our inability to pass aesthetic judgment in the given case.

Some further considerations upon unequal quality and decadence in art may be submitted, by decadence "characteristic imperfection" being meant rather than the opposite of "progress." Any lack of temporal perfection in a work of art is a betrayal of the imperfection of the artist, such perfection as is possible to human work being a product of the will. It is obvious that the workman's first consideration should have been the good of the work to be done, for it is only so that he can praise his theme; and as to whether the work is in this sense good, we ought to be guided by a proper and ruthless critical faculty. But it should not be overlooked that even in outwardly imperfect works, whether originally so or having become so through damage, the image may remain intact; for in the first case the image, which was not of the artist's own invention but inherited, can still be recognized in its imperfect embodiment, and in the second the form by which the art was moved must have been immanent in every part of it, and is thus present in what survives of it, and this is why such works may be adequate to evoke in a strong-minded spectator a true aesthetic experience, such a one supplying by his own imaginative energy all that is lacking in the original production. More often, of course, what passes for an appreciation of decadent or damaged work is merely a sentimental pleasure based on associated ideas, *vāsanā qua* nostalgia.

There are two distinguishable modes of decadence in art, one corresponding to a diminished sensuality, the other reflecting, not an animal attachment to sensation, but a senescent refinement. It is essential to distinguish this attenuation or overrefinement of what was once a classical art from the austerity of primitive forms which may be less seductive, but express a high degree of intellectuality. Overrefinement and elaboration of apparatus in the arts are well illustrated in modern dramatic and concert production, and in the quality of trained voices and instruments such as the piano. All these means at the disposal of the artist are the means of his undoing, except in the rare cases where he can still by a real devotion to his theme make us forget them. Those accustomed to such comfortable arts as these are in real danger of rejecting less highly finished or less elaborate products, not at all on aesthetic grounds, but out of pure laziness and love of comfort. One thinks by contrast of the Bengālī *Yātrās* that "without scenery, without the artistic display of costumes, could rouse emotions which nowadays we scarcely experience," or on the other hand, of utterly sophisticated arts like the Nō plays of Japan, in which the means have been reduced to a minimum, and though they have been brought to that high pitch of perfection that the theme demands, are yet entirely devoid of any element of luxury. These points of view have been discussed by Rabindranath Tagore in connection with the rendition of Indian music. "Our master singers," he says, "never take the least trouble to make their voice and manner attractive. . . . Those of the audience . . . whose senses have to be satisfied as well are held to be beneath the notice of any self-respecting artist," while "those of the audience who are appreciative are content to perfect the song in their own mind by the force of their own feeling." In other words, while the formal beauty is the essential in art, loveliness and convenience are, not indeed fortuitous, but in the proper sense of the word, accidents of art, happy or unhappy accidents as the case may be.

We are now in a position to describe the peculiarities of Oriental art with greater precision. The Indian or Far Eastern icon, carved or painted, is neither a memory image nor an idealization, but a visual symbolism, ideal in the mathematical sense. The "anthropomorphic" icon is of the same kind as a *yantra,* that is, a geometrical representation of a deity, or a *mantra,* that is, an auditory representation of a deity. The peculiarity of the icon depends immediately upon these conditions, and could not be otherwise explained, even were we unaware that in actual practice it *is* the *mantra* and not the eye's intrinsic faculty that originates the image. Accordingly, the Indian icon fills the whole field of vision at once, all is equally clear and equally essential; the eye is not led to range from one point to another, as in empirical vision, nor to seek a concentration of meaning in one part more than in another, as in a more "theatrical" art. There is no feeling of texture or flesh, but only of stone, metal, or pigment, the object being an image in one or other of these materials, and not a deceptive replica (*savarṇa*) of any objective cause of sensation. The parts of the icon are not organically related, for it is not contemplated that they should function biologically, but ideally related, being the required component parts of a given type of activity stated in terms of the visible and tangible medium. This does not mean that the various parts are not related, or that the whole is not a unity, but that the relation is mental rather than functional. These principles will apply as much to landscape as to iconography.

In Western art the picture is generally conceived as seen in a frame or through a window, and so brought toward the spectator; but the Oriental image really exists only in our own mind and heart and is thence projected or reflected onto space. The Western presentation is designed as if seen from a fixed point of view, and must be optically plausible; Chinese landscape is typically represented as seen from more than one point of view, or in any case from a conventional, not a "real," point of view, and here it is not plausibility but intelligibility that is essential. In painting generally there is relievo (*natôn-nata, nimnônnata*), that is to say modeling in abstract light, painting being thought of as a constricted *mode* of sculpture; but never before the European influence in the seventeenth century any use of cast shadows, chiaroscuro, *chāyâtapa*, "shade and shine." Methods of representing space in art will always correspond more or less to contemporary habits of vision, and nothing more than this is required for art; perspective is nothing but the means employed to convey to the spectator the idea of three-dimensional space, and among the different kinds of perspective that have been made use of, the one called "scientific" has no particular advantage from the aesthetic point of view. On this point, Asaṅga, *Mahāyāna Sūtrâlaṁkāra*, XIII, 17, is illuminating: "*citre . . . natôn-nataṁ nâsti ca, dṛṣyate atha ca*," "there is no actual relief in a painting, and yet we see it there," an observation which is repeated from the same point of view in the *Laṅkâvatāra Sūtra*, Nanjio's ed., p. 91. It would be thus as much beside the mark to conceive of a progress in art as revealed by a development in *Raumdarstellung* as to seek to establish a stylistic sequence on a supposed more or less close observation of Nature. Let us not forget that the mind is a part, and the most important part, of our knowledge of Nature, and that this point of view, though it may have been forgotten in Europe, has been continuously current in Asia for more than two thousand years.

Where European art naturally depicts a moment of time,

an arrested action or an effect of light, Oriental art represents a continuous condition. In traditional European terms, we should express this by saying that modern European art endeavors to represent things as they are in themselves, Asiatic and Christian art to represent things more nearly as they are in God, or nearer to their source. As to what is meant by representing a continuous condition, for example, the Buddha attained Enlightenment countless ages since, his manifestation is still accessible, and will so remain; the Dance of Śiva takes place, not merely in the Tāraka forest, nor even at Cidambaram, but in the heart of the worshipper; the Kṛṣṇa Līlā is not a historical event, of which Nīlakaṇṭha reminds us, but, using Christian phraseology, a "play played eternally before all creatures." This point of view, which was by no means unknown to the European schoolmen and is still reflected in India's so-called lack of any historical sense, Islam and China being here nearer to the world than India, though not so enmeshed in the world as modern Europe, constitutes the a priori explanation of the Indian adherence to types and indifference to transient effects. One might say, not that transient effects are meaningless, but that their value is not realized except to the degree that they are seen *sub specie aeternitatis,* that is *formaliter.* And where it is not the event but the type of activity that constitutes the theme, how could the East have been interested in cast shadows? Or how could the Śūnyavādin, who may deny that any Buddha ever really existed, or that any doctrine was ever actually taught, and so must be entirely indifferent as to the historicity of the Buddha's life, have been curious about the portraiture of Buddha? It would indeed be irrelevant to demand from any art a solution of problems of representation altogether remote from contemporary interest.

Little as it might have been foreseen, the concept of types prevails also in the portraiture of individuals, where the model is present (*pratyakṣa*) to the eye or memory. It is true that classical Indian portraits must have been recognizable, and even admirable, likenesses. We have already seen that *sādṛśya,* conformity of sense and substance, is essential in painting, and it has been pointed out that different, though closely related, terms, viz. *sadṛśī* and *susadṛśī,* are employed when the idea of an exact or speaking likeness is to be expressed. The painted portrait (*pratikṛti, ākṛti*) functioned primarily as a substitute for the living presence of the original. One of the oldest treatises, the Tanjur *Citralakṣaṇa,* refers the origin of painting in the world to this requirement, and yet actually treats only the physiognomical peculiarities (*lakṣaṇa*) of types. Even more instructive is a later case, occurring in one of the *Vikramacarita* stories: here the King is so much attached to the Queen that he keeps her at his side, even in council, but this departure from custom and propriety is disapproved of by the courtiers, and the King consents to have a portrait painted, as a substitute for the Queen's presence. The court painter is allowed to see the Queen; he recognizes that she is a *padminī*, that is, a "Lotus-lady," one of the four types under which women are classed according to physiognomy and character by Hindu rhetoricians. He paints her accordingly *padminī-lakṣaṇa-yuktam*, "with the characteristic marks of a Lotus-lady," and yet the portrait is spoken of not merely as *rūpam*, a figure, but even as *svarūpam*, "her intrinsic aspect." We know also, both in China and in India, of ancestral portraits, but these were usually prepared after death, and so far as preserved have the character of effigies (Chinese *ying-tu*, "diagram of a shade") rather than of speaking likenesses. In the *Pratimānāṭaka*, the hero, marveling at the execution of the statues in an ancestral chapel, does not recognize them as those of his parents, and wonders if they are representations of deities. We even find a polemic against portraiture: "images of the angels are productive of good, and heavenward-leading, but those of men or other mortal beings lead not to heaven nor work weal," *Śukranītisāra*, IV, 4, 75 and 76. Chinese ancestral portraits are not devoid of individual characterization, but this represents only a slight, not an essential, modification of general formulas; the books on portraiture (*fu shên*, "depicting soul") refer only to types of features, canons of proportion, suitable accessories, and varieties of brushstroke proper for the draperies; the essence of the subject must be portrayed, but there is nothing said about anatomical accuracy. The painter Kuo Kung-ch'ên was praised for his rendering of very soul (*ching shên*, 2133, 9819) and mind (*i ch'u*, 5367, 3120) in a portrait; but there cannot be adduced from the whole of Asia such a thing as a treatise on anatomy designed for use by artists.

The first effect produced on a modern Western spectator by these scholastic qualities of Oriental art is one of monotony. In literature and plastic art, persons are not so much distinguished as individuals as by what they do, in which connection it may be remembered that orthodoxy, for the East, is determined by what a man does, and not by his beliefs. Again, the productions of any one period are characterized far more by what is common to them all than by the personal variations. Because of their exclusively professional character and formal control, and the total absence of the conception of private property in ideas, the range of quality and theme that can be found in Oriental works of one and the same age or school is less than that which can be seen in European art at the present day, and besides this, identical themes and formulas have been adhered to during long periods. Where the modern student, accustomed to an infinite variety of choice in themes, and an infinite variety and tolerance of personal mannerisms, has neither accustomed himself to the idea of a unanimous style, nor to that of themes determined by general necessities and unanimous demand, nor learned to distinguish nuances in the unfamiliar stylistic sequences, his impatience can hardly be wondered at; but this impatience, which is not a virtue, must be outgrown. Here is involved the whole question of the distinction between originality or novelty and intensity or energy; it should be enough to say that when there is realization, when the themes are felt and art *lives*, it is of no moment whether or not the themes are new or old.

Life itself—the different ways in which the difficult problems of human association have been solved—represents the ultimate and chief of the arts of Asia; and it must be stated once for all that the forms assumed by this life are by no means empirically determined, but designed as far as possible according to a metaphysical tradition, on the one hand conformably to a divine order, and on the other with a view to facilitating the attainment by each individual of approximate perfection in his kind, that is, permitting him, by an exact adjustment of opportunity to potentiality, to achieve such realization of his entire being as is possible to him. Even town planning depends in the last analysis upon considerations of this kind. Neither the society nor the specific arts can be rationally enjoyed without a recognition of the metaphysical principles to which they are thus related, for things can be enjoyed only in proportion to their intelligibility, speaking, that is, humanly and not merely functionally.

Oriental life is modeled on types of conduct sanctioned by tradition. For India, Rāma, and Sītā represent ideals still potent, the *svadharma* of each caste is a *mode* of behavior, good form being *à la mode;* and until recently every Chinese accepted as a matter of course the concept of manners established by Confucius. The Japanese word for rudeness means "acting in an unexpected way." Here, then, life is designed like a garden, not allowed to run wild. All this formality, for a cultured spectator, is far more attractive than can be the variety of imperfection so freely displayed by the plain and blunt, or as he thinks, "more sincere," European. This external conformity, whereby a man is lost in the crowd as true architecture seems to be a part of its native landscape, constitutes for the Oriental himself a privacy within which the individual character can flower unhampered. This is most of all true in the case of women, whom the East has so long sheltered from necessities of self-assertion; one may say that for women of the aristocratic classes in India or Japan there has existed no freedom whatever in the modern sense, yet these same women, molded by centuries of stylistic living, achieved an absolute perfection in their kind, and perhaps Asiatic art can show no higher achievement than this. In India, where the "tyranny of caste" strictly governs marriage, diet, and every detail of outward conduct, there exists and has always existed unrestricted freedom of thought as to modes of belief or thought; a breach of social etiquette may involve excommunication from society, but religious intolerance is practically unknown, and it is a perfectly normal thing for different members of the same family to choose for themselves the particular deity of their personal devotion.

It has been well said that civilization is style. An immanent culture in this sense endows every individual with an outward grace, a typological perfection, such as only the rarest beings can achieve by their own effort, a kind of perfection which does not belong to genius; whereas a democracy, which requires of every man to save his own "face" and soul, actually condemns each to an exhibition of his own irregularity and imperfection, and this implicit acceptance of formal imperfection only too easily passes over into an exhibitionism which makes a virtue of vanity and is complacently described as self-expression.

We have so far discussed the art of Asia in its theological aspect, that is with reference to the scholastic organization of thought in terms of types of activity, and the corresponding arts of symbolism and iconography, in which the elements of form presented by Nature and redeemed by art are used as means of communication. The classical developments of this kind of art belong mainly to the first millennium of the Christian era. Its later prolongations tend to decadence, the formal elements retaining their edifying value, in design and composition, but losing their vitality, or surviving only in folk art, where the intensity of an earlier time expressing a more conscious will is replaced by a simpler harmony of style prevailing throughout the whole man-made environment. Eighteenth-century Siam and Ceylon provide us with admirable examples of such a folk style based on classical tradition, this condition representing the antithesis of that now realized in the West, where in place of vocation as the general type of activity we find the types of individual genius on the one hand, and that of unskilled labor on the other.

Another kind of art, sometimes called romantic or idealistic, but better described as imagist or mystical, where denotation and connotation cannot be divided, is typically developed throughout Asia in the second millennium. In this kind of art no distinction is felt between what a thing "is" and what it "signifies." However, in thus drawing a distinction between symbolic and imagist art it must be very strongly emphasized that the two kinds of art are inseverably connected and related historically and aesthetically; for example, Kamakura Buddhist painting in the twelfth or thirteenth century is still iconographic, in Sung landscape and animal painting there is always an underlying symbolism, and, on the other hand, Indian animal sculpture at Māmallapuram in the seventh century is already romantic, humorous, and mystical. A more definite break between the two points of view is illustrated in the well-known story of the Zen priest Tan-hsia, who used a wooden image of the Buddha to make his fire—not however, as iconoclast, but simply because he was cold. The two kinds of art are most closely connected by the philosophy and practice of Yoga; in other words, a self-identification with the theme is always prerequisite. But whereas the theological art is concerned with types of power, the mystical art is concerned with only one power. Its ultimate theme is that single and undivided principle which reveals itself in every form of life whenever the light of the mind so shines on anything that the secret of its inner life is realized, both as an end in itself unrelated to any human purpose, and as no other than the secret of one's own innermost being. "When thou seest an eagle, thou seest a portion of genius"; "the heavens declare the glory of God"; "a mouse is miracle enough," these are European analogies; or St. Bernard's *"Ligna et lapides docebunt te, quod a magistris audire non posse."*

Here, then, the proximate theme may be any aspect of Nature whatsoever, not excluding human nature but "wherever the mind attaches itself," every aspect of life having an equal value in a spiritual view. In theory this point of view could be applied in justification of the greatest possible variety of individual choice, and interpreted as a "liberation" of the artist from associated ideas. However, in the more practical economy of the great living traditions we find, as before, that certain restricted kinds or groups of themes are adhered to generation after generation in a given area, and that the technique is still controlled by most elaborate rules, and can only be acquired in long years of patient practice (*abhyāsa*). Historical conditions and environment, an inheritance of older symbolisms, specific racial sensibilities, all these provide a better than private determination of the work to be done; for the artist or artisan, who "has his art which he is expected to practice," this is a means to the conservation of energy; for man generally, it secures a continued comprehensibility of art, its value as communication.

The outstanding aspects of the imagist or mystical art of Asia are the Ch'an or Zen art of China and Japan, in which the theme is either landscape or plant or animal life; Vaiṣṇava

painting, poetry, and music in India, where the theme is
sexual love; and Ṣūfī poetry and music in Persia, devoted to
the praise of intoxication.

The nature of Ch'an-Zen is not easy to explain. Its sources
are partly Indian, partly Taoist, its development both Chinese
and Japanese. Chinese Buddhist art is *like* Indian in general
aspect, differing only in style; Ch'an-Zen art provides us with
a perfect example of that kind of real assimilation of new
cultural ideas which results in a development formally *unlike*
the original. This is altogether different from that hybridiza-
tion which results from "influences" exerted by one art upon
another; influences in this last sense, though historians of art
attach great importance to them, are almost always manifested in unconscious parody—one thinks of Hellenistic art in
India, or *chinoiseries* in Europe—and in any case belong to
the history of taste rather than to the history of art. At the
same time that we recognize Indian sources of Ch'an-Zen art,
it is to be remembered that Zen is also deeply rooted in
Taoism; it is sufficiently shown by the saying of Chuang Tzǔ,
"The mind of the sage, being in repose, becomes the mirror
of the universe, the speculum of all creation," that China had
always and independently been aware of the true nature of
imaginative vision.

The Ch'an-Zen discipline is one of activity and order; its
doctrine the invalidity of doctrine, its end an illumination by
immediate experience. Ch'an-Zen art, seeking realization of
the divine being in man, proceeds by way of opening his eyes
to a like spiritual essence in the world of Nature external to
himself; the scripture of Zen "is written with the characters
of heaven, of man, of beasts, of demons, of hundreds of blades
of grass, and of thousands of trees" (Dōggen), "every flower
exhibits the image of Buddha" (Dugō). A good idea of Ch'en-
Zen art can be obtained from the words of a twelfth-century
Chinese critic, writing on animal painting; after alluding to
the horse and bull as symbols of Heaven and Earth, he continues: "But tigers, leopards, deer, wild swine, fawns, and
hares—creatures that cannot be inured to the will of man
—these the painter chooses for the sake of their skittish gam-
bols and swift shy evasions, loves them as things that seek the
desolation of great plains and wintry snows, as creatures that
will not be haltered with a bridle, nor tethered by the foot.
He would commit to brushwork the gallant splendor of their
stride; *this he would do and no more.*" But the Ch'an-Zen
artist no more paints from Nature than the poet writes from
Nature; he has been trained according to treatises on style so
detailed and explicit that there would seem to be no room left
for the operation of personality. A Japanese painter once said
to me, "I have had to concentrate on the bamboo for many,

many years, still a certain technique for the rendering of the tips of bamboo leaves eludes me." And yet immediacy or spontaneity has been more nearly perfectly attained in Ch'an-Zen art than anywhere else. Here there is no formal iconography, but an intuition that has to be expressed in an ink painting where no least stroke of the brush can be erased or modified; the work is as irrevocable as life itself. There is no kind of art that comes nearer to "grasping the joy as it flies," the winged life that is no longer life when we have taken thought to remember and describe it; no kind of art more studied in method, or less labored in effect. Every work of Ch'an-Zen art is unique, and in proportion to its perfection inscrutable.

But Ch'an-Zen is by no means only a way to perfect experience, it is also a way to the perfecting of character. Ch'an-Zen represents all and more than we now mean by the word "culture": an active principle pervading every aspect of human life, becoming now the chivalry of the warrior, now the grace of the lover, now the habit of the craftsman. The latter point may be illustrated by Chuang Tzŭ's story of the wheelwright who ventured to criticize a nobleman for reading the works of a dead sage. In excusing his temerity, he explained: "Your humble servant must regard the matter from the point of view of his own art. In making a wheel, if I proceed too gently, that is easy enough, but the work will not stand fast; if I proceed too violently, that is not only toilsome, but the parts will not fit well together. It is only when the movements of my hand are neither too gentle nor too violent that the idea in my mind can be realized. Still, I cannot explain this in words; there is a skill in it which I cannot teach my son, nor can he learn it from me." The wheelwright pointed out, in other words, that perfection cannot be achieved by reading about it, but only in direct action.

Thus Ch'an-Zen is by no means an asceticism divorced from life, though there are many great Ch'an-Zen monasteries; Ch'an-Zen art presents no exception to the general rule in Asia, that all works of art have definite and commonly understood meanings, apart from any aesthetic perfection of the work itself. The meanings of Ch'an-Zen themes are such as have sometimes been expressed in European art by means of allegorical figures. Dragon and tiger, mist and mountain, horse and bull, are types of Heaven and Earth, spirit and matter; the gentle long-armed gibbon suggests benevolence, the peacock is symbolic of longevity, the lotus represents an immaculate purity. Let us consider the case of the pine tree and the morning-glory, both favorite themes of Japanese art: "The morning-glory blossoms only for an hour, and yet it differs not at heart from the pine, which may endure for a thousand years." What is to be understood here is not an obvious allegory of time and eternity, but that the pine no more takes thought of its thousand years than the morning-glory of its passing hour; each fullfils its destiny and is content; and Matsunaga, the author of the poem, wished that his heart might be like theirs. If such associations add nothing directly to aesthetic quality, neither do they in any way detract from it. When at last Zen art found expression in scepticism,

> Granted this dewdrop world is but a dewdrop world,
>   This granted, yet . . .

there came into being the despised popular and secular Ukiyoye art of Japan. But here an artistic tradition had been so firmly established, the vision of the world so *approfondi*, that in a sphere corresponding with that of the modern picture post card—Ukiyoye illustrated the theater, the *Yoshiwara*, and the *Aussichtspunkt*—there still survived a purity and charm of conception that sufficed, however slight their essence, to win acceptance in Europe, long before the existence of a more serious and classical art had been suspected.

A mystical development took place in India somewhat later, and on different lines. In the anthropocentric European view of life, the nude human form has always seemed to be peculiarly significant, but in Asia, where human life has been thought of as differing from that of other creatures, or even from that of the "inanimate" creation only in degree, not in kind, this has never been the case. On the other hand, in India, the conditions of human love, from the first meeting of eyes to ultimate self-oblivion, have seemed spiritually significant, and there has always been a free and direct use of sexual imagery in religious symbolism. On the one hand, physical union has seemed to present a self-evident image of spiritual unity; on the other, operative forces, as in modern scientific method, are conceived as male and female, positive and negative. It was thus natural enough that later Vaiṣṇava mysticism, speaking always of devotion, *bhakti*, should do so in the same terms; the true and timeless relation of the soul to God could now only be expressed in impassioned epithalamia celebrating the nuptials of Rādhā and Kṛṣṇa, milkmaid and herdsman, earthly Bride and heavenly Bridegroom. So there came into being songs and dances in which at one and the same time sensuality has spiritual significance, and spirituality physical substance, and painting that depicts a transfigured world, where all men are heroic, all women beautiful and passionate and shy, beasts and even trees and rivers are aware of the presence of the Beloved—a world of imagination and reality, seen with the eyes of Majñūn. If in the dance ("nautch") the mutual relations of hero and heroine imitated by the players display an esoteric meaning, this is not by arbitrary interpretation or as allegory, but by a mutual introsusception. If in painting and poetry the daily life of peasants seemed to reflect conditions ever present in the pastoral Heaven of the Divine Cowherd, this is not a sentimental or romantic symbolism, but born of the conviction that "all the men and women of the world are His living forms" (Kabīr), that reality is here and now tangibly and visibly accessible. Here the scent of the earth is ever present: "If he has no eyes, nor nose, nor mouth, how could he have stolen and eaten curd? Can we abandon our love of Kṛṣṇa, to worship a figure painted on a wall?" (Sūr Dās). Realities of experience, and neither a theory of design nor inspiration coming none knows whence, are the sources of this art; and those who cannot at least in fancy (*vāsanā*) experience the same emotions and sense their natural operation cannot expect to be able to understand the art by any other and more analytical processes. For no art can be judged until we place ourselves at the point of view of the artist; so only can the determination be known by which its design and execution are entirely controlled.

A formal theory of art based on the facts as above outlined has been enunciated in India in a considerable literature on Rhetoric (*alaṁkāra*). It is true that this theory is mainly developed in connection with poetry, drama, dancing, and music, but it is immediately applicable to art of all kinds, much of its terminology employs the concept of color, and we have evidence that the theory was also in fact applied to painting. Accordingly, in what follows we have not hesitated to give an extended interpretation to terms primarily employed in connection with poetry, or rather literature (*kāvya*), considered as the type of art. The justification of art is then made with reference to use (*prayojana*) or value (*puruṣârtha*) by pointing out that it subserves the Four Purposes of Life, viz. Right Action (*dharma*), Pleasure (*kāma*), Wealth (*artha*), and Spiritual Freedom (*mokṣa*). Of these, the first three represent the proximate, the last the ultimate, ends of life; the work of art is determined (*prativihita*) in the same way, proximately with regard to immediate use, and ultimately with regard to aesthetic experience. Art is then defined as follows: VAKYAṀ RASÂTMAKAṀ KÁVYAM, that is, "ART IS EXPRESSION INFORMED BY IDEAL BEAUTY." Mere narration (*nirvāha, itihāsa*), bare utility, are not art, or are only art in a rudimentary sense. Nor has art as such a merely informative value confined to its explicit meaning (*vyutpatti*): only the man of little wit (*alpabuddhi*) can fail to recognize that art is by nature a wellspring of delight (*ānanda-*

niṣyanda), whatever may have been the occasion of its appearance. On the other hand, there cannot be imagined an art without meaning or use. The doctrine of art for art's sake is disposed of in a sentence quoted in the *Sāhitya Darpaṇa,* V, 1, Commentary: "All expressions [*vākya*], human or revealed, are directed to an end beyond themselves [*kārya-param*, 'another *factibile*']; or if not so determined [*atat-paratve*], are thereby comparable only to the utterances of a madman." Therefore, "let the purpose [*kṛtârthatā*] of skill [*vaidagdhya*] be attained," *Mālatīmādhava,* I, 32 f. Again, the distinction of art (controlled workmanship, things well and truly made) from Nature (functional expression, *sattva-bhāva*) is made as follows: "the work [*karma*] of the two hands is an otherwise-determined [*parastāt-prativihitā*] element of natural being [*bhūta-mātrā*]," *Kauṣītaki Upaniṣad,* III, 5.

In this theory of art, the most important term is RASA, rendered above "Ideal Beauty," but meaning literally "tincture" or essence, and generally translated in the present connection as "flavor"; aesthetic experience being described as the tasting of flavor (*rasâsvādana*) or simply as tasting (*svāda, āsvāda*), the taster as *rasika,* the work of art as *rasavat.* It should also be observed that the word *rasa* is used (1) relatively, in the plural, with reference to the various, usually eight or nine, emotional conditions which may constitute the burden of a given work, love (*śṛṅgāra-rasa*) being the most significant of these, and (2) absolutely, in the singular, with reference to the interior act of tasting flavor unparticularized. In the latter sense, which alone need be considered here, the idea of an aesthetic beauty to be tast*ed,* and knowable only in the activity of tast*ing,* is to be clearly distinguished from the relative beauties or lovelinesses of the separate parts of the work, or of the work itself considered merely as a surface, the appreciation of all which is a matter of taste (*ruci*) or predilection. The latter relative beauties will appear in the theme and aesthetic surfaces, in all that has to do with the proximate determination of the work to be done, its ordering to use; the formal beauty will be sensed in vitality and unity, design and rhythm, in no way depending on the nature of the theme, or its component parts. It is indeed very explicitly pointed out that any theme whatever, "lovely or unlovely, noble or vulgar, gracious or frightful, etc.," may become the vehicle of *rasa.*

The definition of aesthetic experience (*rasâsvādana*) given in the *Sāhitya Darpaṇa,* III, 2–3, is of such authority and value as to demand translation *in extenso;* we offer first, a very literal version with brief comment, then a slightly smoother rendering avoiding interruptions. Thus, (1) "Flavor (*rasaḥ*) is tasted (*āsvādyate*) by men having an innate knowledge of absolute values (*kaiścit-pramātṛbhiḥ*), in exaltation of the pure consciousness (*sattvôdrekāt*), as self-luminous (*svaprakāśaḥ*), in the mode at once of ecstasy and intellect (*ānanda-cin-mayaḥ*), void of contact with things knowable (*vedyântara-sparśa-śūnyaḥ*), twin brother to the tasting of Brahma (*brahmâsvāda-sahôdaraḥ*), whereof the life is a super-worldly lightning-flash (*lokôttara-camatkāra-prânaḥ*), as intrinsic aspect (*svâkāravat = svarūpavat*), in indivisibility (*abhin-natve*)"; and (2) "Pure aesthetic experience is theirs in whom the knowledge of ideal beauty is innate; it is known intuitively, in intellectual ecstasy without accompaniment of ideation, at the highest level of conscious being; born of one mother with the vision of God, its life is as it were a flash of blinding light of transmundane origin, impossible to analyze, and yet in the image of our very being."

Neither of the foregoing renderings embodies any foreign matter. On the other hand, only an extended series of alternative renderings would suffice to develop the full reference of the original terms. *Pramātṛ* (from the same root as *pramāṇa*, present also in English "meter") is *quis rationem artis intelligit;* here not as one instructed, but by nature. The notion of innate genius may be compared with Blake's "Man is born like a garden ready planted and sown," and "The knowledge of Ideal Beauty cannot be acquired, it is born with us." But it must be understood that from the Indian point of view, genius is not a fortuitous manifestation, but the necessary consequence of a rectification of the whole personality, accomplished in a previous condition of being; cf. the notion of an absolute *pramāṇa* natural to the Comprehensor, to the Buddha. The "exaltation of *sattva*" implies, of course, abstraction from extension, operation, local motion (*rajas*), and from indetermination or inertia (*tamas*). Aesthetic experience is a transformation not merely of feeling (as suggested by the word *aesthesis,* per se), but equally of understanding; cf. the state of "Deep Sleep," characterized by the expression *prajñāna-ghana-ānanda-mayi,* "a condensed understanding in the mode of ecstasy." The level of pure aesthetic experience is indeed that of the pure angelic understanding, proper to the Motionless Heaven, Brahmaloka. With "like a flash of lightning," cf. *Bṛhadāraṇyaka Upaniṣad,* II, 3, 6 and *Kena Upaniṣad,* 29, where the vision of Brahman is compared to a "sudden flash of lightning," or "What flashes in the lightning." The vision is our very Being, *Ding an Sich, svâkāra,* and like our Being, beyond our individually limited grasp (*grahaṇa*) or conception (*saṁkalpa*); "you cannot see the seer of seeing," *Bṛhadāraṇyaka Upaniṣad,* III, 4, 2.

In any case, "It is the spectator's own energy (*utsāha*) that is the cause of tasting, just as when children play with clay elephants"; the permanent mood (*sthāyi-bhāva*) is brought to life as *rasa* because of the spectator's own capacity for tasting, "not by the character or actions of the hero to be imitated (*anukārya*), nor by the deliberate ordering of the work to that end (*tatparatvataḥ*)." Those devoid of the required capacity or energy are no better than the wood or masonry of the gallery. Aesthetic experience is thus only accessible to those competent (*pramātṛ, rasika, sahṛdaya*). Competence depends "on purity or singleness (*sattva*) of heart and on an inner character (*antara-dharma*) or habit of obedience (*anuśīla*) tending to aversion of attention from external phenomena; this character and habit, not to be acquired by mere learning, but either innate or cultivated, depends on an ideal sensibility (*vāsanā*) and the faculty of self-identification (*yogyatā*) with the forms (*bhavana*) depicted (*varnanīya*)." Just as the original intuition arose from a self-identification of the artist with the appointed theme, so aesthetic experience, reproduction, arises from a self-identification of the spectator with the presented matter; criticism repeats the process of creation. An interesting case is that of the actor, or any artist, who must not be naturally moved by the passions he depicts, though he may obtain aesthetic experience from the spectacle of his own performance.

Notwithstanding that aesthetic experience is thus declared to be an inscrutable and uncaused spiritual activity, that is virtually ever-present and potentially realizable, but not possible to be realized unless and until all effective and mental barriers have been resolved, all knots of the heart undone, it is necessarily admitted that the experience arises in relation to some specific representation. The elements of this representation, the work of art itself, can be and are discussed by the Hindu rhetoricians at great length, and provide the material and much of the terminology of analysis and criticism. For present purposes it will suffice to present these constituents of the work of art in a brief form; but it must not be forgotten that here only is to be found the tangible (*grāhya*) matter of the work of art, all that can be explained and accounted for in it, and that this all includes precisely that a priori knowledge which the spectator must possess or come to possess before he can pretend to competence in the sense above defined. The elements of the work of art are, then:

(1) Determinants (*vibhāva*), viz. the physical stimulants to aesthetic reproduction, particularly the theme and its parts, the indications of time and place, and other apparatus of representation—the whole *factibile*. The operation of the Determinants takes place by the operation of an ideal-

sympathy (*sādhāraṇya*), a self-identification with the imagined situation.

(2) Consequents (*anubhāva*), the specific and conventional means of "registering" (*sūcanā*) emotional states, in particular gestures (*abhinaya*).

(3) Moods (*bhāva*), the conscious emotional states as represented in art. These include thirty-three Fugitive or Transient (*vyabhicāri*) Moods such as joy, agitation, impatience, etc., and eight or nine Permanent (*sthāyi*) Moods, the Erotic, Heroic, etc., which in turn are the vehicles of the specific *rasas* or emotional colorings. In any work, one of the Permanent Moods must constitute a master motif to which all the others are subordinate; for "the extended development of a transient emotion becomes an inhibition of *rasa*," or, as we should now express it, the work becomes sentimental, embarrassing rather than moving.

(4) The representation of involuntary physical reactions (*sattva-bhāva*), for example fainting.

All of these determinants and symbols are recognized collectively and indivisibly in aesthetic experience, the work of art being as such a unity; but they are recognized separately in subsequent analysis.

According to the related School of Manifestation (*Vyakti-vāda*) the essential or soul of poetry is called *dhvani*, "the reverberation of meaning arising by suggestion [*vyañjanā*]." In grammar and logic, a word or other symbol is held to have two powers only, those of denotation (*abhidhā*) and connotation (*lakṣaṇā*); for example *gopāla* is literally "cowherd," but constantly signifies Kṛṣṇa. The rhetoricians assume for a word or symbol a third power, that of suggestion (*vyañjanā*), the matter suggested, which we should call the real content of the work, being *dhvani*, with respect to either the theme (*vastu*), any metaphor or other ornament (*alaṁkāra*), or, what is more essential, one of the specific *rasas*. In other words, *abhidhā*, *lakṣaṇā*, and *vyañjanā* correspond to literal, allegorical, and anagogic significance. *Dhvani*, as overtone of meaning, is thus the immediate vehicle of single *rasa* and means to aesthetic experience. Included in *dhvani* is *tātparyārtha*, the meaning conveyed by the whole sentence or formula, as distinct from the mere sum of meanings of its separate parts. The School of Manifestation is so called because the perception (*pratīti*) of *rasa* is thought of simply as the manifestation of an inherent and already existing intuitive condition of the spirit, in the same sense that Enlightenment is virtually ever-present though not always realized. The *pratīti* of *rasa*, as it were, breaks through the enclosing walls (*varaṇa*, *āvaraṇa*) by which the soul, though predisposed by ideal sympathy (*sādhāraṇya*) and sensibility (*vāsanā*), is still immured and restricted from shining forth in its true character as the taster of *rasa* in an aesthetic experience which is as aforesaid the very twin brother of the experience of the unity of Brahman.

In the later and otherwise more synthetic scheme of the *Sāhitya Darpaṇa*, the *rasa* and *dhvani* theories are not quite so closely linked, *dhvani* being now not so much the soul of all poetry as characteristic of the superior sort of poetry in which what is suggested outweighs what is literally expressed.

For the sake of completeness there need only be mentioned two earlier theories in which Ornament or Figures (*alaṁkāra*) and Style or Composition (*rīti*) are regarded respectively as the essential elements in art. These theories, which have not held their own in India, may be compared to the minor European conceptions of art as dexterity, or as consisting merely of aesthetic surfaces which are significant only as sources of sensation. This last point of view can be maintained consistently in India only from the standpoint of the naive realism which underlies a strictly monastic prejudice against the world.

It remains to be pointed out that the *rasa* and *dhvani* theories are essentially metaphysical and Vedântic in method and conclusion, though they are expressed not so much in terms of the pure Vedânta of the Upaniṣads as in those of a later Vedânta combined with other systems, particularly the Yoga. The fully evolved Indian theory of beauty is in fact hardly to be dated before the tenth or eleventh century, though the doctrine of *rasa* is already clearly enunciated in Bharata's *Nāṭya Śastra*, which may be anterior to the fifth century and itself derives from still older sources.

In any case, the conception of the work of art as determined outwardly to use and inwardly to a delight of the reason; the view of its operation as not intelligibly causal, but by way of a destruction of the mental and affective barriers behind which the natural manifestation of the spirit is concealed; the necessity that the soul should be already prepared for this emancipation by an inborn or acquired sensibility; the requirement of self-identification with the ultimate theme, on the part of both artist and spectator, as prerequisite to visualization in the first instance and reproduction in the second; finally, the conception of ideal beauty as unconditioned by natural affections, indivisible, supersensual, and indistinguishable from the gnosis of God—all these characteristics of the theory demonstrate its logical connection with the predominant trends of Indian thought, and its natural place in the whole body of Indian philosophy.

Consequently, though it could not be argued that any aesthetic theory is explicitly set forth in the Upaniṣads, it will not surprise us to find that the ideas and terminology of the later aesthetic are there already recognizable. For example, in the *Bṛhadāraṇyaka Upaniṣad*, I, 4, 7, the world is said to be differentiated or known in plurality by, and only by, means of name and aspect, *nāmarūpa*, idea and image; ibid., III, 2, 3, and 5, "Voice [*vāc*] is an apprehender [*graha*]; it is seized by the idea [*nāma*] as an over-apprehender, then indeed by voice [*vāc*] one utters thoughts [*nāmāni*]," and similarly "Sight [*cakṣu*] is an apprehender; it is seized by aspect [*rūpa*] as an over-apprehender, then indeed by the eye [*cakṣu*] one sees things [*rūpāṇi*]." Further, ibid., III, 9, 20, "on the heart [*hṛdaya*] are aspects [*rūpāṇi*] based," and similarly in the case of speech. As to the heart, "it is the same as Prajāpati, it is Brahman," ibid., V, 3, and "other than that Imperishable, there is none that (really) sees," ibid., III, 8, 11. Actual objects (*rūpāṇi*) seen in space are really seen not as such, but only as colored areas, the concept of space being altogether mental and conventional.

The Indian theory, in origins and formulation, seems at first sight to be *sui generis*. But merely because of the specific idiomatic and mythical form in which it finds expression, it need not be thought of as otherwise than universal. It does not in fact differ from what is implicit in the Far Eastern view of art, or on the other hand in any essentials from the scholastic Christian point of view, or what is asserted in the aphorisms of Blake; it does differ essentially from the modern nonintellectual interpretations of art as sensation. What are probably the most significant elements in the Asiatic theory are the views (1) that aesthetic experience is an ecstasy in itself inscrutable, but insofar as it can be defined, a delight of the reason, and (2) that the work of art itself, which serves as the stimulus to the release of the spirit from all inhibitions of vision, can only come into being and have being as a thing ordered to specific ends. Heaven and Earth are united in the analogy (*sādṛśya*, etc.) of art, which is an ordering of sensation to intelligibility and tends toward an ultimate perfection in which the seer perceives all things imaged in himself.

AMERICA AND ART *

Louis Kronenberger

The compelling fact about art in America is that it is not
organic. It has almost no share in shaping our life; it offers,
rather, compensation for the shapelessness. And just because
we prescribe a certain amount of art for ourselves as a kind
of corrective—being "deficient" in art as we might be in
calcium or iron—we regard it less as ordinary nourishment
than as a tonic, something we gulp rather than sip, regard
with esteem and yet suspicion, and either require to be made
up with a pleasant taste or exult in because it tastes unpleasant. The American feeling, or lack of feeling, for art
has been immemorially easy to satirize, whether at the one
extreme of Babbittry or at the other of Bohemia. All the same,
for whatever reasons, such feeling has long been part of the
American character—which is to say that the American bent,
the American genius, has honestly moved in other directions.
Like the Romans and the Germans, we are not an artistic
people. This may be partly the result of our so long being
able to reach out, rather than having to turn inward; of our
possessing a vast continent to traverse, subdue, explore, develop, grow rich on, so that there was no husbanding or skilled
handling of resources, no modifying what we started with or
were saddled with into something gracious and expressive. A
race, like an individual, develops a style in part through
what it has uniquely, in part through what it has too little of.
French prose owes its dry, neat lucidity to the same things
that produced a general lack of magic in French poetry;
French women owe their chic, I would think, to their general
lack of girlish beauty. Americans have suffered from over-
abundance—from not needing to substitute art for nature,
form for substance, method for materials. At the very point
where a patina might begin to appear, or mellowness to suffuse, we have abandoned what we made for something
newer, brisker, shinier; and with each such act we have
become a little less "artistic" in our approach. But of course
there is more to it than that. An artistic people—the French,
the Chinese, the ancient Greeks—is one whose necessities are
made the comelier by its dreams, but whose dreaming is
equally controlled by its necessities: the two are integrated,

* [From *Company Manners*, by Louis Kronenberger. Copyright
1951-1953-1954; used by special permission of the publishers,
The Bobbs-Merrill Company, Inc.]

are never so harshly at odds that the dreaming must serve as a lurid compensation. With an artistic people a kind of good sense regulates both its acquisitive side and its aspiring one; and from deprecating excess on a large scale, it eventually does so in small ways as well. Hence the design of existence stands forth more powerfully than the décor; and because design, unlike décor, affects a whole society, the national traits and instincts and responses get beyond cost or size or class, and equally characterize the rich and the poor, the cultivated and the unlettered. There is always a sense of bone structure about an artistic people—think of the Spaniards—a touch of severity, of economy. There is, I suppose, something rather classic than romantic—a sense of the ancestor as well as the individual.

An artistic people need not (and very likely will not) be profoundly poetic or mystical, as the English and the Germans are. It is plainly because the English and the Germans lead such double lives, because one extreme must almost atone for the other, because dreaming grows out of repressions or helps to stamp out reality, that two nations so given to vulgar instincts and material aims should be capable of such splendid intensities—intensities which, for all that, do constitute excesses. And we too, as a people, are driven to compensate; are so excessively aspiring for being so excessively acquisitive; come back to God through guilt or satiety; go on binges with Beauty because it is no part of our daily life— and we somehow think the extent of the undertaking will make up for the quality. Our magnates are always giving away millions not too shiningly acquired; our aging plutocrats leave a spendthrift order for art like the flashy sports who buy their women ten dozen American Beauty roses. Nothing amuses or appalls us more than a gangster's funeral with its carloads of flowers and wreaths; and nothing teaches us less. The gangster's funeral is actually the model for Broadway's supermusicals, for the murals on civic architecture, for Florida's luxury resorts; and the gangster's funeral is itself a late development, the descendant of the Newport "cottage" —the only difference being that at Newport conspicuous waste was confined to living, where in Chicago it specialized in death.

But it is not just the excesses born of wealth that have failed to make us an artistic people. After all, corsairs and conquistadors are the ancestors of *most* cultures; and French châteaux and Italian *palazzi* of even the best periods stress sheer display quite as much as they stress beauty. We may just come near enough to being an artistic people to explain why we *are* not and perhaps *cannot be* one. We are an inventive and adaptive people; and thus our whole effort, our

whole genius, is to modify rather than mold, to make more efficient rather than more expressive. We are dedicated to
improvement—to improving our minds and our mousetraps,
our inventions and our diets. We are so dedicated to improvement that we neither ask nor care whether a thing needs
to be improved, is able to be improved, or, qualifying as an
improvement, will necessarily seem a benefit. We never seem
to wonder whether we may not be complicating things by
simplifying them, or making them useless by so constantly
making them over. But the ability to invent, the desire to
improve, may partly spring from our having got so much later
a start than other civilizations—from our being at a log-cabin
and homespun stage when Europe had long achieved silks
and marble—and then lagging for so long behind them. We
first were made competitive from a sense of our marked in-
feriority to others; we then became, from our sense of our
natural wealth and resources, competitive among ourselves;
and we are now, of course, inventive *because* we are competitive: last year's model must be disparaged so that this
year's model can be sold. But no matter how genuine was
the original impulse, or how sheerly commercial it is today,
inventiveness has become ingrained in our practice, and our
source of constant pride; and even among the best of us—
unless we are extremely vigilant—it is now an influence on our
taste. Abroad, avant-gardism expressed the crying need among
old cultures for new forms and feelings; here, we often seem
to be breaking with tradition before establishing it; here,
experiment has a gadget air, a will-to-invent about it, as
often as a sense of rebellion or release.

This gadget aspect crops up everywhere, in the most unexpected places. Thus our highbrow criticism is constantly
inventing and amending a vocabulary—one that somehow will
seem a special, up-to-the-minute possession for critics, exactly
as the latest models in cars or television sets will seem a
special, up-to-the-minute possession of prosperous businessmen. The actual character, too, of our present-day literary
jargon—so much of it psychiatric and sociological—is that of a
profoundly inartistic, indeed, an aesthetically quite barbarous,
yet irrepressibly inventive people. Take just one simple example. In the entire language I doubt whether there exists
an uglier word, or one less needed for the use it has been
put to, than the word *sensitivity*. One special and particular
meaning could be allowed it—the sensitivity, let us say, of a
photographic plate to light. But even among critics with a
historical sense and a cultivated ear, it has almost completely
ousted the two words that for centuries so happily shouldered,
and so neatly divided, the burden: *sensibility* and *sensitive-
ness*. But the whole highbrow vocabulary, the whole need for

new spring-and-fall models in literary language—*subsume* one year, *mystique* the next, *exfoliate* the year after—exhibits our national need to adapt and amend and apply at any cost, with no great concern for the urgency, and perhaps even less for the rightness, of the words themselves. And even more indicative than their original "coinage" is the indecent speed with which they become almost unbearable clichés; even more, also, than their coinage itself is the fact that they are so uniformly pretentious, so very rarely picturesque. If only critics would read Dr. Johnson for his wisdom and not for his unhappier choices in words. We are inartistic, indeed, in our very approach to art.

We have never as a people regarded art as something to live with, to freely delight in, to call by its first name. Perhaps this derives from something beyond an inventive streak that keeps us restless, or an awe that makes us uncomfortable: perhaps had we had more opportunity to live with art, we might have acquired a more relaxed attitude toward it. It has never been on our doorstep; we have had to go in search of it, go doubly in search—as much to discover what it is as where it is. The journeys have had a little of the air of pilgrimages; the works of art, a great deal of the sanctity of shrines. The whole burden of our criticism, our constant cultural plaint, is how scant, and impure, and imperfect, and isolated, art in America has been—which, inevitably, has conditioned our approach to it. We insist on strong, emphatic, unmistakable reactions; we either swoon or snub, analyze at tedious length or dismiss with a mere wave of the hand. We go at art, in other words, not like casual, cultivated shoppers, but like a race of antique-shop dealers for whom everything is either magnificently authentic or the merest fake; and the result—though of course there are other reasons, too—is that we cannot take art in our stride. So belated and uneasy an approach has made us about art what Prohibition made my whole generation about wine: either frank, unblushing ignoramuses or comically solemn snobs. Different levels of Americans reveal very different attitudes toward art; but what is perhaps most significant is that they all reveal one marked kind of attitude or another. They either tend to hold back lest they commit howlers; or to go into raptures lest they be taken for clods; or to pooh-pooh the whole business lest they seem longhaired and sissified; or to purse their lips and utter pronunciamentos lest they seem just vulgarly susceptible or humanly responsive.

If classifying them as fence-straddlers or as poseurs or as philistines or as prigs is to simplify and even travesty the matter, it may yet help account for the fact that we are not a people for whom, at any level, art is just a natural and congenial aspect of existence. The very "uselessness" of it— the fact that art, like virtue, is its own reward; again, the very magic of it—the fact that it cannot be reduced to a formula or equation; the utter arrogance of it—the fact that money cannot buy it nor American salesmanship or elbow grease achieve it: these are, at the very outset, reasons for mystification and distrust. *Its* kind of arrogance, of refusal to be won on extrinsic terms—as of a high-mettled, beautiful girl whom no suitor can win on the strength of his bank account, his family background, or his sober, industrious habits—seems improper, even unethical, to a people who can respect putting a high price on something, who can approve and even enjoy a hard tussle till things are won, but who can no more understand than they can approve that something is beyond negotiations, is just not to be bought. Art to their minds is not a high-mettled girl, but an extremely unreasonable woman. Art's kind of magic again—art's refusal to be achieved through laboratory methods, through getting up charts or symposiums or sales conferences, through looking at smears under the microscope—its magic seems behind the times, almost downright retarded, to a people with a genius for the synthetic. Art's kind of uselessness, finally—its non-vitamin-giving health, its non-pep-you-up modes of pleasure, its non-materialistic enrichment—quite genuinely confuses a people who have been educated to have something to show for their efforts, if only a title or a medal or a diploma. Art, for most Americans, is a very queer fish—it can't be reasoned with, it can't be bribed, it can't be doped out or duplicated; above all, it can't be cashed in on.

Someone, Max Beerbohm perhaps, once defined a Bohemian as a person who uses things for what they're not intended—a window drapery, let us say, for a ball dress, or a goldfish bowl for a soup tureen. And this just a little defines the American sense of the artistic. We must endow everything with a new twist, an added value, an extra function. We literally cannot let well enough alone; hence we very often make it worse—and never more, perhaps, than when we also make it better. The new element, the new effect, the new use to which an art form is put, very often has to do with achieving something more tractable or palatable or painless or time- or labor-saving; with offering, at the very least, old wine in new bottles, and much more to our satisfaction, old wine in plastic containers or ice cream cones. Thus we have Somerset Maugham re-edit and abridge the classics; we get a present-day version of Buckingham's *The Rehearsal*, a Negro *Juno and the Paycock*, a *Cherry Orchard* laid in Mississippi; we have Mr. Orson Welles telescoping five of Shakespeare's plays into one; we have something written for the piano performed on the violin, something intended for men taken over by women. We're not, to be sure, the only nation that does such things, but I think we're the only nation that feels a compulsive urge to do them. Where the Germans have a particular genius for ersatz, for substitutions, we have one for new twists and gimmicks, new mixtures and combinations. We simply *have* to tamper: if we don't cut the words, we must add to the music; if we don't change the story, we must shift the locale. Nowhere else, surely, can there be such a compulsion to make plays out of books, musicals out of plays, *Aida*'s into *My Darlin' Aida*'s; to insert scenes, delete characters, include commentators; to turn gas stations into cathedrals, or churches into dance halls. Out of Plato and Berkeley we get Transcendentalism; out of Transcendentalism we concoct Christian Science; and then, almost immediately, Jewish Science out of Christian. Many nations have discovered the devil in dancing, but we are perhaps the first to find God through calisthenics.

And no doubt we create, from all this, the illusion that we are notably experimental in the arts, ever seeking new forms, contriving new functions, establishing new perspectives. But, even ignoring the material or commercial side of it all, our contrivance of so many artful blends and twists and variants is really our avoidance of art itself, exactly as our craving for sensations argues a distaste or fear of experiences. Our whole artistic effort, if it does not parallel, at least involves our genius for concocting the mixed drink and for putting the packaging ahead of the product. The result— from which almost all of us suffer more than we realize—is a kind of vulgarization, and one that can take place at high levels no less than at low ones. Our stressing significance in art rather than intensity, our present search for symbolic figures and concealed meanings and multiple levels: isn't this part of our compulsion to introduce something new, add something extra, offer something unprecedented? Does it not bear witness, also, to our intellectual ingenuity rather than our aesthetic responsiveness? Hasn't the new multi-level *Pierre* or *Confidence Man* a kinship with the new split-level house, or the concealed meanings with the concealed plumbing, or the indirect approach with the indirect lighting, or the taste for knotty problems with the taste for knotty pine? I do not think I am being anti-intellectual when I say that in America the intellect itself is being overused and misused in the world of art, where—after all—the most thoughtful elucidation avails nothing without the right, pure, instinctive response; for in art the reverse of Wordsworth's saying is also true and immensely important: in art, there are tears that do often lie too deep for thoughts.

Given our inventiveness, such endless and manifold vulgarization is inevitable. No race can make an idea go farther than we can. Wet get the last ounce of derivable income from it; we carry it, indeed, to distances that virtually obscure the original starting point. From the classic sandwich made with bread we evolve the triple-decker made with ice cream; from the first motel, that could hardly have competed with a bathhouse, we are now contriving structures that will outdo—if not soon outmode—the Ritz. And quite beyond our double-barreled desire to make things profitable as well as attractive, all this technical skill and inventive cleverness must in the end conspire as much against our creative instincts as against our artistic ones. A nation that can so marvelously concoct must less and less feel any need to create. We are developing a genius for rewrite at the expense of one for writing, for stage directors who shall do the work of dramatists, for orchestrators who shall do the work of composers. Everything today must carefully and exactly conform to public taste, yet offer a new wrinkle into the bargain—we insist on what might be called a kind of Murphy-bed of Procrustes.

The effect of this vulgarization is almost sure to be pervasive and permanent. There is something disarming, often indeed unnoticeable, about vulgarization itself. Sheer vulgarity quickly stands self-condemned, hence tends quickly to correct itself. Or where it persists—as representing something congenial to a particular social milieu or human type—it is so blatant as to isolate itself and proclaim its own quarantine. So long as what is "wrong" can be quickly spotted, and thereafter vividly contrasted with what is "right," whether or not it continues to exist, it can no longer triumph. The most insidious aspect of vulgarity, I would think, concerns not those to whom its appeal is obvious and immediate, but those, rather, whom it gradually and imperceptibly manages to win over, those who in the beginning are partly superior to it and who only by habituation sink to its level. A vulgarity that can thus contaminate won't often, it seems clear, be of a primitive or glaring sort; it will be, rather, a worm in the apple, a sort of Greek bearing gifts. In the world of art, such vulgarity may boast that it does far more good than it does harm, that it makes many people respond to what they might otherwise pass by. I'm not speaking of the out-and-out popularization, but rather of such things as the movie version of *Henry V* or Stokowski's arrangements of Bach—of things offered under the auspices of culture and aimed at reasonably cultured people. This form of vulgarization will by no means altogether misrepresent or even too greatly discolor. And though a severe taste may resist or reject it at once, a fairly sensitive taste—what I suppose is most conveniently called a middlebrow taste that, if left alone, might come to appreciate Bach or Shakespeare "neat"—will not resist or reject the adulteration, will soon, in fact, come to prefer and eventually to require it.

Vulgarization isn't always a matter of making things pleasanter to the taste, or easier to swallow; it can also consist—which can constitute the highbrow maneuver—in making them more difficult and abstruse, rather resembling the homely girl who goes out of her way to accentuate her homeliness. It is as possible to defeat the primary end of art, the sense of beauty, by minimizing it as by roughing it up. Short cuts represent one kind of vulgarization, labyrinths represent another. The highbrow procedure, if we were to raid the vocabulary that accompanies it, might be called countervulgarization. It constitutes, in any case, no cure or corrective for the middlebrow ailment, but rather a different kind of disease; and though its very lack of cheap allure will cause it to render art far less of a disservice than the rouge-and-syrup process, it is yet equally a barrier to our becoming an artistic people. What with art being something, on the one side, that slides smoothly down our gullets and, on the other, something to be chewed long after any flavor is left, we can seldom any longer, I think, get the fine, sharp, vivid, simple first experience of art that must be the preliminary to any more complex one. Something is always doused over it or drained out of it, hiding the flavor or heightening it, removing gristle or adding lumps; or the thought or look of the thing, before we even bite into it, conditions us. A man can no longer even read, let us say, the "Ode to a Nightingale" without the slightly guilty or, at any rate, self-conscious feeling that it is "romantic poetry."

As a result of the vulgarizing effort to make things palatable, and of a countervulgarization that renders things parched, there is being beggared out of existence a high yet workable cultural ideal, a climate in which a *sense* of art can flourish. And it seems to me that the lack of a proper climate for art is a much more serious shortcoming in America than the actual number of works of art themselves. Culture—in the old-fashioned, well-rounded sense of something civilized and civilizing alike—has not simply failed as a reality in America, but is fast fading as an ideal. Such a culture stands in relation to formal education as good wine to the grape: it is a fermentation, a mellowing, a very special and at the same time wholly characterizing element; and it permeates society in terms of its sensibilities no less than its art. One can, of course, all too easily exalt such a culture as a way of disparaging much that is essential and even healthful in modern life; and one can sigh for it on a sentimental basis, in standpat terms.

All the same, any way of life that lacks its best qualities can scarcely be looked upon as cultivated at all; at any rate, no amount of education or knowledge or skill can begin to mean the same thing. And actually the climate I desiderate is no more than a salubrious, breeze-swept temperate zone; it is not forbidding, nor oppressively patrician, nor strenuously democratic. A cool, dry judgment is mingled there with gusto and generous appreciation; the people there are no more mired in the past than running wild in the present; its tone is altogether urbane without being even faintly genteel; it boasts neither untouchables nor sacred cows; it displays a constant corrective irony and perhaps not overmuch virtue; and everyone there is just sufficiently wrongheaded and prejudiced and inconsistent to be attractively human.

2

Being a curiously inartistic and ingenious people; being, also, too serious-minded to look on pleasure bare, and so commercialized as to put a price tag on Beauty, we approach art by many routes, but never by the most direct. Most frequently vulgarization sets in, the point of the story is sacrificed to the plot, Shakespeare is streamlined or Chekhov fattened up. Among the overserious there is often a process of dehydration, with only such fluid retained as has medicinal properties; or the work of art is converted from thoroughbred to packhorse and forced to stagger under a heavy sociological and psychiatric load.

Although what frankly seem to me the most delightful and rewarding qualities of art are precisely these that are slighted in many highbrow ranks today, I must admit that it is not done altogether without reason. The slighting constitutes a form of dissociation, even of protest. The sight of panders everywhere must inevitably call forth the prig; the sight of art being everywhere rouged and perfumed, groomed and tricked out for harlotry, must inspire a violent contrary wish—a wish to have art, like an Orthodox Jewish bride, shorn of her locks and made as unalluring as possible. Middlebrow adulteration, its slight softening of every texture, its faint sweetening of every taste, have clearly had a hand in creating the current highbrow distrust of charms and graces. This isn't to say there need be an abundance of such qualities or that, in an age like ours, there can be. In this unquiet age, an age not even of scars but of outright wounds, clearly very little that is charming or delightful will seem central or germane. Yet though there is truth in such a statement, there is also cant. It is perhaps not necessary to dance on the edge of volcanoes; but need one ignore, or even disapprove of, the sunset because the sky may soon grow dark with bomber planes? Again, is shaving off the hair an answer to overrouging the cheeks, or a desert the corrective to a swamp? Even so, one might agree that one kind of excess tends, not unprofitably, to breed another—did not highbrow criticism, in the very act of professing to probe the tensions of contemporary life, seem so pedagogically remote from them. Art is not something marketable but neither is it something mummified; and indeed, if it is not chiefly and most palpably a form of transcendence and release, pray then what is? If the impress of style, the vivid air of distinction, the artist's ability to be uniquely expressive and intense—if these do not invite, do not indeed impose, some immediate, electrical response, can the result—however rich in cerebral or moral mineral matter—really have much to do with art itself?

I was not surprised, reading an Inquiring Reporter column on "What Is Charm?" to find a sculptor identifying charm with the prettier examples of eighteenth-century painting. It was to be assumed that charm's status would be relatively low, its character rigorously limited; that it would be equated with Sir Joshua Reynolds's children or, by extension, with Sir James M. Barrie's grownups; that it would at most signify Watteau and Fragonard, minuets and romantic ballets, Hans Andersen or Charles Lamb. No doubt the word itself has acquired vapid and even repellent connotations; and plainly writers who spray charm about without discretion are like women who mistreat an atomizer. Moreover, charm can be a strong ally of gentility and a quite conscienceless weapon of fraud: we usually do right, I think, to ask to see its credentials. But that is very far from trying to have it deported; and to suggest that, because many writers misuse charm, there is no virtue to fragrance is to come closer, I would think, to the gospel of unyielding naturalism than to any goal of truth. Ignoring such obvious charmers as Poulenc or Dufy or Walter de la Mare, if contemporary artists so unlike as Picasso, E. E. Cummings, and Marianne Moore haven't, among other things, a very decided charm, what have they? Art, today, sometimes seems in danger of acquiring all the vices of science without any of the virtues. What with being anthropology's fieldworker and psychiatry's receptionist, art is quite prevented from cultivating its own garden.

Charm is by now too ambiguous, too merely decorative a word to be made the symbol of my own dissatisfaction. But it is clear that all the old, traditional, taken-for-granted "surface" qualities of art—distinction, fragrance, elegance, gaiety, style: those things for which we prize a Mendelssohn or a Vermeer, a Tennyson or a Congreve—such qualities, it is clear, are being slighted or ignored. No doubt *The Tempest* can be profitably viewed as something more than a masque; but to interpret it as something quite other, to regard it as principally a study in expiation, seems to me to make Shakespeare very much of an age—and an age, moreover, not his own. Possibly we are falling into the shallowness of despising the "shallow." He was the mightiest of puritans no less than of philistines who first insisted that beauty is only skin deep. Depth, and its stepdaughter Complexity, and its handmaiden Symbolism, are so much revered today, so much courted and curtsied to, as almost to obscure the fact of exactly what we mean by them, or whether—on the terms set—they aren't properly associated with philosophy rather than art. Perhaps the greatest of all our critics remarked that "poetry gives most pleasure when only generally and not perfectly understood," and he offered it as a principle to honor, not as a puzzle to resent. But so pressing now has become the critical obligation to explain or reinterpret that it is almost mandatory to pitch on something either obscure enough to need explaining or misunderstood enough by all previous critics to need to be straightened out. And since no one can burrow deep where the author happens to be shallow, we must make canyons out of moleholes; we must everywhere find size and significance, those idols so much less of art than of America; and more and more our criticism suggests the tread of elephants approaching a temple.

Given our feeble artistic sense, the whole present tendency isn't too hard to grasp. Anything journalistic must be outlawed—which could be a virtue; but outlawed in terms of the pedagogical, which is almost always a vice. Everywhere people reappraise some simple classic for the small ingenious theory that isn't worth the paper that is written on it. All too frequently the creative is turned into the intellectual, soaring is replaced by delving; while art, which has always constituted the highest and noblest form of release, is more and more tinged with something so gnawing and anxious as to seem more like remorse. But surely one very great characteristic of any inherently artistic people is a sense of play—play of mind, most of all, not mere prankishness—and a natural sense of irony. The reigning current mood has quite ousted all sense of play and exhibits no working sense of irony. To be sure, irony is a much approved and discussed and dissected quality in today's approach to literature, and wherever possible, and perhaps sometimes where not, critics isolate and decipher it; but it doesn't seem very contagious.

Mr. Richard Chase, in his recent book on Emily Dickinson, deplores what he calls the rococo element in her poetry—the minor, dainty, toylike, *bibelot* aspect. And in anyone who at her best is so deeply imaginative and intense an artist as

Emily Dickinson, the persistence of this merely whimsical and fanciful streak causes real injury, becomes a real misfortune. We could similarly wish that the English Metaphysicals had indulged in much fewer conceits, or that Sterne, or even Shakespeare himself—but I needn't dig for other examples. Yet where the superior artist is harmed by not rising above what we may call, with Mr. Chase, the rococo, a nation is very often harmed by not reaching up to it. The artist can dispense with the small forms of beauty, but the public cannot. The artist can function largely in a world of his own making—too much culture is perhaps even "weakening" for genius, and beautiful material objects may in a sense be the enemy of beauty. But nonartists, noncreative people, the world at large, need the atmosphere, the ornaments, the décor of culture. A predominantly *bibelot*-like culture could only, of course, be frivolous, dilettantish, effeminate. But a purely functional, no-nonsense, always-abreast-of-the-times culture, where in one's bookcase Toynbee leans only on Schweitzer and Schweitzer leans only on Freud—does this bespeak anything temperamental or personal, or is it only a part of the times? It's not a question of Old Guard and avant-garde, or whether a Canaletto print does more for a home than a Mexican primitive, or oldish things made of mahogany more than brand-new things made of metal, but whether there are not amenities and graces of the spirit; whether there are not cultures, as well as cups, that cheer. I don't contend that Jung or Margaret Mead or Frank Lloyd Wright aren't more central to our time than Osvald Sirén or Sir Charles Singer; or that in order to be cultured, or well adjusted, or happy, one need be able to distinguish R. L. from G. B. Hobson, A. W. from A. F. Pollard, Oliver from André Simon, Vincent from Gertrude, or Gertrude from T. E., or T. E. from W. W., or W. W. from W. J., or W. J. from D. H. Lawrence. But for every ten educated people who have read Margaret Mead, is there one who knows which Hobson was the great authority on bindings and which on Chinese art?

Much of our own antirococoism stems, I think, from something puritan in us. We are only given to a kind of love of the graces, a feeling for the charming in culture, when the wind is blowing from Europe; and it hasn't blown steadily from there since the 1920's. The twenties, of course, have latterly been as much romanticized as they were formerly run down. The mood of the twenties was made up of many things—not least, of that sense of promise in life, and of profusion in literature, that made us emotionally both spendthrift and carefree. But upstart and disordered and excessive though the twenties were, they were in impulse genuinely antibourgeois, antipuritan, antipedagogical: they reacted to

the creative, they relished the creative, they aspired passion-
ately to create. We lacked, then, the measure and control, the
ability to select, delete, hew to the line, that constitute an
artistic people; but we had, at any rate, the capacity to
absorb and participate, to feel release and indulge in appreciation. We lacked the discipline, but we had the positive
qualities that needed disciplining. The mood of the twenties
had to pass, Depression or not; while, granted the Depression,
the mood of the thirties had to be what it was. But the en-
during significance of the thirties is less the purpose and
propaganda that writers put into their work than the high
spirits they took out of it. For the propaganda has been long
discredited, but the joyousness has never been restored.

The present age is in the strong grip of cultural authori-
tarianism and of the most dogmatic kind. For great natural
cultural lawgivers of Dr. Johnson's type there is much to be
said, though even here "there is much to be said on both
sides." And of course today there are not only all those who
would legislate and lead, there are all the many more who
hunger to be led, who crave to cry "Master." Lionel Trilling
has rather chided E. M. Forster—in an age so generally con-
trariwise—for his "refusal to be great." One knows what Mr.
Trilling means, one knows what is valid in what he means—
whether with Forster specifically or with intellectuals and
artists in general. A "refusal to be great" can mask a certain
evasion of moral responsibility, of final decisions and alle-
giances. It can reflect too a certain self-consciousness, on the
refuser's part, that is mere vanity; it can constitute a special,
perhaps quite extreme, form of egoism. And Forster himself
seems at times not merely casual but playful and frivolous.
All the same, whatever personal shortcomings or debatable
human traits may lodge with this attitude, it yet seems the
backbone of a very notable, a very much honored, tradition—
of that indeed very great tradition of skeptical humanism.
It is a tradition that having said *Thus I think* next always asks
What do I know?, a tradition that forces the very bringer of
light to assay the right he brings as sharply as the darkness he
dispels. In the history of thought and culture the dark nights
have perhaps in some ways cost mankind less grief than the
false dawns; the prison houses in which hope persists, less
grief than the Promised Lands where hope expires. Skeptical
humanism is no enemy of positive values or even of resolute
action; but men bred to that tradition will continue to feel
that their values must be exhibited, warts and all, and must
in the end be made to speak for themselves. About any other
method, including the acceptance of greatness, there is always
at least a touch of *force majeure* and perhaps even a drop or
two of patent medicine. Today anyone's refusal to be great

seems the more formulated for being so out of line with pre-vailing thought. The Great Men, the Strong Men, of liter-ature today are men of fierce passions and strong convictions, men playing the role of prophet, teacher, moralist, martyr, saint, sinner, seer—the Melvilles, Nietzsches, Kierkegaards, the Gides, Dostoevskys, D. H. Lawrences. Some of these men are as individual, one or two are now and then as skepti-cal, as Forster; but the real point is, to what degree have they encouraged independence, individualism, skepticism, the relaxed will, in others?

If only because the tide has been running strong against the old humanist attitude, the Forsters with their relaxed wills and their refusals to be great must take on a special value. The tradition of Socrates, of Montaigne and Erasmus, of Hume, and of the Enlightenment, all the more because it never flourishes *below* the cultured classes, is immensely vital to them, is what we might almost call their claim to culture. It seems to me an absolutely essential tradition for societies and nations in needs of something equable as well as affirmative, in need of lasting daylight as well as glowing dawns. It is a tradition that has never really established itself in America—a corollary, I think, to our being an inartistic people; it is a tradition, at any rate, at variance with a people who love the *idea* of greatness, who love panaceas, and formulas, and solutions, and absolutions, and reassuring answers. To a nation that worships God and Mammon both there must be something profoundly uncongenial in an at-titude that blindly worships nothing. From the failure of the humanist tradition to participate fully or to act decisively, civilization may perhaps crumble or perish at the hands of barbarians. But unless the humanist tradition itself in some form survives, there can really be no civilization at all.

II
STYLE: FORM-and-CONTENT
INTRODUCTION

In an essay on the history of modern German aesthetics,[*] Professor Ernest K. Mundt has pointed out that Immanuel Kant was the forefather of theories that separate "form" from "content." For a century and a half, Kant's interpretation of Intellectualism and Sensationism has had the following effects: his category of (1) Desire has been used for such theories of sensualism and empathy as Vischer's, Lipps', and Worringer's; his category of (2) Pleasure and Displeasure has led to the formalism and "pure visibility" of Herbart, Zimmermann, Fiedler, Hildebrand, and Wölfflin; his category of (3) Knowledge has yielded theories of idealism that are currently maintained in terms of iconology by Panofsky. The writings of Alois Riegl may have acted as a catalytic agent among the twentieth-century German aestheticians, but—seconded only by Nietzsche's division of the arts into those having Dionysian and those having Apollonian characteristics—Kant's separation of form from subject matter is the primary principle for or against which most theories of aesthetics have been written since his day, in England, France, and Italy, as well as in Germany.

In his interpretation of the concept of style, Meyer Schapiro, dean of American art historians, offers an alternative position to this division between form and content. Approaching style in the context of its broad usefulness for cultural history, Professor Schapiro points out that although there is no agreement concerning typologies of style, "the description of a style refers to three aspects of art: form elements or motives, form relationships, and qualities (including an over-all quality which we may call the 'expression')." The results of such analyses have been the movements toward correlating form and content—with each other, and with a variety of other factors. In the course of his encyclopedic study, Professor Schapiro casts revealing light on a number of theories of styles, such as the organic, cyclical, polar, material, and dominant-personality, and on efforts to correlate the style patterns of a given art with those of other arts of the same time-place, with a given social structure, or with a cultural group. The scope of his study extends to the farthest reaches of a supremely curious and erudite mind, and his

[*] See Bibliography.

generalizations are as sound as his insights are illuminating. "Not the content as such," he writes, "but the content as part of a dominant set of beliefs, ideas, and interests, supported by institutions and the forms of everyday life, shapes the common style."

By contrast with the great inclusiveness of Schapiro's essay, the following two selections—E. H. Gombrich's sketch for a theory of the *roots* of artistic form,* and Ortega y Gasset's notes on "point of view" in the arts—will seem considerably limited or specialized; but each one in its way is an excellent and important study.

Gombrich suggests that form, as one aspect of style, should be conceived, not in terms of reference to something else (representation) or by degree of differentiation from a model (abstraction), but as a symbolic *substitute* for a specific function. "An 'image,'" he writes, "is not an imitation of an object's external form [shape] but an imitation of certain privileged or relevant aspects . . . certain privileged motifs in our world." And such a privilege is relevant to a social system of values and uses.

Ortega y Gasset is directly concerned with such systems and their effects. He deals with "point of view in the arts," as both a literal and a metaphoric expression, in order to show that the conceptual point of view conditions the optical point of view by way of the psychology of attention, interest, and understanding. In effect, he is saying that there are appearances which are optically privileged for certain theoretical reasons, a statement comparable to Gombrich's ideas that there are appearances privileged for certain functional reasons. In the end, Ortega tries to draw a parallel between certain styles in painting and the styles of philosophy contemporary with them.

It is a pleasure to point out that each of these three thinkers, whose writings—clear, concise, and charming—make up this section on style, is himself a masterful prose stylist.

* Many of the topics of this essay are extensively developed in the author's recent book *Art and Illusion: A Study in the Psychology of Pictorial Representation* (New York: Pantheon Books, 1960).

STYLE *

Meyer Schapiro

By style is meant the constant form—and sometimes the constant elements, qualities, and expression—in the art of an individual or a group. The term is also applied to the whole activity of an individual or society, as in speaking of a "life-style" or the "style of a civilization."

For the archaeologist, style is exemplified in a motive or pattern, or in some directly grasped quality of the work of art, which helps him to localize and date the work and to establish connections between groups of works or between cultures. Style here is a symptomatic trait, like the nonaesthetic features of an artifact. It is studied more often as a diagnostic means than for its own sake as an important constituent of culture. For dealing with style, the archaeologist has relatively few aesthetic and physiognomic terms.

To the historian of art, style is an essential object of investigation. He studies its inner correspondences, its life-history, and the problems of its formation and change. He, too, uses style as a criterion of the date and place of origin of works, and as a means of tracing relationships between schools of art. But the style is, above all, a system of forms with a quality and a meaningful expression through which the personality of the artist and the broad outlook of a group are visible. It is also a vehicle of expression within the group, communicating and fixing certain values of religious, social, and moral life through the emotional suggestiveness of forms. It is, besides, a common ground against which innovations and the individuality of particular works may be measured. By considering the succession of works in time and space and by matching the variations of style with historical events and with the varying features of other fields of culture, the historian of art attempts, with the help of common-sense psychology and social theory, to account for the changes of style or specific traits. The historical study of individual and group styles also discloses typical stages and processes in the development of forms.

For the synthesizing historian of culture or the philosopher of history, the style is a manifestation of the culture as a whole, the visible sign of its unity. The style reflects or projects the "inner form" of collective thinking and feeling.

* [Reprinted from *Anthropology Today,* edited by A. L. Kroeber, by permission of The University of Chicago Press. Copyright 1953, by the University of Chicago.]

What is important here is not the style of an individual or of a single art, but forms and qualities shared by all the arts of a culture during a significant span of time. In this sense one speaks of Classical or Medieval or Renaissance Man with respect to common traits discovered in the art styles of these epochs and documented also in religious and philosophical writings.

The critic, like the artist, tends to conceive of style as a value term; style as such is a quality and the critic can say of a painter that he has "style" or of a writer that he is a "stylist." Although "style" in this normative sense, which is applied mainly to individual artists, seems to be outside the scope of historical and ethnological studies of art, it often occurs here, too, and should be considered seriously. It is a measure of accomplishment and therefore is relevant to understanding of both art and culture as a whole. Even a period style, which for most historians is a collective taste evident in both good and poor works, may be regarded by critics as a great positive achievement. So the Greek classic style was, for Winckelmann and Goethe, not simply a convention of form but a culminating conception with valued qualities not possible in other styles and apparent even in Roman copies of lost Greek originals. Some period styles impress us by their deeply pervasive, complete character, their special adequacy to their content; the collective creation of such a style, like the conscious shaping of a norm of language, is a true achievement. Correspondingly, the presence of the same style in a wide range of arts is often considered a sign of the integration of a culture and the intensity of a high creative moment. Arts that lack a particular distinction or nobility of style are often said to be style-less, and the culture is judged to be weak or decadent. A similar view is held by philosophers of culture and history and by some historians of art.

Common to all these approaches are the assumptions that every style is peculiar to a period of a culture and that, in a given culture or epoch of culture, there is only one style or a limited range of styles. Works in the style of one time could not have been produced in another. These postulates are supported by the fact that the connection between a style and a period, inferred from a few examples, is confirmed by objects discovered later. Whenever it is possible to locate a work through nonstylistic evidence, this evidence points to the same time and place as do the formal traits, or to a culturally associated region. The unexpected appearance of the style in another region is explained by migration or trade. The style is therefore used with confidence as an independent clue to the time and place of origin of a work of art. Building upon these assumptions, scholars have constructed a systematic, although not complete, picture of the temporal and spatial distribution of styles throughout large regions of the globe. If works of art are grouped in an order corresponding to their original positions in time and space, their styles will show significant relationships which can be co-ordinated with the relationships of the works of art to still other features of the cultural points in time and space.

2

Styles are not usually defined in a strictly logical way. As with languages, the definition indicates the time and place of a style or its author, or the historical relation to other styles, rather than its peculiar features. The characteristics of styles vary continuously and resist a systematic classification into perfectly distinct groups. It is meaningless to ask exactly when ancient art ends and medieval begins. There are, of course, abrupt breaks and reactions in art, but study shows that here, too, there is often anticipation, blending, and continuity. Precise limits are sometimes fixed by convention for simplicity in dealing with historical problems or in isolating a type. In a stream of development the artificial divisions may even be designated by numbers—Styles I, II, III. But the single name given to the style of a period rarely corresponds to a clear and universally accepted characterization of a type. Yet direct acquaintance with an unanalyzed work of art will often permit us to recognize another object of the same origin, just as we recognize a face to be native or foreign. This fact points to a degree of constancy in art that is the basis of all investigation of style. Through careful description and comparison and through formation of a richer, more refined typology adapted to the continuities in development, it has been possible to reduce the areas of vagueness and to advance our knowledge of styles.

Although there is no established system of analysis and writers will stress one or another aspect according to their viewpoint or problem, in general the description of a style refers to three aspects of art: form elements or motives, form relationships, and qualities (including an all-over quality which we may call the "expression").

This conception of style is not arbitrary but has arisen from the experience of investigation. In correlating works of art with an individual or culture, these three aspects provide the broadest, most stable, and therefore most reliable criteria. They are also the most pertinent to modern theory of art, although not in the same degree for all viewpoints. Technique, subject matter, and material may be characteristic of certain groups of works and will sometimes be included in definitions;

but more often these features are not so peculiar to the art of a period as the formal and qualitative ones. It is easy to imagine a decided change in material, technique, or subject matter accompanied by little change in the basic form. Or, where these are constant, we often observe that they are less responsive to new artistic aims. A method of stone-cutting will change less rapidly than the sculptor's or architect's forms. Where a technique does coincide with the extension of a style, it is the formal traces of the technique rather than the operations as such that are important for description of the style. The materials are significant mainly for the textural quality and color, although they may affect the conception of the forms. For the subject matter, we observe that quite different themes—portraits, still lifes, and landscapes—will appear in the same style.

It must be said, too, that form elements or motives, although very striking and essential for the expression, are not sufficient for characterizing a style. The pointed arch is common to Gothic and Islamic architecture, and the round arch to Roman, Byzantine, Romanesque, and Renaissance buildings. In order to distinguish these styles, one must also look for features of another order and, above all, for different ways of combining the elements.

Although some writers conceive of style as a kind of syntax or compositional pattern, which can be analyzed mathematically, in practice one has been unable to do without the vague language of qualities in describing styles. Certain features of light and color in painting are most conveniently specified in qualitative terms and even as tertiary (intersensory) or physiognomic qualities, like cool and warm, gay and sad. The habitual span of light and dark, the intervals between colors in a particular palette—very important for the structure of a work—are distinct relationships between elements, yet are not comprised in a compositional schema of the whole. The complexity of a work of art is such that the description of forms is often incomplete on essential points, limiting itself to a rough account of a few relationships. It is still simpler, as well as more relevant to aesthetic experience, to distinguish lines as hard and soft than to give measurements of their substance. For precision in characterizing a style, these qualities are graded with respect to intensity by comparing different examples directly or by reference to a standard work. Where quantitative measurements have been made, they tend to confirm the conclusions reached through direct qualitative description. Nevertheless, we have no doubt that, in dealing with qualities, much greater precision can be reached.

Analysis applies aesthetic concepts current in the teaching, practice, and criticism of contemporary art; the development of new viewpoints and problems in the latter directs the attention of students to unnoticed features of older styles. But the study of works of other times also influences modern concepts through discovery of aesthetic variants unknown in our own art. As in criticism, so in historical research, the problem of distinguishing or relating two styles discloses unsuspected, subtle characteristics and suggests new concepts of form. The postulate of continuity in culture—a kind of inertia in the physical sense—leads to a search for common features in successive styles that are ordinarily contrasted as opposite poles of form; the resemblances will sometimes be found not so much in obvious aspects as in fairly hidden ones—the line patterns of Renaissance compositions recall features of the older Gothic style, and in contemporary abstract art one observes form relationships like those of Impressionist painting.

The refinement of style analysis has come about in part through problems in which small differences had to be disengaged and described precisely. Examples are the regional variations within the same culture; the process of historical development from year to year; the growth of individual artists and the discrimination of the works of master and pupil, originals and copies. In these studies the criteria for dating and attribution are often physical or external—matters of small symptomatic detail—but here, too, the general trend of research has been to look for features that can be formulated in both structural and expressive-physiognomic terms. It is assumed by many students that the expression terms are all translatable into form and quality terms, since the expression depends on particular shapes and colors and will be modified by a small change in the latter. The forms are correspondingly regarded as vehicles of a particular affect (apart from the subject matter). But the relationship here is not altogether clear. In general, the study of style tends toward an ever stronger correlation of form and expression. Some descriptions are purely morphological, as of natural objects —indeed, ornament has been characterized, like crystals, in the mathematical language of group theory. But terms like "stylized," "archaistic," "naturalistic," "mannerist," "baroque," are specifically human, referring to artistic processes, and imply some expressive effect. It is only by analogy that mathematical figures have been characterized as "classic" and "romantic."

3

The analysis and characterization of the styles of primitive and early historical cultures have been strongly influenced by the standards of recent Western art. Nevertheless, it may be said that the values of modern art have led to a more sympathetic and objective approach to exotic arts than was possible fifty or a hundred years ago.

In the past, a great deal of primitive work, especially representation, was regarded as artless even by sensitive people; what was valued were mainly the ornamentation and the skills of primitive industry. It was believed that primitive arts were childlike attempts to represent nature—attempts distorted by ignorance and by an irrational content of the monstrous and grotesque. True art was admitted only in the high cultures, where knowledge of natural forms was combined with a rational ideal which brought beauty and decorum to the image of man. Greek art and the art of the Italian High Renaissance were the norms for judging all art, although in time the classic phase of Gothic art was accepted. Ruskin, who admired Byzantine works, could write that in Christian Europe alone "pure and precious ancient art exists, for there is none in America, none in Asia, none in Africa." From such a viewpoint careful discrimination of primitive styles or a penetrating study of their structure and expression was hardly possible.

With the change in Western art during the last seventy years, naturalistic representation has lost its superior status. Basic for contemporary practice and for knowledge of past art is the theoretical view that what counts in all art are the elementary aesthetic components, the qualities and relationships of the fabricated lines, spots, colors, and surfaces. These have two characteristics: they are intrinsically expressive, and they tend to constitute a coherent whole. The same tendencies to coherent and expressive structure are found in the arts of all cultures. There is no privileged content or mode of representation (although the greatest works may, for reasons obscure to us, occur only in certain styles). Perfect art is possible in any subject matter or style. A style is like a language, with an internal order and expressiveness, admitting a varied intensity or delicacy of statement. This approach is a relativism that does not exclude absolute judgments of value; it makes these judgments possible within every framework by abandoning a fixed norm of style. Such ideas are accepted by most students of art today, although not applied with uniform conviction.

As a result of this new approach, all the arts of the world, even the drawings of children and psychotics, have become accessible on a common plane of expressive and form-creating activity. Art is now one of the strongest evidences of the basic unity of mankind.

This radical change in attitude depends partly on the development of modern styles, in which the raw material and distinctive units of operation—the plane of the canvas, the trunk of wood, toolmarks, brushstrokes, connecting forms, schemas, particles and areas of pure color—are as pronounced as the elements of representation. Even before nonrepresentative styles were created, artists had become more deeply conscious of the aesthetic-constructive components of the work apart from denoted meanings.

Much in the new styles recalls primitive art. Modern artists were, in fact, among the first to appreciate the works of natives as true art. The development of Cubism and Abstraction made the form problem exciting and helped to refine the perception of the creative in primitive work. Expressionism, with its high pathos, disposed our eyes to the simpler, more intense modes of expression, and together with Surrealism, which valued, above all, the irrational and instinctive in the imagination, gave a fresh interest to the products of primitive fantasy. But, with all the obvious resemblances, modern paintings and sculptures differ from the primitive in structure and content. What in primitive art belongs to an established world of collective beliefs and symbols arises in modern art as an individual expression, bearing the marks of a free, experimental attitude to forms. Modern artists feel, nevertheless, a spiritual kinship with the primitive, who is now closer to them than in the past because of their ideal of frankness and intensity of expression and their desire for a simpler life, with more effective participation of the artist in collective occasions than modern society allows.

One result of the modern development has been a tendency to slight the content of past art; the most realistic representations are contemplated as pure constructions of lines and colors. The observer is often indifferent to the original meanings of works, although he may enjoy through them a vague sentiment of the poetic and religious. The form and expressiveness of older works are regarded, then, in isolation, and the history of an art is written as an immanent development of forms. Parallel to this trend, other scholars have carried on fruitful research into the meanings, symbols, and iconographic types of Western art, relying on the literature of mythology and religion; through these studies the knowledge of the content of art has been considerably deepened, and analogies to the character of the styles have been discovered in the content. This has strengthened the view that the development of forms is not autonomous but is connected with changing attitudes and interests that appear more or less clearly in the subject matter of the art.

4

Students observed early that the traits which make up a style have a quality in common. They all seem to be marked by the expression of the whole, or there is a dominant feature to which the elements have been adapted. The parts of a Greek temple have the air of a family of forms. In Baroque art, a taste for movement determines the loosening of boundaries, the instability of masses, and the multiplication of large contrasts. For many writers a style, whether of an individual or a group, is a pervasive, rigorous unity. Investigation of style is often a search for hidden correspondences explained by an organizing principle which determines both the character of the parts and the patterning of the whole.

This approach is supported by the experience of the student in identifying a style from a small random fragment. A bit of carved stone, the profile of a molding, a few drawn lines, or a single letter from a piece of writing often possesses for the observer the quality of the complete work and can be dated precisely; before these fragments, we have the conviction of insight into the original whole. In a similar way, we recognize by its intrusiveness an added or repaired detail in an old work. The feel of the whole is found in the small parts.

I do not know how far experiments in matching parts from works in different styles would confirm this view. We may be dealing, in some of these observations, with a microstructural level in which similarity of parts only points to the homogeneity of a style or a technique, rather than to a complex unity in the aesthetic sense. Although personal, the painter's touch, described by constants of pressure, rhythm, and size of strokes, may have no obvious relation to other unique characteristics of the larger forms. There are styles in which large parts of a work are conceived and executed differently, without destroying the harmony of the whole. In African sculpture an exceedingly naturalistic, smoothly carved head rises from a rough, almost shapeless body. A normative aesthetic might regard this as imperfect work, but it would be hard to justify this view. In Western paintings of the fifteenth century, realistic figures and landscapes are set against a gold background, which in the Middle Ages had a spiritualistic sense. In Islamic art, as in certain African and Oceanic styles, forms of great clarity and simplicity in three dimensions—metal vessels and animals or the domes of buildings—have surfaces spun with rich mazy patterns; in Gothic and Baroque art, on the contrary, a complex surface treatment is associated with a correspondingly complicated silhouette of the whole. In Romanesque art the proportions of figures are not submitted to a single canon, as in Greek art, but two or three distinct systems of proportioning exist even within the same sculpture, varying with the size of the figure.

Such variation within a style is also known in literature, sometimes in great works, like Shakespeare's plays, where verse and prose of different texture occur together. French readers of Shakespeare, with the model of their own classical drama before them, were disturbed by the elements of comedy in Shakespeare's tragedies. We understand this contrast as a necessity of the content and the poet's conception of man—the different modes of expression pertain to contrasted types of humanity—but a purist classical taste condemned this as inartistic. In modern literature both kinds of style, the rigorous and the free, coexist and express different viewpoints. It is possible to see the opposed parts as contributing elements in a whole that owes its character to the interplay and balance of contrasted qualities. But the notion of style has lost in that case the crystalline uniformity and simple correspondence of part to whole with which we began. The integration may be of a looser, more complex kind, operating with unlike parts.

Another interesting exception to the homogeneous in style is the difference between the marginal and the dominant fields in certain arts. In early Byzantine works, rulers are represented in statuesque, rigid forms, while the smaller accompanying figures, by the same artist, retain the liveliness of an older episodic, naturalistic style. In Romanesque art this difference can be so marked that scholars have mistakenly supposed that certain Spanish works were done partly by a Christian and partly by a Moslem artist. In some instances the forms in the margin or in the background are more advanced in style than the central parts, anticipating a later stage of the art. In medieval work the unframed figures on the borders of illuminated manuscripts or on cornices, capitals, and pedestals are often freer and more naturalistic than the main figures. This is surprising, since we would expect to find the most advanced forms in the dominant content. But in medieval art the sculptor or painter is often bolder where he is less bound to an external requirement; he even seeks out and appropriates the regions of freedom. In a similar way an artist's drawings or sketches are more advanced than the finished paintings and suggest another side of his personality. The execution of the landscape backgrounds behind the religious figures in paintings of the fifteenth century is sometimes amazingly modern and in great contrast to the precise forms of the large figures. Such observations teach us the importance of considering in the description and explanation of a style the unhomogeneous, unstable aspect, the obscure tendencies toward new forms.

If in all periods artists strive to create unified works, the strict ideal of consistency is essentially modern. We often observe in civilized as well as primitive art the combination of works of different style into a single whole. Classical gems were frequently incorporated into medieval reliquaries. Few great medieval buildings are homogeneous, since they are the work of many generations of artists. This is widely recognized by historians, although theoreticians of culture have innocently pointed to the conglomerate cathedral of Chartres as a model of stylistic unity, in contrast to the heterogeneous character of stylelessness of the arts of modern society. In the past it was not felt necessary to restore a damaged work or to complete an unfinished one in the style of the original. Hence the strange juxtapositions of styles within some medieval objects. It should be said, however, that some styles, by virtue of their open, irregular forms, can tolerate the unfinished and heterogeneous better than others.

Just as the single work may possess parts that we would judge to belong to different styles, if we found them in separate contexts, so an individual may produce during the same short period works in what are regarded as two styles. An obvious example is the writing of bilingual authors or the work of the same man in different arts or even in different genres of the same art—monumental and easel painting, dramatic and lyric poetry. A large work by an artist who works mainly in the small, or a small work by a master of large forms, can deceive an expert in styles. Not only will the touch change, but also the expression and method of grouping. An artist is not present in the same degree in everything he does, although some traits may be constant. In the twentieth century, some artists have changed their styles so radically during a few years that it would be difficult, if not impossible, to identify these as works of the same hand, should their authorship be forgotten. In the case of Picasso, two styles—Cubism and a kind of classicizing naturalism—were practiced at the same time. One might discover common characters in small features of the two styles—in qualities of the brushstroke, the span of intensity, or in subtle constancies of the spacing and tones— but these are not the elements through which either style would ordinarily be characterized. Even then, as in a statistical account small and large samples of a population give different results, so in works of different scale of parts by one artist the scale may influence the frequency of the tiniest elements or the form of the small units. The modern experience of stylistic variability and of the unhomogeneous within an art style will perhaps lead to a more refined conception of style. It is evident, at any rate, that the conception of style as a visibly unified constant rests upon a particular norm of stability of style and shifts from the large to the small forms, as the whole becomes more complex.

What has been said here of the limits of uniformity of structure in the single work and in the works of an individual also applies to the style of a group. The group style, like a language, often contains elements that belong to different historical strata. While research looks for criteria permitting one to distinguish accurately the works of different groups and to correlate a style with other characteristics of a group, there are cultures with two or more collective styles of art at the same moment. This phenomenon is often associated with arts of different function or with different classes of artists. The arts practiced by women are of another style than those of the men; religious art differs from profane, and civic from domestic; and in higher cultures the stratification of social classes often entails a variety of styles, not only with respect to the rural and urban, but within the same urban community. This diversity is clear enough today in the coexistence of an official-academic, a mass-commercial, and a freer avant-garde art. But more striking still is the enormous range of styles within the latter—although a common denominator will undoubtedly be found by future historians.

While some critics judge this heterogeneity to be a sign of an unstable, unintegrated culture, it may be regarded as a necessary and valuable consequence of the individual's freedom of choice and of the world scope of modern culture, which permits a greater interaction of styles than was ever possible before. The present diversity continues and intensifies a diversity already noticed in the preceding stages of our culture, including the Middle Ages and the Renaissance, which are held up as models of close integration. The unity of style that is contrasted with the present diversity is one type of style formation, appropriate to particular aims and conditions; to achieve it today would be impossible without destroying the most cherished values of our culture.

If we pass to the relation of group styles of different visual arts in the same period, we observe that, while the Baroque is remarkably similar in architecture, sculpture, and painting, in other periods, e.g., the Carolingian, the early Romanesque, and the modern, these arts differ in essential respects. In England, the drawing and painting of the tenth and eleventh centuries—a time of great accomplishment, when England was a leader in European art—are characterized by an enthusiastic linear style of energetic, ecstatic movement, while the architecture of the same period is inert, massive, and closed and is organized on other principles. Such variety has been explained as a sign of immaturity; but one can point to similar contrasts between two arts in later times, for example, in Holland in the seventeenth century where Rembrandt and his school were contemporary with classicistic Renaissance buildings.

When we compare the styles of arts of the same period in different media—literature, music, painting—the differences are no less striking. But there are epochs with a far-reaching unity, and these have engaged the attention of students more than the examples of diversity. The concept of the Baroque has been applied to architecture, sculpture, painting, music, poetry, drama, gardening, script, and even philosophy and science. The Baroque style has given its name to the entire culture of the seventeenth century, although it does not exclude contrary tendencies within the same country, as well as a great individuality of national arts. Such styles are the most fascinating to historians and philosophers, who admire in this great spectacle of unity the power of a guiding idea or attitude to impose a common form upon the most varied contexts. The dominant style-giving force is identified by some historians with a world outlook common to the whole society; by others with a particular institution, like the church or the absolute monarchy, which under certain conditions becomes the source of a universal viewpoint and the organizer of all cultural life. This unity is not necessarily organic; it may be likened also, perhaps, to that of a machine with limited freedom of motion; in a complex organism the parts are unlike and the integration is more a matter of functional interdependence than of the repetition of the same pattern in all the organs.

Although so vast a unity of style is an impressive accomplishment and seems to point to a special consciousness of style—the forms of art being felt as a necessary universal language—there are moments of great achievement in a single art with characteristics more or less isolated from those of the other arts. We look in vain in England for a style of painting that corresponds to Elizabethan poetry and drama; just as in Russia in the nineteenth century there was no true parallel in painting to the great movement of literature. In these instances we recognize that the various arts have different roles in the culture and social life of a time and express in their content as well as style different interests and values. The dominant outlook of a time—if it can be isolated—does not affect all the arts in the same degree, nor are all the arts equally capable of expressing the same outlook. Special conditions within an art are often strong enough to determine a deviant expression.

5

The organic conception of style has its counterpart in the search for biological analogies in the growth of forms. One view, patterned on the life-history of the organism, attributes to art a recurrent cycle of childhood, maturity, and old age, which coincides with the rise, maturity, and decline of the culture as a whole. Another view pictures the process as an unfinished evolution from the most primitive to the most advanced forms, in terms of a polarity evident at every step.

In the cyclical process each stage has its characteristic style or series of styles. In an enriched schema, for which the history of Western art is the model, the archaic, classic, baroque, impressionist, and archaistic are types of style that follow in an irreversible course. The classic phase is believed to produce the greatest works; the succeeding ones are a decline. The same series has been observed in the Greek and Roman world and somewhat less clearly in India and the Far East. In other cultures this succession of styles is less evident, although the archaic type is widespread and is sometimes followed by what might be considered a classic phase. It is only by stretching the meaning of the terms that the baroque and impressionist types of style are discovered as tendencies within the simpler developments of primitive arts.

(That the same names, "baroque," "classic," and "impressionist," should be applied both to a unique historical style and to a recurrent type or phase is confusing. We will distinguish the name of the unique style by a capital, e.g., "Baroque." But this will not do away with the awkwardness of speaking of the late phase of the Baroque style of the seventeenth century as "baroque." A similar difficulty exists also with the word "style," which is used for the common forms of a particular period and the common forms of a phase of development found in many periods.)

The cyclical schema of development does not apply smoothly even to the Western world from which it has been abstracted. The classic phase in the Renaissance is preceded by Gothic, Romanesque, and Carolingian styles, which cannot all be fitted into the same category of the archaic. It is possible, however, to break up the Western development into two cycles—the medieval and the modern—and to interpret the late Gothic of northern Europe, which is contemporary with the Italian Renaissance, as a style of the baroque type. But contemporary with the Baroque of the seventeenth century is a classic style which in the late eighteenth century replaces the Baroque.

It has been observed, too, that the late phase of Greco-Roman art, especially in architecture, is no decadent style marking a period of decline, but something new. The archaistic trend is only secondary beside the original achievement of late imperial and early Christian art. In a similar way, the complex art of the twentieth century, whether regarded as the end of an old culture or the beginning of a new, does not correspond to the categories of either a declining or an archaic art.

Because of these and other discrepancies, the long-term cyclical schema, which also measures the duration of a culture, is little used by historians of art. It is only a very rough approximation to the character of several isolated moments in Western art. Yet certain stages and steps of the cycle seem to be frequent enough to warrant further study as typical processes, apart from the theory of a closed cyclical form of development.

Some historians have therefore narrowed the range of the cycles from the long-term development to the history of one or two period styles. In Romanesque art, which belongs to the first stage of the longer Western cycle and shares many features with early Greek and Chinese arts, several phases have been noted within a relatively short period that resemble the archaic, the classic, and the baroque of the cyclical scheme; the same observation has been made about Gothic art. But in Carolingian art the order is different; the more baroque and impressionistic phases are the earlier ones, the classic and archaic come later. This may be due in part to the character of the older works that were copied then; but it shows how difficult it is to systematize the history of art through the cyclical model. In the continuous line of Western art, many new styles have been created without breaks or new beginnings occasioned by the exhaustion or death of a preceding style. In ancient Egypt, on the other hand, the latency of styles is hardly confirmed by the slow course of development; an established style persists here with only slight changes in basic structure for several thousand years, a span of time during which Greek and Western art run twice through the whole cycle of stylistic types.

If the exceptional course of Carolingian art is due to special conditions, perhaps the supposedly autonomous process of development also depends on extra-artistic circumstances. But the theorists of cyclical development have not explored the mechanisms and conditions of growth as the biologists have done. They recognize only a latency that conditions might accelerate or delay but not produce. To account for the individuality of the arts of each cycle, the evident difference between a Greek, a western European, and a Chinese style of the same stage, they generally resort to racial theory, each cycle being carried by a people with unique traits.

In contrast to the cyclical organic pattern of development, a more refined model has been constructed by Heinrich Wölfflin, excluding all value judgment and the vital analogy of birth, maturity, and decay. In a beautiful analysis of the art of the High Renaissance and the seventeenth century, he devised five pairs of polar terms, through which he defined the opposed styles of the two periods. These terms were applied to architecture, sculpture, painting, and the so-called "decorative arts." The linear was contrasted with the picturesque or painterly (*malerisch*), the parallel surface form with the diagonal depth form, the closed (or tectonic) with the open (or a-tectonic), the composite with the fused, the clear with the relatively unclear. The first terms of these pairs characterize the classic Renaissance stage, the second belong to the Baroque. Wölfflin believed that the passage from the first set of qualities to the others was not a peculiarity of the development in this one period, but a necessary process which occurred in most historical epochs. Adama van Scheltema applied these categories to the successive stages of northern European arts from the prehistoric period to the age of the migrations. Wölfflin's model has been used in studies of several other periods as well, and it has served the historians of literature and music and even of economic development. He recognized that the model did not apply uniformly to German and Italian art; and, to explain the deviations, he investigated peculiarities of the two national arts, which he thought were "constants"—the results of native dispositions that modified to some degree the innate normal tendencies of development. The German constant, more dynamic and unstable, favored the second set of qualities, and the Italian, more relaxed and bounded, favored the first. In this way, Wölfflin supposed he could explain the precociously *malerisch* and baroque character of German art in its classic Renaissance phase and the persistent classicism in the Italian Baroque.

The weaknesses of Wölfflin's system have been apparent to most students of art. Not only is it difficult to fit into his scheme the important style called "Mannerism" which comes between the High Renaissance and the Baroque; but the pre-Classic art of the fifteenth century is for him an immature, unintegrated style because of its inaptness for his terms. Modern art, too, cannot be defined through either set of terms, although some modern styles show features from both sets —there are linear compositions which are open and painterly ones which are closed. It is obvious that the linear and painterly are genuine types of style, of which examples occur, with more or less approximation to Wölfflin's model, in other periods. But the particular unity of each set of terms is not a necessary one (although it is possible to argue that the Classic and Baroque of the Renaissance are "pure" styles in which basic processes of art appear in an ideally complete and legible way). We can imagine and discover in history other combinations of five of these ten terms. Mannerism, which had been ignored as a phenomenon of decadence, is now described as a type of art that appears in other periods. Wölfflin cannot be right, then, in supposing that, given the first type of art—the classic phase—the second will follow. That depends perhaps on special circumstances which have been effective in some epochs, but not in all. Wölfflin, however, regards the development as internally determined; outer conditions can only retard or facilitate the process, they are not among its causes. He denied that his terms have any other than artistic meaning; they describe two typical modes of seeing and are independent of an expressive content; although artists many choose themes more or less in accord with these forms, the latter do not arise as a means of expression. It is remarkable, therefore, that qualities associated with these pure forms should be attributed also to the psychological dispositions of the Italian and German people.

How this process could have been repeated after the seventeenth century in Europe is a mystery, since that required—as in the passage from Neo-Classicism to Romantic painting—a reverse development from the Baroque to the Neo-Classic.

In a later book Wölfflin recanted some of his views, admitting that these pure forms might correspond to a world outlook and that historical circumstances, religion, politics, etc., might influence the development. But he was unable to modify his schemas and interpretations accordingly. In spite of these difficulties, one can only admire Wölfflin for his attempt to rise above the singularities of style to a general construction that simplifies and organizes the field.

To meet the difficulties of Wölfflin's schema, Paul Frankl has conceived a model of development which combines the dual polar structure with a cyclical pattern. He postulates a recurrent movement between two poles of style—a style of Being and a style of Becoming; but within each of these styles are three stages: a preclassic, a classic, and a postclassic; and in the first and third stages he assumes alternative tendencies which correspond to those historical moments, like Mannerism, that would be anomalous in Wölfflin's scheme. What is most original in Frankl's construction—and we cannot begin to indicate its rich nuancing and complex articulation—is that he attempts to deduce this development and its phases (and the many types of style comprehended within his system) from the analysis of elementary forms and the limited number of possible combinations, which he has investigated with great care. His scheme is not designed to describe the actual historical development—a very irregular affair—but to provide a model or ideal plan of the inherent or normal tendencies of development, based on the nature of forms. Numerous factors, social and psychological, constrain or divert the innate tendencies and determine other courses; but the latter are unintelligible, according to Frankl, without reference to his model and his deduction of the formal possibilities.

Frankl's book—a work of over a thousand pages—appeared unfortunately at a moment (1938) when it could not receive the attention it deserved; and since that time it has been practically ignored in the literature, although it is surely the most serious attempt in recent years to create a systematic foundation for the study of art forms. No other writer has analyzed the types of style so thoroughly.

In spite of their insights and ingenuity in constructing models of development, the theoreticians have had relatively little influence on investigation of special problems, perhaps because they have provided no adequate bridge from the model to the unique historical style and its varied developments. The principles by which are explained the broad similarities in development are of a different order from those by which the singular facts are explained. The normal motion and the motion due to supposedly perturbing factors belong to different worlds; the first is inherent in the morphology of styles, the second has a psychological or social origin. It is as if mechanics had two different sets of laws, one for irregular and the other for regular motions; or one for the first and another for the second approximation, in dealing with the same phenomenon. Hence those who are most concerned with a unified approach to the study of art have split the history of style into two aspects which cannot be derived from each other or from some common principle.

Parallel to the theorists of cyclical development, other scholars have approached the development of styles as a continuous, long-term evolutionary process. Here, too, there are poles and stages and some hints of a universal, though not cyclical, process; but the poles are those of the earliest and latest stages and are deduced from a definition of the artist's goal or the nature of art or from a psychological theory.

The first students to investigate the history of primitive art conceived the latter as a development between two poles, the geometrical and the naturalistic. They were supported by observation of the broad growth of art in the historical cultures from geometric or simple, stylized forms to more natural ones; they were sustained also by the idea that the most naturalistic styles of all belonged to the highest type of culture, the most advanced in scientific knowledge, and the most capable of representing the world in accurate images. The process in art agreed with the analogous development in nature from the simple to the complex and was paralleled by the growth of the child's drawings in our own culture from schematic or geometrical forms to naturalistic ones. The origin of certain geometrical forms in primitive industrial techniques also favored this view.

It is challenging and amusing to consider in the light of these arguments the fact that the Paleolithic cave paintings, the oldest known art, are marvels of representation (whatever the elements of schematic form in those works, they are more naturalistic than the succeeding Neolithic and Bronze Age art) and that in the twentieth century naturalistic forms have given way to "abstraction" and so-called "subjective" styles. But, apart from these paradoxical exceptions, one could observe in historical arts—e.g., in the late classic and early Christian periods—how free naturalistic forms are progressively stylized and reduced to ornament. In the late nineteenth century, ornament was often designed by a method of stylization, a geometrizing of natural motives; and those who knew contemporary art were not slow to discern in the geometrical styles of existing primitives the traces of an older more naturalistic model. Study shows that both processes occur in history; there is little reason to regard either one as more typical or more primitive. The geometrical and the naturalistic forms may arise independently in different contexts and coexist within the same culture. The experience of the art of the last fifty years suggests further that the degree of naturalism in art is not a sure indication of the technological or intellectual level of a culture. This does not mean that style is independent of that level but that other concepts than those of the naturalistic and the geometrical must be applied in considering such relationships. The essential opposition is not of the natural and the geometric but of certain modes of composition of natural and geometric motives. From this point of view, modern "abstract" art in its taste for open, asymmetrical, random, tangled, and incomplete forms is much closer to the compositional principles of realistic or Impressionist painting and sculpture than to any primitive art with geometrical elements. Although the character of the themes, whether "abstract" or naturalistic, is important for the concrete aspect of the work of art, historians do not operate so much with categories of the naturalistic and geometrical as with subtler structural concepts, which apply also to architecture, where the problem of representation seems irrelevant. It is with such concepts that Wölfflin and Frankl have constructed their models.

Nevertheless, the representation of natural forms has been a goal in the arts of many cultures. Whether we regard it as a spontaneous common idea or one that has been diffused from a single prehistorical center, the problem of how to represent the human and animal figure has been attacked independently by various cultures. Their solutions present not only similar features in the devices of rendering but also a remarkable parallelism in the successive stages of the solutions. It is fascinating to compare the changing representation of the eyes or of pleated costume in succeeding styles of Greek, Chinese, and medieval European sculpture. The development of such details from a highly schematic to a naturalistic type in the latter two can hardly be referred to a direct influence of Greek models; for the similarities are not only of geographically far separated styles but of distinct series in time. To account for the Chinese and Romanesque forms as copies of the older Greek, we would have to assume that at each stage in the post-Greek styles the artists had recourse to Greek works of the corresponding stage and in the same order. Indeed, some of the cyclical schemas discussed above are, in essence, descriptions of the stages in the development of representation; and it may be asked whether the formal schemas, like Wölfflin's, are not veiled categories of representation, even though they are applied to architecture as well as to sculpture and painting; for the standards of representation in the latter may conceivably determine a general norm of plasticity and structure for all the visual arts.

This aspect of style—the representation of natural forms —has been studied by the classical archaeologist Emmanuel Löwy; his little book on *The Rendering of Nature in Early Greek Art,* published in 1900, is still suggestive for modern research and has a wider application than has been recognized. Löwy has analyzed the general principles of representation in early arts and explained their stages as progressive steps in a steady change from conceptual representation, based on the memory image, to perspective representation, according to direct perception of objects. Since the structure of the memory image is the same in all cultures, the representations based on this psychological process will exhibit common features: (1) The shape and movement of figures and their parts are limited to a few typical forms; (2) the single forms are schematized in regular linear patterns; (3) representation proceeds from the outline, whether the latter is an independent contour or the silhouette of a uniformly colored area; (4) where colors are used, they are without gradation of light and shadow; (5) the parts of a figure are presented to the observer in their broadest aspect; (6) in compositions the figures, with few exceptions, are shown with a minimum of overlapping of their main parts; the real succession of figures in depth is transformed in the image into a juxtaposition on the same plane; (7) the representation of the three-dimensional space in which an action takes place is more or less absent.

Whatever criticisms may be made of Löwy's notion of a memory image as the source of these peculiarities, his account of archaic representation as a universal type, with a characteristic structure, is exceedingly valuable; it has a general application to children's drawings, to the work of modern untrained adults, and to primitives. This analysis does not touch on the individuality of archaic styles, nor does it help us to understand why some cultures develop beyond them and others, like the Egyptian, retain the archaic features for many centuries. Limited by an evolutionary view and a natu- ralistic value norm, Löwy ignored the perfection and expres- siveness of archaic works. Neglecting the specific content of the representations, this approach fails to recognize the role of the content and of emotional factors in the proportioning and accentuation of parts. But these limitations do not lessen the importance of Löwy's book in defining so clearly a wide- spread type of archaic representation and in tracing the stages of its development into a more naturalistic art.

I may mention here that the reverse process of the conver- sion of naturalistic to archaic forms, as we see it wherever works of an advanced naturalistic style are copied by primi- tives, colonials, provincials, and the untrained in the high cultures, can also be formulated through Löwy's principles.

We must mention, finally, as the most constructive and imaginative of the historians who have tried to embrace the whole of artistic development as a single continuous process, Alois Riegl, the author of *Stilfragen* and *Die spätrömische Kunstindustrie.*

Riegl was especially concerned with transitions that mark the beginning of a world-historical epoch (the Old Oriental to the Hellenic, the ancient to the medieval). He gave up not only the normative view that judges the later phases of a cycle as a decline but also the conception of closed cycles. In late Roman art, which was considered decadent in his time, he found a necessary creative link between two great stages of an open development. His account of the process is like Wölfflin's, however, though perhaps independent; he formu- lates as the poles of the long evolution two types of style, the "haptic" (tactile) and the "optic" (or painterly, impression- istic), which coincide broadly with the poles of Wölfflin's shorter cycles. The process of development from the haptic to the optic is observable in each epoch, but only as part of a longer process, of which the great stages are millennial and correspond to whole cultures. The history of art is, for Riegl, an endless necessary movement from representation based on vision of the object and its parts as proximate, tangible, dis- crete, and self-sufficient, to the representation of the whole perceptual field as a directly given, but more distant, con- tinuum with merging parts, with an increasing role of the spatial voids, and with a more evident reference to the know- ing subject as a constituting factor in perception. This artistic process is also described by Riegl in terms of a faculty psy- chology; will, feeling, and thought are the successive dominants in shaping our relations to the world; it corresponds in philosophy to the change from a predominantly objective to a subjective outlook.

Riegl does not study this process simply as a development of naturalism from an archaic to an impressionistic stage. Each phase has its special formal and expressive problems, and Riegl has written remarkably penetrating pages on the intimate structure of styles, the principles of composition, and the relations of figure to ground. In his systematic account of ancient art and the art of the early Christian period, he has observed common principles in architecture, sculpture, painting, and ornament, sometimes with surprising acuteness. He has also succeeded in showing unexpected relationships between different aspects of a style. In a work on Dutch group portraiture of the sixteenth and seventeenth centuries, a theme that belongs to art and social history, he has carried through a most delicate analysis of the changing relations between the objective and the subjective elements in portraiture and in the correspondingly variable mode of unifying a represented group which is progressively more attentive to the observer.

His motivation of the process and his explanation of its shifts in time and space are vague and often fantastic. Each great phase corresponds to a racial disposition. The history of Western man from the time of the Old Oriental kingdoms to the present day is divided into three great periods, characterized by the successive predominance of will, feeling, and thought, in Oriental, Classical, and Western Man. Each race plays a prescribed role and retires when its part is done, as if participating in a symphony of world history. The apparent deviations from the expected continuities are saved for the system by a theory of purposive regression which prepares a people for its advanced role. The obvious incidence of social and religious factors in art is judged to be simply a parallel manifestation of a corresponding process in these other fields rather than a possible cause. The basic, immanent development from an objective to a subjective standpoint governs the whole of history, so that all contemporary fields have a deep unity with respect to a common determining process.

This brief summary of Riegl's ideas hardly does justice to the positive features of his work, and especially to his conception of art as an active creative process in which new forms arise from the artist's will to solve specifically artistic problems. Even his racial theories and strange views about the historical situation of an art represent a desire to grasp large relationships, although distorted by an inadequate psychology and social theory; this search for a broad view has become rare in the study of art since his time. And still rarer is its combination with the power of detailed research that Riegl possessed to a high degree.

To summarize the results of modern studies with respect to the cyclical and evolutionary theories:

(1) From the viewpoint of historians who have tried to reconstruct the precise order of development, without presuppositions about cycles, there is a continuity in the Near East and Europe from the Neolithic period to the present —perhaps best described as a tree with many branches—in which the most advanced forms of each culture are retained, to some extent, in the early forms of succeeding cultures.

(2) On the other hand, there are within that continuity at least two long developments—the ancient Greek and the Western European medieval-modern—which include the broad types of style described in various cyclical theories. But these two cycles are not unconnected; artists in the second cycle often copied surviving works of the first, and it is uncertain whether some of the guiding principles in Western art are not derived from the Greeks.

(3) Within these two cycles and in several other cultures (Asiatic and American) occur many examples of similar short developments, especially from an archaic linear type of representation to a more "pictorial" style.

(4) Wherever there is a progressive naturalistic art, i.e., one which becomes increasingly naturalistic, we find in the process stages corresponding broadly to the line of archaic, classic, baroque, and impressionist in Western art. Although these styles in the West are not adequately described in terms of their method of representation, they embody specific advances in range or method of representation from a first stage of schematized, so-called "conceptual," representation of isolated objects to a later stage of perspective representation in which continuities of space, movement, light and shadow, and atmosphere have become important.

(5) In describing the Western development, which is the model of cyclical theories, historians isolate different aspects of art for the definition of the stylistic types. In several theories the development of representation is the main source of the terms; in others formal traits, which can be found also in architecture, script, and pottery shapes, are isolated; and, in some accounts, qualities of expression and content are the criteria. It is not always clear which formal traits are really independent of representation. It is possible that a way of seeing objects in nature—the perspective vision as distinguished from the archaic conceptual mode—also affects the design of a column or a pot. But the example of Islamic art, in which representation is secondary, suggests that the devel-

opment of the period styles in architecture and ornament need not depend on a style of representation. As for expression, there exist in the Baroque art of the seventeenth century intimate works of great tragic sensibility, like Rembrandt's, and monumental works of a profuse splendor; either of these traits can be paralleled in other periods in forms of non-baroque type. But a true counterpart of Rembrandt's light and shadow will not be found in Greek or Chinese painting, although both are said to have baroque phases.

6

We shall now consider the explanations of style proposed without reference to cycles and polar developments.

In accounting for the genesis of a style, early investigators gave great weight to the technique, materials, and practical functions of an art. Thus wood carving favors grooved or wedge-cut relief, the column of the tree trunk gives the statue its cylindrical shape, hard stone yields compact and angular forms, weaving begets stepped and symmetrical patterns, the potter's wheel introduces a perfect roundness, coiling is the source of spirals, etc. This was the approach of Semper and his followers in the last century. Boas, among others, identified style, or at least its formal aspect, with motor habits in the handling of tools. In modern art this viewpoint appears in the program of functionalist architecture and design. It is also behind the older explanation of the Gothic style of architecture as a rational system derived from the rib construction of vaults. Modern sculptors who adhere closely to the block, exploiting the texture and grain of the material and showing the marks of the tool, are supporters of this theory of style. It is related to the immense role of the technological in our own society; modern standards of efficient production have become a norm in art.

There is no doubt that these practical conditions account for some peculiarities of style. They are important also in explaining similarities in primitive and folk arts which appear to be independent of diffusion or imitation of styles. But they are of less interest for highly developed arts. Wood may limit the sculptor's forms, but we know a great variety of styles in wood, some of which even conceal the substance. Riegl observed long ago that the same forms occurred within a culture in works of varied technique, materials, and use; it is this common style that the theory in question has failed to explain. The Gothic style is, broadly speaking, the same in buildings; sculptures of wood, ivory, and stone; panel paintings; stained glass; miniatures; metalwork, enamels, and textiles. It may be that in some instances a style created in one art under the influence of the technique, material, and function of particular objects has been generalized by application to all objects, techniques, and materials. Yet the material is not always prior to the style but may be chosen because of an ideal of expression and artistic quality or for symbolism. The hard substances of Old Egyptian art, the use of gold and other precious luminous substances in arts of power, the taste for steel, concrete, and glass in modern design, are not external to the artist's first goal but parts of the original conception. The compactness of the sculpture cut from a tree trunk is a quality that is already present in the artist's idea before he begins to carve. For simple compact forms appear in clay figures and in drawings and paintings where the matter does not limit the design. The compactness may be regarded as a necessary trait of an archaic or a "haptic" style in Löwy's or Riegl's sense.

Turning away from material factors, some historians find in the content of the work of art the source of its style. In the arts of representation, a style is often associated with a distinct body of subject matter, drawn from a single sphere of ideas or experience. Thus in Western art of the fourteenth century, when a new iconography of the life of Christ and of Mary was created in which themes of suffering were favored, we observe new patterns of line and color, which possess a more lyrical, pathetic aspect than did the preceding art. In our own time, a taste for the constructive and rational in industry has led to the use of mechanical motives and a style of forms characterized by coolness, precision, objectivity, and power.

The style in these examples is viewed by many writers as the objective vehicle of the subject matter or of its governing idea. Style, then, is the means of communication, a language not only as a system of devices for conveying a precise message by representing or symbolizing objects and actions but also as a qualitative whole which is capable of suggesting the diffuse connotations as well and intensifying the associated or intrinsic affects. By an effort of imagination based on experience of his medium, the artist discovers the elements and formal relationships which will express the values of the content and look right artistically. Of all the attempts made in this direction, the most successful will be repeated and developed as a norm.

The relationship of content and style is more complex than appears in this theory. There are styles in which the correspondence of the expression and the values of the typical subjects is not at all obvious. If the difference between pagan and Christian art is explained broadly by the difference in religious content, there is nevertheless a long period of time —in fact, many centuries—during which Christian subjects are represented in the style of pagan art. As late as 800, the *Libri Carolini* speak of the difficulty of distinguishing images of

Mary and Venus without the labels. This may be due to the fact that a general outlook of late paganism, more fundamental than the religious doctrines, was still shared by Christians or that the new religion, while important, had not yet transformed the basic attitudes and ways of thinking. Or it may be that the function of art within the religious life was too slight, for not all concepts of the religion find their way into art. But even later, when the Christian style had been established, there were developments in art toward a more naturalistic form and toward imitation of elements of ancient pagan style which were incompatible with the chief ideas of the religion.

A style that arises in connection with a particular content often becomes an accepted mode governing all representations of the period. The Gothic style is applied in religious and secular works alike; and, if it is true that no domestic or civil building in that style has the expressiveness of a cathedral interior, yet in painting and sculpture the religious and secular images are hardly different in form. On the other hand, in periods of a style less pervasive than the Gothic, different idioms or dialects of form are used for different fields of content; this was observed in the discussion of the concept of stylistic unity.

It is such observations that have led students to modify the simple equation of style and the expressive values of a subject matter, according to which the style is the vehicle of the main meanings of the work of art. Instead, the meaning of content has been extended, and attention has been fixed on broader attitudes or on general ways of thinking and feeling, which are believed to shape a style. The style is then viewed as a concrete embodiment or projection of emotional dispositions and habits of thought common to the whole culture. The content as a parallel product of the same viewpoint will therefore often exhibit qualities and structures like those of the style.

These world views or ways of thinking and feeling are usually abstracted by the historian from the philosophical systems and metaphysics of a period or from theology and literature and even from science. Themes like the relation of subject and object, spirit and matter, soul and body, man and nature or God, and conceptions of time and space, self and cosmos are typical fields from which are derived the definitions of the world view (or *Denkweise*) of a period or culture. The latter is then documented by illustrations from many fields, but some writers have attempted to derive it from the works of art themselves. One searches in a style for qualities and structures that can be matched with some aspect of thinking or a world view. Sometimes it is based on a priori deduction of possible world views, given the limited number of solutions of metaphysical problems; or a typology of the possible attitudes of the individual to the world and to his own existence is matched with a typology of styles. We have seen how Riegl apportioned the three faculties of will, feeling, and thought among three races and three major styles.

The attempts to derive style from thought are often too vague to yield more than suggestive *aperçus;* the method breeds analogical speculations which do not hold up under detailed critical study. The history of the analogy drawn between the Gothic cathedral and scholastic theology is an example. The common element in these two contemporary creations has been found in their rationalism and in their irrationality, their idealism and their naturalism, their encyclo-pedic completeness and their striving for infinity, and recently in their dialectical method. Yet one hesitates to reject such analogies in principle, since the cathedral belongs to the same religious sphere as does contemporary theology.

It is when these ways of thinking and feeling or world views have been formulated as the outlook of a religion or dominant institution or class of which the myths and values are illustrated or symbolized in the work of art that the general intellectual content seems a more promising field for explana-tion of style. But the content of a work of art often belongs to another region of experience than the one in which both the period style and the dominant mode of thinking have been formed; an example is the secular art of a period in which religious ideas and rituals are primary, and, conversely, the religious art of a secularized culture. In such cases we see how important for a style of art is the character of the dominants in culture, especially of institutions. Not the con-tent as such, but the content as part of a dominant set of beliefs, ideas, and interests, supported by institutions and the forms of everyday life, shapes the common style.

Although the attempts to explain styles as an artistic ex-pression of a world view or mode of thought are often a drastic reduction of the concreteness and richness of art, they have been helpful in revealing unsuspected levels of meaning in art. They have established the practice of interpreting the style itself as an inner content of the art, especially in the nonrepresentational arts. They correspond to the conviction of modern artists that the form elements and structure are a deeply meaningful whole related to metaphysical views.

7

The theory that the world view or mode of thinking and feeling is the source of long-term constants in style is often formulated as a theory of racial or national character. I have already referred to such concepts in the work of Wölfflin and Riegl. They have been common in European writing on art for over a hundred years and have played a significant role in promoting national consciousness and race feeling; works of art are the chief concrete evidences of the affective world of the ancestors. The persistent teaching that German art is by nature tense and irrational, that its greatness depends on fidelity to the racial character, has helped to produce an acceptance of these traits as a destiny of the people.

The weakness of the racial concept of style is evident from analysis of the history and geography of styles, without reference to biology. The so-called "constant" is less constant than the racially (or nationally) minded historians have assumed. German art includes Classicism and the Biedermeier style, as well as the work of Grünewald and the modern Expressionists. During the periods of most pronounced Germanic character, the extension of the native style hardly coincides with the boundaries of the preponderant physical type or with the recent national boundaries. This discrepancy holds for the Italian art which is paired with the German as a polar opposite.

Nevertheless, there are striking recurrences in the art of a region or nation which have not been explained. It is astonishing to observe the resemblances between German migrations art and the styles of the Carolingian, Ottonian, and late Gothic periods, then of German rococo architecture, and finally of modern Expressionism. There are great gaps in time between these styles during which the forms can scarcely be described in the traditional German terms. To save the appearance of constancy, German writers have supposed that the intervening phases were dominated by alien influences or were periods of preparation for the ultimate release, or they conceived the deviant qualities as another aspect of German character: the Germans are both irrational and disciplined.

If we restrict ourselves to more modest historical correlations of styles with the dominant personality types of the cultures or groups that have created the styles, we meet several difficulties; some of these have been anticipated in the discussion of the general problem of unity of style.

(1) The variation of styles in a culture or group is often considerable within the same period.

(2) Until recently, the artists who create the style are generally of another mode of life than those for whom the arts are designed and whose viewpoint, interests, and quality of life are evident in the art. The best examples are the arts of great monarchies, aristocracies, and privileged institutions.

(3) What is constant in all the arts of a period (or of

several periods) may be less essential for characterizing the style than the variable features; the persistent French quality in the series of styles between 1770 and 1870 is a nuance which is hardly as important for the definition of the period style as the traits that constitute the Rococo, Neo-Classic, Romantic, Realistic, and Impressionist styles.

To explain the changing period styles, historians and critics have felt the need of a theory that relates particular forms to tendencies of character and feeling. Such a theory, concerned with the elements of expression and structure, should tell us what affects and dispositions determine choices of forms. Historians have not waited for experimental psychology to support their physiognomic interpretations of style but, like the thoughtful artists, have resorted to intuitive judgments, relying on direct experience of art. Building up an unsystematic, empirical knowledge of forms, expressions, affects, and qualities, they have tried to control these judgments by constant comparison of works and by reference to contemporary sources of information about the content of the art, assuming that the attitudes which govern the latter must also be projected in the style. The interpretation of Classical style is not founded simply on firsthand experience of Greek buildings and sculptures; it rests also on knowledge of Greek language, literature, religion, mythology, philosophy, and history, which provide an independent picture of the Greek world. But this picture is, in turn, refined and enriched by experience of the visual arts, and our insight is sharpened by knowledge of the very different arts of the neighboring peoples and of the results of attempts to copy the Greek models at later times under other conditions. Today, after the work of nearly two centuries of scholars, a sensitive mind, with relatively little information about Greek culture, can respond directly to the "Greek mind" in those ancient buildings and sculptures.

In physiognomic interpretations of group styles, there is a common assumption that is still problematic: that the psychological explanations of unique features in a modern individual's art can be applied to a whole culture in which the same or similar features are characteristics of a group or period style.

If schizophrenics fill a sheet of paper with closely crowded elements in repeat patterns, can we explain similar tendencies in the art of a historic or primitive culture by a schizophrenic tendency or dominant schizoid personality type in that culture? We are inclined to doubt such interpretations for two reasons. First, we are not sure that this pattern is uniquely schizoid in modern individuals; it may represent a component of the psychotic personality which also exists in other temperaments as a tendency associated with particular emotional contents or problems. Secondly, this pattern, originating in a single artist of schizoid type, may crystallize as a common convention, accepted by other artists and the public because it satisfies a need and is most adequate to a special problem of decoration or representation, without entailing, however, a notable change in the broad habits and attitudes of the group. This convention may be adopted by artists of varied personality types, who will apply it in distinct ways, filling it with an individual content and expression.

A good instance of this relationship between the psychotic, the normal individual, and the group is the practice of reading object forms in relatively formless spots—as in hallucination and in psychological tests. Leonardo da Vinci proposed this method to artists as a means of invention. It was practiced in China, and later in Western art; today it has become a standard method for artists of different character. In the painter who first introduced the practice and exploited it most fully, it may correspond to a personal disposition; but for many others it is an established technique. What is personally significant is not the practice itself but the kinds of spots chosen and what is seen in them; attention to the latter discloses a great variety of individual reactions.

If art is regarded as a projective technique—and some artists today think of their work in these terms—will interpretation of the work give the same result as a projective test? The tests are so designed as to reduce the number of elements that depend on education, profession, and environment. But the work of art is very much conditioned by these factors. Hence, in discerning the personal expression in a work of art, one must distinguish between those aspects that are conventional and those that are clearly individual. In dealing with the style of a group, however, we consider only such superindividual aspects, abstracting them from the personal variants. How, then, can one apply to the interpretation of the style concepts from individual psychology?

It may be said, of course, that the established norms of a group style are genuine parts of an artist's outlook and response and can be approached as the elements of a modal personality. In the same way the habits and attitudes of scientists that are required by their profession may be an important part of their characters. But do such traits also constitute the typical ones of the culture or the society as a whole? Is an art style that has crystallized as a result of special problems necessarily an expression of the whole group? Or is it only in the special case where the art is open to the common outlook and everyday interests of the entire group that its content and style can be representative of the group?

A common tendency in the physiognomic approach to

group style has been to interpret all the elements of representation as expressions. The blank background or negative features like the absence of a horizon and of consistent perspective in paintings are judged to be symptomatic of an attitude to space and time in actual life. The limited space in Greek art is interpreted as a fundamental trait of Greek personality. Yet this blankness of the background, we have seen, is common to many styles; it is found in prehistoric art, in Old Oriental art, in the Far East, in the Middle Ages, and in most primitive painting and relief. The fact that it occurs in modern children's drawings and in the drawings of untrained adults suggests that it belongs to a universal primitive level of representation. But it should be observed that this is also the method of illustration in the most advanced scientific work in the past and today.

This fact does not mean that representation is wholly without expressive personal features. A particular treatment of the "empty" background may become a powerful expressive factor. Careful study of so systematic a method of representation as geometrical perspective shows that within such a scientific system there are many possible choices; the position of the eye-level, the intensity of convergence, the distance of the viewer from the picture plane—all these are expressive choices within the conditions of the system. Moreover, the existence of the system itself presupposes a degree of interest in the environment which is already a cultural trait with a long history.

The fact that an art represents a restricted world does not allow us to infer, however, a corresponding restriction of interests and perceptions in everyday life. We would have to suppose, if this were true, that in Islam people were unconcerned with the human body, and that the present vogue of "abstract" art means a general indifference to the living.

An interesting evidence of the limitations of the assumed identities of the space or time structure of works of art and the space or time experience of individuals is the way in which painters of the thirteenth century represented the new cathedrals. These vast buildings with high vaults and endless vistas in depth are shown as shallow structures, not much larger than the human beings they enclose. The conventions of representation provided no means of re-creating the experience of architectural space, an experience that was surely a factor in the conception of the cathedral and was reported in contemporary descriptions. (It is possible to relate the architectural and pictorial spaces; but the attempt would take us beyond the problems of this paper.) The space of the cathedrals is intensely expressive, but it is a constructed, ideal space, appealing to the imagination, and not an attempt to transpose the space of everyday life. We will understand it better as a creation adequate to a religious conception than as one in which an everyday sentiment of space has been embodied in architecture. It is an ideological space, too, and, if it conveys the feelings of the most inspired religious personalities, it is not a model of an average, collective attitude to space in general, although the cathedral is used by everyone.

The concept of personality in art is most important for the theory that the great artist is the immediate source of the period style. This little-explored view, implicit in much historical research and criticism, regards the group style as an imitation of the style of an original artist. Study of a line of development often leads to the observation that some individual is responsible for the change in the period form. The personality of the great artist and the problems inherited from the preceding generation are the two factors studied. For the personality as a whole is sometimes substituted a weakness or a traumatic experience which activates the individual's will to create. Such a view is little adapted to the understanding of those cultures or historical epochs that left us no signed works or biographies of artists; but it is the favored view of many students of the art of the last four centuries in Europe. It may be questioned whether it is applicable to cultures in which the individual has less mobility and range of personal action and in which the artist is not a deviant type. The main difficulty, however, arises from the fact that similar stylistic trends often appear independently in different arts at the same time; that great contemporary artists in the same field—Leonardo, Michelangelo, Raphael—show a parallel tendency of style, although each artist has a personal form; and that the new outlook expressed by a single man of genius is anticipated or prepared in preceding works and thought. The great artists of the Gothic period and the Renaissance constitute families with a common heritage and trend. Decisive changes are most often associated with original works of outstanding quality; but the new direction of style and its acceptance are unintelligible without reference to the conditions of the moment and the common ground of the art.

These difficulties and complexities have not led scholars to abandon the psychological approach; long experience with art has established as a plausible principle the notion that an individual style is a personal expression; and continued research has found many confirmations of this, wherever it has been possible to control statements about the personality, built upon the work, by referring to actual information about the artist. Similarly, common traits in the art of a culture or nation can be matched with some features of social life, ideas, customs, general dispositions. But such correlations have been of single elements or aspects of a style with single traits of a people; it is rarely a question of wholes. In our own culture, styles have changed very rapidly, yet the current notions about group traits do not allow sufficiently for corresponding changes in the behavior patterns or provide such a formulation of the group personality that one can deduce from it how that personality will change under new conditions.

It seems that for explanation of the styles of the higher cultures, with their great variability and intense development, the concepts of group personality current today are too rigid. They underestimate the specialized functions of art which determine characteristics that are superpersonal. But we may ask whether some of the difficulties in applying characterological concepts to national or period styles are not also present in the interpretation of primitive arts. Would a psychological treatment of Sioux art, for example, give us the same picture of Sioux personality as that provided by analysis of Sioux family life, ceremony, and hunting?

8

We turn last to explanations of style by the forms of social life. The idea of a connection between these forms and styles is already suggested by the framework of the history of art. Its main divisions, accepted by all students, are also the boundaries of social units—cultures, empires, dynasties, cities, classes, churches, etc.—and periods which mark significant stages in social development. The great historical epochs of art, like antiquity, the Middle Ages, and the modern era, are the same as the epochs of economic history; they correspond to great systems, like feudalism and capitalism. Important economic and political shifts within these systems are often accompanied or followed by shifts in the centers of art and their styles. Religion and major world views are broadly coordinated with these eras in social history.

In many problems the importance of economic, political, and ideological conditions for the creation of a group style (or of a world view that influences a style) is generally admitted. The distinctiveness of Greek art among the arts of the ancient world can hardly be separated from the forms of Greek society and the city-state. The importance of the burgher class, with its special position in society and its mode of life, for the medieval and early Renaissance art of Florence and for Dutch art of the seventeenth century, is a commonplace. In explaining Baroque art, the Counter-Reformation and the absolute monarchy are constantly cited as the sources of certain features of style. We have interesting studies on a multitude of problems concerning the relationship of particular styles and contents of art to institutions and historical situations. In these studies ideas, traits, and values arising from the conditions of economic, political, and civil life are matched with the new characteristics of an art. Yet, with all this experience, the general principles applied in explanation and the connection of types of art with types of social structure have not been investigated in a systematic way. By the many scholars who adduce piecemeal political or economic facts in order to account for single traits of style or subject matter, little has been done to construct an adequate comprehensive theory. In using such data, scholars will often deny that these "external" relationships can throw any light on the artistic phenomenon as such. They fear "materialism" as a reduction of the spiritual or ideal to sordid practical affairs.

Marxist writers are among the few who have tried to apply a general theory. It is based on Marx's undeveloped view that the higher forms of cultural life correspond to the economic structure of a society, the latter being defined in terms of the relations of classes in the process of production and the technological level. Between the economic relationships and the styles of art intervenes the process of ideological construction, a complex imaginative transposition of class roles and needs, which affects the special field—religion, mythology, or civil life—that provides the chief themes of art.

The great interest of the Marxist approach lies not only in the attempt to interpret the historically changing relations of art and economic life in the light of a general theory of society but also in the weight given to the differences and conflicts within the social group as motors of development, and to the effects of these on outlook, religion, morality, and philosophical ideas.

Only broadly sketched in Marx's works, the theory has rarely been applied systematically in a true spirit of investigation, such as we see in Marx's economic writings. Marxist writing on art has suffered from schematic and premature formulations and from crude judgments imposed by loyalty to a political line.

A theory of style adequate to the psychological and historical problems has still to be created. It waits for a deeper knowledge of the principles of form construction and expression and for a unified theory of the processes of social life in which the practical means of life as well as emotional behavior are comprised.

MEDITATIONS ON A HOBBY HORSE OR THE ROOTS OF ARTISTIC FORM *

E. H. Gombrich

The subject of this article is a very ordinary hobby horse. It is neither metaphorical nor purely imaginary, at least not more so than the broomstick on which Swift wrote his meditations. It is usually content with its place in the corner of the nursery and it has no aesthetic ambitions. Indeed it abhors frills. It is satisfied with its broomstick body and its crudely carved head which just indicates the upper end and serves as holder for the reins. How should we address it? Should we describe it as an "image of a horse"? The compilers of the *Oxford Pocket Dictionary* would hardly have agreed. They defined *image* as "imitation of object's external form" and the "external form" of a horse is surely not "imitated" here. So much the worse, we might say, for the "external form," that elusive remnant of the Greek philosophical tradition which has dominated our aesthetic language for so long. Luckily there is another word in the *Dictionary* which might prove more accommodating: *representation*. To *represent,* we read, can be used in the sense of "call up by description or portrayal or imagination, figure, place likeness of before mind or senses, serve or be meant as likeness of . . . stand for, be specimen of, fill place of, be substitute for." A portrayal of a horse? Evidently not. A substitute for a horse? Yes. That it is. Perhaps there is more in this formula than meets the eye.

1

Let us first ride our wooden steed into battle against a number of ghosts which still haunt the language of art criticism. One of them we even found entrenched in the *Oxford Dictionary.* The implication of its definition of an image is that the artist "imitates" the "external form" of the object in front of him, and the beholder, in his turn, recognizes the "subject" of the work of art by its "form." This is what might be called the traditional view of representation. Its corollary is that a work of art will either be a faithful copy, in fact a complete replica, of the object represented or that it consti-

---

* [From *Aspects of Form,* edited by Lancelot Law Whyte (London: Lund Humphries, 1951). Reprinted by permission of the author, the editor, and the publisher.]

tutes a degree of "abstraction." The artist, we read, abstracts the "form" from the object he sees. The sculptor usually abstracts the three-dimensional form and abstracts *from* color, the painter abstracts contours and colors, and *from* the third dimension. In this context one hears it said that the draftsman's line is a "tremendous feat of abstraction" because it does not "occur in nature." A modern sculptor of Brancusi's persuasion may be praised or blamed for "carrying abstraction to its logical extreme." Finally the label of "abstract art" for the creation of pure forms carries with it the same implications. Yet we need only look at our hobby horse to see that the very idea of abstraction as a complicated mental act lands us in curious absurdities. There is an old music hall joke describing a drunkard who politely lifts his hat to every lamppost he passes. Should we say that the liquor has so increased his power of abstraction that he is now able to isolate the formal quality of uprightness from both lamppost and the human figure? Our mind, of course, works by differentiation rather than by generalization, and the child will for long call all four-footers of a certain size "gee-gee" before it learns to distinguish breeds and "forms"! [1]

2

Then there is that age-old problem of universals as applied to art. It has received its classical formulation in the Platonizing theories of the Academicians. "A history-painter," says Reynolds, "paints man in general; a portrait-painter a particular man, and therefore a defective model." [2] This, of course, is the theory of abstraction applied to one specific problem. The implications are that the portrait, being an exact copy of a man's "external form" with all "blemishes" and "accidents," refers to the individual person exactly as does the proper name. The painter, however, who wants to "elevate his style" disregards the particular and "generalizes the forms." Such a picture will no longer represent a particular man but rather the class or concept "man." There is a deceptive simplicity in this argument but it makes at least one unwarranted assumption: that every image of this kind necessarily refers to something outside itself—be it individual or class. But no such reference need be implied if we point to an image and say "this is a man." Strictly speaking that statement may be interpreted to mean that the image itself is a member of the class "man." Nor is that interpretation as farfetched as it may sound. In fact our hobby horse would submit to no other interpretation. By the logic of Reynolds's reasoning it would have to represent the most generalized idea of horseness. But if the child calls a stick a horse it obviously means nothing of the kind. It does not think in terms of reference at all. The stick is neither a sign signifying the concept horse nor is it a portrait of an individual horse. By its capacity of serving as a "substitute" the stick becomes a horse in its own right, it may graduate into the class of "gee-gees" and even receive a proper name of its own.

When Pygmalion blocked out a figure from his marble he did not at first represent a "generalized" human form, and then gradually a particular woman. For as he chipped away and made it more lifelike the block was not turned into a portrait—not even in the unlikely case that he used a live model. So when his prayers were heard and the statue came to life she was Galatea and no one else—and that regardless of whether she had been fashioned in an archaic, idealistic, or naturalistic style. The question of reference, in fact, is totally independent of the degree of differentiation. The witch who made a "generalized" wax dummy of an enemy may have meant it to refer to someone in particular. She would then pronounce the right spell to establish this link—much as we may write a caption under a generalized picture to do the same. But even those proverbial replicas of nature, Madam Tussaud's effigies, need the same treatment. Those in the galleries which are labeled are "portraits of the great." The figure on the staircase made to hoax the visitor simply represents "an" attendant, a class. It stands there as a "substitute" for the expected guard—but it is not more "generalized" in Renyolds's sense.

3

The idea that art is "creation" rather than "imitation" is sufficiently familiar. It has been proclaimed in various forms from the time of Leonardo, who insisted that the painter is "Lord of all Things," [3] to Klee, who wanted to create as Nature does.[4] But the more solemn overtones of metaphysical power disappear when we leave art for toys. The child "makes" a train either of a few blocks or with pencil on paper. Surrounded as we are by posters and newspapers carrying illustrations of commodities or events, we find it difficult to rid ourselves of the prejudice that all images should be "read" as referring to some imaginary or actual reality. Only the historian knows how hard it is to look at Pygmalion's work without comparing it with nature. But recently have we been made aware how thoroughly we misunderstand primitive or Egyptian art whenever we make the assumption that the artist "distorts" his motif or that he even wants us to see in his work the record of any concrete experience.[5] In many cases these images "represent" in the sense of "substitution." The clay horse or servant buried in the tomb of the mighty takes the place of the living. The idol takes the place of the God.

The question whether it represents the "external form" of the particular divinity or, for that matter, of a class of demons does not come in at all. The idol serves as the substitute of the God in worship and ritual—it is a man-made God in precisely the sense that the hobby horse is a man-made horse; to question it further means to court deception.[6]

There is another misunderstanding to be guarded against. We often try instinctively to save our idea of "representation" by shifting it to another plane. Where we cannot refer the image to a motif in the outer world we take it to be a portrayal of a motif in the artist's inner world. Much critical (and uncritical) writing on both primitive and modern art betrays this assumption. But to apply the naturalistic idea of portrayal to dreams and visions—let alone to unconscious images—begs a whole number of questions.[7] The hobby horse does not portray our idea of a horse. The fearsome monster or funny face we may doodle on our blotting pad is not projected out of our mind as paint is "ex-pressed" out of a paint tube. Of course any image will be in some way symptomatic of its maker, but to think of it as of a photograph of a pre-existing reality is to misunderstand the whole process of image-making.

4

Can our substitute take us further? Perhaps, if we consider how it could become a substitute. The "first" hobby horse (to use eighteenth-century language) was probably no image at all. Just a stick which qualified as a horse because one could ride on it (Figure 1).* The *tertium comparationis,* the common factor, was function rather than form. Or, more precisely, that formal aspect which fulfilled the minimum requirement for the performance of the function—for any "ridable" object could serve as a horse. If that is true we may be enabled to cross a boundary which is usually regarded as closed and sealed. For in this sense "substitutes" reach deep into biological layers that are common to man and animal. The cat runs after the ball as if it were a mouse. The baby sucks its thumb as if it were the breast. In a sense the ball "represents" a mouse to the cat, the thumb a breast to the baby. But here too "representation" does not depend on formal, that is geometrical, qualities beyond the minimum requirements of function. The ball has nothing in common with the mouse except that it is chasable. The thumb nothing with the breast except that it is suckable. As "substitutes" they fulfill certain demands of the organism. They are keys which happen to fit into biological or psychological locks, or counterfeit coins which make the machine work when dropped into the slot.

* [Additional illustrations originally accompanying this essay have been deleted.]

Fig. 1. The Hobby Horse. Engraving by Israel van Meckenem
(about 1500).

In the language of the nursery the psychological function of
"representation" is still recognized. The child will reject a
perfectly naturalistic doll in favor of some monstrously "abstract" dummy which is "cuddly." It may even dispose of
the element of "form" altogether and take to a blanket or an
eiderdown as its favorite "comforter"—a substitute on which
to bestow its love. Later in life, as the psychoanalysts tell us,
it may bestow this same love on a worthy or unworthy living
substitute. A teacher may "take the place" of the mother, a
dictator or even an enemy may come to "represent" the
father. Once more the common denominator between the
symbol and the thing symbolized is not the "external form"
but the function; the mother symbol should be lovable, the
father-imago fearable, or whatever the case may be.

Now this psychological concept of symbolization seems to
lead enormously far away from the more precise meaning
which the word "representation" has acquired in the figurative arts. Can there be any gain in throwing all these meanings together? Possibly there is. For anything seems worth
trying to get the function of symbolization out of its isolation.

The "origin of art" has ceased to be a popular topic. But the origin of the hobby horse may be a permitted subject for speculation. Let us assume that the owner of the stick on which he proudly rode through the land decided in a playful or magic mood—and who could always distinguish between the two?—to fix "real" reins and that finally he was even tempted to "give" it two eyes near the top end. Some grass could have passed for a mane. Thus our archartist "had a horse." He had made one. Now there are two things about this fictitious event which have some bearing on the idea of the figurative arts. One is that, contrary to what is sometimes said, communication need not come into this process at all. He may not have wanted to show his horse to anyone. It just served as a focus for his fantasies as he galloped along —though more likely than not it fulfilled this same function to a tribe to which it "represented" some horse-demon of fertility and power.[8] We may sum up the moral of this "Just So Story" by saying that substitution may precede portrayal, and creation communication. It remains to be seen how such a general theory can be tested. If it can, it may really throw light on some concrete questions. Even the origin of language, that notorious problem of speculative history,[9] might be investigated from this angle. For what if the "pow-wow" theory, which sees the root of language in imitation, and the "pooh-pooh" theory which sees it in emotive interjection, were to be joined by yet another? We might term it the "niam-niam" theory postulating the primitive hunter lying awake in hungry winter nights and making the sound of eating, not for communication but as a substitute for eating—being joined, perhaps, by a ritualistic chorus trying to conjure up the phantasm of food.

5

There is one sphere in which the investigation of "representational" functions of forms has made considerable progress of late, that of animal psychology. Pliny, and innumerable writers after him, have regarded it as the greatest triumph of naturalistic art for a painter to have deceived sparrows or horses. The implication of these anecdotes is that a human beholder easily recognizes a bunch of grapes in a painting because for him recognition is an intellectual act. But for the birds to fly at the painting is a sign of a complete "objective" illusion. It is a plausible idea, but a wrong one. The merest outline of a cow seems sufficient for a tsetse trap, for somehow it sets the apparatus of attraction in motion and "deceives" the fly. To the fly, we might say, the crude trap has the "significant" form—biologically significant, that is. It appears that visual stimuli of this kind play an important part in the animal world. By varying the shapes of "dummies" to which animals were seen to respond, the "minimum image" that still sufficed to release a specific reaction has been ascertained.[10] Thus little birds will open their beak when they see the feeding parent approaching the nest but they will also do so when they are shown two darkish roundels of different size "representing" the silhouette of the head and body of the bird in its most "generalized" form. Certain young fishes can even be deceived by two simple dots arranged horizontally, which they take to be the eyes of the mother fish in whose mouth they are accustomed to shelter against danger. The fame of Zeuxis will have to rest on other achievements than his deception of birds.

An "image" in this biological sense, then, is not an imitation of an object's external form but an imitation of certain privileged or relevant aspects. It is here that a wide field of investigation would seem to open. For man is not exempt from this type of reaction.[11] The artist who goes out to represent the visible form is not simply faced with a neutral medley of forms he seeks to "imitate." Ours is a structured universe whose main lines of force are still bent and fashioned by our biological and psychological needs, however much they may be overlaid by cultural influences. We know that there are certain privileged motifs in our world to which we respond almost too easily. The human face may be outstanding among them. Whether by instinct or by very early training, we certainly are ever disposed to single out the expressive features of a face from the chaos of sensations that surrounds it and to respond to its slightest variations with fear or joy. Our whole perceptive apparatus is somehow hypersensitized in this direction of physiognomic vision [12] and the merest hint suffices for us to create an expressive physiognomy that "looks" at us with surprising intensity. In a heightened state of emotion, in the dark, or in a feverish spell the looseness of this trigger may assume pathological forms. We may see faces in the pattern of a wallpaper, and three apples arranged on a plate may stare at us like two eyes and a clownish nose. What wonder that it is so easy to "make" a face with two dots and a stroke even though their geometrical constellation may be greatly at variance with the "external form" of a real head? The well-known graphic joke of the "reversible face" might well be taken as a model for experiments which could still be made in this direction. It shows to what extent the group of shapes that can be read as a physiognomy has priority over all other readings. It turns the side which is the right way up into a convincing face and disintegrates the one that is upside down into a mere jumble of forms which is accepted as a strange headgear.[13] In good pictures of this kind it needs a real effort to see both faces at the same time. Our automatic response is stronger than our intellectual awareness.

Seen in the light of the biological examples discussed above there is nothing surprising in this observation. We may venture the guess that this type of automatic recognition is dependent on the two factors of resemblance and biological relevance and that the two may stand in some kind of inverse ratio. The greater the biological relevance an object has to us the more will we be attuned to its recognition—and the more tolerant will therefore be our standards of formal correspondence. In an erotically charged atmosphere the merest hint of formal similarity with sexual functions creates the desired response and the same is true of the dream symbols investigated by Freud. The hungry man will be similarly attuned to the discovery of food—he will scan the world for sensations likely to satisfy his urge. The starving may even project food into all sorts of dissimilar objects—as Chaplin does in *Gold Rush* when his huge companion suddenly appears to him as a chicken. Can it have been some such experience which stimulated our "niam-niam" chanting hunters to see their longed-for prey in the patches and irregular shapes on the dark cave walls? Could they perhaps gradually have sought this experience in the deep mysterious recesses of the rocks, much as Leonardo sought out crumbling walls to aid his visual fantasies? Could they finally have been prompted to fill in such "readable" outlines with colored earth—to have at least something "spearable" at hand which might "represent" the eatable in some magic fashion? There is no way of testing such a theory, but if it is true that cave artists often "exploited" the natural formations of the rocks,[14] this, together with the "eidetic" character of their works,[15] would at least not contradict our fantasy. The great naturalism of cave paintings may after all be a very late flower. It may correspond to our late, derivative, and naturalistic hobby horse.

6

It needed two conditions, then, to turn a stick into our hobby horse: first, that its form made it just possible to ride on it; secondly—and perhaps decisively—that riding mattered. Fortunately it still needs no great effort of the imagination to understand how the horse could become such a focus of desires and aspirations, for our language still carries the metaphors molded by a feudal past when to be chival-rous was to be horsy. The same stick that had to represent a horse in such a setting would have become the substitute of something else in another. It might have become a sword, scepter, or—in the context of ancestor worship—a fetish representing a dead chieftain. Seen from the point of view of "abstraction," such a convergence of meanings onto one shape offers considerable difficulties, but from that of psychological "projection" of meanings it becomes more easily intelligible. After all a whole diagnostic technique has been built up on the assumption that the meanings read into identical forms by different people tell us more about the readers than about the forms. In the sphere of art it has been shown that the same triangular shape which is the favorite pattern of many adjoining American Indian tribes is given different meanings reflecting the main preoccupations of the peoples concerned.[16] To the student of styles this discovery that one basic form can be made to represent a variety of objects may still become significant. For while the idea of realistic pictures being deliberately "stylized" seems hard to swallow, the opposite idea of a limited vocabulary of simple shapes being used for the building and making of different representations would fit much better into what we know of primitive art.

7

Once we get used to the idea of "representation" as a two-way affair rooted in psychological dispositions we may be able to refine a tool which has proved quite indispensable to the historian of art and which is nevertheless rather unsatisfactory: the notion of the "conceptual image." By this we mean the mode of representation which is more or less common to children's drawings and to various forms of primitive and primitivist art. The remoteness of this type of imagery from any visual experience has often been described.[17] The explanation of this fact which is most usually advanced is that the child (and the primitive) do not draw what they "see" but what they "know." According to this idea the typical children's drawing of a manikin is really a graphic enumeration of those human features the child remembered.[18] It represents the content of the childish "concept" of man. But to speak of "knowledge" or "intellectual realism" (as the French do) [19] brings us dangerously near to the fallacy of "abstraction." So back to our hobby horse. Is it quite correct to say that it consists of features which make up the "concept" of a horse or that it reflects the memory image of horses seen? No—because this formulation omits one factor: the stick. If we keep in mind that representation is originally the creation of substitutes out of given material we may reach safer ground. The greater the wish to ride, the fewer may be the features that will do for a horse. But at a certain stage it must have eyes—for how else could it see? At the most primitive layer, then, the conceptual image might be identified with what we have called the minimum image—that minimum, that is, which will make it fit into a psychological lock. The form of the key depends on the material out of which it is fashioned, and on the lock. It would be a dangerous mistake, however, to equate the "conceptual image" as we find it used in the historical styles with this psychologically grounded minimum image. On the contrary. One has the impression that the presence of these schemata is always felt but that they are as much avoided as exploited.[20] We must reckon with the possibility of a "style" being a set of convictions born out of complex tensions. The man-made image must be complete. The servant for the grave must have two hands and two feet. But he must not become a double under the artist's hands. Image-making is beset with dangers. One false stroke and the rigid mask of the face may assume an evil leer. Strict adherence to conventions alone can guard against such dangers. And thus primitive art seems often to keep on that narrow ledge that lies between the lifeless and the uncanny. If the hobby horse became too lifelike it might gallop away on its own.[21]

8

The contrast between primitive art and "naturalistic" or "illusionist" art can easily be overdrawn.[22] All art is "image-making" and all image making is rooted in the creation of substitutes. Even the artist of an "illusionist" persuasion must make the man-made, the "conceptual" image of convention his starting point. Strange as it may seem he cannot simply "imitate an object's external form" without having first learned how to construct such a form. If it were otherwise there would be no need for the innumerable books on "how to draw the human figure" or "how to draw ships." Wölfflin once remarked that all pictures owe more to other pictures than they do to nature.[23] It is a point which is familiar to the student of pictorial traditions but which is still insufficiently understood in its psychological implications. Perhaps the reason is that contrary to the hopeful belief of many artists the "innocent eye" which should see the world afresh would not see it at all. It would smart under the painful impact of a chaotic medley of forms and colors.[24] In this sense the conventional vocabulary of basic forms is still indispensable to the artist as a starting point, as a focus of organization.

How, then, should we interpret that great divide which runs through the history of art and sets off the few islands of illusionist styles, of Greece, of China, and of the Renaissance, from the vast ocean of "conceptual" art?

One difference, undoubtedly, lies in a change of function. In a way the change is implicit in the emergence of the idea of the image as a "representation" in our modern sense of the word. As soon as it is generally understood that an image

need not exist in its own right, that it refers to something outside itself and is therefore the record of a visual experience
rather than the creation of a substitute, the basic rules of
primitive art can be transgressed with impunity. No longer
is there any need for that completeness of essentials which
belongs to the conceptual style, no longer is there the fear
of the casual which dominates the archaic conception of art.
The picture of a man on a Greek vase no longer needs a hand
or a foot in full view. We know it is meant as a shadow, a
mere record of what the artist saw and we are quite ready
to join in the game and to supplement in our imagination
what the real motif undoubtedly possessed. Once this idea of
the picture as a sign referring to something outside itself is
accepted in all its implications—and this certainly did not
happen overnight—we are indeed forced to let our imagination
play around it. We endow it with "space" around the figure,
which is only another way of saying that we understand
that the reality to which it referred was three-dimensional,
that the man could move and that even the aspect momen-
tarily hidden "was there."[25] When medieval art broke away
from that narrative conceptual symbolism into which the
formulas of classical art had been frozen, Giotto made particular use of the figure seen from behind which stimulates our
"tactile" imagination by forcing us to imagine it in the round.

Thus the idea of the picture as a representation of a reality
outside itself leads to an interesting paradox. On the one hand
it compels us to refer every figure and every object shown to
that imaginary reality which is "meant." This mental operation can only be completed if the picture allows us to infer
not only the "external form" of every object represented but
also its relative size and position. It leads thus to that "ra-
tionalization of space" we call scientific perspective by which
the picture plane becomes a window pane through which we
look into the imaginary world the artist creates there for us.
In theory, at least, painting becomes synonymous with geometrical projection.[26]

The paradox of the situation is that once the whole picture
is conceived as the representation of a slice of reality, a new
context is created in which the conceptual image plays a
different part. For the first consequence of the "window"
idea is that we cannot conceive of any spot on the panel which
is not "significant," which does not represent something. The
empty patch thus comes easily to signify light, air, and atmosphere, and the vague form is interpreted as enveloped
by air. It is this confidence in the representational context
which is given by the very convention of the frame which
makes the development of impressionist methods possible.
The artists who tried to rid themselves of their conceptual

knowledge, who conscientiously became beholders of their own work and never ceased matching their created images against their impressions by stepping back and comparing the two—these artists could only achieve their aim by shifting something of the load of creation on to the beholder. For what else does it mean if we are enjoined to step back in turn and watch the colored patches of an impressionist landscape "spring to life"? It means that the painter relies on our readiness to take hints, to read contexts, and to call up our conceptual image under his guidance. The blob in the painting by Manet which stands for a horse is no more an imitation of its external form than is our hobby horse. But he has so cleverly contrived it that it evokes the image in us—provided, of course, we collaborate.

Here there may be another field for independent investigation. For those "privileged" objects which play their part in the earliest layers of image-making recur—as was to be expected—in that of image-reading. The more vital the feature that is indicated by the context and yet omitted, the more intense seems to be the process that is started off. On its lowest level this method of "suggestive veiling" is familiar to erotic art. Not, of course, to its Pygmalion phase, but to its illusionist applications. What is here a crude exploitation of an obvious biological stimulus may have its parallel, for instance, in the representation of the human face. Leonardo achieved his greatest triumphs of lifelike expression by blurring precisely the features in which expression resides, thus compelling us to complete the act of creation. Rembrandt could dare to leave the eyes of his most moving portraits in the shade because we are thus stimulated to supplement them.[27] The "evocative" image, like its "conceptual" counterpart, should be studied against a wider psychological background.

9

My hobby horse is not art. At best it can claim the attention of iconology, that emerging branch of study which is to art criticism what linguistics is to the criticism of literature. But has not modern art experimented with the primitive image, with the "creation" of forms, and the exploitation of deep-rooted psychological forces? It has. But whatever the nostalgic wish of their makers the meaning of these forms can never be the same as that of their primitive models. For that strange precinct we call "art" is like a hall of mirrors or a whispering gallery. Each form conjures up a thousand memories and afterimages. No sooner is an image presented as art than, by this very act, a new frame of reference is created which it cannot escape. It becomes part of an institution as surely as does the toy in the nursery. If—as might be conceivable—a Picasso would turn from pottery to hobby horses and send the products of this whim to an exhibition, we might read them as demonstrations, as satirical symbols, as a declaration of faith in humble things or as self-irony— but one thing would be denied even to the greatest of contemporary artists: he could not make the hobby horse mean to us what it meant to its first creator. This way is barred by the angel with a flaming sword.

NOTES

1. In the sphere of art this process of differentiation rather than abstraction is wittily described by Oliver Wendell Holmes in the essay "*Cacoethes Scribendi,*" from *Over the Teacups* (London: 1890): "It's just my plan . . . for teaching drawing. . . . A man at a certain distance appears as a dark spot —nothing more. Good. Anybody . . . can make a dot. . . . Lesson No. 1. Make a dot; that is, draw your man, a mile off. . . . Now make him come a little nearer. . . . The dot is an oblong figure now. Good. Let your scholar draw an oblong figure. It is as easy as to make a note of admiration. . . . So by degrees the man who serves as a model approaches. A bright pupil will learn to get the outline of a human figure in ten lessons, the model coming five hundred feet nearer every time."

2. *Fourth Discourse* (Everyman Edition), p. 55. I have discussed the historical setting of this idea in "*Icones Symbolicae,*" *Journal of the Warburg and Courtauld Institutes*, XI (1948), p. 187, and some of its more technical aspects in a review of Charles Morris, *Signs, Language, and Behavior* (New York: 1946) in *The Art Bulletin*, March 1949. In Morris's terminology these present meditations are concerned with the status and origin of the "iconic sign."

3. Leonardo da Vinci, *Paragone,* edited by I. A. Richter (London: 1949), p. 51.

4. Paul Klee, *On Modern Art* (London, 1948). For the history of the idea of *deus artifex* cf. E. Kris and O. Kurz, *Die Legende vom Künstler* (Vienna: 1934).

5. H. A. Groenewegen-Frankfort, *Arrest and Movement: An Essay on Space and Time in the Representational Art of the Ancient Near East* (London: 1951).

6. Perhaps it is only in a setting of realistic art that the problem I have discussed in "*Icones Symbolicae,*" loc. cit., becomes urgent. Only then the idea can gain ground that the allegorical

image of, say, Justice, must be a portrait of Justice as she dwells in heaven.

7. For the history of this misinterpretation and its consequences, cf. my article on "Art and Imagery in the Romantic Period," *The Burlington Magazine,* June 1949.

8. This, at least, would be the opinion of Lewis Spence, *Myth and Ritual in Dance, Game, and Rhyme* (London: 1947). And also of Ben Jonson's Busy, the Puritan: "Thy Hobby-horse is an Idoll, a feirce and rancke Idoll: And thou, the *Nabuchadnezzar* . . . of the *Faire,* that set'st it up, for children to fall downe to, and worship." (*Bartholomew Fair,* Act. III, Scene 6).

9. Cf. Géza Révész, *Ursprung und Vorgeschichte der Sprache* (Berne: 1946).

10. Cf. Konrad Lorenz, *"Die angeborenen Formen möglicher Erfahrung,"* Zeitschrift für Tierpsychologie V (1943), and the discussion of these experiments in E. Grassi and Th. von Uexküll, *Vom Ursprung und von den Grenzen der Geisteswissenschaften und Naturwissenschaften* (Bern: 1950).

11. K. Lorenz, loc. cit. The citation of this article does not imply support of the author's moral conclusions. On these more general issues see K. R. Popper, *The Open Society and Its Enemies,* esp., I, pp. 59 ff. and p. 268.

12. F. Sander, *"Experimentelle Ergebnisse der Gestaltpsychologie," Berichte über den 10. Kongress für Experimentelle Psychologie* (Jena: 1928), p. 47, has shown that the distance of two dots is much harder to estimate in its variations when these dots are isolated than when they are made to represent eyes in a schematic face and thus attain physiognomic significance.

13. For a large collection of such faces cf. Laurence Whistler, *Oho! The Drawings of Rex Whistler* (London: 1946).

14. G. H. Luquet, *The Art and Religion of Fossil Man* (London: 1930), pp. 141 f.

15. G. A. S. Snijder, *Kretische Kunst* (Berlin: 1936), pp. 68 f.

16. Franz Boas, *Primitive Art* (Oslo: 1927), pp. 118–28.

17. E.g., E. Löwy, *The Rendering of Nature in Early Greek Art* (London: 1907), H. Schaefer, *Von aegyptischer Kunst* (Leipzig: 1930), Mr. Verworn, *Ideoplastische Kunst* (Jena: 1914).

18. Karl Buehler, *The Mental Development of the Child* (London: 1930), pp. 113–17, where the connection with the linguistic faculty is stressed. A criticism of this idea was advanced by R. Arnheim, "Perceptual Abstraction and Art," *Psychological Review,* LVI, 1947.

19. G. H. Luquet, *L'Art primitif* (Paris: 1930).

20. The idea of avoidance (of sexual symbols) is stressed by A. Ehrenzweig, "Unconscious Form-creation in Art," *The British Journal of Medical Psychology,* XXI (1948) and XXII (1949).

21. E. Kris and O. Kurz, loc. cit., have collected a number of

legends reflecting this age-old fear: Thus a famous Chinese master was said never to have put the light into the eyes of his painted dragons lest they would fly away.

22. It was the intellectual fashion in German art history to work with contrasting pairs of concepts such as haptic-optic (Riegl), paratactic-hypotactic (Coellen), abstraction-empathy (Worringer), idealism-naturalism (Dvorak), physioplastic-ideoplastic (Verworn), multiplicity-unity (Wölfflin), all of which could probably be expressed in terms of "conceptual" and "less conceptual" art. While the heuristic value of this method of antithesis is not in doubt it often tends to introduce a false dichotomy. In my book *The Story of Art* (London: 1950) I have attempted to stress the continuity of tradition and the persistent role of the conceptual image.

23. H. Wölfflin, *Principles of Art History* (New York: 1932).

24. Cf. the Reith Lecture by J. Z. Young, "Doubt and Certainty in Science," reprinted in *The Listener*, November 23, 1950. The fallacy of a passive idea of perception is also discussed in detail by E. Brunswik, *Wahrnehmung und Gegenstandswelt* (Vienna: 1934). In its application to art the writings of K. Fiedler contain many valuable hints; cf. also A. Ehrenzweig, loc. cit., for an extreme and challenging presentation of this problem.

25. This may be meant in the rather enigmatic passage on the painter Parrhasius in Pliny's *Natural History*, XXXV, 67, where it is said that "the highest subtlety attainable in painting is to find an outline . . . which should appear to fold back and to enclose the object so as to give assurance of the parts behind, thus clearly suggesting even what it conceals."

26. Cf. E. Panofsky, "The Codex Huygens and Leonardo da Vinci's Art Theory," *Studies of the Warburg Institute*, XIII (London: 1940), pp. 90 f.

27. Cf. J. V. Schlosser, *"Gespräch von der Bildniskunst,"* *Praludien* (Vienna: 1927), where, incidentally, the hobby horse also makes its appearance.

ON POINT OF VIEW IN THE ARTS *

José Ortega y Gasset

When history is what it should be, it is an elaboration of cinema. It is not content to install itself in the successive facts and to view the moral landscape that may be perceived from here; but for this series of static images, each enclosed within itself, history substitutes the image of a movement. "Vistas" which had been discontinuous appear to emerge one from another, each prolonging the other without interruption. Reality, which for one moment seemed an infinity of crystallized facts, frozen in position, liquefies, springs forth, and flows. The true historical reality is not the datum, the fact, the thing, but the evolution formed when these materials melt and fluidify. History moves; the still waters are made swift.

2

In the museum we find the lacquered corpse of an evolution. Here is the flux of that pictorial anxiety which has budded forth from man century after century. To conserve this evolution, it has had to be undone, broken up, converted into fragments again, and congealed as in a refrigerator. Each picture is a crystal with unmistakable and rigid edges, separated from the others, a hermetic island.

And, nonetheless, it is a corpse we could easily revive. We would need only to arrange the pictures in a certain order and then move the eye—or the mind's eye—quickly from one to the other. Then, it would become clear that the evolution of painting from Giotto to our own time is a unique and simple action with a beginning and an end. It is surprising that so elementary a law has guided the variations of pictorial art in our Western world. Even more curious, and most disturbing, is the analogy of this law with that which has directed the course of European philosophy. This parallel between the two most widely separated disciplines of culture permits us to suspect the existence of an even more general principle which has been active in the entire evolution of the European mind. I am not, however, going to prolong our adventure to this remote arcana, and will content myself, for the present, with interpreting the visage of six centuries that has been Occidental painting.

* [Translated from the Spanish by Paul Snodgress and Joseph Frank. Copyright, August 1949, by *Partisan Review*. Reprinted by permission of *Partisan Review*.]

3

Movement implies a mover. In the evolution of painting, what is it that moves? Each canvas is an instant in which the mover stands fixed. What is this? Do not look for something very complicated. The thing that varies, the thing that shifts in painting, and which by its shifts produces the diversity of aspects and styles, is simply the painter's point of view.

It is natural enough. An abstract idea is ubiquitous. The isosceles triangle presents the same aspect on Earth as on Sirius. On the other hand, a sensuous image bears the indelible mark of its localization, that is, the image presents something seen from a definite point of view. This localization of the sensible may be strict or vague, but it is inevitable. A church spire, a sail at sea, present themselves to us at a distance that for practical purposes we may estimate with some accuracy. The moon or the blue face of heaven are at a distance essentially imprecise, but quite characteristic in their imprecision. We cannot say that they are so many miles away; their localization in distance is vague, but this vagueness is not indetermination.

Nonetheless, it is not the geodetic *quantity* of distance which decisively influences the painter's point of view, but its optical *quality*. "Near" and "far" are relative, metrically, while to the eye they may have a kind of absolute value. Indeed, the *proximate vision* and the *distant vision* of which physiology speaks are not notions that depend chiefly on measurable factors, but are rather two distinct ways of seeing.

If we take up an object, an earthen jar, for example, and bring it near enough to the eyes, these converge on it. Then, the field of vision assumes a peculiar structure. In the center there is the favored object, fixed by our gaze; its form seems clear, perfectly defined in all its details. Around the object, as far as the limits of the field of vision, there is a zone we do not look at, but which, nevertheless, we see with an indirect, vague, inattentive vision. Everything within this zone seems to be situated behind the object; this is why we call it the "background." But, moreover, this whole background is blurred, hardly identifiable, without accented form, reduced to confused masses of color. If it is not something to which we are accustomed, we cannot say what it is, exactly, that we see in this indirect vision.

The proximate vision, then, organizes the whole field of vision, imposing upon it an optical hierarchy: a privileged central nucleus articulates itself against the surrounding area. The central object is a luminous hero, a protagonist standing out against a "mass," a visual *plebs,* and surrounded by a cosmic chorus.

Compare this with distant vision. Instead of fixing a proximate object, let the eye, passive but free, prolong its line of vision to the limit of the visual field. What do we find then? The structure of our hierarchized elements disappears. The ocular field is homogeneous; we do not see one thing clearly and the rest confusedly, for all are submerged in an optical democracy. Nothing possesses a sharp profile; everything is background, confused, almost formless. On the other hand, the duality of proximate vision is succeeded by a perfect unity of the whole visual field.

4

To these different modes of seeing, we must add another more important one.

In looking close-up at our earthen jar, the eyebeam strikes the most prominent part of its bulge. Then, as if shattered at this point of contact, the beam is splintered into multiple lines which glide around the sides of the vase and seem to embrace it, to take possession of it, to emphasize its rotundity. Thus the object seen at close range acquires the indefinable corporeality and solidity of filled volume. We see it "in bulk," convexly. But this same object placed farther away, for distant vision, loses this corporeality, this solidity and plenitude. Now it is no longer a compact mass, clearly rotund, with its protuberance and curving flanks; it has lost "bulk," and become, rather, an insubstantial surface, an unbodied specter composed only of light.

Proximate vision has a tactile quality. What mysterious resonance of touch is preserved by sight when it converges on a nearby object? We shall not now attempt to violate this mystery. It is enough that we recognize this quasi-tactile density possessed by the ocular ray, and which permits it, in effect, to embrace, to touch, the earthen jar. As the object is withdrawn, sight loses its tactile power and gradually becomes pure vision. In the same way, things, as they recede, cease to be filled volumes, hard and compact, and become mere chromatic entities, without resistance, mass, or convexity. An age-old habit, founded in vital necessity, causes men to consider as "things," in the strict sense, only such objects solid enough to offer resistance to their hands. The rest is more or less illusion. So in passing from proximate to distant vision an object becomes illusory. When the distance is great, there on the confines of a remote horizon—a tree, a castle, a mountain range—all acquire the half-unreal aspect of ghostly apparitions.

5

A final and decisive observation.

When we oppose proximate to distant vision, we do not

mean that in the latter the object is farther away. To look means here, speaking narrowly, to focus both ocular rays on a point which, thanks to this, becomes favored, optically privileged. In distant vision we do not fix the gaze on any point, but rather attempt to embrace the whole field, including its boundaries. For this reason, we avoid focusing the eyes as much as possible. And then we are surprised to find that the object just perceived—our entire visual field—is concave. If we are in a house the concavity is bordered by the walls, the roof, the floor. This border or limit is a surface that tends to take the form of a hemisphere viewed from within. But where does the concavity begin? There is no possibility of doubt: it begins at our eyes themselves.

The result is that what we see at a distance is hollow space as such. The content of perception is not strictly the surface in which the hollow space terminates, but rather the whole hollow space itself, from the eyeball to the wall or the horizon.

This fact obliges us to recognize the following paradox: the object of sight is not farther off in distant than in proximate vision, but on the contrary is nearer, since it begins at our cornea. In pure distant vision, our attention, instead of being directed farther away, has drawn back to the absolutely proximate, and the eyebeam, instead of striking the convexity of a solid body and staying fixed on it, penetrates a concave object, glides into a hollow.

6

Throughout the history of the arts in Europe, then, the painter's point of view has been changing from proximate to distant vision, and painting, correspondingly, which begins with Giotto as painting of bulk, turns into painting of hollow space.

This means there has been nothing capricious in the itinerary followed by the painter's shift of attention. First it is fixed upon the body or volume of an object, then upon what lies between the body of the object and the eye, that is, the hollow space. And since the latter is in front of the object, it follows that the journey of the pictorial gaze is a retrogression from the distant—although close by—toward what is contiguous to the eye.

According to this, the evolution of Western painting would consist in a retraction from the object toward the subject, the painter.

The reader may test for himself this law that governs the movement of pictorial art by a chronological review of the history of painting. In what follows, I limit myself to a few examples that are, as it were, stages on such a journey.

7   THE QUATTROCENTO

The Flemish and the Italians cultivate with passion the painting of bulk. One would say they paint with their hands. Every object appears unequivocally solid, corporeal, tangible. Covering it is a polished skin, without pores or growths, which seems to delight in asserting its own rounded volume. Objects in the background receive the same treatment as those of the foreground. The artist contents himself with representing the distant as smaller than the proximate, but he paints both in the same way. The distinction of planes is, then, merely abstract, and is obtained by pure geometrical perspective. Pictorially, everything in these pictures is in one plane, that is, everything is painted from close-up. The smallest figure, there in the distance, is as complete, spherical, and detached as the most important. The painter seems to have gone to the distant spot where they are, and from near at hand to have painted them as distant.

But it is impossible to see several objects close-up at the same time. The proximate gaze must shift from one to the other to make each in turn the center of vision. This means that the point of view in a primitive picture is not single, but as many points of view as there are objects represented. The canvas is not painted as a unity, but as a plurality. No part is related to any other; each is perfect and separate. Hence the best means of distinguishing the two tendencies in pictorial art—painting of bulk and painting of hollow space—is to take a portion of the picture and see whether, in isolation, it is enough to represent something fully. On a canvas of Velázquez, each section contains only vague and monstrous forms.

The primitive canvas is, in a certain sense, the sum of many small pictures, each one independent and each painted from the proximate view. The painter has directed an exclusive and analytic gaze at each one of the objects. This accounts for the diverting richness of these *quattrocento* catalogues. We never have done with looking at them. We always discover a new little interior picture that we had not observed closely enough. On the other hand, they cannot be seen as a whole. The pupil of our eye has to travel step by step along the canvas, pausing in the same point of view that the painter successively took.

8   RENAISSANCE

Proximate vision is exclusive, since it apprehends each object in itself and separates it from the rest. Raphael does not modify this point of view, but introduces in the picture an abstract element that affords it a certain unity; this is composition, or architecture. He continues to paint one object after another, like a primitive; his visual apparatus functions on the same principle. But instead of limiting himself, like the primitive, to paint what he sees as he sees it, he submits everything to an external force: the geometrical idea of unity. Upon the analytic form of objects, there is imperatively fixed the synthetic form of composition, which is not the visible form of an object, but a pure rational schema. (Leonardo, too, for example in his triangular canvases.)

Raphael's pictures, then, do not derive from, and cannot be viewed in, a unified field of vision. But there is already in them the rational basis of unification.

9 TRANSITION

If we pass from the primitives and the Renaissance toward Velázquez, we find in the Venetians, but especially in Tintoretto and El Greco, an intermediate stage. How shall we define it?

In Tintoretto and El Greco two epochs meet. Hence the anxiety, the restlessness that marks the work of both. These are the last representatives of painting in bulk, and they already sense the future problems of painting in hollow space without, however, coming to grips with them.

Venetian art, from the beginning, tends to a distant view of things. In Giorgione and Titian, the bodies seem to wish to lose their hard contours, and float like clouds or some diaphanous fabric. However, the will to abandon the proximate and analytic point of view is still lacking. For a century, there is a struggle between both principles, with victory for neither. Tintoretto is an extreme example of this inner tension, in which distant vision is already on the point of victory. In the canvases of the Escorial he constructs great empty spaces. But in this undertaking he is forced to lean on architectonic perspective as on a crutch. Without those columns and cornices that flee into the background, Tintoretto's brush would fall into the abyss of that hollow space he aspired to create.

El Greco represents something of a regression. I believe that his modernity and his nearness to Velázquez has been exaggerated. El Greco is still chiefly preoccupied with volume. The proof is that he may be accounted the last great foreshortener. He does not seek empty space; in him there remains the intention to capture the corporeal, filled volume. While Velázquez, in "The Ladies in Waiting" and "The Spinners," groups his human figures at the right and left, leaving the central space more or less free—as if space were the true protagonist—El Greco piles up solid masses over the whole canvas that completely displace the air. His works are usually stuffed with flesh.

However, pictures like "The Resurrection," "The Crucified" (Prado), and "Pentecost," pose the problems of painting
in depth with rare power.

But it is a mistake to confuse the painting of depth with
that of hollow space or empty concavity. The former is only
a more learned way of asserting volume. On the other hand,
the latter is a total inversion of pictorial intention.

What we find in El Greco is that the architectonic principle has completely taken over the represented objects and
forced these, with unparalleled violence, to submit to its ideal
schema. In this way, the analytic vision, which seeks volume
by emphasizing each figure for its own sake, is mitigated and
neutralized, as it were, by the synthetic intention. The formal
dynamic schema that dominates the picture imposes on it a
certain unity and fosters the illusion of a single point of view.

Furthermore, there appears already in the work of El
Greco another unifying element: chiaroscuro.

10 THE CHIAROSCURISTS

Raphael's composition, El Greco's dynamic schema, are
postulates of unity that the artist throws upon his canvas—
but nothing more. Every object in the picture continues as
before to assert its volume, and consequently, its independence
and particularism. These unities, then, are of the same abstract
lineage as the geometrical perspective of the primitives. Derived from pure reason, they show themselves incapable of
giving form to the materials of the picture as a whole; or in
other words, they are not pictorial principles. Each section of
the picture is painted without their intervention.

Compared to them, chiaroscuro signifies a radical and more
profound innovation.

When the eye of the painter seeks the body of things, the
objects placed in the painted area will demand, each for itself,
an exclusive and privileged point of view. The picture will
possess a feudal constitution in which every element will
maintain its personal rights. But here, slipping between them,
is a new object gifted with a magic power that permits it—
even more—obliges it to be ubiquitous and occupy the whole
canvas without having to dispossess the others. This magic
object is light. It is everywhere single and unique throughout
the composition. Here is a principle of unity that is not
abstract but real, a thing among other things, not an idea
or schema. The unity of illumination or chiaroscuro imposes
a unique point of view. The painter must now see his entire
work as immersed in the ample element of light.

Thus Ribera, Caravaggio, and the young Velázquez ("The
Adoration of the Magi"). They still seek for corporeality according to accepted practice. But this no longer interests them

primarily. The object in itself begins to be disregarded and have no other role than to serve as support and background for the light playing upon it. One studies the trajectory of light, emphasizing the fluidity of its passage over the face of volumes, over bulkiness.

Is it not clear what shift in the artist's point of view is implied by this? The Velázquez of "The Adoration of the Magi" no longer fixes his attention upon the object as such but upon its surface, where the light falls and is reflected. There has occurred, then, a retraction of vision, which has stopped being a hand and released its grasp of the rounded body. Now, the visual ray halts at the point where the body begins and light strikes resplendently; from there it seeks another point on another object where the same intensity of illumination is vibrating. The painter has achieved a magic solidarity and unification of all the light elements in contrast to the shadow elements. Things of the most disparate form and condition now become equivalent. The individualistic primacy of objects is finished. They are no longer interesting in themselves, and begin to be only a pretext for something else.

11 VELÁZQUEZ

Thanks to chiaroscuro, the unity of the picture becomes internal, and not merely obtained by extrinsic means. However, under the light, volumes continue to lurk, the painting of bulk persists through the refulgent veil of light.

To overcome this dualism, art needed a man of disdainful genius, resolved to have no interest in bodies, to deny their pretensions to solidity, to flatten their petulant bulk. This disdainful genius was Velázquez.

The primitive, enamored of objective shapes, seeks them arduously with his tactile gaze, touches them, embraces them. The chiaroscurist, already less taken with corporeality, lets his ray of vision travel, as along a railway track, with the light ray that migrates from one surface to the next. Velázquez, with formidable audacity, executes the supreme gesture of disdain that calls forth a whole new painting: he halts the pupil of the eye. Nothing more. Such is this gigantic revolution.

Until then, the painter's eye had Ptolemaically revolved about each object, following a servile orbit. Velázquez despotically resolves to fix the one point of view. The entire picture will be born in a single act of vision, and things will have to contrive as best they may to move into the line of vision. It is a Copernican revolution, comparable to that promoted by Descartes, Hume, and Kant in philosophic thought. The eye of the artist is established as the center of the plastic cosmos, around which revolve the forms of objects. Rigidly, the ocular apparatus casts its ray directly forward, without deviating to one side or the other, without preference for any object. When it lights on something, it does not fix upon it, and consequently, that something is converted, not into a round body, but into a mere surface that intercepts vision.[1]

The point of view has been retracted, has placed itself farther from the object, and we have passed from proximate to distant vision, which, strictly speaking, is the more proximate of the two kinds of vision. Between the eye and the bodies is interposed the most immediate object: hollow space, air. Floating in the air, transformed into chromatic gases, formless pennons, pure reflections, things have lost their solidity and contour. The painter has thrown his head back, half-closed his eyelids, and between them has pulverized the proper form of each object, reducing it to molecules of light, to pure sparks of color. On the other hand, his picture may be viewed from a single point of view, as a whole and at a glance.

Proximate vision dissociates, analyzes, distinguishes—it is feudal. Distant vision synthesizes, combines, throws together —it is democratic. The point of view becomes synopsis. The painting of bulk has been definitively transformed into the painting of hollow space.

12 IMPRESSIONISM

It is not necessary to remark that, in Velázquez, the moderating principles of the Renaissance persisted. The innovation did not appear in all its radicalism until the impressionists and postimpressionists.

The premises formulated in our first paragraphs may seem to imply that the evolution had terminated when we arrive at the painting of hollow space. The point of view, transforming itself from the multiple and proximate to the single and distant, appears to have exhausted its possible itinerary. Not at all! We shall see that it may retreat even closer to the subject. From 1870 until today, the shift of viewpoint has continued, and these latest stages, precisely because of their surprising and paradoxical character, confirm the fatal law to which I alluded at the beginning. The artist, starting from the world about him, ends by withdrawing into himself.

I have said that the gaze of Velázquez, when it falls on an object, converts it into a surface. But, meanwhile, the visual ray has gone along its path, enjoying itself by perforating the air between the cornea and distant things. In "Ladies in Waiting" and "The Spinners," we see the satisfaction with which the artist has accentuated hollow space as such. Velázquez looks straight to the background; thus, he encounters the enormous mass of air between it and the boundary of his eye. Now, to look at something with the central ray of the eye is what is known as direct vision or vision *in modo recto*. But behind the axial ray the pupil sends out many others at oblique angles, enabling us to see *in modo obliquo*. The impression of concavity is derived from the *modo recto*. If we eliminate this—for example, by blinking the eyes—we have only oblique vision, those side views "from the tail of the eye" which represent the height of disdain. Thus, the third dimension disappears and the field of vision tends to convert itself entirely into surface.

This is what the successive impressionisms have done. Velázquez's background has been brought forward, and so of course ceases to be background since it cannot be compared with a foreground. Painting tends to become planimetric, like the canvas on which one paints. One arrives, then, at the elimination of all tactile and corporeal resonance. At the same time, the atomization of things in oblique vision is such that almost nothing remains of them. Figures begin to be unrecognizable. Instead of painting objects as they are seen, one paints the experience of seeing. Instead of an object an impression, that is, a mass of sensations. Art, with this, has withdrawn completely from the world and begins to concern itself with the activity of the subject. Sensations are no longer things in any sense; they are subjective states through which and by means of which things appear.

Let us be sure we understand the extent of this change in the point of view. It would seem that in fixing upon the object nearest the cornea, the point of view is as close as possible to the subject and as far as possible from things. But no—the inexorable retreat continues. Not halting even at the cornea, the point of view crosses the last frontier and penetrates into vision itself, into the subject himself.

13   CUBISM

Cézanne, in the midst of his impressionist tradition, discovers volume. Cubes, cylinders, cones begin to emerge on his canvases. A careless observer might have supposed that, with its evolution exhausted, pictorial art had begun all over again and that we had relapsed back to the point of view of Giotto. Not at all! In the history of art there have always been eccentric movements tending toward the archaic. Nevertheless, the main stream flows over them and continues its inevitable course.

The cubism of Cézanne and of those who, in effect, were cubists, that is, stereometrists, is only one step more in the internalizing of painting. Sensations, the theme of impressionism, are subjective states; as such, realities, effective modifications of the subject. But still further within the subject are found the ideas. And ideas, too, are realities present in the individual, but they differ from sensations in that their content—the ideated—is unreal and sometimes even impossible. When I conceive a strictly geometrical cylinder, my *thought* is an effective act that takes place in me; but the geometric cylinder of which I think is unreal. Ideas, then, are subjective realities that contain virtual objects, a whole specific world of a new sort, distinct from the world revealed by the eye, and which emerges miraculously from the psychic depths.

Clearly, then, there is no connection between the masses evoked by Cézanne and those of Giotto; they are, rather, antagonists. Giotto seeks to render the actual volume of each thing, its immediate and tangible corporeality. Before his time, one knew only the Byzantine two-dimensional image. Cézanne, on the other hand, substitutes for the bodies of things nonexistent volumes of his own invention to which real bodies have only a metaphorical relationship. After Cézanne, painting only paints ideas—which, certainly, are also objects, but ideal objects, immanent to the subject or intrasubjective.

This explains the hodge-podge that, in spite of misleading interpretations, is inscribed on the muddy banner of so-called *cubism*. Together with volumes that seem to accord major emphasis to the rotundity of bodies, Picasso, in his most typical and scandalous pictures, breaks up the closed form of an object and, in pure Euclidian planes, exhibits their fragments—an eyebrow, a mustache, a nose—without any purpose other than to serve as a symbolic cipher for ideas.

This equivocal cubism is only a special manner within contemporary expressionism. In the impression, we reached the minimum of exterior objectivity. A new shift in the point of view was possible only if, leaping behind the retina—a tenuous frontier between the external and internal—painting completely reversed its function and, instead of putting us within what is outside, endeavored to pour out upon the canvas what is within: ideal invented objects. Note how, by a simple advance of the point of view along the same trajectory it has followed from the beginning, it arrives at an inverse result. The eyes, instead of absorbing things, are converted into projectors of private flora and fauna. Before, the real world drained off into them; now, they are reservoirs of irreality.

It is possible that present-day art has little aesthetic value; but he who sees in it only a caprice may be very sure indeed that he has not understood either the new art or the old. Evolution has conducted painting—and art in general—inexorably, fatally, to what it is today.

14

The guiding law of the great variations in painting is one of disturbing simplicity. First, things are painted; then, sensations; finally, ideas. This means that in the beginning the artist's attention was fixed on external reality; then, on the subjective; finally, on the intrasubjective. These three stages are three points on a straight line.

Now, Occidental philosophy has followed an identical route, and this coincidence makes our law even more disturbing.

Let us annotate briefly this strange parallelism.

The painter begins by asking himself what elements of the universe ought to be translated onto canvas, that is, what class of phenomena are pictorially essential. The philosopher, for his part, asks what class of objects is fundamental. A philosophical system is an effort to reconstruct the universe conceptually, taking as a point of departure a certain type of fact considered as the firmest and most secure. Each epoch of philosophy has preferred a distinct type, and upon this has built the rest of the construction.

In the time of Giotto, painter of solid and independent bodies, philosophy believed that the ultimate and definitive reality were individual substances. Examples given of such substances in the schools were: this horse, this man. Why did one believe to have discovered in these the ultimate metaphysical value? Simply because in the practical and natural idea of the world, every horse and every man seems to have an existence of his own, independent of other things and of the mind that contemplates them. The horse lives by himself, complete and perfect, according to his mysterious inner energy; if we wish to know him, our senses, our understanding must go to him and turn humbly, as it were, in his orbit. This, then, is the substantialist realism of Dante, a twin brother to the painting of bulk initiated by Giotto.

Let us jump to the year 1600, the epoch in which the painting of hollow space began. Philosophy is in the power of Descartes. What is cosmic reality for him? Multiple and independent substances disintegrate. In the foreground of metaphysics there is a single substance—an empty substance—a kind of metaphysical hollow space that now takes on a magical creative power. For Descartes, the *real* is space, as for Velázquez it is hollow space.

After Descartes, the plurality of substance reappears for a moment in Leibnitz. These substances are no longer corporeal principles, but quite the reverse: the monads are subjects, and the role of each—a curious symptom—is none other than to represent a *"point de vue."* For the first time in the history of philosophy we hear a formal demand that science be a system which submits the universe to a point of view. The monad does nothing but provide a metaphysical situs for this unity of vision.

In the two centuries that follow, subjectivism becomes increasingly radical, and toward 1880, while the impressionists were putting pure sensations on canvas, the philosophers of extreme positivism were reducing universal reality to pure sensations.

The progressive dis-realization of the world, which began in the philosophy of the Renaissance, reaches its extreme consequences in the radical sensationalism of Avenarius and Mach. How can this continue? What new philosophy is possible? A return to primitive realism is unthinkable; four centuries of criticism, of doubt, of suspicion, have made this attitude forever untenable. To remain in our subjectivism is equally impossible. Where shall we find the material to reconstruct the world?

The philosopher retracts his attention even more and, instead of directing it to the subjective as such, fixes on what up to now has been called "the content of consciousness," that is, the intrasubjective. There may be no corresponding reality to what our ideas project and what our thoughts think; but this does not make them purely subjective. A world of hallucination would not be real, but neither would it fail to be a world, an objective universe, full of sense and perfection. Although the imaginary centaur does not really gallop, tail and mane in the wind, across real prairies, he has a peculiar independence with regard to the subject that imagines him. He is a virtual object, or as the most recent philosophy expresses it, an ideal object.[2] This is the type of phenomena which the thinker of our times considers most adequate as a basis for his universal system. Can we fail to be surprised at the coincidence between such a philosophy and its synchronous art, known as expressionism or cubism?

NOTES

1. If we look at an empty sphere from without, we see a solid volume. If we enter the sphere, we see about us a surface that limits the interior concavity.
2. The philosophy to which Ortega refers, but which unfortunately he neglects to name, is obviously Husserlian phenomenology. (Translator's note—J. F.)

III
EXPRESSION AND COMMUNICATION
INTRODUCTION

Among the basic issues concerned with understanding the nature of art are the classic questions: Does a work of art express something other than the objects of which it consists? What is the nature of such expressions? and, What is the artist trying to communicate to his audience?

Professor O. K. Bouwsma is a linguistic-analysis philosopher whose study, "The Expression Theory of Art," is intended to expose the ambiguities and inadequacies of that theory. He applies Wittgenstein's method of examining the ways that terms are currently used in order to discover their meanings. He concludes that emotion is not a separable entity expressed by a work of art; it is "in" the object. In much of this essay the author examines misleading contexts that determine the use of the word "expression." His examples are drawn from the language of emotion and from language about language. His solution may puzzle many, but his position is important in that it represents a quantitatively large proportion of professional philosophic thought today.

It might be helpful to think of the linguistic-analysis school as being for philosophy what behaviorism is to psychology: a study of "external" phenomena. Bouwsma's essay reads as if it were written in a void where depth psychology had never been heard of, just as Kinsey's study of sexual behavior reads like statistical data compiled by men who had never heard of motivation, ambivalence, "acting-out," or the theory of the unconscious. Bouwsma makes frequent reference to the word "emotion," but it would be difficult to see from his essay whether he is referring to any theory of emotion more subtle than that of René Descartes. Perhaps, more than any other single element, it is this disregard of contemporary psychology by the philosophers of language-analysis that gives to their writings the quality of "quaintness."

Leonard B. Meyer considers the possibility of explicating some of the expression-questions about art by using the idea that art is *like* language. But he does so in a context rich with references to Keats, G. H. Mead, Freud, and Wiener, to information theory, semantics, and the history of culture. In a word, his thesis is sophisticated, having the worldliness of a highly civilized mind and the sympathies of a spirit of broad humanistic inclusiveness. His conclusions may be highly debatable, but his position is far more competent to deal with the syntactical meanings as well as the sensuous and associative aspects of aesthetic enjoyment than is Bouwsma's linguistic puritanism.

Rudolf Arnheim writes of the "dynamics of appearance" so as to apply his conclusions to all perceptual patterns. *What* is expressed need not be limited to emotion, since not all expressive objects are works of art. "It is the kind of directed tension or 'movement' . . . transmitted by the visible patterns that is perceived as expression." Such perceived forces, making their impact on the nervous system of the observer, are "inherent characteristics" of the objects perceived. References to Köhler and Wertheimer within the Arnheim selection underline the debt to Gestalt psychology which the theory maintains. *Art and Visual Perception,* the great study from which this chapter is taken, is a thoroughgoing application of Gestalt theory to our appreciation of plastic and graphic art. This book is one of the most striking accomplishments of twentieth-century aesthetics—for our understanding of the nature of "expression," even if it is not the last word on the meaning of that concept.

Suzanne K. Langer is conspicuous by her absence from this section. Her various efforts to contribute to aesthetics are founded on the assumption that what one experiences in a work of art is *feeling* in a beautiful and integral *form.* In other words, the art object is "symbolic" insofar as its "expressive form" expresses feeling that it contains directly. In this respect art is not *like* language, it *is* a language; a language that one does not learn, but comprehends immediately by the "peculiar impression" it always makes.

Happy as one would be to report that we are now in a position to correlate language and emotion as neatly as Mrs. Langer would have it, the fact is that we still know too little about the nature of language, to say nothing of the unsolved problems concerned with the nature of "feeling." Nevertheless, the reader is recommended to consult Mrs. Langer's books for suggestive opinions.

THE EXPRESSION THEORY OF ART *

O. K. Bouwsma

The expression theory of art is, I suppose, the most commonly held of all theories of art. Yet no statement of it seems to satisfy many of those who expound it. And some of us find all statements of it baffling. I propose in what follows to examine it carefully. In order to do this, I want first of all to state the question which gives rise to the theory and then to follow the lead of that question in providing an answer. I am eager to do this without using the language of the expression theory. I intend then to examine the language of that theory in order to discover whether it may reasonably be interpreted to mean what is stated in my answer. In this way I expect to indicate an important ambiguity in the use of the word "expression," but more emphatically to expose confusions in the use of the word "emotion." This then may explain the bafflement.

1

And now I should like to describe the sort of situation out of which by devious turnings the phrase "expression of emotion" may be conceived to arise.

Imagine then two friends who attend a concert together. They go together untroubled. On the way they talk about two girls, about communism and pie on earth, and about a silly joke they once laughed at and now confess to each other that they never understood. They were indeed untroubled, and so they entered the hall. The music begins, the piece ends, the applause intervenes, and the music begins again. Then comes the intermission and time for small talk. Octave, a naive fellow, who loves music, spoke first. "It was lovely, wasn't it? Very sad music, though." Verbo, for that was the other's name, replied: "Yes, it was very sad." But the moment he said this he became uncomfortable. He fidgeted in his seat, looked askance at his friend, but said no more aloud. He blinked, he knitted his brows, and he muttered to himself. "Sad music, indeed! Sad? Sad music?" Then he looked gloomy and shook his head. Just before the conductor returned, he was muttering to himself, "Sad music, crybaby, weeping willows, tear urns, sad grandma, sad, your grandmother!" He

* [From *Aesthetics and Language*, edited by William Elton (New York: Philosophical Library, 1954). Reprinted by permission of the author and the publisher.]

was quite upset and horribly confused. Fortunately, about this time the conductor returned and the music began. Verbo was upset but he was a good listener, and he was soon reconciled. Several times he perked up with "There it is again," but music calms, and he listened to the end. The two friends walked home together but their conversation was slow now and troubled. Verbo found no delight in two girls, in pie on earth, or in old jokes. There was a sliver in his happiness. At the corner as he parted with Octave, he looked into the sky, "Twinkling stars, my eye! Sad music, my ear!" and he smiled uncomfortably. He was miserable. And Octave went home, worried about his friend.

So Verbo went home and went to bed. To sleep? No, he couldn't sleep. After four turns on his pillow, he got up, put a record on the phonograph, and hoped. It didn't help. The sentence "Sad, isn't it?" like an imp, sat smiling in the loud-speaker. He shut off the phonograph and paced the floor. He fell asleep, finally, scribbling away at his table, like any other philosopher.

This then is how I should like to consider the use of the phrase "expression of emotion." It may be thought of as arising out of such situations as that I have just described. The use of emotional terms—sad, gay, joyous, calm, restless, hopeful, playful, etc.—in describing music, poems, pictures, etc., is indeed common. So long as such descriptions are accepted and understood in innocence, there will be, of course, no puzzle. But nearly everyone can understand the motives of Verbo's question "How can music be sad?" and of his impulsive "It can't, of course."

Let us now consider two ways in which one may safely escape the expression theory.

Imagine Verbo at his desk, writing. This is what he now writes and this gives him temporary relief. "Every time I hear that music I hear that it's sad. Yet I persist in denying it. I say that it cannot be sad. And now what if I were wrong? If every day I met a frog, and the frog said to me that he was a prince, and that there were crown jewels in his head ('wears yet a precious jewel in his head'), no doubt I should begin by calling him a liar. But the more I'd consider this the more troubled I should be. If I could only believe him, and then treat him like a prince, I'd feel so much better. But perhaps *this* would be more like the case of this music: Suppose I met the frog and every day he said to me, 'I can talk,' and then went on talking and asked me, 'Can I talk?' then what would I do? And that's very much how it is with the music. I hear the music, and there it is again, sad, weeping. It's silly to deny this. See now, how it is? There's a little prince, the soul of a prince, in the frog, and so there's the soul in this music, a princess, perhaps. See then how rude I was denying this princess her weeping. Why shouldn't music have a soul too? Why this prejudice in favor of lungs and livers? And it occurs to me that this is precisely how people have talked about music and poems. Art lives, doesn't it? And how did Milton describe a good book? Didn't Shelley pour out his soul? And isn't there soul and spirit in the music? I remember now that the poet Yeats recommended some such thing. There are spirits; the air is full of them. They haunt music, cry in it. They dance in poems, and laugh. Panpsychism for the habitation of all delicacies! So this is how it is, and there is neither joke nor puzzle in this sad music. There's a sad soul in it."

And then it was that Verbo fell asleep. His resistance to the music had melted away as soon as he gave up his curious prejudice in favor of animal bodies, as soon as he saw that chords and tones, like rhymes and rhythms, may sigh and shed invisible tears. Tears without tear glands—oh, I know the vulgar habit! But surely tones may weep. Consider now how reasonable all this is. Verbo is suddenly surprised to discover something which he has always known; namely, that music is sad. And the discovery startles him. Why? Because in connection with this, he thinks of his sister Sandra (Cassie to all who saw her cry). And he knows what her being sad is like. She sobs, she wipes her eyes, and she tells her troubles. Cassie has a soul, of course. So Cassie is sad and the music is sad. So the question for Verbo is, How can the music be like Cassie? and he gives the answer: "Why shouldn't there be a soul of the music, that flits in and flits out (People die too!) and inhabits a sonata for a half-hour? Or why shouldn't there be a whole troupe of them? 'The music is sad' is just like 'Cassie is sad,' after all. And Octave who was not disturbed was quite right for he must have a kind of untroubled belief in spirits. He believes in the frog-prince, in the nymphs in the wood, and in the Psyche of the sonnet."

This then is one way of going to sleep. But there is another one, and it is based upon much the same sort of method. Both accept as the standard meaning for "The music is sad," the meaning of "Cassie is sad." We saw how Verbo came to see that the meaning is the same, and how then it was true in the case of the music. He might however have decided that the meaning certainly was the same, but that as applied to the music it simply made no sense at all, or was plainly false. Souls in sonnets Don't be silly. There is the story about Parmenides, well known to all readers of Dionoges,[1] which will illustrate the sort of thing I have in mind. According to the story, Parmenides and his finicky friend Zeno once went to a chariot race. The horses and chariots had been whizzing past and the race had been quite exciting. During the third round, at one turn a chariot broke an axle and horse and chariot and rider went through the fence. It was a marvelous exhibition of motion done to a turn at a turn. Parmenides was enjoying himself thoroughly. He clutched at the railing and shouted at the top of his voice, "Go, Buceph! Run!" The race is close. But at about the seventh round, with Buceph now some part of a parasang behind, Parmenides began to consider: "Half the distance in half the time; a quarter of the length of a horse in a quarter of the pace it takes . . ." Suddenly, before the race was half over, Parmenides turned to Zeno. "Zeno," he said, "this is impossible." Zeno, who was ready for his master, retorted, "I quit looking a long time ago." So they left the chariot race, a little embarrassed at their non-existence showing as they walked, but they did not once look back to see how Buceph was doing.

This then is the story about Parmenides. It may be, of course, that this story is not true; it may be one of Dionoges' little jokes. But our concern is not with Parmenides. The point is that it illustrates a certain way of disposing of puzzles. Parmenides has been disciplined to a certain use of such words as "run," "go," "turn," "walk," etc., so that when he is thoughtful and has all his careful wits about him, he never uses those words. He is then fully aware that all forms of motion are impossible. Nevertheless, the eyes are cunning tempters. In any case, as soon as Parmenides reflects, he buries himself in his tight-fitting vocabulary, and shuts out chariots and horses, and Buceph, as well. "Motion is impossible, so what am I doing here? Less than nothing. *N'est pas* is not." This disposition of the puzzle is, of course, open only to very strong men. Not many of those people who believe in the impossibility of motion are capable of leaving a horse race, especially when some fleet favorite is only a few heads behind.

Now something like this was a possibility also for Verbo. When, puzzled as he was, asking "How can that be?" he hit upon the happy solution "Why not?" But he might surely have said, stamping his foot, "It can't be." And in order then to avoid the pain of what can't be, he might have sworn off music altogether. No more concerts, no more records! The more radical decision is in such cases most effective. One can imagine Parmenides, for instance, sitting out the race, with his eyes closed, and every minute blinking and squinting, hoping he'd see nothing. So too Verbo might have continued to listen to music, but before every hearing invigorating his resolution never to say that the music was sad. Success in this latter enterprise is not likely to be successful, and for anyone who has already been puzzled it is almost certainly futile.

We have now noticed two ways in which one may attempt to rid oneself of the puzzle concerning "The music is sad," but incidentally we have also noticed the puzzle. The puzzle is identified with the question, How can music be sad? We have also noticed how easy it is, once having asked the question, to follow it with "Well, it can't." I want now to go on to consider the expression theory in the light of the question, How can it be? In effect, the expression theory is intended to relieve people who are puzzled by music, etc. They listen and they say that the music is sad. They ask, troubled and shaking their heads, How can it be? Then along comes the expression theory. It calms them, saying, "Don't you see that the music expresses sadness and that this is what you mean by its being sad?" The puzzled one may be calmed too, if he isn't careful. In any case, I propose to consider the question "How can it be?" before going on further.

This question, "How can it be?" is apparently then not a question primarily about the music. One listens to the music and hears all that there is to hear. And he is sure that it is sad. Nevertheless, when he notices this and then returns to the music to identify just what is sad in it, he is baffled. If someone, for instance, had said that there is a certain succession of four notes on the flute, in this music, and he now sought to identify them, he could play the music, and when they came along, he would exclaim, "There they are," and that would be just what he aimed at. Or again if someone had said that a certain passage was very painful, and he explained that he meant by this that when it is heard one feels a stinging at one's finger tips, then again one could play the music and wait for the stinging. Neither is it like the question which leaped out of the surprise of the farmer at the birth of his first two-headed calf. He looked, amazed, and exclaimed, "Well, I'll be switched! How can that be?" He bedded the old cow, Janus, tucked in the calf, and went to consult his book. He did not stand muttering, looking at the calf, as Verbo did listening to the record on the phonograph. He took out his great book, *The Cow*, and read the chapter entitled "Two Heads Are Better than One?" He read statistics and something about the incidence of prenatal collusion and decided to keep an eye on collaborators among his herd. And that was all. When now it comes to "The music is sad," there's no such easy relief. What is there to listen for? What statistics are there?

We have noticed before how Verbo settled his difficulty. He did this, but not by examining the music any further. He simply knew that the music was sad, and supplied the invisible tears, the unheard sobs, the soul of the music. If you had asked him to identify the tears, the unheard sobs, the soul of the music, he could have done this. He might have tried, of course, and then he would have been baffled too. But the point is that he tries to think of the sadness of the music in the way in which he thinks of Cassie's sadness. Now we may be ready to explain the predicament, the bafflement. It arises from our trying to understand our use of the sentence "The music is sad" in terms of our uses of other sentences very much like this. So Verbo understands in terms of the sentence "Cassie is sad." One can imagine him saying to himself, "I know what sadness is, of course, having Cassie in the house, so that must be how it is with the music." Happily, as in the case of Parmenides, he thought of only one use, and as with a sharp knife he cut the facts to suit the knife. But suppose now that there are several uses of sentences much like "The music is sad"; what then? Is it like this use or this use or this use? And suppose that sometimes it's like this and at other times like this, and sometimes like both. Suppose further that one is only vaguely aware that this is so, and that one's question "How can that be?" is not stated in such a way as to make this possibility explicit, would it then be any wonder that there is bafflement?

Let us admit then that the use of "The music is sad" is baffling, and that without some exploration, the question "How can that be?" cannot be dealt with. Merely listening to the music will not suffice. We must then explore the uses of other sentences which are or may be similar to this, and we may hope that in this process we may see the expression theory emerge. At any rate, we'll understand what we are about.

2

What now are some of these other types of sentences which might be helpful? Well, here are a few that might serve: "Cassie is sad," "Cassie's dog is sad," "Cassie's book is sad," "Cassie's face is sad." Perhaps, one or the other of these will do.

Though we have already noticed how Verbo came to use "Cassie is sad," I should like to consider that sentence further. Verbo understood this. When, as he remembered so well, the telephone call came and little Cassie answered—she had been waiting for that call—she was hurt. Her voice had broken as she talked, and he knew that the news had been bad. But he did not think she would take it so hard. And when she turned to him and he asked her what the man had said, at first her chin quivered and she didn't speak. Then she moved toward him and fell into his arms, sobbing: "Poor Felicia, poor Felicia!" He stroked her hair and finally, when she was calm, she began to pour out her confidences to him. She loved her cat so; they had been brought up together, had had their milk from the same bottle, and had kept no secrets from each other. And now the veterinary had called to say that she had had another fit. And she burst into tears again. This was some years ago. Cassie is older now.

But this is not the only way in which "Cassie is sad" is used. Verbo had often heard his father and mother remark that it was good that Cassie could cry. They used to quote some grandmother who made a proverb in the family. It went: "Wet pillows are best." She had made this up many years ago when some cousin came to sudden grief. This cousin was just on the verge of planned happiness, when the terrible news came. (Her picture is the third in the album.) She received the news in silence and never spoke of it or referred to it as long as she washed the dishes in her father's house, for, as you may have guessed, she never married. She never cried either. No one ever heard her sniffling in the middle of the night. She expressed no regrets. And she never told cat or mirror anything. Once she asked for a handkerchief, but she said she had a cold. All the family knew what had happened, of course, and everyone was concerned, but there was nothing to do. And so she was in many ways changed. She was drooping, she had no future, and she tried to forget her past. She was not interested. They all referred to her as their sad cousin, and they hoped that she would melt. But she didn't. Yet how can Cassie's cousin be sad if she never cries?

Well, there is a third use of "Cassie is sad." Tonight Cassie, who is eighteen now, quite a young lady, as the neighbors say, goes up to her room with her cat, her big book, and a great bowl of popcorn. She settles into her chair, tells kitty to get down, munches buttery corn, and reads her book. Before very long she is quite absorbed in what she reads and feels pretty bad. Her eyes fill with tears and the words on the page swim in the pool. It's so warm and so sweet and so sad! She would like to read this aloud, it's so wonderful, but she knows how the sadness in her throat would break her words in two. She's so sorry; she's so sad. She raises her eyes, closes them, and revels in a deep-drawn sigh. She takes up a full hand of popcorn and returns to her sadness. She reads on and eats no more corn. If she should sob in corn, she might choke. She does sob once, and quite loud, so that she is startled by it. She doesn't want to be heard sobbing over her book. Five minutes later she lays her book aside, and in a playful mood, twits her cat, pretending she's a little bird. Then, walking like old Mother Hubbard, she goes to the cupboard to get her poor cat a milk.

Cassie is sad, isn't she? Is she? Now that you consider it, she isn't really sad, is she? That cosy chair, that deliberate popcorn, that playing sparrow with her cat, that old Mother Hubbard walk—these are not the manners of a sad girl. She hasn't lost her appetite. Still one can see at once how we come to describe her in this way. Those are not phony tears, and she's as helpless in her sobs and in keeping her voice steady and clear as she was years ago when her dear cat had that fit. And she can, if you are so curious, show you in the book just what made her feel so sad. So you see it is very much like the case in which Cassie was sad. There's an obvious difference, and a similarity too. And now if you balk at this and don't want to say that Cassie in this situation is sad, your objection is intelligible. On the other hand, if Cassie herself laughingly protests, "Oh, yes, I was sad," that will be intelligible too. This then may serve as an illustration of the way in which a puzzle which might become quite serious is fairly easily dealt with. How can Cassie be sad, eating popcorn and playing she's a sparrow?

In order to make this clear, consider Cassie now a grown woman, and an accomplished actress. She now reads that same passage which years ago left her limp as a willow, but her voice is steady and clear, and there are no tears. She understands what she reads and everyone says that she reads it with such feeling—it's so sad!—but there isn't a sign of emotion except for the reading itself, which, as I said, goes along smoothly and controlled even to each breath and syllable. So there are no wet eyes, no drunken voice, and not a sob that isn't in the script. So there. Is she sad? I take it not. The spoken words are not enough. Tears, real tears, a voice that breaks against a word, sighs that happen to one, suffered sobs —when the reading occasions these, then you might say that Cassie was sad. Shall we say, however, that the reading is sad? How can that be? Well, you see, don't you?

Let us now attend to a sentence of a different type: "Cassie's dog is sad." Can a dog be sad? Can a dog hope? Can a dog be disappointed? We know, of course, how a Cartesian would answer. He might very well reply with this question: "Can a locomotive be sad?" Generous, he might allow that a locomotive might look sad, and so give you the benefit of a sad look for your dog. But can a dog be sad? Well, our dog can. Once during the summer when Cassie left her for three weeks, you should have seen her. She wouldn't look at the meatiest bone. She'd hang her head and look up at you as woebegone as a cow. And she'd walk as though her four hearts would break. She didn't cry, of course, and there were no confidences except those touching ones that come by way of petting and snuggling and looking into those wailing eyes. In any case, our dog acted very much like that sad cousin who couldn't cry. She had plenty of reason, much too much, but she kept her wellings-up down. It's clear, in any case, what I mean when I say that our dog was sad. You mustn't expect everything from a sad dog.

So we pass to another type of sentence: "Cassie's book is sad." Well, obviously books don't cry. Books do not remember happier days nor look upon hopes snuffed out. Still, books that are sad must have something to do with sadness, so there must be sadness. We know, of course. Books make people sad. Cassie reads her book and in a few minutes, if she's doing well, she's sad. Not really sad, of course, but there are real tears, and one big sob that almost shook the house. It certainly would be misleading to say that it was imaginary sadness, for the sadness of Cassie isn't imagined by anyone, not even by herself. What she reads, on the other hand, is imaginary. What she reads about never happened. In this respect it's quite different from the case in which she is overwhelmed by the sad news over the telephone. That was not imaginary, and with the tears and sobs there was worry, there was distress. She didn't go twittering about, pretending she was a little bird five minutes after that happened. So a sad book is a book that makes Cassie, for instance, sad. You ask, "Well, what are you crying about?" And she says, "Booh, you just read this." It's true that that is how you will find out, but you may certainly anticipate too that it will be a story about a little boy who died, a brave little boy who had stood up bravely for his father, about a new love and reconciliation come almost too late, about a parting of friends and tender feelings that will die, and so on. At any rate, if this is what it is like, you won't be surprised. It's a sad book.

There is one further sentence to consider: "Cassie's face is sad." The same sort of thing might be said about her speaking, about her walk, about her eyes, etc. There is once again an obvious way of dealing with this. What makes you say her face is sad? Anyone can tell. See those tear stains and those swollen eyes. And those curved lines, they all turn down. Her face is like all those sad faces in simple drawings where with six strokes of my neighbor's pencil I give you "Sad-Eye, the Sorry Man." The sad face is easily marked by these few unmistakable signs. Pull a sad face, or droop one, and then study it. What have you done? In any case, I am supposing that there is another use of "Cassie's face is sad," where this simplicity is absent. Oh, yes, there may be certain lines, but if you now ask, "And is this all you mean by Cassie's

face being sad?" the answer may very well be "No." Where
then is the sadness? Take a long look and tell me. Cassie,
hold still. The sadness is written all over her face, and I can't
tell you it's here and not there. The more I look, the more I
see it. The sadness in this case is not identified with some gross
and simple signs. And you are not likely to find it there in
some quick glance. Gaze into that face, leisurely, quietly,
gently. It's as though it were composed not of what is sad
in all sad faces, but rather of what is sad only in each sad
face you've ever known. This sad face is sad but when you try
now to tell someone what is sad in it, as you might with the
drawing I made, you will have nothing to say. But you may
say, "Look, and you will see." It is clear, of course, that when
Cassie's face is sad, she need not be sad at all. And certainly
when you look as you do, you need not be sad.

We have noticed briefly several types of sentences similar
to "The music is sad," and we have seen how in respect to
several of these the same sort of puzzling might arise that
arose in respect to "The music is sad." We have also seen how
in respect to these more obvious cases this puzzling is relieved.
The puzzling is relieved by discerning the similarity between
the offending use and some other use or uses. And now I
should like to ask whether the puzzle concerning "The music
is sad" might not also be relieved in some similar fashion.
Is there not a use of some type of sentence, familiar and
relatively untroubled, which is like the use of "The music is
sad"?

We have these types of sentences now ready at our disposal: There are two uses of "Cassie is sad," in the first of
which she is concerned about her cat, and in the second of
which she is cosy and tearful, reading her book. We have
"Cassie's cousin is sad," in which Cassie's cousin has real
cause but no tears, and "Cassie's dog is sad," in which her
dog is tearless as her cousin, but with a difference of course.
You could scarcely say that Fido restrained his tears. Then
there were the uses of "Cassie's face is sad" and "Cassie's
reading is sad." And, of course, there is the use of "Cassie's
book is sad." I am going to take for granted that these uses
are also intelligible. Now then is the use of "The music is
sad" similar to any of these?

I suppose that if the question is stated in this way, one
might go on by pointing out a similarity between it and each
one of these other types of sentences. But what we must
discover is enough similarity, enough to relieve the puzzle.
So the question is, To which use is the use of "The music is
sad" most similar? Certainly not to "Cassie is sad (about her
cat)," nor to "Cassie's cousin is sad," nor to "Cassie's dog
is sad."

There are two analogies that one may hopefully seize upon. The first is this: "Cassie is sad, reading a book," is very much like "Verbo is sad, listening to music." And this first is also very much like "Cassie is sad, hearing the news over the telephone." And just as the first involves "The book is sad," so the second involves "The music is said," and the third involves "The news is sad." Now let us consider the first. Reading the book is one thing, and feeling sad is quite another, and when you say that the book is sad, you mean by this something like this: When Cassie reads, she feels sad about what she reads. Her feeling sad refers to her tears, her sobs, etc. So too listening to the music and hearing it is one thing, and feeling sad is another, and when you say that the music is sad, you mean that while Verbo listens to the music, he feels sad. And shall we add that he feels sad about it? This might, if you like, refer to something like his half-tears, sub-sobs, etc.

Suppose now we try to relieve Verbo in this way. We say: "Don't you see? 'This music is sad' is like 'The book is sad.' You understand that. That's very much like 'The news is sad.'" Will that satisfy him? I think that if he is very sharp, it won't. He may say: "I can see how 'The book is sad' is like 'The news is sad.' But when it comes to these you can easily point out the disturbance, the weeping, but the music—that's different. Still there might be something." What now bothers him?

I think what bothers him may be explained in this way. When you say that a book is sad, or a certain passage in a book is sad, you may mean one or other or both of two things. You may mean what has already been defined by the analogy above. But you may also mean something else. The following illustration may exhibit this. Imagine Cassie, then, in her big chair, reading, and this is the passage she reads:

"I say this in case we become bad," Alyosha went on, "but there's no reason why we should become bad, is there, boys? Let us be, first and above all, kind, then honest, and let us never forget each other! I say that again. I give you my word, for my part, that I'll never forget one of you. Every face looking at me now I shall remember even for thirty years. Just now Kolya said to Kartashov that he did not care to know whether he exists or not. But I cannot forget that Kartashov exists and that he is blushing now as he did when he discovered the founders of Troy, but is looking at me with his jolly, kind, dear little eyes. Boys, my dear boys, let us all be generous and brave like Ilusha, clever, brave and generous like Kolya (though he will be ever so much cleverer when he grows up), and let us all be as modest, as clever and sweet as Kartashov. But why am I talking about those two! You are all dear to me, boys, from this day forth I have a place in my heart for you all, and I beg you to keep a place in your hearts for me! Well, and who has united us in this kind, good feeling which we shall remember, and intend to remember all our lives? Who, if not Ilusha, the good boy, the dear boy, precious to us for ever! Let us never forget him. May his memory live for ever in our hearts from this time forth."

Cassie reads this and Cassie cries. Let us call this Cassie's sadness. But is there now any other emotion, any other sadness, present? Well, there may very well be. There may be the Alyosha emotion. Whether that is present, however, depends upon how the passage in question is read. It may be read in such a way, that though Cassie understands all she reads, and so knows about the Alyosha emotion, yet she will miss it. This will be the case if she cries through the reading of it. If she reads the passage well, controlled, clear, unfalteringly, with feeling, as we say, which does not mean with crying, then the Alyosha emotion will be present. Otherwise only signs of it will be present. Anyone who has tried to read such a passage well, and who has sometimes failed and sometimes succeeded, will understand what I have in mind. Now then we have distinguished the Cassie emotion and the Alyosha emotion. They may be present together, but only, I think, when the Cassie emotion is relatively weak. And so when someone says that the passage in question is sad, then in order to understand we must ask, Is it sad in the Cassie emotion or is it sad in the Alyosha emotion?

And now we are prepared again to examine the analogy: "The music is sad" is like "The book is sad," where it is sad with the Alyosha emotion. This now eliminates the messiness of tears. What we mean by Alyosha's emotion involves no tears, just as the sadness of the music involves no tears. And this now may remind us of Cassie reading the passage, cool, collected, reading with feeling. But more to the point it suggests the sentence "Cassie's face is sad." For see, when the music is sad, there are no tears, and when the passage is read, well read, there are no tears. And so when I look into this face and find it sad, there are no tears. The sadness in all these cases may be unmistakable, and yet in none of these is there anything to which I might now draw your attention, and say, "That's how I recognize it as sad." Even in the case of the reading, it isn't the sentences, it isn't the subject, that make it sad. The sadness is in the reading. Like a musical score, it too may be played without feeling. And it isn't now as though you both read and have these feelings. There is nothing but the reading, and the feeling is nothing apart from this. Read the passage with and without feeling, and see that the difference consists in a difference in the reading. What baffles in these cases is that when you use the word "sadness" and the phrase "with feeling," you are certain to anticipate sadness and feeling in the ordinary sense. But if the sadness is in the sounds you make, reading or playing, and in the face, once you are forewarned you need no longer anticipate anything else. There is sadness which is heard and sadness which is seen.

This then is my result. "The music is sad" is like "The book is sad," where "The book is sad" is like "The face is sad." But "The music is sad" is sometimes also like "The book is sad," where "The book is sad" is like "The news is sad." If exhibiting these analogies is to be helpful, then, of course, this depends on the intelligibility of such sentences as "The book is sad," "The face is sad," "The news is sad," etc.

3

So far I have tried to do two things. I have tried to state the problem to which the expression theory is addressed, and then I have gone on to work at the solution of that problem in the way in which this statement of the problem itself suggests that it be worked out. In doing this I have sought deliberately to avoid the language of the expression theory.

Here then is the phrase to be studied. The expression theory maintains: "The music is sad" means "The music is the expression of sadness or of a certain sadness." The crucial word is the word "expression." There are now at least two contexts which determine the use of that word, one is the language of emotion, and the other is the language of or about language.

Let us consider first the use of the word "expression" in the language of emotion. In the discussion of the types of sentences above, it will be remembered that Cassie's cousin is sad, but doesn't cry. She does not "express" her emotion. Cassie, on the other hand, carries on, crying, sobbing, and confiding in everyone. She "expresses" her emotion, and the expression of her emotion is tears, noises, talk. That talk is all about her cat, remember. When she reads her book, she carries on in much the same way. In this latter case, there was some question as to whether there was really any emotion. She was so sad, remember, and ate popcorn. But in terms of what we just now said, whether there is emotion or not, there certainly is "expression" of emotion. These tears are just as wet as other tears, and her sobs are just as wet too. So in both cases there is expression of emotion, and in the first case there is emotion, thick as you please, but in the second case, it's not that thick. It appears, then, that you might find it quite natural to say that there is expression of emotion but no emotion, much as you might say that there was the thought of an elephant, but no elephant. This may not seem so strange, however, if we reflect that as in the case of Cassie's cousin, there may be emotion, but no or very little expression of emotion.

In order to probe the further roots of the uses of this phrase, it may be useful to notice that the language of emotion is dominantly the language of water. So many of our associations with the word "emotion" are liquid. See then: Emotions well up. Children and young girls bubble over. There are springs of emotion. A sad person is a deep well. Emotions come in waves; they are like the tides; they ebb and flow. There are floods and "seas of passion." Some people gush; some are turbulent. Anger boils. A man blows up like a boiler. Sorrow overwhelms. The dear girl froze. We all know the theory of humors. In any case, it is easy enough, in this way, to think of a human being as like a reservoir and an ever-flowing pool and stream of emotions. All flow on toward a dam, which may be raised or lowered, and over and through which there is a constant trickle. Behind the dam are many currents, hot, cold, lukewarm, swift, slow, steady, rippling, smooth. And there are many colors. Perhaps we should say that currents are never exhausted and do not altogether trickle away. Emotions, like our thoughts, are funded, ready to be tapped, to be rippled, to be disturbed.

Let us see how the term "expression" fits into this figure. How was it with Cassie's cousin? Well, once there was a clear, smooth-flowing current of affection, and it flowed, trickle, trickle, over the dam in happy anticipation and a chestful of hope's kitchen and linen showers. And suddenly a planet falls, in the form of a letter, into that deep and flowing pool. Commotion follows, waves leap, eddies swirl. The current rushes on to the dam. And what happens? The dam rises. Cassie's cousin resists, bites her lip, intensifies her fist. She keeps the current back. Her grief is impounded. She does not "express" her emotion. And what happened to Cassie, when she felt so bad about the cat? That's easy. Then too there was a disturbance. The current came down, splashed over the dam which did not rise at all, and it flowed away in a hurly-burly of "Oh! It's awful! My poor kitty!" Cassie let herself go. She "expressed" her emotion.

The use of the word "expression" in the light of this figure is, I take it, clear enough. And the use of the word in this way describes a familiar difference in the way in which good news and bad news may affect us. And now we may ask, And is it something like this that people have in mind when they say that art is the expression of emotion? Certainly something like this, at least part of the time. Consider how Wordsworth wrote about poetry: "Poetry is the spontaneous overflow of powerful emotions." Overflow! This suggests the pool and the dam and the "powerful" current. An emotion, lying quiet, suddenly gets going and goes over. There is spontaneity, of course. No planet falls and no cat is sick. The emotion is unprovoked. There is also the common view that artists are people who are more emotional than other people. They are temperamental. This once again suggests the idea that they have particular need of some overflow. Poetry is a little like blowing off steam. Write poetry or explode!

This isn't all that Wordsworth said about poetry. In the same context he said: "Poetry is emotion recollected in tranquillity." Again this suggests a hiding place of emotion, a place where past heartaches are stored, and may be taken up again, "recollected." We store ideas. We also put away emotions. So we have the pool as we had the pool before in describing Cassie's cousin and Cassie. But now we have something else, "the spontaneous overflow" and the "recollection in tranquillity."

Let us consider this for a moment, again in order to notice the use of the word "expression." Cassie hears bad news and cries. She "expresses" her emotion. The emotion is aroused and out it flows. What now happens in the case of the poet? Ostensibly in his case too emotions are aroused, but they do not flow out. Poets do not cry enough. Emotions are stored up, blocked. Emotions accumulate. And what happens now? Well, one of two things may happen. Emotions may quite suddenly leap up like spray, and find a way out, or again a poet may dip into the pool with his word dipper, and then dip them out. It's as though the emotions come over the dam in little boats (the poems) and the little boats may be used over and over again to carry over new surges. And this too may be described in this way: The poet "expresses" his emotion. Cassie cries. The real incident is sufficient. The poet does not cry. The real incident is not sufficient. He's got to make poems in order to cry. All men must cry. This may seem a bit fantastic, but this sort of fantasy is common in explaining something as old, for instance, as Aristotle's use of the word "catharsis."

The analogy which we have tried to exhibit now is this one: As Cassie "expresses" her emotion at hearing the news, so the poet or reader "expresses" his emotion at reading the poem. The news and the poem arouse or evoke the respective emotions. Now most people who expound the expression theory are not content with this analogy. They say that Cassie merely vents or discharges her emotion. This is not "expression" of emotion. Cassie merely gets rid of her emotion. And what does the poem do? Perhaps in terms of our figure we may say: It ripples it, blows a gentle wind over it, like a bird skimming the water. At any rate the emotion stays. And so the theory seeks a more suitable analogy and finds it conveniently in the language about language.

I should like first to notice certain distinctions which lead to this shift from the first to the second analogy. In the first place poems and music are quite different from the occasions that make Cassie and Cassie's cousin so sad. Tones on a piano and a faithless lover or a dying cat are not much alike, and this is enough to disturb the analogy. But there is also an unmistakable difference in the use of the word "emotion" in the two cases. An "emotion recollected in tranquillity" is, after all, as I suggested before, more like a ripple than like a tempest. It is, accordingly, these distinctions that determine the shift. It may be useful to notice that the general form of the first analogy is retained in the second. For the poem and the music are still conceived as "arousing," as "evoking," the emotion.

The new analogy accordingly is this one: Music "expresses" sadness (art expresses emotion) as sentences "express" ideas. And now, I think, it is easy to see why this analogy should have been seized upon. In the first place so much of art involves symbols, sentences themselves, and representations. There are horses in pictures. It is quite easy then to fall into regarding art as symbolic; that is, as like sentences. And now just as sentences symbolize ideas and serve to evoke them as distinguished from real things, of which ideas are more like shadows, so too music and poems serve to evoke emotions of a peculiar sort, emotions which are like the shadows of real emotions. So this analogy is certainly an improvement. Art is after all an artifice, like sentences, and the emotions involved are related to the real things in much the way that ideas are to real things, faint copies. All this fits in very well with the idea that art is like a dream, a substitute of real life, a vicarious more of what you cannot have, a shadowland.

And now how does this analogy succeed?

Before answering this question, I should like to notice the use of the words "evoking" and "arousing." Sentences "evoke" ideas. As one spieler I know says: "When I read a sentence, an idea pops into my head." Pops! This is something like what, according to the analogy, is meant by sentences "expressing" ideas. I am not interested in criticizing this at this point. I wish only to clarify ideas. Pop! Consider the sentence "The elephant ate a jumbo peanut." If at the moment when you read this sentence you see in your mind's eye a big elephant nuzzling around a huge peanut, this will illustrate what "evoking" is like. The sentence evokes; the idea pops. There is the sentence and there is this unmistakable seeing in your mind's eye. And if this happened, surely you would have got the idea. What I wish to point out is that it is this view or some similar view of how sentences work, that underlies this present analogy. They "evoke." But the word "evoke" has other contexts. It suggests spirits, witchcraft. The spirit of Samuel appearing at the behest of the witch of Endor is an "evocation." Spiritualistic mediums "evoke" the living spirits of the dead. And the point of this association is that the spirits are waiting, in the second or third canto of Dante's *Comedy,* perhaps, to be called. They are in storage like our ideas, like our emotions. And the word "arouse" is like the word "evoke." Whom do you arouse? The sleeper. And so, sleeping ideas and sleeping emotions lie bedded in that spacious dormitory—hush!—we call the mind. Waiting to be called! And why now have I made a point of this? Because this helps to fill out this analogy by which in particular we are led to use the word "feeling" or "emotion" in the language of the expression theory. The music "evokes," "arouses" feelings.

Now then, do poems and music and pictures evoke emotions as sentences evoke images? I think that they frequently do. Cassie reading her book may be cited as an instance. This seems to me a very common type of experience. It happens at the movies, in reading novels, and even in listening to music. People are moved to tears. If, accordingly, the expression theory were intended merely to describe experience of this sort, I should say, "Very well." In that case there would be no particular puzzle, beyond presenting this analogy clearly. But I, at least, am convinced that this is not all.

The difficulty, then, does not arise concerning experiences of this sort. The puzzle arises and remains most stubbornly where the sadness is dry-eyed. And here the analogy with language seems, at least, to be of no use. Cassie may read the passage with feeling, but without the flicker of an eyelash. And she may listen to sad music as cool and intent as she is gazing at a butterfly. She might say that it was more like watching, fascinated, the pain in a suffering face, herself quite undistressed. Santayana identifies the experience in this way: "Not until I confound the impressions (the music, the sentences) and suffuse the symbols with the emotions they arouse, and find joy and sweetness in the very words I hear, will the expressiveness constitute a beauty." [2] I propose now to study this sentence.

Now notice how curious this is. Once more we have the sentences or the music. And these arouse emotion. This describes Cassie reading her book. So we might expect that Cassie would cry and would sob and so on. But this isn't all. Cassie is confused. Actually she is crying but she thinks the words are crying. She wipes her tears off those words. She sighs but the words heave. The sentence of Santayana suggests that she sees the sentences she reads through her tears and now her tears misserve her much as blue moods or dark glasses do. So Cassie looks through sadness and the sentence is tearful. What a pathetic fallacy! From confusion to suffusion! Are there misplaced emotions? Imagine what this would be like where sentences aroused not emotions but a toothache. And now you confused the toothache with the sentence, and before someone prevented you, you sent the sentence to the dentist.

Nevertheless, Santayana has almost certainly identified an experience that is different from that in which Cassie is sad over her book. We find "joy and sweetness in the very words" we hear. Clearly, too, Santayana has been misled by these words "joy and sweetness." For if there is joy and sweetness, where should these be but where they usually are? Where is joy then and where is sweetness? In the human breast, in the heart ("my heart leaps up when I behold"), in the eye. And if you say this, then indeed there must be some illusion. The sentence is like a mirror that catches and holds what is in the heart. And so artful are poets' sentences that the best readers are the best confused. I want now, however, to suggest that indeed joy and sweetness, and sadness too, are in the very words you hear. But in that case, joy and sweetness must be of the sort that can be in sentences. We must, accordingly, try to figure out what this "joy and sweetness in the very words" is like. For even though, making a mistake, one imagined they were in the words, their being there must make some sense. And Santayana too does not imagine that sentences cry.

Let me return now to the analogy: "The music is sad" is like "The sentence expresses an idea." We saw before how the sentence "The elephant ate a jumbo peanut" might be accompanied by an image and how this was like sentences or music arousing emotions. We want now to see how we might use the phrase "joy and sweetness in the very words." Do we have a meaning for "The idea in the very words you hear." Where is the idea of the elephant eating a jumbo peanut? Suppose we say: "It's in the very words you hear." Have you ever seen, in your mind's eye, that is, an elephant eating a peanut in the very words you hear? A sentence is like a circus tent? I do not suppose that anyone who said that joy and sweetness are in the very words you hear would be likely to say that this was like the way in which you might also see an image in the very sentence which you hear—a bald head in the word "but." I should like in any case to try something different.

I do not intend to abandon the analogy with language yet.

Music is expression of emotion as sentences are expression of ideas. But now how do sentences express ideas? We have noticed one way in which sentences do sometimes have meaning. Sentences, however, have been described in many ways. Sentences are like buzzers, like doorbells, like electric switches. Sentences are like mirrors, like maps, like pictures; sentences are like road signs, with arrows pointing the way. And so we might go on to ask, Is music like buzzers, like pictures, like road sign arrows? I do not however intend to do this. It will be noticed that the same analogy by which we have been trying to understand music, art, etc., may serve us also to understand what language is like. The analogy presupposes that we do know something about music, and so turning the analogy to this use may be fruitful. It might show us just how enlightening and how unenlightening the analogy is.

In order to study the analogy between music and the sentence and to try in this way to find out what the sentence is like, I now intend to offer a foolish theory. This may throw into clearer relief what Santayana says. What is understanding a sentence like? Understanding a sentence is speaking the sentence in a certain way. You can tell, listening to yourself talk, that you are understanding the sentence, and so can anyone else who hears you speak. Understanding has its rhythm. So the meaning of the sentence consists in a certain reading of the sentence. If, in this case, a sentence is spoken and not understood by someone, there would be only one thing to do; namely, speak the sentence again. Obviously this account will not do, for there are other ways of clarifying what we mean. Nevertheless, in some cases it may be all that is necessary.

Now notice. If this were what the meaning of a sentence is like, we should see at once what was meant if someone said that the meaning or the idea is in the sentence. For if there is meaning, where could it be but in the sentence, since the sentence is all there is? Of course, it is true that the sentence would have to be spoken and, of course, spoken in some way or other. And with every variation in reading it might then be said to have a different meaning. If anyone asked, "And what does the sentence mean?" expecting you to point to something or to elaborate the matter in gestures or to translate, it would be clear that he quite misunderstood what meaning is like. One might even correct him, saying it is even misleading to say that the meaning is in the sentence, as though it were only a part of the sentence, or tucked away somehow under overlapping syllables. A sentence having meaning in a case like this would be something like a living thing. Here too one might ask, Where is the life in a squirrel and in a geranium? Truly the life is the squirrel and is the geranium, and is no part of either nor tucked away in some hidden fold or tiny vein. And so it is with the sentence, according to our imaginary theory. We might speak of the sentence as like a living thing.

And now let us see whether we have some corresponding use for "The joy and sweetness are in the very words you hear." People do ask about the meaning of poems and even about the meaning of music. Let us first of all say that the meaning is "the joy and sweetness," and the sadness. And where are these? In the very words you hear, and in the music. And now notice that what was admittedly a foolish theory in respect to sentences is not a foolish theory in respect to poems or music. Do you get the poem? Do you get the music? If you do not, pointing, gestures, translations will not help. (Understanding the words is presupposed.) There will be only one thing to do; namely, read the verses again, play the music once more. And what will the joy and sweetness and the sadness be like? They will be like the life in the living thing, not to be distinguished as some one part of the poem or music and not another part, or as some shadow that follows the sounded words or tones. "In the very words you hear," like the squirrel in fur!

I infer now that the analogy between the "joy and sweetness" in words and the meaning in sentences is misleading and is not likely to be helpful. The meaning of sentences is translatable, but the "meaning" of poems, of music, is not. We have seen how this is so. There may, of course, be something in the sounding of all sentences which is analogous to the "joy and sweetness in the very words," but it is not the meaning of those sentences. And now this is an interesting consequence. It makes sense to ask, What does the sentence express? It expresses a meaning, of course, and you may have some way of showing what this is, without using the sentence to do so. But now it makes no sense to ask, What does the poem express? or What does the music express? We may say, if we like, that both are expressive, but we must beware of the analogy with language. And we may prevent the helpless searching in this case, by insisting that they "express" nothing, nothing at all.

And now let us review. My assumption has been that the expression theory is plagued with certain analogies that are not clearly distinguished, and none of which finally is helpful without being misleading. The first analogy is that in terms of which we commonly think of emotions. The second is that in terms of which we think of language, the doorbell view. Besides this there are two different types of experience that arise in connection with art. One of these types may be fairly well described by the analogy with doorbell language. The similarity of our language, however, in respect to both these types of experience, conceals the difference between those two types. Santayana's sentence reveals the agony that follows the recognition of this difference in these types of experience and the attempt to employ the language which describes the one to describe the other. The language requires very interesting translation. My conclusion, accordingly, is this: The analogy drawn from language may be useful in describing one type of experience. It is practically useless in describing the other. Since, then, these two analogies dominate the use of the word "expression," I suggest that, for the sake of clarity and charity, they be abandoned in seeking to describe that "expressiveness" which Santayana says constitutes "a beauty."

If we now abandon these analogies, are we also to abandon the use of the word "expression"? Not unless we please to do so. But we do so at our risk, for these analogies are not easily abandoned. We may, however, fortify our use of this word by considerations such as these. We use the word "expressive" to describe faces. And we use "expressive" in much the same way that we use the phrase "has character." A face that is expressive "has character." But when we now say that a face has character, this may remind us that the letters of the alphabet are characters. Let us suppose for a moment that this is related to "He's a character!" I suppose that he's a character and he has a character do not mean quite the same thing. There are antics in he's a character. Try again: The zigzag line has character and the wavy line has character. Each letter of the alphabet is a character, but also has character. The number tokens, 1 2 3 4 5 6 7 8 9—each has its character. In the same way sounds have character. Let me see whether we can explain this further. You might say that if some dancing master were to arrange a dance for each of the numbers, you might see how a dance for the number one would not do at all for number five. Or again if the numbers were to be dressed in scarves, again a certain color and a certain flimsy material would do for six but would not suit five at all. Now something of the same sort is true of words, and particularly of some. Words have character. I am tempted to say that all these things have their peculiar feel, but this then must be understood on the analogy with touch. If we, for instance, said that all these things have their peculiar feeling, then once again it might be supposed that in connection with them there is a feeling which is aroused by them.

Let your ears and your eyes, perhaps, too, feel these familiar bits of nonsense:

> Hi diddle diddle!
> Fee! fi, fo, fum!
> Intery, mintery.
> Abra ca da bra.

Each has its character. Each is, in this sense, expressive. But to ask now What is its character or what does it express? is to fall into the pit. You may, of course, experiment to exhibit more clearly just what the character, in each case, is. You may, for instance, contrast the leaping, the stomping, the mincing, the shuffle, with what you get if you change the vowels. Try:

> Ho! doodle doodle!
> Fa, fo, fu, fim!
> Untery, muntery.
> Ay bray cay day bray.

One might also go on to change consonants in order again to exhibit character by giving the words new edges and making their sides steeper or smoothing them down.

I do not intend, in proposing illustrations of this sort, to suggest that art is nonsense and that its character is simple as these syllables are. A face, no doubt may bear the impress, the character, of a life's torment and of its hope and victory. So too words and phrases may come blazing out of the burning past. In art the world is born afresh, but the travail of the artist may have had its beginnings in children's play. My only point is that once the poem is born it has its character as surely as a cry in the night or intery, mintery. And this character is not something that follows it around like a clatter in a man's insides when he reads it. The light of the sun is in the sun, where you see it. So with the character of the poem. Hear the words and do not imagine that in hearing them you gulp a jigger to make yourself foam. Rather suppose that the poem is as hard as marble, ingrained, it may be, with indelible sorrow.

If, accordingly, we now use the sentence "Art is expression," or "Art is expressive," and the use of this sentence is determined by elucidations such as I have just now set out, then, I think that our language may save us from some torture. And this means that we are now prepared to use freely those sentences that the expression theory is commonly inclined to correct. For now, unabashed, we shall say that the music is sad, and we shall not go on to say that this means that the music expresses sadness. For the sadness is to the music rather like the redness to the apple, than it is like the burp to the cider. And above all we shall not, having heard the music or read the poem, ask, What does it express?

4

And now it's many words ago since we left Verbo and his friend at the corner. Verbo was trying to figure out, you remember, how the music was related to his grandmother. How can music be sad? I suggested then that he was having word trouble, and that it would be necessary to probe his sentences. And so we probed. And now what shall we tell Verbo?

"Verbo," we will say, "the music is sad." And then we will remind him that the geranium is living, and that the sun is light. We will say these things so that he will not look away from the music to discover the sadness of it. Are you looking for the life in the geranium? Are you looking for the light in the sun? As then the life and the light describe the geranium and the sun, so too does sadness describe the music. And then we shall have to go on to tell him about these fearful analogies, and about Santayana's wrestle on the precipice. And about how we cut the ropes! And you may be sure that just as things are going along so well, Verbo will ask, flicking the ashes from his cigarette, "And what about the sadness?"

And now it's time to take the cat out of the bag, for so far all that has been exposed is the bag. The sadness is a quality of what we have already described as the character, the expressive. One piece of music is like and unlike some other pieces of music. These similarities and these differences may be perceived. Now then, we have a class of sad music. But why sad; that is, why use this word? It must be remembered, of course, that the use of this word is not precise. So there may be some pieces of music which are unmistakably sad, and others which shade off in gradations to the point where the question, Is it sad? is not even asked. Suppose we ask our question, Why sad? in respect to the unmistakable cases. Then, perhaps, some such answer as this will do. Sad music has some of the characteristics of people who are sad. It will be slow, not tripping: it will be low, not tinkling. People who are sad move more slowly, and when they speak, they speak softly and low. Associations of this sort may, of course, be multiplied indefinitely. And this now is the kitten in whose interest we made so much fuss about the bag. The kitten has, I think, turned out to be a scrawny little creature, not worth much. But the bag was worth it.

The bag was worth it? What I have in mind is that the identification of music as the expressive, as character, is crucial. That the expressive is sad serves now only to tag the music. It is introspective or, in relation to the music, an aside. It's a judgment that intervenes. Music need not be sad, nor joyous, nor anything else. Aestheticians usually account for this by inventing all sorts of emotions without names, an emotion for every piece of music. Besides, bad music, characterless music, the unexpressive, may be sad in quite the same way that good music may be. This is no objection, of course, to such classifications. I am interested only in clarifying the distinction between our uses of these several sentences.

And now that I have come to see what a thicket of tangle-words I've tried to find my way through, it seems to me that I am echoing such words as years ago I read in Croce, but certainly did not then understand. Perhaps if I read Croce again now I shouldn't understand them either. "Beauty is expression."

NOTES

1. An author of no repute at all, not to be confused with Diogenes.
2. *Sense of Beauty* (1896), p. 149.

SOME REMARKS ON VALUE AND
GREATNESS IN MUSIC *

Leonard B. Meyer

As every musician must, I have been concerned with the
nature of value in music and have in moments of impetuous
rashness even asked myself the $64,000 question: What makes
music great? In grappling with these perplexing problems I
have changed my mind many times, testing first this view then
that; finding this objection then another to what I thought
at first to be tenable positions. Nor have I as yet arrived at
any fixed opinions or final conclusions.

Indeed, instead of providing positive answers neatly confined to the area of aesthetics (as I should have preferred),
my attempts to understand the nature of value in music have
led to still further questions as to the nature of value in general and ultimately to the rarefied realm of metaphysics. Since
my ideas on these matters are still in flux, I shall present
neither an explicit theory of value nor a definitive account of
greatness. Rather, in pointing out relationships and correlations between value in music and value in other areas, I shall
hope to suggest viewpoints and avenues of approach which
will perhaps provide fruitful insights and may later lead to
plausible conclusions.

Whatever the difficulties, uncertainties, and hazards may
be, the question "What makes music great?" is one that anyone deeply concerned with his art must attempt at least to
answer. And if some scholars make a point of avoiding such
questions altogether as the positivists do, or throw them into
the vast nets of cultural context as the social scientists have
often done, or surreptitiously substitute the plausibility of
technical jargon for basic questionings as humanists sometimes
do—so much the worse for them. We cannot—nor can they for
all their rationalizations—really escape from the problem of
value.

This is true in two senses. The first is perhaps obvious, yet
nonetheless important. We are in fact continually making
value judgments both for ourselves and others. As an individual I can listen to and study only a limited number of
musical works during my lifetime. I must choose between
works, exercising value judgments. As a teacher I decide to
use this work for teaching rather than that. And though I may
select the work for didactic reasons rather than because I

* [From *The Journal of Aesthetics and Art Criticism*, Vol. XVII,
No. 4 (June 1959). Reprinted by permission of the author and
The Journal of Aesthetics and Art Criticism.]

think it is a masterpiece, even as I choose it for this reason I am aware of the distinction between a work which is great in its own terms and one which will serve to illustrate a given point clearly.

The second reason why the problem of value is inescapable for someone concerned with music—or any art for that matter —is that a system or ordering of values is implicit in his account of how and what art communicates. Indeed, as soon as we say it communicates, we introduce values into the discussion. At one time I subscribed to I. A. Richards's statement that "The two pillars upon which a theory of criticism must rest are an account of value and an account of communication." [1] However, it has seemed increasingly clear that these two are as inextricably linked to one another as are means and ends. When you discuss one you are of necessity implying the other. For instance, if your account of musical communication is primarily in terms of the referential and associative states which music can arouse, then your judgments as to value are going to be different from those which would arise out of an account of communication which emphasized the more exclusively intra-musical meanings which I shall call embodied or syntactical. In a sense, then, this paper is an attempt to make explicit the scheme of values implicit in the analysis of musical communication given in *Emotion and Meaning in Music*.[2]

At first it would seem that the problem is not really very difficult. After all there are certain technical criteria for excellence in a piece of music. A good piece of music must have consistency of style: that is, it must employ a unified system of expectations and probabilities; it should possess clarity of basic intent; it should have variety, unity, and all the other categories which are so easy to find after the fact. But these are, I think, only necessary causes. And while they may enable us to distinguish a good or satisfactory piece from a downright bad one, they will not help us very much when we try to discriminate between a pretty good work and a very good one, let alone distinguish the characteristics of greatness.

Indeed the tune "Twinkle, Twinkle, Little Star" possesses style, unity, variety, and so forth. And if we then ask is Bach's B Minor Mass better than "Twinkle, Twinkle"—using *only* these technical categories—we shall, I am afraid, be obliged to answer that they are equally good, adding perhaps, "each in its own way." I shall return to the "each in its own way" argument presently. But for now, it seems to me that, granting listeners who have learned to respond to and understand both works, the statement that these works are equally good is preposterous and false.

Nor are length, size, or complexity *as such* criteria of value, though as we shall see, complexity does have something to do with excellence. Thus some of Brahms's smaller piano pieces are often considered to be better works than, for instance, his Fourth Symphony. And I am sure that each of us can cite instances of this for himself. Perhaps it would be well at this point to turn to particular musical examples to see what we can learn from them.

Because a relatively thorough examination of even two brief pieces would involve a complex and lengthy analysis, I have chosen to discuss, briefly, two fugue subjects: the first by Geminiani, the second by Bach. Since only the themes will be discussed, it should be pointed out that good themes do not necessarily give rise to good total works. And though it is difficult to write a good fugue on a really poor subject, an unprepossessing theme—such as that of Bach's Fugue in C-sharp Minor (W.T.C.,I)—may act as the basis for a very fine work.

Even though it goes against critical canon I intend to treat the themes as entities in their own right, but as themes, not as complete works. For considered in themselves they will serve to raise some of the basic considerations which are involved in value and ultimately in greatness. And these considerations apply with equal force to complete works, even those of the greatest magnitude. In short, reversing the procedure of Plato, who inquired as to the principles of justice in the individual by considering the nature of justice in the State, we shall try to learn something about the value of whole works by considering the nature of value in a small segment.

Here then are the two themes:

Example 1

They are certainly not equally good. And at first glance we observe that the Bach theme has more rhythmic and motivic variety, that it covers a larger range, and so forth, than Geminiani's theme. However, there are good themes which lack obvious variety. In any case, it would seem safe to say that variety is a means to an end, not an end in itself.

Looking at these two themes more closely, we see that they are quite similar in their basic melodic structure. Both begin on the fifth degree of the scale, move to the tonic (in the case of the Bach, through the third of the scale), and then skip an octave. This skip creates a structural gap, a sense of incompleteness. We expect that the empty space thus outlined will be filled in, made complete. This melodic incompleteness is complemented by the rhythmic instability of this first musical shape. That is, the first separable musical events in both themes are up-beats which are oriented toward the stability of down-beats.

In a sense the structural gap and the rhythmic up-beats have established musical goals to be reached. We expect the melodic line to descend and ultimately to come to rest on the tonic note, reaching a clear organizing accent in the course of this motion. And so in fact they both do. *But* with crucial differences. The Bach theme moves down slowly with delays and temporary diversions through related harmonic areas. It establishes various levels of melodic activity with various potentials to be realized. Furthermore, these delays are rhythmic as well as melodic (see analysis under Example 1). The Geminiani theme, on the other hand, moves directly—or almost directly—to its goal. The second measure is chromatic and contains a potential for different modes of continuation. Of these the return to the B is certainly the most probable, but only slightly so. However, once the B is reached, the descent to E seems almost inevitable. And when the theme falls to this obvious consequent with neither delay nor diversion, it seems like a blatant platitude, a musical cliché. Nor are there any rhythmic resistances. The initial up-beat perpetuates itself without marked disturbance down to the final note which arrives on the obvious down-beat.

Thus it would seem that in this case at least value has something to do with the activation of a musical impulse having tendencies toward a more or less definite goal and with the temporary resistance or inhibition of these tendencies. The importance of the element of resistance can be made even more apparent if we rewrite the Bach theme in such a way that this element is eliminated.

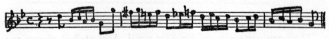

Example 2

The theme is now as banal as Geminiani's.

From these considerations it follows (1) that a melody or a work which establishes no tendencies, if such can be imagined, will from this point of view (and others are possible) be of no value. Of course, such tendencies need not be powerful at the outset, but may be developed during the course of musical progress. (2) If the most probable goal is reached in the most immediate and direct way, given the stylistic context, the musical event taken in itself will be of little value. And (3) if the goal is never reached or if the tendencies activated become dissipated in the press of over-elaborate or irrelevant diversions, then value will tend to be minimal.

The notion that the inhibition of goal-oriented tendencies is related to value is not a new one. Robert Penn Warren writes that "a poem, to be good, must earn itself. It is a motion toward a point of rest, but if it is not a resisted motion, it is a motion of no consequence. For example, a poem which depends upon stock materials and stock responses is simply a toboggan slide, or a fall through space.[3] Dewey's position is quite similar. "Impulsion forever boosted on its forward way would run its course thoughtless, and dead to emotion . . . . The only way it can become aware of its nature and its goal is by obstacles surmounted and means employed." [4]

More recently information theory has developed concepts in which the relationship between resistance and value seems to be implicit. In order to understand how information theory relates to these considerations, it is necessary to examine the nature of goal-tendency processes in more detail.

Musical events take place in a world of stylistic probability. If we hear only a single tone, a great number of different tones could follow it with equal probability. If a sequence of two tones is heard the number of probable consequent tones is somewhat reduced—how much depends upon the tones chosen and the stylistic context—and hence the probability of the remaining alternatives is somewhat increased. As more tones are added and consequently more relationships between tones established, the probabilities of a particular goal become increased. Thus in Bach's theme the probability of any particular tone following the first D is very small, for the number of possible consequents is very large. As the line moves downward through the B-flat and the A, the probabilities of the G become very high and it is the satisfaction of this motion which closes out the first pattern as a musical event. This pattern, after the octave skip, now becomes the unit of motion and becomes the basis for probability estimates on a higher architectonic level. Note that the variety of events in this theme, as well as the delays already noted, make the particular sequence of events seem much less probable than the sequence of events in the Geminiani theme.

Here information theory becomes relevant.[5] It tells us that if a situation is highly organized so that the possible consequents have a high degree of probability, then if the probable occurs, the information communicated by the message (what we have been calling a musical event) is minimal. If, on the other hand, the musical situation is less predictable so that the antecedent-consequent relationship does *not* have a high degree of probability, then the information contained in the musical message will be high. Norbert Wiener has put the matter succinctly: "the more probable the message, the less its information. Clichés, for example, are less illuminating than great poems." [6]

Since resistances, or more generally deviations, are by definition disturbances in the goal-oriented tendencies of a musical impulse, they lower the probability not only of a particular consequent but of the musical event as a whole. In so doing they create or increase information. And it does not seem a rash step to conclude that what creates or increases the information contained in a piece of music increases its value.

(Of course in either linguistic or musical communication a completely random series of stimuli will in all likelihood communicate nothing. For language and music depend upon the existence of an ordered probability system, a stochastic process, which serves to make the several stimuli or events mutually relevant to one another. Thus the probability of any particular musical event depends in part upon the probabilistic character of the style employed. Randomness of choice is limited by the fact of musical style.)

The concepts of information theory suggest that the notion of resistance can be generalized by relating it through probability to uncertainty. For the lower the probability that any particular sequence of events will take place—that is, the lower the probability that the total message will be any particular one—the greater the uncertainty as to what the events and the message will actually be. And also the greater the information contained in the total event. Thus greater uncertainty and greater information go hand in hand.[7]

The relationship between resistance and uncertainty is not difficult to discover. Whenever a tendency is inhibited—or more generally, when deviation takes place—slight though perhaps unconscious uncertainty is experienced. What seemed perhaps so probable that alternative consequents were not considered, now seems less so. For the mind, attempting to account for and understand the import of the deviation, is made aware of the possibility of less probable, alternative consequents.

A distinction must be made between desirable and undesirable uncertainty. Desirable uncertainty is that which arises as a result of the structured probabilities of a musical style. Information is a function of such uncertainty. Undesirable uncertainty arises when the probabilities are not known, either because the listener's habit responses are not relevant to the style (which I have called "cultural noise") [8] or because external interference obscures the structure of the situation in question (i.e., acoustical noise).

It seems further that uncertainty should be distinguished from vagueness, though the distinction is by no means clear-cut. Uncertainty evidently presumes a basic norm of clear probability patterns such that even the ambiguous is felt to be goal-oriented. Vagueness, on the other hand, involves a weakening of the transitive, kinetic character of syntactic relationships and as a result the sense of musical tendency is enervated. When this occurs, attention becomes focused upon the nuances and refinements of phrases, timbres, textures, and the like. And impressionism tends in this respect to be the sensitive projection of the sensuous. We shall return to another aspect of the relationship between value and uncertainty a bit later. Now we must briefly consider the nature of the unexpected, or more particularly, the surprising in relation to information theory.

All deviation involves the less probable. However, because in most cases the less probable grows gradually out of the more probable or because in some cases the musical context is one in which deviation is more or less expected, listeners are as a rule aware of the possibility of deviation. They are set and ready for the less probable, though often unconsciously so. In the case of the unexpected the probability of a given music event seems so high that the possibility of alternative consequent is not considered. It seems as though the message involves a minimum of uncertainty and that, when completed, it will have contained little information. But when at the last moment the improbable abruptly arrives, the listener discovers that his estimates of probability and uncertainty were wrong and that the event or message actually contained more information than it was presumed to contain.

Let us consider these matters in relation to an example from language and in relation to Geminiani's fugue subject. Take the phrase "she is as tall." First off, we can talk about the sequence of sounds in terms of probability, uncertainty, and information. The uncertainty of what will follow the sound "sh" is very high indeed, though clearly some sounds will be less probable than others, given the stylistic context we call English. Thus the sound or "word" *shvin* is highly improbable in an English sentence. But it is not impossible—witness the fact that it has just occurred in one.[9] The uncertainties are reduced and the probabilities increased when the sound "i" (e) arrives. But the pause which actually follows is only one of the possible sequels to the sound "she." The word might have become "sheep." Thus both the sound "i" and the pause add considerable information. And please note that silence is a part of information, musical as well as linguistic.

Now the same kind of analysis is possible for the first event in Geminiani's theme. Considering the notes B and E, for the sake of comparison, as being equivalent to the sound "sh," it is clear that the number of possible consequents is very high. The event could have continued in many different ways, though again some (Example 3,a) are more probable, given the stylistic context and the fact that this is the beginning of a work, than others (Example 3,b). The high E, like the sound "i" (e), thus adds a great deal of information to the musical message (see Example 1).

Example 3

The turning of the melodic line downward and the arrival of a clear down-beat—these complement one another—make it clear in retrospect that a musical event has been completed. Had the melodic line not been articulated by a change of motion or had the down-beat been suppressed, the musical event would have been different. That is, just as the sound "she" could have become part of the linguistic event "sheep," so the first three notes of this theme could have become part of the events presented in Example 3, parts c and d.

Of course these events, both the musical and the linguistic ones, exist only on the lowest architectonic level. They cannot stand alone, but are parts of larger wholes. That is, the musical event is part of a syntactical unit we call a theme, the linguistic event part of a syntactical unit we call a sentence or phrase. And these larger units, which are events on higher architectonic levels, are but parts of still larger musical sections or linguistic paragraphs or stanzas. These in turn are parts of whole pieces of music or works of literature.

Turning now to the partial phrase "She is as tall," it is evident that there is one highly probable syntactical consequent.

That is, we expect that the phrase will be followed by the word "as" and then by a proper noun or a pronoun. And we would be surprised to find an adjective following either the word "tall" or the words "tall as." For instance, the phrases "she is as tall blue" or "she is as tall as blue" are rather improbable, though not impossible. The first of these alternatives might continue "she is as tall blue lilacs are," and the simile being improbable increases information considerably.

If we take a more probable consequent, "she is as tall as Bill," we have acquired information, but syntactically speaking not very much. Notice incidentally that we actually leave out that part of the construction which is the most probable. That is, we omit the implicit "as Bill *is tall*" because in the context these words contribute no information and hence are unnecessary. Now if we look at the first part of the Geminiani theme we might say, by analogy, that the half-phrase up to the B corresponds to the part-phrase "she is as tall" and that the descent to the E corresponds to the most probable syntactical completion just as the words "as Bill is tall" do. Both completions are obvious and neither is very good. However, this does *not* assert that taken in the context of a larger whole, these phrases might not become part of a meaningful, valuable work.

Before leaving this comparison between musical and linguistic behavior, it might be amusing to construct examples involving the unexpected. Observe, first of all, that since the phrase "she is as tall" is syntactically incomplete, we are alert to the possibility of alternative consequents and that if the word "blue" follows (as in the phrase "she is as tall blue lilacs are"), it seems improbable but in a sense not unexpected. But if we take the phrase "she is as tall as Bill is," we assume our information is complete and are not ready for new information. And so if we add the word "wide" instead of the understood "tall," it is both improbable and unexpected. And the whole message contains more information than we presumed it to contain.

In a similar manner we can add to the Geminiani theme so that what at first seems to be a point of completion ceases to be so and becomes part of an unexpected twist of meaning (Example 4).

Example 4

Notice that not only is information increased in this variant, but that the meaning of the descent from B is in retrospect *literally* different. For its obviousness now seems to have been a means of deception as to the ultimate intent of the theme.

To summarize what we have learned from this excursion into the relationship of information theory to music and to value: first of all, we have found that resistance, or more broadly deviation, is a correlative of information. And since information is valuable—as tautology is not—our hypothesis as to the importance of deviation has received confirmation. Secondly, our inquiry has pointed to a relationship between information and deviation on the one hand, and uncertainty on the other. This implies that uncertainty is somewhat related to value. This apparently paradoxical pairing will be considered presently.

2

Hypotheses gain in plausibility not only through the corroboration of other investigators and through correlation with other fields of inquiry, but also by accounting for facts observed but hitherto unexplained theoretically. Our hypothesis can do this in explaining the difference between primitive music and art music. In so doing it is hoped that another aspect of the relationship between tendency inhibition and value will be revealed.

If we ask, What is the fundamental difference between sophisticated art music and primitive music? (and I do not include under the term "primitive" the highly sophisticated music which so-called primitives often play), then we can point to the fact that primitive music generally employs a smaller repertory of tones, that the distance of these notes from the tonic is smaller, that there is a great deal of repetition, though often slightly varied repetition, and so forth. But these are the symptoms of primitivism in music, not its causes.

The differentia between art music and primitive music lies in speed of tendency gratification. The primitive seeks almost immediate gratification for his tendencies whether these be biological or musical. Nor can he tolerate uncertainty. And it is because distant departures from the certainty and repose of the tonic note and lengthy delays in gratification are insufferable to him that the tonal repertory of the primitive is limited, not because he can't think of other tones. It is not his mentality that is limited, it is his maturity. Note, by the way, that popular music can be distinguished from real jazz on the same basis. For while "pop" music whether of the tin-pan-alley or the Ethelbert Nevin variety makes use of a fairly large repertory of tones, it operates with such conventional clichés that gratification is almost immediate and uncertainty is minimized.

One aspect of maturity both of the individual and of the culture within which a style arises consists then in the willingness to forgo immediate, and perhaps lesser gratification, for the sake of future ultimate gratification. Understood generally, not with reference to any specific musical work, self-imposed tendency-inhibition and the willingness to bear uncertainty are indications of maturity. They are signs, that is, that the animal is becoming a man. And this, I take it, is not without relevance to considerations of value.

"This is all very well and more or less plausible," someone will say, "but in the last analysis isn't music valuable for a variety of reasons rather than just for the rather puritanical ones which you have been hinting at? What of the sensuous pleasure of beautiful sound? What of the ability of music to move us through the deep-seated associations it is able to evoke? Are these without value?"

The problems raised by these questions—that of the relation of pleasure to value and that of the ordering of values—have concerned philosophy from its very beginnings, and I shall not presume to give definite answers to them. What follows must therefore be taken as provisional. At first blush it would seem that we do in fact distinguish between what is *pleasurable* and what is *good*. Indeed the difference between them seems to parallel the distinction drawn above between immediate gratification and delayed gratification. But even as we state it, the distinction breaks down, even linguistically. For delayed gratification too is pleasurable; not only in the sense that it does culminate in ultimate and increased satisfaction, but also in the sense that it involves pleasures related to the conquest of difficulties—to control and power.[10]

Two points should be noted in this connection. In the first place, both immediate gratification and delayed gratification are pleasurable and both are valuable, though they are not necessarily equally valuable. Secondly, value refers to a quality of musical experience. It is inherent neither in the musical object per se nor in the mind of the listener per se. Rather value arises as the result of a transaction, which takes place within an objective tradition, between the musical work and a listener. This being the case, the value of any particular musical experience is a function both of the listener's ability to respond—his having learned the style of the music—and of his mode of response.

Three aspects of musical enjoyment may be distinguished: the sensuous, the associative-characterizing, and the syntactical. And though every piece of music involves all three to some extent, some pieces tend to emphasize one aspect and minimize others. Thus at one end of what is obviously a continuum is the immediate gratification of the sensuous and the exclamatory outburst of uncontrolled, pent-up energy. At the other end of the continuum is the delayed gratification arising out of the perception of and response to the syntactical relationships which shape and mold musical experience, whether intellectual or emotional. The associative may function with either. It may color our sensuous pleasures with the satisfactions of wish-fulfillment. Or it may shape our expectations as to the probabilities of musical progress by characterizing musical events. For just as our estimate of the character of an individual influences our expectations as to his probable behavior, so our estimate of the character of a theme or musical event shapes our expectations as to how it will behave musically. And conversely, the way in which a musical event behaves—involves regular, deviant, or surprising progressions —influences our opinion as to its character. Thus the syntactical and characterizing facets of musical communication are inextricably linked.

The question of the ordering of values still remains. Are the different aspects of musical enjoyment equally valuable? Is a piece of music which appeals primarily to sensuous-associative pleasure as good as one which appeals to syntactical-associative enjoyment? If we put the matter as crudely as possible—if we ask, Is the best arrangement of the best pop tune as good as Beethoven's Ninth Symphony?"—then the answer seems easy. But if we put a similar question using less polar works and ask, Is Debussy's *Afternoon of a Faun* as good as the Ninth Symphony? we have qualms about the answer.

At this point some of our social scientist friends, whose blood pressure has been steadily mounting, will throw up their hands in relativistic horror and cry: "You can't do this! You can't compare baked Alaska with roast beef. Each work is good of its kind and there's the end of it." Now granting both that we can enjoy a particular work for a variety of reasons and also that the enjoyment of one kind of music does not preclude the enjoyment of others—that we can enjoy both Debussy and Beethoven—this does not mean that they are equally good. Nor does it mean that all modes of musical enjoyment are equally valuable. In fact, when you come right down to it, the statement that "each is good of its kind" is an evasion of the problem, not a solution of it. And so we are still driven to ask: are all kinds equally good?

3

To begin the next stage of our inquiry, let us recall an idea brought out in our discussion of the difference between primitive music and sophisticated music. I refer to the observation that willingness to inhibit tendencies and tolerate uncertainties is a sign of maturity. Note, however, that the converse of this is also true. For maturation and individualization are themselves products of the resistances, problems, and uncertainties with which life confronts us. As George Herbert Mead has pointed out, it is only by coming to grips with these difficulties and overcoming them and by making the choices and decisions which each of us must make that the self becomes aware of itself, becomes a self.[11] Only through our encounters with the world, through what we suffer, do we achieve self-realization as particular men and women.

It is because the evaluation of alternative probabilities and the retrospective understanding of the relationships among musical events as they actually occurred leads to self-awareness and individualization that the syntactical response is more valuable than those responses in which the ego is dissolved, losing its identity in voluptuous sensation or in the reverie of daydreams. And for the same reasons works involving deviation and uncertainty are better than those offering more immediate satisfaction. I am not contending that other modes of enjoyment are without value, but rather that they are of a lesser order of value.

The difficulty is that, aside from the most primitive forms of musical-emotional outburst and the most blatant appeals to the sensuous such as one finds in the cheapest pop arrangements, there are no musical works of art in which syntactical relationships do not play a significant role. Nor will it do to try to arrange musical works in order of their syntactical vs. their sensuous-associative appeals. For even a work such as Debussy's *Afternoon of a Faun*, which strongly emphasizes the sensuous, is syntactically complex—as complex, for instance, as the first movement of Mozart's famous Piano Sonata in C Major, which is predominantly syntactical.[12]

Thus it would seem that while the contrast between the sensuous-associative and the syntactical may provide a basis for evaluating the responses of listeners, it does not provide a basis for judging the value of most pieces of music. The sensuous-associative is of minor importance in the consideration of value.[13] Music must be evaluated syntactically. And indeed it is so. For who is to say which of two works has greater sensuous appeal or evokes more poignant associations? The matter is by definition completely subjective. And if we ask, Why is Debussy's music superior to that of Delius? the answer lies in the syntactical organization of his music, not in its superior sensuousness.

What then are the determinants of value from the syntactical viewpoint? We noted earlier that complexity, size, and length are not in themselves virtues. For as we all know from sad experience, a large complex work can be pretentious and bombastic, dull and turgid, or a combination of these. Yet insofar as the intricate and subtle interconnections between musical events, whether simultaneous or successive, of a complex work involve considerable resistance and uncertainty—and presumably information—value is thereby created. This viewpoint seems more plausible when we consider that as we become more familiar with a complex work and are therefore better able to comprehend the permutations and interrelations among musical events, our enjoyment is increased. For the information we get out of the work is increased.

Obviously neither information nor complexity refer to the mere accumulation of a heterogeneous variety of events. If the events are to be meaningful, they must arise out of a set of probability relationships, a musical style. Moreover, the capacity of the human mind to perceive and relate patterns to one another and to remember them would appear to limit complexity. For if a work is so complex that the musical events eclipse one another, then value will be diminished. Or, as mentioned earlier, if complexity and length are such that tendencies become dissipated in the course of overelaborate deviations, then meanings will be lost as relationships become obscure. Of course if listeners are unable to remember the musical events, whether because of the magnitude of a work or because it involves stylistic innovations, then the piece of music may seem overcomplex when it is not so. This is why music at first found unintelligible and empty may later become understandable and rewarding.

We have been so conditioned by the nineteenth-century notion that great art is simple that the association of complexity with value is repugnant. Yet, while complexity is not the sufficient cause of value, the implication that the two are in no way related is simply not true. Can one seriously argue that the complexity of Bach's B Minor Mass has nothing to do with its excellence relative to the tune "Twinkle, Twinkle, Little Star"? Or think of some of the masterpieces of Western art: "The Last Judgment" by Michelangelo, Picasso's "Guernica," *The Iliad,* Joyce's *Ulysses,* Mozart's *Jupiter Symphony,* Stravinsky's *Symphony of Psalms.*

Nevertheless one is reluctant. What of a relatively simple but touching work such as Schubert's song, *"Das Wandern"?* Is it not perfect of its kind? Is it not enchanting precisely *because* of its simplicity? Without arguing the point, it seems probable that the charm of simplicity as such is associative rather than syntactical; that is, its appeal is to childhood, remembered as untroubled and secure. However, a direct, one-to-one correspondence between complexity and value will not stand up. For we are all aware that relatively simple pieces such as some of Schubert's songs or Chopin's preludes are better—more rewarding—than some large and complex works, such as, for instance, Strauss's *Don Quixote*.

This is the case because information is judged not in absolute, but in relative terms. For we evaluate not only the amount of information in a work but also the relationship between the stimulus "input" and the actual informational "output." Evidently the operation of some "principle of psychic economy" makes us compare the ratio of musical means invested to the informational income produced by this investment. Those works are judged good which yield a high return. Those works yielding a low return are found to be pretentious and bombastic.

Musical information is then evaluated both quantitatively and qualitatively. Hence two pieces might, so to speak, yield the same amount of information but not be equally good because one is less elegant and economical than the other. On the other hand, a piece which is somewhat deficient in elegance may be better than a more economical piece because it contains substantially more information and hence provides a richer musical experience.

4

Musical communication is qualitative not only in this syntactical sense. The content of musical experience is also an important aspect of its quality. With the introduction of "content" we not only leave the concepts of information theory, which is concerned only with the syntactical nature of music, but we also part company from those aestheticians who contend that musical experience is devoid of any content whatsoever. And we move from the consideration of value per se to the consideration of greatness.

For when we talk of greatness, we are dealing with a quality of experience which transcends the syntactical. We are considering another order of value in which self-awareness and individualization arise out of the cosmic uncertainties that pervade human existence; where man's sense of the inadequacy of reason in a capricious and inscrutable universe, his feeling of terrible isolation in a callous and indifferent, if not hostile, nature, and his awareness of his own insignificance and impotence in the face of the magnitude and power of creation, all lead to those ultimate and inescapable questions which Pascal posed when he wrote:

I see the formidable regions of the universe which enclose me, and I find myself penned in one corner of this vast expanse, without knowing why I am set in this spot rather than another, nor why the little span of life granted me is assigned to this point of time rather than another of the whole eternity which went before or which shall follow after. I see nothing but infinities on every hand, closing me in as if I were an atom or a shadow which lasts but a moment and returns no more. All I know is that I must shortly die, but what I know least of all about is this very death which I cannot escape.[14]

These ultimate uncertainties—and at the same time ultimate realities—of which great music makes us aware result not from syntactical relationships alone, but from the interaction of these with the associative aspect of music. This interaction, at once shaping and characterizing musical experience, gives rise to a profound wonderment—tender, yet awful—at the mystery of existence.[15] And in the very act of sensing this mystery, we attain a new level of consciousness, of individualization. The nature of uncertainty too has changed. It has become a means to an end rather than an end to be suffered.

The reasons for contending that Beethoven's Ninth Symphony is a great work, while Debussy's *Afternoon of a Faun* is only excellent should now be clear.[16] If we ask further about value per se, apart from considerations of greatness, it would seem that the Debussy may be the more elegant work, but the Beethoven is better. On the other hand, *The Afternoon of a Faun* is clearly a better work than the Mozart C Major Piano Sonata. And the greatest works would be those which embody value of the highest order with the most profound —and I use the word without hesitation—content.[17]

In her book, *The Greek Way to Western Civilization,* Edith Hamilton finds that the essence of tragedy springs from the fact of human dignity and she goes on to say that "it is by our power to suffer, above all, that we are of more value than the sparrows."[18] This, I think, carries the insight only part way. Rather it is because tragic suffering, arising out of the ultimate uncertainties of human existence, is able to individualize and purify our wills that we are of more value than the sparrows.

But are not war, poverty, disease, old age, and all other forms of suffering evil? As a general rule they are. For in most cases they lead to the degradation and dissolution of the self. The individual will is lost in the primordial impulses of the group which, as Freud has pointed out, "cannot tolerate any delay between its desires and the fulfillment of what it desires."[19] In short, suffering is regarded as evil because, generally speaking, it brings about a regression toward the immaturity of primitivism.

However, in instances where the individual is able to master it through understanding, as Job did, suffering may ultimately be good. For though, like medical treatment, it is painful, suffering may lead to a higher level of consciousness and a more sensitive, realistic awareness of the nature and meaning of existence. Indeed all maturation, all self-discovery, is in the last analysis more or less painful. And the wonder of great art is this: that through it we can approach this highest level of consciousness and understanding without paying the painful price exacted in real life and without risking the dissolution of the self which real suffering might bring.

One must therefore distinguish between moral values and individual values. Moral values deal with what will probably be good or bad for men taken as a group. Individual values are concerned with experience as it relates to particular men and women. The two should not be confused. For a concern with moral values such as the social sciences exhibit (and their inductive-statistical method makes this all but inevitable) leads to a normative, relativistic view in which values change from culture to culture and from group to group within the culture. A concern with individual values such as one finds in the humanities leads, on the other hand, to a universal view of value, though recognizing that ultimate value-goals may be reached by somewhat different means in different cultures. Indeed it is because the individual dimension of value is universal that, where translation is possible (as it is not in music), one is able to enjoy and value art works of another culture. Lastly, in contending that the ultimate value of art lies in its ability to individualize the self, I am conscious of my opposition to those who like Plato, Tolstoy, and the Marxists, would make aesthetic value a part of moral value.

It is clear then that our hypothesis as to the relation of resistance and uncertainty to value transcends the realm of aesthetics. For the choice to be made, the question to be asked, is in the final analysis metaphysical. It is this: What is the meaning and purpose of man's existence? And though one's answer can be rationalized and explained—though one can assert that it is through self-realization that man becomes differentiated from the beasts—it cannot be proved. Like an axiom, it must be self-evident.

In closing, I should like to quote from a letter written by a man who suffered greatly and who in so doing came to understand the meaning of suffering. The letter, dated February 14, 1819, two years before he died, is by John Keats.

Man is originally a poor forked creature subject to the same mischances as the beasts of the forest, destined to hardships and disquietude of some kind or other. . . . The common cognomen of this world among the misguided and superstitious is "a vale of tears" from which we are to be redeemed by a certain arbitrary interposition of God and taken to heaven. What a little circumscribed straightened notion! Call the world if you please "the vale of Soul-making." Then you will find out the use of the world. . . . I say *"soul making"*—Soul as distinguished from Intelligence. There may be intelligences or sparks of the divinity in millions—but they are not souls till they acquire identities, till each one is personally itself. . . . How then are Souls made? . . . How but by the medium of a world like this? . . . I will call the *world* a School instituted for the purpose of teaching little children how to read—I will call the *human heart* the *horn book* read in that school—and I will call the *Child able to read,* the Soul made from that *School* and its *horn book.* Do you not see how necessary a World of Pains and troubles is to school an Intelligence and make it a soul? A place where the heart must feel and suffer in a thousand diverse ways. . . . As various as the Lives of Men are—so various become their souls, and thus does God make individual beings.[20]

NOTES

1. I. A. Richards, *Principles of Literary Criticism* (London: Kegan Paul & Co., 1947), p. 25.

2. Leonard B. Meyer, *Emotion and Meaning in Music* (Chicago: The University of Chicago Press, 1956).

3. Robert Penn Warren, "Pure and Impure Poetry," *Kenyon Review,* V (1943), p. 251.

4. John Dewey, *Art as Experience* (New York: Minton, Balch & Co., 1954), p. 59.

5. For a clear discussion of information theory see Warren Weaver, "Recent Contributions to the Mathematical Theory of Communication," *Etc.: A Review of General Semantics,* X (1953), pp. 261–81.

6. Norbert Wiener, *The Human Use of Human Beings* (New York: Doubleday Anchor Books, 1954), p. 21.

7. In part uncertainty is inherent in the nature of the probability process, in part it is intentionally introduced by the composer. See the discussion of Markoff process, systemic uncertainty, and designed uncertainty in Leonard B. Meyer, "Meaning in Music and Information Theory," *JAAC,* XV (1957), pp. 418–19.

8. Ibid., pp. 420–1.

9. This "gimmick" is borrowed from Weaver, op. cit., p. 267.

10. This does not, of course, assert that all experience is either good or pleasurable. Total quiescence—the absence of any stimulation whatever—is both unpleasant and valueless; as is its opposite, the complete frustration of a strong tendency which can find no substitute outlet. In connection with the former, it would seem that information is a basic need of the mind. See Woodburn Heron, "The Pathology of Boredom," *Scientific American,* CLXXXXVI (Jan. 1957), pp. 52–6.

11. George H. Mead, *Mind, Self and Society* (Chicago: The University of Chicago Press, 1934). See in particular Parts ii and iii.

12. In this connection it should be observed that instrumentation, texture, tempo, and dynamics which are often thought of as contributing most to the sensuous-associative aspect of music may, and in the work of fine composers do, function syntactically.

13. The sensuous-associative may, however, be of importance in accounting for individual musical preferences.

14. Pascal, *Pensées,* trans., H. F. Stewart (New York: Pantheon Books, Inc., 1950), pp. 105–7.

15. What I have been calling "greatness" is clearly related to what some philosophers have distinguished as the "sublime."

16. It seems possible that there is a correspondence between the several aspects of musical communication and the several levels of consciousness; that is, that the sensuous-associative, the syntactical, and the "sublime" give rise to different levels of awareness and individualization.

17. The distinction between *excellence* as syntactical and *greatness* which involves considerations of content makes it clear why we can speak of a "great work" that doesn't quite "come off." For there are works which seek to make us aware of ultimate uncertainties, but which fail in execution. Furthermore, this distinction makes clear the difference between a masterpiece and a great work. Some of Bach's Inventions are masterpieces, but they are not great works.

18. Edith Hamilton, *The Greek Way to Western Civilization* (New York: Mentor Books, 1948), p. 168.

19. Sigmund Freud, *Group Psychology and the Analysis of the Ego* (London: The International Psycho-Analytical Press, 1922), p. 15.

20. John Keats, *Letters,* ed., Maurice Buxton Forman (New York: Oxford University Press, 1935), pp. 335–6.

EXPRESSION *

Rudolf Arnheim

Every work of art must express something. This means, first of all, that the content of the work must go beyond the presentation of the individual objects of which it consists. But such a definition is too large for our purpose. It broadens the notion of "expression" to include any kind of communication. True, we commonly say, for example, that a man "expresses his opinion." Yet artistic expression seems to be something more specific. It requires that the communication of the data produce an "experience," the active presence of the forces that make up the perceived pattern. How is such an experience achieved?

INSIDE LINKED TO OUTSIDE

In a limited sense of the term, expression refers to features of a person's external appearance and behavior that permit us to find out what the person is feeling, thinking, striving for. Such information may be gathered from a man's face and gestures, the way he talks, dresses, keeps his room, handles a pen or a brush, as well as from the opinions he holds, the interpretation he gives to events. This is less and also more than what I mean here by expression: less, because expression must be considered even when no reference is made to a mind manifesting itself in appearance; more, because much importance cannot be attributed to what is merely inferred intellectually and indirectly from external clues. Nevertheless this more familiar meaning of the term must be discussed briefly here.

We look at a friend's face, and two things may happen: we understand what his mind is up to, and we find in ourselves a duplicate of his experiences. The traditional explanation of this accomplishment may be gathered from a playful review of Lavater's *Physiognomic Fragments for the Advancement of the Knowledge and Love of Our Fellow Man* written by the poet Matthias Claudius around 1775.

Physiognomics is a science of faces. Faces are *concreta* for they are related *generaliter* to natural reality and *specialiter* are firmly attached to people. Therefore the

* [From *Art and Visual Perception* (Berkeley and Los Angeles: University of California Press, 1957). Reprinted by permission of the publisher. The notes to this selection (Ch. x) may be found in the original edition.]

question arises whether the famous trick of the "abstractio" and the "methodus analytica" should not be applied here, in the sense of watching out whether the letter *i*, whenever it appears, is furnished with a dot and whether the dot is never found on top of another letter; in which case we should be sure that the dot and the letter are twin brothers so that when we run into Castor we can expect Pollux not to be far away. For an example we posit that there be one hundred gentlemen, all of whom are very quick on their feet, and they had given sample and proof of this, and all of these hundred gentlemen had a wart on their noses. I am not saying that gentlemen with a wart on their noses are cowards but am merely assuming it for the sake of the example. . . . Now *ponamus* there comes to my house a fellow who calls me a wretched scribbler and spits me into the face. Suppose I am reluctant to get into a fist fight and also cannot tell what the outcome would be, and I am standing there and considering the issue. At that moment I discover a wart on his nose, and now I cannot refrain myself any longer, I go after him courageously and, without any doubt, get away unbeaten. This procedure would represent, as it were, the royal road in this field. The progress might be slow but just as safe as that on other royal roads.

In a more serious vein, the theory was stated early in the eighteenth century by the philosopher Berkeley. In his essay on vision he speaks about the way in which the observer sees shame or anger in the looks of a man. "Those passions are themselves invisible: they are nevertheless let in by the eye along with colors and alterations of countenance, which are the immediate object of vision, and which signify them for no other reason than barely because they have been observed to accompany them: without which experience, we should no more have taken blushing for a sign of shame than gladness." Charles Darwin, in his book on the expression of emotions, devoted a few pages to the same problem. He believed that external manifestations and their psychical counterparts are connected by the observer either on the basis of an inborn instinct or of learning. "Moreover, when a child cries or laughs, he knows in a general manner what he is doing and what he feels; so that a very small exertion of reason would tell him what crying or laughing meant in others. But the question is, do our children acquire their knowledge of expression solely by experience through the power of association and reason? As most of the movements of expression must have been gradually acquired, afterwards becoming instinctive, there seems to be some degree of *a priori* probability that their recognition would likewise have become instinctive."

Recently a new version of the traditional theory has developed from a curious tendency on the part of many social scientists to assume that when people agree on some fact it is probably based on an unfounded convention. According to this view, judgments of expression rely on "stereotypes," which individuals adopt ready-made from their social group. For example, we have been told that aquiline noses indicate courage and that protruding lips betray sensuality. The promoters of the theory generally imply that such judgments are wrong, as though information not drawn from the individual's firsthand experience could never be trusted. The real danger does not lie in the social origin of the information, but rather in the fact that people have a tendency to acquire simply structured concepts on the basis of insufficient evidence, which may have been gathered firsthand or secondhand, and to preserve these concepts unchanged in the face of contrary experience. Whereas this may make for many one-sided or entirely wrong evaluations of individuals and groups of people, the existence of stereotypes does not explain the origin of physiognomic judgments. If these judgments stem from tradition, what is the tradition's source? Are they right or wrong? Even though often misapplied, traditional interpretations of physique and behavior may still be based on sound observation. In fact, perhaps they are so hardy because they are so true.

Within the framework of associationist thinking, a step forward was made by Lipps, who pointed out that the perception of expression involves the activity of forces. His theory of "empathy" was designed to explain why we find expression even in inanimate objects, such as the columns of a temple. The reasoning was as follows. When I look at the columns, I know from past experience the kind of mechanical pressure and counterpressure that occurs in them. Equally from past experience, I know how I should feel myself if I were in the place of the columns and if those physical forces acted upon and within my own body. I project my own kinesthetic feelings into the columns. Furthermore, the pressures and pulls called up from the stores of memory by the sight tend to provoke responses also in other areas of the mind. "When I project my strivings and forces into nature I do so also as to the way my strivings and forces make me feel, that is, I project my pride, my courage, my stubbornness, my lightness, my playful assuredness, my tranquil complacence. Only thus my empathy with regard to nature becomes truly aesthetic empathy."

The characteristic feature of traditional theorizing in all

its varieties is the belief that the expression of an object is not inherent in the visual pattern itself. What we see provides only clues for whatever knowledge and feelings we may mobilize from memory and project upon the object. The visual pattern has as little to do with the expression we confer upon it as words have to do with the content they transmit. The letters "pain" mean "suffering" in English and "bread" in French. Nothing in them suggests the one rather than the other meaning. They transmit a message only because of what we have learned about them.

EXPRESSION EMBEDDED IN STRUCTURE

William James was not so sure that body and mind have nothing intrinsically in common. "I cannot help remarking that the disparity between motions and feelings, on which these authors lay so much stress, is somewhat less absolute than at first sight it seems. Not only temporal succession, but such attributes as intensity, volume, simplicity or complication, smooth or impeded change, rest or agitation, are habitually predicated of both physical facts and mental facts." Evidently James reasoned that although body and mind are different media—the one being material, the other not—they might still resemble each other in certain structural properties.

This point was greatly stressed by Gestalt psychologists. Particularly Wertheimer asserted that the perception of expression is much too immediate and compelling to be explainable merely as a product of learning. When we watch a dancer, the sadness or happiness of the mood seems to be directly inherent in the movements themselves. Wertheimer concluded that this was true because formal factors of the dance reproduced identical factors of the mood. The meaning of this theory may be illustrated by reference to an experiment by Binney in which members of a college dance group were asked individually to give improvisations of such subjects as sadness, strength, or night. The performances of the dancers showed much agreement. For example, in the representation of sadness the movement was slow and confined to a narrow range. It was mostly curved in shape and showed little tension. The direction was indefinite, changing, wavering, and the body seemed to yield passively to the force of gravitation rather than being propelled by its own initiative. It will be admitted that the physical mood of sadness has a similar pattern. In a depressed person the mental processes are slow and rarely go beyond matters closely related to immediate experiences and interests of the moment. In all his thinking and striving are softness and a lack of energy. There is little determination, and activity is often controlled by outside forces.

Naturally there is a traditional way of representing sadness in a dance, and the performances of the students may have been influenced by it. What counts, however, is that the movements, whether spontaneously invented or copied from other dancers, exhibited a formal structure so strikingly similar to that of the intended mood. And since such visual qualities as speed, shape, or direction are immediately accessible to the eye, it seems legitimate to assume that they are the carriers of an expression directly comprehensible to the eye.

If we examine the facts more closely, we find that expression is conveyed not so much by the "geometric-technical" properties of the percept as such, but by the forces they can be assumed to arouse in the nervous system of the observer. Regardless of whether the object moves (dancer, actor) or is immobile (painting, sculpture), it is the kind of directed tension or "movement"—its strength, place, and distribution —transmitted by the visible patterns that is perceived as expression.

Many already cited examples have illustrated the expressive meaning of visual forces. In Giotto's "Lamentation" the upsurge of the diagonal expressed the dynamic motif of the Resurrection, and the retreat and rise of the curve formed by the row of the mourners expressed awe and despair. It may be worth while to add here two examples of abstract form in order to demonstrate that expression is contained in the pattern itself without necessary reference to objects of nature.

In comparing two curves—one a part of a circle, the other a part of a parabola—it will be found that the circular curve looks more rigid, the parabolic one more gentle. What is the cause of this difference? Instead of looking around for objects of nature with which the two objects might be associated, examine the structure of the curves themselves. Geometrically, the constant curvature of the circle is the result of only one structural condition: it is the locus of all points that are equally distant from one center. A parabola satisfies two such conditions and therefore is of variable curvature. It is the locus of all points that have equal distance from one point and one straight line. The parabola may be called a compromise between two structural demands. Either structural condition yields to the other. In other words, the rigid hardness of the circular line and the gentle flexibility of the parabola can be derived from the inherent make-up of the two curves.

Now for a somewhat similar example from architecture. In the outlines of the dome that Michelangelo designed for St. Peter's in Rome, we admire the synthesis of massive heaviness and free rising. This expressive effect is obtained in the following way. The two contours that make up the section of the outer cupola (Figure 1) are parts of circles, and thus possess the firmness of circular curves. But they are not parts of the same circle. They do not form a hemisphere. The right contour is described around the center *a*, and left around *b*. In a Gothic arch the crossing of the curves would be visible at the apex. The cupola hides it by the gallery and the lantern on top of it. In consequence both contours appear as part of one and the same curve, which, however, does not have the rigidity of a hemisphere. It represents a compromise between two different curvatures, and thus appears flexible while at the same time preserving circular hardness in its elements. The total contour of the dome appears as a deviation from a hemisphere, which has been stretched upward. Hence the effect of vertical striving. It will also be seen that line *A* contains the horizontal diameters of the circles for both contours of the section. Therefore at the intersection with *A* the contours would reach verticality. This would give the cupola a stable, rather static orientation. Now this verticality is hidden by the drum between *B* and *A*. The cupola rests on *B* rather than on *A*. This means that the contours meet the base at an oblique rather than a right angle. Instead of moving straight upward, the cupola tilts inward, which produces an oblique sagging—that is, the effect of heaviness. The delicate balancing of all these dynamic factors produces the

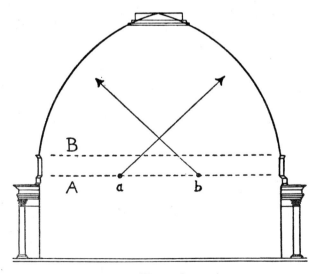

Figure 1

complex and at the same time unified expression of the whole. "The symbolic image of weight," says Wölfflin, "is maintained, yet dominated by the expression of spiritual liberation." Michelangelo's dome thus embodies "the paradox of the Baroque spirit in general."

THE PRIORITY OF EXPRESSION

The impact of the forces transmitted by a visual pattern is an intrinsic part of the percept, just as shape or color. In fact, expression can be described as the primary content of vision. We have been trained to think of perception as the recording of shapes, distances, hues, motions. The awareness of these measurable characteristics is really a fairly late accomplishment of the human mind. Even in the Western man of the twentieth century it presupposes special conditions. It is the attitude of the scientist and the engineer or of the salesman who estimates the size of a customer's waist, the shade of a lipstick, the weight of a suitcase. But if I sit in front of a fireplace and watch the flames, I do not normally register certain shades of red, various degrees of brightness, geometrically defined shapes moving at such and such a speed. I see the graceful play of aggressive tongues, flexible striving, lively color. The face of a person is more readily perceived and remembered as being alert, tense, concentrated rather than as being triangularly shaped, having slanted eyebrows, straight lips, and so on. This priority of expression, although somewhat modified in adults by a scientifically oriented education, is striking in children and primitives, as has been shown by Werner and Köhler. The profile of a mountain is soft or threateningly harsh; a blanket thrown over a chair is twisted, sad, tired.

The priority of physiognomic properties should not come as a surprise. Our senses are not self-contained recording devices operating for their own sake. They have been developed by the organism as an aid in properly reacting to the environment. The organism is primarily interested in the forces that are active around it—their place, strength, direction. Hostility and friendliness are attributes of forces. And the perceived impact of forces makes for what we call expression.

If expression is the primary content of vision in daily life, the same should be all the more true for the way the artist looks at the world. The expressive qualities are his means of communication. They capture his attention, through them he understands and interprets his experiences, and they determine the form patterns he creates. Therefore the training of art students should be expected to consist basically in sharpening their sense of these qualities and in teaching them to look to expression as the guiding criterium for every stroke of the pencil, brush, or chisel. In fact many good art teachers do precisely this. But there are also plenty of times when the spontaneous sensitivity of the student to expression not only is not developed further, but is even disturbed and suppressed. There is, for example, an old-fashioned but not extinct way of teaching students to draw from the model by asking them to establish the exact length and direction of contour lines, the relative position of points, the shape of masses. In other words, students are to concentrate on the geometric-technical qualities of what they see. In its modern version this method consists in urging the young artist to think of the model or of a freely invented design as a configuration of masses, planes, directions. Again interest is focused on geometric-technical qualities.

This method of teaching follows the principles of scientific definition rather than those of spontaneous vision. There are, however, other teachers who will proceed differently. With a model sitting on the floor in a hunched-up position, they will not begin by making the students notice that the whole figure can be inscribed in a triangle. Instead they will ask about the expression of the figure; they may be told, for example, that the person on the floor looks tense, tied together, full of potential energy. They will suggest, then, that the student try to render this quality. In doing so the student will watch proportions and directions, but not as geometric properties in themselves. These formal properties will be perceived as being functionally dependent upon the primarily observed expression, and the correctness and incorrectness of each stroke will be judged on the basis of whether or not it captures the dynamic "mood" of the subject. Equally, in a lesson of design, it will be made clear that to the artist, just as to any unspoiled human being, a circle is not a line of constant curvature, whose points are all equally distant from a center, but first of all a compact, hard, restful thing. Once the student has understood that roundness is not identical with circularity, he may try for a design whose structural logic will be controlled by the primary concept of something to be expressed. For whereas the artificial concentration on formal qualities will leave the student at a loss as to which pattern to select among innumerable and equally acceptable ones, an expressive theme will serve as a natural guide to forms that fit the purpose.

It will be evident that what is advocated here is not the so-called self-expression. The method of self-expression plays down, or even annihilates, the function of the theme to be represented. It recommends a passive, "projective" pouring-out of what is felt inside. On the contrary, the method discussed here requires active, disciplined concentration of all organizing powers upon the expression that is localized in the object of representation.

It might be argued that an artist must practice the purely formal technique before he may hope to render expression successfully. But that is exactly the notion that reverses the natural order of the artistic process. In fact all good practicing is highly expressive. The first occurred to me many years ago when I watched the dancer Gret Palucca perform one of her most popular pieces, which she called "Technical Improvisations." This number was nothing but the systematic exercise that the dancer practiced every day in her studio in order to loosen up the joints of her body. She would start out by doing turns of her head, then move her neck, then shrug her shoulders, until she ended up wriggling her toes. This purely technical practice was a success with the audience because it was thoroughly expressive. Forcefully precise and rhythmical movements presented, quite naturally, the entire catalogue of human pantomime. They passed through all the moods from lazy happiness to impertinent satire.

In order to achieve technically precise movements, a capable dance teacher may not ask students to perform "geometrically" defined positions, but to strive for the muscular experience of uplift, or attack, or yielding, that will be created by correctly executed movements. (Comparable methods are nowadays applied therapeutically in physical rehabilitation work. For example, the patient is not asked to concentrate on the meaningless, purely formal exercise of flexing and stretching his arm, but on a game or piece of work that involves suitable motions of the limbs as a means to a sensible end.)

THE PHYSIOGNOMICS OF NATURE

The perception of expression does not therefore necessarily —and not even primarily—serve to discover the state of mind of another person by way of externally observable manifestations. Köhler has pointed out that people normally deal with and react to expressive physical behavior in itself rather than being conscious of the physical experiences reflected by such behavior. We perceive the slow, listless, "droopy" movements of one person as contrasted to the brisk, straight, vigorous movements of another, but do not necessarily go beyond the meaning of such appearance by thinking explicitly of the psychical weariness or alertness behind it. Weariness and alertness are already contained in the physical behavior itself; they are not distinguished in any essential way from the weariness of slowly floating tar or the energetic ringing of the telephone bell. It is true, of course, that during a business conversation one person may be greatly concerned with trying to read the other's thoughts and feelings through what can be seen in his face and gestures. "What is he up to? How is he taking it?" But in such circumstances we clearly go beyond what is apparent in the perception of expression itself, and secondarily apply what we have seen to the mental processes that may be hidden "behind" the outer image.

Particularly the content of the work of art does not consist in states of mind that the dancer may pretend to be experiencing in himself or that our imagination may bestow on a painted Mary Magdalen or Sebastian. The substance of the work consists in what appears in the visible pattern itself. Evidently, then, expression is not limited to living organisms that we assume to possess consciousness. A steep rock, a willow tree, the colors of a sunset, the cracks in a wall, a tumbling leaf, a flowing fountain, and in fact a mere line or color or the dance of an abstract shape on the movie screen have as much expression as the human body, and serve the artist equally well. In some ways they serve him even better, for the human body is a particularly complex pattern, not easily reduced to the simplicity of shape and motion that transmits compelling expression. Also it is overloaded with nonvisual associations. The human figure is not the easiest, but the most difficult, vehicle of artistic expression.

The fact that nonhuman objects have genuine physiognomic properties has been concealed by the popular assumption that they are merely dressed up with human expression by an illusory "pathetic fallacy," by empathy, anthropomorphism, primitive animism. But if expression is an inherent characteristic of perceptual patterns, its manifestations in the human figure are but a special case of a more general phenomenon. The comparison of an object's expression with a human state of mind is a secondary process. A weeping willow does not look sad because it looks like a sad person. It is more adequate to say that since the shape, direction, and flexibility of willow branches convey the expression of passive hanging, a comparison with the structurally similar state of mind and body that we call sadness imposes itself secondarily. The columns of a temple do not strive upward and carry the weight of the roof so dramatically because we put ourselves in their place, but because their location, proportion, and shape are carefully chosen in such a way that their image contains the desired expression. Only because and when this is so, are we enabled to "sympathize" with the columns, if we so desire. An inappropriately designed temple resists all empathy.

To define visual expression as a reflection of human feelings would seem to be misleading on two counts: first, because it makes us ignore the fact that expression has its origin in the perceived pattern and in the reaction of the brain field of vision to this pattern; second, because such a description unduly limits the range of what is being expressed. We found as the basis of expression a configuration of forces. Such a configuration interests us because it is significant not only for the object in whose image it appears, but for the physical and mental world in general. Motifs like rising and falling, dominance and submission, weakness and strength, harmony and discord, struggle and conformance, underlie all existence. We find them within our own mind and in our relations to other people, in the human community and in the events of nature. Perception of expression fulfills its spiritual mission only if we experience in it more than the resonance of our own feelings. It permits us to realize that the forces stirring in ourselves are only individual examples of the same forces acting throughout the universe. We are thus enabled to sense our place in the whole and the inner unity of that whole.

Some objects and events resemble each other with regard to the underlying patterns of forces; others do not. Therefore, on the basis of their expressive appearance, our eye spontaneously creates a kind of Linnaean classification of all things existing. This perceptual classification cuts across the order suggested by other kinds of categories. Particularly in our modern Western civilization we are accustomed to distinguishing between animate and inanimate things, human and nonhuman creatures, the mental and the physical. But in terms of expressive qualities, the character of a given person may resemble that of a particular tree more closely than that of another person. The state of affairs in a human society may be similar to the tension in the skies just before the outbreak of a thunderstorm. Further, our kind of scientific and economic thinking makes us define things by measurements rather than by the dynamics of their appearance. Our criteria for what is useful or useless, friendly or hostile, have tended to sever the connections with outer expression, which they possess in the minds of children or primitives. If a house or a chair suits our practical purposes, we may not stop to find out whether its appearance expresses our style of living. In business relations we define a man by his census data, his income, age, position, nationality, or race—that is, by categories that ignore the inner nature of the man as it is manifest in his outer expression.

Primitive languages give us an idea of the kind of world that derives from a classification based on perception. Instead of restricting itself to the verb "to walk," which rather abstractly refers to locomotion, the language of the African Ewe takes care to specify in every kind of walking the particular expressive qualities of the movement. There are expressions for "the gait of a little man whose limbs shake very much, to walk with a dragging step like a feeble person, the gait of a long-legged man who throws his legs forward, of a corpulent man who walks heavily, to walk in a dazed fashion without looking ahead, an energetic and firm step," [1] and many others. These distinctions are not made out of sheer aesthetic sensitivity, but because the expressive properties of the gait are believed to reveal important practical information on what kind of man is walking and what is his intent at the moment.

Although primitive languages often surprise us by their wealth of subdivisions for which we see no need, they also reveal generalizations that to us may seem unimportant or absurd. For example, the language of the Klamath Indians has prefixes for words referring to objects of similar shape or movement. Such a prefix may describe "the outside of a round or spheroidal, cylindrical, discoid or bulbed object, or a ring; also voluminous; or again, an act accomplished with an object which bears such a form; or a circular or semi-circular or waving movement of the body, arms, hands, or other parts. Therefore this prefix is to be found connected with clouds, celestial bodies, rounded slopes on the earth's surface, fruits rounded or bulbed in shape, stones and dwellings (these last being usually circular in form). It is employed, too, for a crowd of animals, for enclosures, social gatherings (since an assembly usually adopts the form of a circle), and so forth." [2]

Such a classification groups things together that to our way of thinking belong in very different categories and have little or nothing in common. At the same time, these features of primitive language remind us that the poetical habit of uniting practically disparate objects by metaphor is not a sophisticated invention of artists, but derives from and relies on the universal and spontaneous way of approaching the world of experience.

Georges Braque advises the artist to seek the common in the dissimilar. "Thus the poet can say: The swallow knifes the sky, and thereby makes a knife out of a swallow." It is the function of the metaphor to make the reader penetrate the concrete shell of the world of things by combinations of objects that have little in common but the underlying pattern. Such a device, however, would not work unless the reader of poetry was still alive, in his own daily experience, to the symbolic or metaphoric connotation of all appearance and activity. For example, hitting or breaking things normally evokes, if ever so slightly, the overtone of attack and de-struction. There is a tinge of conquest and achievement to all rising—even the climbing of a staircase. If the shades are pulled in the morning and the room is flooded with light, more is experienced than a simple change of illumination. One aspect of the wisdom that belongs to a genuine culture is the constant awareness of the symbolic meaning expressed in concrete happening, the sensing of the universal in the particular. This gives significance and dignity to all daily pursuits, and prepares the ground on which the arts can grow. In its pathological extreme this spontaneous symbolism manifests itself in what is known to the psychiatrist as the "organ speech" of psychosomatic and other neurotic symptoms. There are people who cannot swallow because there is something in their lives they "cannot swallow" or whom an unconscious sense of guilt compels to spend hours every day on washing and cleaning.

SYMBOLS IN ART

In the more popular sense of the term, we do not call a work of art symbolic unless the individual facts it represents can be understood only by reference to an underlying idea. A Dutch genre painting that shows a group of peasants around the inn table may be called devoid of symbolism. But when Titian paints a picture in which two women, one fully dressed and one almost naked, are placed symmetrically on a well, or when in one of Dürer's engravings a winged woman with a goblet in her hand stands on a sphere that moves through the clouds, we are convinced that the mysterious scene has been invented to convey an idea. Such symbolism may be standardized to the kind of picture language that is found, for example, in the allegories of religious art. A lily stands for the virginity of Mary, lambs are disciples, or two deer drinking from a pond show the re-creation of the faithful.

But symbolic meaning is expressed only indirectly by what our reasoning or learning tells us about the subject matter. In the great works of art the deepest significance is transmitted to the eye with powerful directness by the perceptual characteristics of the compositional pattern. The "story" of Michelangelo's "Creation of Adam," on the ceiling of the Sistine Chapel in Rome (Figure 2), is understood by every reader of the book of Genesis. But even the story is modified in a way that makes it more comprehensible and impressive to the eye. God, instead of breathing a living soul into the body of clay—a motif not easily translatable into an expressive pattern—reaches out toward the arm of Adam as though an animating spark, leaping from finger tip to finger tip, was transmitted from the creator to the creature. The bridge of the arm visually connects two separate worlds: the self-contained, complete roundness of the mantle that encloses God and is given forward motion by the diagonal of his body; and the incomplete, flat slice of the earth, whose passivity is expressed by the backward slant of its contour. There is passivity also in the concave curve over which the body of Adam is molded. It is lying on the ground and enabled partly to rise by the attractive power of the approaching creator. The desire and potential capacity to get up and walk are indicated as a subordinate theme in the left leg, which also serves as a support of Adam's arm, unable to maintain itself freely like the energy-charged arm of God.

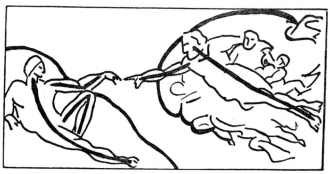

Figure 2

The analysis shows that the structural skeleton of the pictorial composition reveals the dynamic pattern of the story. There is an active power making contact with a passive object, which is being animated by the energy it receives. The essence of the story appears in what strikes the eye of the observer first: the dominant perceptual pattern of the work. And since this pattern is not simply recorded by the nervous system, but presumably arouses a corresponding configuration of forces, the observer's reaction is more than a mere taking cognizance of an outer object. The forces that characterize the meaning of the story become active in the observer, and produce the kind of stirring participation that distinguishes artistic experience from the detached acceptance of information.

But there is more. The structural pattern does not only elucidate the meaning of the individual story presented in the work. The dynamic theme revealed by this pattern is not limited to the Biblical episode at hand, but is valid for any number of situations that may occur in the psychical and the physical world. Not only is the perceptual pattern a means of understanding the story of the creation of man, but the story becomes a means of illustrating a kind of event that is universal and therefore abstract and therefore in need of being clad with flesh and blood so that the eye may see it.

The perceptual pattern of a work of art is neither arbitrary nor a purely formal play of shapes and colors. It is indispensable as a precise interpreter of the idea the work is meant to express. Similarly, the subject matter is neither arbitrary nor unimportant. It is exactly correlated with the formal pattern to supply a concrete application of an abstract theme. The kind of connoisseur who looks only for the pattern does as little justice to the work as the kind of layman who looks only for the subject matter. When Whistler called the portrait of his mother "Arrangement in Grey and Black," he treated his picture as one-sidedly as someone who sees nothing in it but a dignified lady sitting on a chair. Neither the formal pattern nor the subject matter is the final content of the work of art. Both are devices of artistic form. They serve to give body to the invisible universal.

THE PSYCHOANALYTIC WAY

It will be evident why we must hesitate to accept the interpretation of artistic symbols presented by some psychoanalytic writers. In their analyses we find, first of all, a tendency to understand the artistic object as a representation of other objects, such as the womb, the genitals, or the artist's father or mother. Extreme examples are contained in a book, *Man as Symbol*,* by Groddeck. He maintains, for example, that the attitudes of the figures in Rembrandt's "Anatomy," read from the back of the picture toward the front, and the Roman "Laocoön," read from the right to the left of the group, are representations of the male genital in the stages of excitation and slackening. The most common objection to this kind of interpretation points to its one-sidedness, that is, to the presupposition that sex is the most basic and important human experience, to which everything else is spontaneously referred. Psychologists have remarked that this assumption is unproved. At best the theory holds true for certain psychoneurotic individuals or even cultural periods in which "an overemphasized sexuality is piled up behind a dam" of severe moral restrictions and in which other aims of life have been deprived of their weight by an empty existence under unfavorable social conditions. As Jung has remarked in this connection, "It is well known that when we have a bad toothache, we can think of nothing else."

But another objection seems even more pertinent. The psychoanalytic theory describes the visible facts of the work of art as a representation of other, equally concrete and

* [Published, in translation, under the title *The World of Man* (London: 1934).]

individual facts. If after penetrating the work of a master we are left with nothing but references to organs and functions of the human body or to some close relative, we wonder what makes art such a universal and supposedly important creation of the human mind. Its message seems pitifully obvious. A little thought shows that sex is no more final and no less symbolical than other human experiences. It is true that in the arts as well as in common usage "neutral" situations are often employed to point to a veiled sexual meaning, as, for example, when Rabelais warns husbands to be wary of the monks because "the very shadow of an abbey's steeple is fertile." But equally often we find the less refined device of describing "neutral" situations by colorful sexual images. Thus Cézanne was fond of distinguishing between substantial and insubstantial art by the epithets *"bien couillard"* and *"pas couillard."* For our purposes it is especially significant that sex stands often for a highly abstract power. According to Jung: "As was customary throughout antiquity, primitive people today make a free use of phallic symbols, yet it never occurs to them to confuse the phallus, as a ritualistic symbol, with the penis. They always take the phallus to mean the creative *mana*, the power of healing and fertility, 'that which is unusually potent,' to use Lehmann's expression."

Similarly, some psychoanalysts have come recently to interpret narrative plots in a less restricted manner. For example, Fromm says of the Bible story of Jonah: "We find a sequence of symbols which follow one another: going into the ship, going into the ship's belly, falling asleep, being in the ocean, and being in the fish's belly. All these symbols stand for the same inner experience: for a condition of being protected and isolated, of safe withdrawal from communication with other human beings."

Symbolic interpretations that make one concrete object stand for another equally concrete one are almost always arbitrary and unprovable. There is no telling whether a particular association was or is on the conscious or unconscious mind of the artist or beholder unless we obtain direct information, which may require a depth analysis. The work of art itself does not offer the information, except in the case of symbols standardized by convention or in those few individual instances in which the overt content of the work appears strange and unjustified unless it is considered as a representation of different objects of similar appearance. Since the underlying theme of any work of art is so universal that it can fit an infinite number of concrete situations, an observer has no trouble in associating it with any one of them that happens to be on his mind. But whereas the associations produced by someone in reaction to his own dream are valid because the dream is a spontaneous product of his own making, associations to a work of art are often purely personal responses, which lead away from the meaning of the work rather than elucidating it. This is true even for the artist himself. The first concept of a work may be as spontaneously private as that of a dream. But in the course of the creative process the work goes through elaborations that require that the artist distinguish, with severe discipline, between what suits the nature of his subject and what is accidental impulse.

The psychoanalytic approach is somewhat too limited also when it defines, as Fromm has recently, the symbolic language as one "in which the world outside is a symbol of the world inside, a symbol for our souls and our minds." Undoubtedly artists often represent relatively abstract psychical situations through concrete outer themes; and Freud, for example, has atttempted interesting analyses of Shakespeare, the Oedipus legend, and Leonardo's painting "Virgin and Child with St. Anne." We cannot, however, describe art as a mere projection of human personalities without restricting its scope unduly.

Finally, progress has been made beyond Freud's original conviction that symbols serve to camouflage an objectionable content. In an early paper, "The Poet and Fantasy," Freud asserts that the artist makes his "daydreams" acceptable essentially by two devices: he "tones down the character of the egotistic daydream by modifications and concealments and seduces us by purely formal, that is, aesthetic pleasure offered to us in the presentation of his fantasies." In other words, artistic form serves to hide the true content of the work and to sugar-coat the repulsive ingredients of the pill by external "beauty." In opposition to Freud's view of dream symbols, Jung has maintained that symbols reveal rather than veil the message. "When Freud speaks of the 'dream-façade,' he is really speaking not of the dream itself but of its obscurity, and in so doing is projecting upon the dream his own lack of understanding. We say that the dream has a false front only because we fail to see into it."

This reinterpretation opens our eyes to the similarity between the language of the dream and that of the work of art. During sleep the human mind seems to descend to the more elementary level at which life situations are described not by abstract concepts but by significant images. We cannot but admire the creative imagination awakened by sleep in all of us. It is this dormant power of picture language on which the artist also draws for his inventions.

ALL ART IS SYMBOLIC

If art could do nothing better than reproduce the things of nature, either directly or by analogy, or to delight the senses, there would be little justification for the honorable place reserved to it in every known society. Art's reputation must be due to the fact that it helps man to understand the world and himself, and presents to his eyes what he has understood and believes to be true. Now everything in this world is a unique individual; no two things can be equal. But anything can be understood only because it is made up of ingredients not reserved to itself but common to many or all other things. In science, greatest knowledge is achieved when all existing phenomena are reduced to a common law. This is true for art also. The mature work of art succeeds in subjecting everything to a dominant law of structure. In doing so, it does not distort the variety of existing things into uniformity. On the contrary, it clarifies their differences by making them all comparable. Braque has said: "By putting a lemon next to an orange they cease to be a lemon and an orange and become fruit. The mathematicians follow this law. So do we." He fails to remember that the virtue of such correlation is twofold. It shows the way in which things are similar and, by doing so, defines their individuality. By establishing a common "style" for all objects, the artist creates a whole, in which the place and function of every one of them are lucidly defined. Goethe said: "The beautiful is a manifestation of secret laws of nature, which would have remained hidden to us forever without its appearance."

Every element of a work of art is indispensable for the one purpose of pointing out the theme, which embodies the nature of existence for the artist. In this sense we find symbolism even in works that, at first sight, seem to be little more than arrangements of fairly neutral objects. We need only glance at the bare outlines of the two still lifes sketched in Figure 3 to experience two different conceptions of reality. Cézanne's picture (*a*) is dominated by the stable framework of verticals and horizontals in the background, the table, and the axes of bottles and glass. This skeleton is strong enough to give support even to the sweeping folds of the fabric. A simple order is conveyed by the upright symmetry of each bottle and that of the glass. There is abundance in the swelling volumes and emphasis on roundness and softness even in the inorganic matter. Compare this image of prosperous peace with the catastrophic turmoil in Picasso's work (*b*). Here we find little stability. The vertical and horizontal orientations are avoided. The room is slanted, the right angles of the table, which is turned over, are either hidden by oblique position or distorted. The four legs do not run parallel, the bottle topples, the desperately sprawling corpse of the bird is about to fall off the table. The contours tend to be hard, sharp, lifeless, even in the body of the animal.

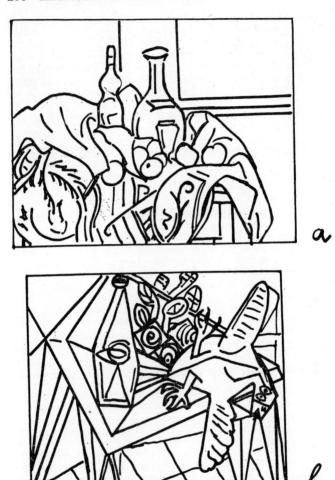

Figure 3

Since the basic perceptual pattern carries the theme, we must not be surprised to find that art continues to fulfill its function even when it ceases to represent objects of nature. "Abstract" art does in its own way what art has always done. It is not better than representational art, which also does not hide but reveals the meaningful skeleton of forces. It is no less good, for it contains the essentials. It is not "pure form," because even the simplest line expresses visible meaning and is therefore symbolic. It does not offer intellectual abstractions, because there is nothing more concrete than color, shape, and motion. It does not limit itself to the inner life of man, or to the unconscious, because for art the distinctions between the outer and the inner world and the conscious and the unconscious mind are artificial. The human mind receives, shapes, and interprets its image of the outer world with all its conscious and unconscious powers, and the realm of the unconscious could never enter our experience without the reflection of perceivable things. There is no way of presenting the one without the other. But the nature of the outer and the inner world can be reduced to a play of forces, and this "musical" approach is attempted by the misnamed abstract artists.

We do not know what the art of the future will look like. But we know that "abstraction" is not art's final climax. No style will ever be that. It is one valid way of looking at the world, one view of the holy mountain, which offers a different image from every place but can be seen as the same everywhere.

NOTES

1. Lucien Lévy-Bruhl, *How Natives Think* (London: 1926), p. 153.
2. Ibid., pp. 165–6.

IV
ART AND KNOWLEDGE
INTRODUCTION

The positivists and logical empiricists have applied the most devastating corrosive to the idea that art is a means of acquiring knowledge, different from that of science but equally valid in its own way. Totally negative critics of the heuristic value of art, such as Carnap, may be "throwing out the baby with the bathwater." Their position, in general, has been that only verifiable statements of specific empirical sciences can be legitimately conceived as *knowledge* of the "states of nature" or of "matters of fact." The logical sciences offer knowledge of a different order, since they make statements not about matters of fact but only about the definition of terms in their internal "games." When the abstract forms of mathematics or logic are "filled in" by references to the realm of nature we are able to arrive at more accurate knowledge than ever before, but *why* this is so, even the Vienna Circle and its followers have not been able to answer convincingly. Nevertheless, they do not hesitate to state in unqualified terms that *no object in any mode of art can be of any value in acquiring new knowledge*. Whatever we take to be the knowledge derived from a work of art is knowable independent of the art object. The new pattern or over-all unit that such discrete elements of knowledge constitute in an art work does not in itself contribute anything that can be said to yield knowledge.

Art is expressive; science is representative. The empirical sciences make assertions that can be verified or disconfirmed. Art objects do not assert, they express (feelings, moods, dispositions, characters, preferences, etc.), and such expressions are never either true or false. That which cannot be true cannot be knowledge. It may offer emotional or formal pleasure, but it cannot offer intellectual meaning of an original kind. It cannot discover.

This question of what the relations are between art and the concept of knowledge has stimulated some of the most interesting writing during recent years. The issue is by no means resolved to any general agreement. Trilling, Maritain, and Aiken represent three of the most important positions in the debate.

Lionel Trilling asks *what is* The Meaning of a Literary Idea? He answers that the meaning is not rational; it is *"rhetorical."* He may not actually use the word "rhetoric," but that is what his essay spells out, since rhetoric is concerned with convincing rather than with making truthful statements or constructing valid arguments; its purpose is "to win-over." Rhetoric, it should be remembered, is a practical science, not a theoretical one. Neither the Aristotelians nor the contemporary logical empiricists would credit the use of rhetoric with producing new *theoretical knowledge.* It is characterized by the *appearance* of knowledge often incorrectly interpreted or used for the construction of an unwarrantable conclusion. But its practical purpose is to lead an audience to act in a certain way, and for this end, means which are intellectually or scientifically illegitimate are here acceptable.

Trilling finds himself in a peculiar position. Concerning the value of works of literary art, he is as dissatisfied with the attitude of the pure formalists at the one extreme as he is with that of the "logicians" at the opposite extreme. Of the former, he feels the inadequacy of considering art works only as "significant forms" while ignoring the fact that literary statements have persuasive implications as well as formal charms; but in contrast to the latter, he cannot agree that art works should be distilled to yield "the moral of the story" as though each work has only one intelligible "meaning" that is scientifically true or false. Trilling's resolution is that literary works offer the *appearance of thought,* yielding the pleasure of feeling that one is understanding—despite the lack of intellectual comprehension. Trilling refers to this as "cogency," which is the man-in-the-street conception of logical validity, referring not to a logically sound argument, but to the *appearance* of validity in the mind of one who, in all honesty, cannot judge validity but only has "a feel for it," and will *act* in harmony with such "conviction."

This rhetorical appearance of sound thinking is greatly enhanced by the appearance of thinking about *Important Issues.* Trilling considers the ideas of the greatest affective power to be birth, fate, destiny, love, parenthood, incest, and patricide. Therefore, the pleasure taken in great works of literary art is the pleasure of feeling that one is coming to understand matters of weight and consequence, in a way that affects one's practical life. Such understanding is obviously not what is meant by scientific understanding but must be described by the phrase "human understanding," which implies something quite different. Scientific understanding depends on the intellectual abstraction of similarities, and the formulation of generalizations; "human understanding" depends on sympathetic insight into what is special, individual, unique. Thus, the kind of meaning that Trilling ascribes to a literary idea (expressed in the unifying form of an art work rather than in the separable statements that constitute its parts) is emotive meaning. It is the sympathetic response that affects the unconscious rather than the conscious mind, and that leaves one with the sense of a continuing "under the counter" relation with the work.

In most of his critical writings, Trilling talks like a man who goes to literature for *information*. The first lines of his 1943 book *E. M. Forster* say that Forster "is for me the only living novelist who . . . after each reading, gives me . . . the sensation [*sic*] of having learned something." In 1960 Trilling writes: "Lawrence Durrell is the first contemporary novelist in a long time to lead me to believe he is telling me something new." But it is *not* information that actually interests him; it is the special (practical) interpretation that the author makes of the information he presents. And such an interpretation is of a psycho-social nature. It is the "cogency" with which an artist organizes and unifies the information he employs that constitutes the "meaning" to which Trilling refers. Such an organizing form or idea cannot be abstracted and then judged either formally or intellectually; it is an "appearance of thought" to be evaluated pragmatically. It results in an effect that "may be judged by the action it can be thought ultimately to lead to." This is, precisely, the only function that characterizes *rhetoric*. Thus, Trilling leads one to the conclusion that both the intellectual and the formal values of a work of art are indifferent to its rhetorical powers, and that these practical effects must be evaluated in respect to whether they accord with or are in opposition to the commonly accepted views of individual or social life held by its audience. This, naturally, leads us out of aesthetics into social, moral, and ethical debate. Incidentally, this explains why Trilling's "literary criticism" is, in fact, "cultural criticism."

If Trilling's position leads us to the judgment of the heuristic value of art works by the standards of politics and psychology, Jacques Maritain's position leads us to the standards of theology and speculative philosophy. Maritain's erudite and subtle mind is like a kaleidoscope with a specific number of jewellike principles that, with a mere twist of the wrist, can be continually readjusted to yield an infinite number of different combinations, each one a rose window, seen clearly only if illuminated by some source of light outside itself. The source of light necessary to see fully the essay "Concerning Poetic Knowledge" is the Thomistic Catholicism that Maritain has been devoted to formulating during most of the past half century. For Maritain the ultimate principle of our understanding, and the ultimate source of the objects of experience to be understood, is God—as conceived in his Thomism. This God is to Maritain's thought what the Freudian Unconscious is to Trilling's; the essential assumption, the primary principle.

Again, like Trilling's position, Maritain's is not an argument for knowledge derived from art works in terms of rational cognition. However, his conception of poetic knowledge is not rhetorical and pragmatic. He conceives of it as metaphysical and theological, as "knowledge of Reality" inaccessible to rational categories. "Here is a knowledge that is different enough from what we commonly call knowledge, a knowledge which is not expressible in ideas and in judgments, but which is rather experience . . . for it wants to be expressed, and is expressible only in a work [of art]." Thus, while art for Trilling is a means of acquiring *practical knowledge*, for Maritain it is an opportunity for achieving *spiritual insight*. Both of these operate through human understanding or "experience" rather than through rational cognition.

Henry David Aiken's essay is the most philosophically disciplined of the three. He is concerned with exposing the ambiguities, errors, and equivocations of aesthetic sensationalism, and aesthetic perceptualism, in order to justify the scope that cognitive meaning can rightly be understood to have in works of art. "In the case of literary art," he writes, "the predominant power of words to arouse, sustain, and project emotion is a function, not of their quality as sounds, but of their meaning."

The three essays presented here do not show that the logical empiricists have been disproved; rather, they emphasize the necessity to see clearly (1) the function of knowledge as an integral factor in a work of art and (2) the effects of art works in the light of an epistemology giving us a wider comprehension of "knowledge" than the scope to which these positivists would narrowly limit it. If a work of art effects the whole person, not only one's intellect, then not theoretical but *"practical knowledge"* must be the key to understanding it; and our theory of knowledge must be made adequate to accommodate this fact.

THE MEANING OF A LITERARY IDEA *

Lionel Trilling

> Though no great minist'ring reason sorts
> Out the dark mysteries of human souls
> To clear conceiving: yet there ever rolls
> A vast idea before me, and I glean
> Therefrom my liberty. . . .
> > Keats—"Sleep and Poetry"

The question of the relation which should properly obtain between what we call creative literature and what we call ideas is a matter of insistent importance for modern criticism. It did not always make difficulties for the critic, and that it now makes so many is a fact which tells us much about our present relation to literature.

Ever since men began to think about poetry, they have conceived that there is a difference between the poet and the philosopher, a difference in method and in intention and in result. These differences I have no wish to deny. But a solidly established difference inevitably draws the fire of our question; it tempts us to inquire whether it is really essential or whether it is quite so settled and extreme as at first it seems. To this temptation I yield perhaps too easily, and very possibly as the result of an impercipience on my part—it may be that I see the difference with insufficient sharpness because I do not have a proper notion either of the matter of poetry or of the matter of philosophy. But whatever the reason, when I consider the respective products of the poetic and of the philosophic mind, although I see that they are by no means the same and although I can conceive that different processes, even different mental faculties, were at work to make them and to make them different, I cannot resist the impulse to put stress on their similarity and on their easy assimilation to each other.

Let me suggest some of the ways in which literature, by its very nature, is involved with ideas. I can be quite brief because what I say will not be new to you.

The most elementary thing to observe is that literature is of its nature involved with ideas because it deals with man in society, which is to say that it deals with formulations,

---

* [From *The Liberal Imagination,* by Lionel Trilling. Copyright 1949, by Lionel Trilling. Reprinted by permission of The Viking Press, Inc.]

valuations, and decisions, some of them implicit, others explicit. Every sentient organism *acts* on the principle that pleasure is to be preferred to pain, but man is the sole creature who formulates or exemplifies this as an idea and causes it to lead to other ideas. His consciousness of self abstracts this principle of action from his behavior and makes it the beginning of a process of intellection or a matter for tears and laughter. And this is but one of the innumerable assumptions or ideas that are the very stuff of literature.

This is self-evident and no one ever thinks of denying it. All that is ever denied is that literature is within its proper function in bringing these ideas to explicit consciousness, or ever gains by doing so. Thus, one of the matters of assumption in any society is the worth of men as compared with the worth of women; upon just such an assumption, more or less settled, much of the action of the *Oresteia* is based, and we don't in the least question the propriety of this—or not until it becomes the subject of open debate between Apollo and Athene, who, on the basis of an elaborate biological speculation, try to decide which is the less culpable, to kill your father or to kill your mother. At this point we, in our modern way, feel that in permitting the debate Aeschylus has made a great and rather silly mistake, that he has for the moment ceased to be *literary*. Yet what drama does not consist of the opposition of formulable ideas, what drama, indeed, is not likely to break into the explicit exposition and debate of these ideas?

This, as I say, is elementary. And scarcely less elementary is the observation what whenever we put two emotions into juxtaposition we have what we can properly call an idea. When Keats brings together, as he so often does, his emotions about love and his emotions about death, we have a very powerful idea and the source of consequent ideas. The force of such an idea depends upon the force of the two emotions which are brought to confront each other, and also, of course, upon the way the confrontation is contrived.

Then it can be said that the very form of a literary work, considered apart from its content, so far as that is possible, is in itself an idea. Whether we deal with syllogisms or poems, we deal with dialectic—with, that is, a developing series of statements. Or if the word "statements" seems to prejudge the question so far as literature is concerned, let us say merely that we deal with a developing series—the important word is "developing." We judge the value of the development by judging the interest of its several stages and the propriety and the relevance of their connection among themselves. We make the judgment in terms of the implied purpose of the developing series.

Dialectic, in this sense, is just another word for form, and has for its purpose, in philosophy or in art, the leading of the mind to some conclusion. Greek drama, for example, is an arrangement of moral and emotional elements in such a way as to conduct the mind—"inevitably," as we like to say—to a certain affective condition. This condition is a quality of personal being which may be judged by the action it can be thought ultimately to lead to.

We take Aristotle to be a better critic of the drama than Plato because we perceive that Aristotle understood and Plato did not understand that the form of the drama was of itself an idea which controlled and brought to a particular issue the subordinate ideas it contained. The form of the drama *is* its idea, and its idea *is* its form. And form in those arts which we call abstract is no less an idea than is form in the representational arts. Governments nowadays are very simple and accurate in their perception of this—much more simple and accurate than are academic critics and aestheticians—and they are as quick to deal with the arts of "pure" form as they are to deal with ideas stated in discourse: it is as if totalitarian governments kept in mind what the rest of us tend to forget, that "idea" in one of its early significations exactly means form and was so used by many philosophers.

It is helpful to have this meaning before us when we come to consider that particular connection between literature and ideas which presents us with the greatest difficulty, the connection that involves highly elaborated ideas, or ideas as we have them in highly elaborated systems such as philosophy, or theology, or science. The modern feeling about this relationship is defined by two texts, both provided by T. S. Eliot. In his essay on Shakespeare Mr. Eliot says, "I can see no reason for believing that either Dante or Shakespeare did any thinking on his own. The people who think that Shakespeare thought are always people who are not engaged in writing poetry, but who are engaged in thinking, and we all like to think that great men were like ourselves." And in his essay on Henry James, Mr. Eliot makes the well-known remark that James had a mind so fine that no idea could violate it.

In both statements, as I believe, Mr. Eliot permits his impulse to spirited phrase to run away with him, yielding too much to what he conceives to be the didactic necessities of the moment, for he has it in mind to offer resistance to the nineteenth-century way of looking at poetry as a heuristic medium, as a communication of knowledge. This is a view which is well exemplified in a sentence of Carlyle's: "If called to define Shakespeare's faculty, I should say superiority of

Intellect, and think I had included all in that." As between the two statements about Shakespeare's mental processes, I give my suffrage to Carlyle's as representing a more intelligible and a more available notion of intellect than Mr. Eliot's, but I think I understand what Mr. Eliot is trying to do with his—he is trying to rescue poetry from the kind of misinterpretation of Carlyle's view which was once more common than it is now; he is trying to save for poetry what is peculiar to it, and for systematic thought what is peculiar to it.

As for Mr. Eliot's statement about James and ideas, it is useful to us because it gives us a clue to what might be called the sociology of our question. "Henry James had a mind so fine that no idea could violate it." In the context "violate" is a strong word, yet we can grant that the mind of the poet is a sort of Clarissa Harlowe and that an idea is a sort of Colonel Lovelace, for it is a truism of contemporary thought that the whole nature of man stands in danger of being brutalized by the intellect, or at least by some one of its apparently accredited surrogates. A specter haunts our culture—it is that people will eventually be unable to say, "They fell in love and married," let alone understand the language of *Romeo and Juliet,* but will as a matter of course say, "Their libidinal impulses being reciprocal, they activated their individual erotic drives and integrated them within the same frame of reference."

Now this is not the language of abstract thought or of any kind of thought. It is the language of non-thought. But it is the language which is developing from the peculiar status which we in our culture have given to abstract thought. There can be no doubt whatever that it constitutes a threat to the emotions and thus to life itself.

The specter of what this sort of language suggests has haunted us since the end of the eighteenth century. When he speaks of the mind being violated by an idea, Mr. Eliot, like the romantics, is simply voicing his horror at the prospect of life being intellectualized out of all spontaneity and reality.

We are the people of the idea, and we rightly fear that the intellect will dry up the blood in our veins and wholly check the emotional and creative part of the mind. And although I said that the fear of the total sovereignty of the abstract intellect began in the romantic period, we are of course touching here upon Pascal's opposition between two faculties of the mind, of which *l'esprit de finesse* has its heuristic powers no less than *l'esprit de géométrie,* powers of discovery and knowledge which have a particular value for the establishment of man in society and the universe.

But to call ourselves the people of the idea is to flatter ourselves. We are rather the people of ideology, which is a very different thing. Ideology is not the product of thought; it is the habit or the ritual of showing respect for certain formulas to which, for various reasons having to do with emotional safety, we have very strong ties of whose meaning and consequences in actuality we have no clear understanding. The nature of ideology may in part be understood from its tendency to develop the sort of language I parodied, and scarcely parodied, a moment ago.

It is therefore no wonder that any critical theory that conceives itself to be at the service of the emotions, and of life itself, should turn a very strict and jealous gaze upon an intimate relationship between literature and ideas, for in our culture ideas tend to deteriorate into ideology. And indeed it is scarcely surprising that criticism, in its zeal to protect literature and life from the tyranny of the rational intellect, should misinterpret the relationship. Mr. Eliot, if we take him literally, does indeed misinterpret the relationship when he conceives of "thinking" in such a way that it must be denied to Shakespeare and Dante. It must puzzle us to know what thinking is if Shakespeare and Dante did not do it.

And it puzzles us to know what René Wellek and Austin Warren mean when in their admirable *Theory of Literature* they say that literature can make use of ideas only when ideas "cease to be ideas in the ordinary sense of concepts and become symbols, or even myths." I am not sure that the ordinary sense of *ideas* actually is *concepts*, or at any rate concepts of such abstractness that they do not arouse in us feelings and attitudes. And I take it that when we speak of the relationship of literature and ideas, the ideas we refer to are not those of mathematics or of symbolic logic, but only such ideas as can arouse and traditionally have aroused the feelings—the ideas, for example, of men's relation to one another and to the world. A poet's simple statement of a psychological fact recalls us to a proper simplicity about the nature of ideas. "Our continued influxes of feeling," said Wordsworth, "are modified and directed by our thoughts, which are indeed the representatives of all our past feelings." The interflow between emotion and idea is a psychological fact which we do well to keep clearly in mind, together with the part that is played by desire, will, and imagination in philosophy as well as in literature. Mr. Eliot, and Mr. Wellek and Mr. Warren—and in general those critics who are zealous in the defense of the autonomy of poetry—prefer to forget the ground which is common to both emotion and thought; they presume ideas to be only the product of formal systems of philosophy, not remembering, at least on the occasion of their argument, that poets too have their effect in the world of thought. *L'esprit de finesse* is certainly not to be confused with *l'esprit de géométrie,* but neither—which is precisely the point of Pascal's having distinguished and named the two different qualities of mind—is it to be denied its powers of comprehension and formulation.

Mr. Wellek and Mr. Warren tell us that "the artist will be hampered by too much ideology [1] if it remains unassimilated." We note the tautology of the statement—for what else is "too much" ideology except ideology that *is* unassimilated?—not because we wish to take a disputatious advantage over authors to whom we have reason to be grateful, but because the tautology suggests the uneasiness of the position it defends. We are speaking of art, which is an activity which defines itself exactly by its powers of assimilation and of which the essence is the just amount of any of its qualities or elements; of course too much or unassimilated ideology will "hamper" the artist, but so will too much of anything, so will too much metaphor: Coleridge tells us that in a long poem there can be too much *poetry.* The theoretical question is simply being begged, out of an undue anxiety over the "purity" of literature, over its perfect literariness.

The authors of *Theory of Literature* are certainly right to question the "intellectualist misunderstanding of art" and the "confusions of the functions of art and philosophy" and to look for the flaws in the scholarly procedures which organize works of art according to their ideas and their affinities with philosophical systems. Yet on their own showing there has always been a conscious commerce between the poet and the philosopher, and not every poet has been violated by the ideas that have attracted him. The sexual metaphor is forced upon us, not only explicitly by Mr. Eliot but also implicitly by Mr. Wellek and Mr. Warren, who seem to think of ideas as masculine and gross and of art as feminine and pure, and who permit a union of the two sexes only when ideas give up their masculine, effective nature and "cease to be ideas in the ordinary sense and become symbols, or even myths." We naturally ask: symbols of what, myths about what? No anxious exercise of aesthetic theory can make the ideas of, say, Blake and Lawrence other than what they are intended to be—ideas relating to action and to moral judgment.

This anxiety lest the work of art be other than totally self-contained, this fear lest the reader make reference to something beyond the work itself, has its origin, as I have previously suggested, in the reaction from the earlier impulse —it goes far back beyond the nineteenth century—to show that art is justified in comparison with the effective activity of the systematic disciplines. It arises too from the strong contemporary wish to establish, in a world of unremitting action and effectiveness, the legitimacy of contemplation, which it is now no longer convenient to associate with the exercises of religion but which may be associated with the experiences of art. We will all do well to advance the cause of contemplation, to insist on the right to a haven from perpetual action and effectiveness. But we must not enforce our insistence by dealing with art as if it were a unitary thing, and by making reference only to its "purely" aesthetic element, requiring that every work of art serve our contemplation by being wholly self-contained and without relation to action. No doubt there is a large body of literature to which ideas, with their tendency to refer to action and effectiveness, are alien and inappropriate. But also much of literature wishes to give the sensations and to win the responses that are given and won by ideas, and it makes use of ideas to gain its effects, considering ideas—like people, sentiments, things, and scenes —to be indispensable elements of human life. Nor is the intention of this part of literature always an aesthetic one in the strict sense that Mr. Wellek and Mr. Warren have in mind; there is abundant evidence that the aesthetic upon which the critic sets primary store is to the poet himself frequently of only secondary importance.

We can grant that the province of poetry is one thing and the province of intellection another. But keeping the difference well in mind, we must yet see that systems of ideas have a particular quality which is much coveted as their chief effect—let us even say as their chief aesthetic effect—by at least certain kinds of literary works. Say what we will as critics and teachers trying to defend the province of art from the dogged tendency of our time to ideologize all things into grayness, say what we will about the "purely" literary, the purely aesthetic values, we as readers know that we demand of our literature some of the virtues which define a successful work of systematic thought. We want it to have —at least when it is appropriate for it to have, which is by no means infrequently—the authority, the cogency, the completeness, the brilliance, the *hardness* of systematic thought.[2]

Of late years criticism has been much concerned to insist on the indirection and the symbolism of the language of poetry. I do not doubt that the language of poetry is very largely that of indirection and symbolism. But it is not only that. Poetry is closer to rhetoric than we today are willing to admit; syntax plays a greater part in it than our current theory grants, and syntax connects poetry with rational thought, for, as Hegel says, "grammar, in its extended and consistent form"—by which he means syntax—"is the work of thought, which makes its categories distinctly visible therein." And those poets of our time who make the greatest impress upon us are those who are most aware of rhetoric, which is to say, of the intellectual content of their work. Nor is the intellectual content of their work simply the inevitable effect produced by good intelligence turned to poetry; many of these poets—Yeats and Eliot himself come most immediately to mind —have been at great pains to develop consistent intellectual positions along with, and consonant with, their work in poetry.

The aesthetic effect of intellectual cogency, I am convinced, is not to be slighted. Let me give an example for what it is worth. Of recent weeks my mind has been much engaged by two statements, disparate in length and in genre, although as it happens they have related themes. One is a couplet of Yeats:

> We had fed the heart on fantasies,
> The heart's grown brutal from the fare.

I am hard put to account for the force of the statement. It certainly does not lie in any metaphor, for only the dimmest sort of metaphor is to be detected. Nor does it lie in any special power of the verse. The statement has for me the pleasure of relevance and cogency, in part conveyed to me by the content, in part by the rhetoric. The other statement is Freud's short book, his last, *An Outline of Psychoanalysis*, which gives me a pleasure which is no doubt different from that given by Yeats's couplet, but which is also similar; it is the pleasure of listening to a strong, decisive, self-limiting voice uttering statements to which I can give assent. The pleasure I have in responding to Freud I find very difficult to distinguish from the pleasure which is involved in responding to a satisfactory work of art.

Intellectual assent in literature is not quite the same thing as agreement. We can take pleasure in literature where we do not agree, responding to the power or grace of a mind without admitting the rightness of its intention or conclusion— we can take our pleasure from an intellect's *cogency*, without making a final judgment on the correctness or adaptability of what it says.

2

And now I leave these general theoretical matters for a more particular concern—the relation of contemporary American literature to ideas. In order to come at this as directly as possible we might compare modern American prose literature —for American poetry is a different thing—with modern European literature. European literature of, say, the last thirty or forty years seems to me to be, in the sense in which I shall use the word, essentially an active literature. It does not, at its best, consent to be merely comprehended. It refuses to be understood as a "symptom" of its society, although of course it may be that, among other things. It does not submit to being taped. We as scholars and critics try to discover the source of its effective energy and of course we succeed in some degree. But inevitably we become aware that it happily exists beyond our powers of explanation, although not, certainly, beyond our powers of response. Proust, Joyce, Lawrence, Kafka, Yeats, and Eliot himself do not allow us to finish with them; and the refusal is repeated by a great many European writers less large than these. With exceptions that I shall note, the same thing cannot be said of modern American literature. American literature seems to me essentially passive: our minds tend always to be made up about this or that American author, and we incline to speak of him, not merely incidentally but conclusively, in terms of his moment in history, of the conditions of the culture that "produced" him. Thus American literature as an academic subject is not so much a *subject* as an *object* of study: it does not, as a literature should, put the scrutinizer of it under scrutiny but, instead, leaves its students with a too comfortable sense of complete comprehension.

When we try to discover the root of this difference between European and American literature, we are led to the conclusion that it is the difference between the number and weight or force of the ideas which the two literatures embody or suggest. I do not mean that European literature makes use of, as American literature does not, the ideas of philosophy or theology or science. Kafka does not exemplify Kierkegaard, Proust does not dramatize Bergson. One way of putting the relationship of this literature to ideas is to say that the literature of contemporary Europe is in competition with philosophy, theology, and science, that it seeks to match them in comprehensiveness and power and seriousness.

This is not to say that the best of contemporary European literature makes upon us the effect of a rational system of thought. Quite the contrary, indeed; it is precisely its artistic power that we respond to, which I take in part to be its power of absorbing and disturbing us in secret ways. But this power it surely derives from its commerce, according to its own rules, with systematic ideas.

For in the great issues with which the mind has traditionally been concerned there is, I would submit, something *primitive* which is of the highest value to the literary artist. I know that it must seem a strange thing to say, for we are in the habit of thinking of systematic ideas as being of the very essence of the not-primitive, of the highly developed. No doubt they are: but they are at the same time the means by which a complex civilization keeps the primitive in mind and refers to it. Whence and whither, birth and death, fate, free will, and immortality—these are never far from systematic thought; and Freud's belief that the child's first inquiry—beyond which, really, the adult does not go in kind—is in effect a sexual one seems to me to have an empirical support from literature. The ultimate questions of conscious and rational thought about the nature of man and his destiny match easily in the literary mind with the dark *unconscious* and with the most primitive human relationships. Love, parenthood, incest, patricide: these are what the great ideas suggest to literature, these are the means by which they express themselves. I need but mention three great works of different ages to suggest how true this is: *Oedipus, Hamlet, The Brothers Karamazov.*

Ideas, if they are large enough and of a certain kind, are not only not hostile to the creative process, as some think, but are virtually inevitable to it. Intellectual power and emotional power go together. And if we can say, as I think we can, that contemporary American prose literature in general lacks emotional power, it is possible to explain the deficiency by reference to the intellectual weakness of American prose literature.

The situation in verse is different. Perhaps this is to be accounted for by the fact that the best of our poets are, as good poets usually are, scholars of their tradition. There is present to their minds the degree of intellectual power which poetry is traditionally expected to exert. Questions of form and questions of language seem of themselves to demand, or to create, an adequate subject matter; and a highly developed aesthetic implies a matter strong enough to support its energy. We have not a few poets who are subjects and not objects, who are active and not passive. One does not finish quickly, if at all, with the best work of, say, Cummings, Stevens, and Marianne Moore. This work is not exempt from our judgment, even from adverse judgment, but it is able to stay with a mature reader as a continuing element of his spiritual life. Of how many writers of prose fiction can we say anything like the same thing?

The topic which was originally proposed to me for this occasion and which I have taken the liberty of generalizing was the debt of four American writers to Freud and Spengler. The four writers were O'Neill, Dos Passos, Wolfe, and Faulkner. Of the first three how many can be continuing effective elements of our mental lives? I hope I shall never read Mr. Dos Passos without interest nor ever lose the warm though qualified respect that I feel for his work. But it is impossible for me to feel of this work that it is autonomous, that it goes on existing beyond our powers of explanation. As for Eugene O'Neill and Thomas Wolfe, I can respect the earnestness of their dedication, but I cannot think of having a living, reciprocal relation with what they have written. And I believe that this is because these men, without intellectual capital of their own, don't owe a sufficient debt of ideas to anyone. Spengler is certainly not a great mind; at best he is but a considerable dramatist of the idea of world history and of, as it were, the natural history of cultures; and we can find him useful as a critic who summarizes the adverse views of our urban, naturalistic culture which many have held. Freud is a very great mind indeed. Without stopping to specify what actual influence of ideas was exerted by Spengler and Freud on O'Neill, Dos Passos, or Wolfe, or even to consider whether there was any influence at all, we can fairly assume that all are in something of the same ambiance. But if, in that ambiance, we want the sense of the actuality of doom—actuality being one of the qualities we expect of literature—surely we do better to seek it in Spengler himself than in any of the three literary artists, just as, if we want the sense of the human mystery, of tragedy truly conceived in the great terms of free will, necessity, and hope, surely we do far better to seek it directly in Freud himself than in these three literary men.

In any extended work of literature, the aesthetic effect, as I have said, depends in large degree upon intellectual power, upon the amount and recalcitrance of the material the mind works on, and upon the mind's success in mastering the large material. And it is exactly the lack of intellectual power that makes our three writers, after our first response of interest, so inadequate aesthetically. We have only to compare, say, Dos Passos's *USA* to a work of similar kind and intention, Flaubert's *L'Education sentimentale,* to see that in Dos Passos's novel the matter encompassed is both less in amount and less in resistance than in Flaubert's; the energy of the encompassing mind is also less. Or we consider O'Neill's crude, dull notion of the unconscious and his merely elementary grasp of Freud's ideas about sex and we recognize the lamentable signs of a general inadequacy of mind. Or we ask what it is about Thomas Wolfe that always makes us uncomfortable with his talent, so that even his admirers deal with him not as a subject but as an object—an object which must be explained and accounted for—and we are forced to answer that it is the disproportion between the energy of his utterance and his power of mind. It is customary to say of Thomas Wolfe that he is an emotional writer. Perhaps: although it is probably not the most accurate way to describe a writer who could deal with but one single emotion; and we feel that it is a function of his unrelenting, tortured egoism that he could not submit his mind to the ideas that might have brought the variety and interest of order to the single, dull chaos of his powerful self-regard, for it is true that the intellect makes many emotions out of the primary egoistic one.

At this point it may be well to recall what our subject is. It is not merely the part that is played in literature by those ideas which may be derived from the study of systematic, theoretical works; it is the part that is played in literature by ideas in general. To be sure, the extreme and most difficult instance of the general relation of literature to ideas is the relation of literature to highly developed and formulated ideas; and because this is indeed so difficult a matter, and one so often misconceived, I have put a special emphasis upon it. But we do not present our subject adequately—we do not, indeed, represent the mind adequately—if we think of ideas only as being highly formulated. It will bring us back to the proper generality of our subject if I say that the two contemporary writers who hold out to me the possibility of a living reciprocal relationship with their work are Ernest Hemingway and William Faulkner—it will bring us back the more dramatically because Hemingway and Faulkner have insisted on their indifference to the conscious intellectual tradition of our time and have acquired the reputation of achieving their effects by means that have the least possible connection with any sort of intellectuality or even with intelligence.

In trying to explain a certain commendable quality which is to be found in the work of Hemingway and Faulkner—and a certain quality only, not a total and unquestionable literary virtue—we are not called upon by our subject to show that particular recognizable ideas of a certain force or weight are "used" in the work. Nor are we called upon to show that new ideas of a certain force and weight are "produced" by the work. All that we need to do is account for a certain aesthetic effect as being in some important part achieved by a mental process which is not different from the process by which discursive ideas are conceived, and which is to be judged by some of the criteria by which an idea is judged.

The aesthetic effect which I have in mind can be suggested by a word that I have used before—activity. We feel that Hemingway and Faulkner are intensely at work upon the recalcitrant stuff of life; when they are at their best they give us the sense that the amount and intensity of their activity are in a satisfying proportion to the recalcitrance of the material. And our pleasure in their activity is made the more secure because we have the distinct impression that the two novelists are not under any illusion that they have conquered the material upon which they direct their activity. The opposite is true of Dos Passos, O'Neill, and Wolfe; at each point of conclusion in their work we feel that *they* feel that they have said the last word, and we feel this even when they represent themselves, as O'Neill and Wolfe so often do, as puzzled and baffled by life. But of Hemingway and Faulkner we seldom have the sense that they have deceived themselves, that they have misrepresented to themselves the nature and the difficulty of the matter they work on. And we go on to make another intellectual judgment: we say that the matter they present, together with the degree of difficulty which they assume it to have, seems to be very cogent. This, we say, is to the point; this really has something to do with life as we live it; we cannot ignore it.

There is a traditional and aggressive rationalism that can understand thought only in its conscious, developed form and believes that the phrase "unconscious mind" is a meaningless contradiction in terms. Such a view, wrong as I think it is, has at least the usefulness of warning us that we must not call by the name of thought or idea all responses of the human organism whatever. But the extreme rationalist position ignores the simple fact that the life of reason, at least in its most extensive part, begins in the emotions. What comes into being when two contradictory emotions are made to confront each other and are required to have a relationship with each other is, as I have said, quite properly called an idea. Ideas may also be said to be generated in the opposition of ideals, and in the felt awareness of the impact of new circumstances upon old forms of feeling and estimation, in the response to the conflict between new exigencies and old pieties. And it can be said that a work will have what I have been calling cogency in the degree that the confronting emotions go deep, or in the degree that the old pieties are firmly held and the new exigencies strongly apprehended. In Hemingway's stories [3] a strongly charged piety toward the ideals and attachments of boyhood and the lusts of maturity is in conflict not only with the imagination of death but also with that imagination as it is peculiarly modified by the dark negation of the modern world. Faulkner as a Southerner of today, a man deeply implicated in the pieties of his tradition, is of course at the very heart of an exigent historical event which thrusts upon him the awareness of the inadequacy and wrongness of the very tradition he loves. In the work of both men the cogency is a function not of their conscious but of their unconscious minds. We can, if we admire Tolstoy and Dostoevsky, regret the deficiency of consciousness, blaming it for the inadequacy in both our American writers of the talent for generalization.[4] Yet it is to be remarked that the unconscious minds of both men have wisdom and humility about themselves. They seldom make the attempt at formulated solution, they rest content with the "negative capability." And this negative capability, this willingness to remain in uncertainties, mysteries, and doubts, is not, as one tendency of modern feeling would suppose, an abdication of intellectual activity. Quite to the contrary, it is precisely an aspect of their intelligence, of their seeing the full force and complexity of their subject matter. And this we can understand the better when we observe how the unconscious minds of Dos Passos, O'Neill, and Wolfe do not possess humility and wisdom; nor are they fully active, as the intellectual histories of all three men show. A passivity on the part of Dos Passos before the idea of the total corruption of American civilization has issued in his later denial of the possibility of economic and social reform and in his virtually unqualified acceptance of the American status quo. A passivity on the part of O'Neill before the clichés of economic and metaphysical materialism issued in his later simplistic Catholicism. The passivity of Thomas Wolfe before all his experience led him to that characteristic *malice* toward the objects or partners of his experience which no admirer of his ever takes account of, and eventually to that simple affirmation, recorded in *You Can't Go Home Again*, that literature must become the agent of the immediate solution of all social problems and undertake the prompt eradication of human pain; and because his closest friend did not agree that this was a possible thing for literature to do, Wolfe terminated the friendship. These are men of whom it is proper to speak of their having been violated by ideas; but we must observe that it was an excess of intellectual passivity that invited the violence.

In speaking of Hemingway and Faulkner I have used the word "piety." It is a word that I have chosen with some care and despite the pejorative meanings that nowadays adhere to it, for I wished to avoid the word "religion," and piety is not religion, yet I wished too to have religion come to mind as it inevitably must when piety is mentioned. Carlyle says of Shakespeare that he was the product of medieval Catholicism, and implies that Catholicism *at the distance at which Shakespeare stood from it* had much to do with the power of Shakespeare's intellect. Allen Tate has developed in a more particular way an idea that has much in common with what Carlyle here implies. Loosely put, the idea is that religion in its decline leaves a detritus of pieties, of strong assumptions, which afford a particularly fortunate condition for certain kinds of literature; these pieties carry a strong charge of intellect, or perhaps it would be more accurate to say that they tend to stimulate the mind in a powerful way.

Religious emotions are singularly absent from Shakespeare and it does not seem possible to say of him that he was a religious man. Nor does it seem possible to say of the men of the great period of American literature in the nineteenth century that they were religious men. Hawthorne and Melville, for example, lived at a time when religion was in decline, and they were not drawn to support it. But from religion they inherited a body of pieties, a body of issues, if you will, which engaged their hearts and their minds to the very bottom. Henry James was not a religious man and there is not the least point in the world in trying to make him out one. But you need not accept all the implications of Quentin Anderson's thesis that James allegorized his father's religious system to see that Mr. Anderson is right when he says that James was dealing, in his own way, with the questions that his father's system propounded. This will indicate something of why James so catches our imagination today, and why we turn so eagerly again to Hawthorne and Melville.

The piety which descends from religion is not the only possible piety, as the case of Faulkner reminds us, and perhaps also the case of Hemingway. But we naturally mention first that piety which does descend from religion because it is most likely to have in it the quality of transcendence which, whether we admit it or no, we expect literature at its best to have.

The subject is extremely delicate and complex and I do no more than state it barely and crudely. But no matter how I state it, I am sure that you will see that what I am talking about leads us to the crucial issue of our literary culture.

I know that I will not be wrong if I assume that most of us here are in our social and political beliefs consciously liberal and democratic. And I know that I will not be wrong if I say that most of us, and in the degree of our commitment to literature and our familiarity with it, find that the contemporary authors we most wish to read and most wish to admire for their literary qualities demand of us a great agility and ingenuity in coping with their antagonism to our social and political ideals. For it is in general true that the modern European literature to which we can have an active, reciprocal relationship, which is the right relationship to have, has been written by men who are indifferent to, or even hostile to, the tradition of democratic liberalism as we know it. Yeats and Eliot, Proust and Joyce, Lawrence and Gide—these men do not seem to confirm us in the social and political ideals which we hold.

If we now turn and consider the contemporary literature of America, we see that wherever we can describe it as patently liberal and democratic, we must say that it is not of lasting interest. I do not say that the work which is written to conform to the liberal democratic tradition is of no value but only that we do not incline to return to it, we do not establish it in our minds and affections. Very likely we learn from it as citizens; and as citizen-scholars and citizen-critics we understand and explain it. But we do not live in an active reciprocal relation with it. The sense of largeness, of cogency, of the transcendence which largeness and cogency can give, the sense of being reached in our secret and primitive minds— this we virtually never get from the writers of the liberal democratic tradition at the present time.

And since liberal democracy inevitably generates a body of ideas, it must necessarily occur to us to ask why it is that these particular ideas have not infused with force and cogency the literature that embodies them. This question is the most important, the most fully challenging question in culture that at this moment we can ask.

The answer to it cannot of course even be begun here, and I shall be more than content if now it is merely accepted as a legitimate question. But there are one or two things that may be said about the answer, about the direction we must take to reach it in its proper form. We will not find it if we come to facile conclusions about the absence from our culture of the impressive ideas of traditional religion. I have myself referred to the historical fact that religion has been an effective means of transmitting or of generating ideas of a sort which I feel are necessary for the literary qualities we want, and to some this will no doubt mean that I believe religion to be a necessary condition of great literature. I do not believe that; and what is more, I consider it from many points of view an impropriety to try to guarantee literature by religious belief.

Nor will we find our answer if we look for it in the weakness of the liberal democratic ideas in themselves. It is by no means true that the inadequacy of the literature that connects itself with a body of ideas is the sign of the inadequacy of those ideas, although it is no doubt true that some ideas have less affinity with literature than others.

Our answer, I believe, will rather be found in a cultural fact—in the kind of relationship which we, or the writers who represent us, maintain toward the ideas we claim as ours, and in our habit of conceiving the nature of ideas in general. If we find that it is true of ourselves that we conceive ideas to be pellets of intellection or crystallizations of thought, precise and completed, and defined by their coherence and their procedural recommendations, then we shall have accounted for the kind of prose literature we have. And if we find that we do indeed have this habit, and if we continue in it, we can predict that our literature will continue much as it is. But if we are drawn to revise our habit of conceiving ideas in this way and learn instead to think of ideas as living things, inescapably connected with our wills and desires, as susceptible of growth and development by their very nature, as showing their life by their tendency to change, as being liable, by this very tendency, to deteriorate and become corrupt and to work harm, then we shall stand in a relation to ideas which makes an active literature possible.

NOTES

1. The word is used by Mr. Wellek and Mr. Warren, not in the pejorative sense in which I have earlier used it, but to mean simply a body of ideas.
2. Mr. Wellek and Mr. Warren say something of the same sort, but only, as it were, in a concessive way: "Philosophy, ideological content, in its proper context, seems to enhance artistic value because it corroborates several important artistic values: those of complexity and coherence. . . . But it need not be so. The artist will be hampered by too much ideology if it remains unassimilated" (p. 122). Earlier (p. 27) they say: "Serious art implies a view of life which can be stated in philosophical terms, even in terms of systems. Between artistic coherence . . . and philosophic coherence there is some kind of correlation." They then hasten to distinguish between emotion and thinking, sensibility and intellection, etc., and to tell us that art is more complex than "propaganda."
3. It is in the stories rather than in the novels that Hemingway is characteristic and at his best.
4. Although there is more impulse to generalization than is usually supposed. This is especially true of Faulkner, who has never subscribed to the contemporary belief that only concrete words have power and that only the representation of things and actions is dramatic.

CONCERNING POETIC KNOWLEDGE *

Jacques Maritain

The career itself of the word "poetry" seems to me very instructive. It is only in relatively recent times that this word has come to designate *poetry:* previously it designated *art,* the activity of the working reason; it is in this sense that Aristotle and the ancients—and our own classical age—treated of Poetics. One might say that piercing and boring through metaphysical layers the word poetry has little by little traversed the body of the poetic work and arrived at its soul, where it has opened out into the spiritual realm. This phenomenon will not appear very surprising if one admits that poetry has only recently begun (*poets,* that is, have only recently begun) to become self-conscious in an explicit and deliberate way (and this process will never have finished).

This law of progressively becoming conscious of itself is one of the great laws of the historical development of the human being, and it is related to a property of activities of a spiritual order. The distinctive property of spirit is to be able, the ancients said, to return entirely upon itself, to accomplish a perfect reflexion, the essential thing here being not the turning back, but the grasp, the penetration of the self by the self, which is integral to it. Reflexivity is essential to the spirit, which thus grasps itself by means of itself and penetrates itself. Thence the general importance, for everything concerning culture, of the phenomenon of becoming self-conscious.

But because man is a spirit *one* in substance with the flesh, in other words, a seriously incommoded spirit, this phenomenon takes place in him slowly and with difficulty, with extraordinary delays, and it involves errors.

And it is not accomplished without unhappy accidents.

As in each case in which thought attacks a difficult task, it begins, in the conquering of new domains, and especially the interior domains of its own spiritual universe, by bringing on troubles, disasters. The human being seems to disorganize itself, and it happens in fact sometimes that these crises of growth end badly. They are nevertheless crises of growth.

Poetry in France has experienced several of them. The one in our epoch seems to me particularly significant, and never has the need to *know itself* been so violent for poetry. At

* [From *The Situation of Poetry,* by Jacques and Raïssa Maritain (New York: Philosophical Library, 1955). Reprinted by permission of the author and the publisher.]

these moments poetry must accomplish a double task: pursue its creative song, and turn back reflexively upon its own substance. It seems in consequence that a distinction can be made, a very summary one it is true and one which could easily become vulgar if one insisted on it too much, between two families of poets. (I shall not consider those, and they can be very great poets, who in their work carry a past moment in the life of poetry to a higher degree of perfection —which is generally the case with *great men*.)

With this reservation, then, we may say that in epochs like ours there is a family of poets who are more (I say more, I do not say exclusively) concerned with the *interior discovery of themselves* and the process of poetry's becoming self-conscious; these poets are more closely engaged in the activity and the experiments by which poetry is working on itself and renewing itself and yearns to grow in time, but precisely for this reason they are also more concerned with the typical effort of their own time. And there is another family of poets who are more concerned with continuing *poetic action* itself and that effusion of the voice of which David speaks and which goes on from age to age. Less involved in the work of historical growth of poetry, they are, in turn, freer in respect to the particular characteristics of their epoch. It is only a preponderance of aspect that I am pointing to here, and it is variable in a thousand ways; for the one family of poets like the other participates in some fashion, both in the experiments and discoveries of the poetry of its time, and its work of growing, and both continue in some fashion the work of creative song.

But let us close this parenthesis. What I should like to point out is that the phenomenon of becoming self-conscious which we spoke of above is not a simple one, far from it. It occurs in a kind of labyrinthine manner, amid a host of secondary phenomena of acceleration, condensation, regression, survivance, among which genius appears from time to time to complicate things further; and it is a discontinuous phenomenon, in which successive moments may be separated by long delays.

To be sure, even among the men of the Ice Age (certain of whose designs and sculptures reveal the hand of a professional), the artist has always had a certain consciousness of his art; but in comparison with an "explicit" consciousness which is thoroughly awakened by reflexion, the "concomitant" or implicit consciousness remains a kind of sleep. And so there occurs, in the great literatures, a moment when poetry, after having created immortal works as it were in a state of sleep and not aware of itself except as a runner who at certain moments turns his head a little, begins to pass into a state of explicit self-consciousness, into a state of reflexive knowledge of that mysterious operative spiritual virtue that we call art. It is a fleeting moment, an astonishingly privileged moment. It must not be missed; it presupposes a normal and sufficiently autonomous development of civilization, a multitude of social, cultural, and spiritual conditions—and a great poet, the angels of history demand a great poet for such a moment. When one is given to them, that moment is called the moment of Aeschylus and Sophocles, the moment of Virgil, the moment of Dante. It opens the great classical epochs. After it, sometimes with it, come the grammar, the rhetoric, the recipes.

In the literatures of Christian Europe (excepting the first Italian Renaissance, and the miracle of Dante, which crowned the Middle Ages with glory at the instant when they tottered and were metamorphosed—and Petrarch is already a man of letters in the sense in which that term is understood in our day), it seems that the moment of which we have just spoken was more or less obscured by adventitious phenomena resulting from the second Renaissance. In England there was the moment of Shakespeare. In France, the moment which interests us in this connection is spread over a long period. There was, first of all, the time of Ronsard and the Pléiade, then the time of Racine, after an interval full of contrasts.

When has French poetry been richer in the invention of forms, in honest and precise ways of turning a piece of verse, than in the time of Charles of Orléans, of Marot, of Mesnard, and of Ronsard? It was the century of the rondel and the sonnet, of the ballade, of the virelay, of the *rime royale;* the consciousness that poetry then took of itself was the consciousness of the craftsman—a century later it was to be the consciousness of the grammarian.

For the Pléiade the injuries to poetry associated with the progress of becoming self-conscious were those deriving from archaeology, and a surplus of science and verbalism which is still naive but which already causes us to miss Villon. After that, when the French spirit had felt the dangers of over-refinements in art, but reacted in the name of nature and reason, a juridical and very soon a Cartesian reason, not at all in the name of poetry, poetry experienced the greatest danger it had known in France. As a protection against the invasion of the baroque, which has produced so many masterpieces in the world, it was proclaimed: *And now let us not depart from nature by one iota!* And at the same time the consciousness of the grammarian of which I spoke a moment ago, breathing hatred against poetry, undertook, and with what ferocity, with what sureness of its mission, to sacrifice poetry to art, art having withered under this rationalist glance into artifice. It was, however, at this moment of greatest danger that poetry passed athwart grammar as a child of heaven athwart the doctors, with a supple and brilliant infallibility which was to usher in the greatest glory of that great age of prose which was our seventeenth century.

After Racine and La Fontaine, the fall is vertical. "Any man," writes Abbé Terrasson, "who does not think in literary matters as Descartes prescribes that one must think in matters of physics is not worthy of the present age." But in the midst of the general disaster something was acquired, and something that was not to be lost: poetry gained consciousness of itself as art, however miserable the conceptualization made of that gaining of consciousness by the disciples of Abbé Terrasson.

The question *what is art?* is thenceforward a wound in its side. The classicism of the eighteenth century answered that question very badly, denaturing, according to the logic of clear ideas, the ancient notion of art as rectitude of the working reason, as intelligence productive of objects.

French Romanticism answered, in a manner which was primarily a movement of instinctive reaction, by rejecting together the role of the operative intellect and the absurd idea which the preceding age had formed of it. But at the same time the consciousness of art was admirably deepened. The German Romantics came in under the veil of philosophy and metaphysical enigmas, into the proper realm of poetic realities.

At the time of Gérard de Nerval and of Delacroix, then, this is what happened: by force of scrutinizing in themselves the consciousness of art, the poets ended by laying hand upon a voracious thing crouching in the depths, a thing which art does not encompass any more than the world encompasses God, and which seizes you and you no longer know where you are going. The moment arrives, in the course of the nineteenth century, when poetry begins to take consciousness of itself *as poetry*. Then, in a few decades, there is a series of discoveries, defeats, catastrophes, and revelations of which in my opinion one could hardly exaggerate the importance. And that was only the beginning. It required this contact of self-consciousness, of reflexive spirituality, finally to release poetry in France. I believe that what has happened to French poetry since Baudelaire has a historical importance equal in the domain of art to that of the greatest epochs of revolution and renewal of physics and astronomy in the domain of science.

I suppose that the situation of Baudelaire would be indicated precisely enough if one said that he seems to be in continuity with the best of romanticism by virtue of that deepening of the consciousness of *art* to which I just alluded, but that in reality he marks a discontinuity, a formidable mutation, because at the same instant it is *of poetry*, it is *of itself as poetry* that with him poetry becomes conscious.

The importance of this becoming conscious is immense with him, and he often insisted on it himself: "It would be prodigious that a critic should become a poet," he writes, "but it is impossible that a poet should not contain a critic." And the consciousness of poetry, it is that which constantly tortured him; the mystical knowledge of poetry, it is that which was his *abyss, moving with him;* it is that which made for the astonishing magical power of his lines (sometimes prosaic). One knows how he speaks of it many times, in particular in the first poem of *Les Fleurs du mal:*

> *Lorsque par un décret des puissances suprêmes*
> *Le poète apparaît en ce monde ennuyé,*
> *Sa mère épouvantée et pleine de blasphèmes*
> *Crispe ses poings vers Dieu, qui la prend en pitié ...*

or in a celebrated passage almost copied from Edgar Allan Poe, but Baudelaire had the right to consider that between himself and Poe all things were in common:

> It is that immortal instinct for the beautiful which causes us to consider the earth and its spectacles as a glimpse, as a *correspondence* of heaven. The insatiable thirst for all that is beyond what life reveals is the most living proof of our immortality. It is at the same time by means of poetry and by going beyond poetry, by means of and beyond music, that the soul glimpses the splendors that lie beyond the tomb; and when an exquisite poem brings tears to the eyes, those tears are not the proof of an excess of pleasure, they are much rather the witnesses of an irritated melancholy, of an exasperated demand of the nerves, of a nature exiled in the imperfect and wishing to seize immediately, on this very earth, a revealed paradise.

It is to Baudelaire that modern poetry owes its consciousness of the quasi-theological quality, of the despotic spirituality of poetry, which for him was still called Beauty.

"The capital role of Baudelaire and of Rimbaud," we noted in the previous essay,[1] "is to have made modern art pass the frontiers of the spirit. But these are regions of supreme perils, where the hardest metaphysical problems fall upon poetry, where the battle is joined between the good angels and the bad."

I do not think Lautréamont is a good angel; he has nothing of the guardian angel about him. It is in the magic of pride that he excels; later on hate and malice will come also, or rather the spirit, the spiritual quintessence, the active extract of malice. Neither was Rimbaud a good angel, nor Baudelaire, though Baudelaire was infinitely more Christian than the other two, Christian and Jansenist and almost Manichaean. But it is all the same to poetry—poetry is no longer concerned with anything but knowing itself.

We must try to distinguish, naturally in a very schematic manner, different moments in this research with which poetry is henceforth obsessed, and which no longer asks: *what is art?* but *what is poetry?*—that poetry which is to art what grace is to the moral virtues, and which is not the peculiar privilege of poets, nor even of other artists—it can also be found in a boy who knows only how to look and to say *ah, ah, ah,* like Jeremiah, or who intoxicates himself with it to the point of frenzy or suicide without ever having said or done anything in his whole life.

One of the first aspects of poetry's taking consciousness of itself as poetry is related, it seems to me, to what is still a proper function of art, which is the creating of an object. But poetry soon transfigures this function, and this exigency: it is not an object of art that is to be created, as one might have understood the matter in the time of the Parnassians, it is a world—the poem will by itself be a self-sufficient universe, without the need of signifying anything but itself, and in which the soul must allow itself to be enclosed blindfolded, in order to receive as if through the skin, through all the surface of the body, the effluvia of night that penetrate to the heart without one's knowing how. *I am obscure like feeling,* wrote Pierre Reverdy, and his poems have the same obscurity. In order to experience their beauty, which is great, one must consent first to that obscurity. The fact is that such a preliminary consent, I mean a consent to the intentions of the artist, is always required for the understanding of a work of art and the communication which that understanding presupposes.

A second capital moment in the progressive coming to consciousness of poetry is related, I believe, to the essence of the *poetic state;* here we see poetry immersed in an infinity of infra-conscious, supra-conscious mystery to be discovered and come to know.

In a lecture delivered in Buenos Aires in the summer of 1936, Henri Michaux admirably described the disvestiture required by this frantic investigation, and by the pitiless task to which poetry thus feels itself held, to discover, to lay bare the truth of its pure substance and its own inspiration. Rhythm, rhyme, line, stanza, all the clothing of words, of music, of human intelligibility, from which the poem seems to derive its consistency, none of that is what is sought for, all of that constitutes an obstacle to the research being pursued. Are we going to reduce poetry to the impossible in order to test its resistance, and allow only an ultimate sparkling germ at the point of death to survive? Shall we not rather enter into a kind of negative theology in which the hidden essence of poetry will be attained in an incommunicable experience, from which later we shall return among men, all the means of expression now being changed and purified, I mean to say as if burned from within, by a fire which will seem to annihilate them but which will liberate unknown energies in them?

Meanwhile, insofar as it expresses that effort toward achieving consciousness which occupies us, the work itself is subjected to singular conditions of asceticism; it ceases to be a song, which it naturally demands to be, in order to become rather a revelation—secret in itself, and to which nothing remains but to try to touch our hearts in forbidden ways—of the secret functioning of the poetic powers in the substance of the poet.

To do away with words, with all the load of falsehood and the more-or-less, of parasitical associative connotations which they involve, to do away with words, or create new words, or transubstantiate the old ones, is to leave off the ordinary play of ideas and concepts as well as the rational, social, and human life; it is to enter a savage world where there is no longer anything to protect us, and, finally, it is to take leave, in a way, of the human race—*aber ich will kein Mensch sein,* but I do not want to be a man . . .

There is the great night, the night which stirs, and the desire to lose one's being.

We have just spoken of a second aspect or moment in the coming to consciousness of poetry *as poetry,* and which concerns above all the poetic state. I think that one could, at least by abstraction, discern a third, deeper still than the other two, and which would be related rather to *poetic knowledge,* I mean to the knowledge of reality, and of the interior of things, or their reverse side, proper to poetry or to the spirit of poetry.

The more deeply poetry becomes conscious of itself, the more deeply it becomes conscious of its power of *knowing,* and of the mysterious movement by which, as Jules Supervielle put it one day, it approaches the sources of being.

Here we arrive at the crucial point of the debate, and at particularly difficult philosophical questions, but questions which it would be a lack of courage not to want to consider. Before treating them rapidly I should like to remark that the three moments of which I have spoken are related to diverse modalities of the coming to consciousness of poetry, not to diverse chronological instants; they can take place at the same time; and, for example, it is to the ultimate moment, to the moment of *poetic knowledge,* that Rimbaud is carried at the very start, thus entering at once the burning core of the flame.

2

When a philosopher reflects on poetry, he perceives first of all, as we noted above, that poetry is situated in the line of art or creative activity. Now the end of art as such is not to know, but to produce or *create*—not in the mode of nature, as radium produces helium or as a living being engenders another, but in the way of spirit and of liberty; here it is a matter of the productivity of the intellect *ad extra.*[2]

The activity of the intelligence in itself is a kind of manifestation: it produces *within* itself its mental words, which are, for it, its means of knowing, but which are also effects of its spiritual *abundance,* internal expressions or manifestations of what it knows.

And by a natural *superabundance* it tends of itself to express and manifest outside itself, to sing: it abounds not only in its own word, it demands to superabound in a work, a natural desire which, because it will go beyond the frontiers of the intelligence itself, cannot be realized without the movement to which it entices the will and the appetitive powers. These then cause the intellect to go out from itself, in accord with its natural wish, and thus determine its original impulse of movement, and, in an altogether general way, the *poeticity* (in the Aristotelian sense of the word) or the operative practicity of the intellect. After this original determination, the activity of art will develop in a line which is much more purely intellectual—and in which the human will with its own ends will be much less involved—than the line of moral activity (ethical practicity).

Thus we understand that in general, in all practicity of the spirit, the will or appetite has a certain part, a variable one moreover, and that, in the special case of the practicity which issues in the making of objects, that part is less than in the case of ethical practicity, since the "idea" of the work-to-be-made is already a practical idea in and by itself (because in itself it presupposes that primitive movement of the intellect toward some being to be produced, in which the will intervened).

Such is, we believe, reduced to its pure and essential metaphysical exigencies, the primary root of the poetic activity in the sense of *activity of art.* This metaphysical root can be obscured by an immense empirical, psychological, and sociological conditioning, and by the more apparent ends of utility, whether they be for example the magical ends of the most primitive painters or the need of tools which is connatural to man; this metaphysical root is presupposed by these ends and by this conditioning.

Understood thus, the activity of art is not related in itself to a need of communicating *to others* (this need is real and in fact intervenes inevitably in artistic activity, but it does not *define* it); it is related essentially to the need of speaking and manifesting in a work-to-be-made—by virtue of spiritual superabundance and even though there were no one to see or hear (which would in other ways be a cruel anomaly). This is so true that it happens sometimes that the artist suffers more profoundly from that very public with which he wishes to enter into communion when he is "understood" by it than when he is "misunderstood": to be understood diminishes him, puts him out of his element; he wonders if his work does not lack some deeper quality which, if it were there, would not have been communicable. It is not for man that he produces his work, or at least it is for future generations which he conceives of as in some way immaterial because they do not exist. What he wants is not to be understood, it is to endure in history.

What follows from all this, from the point of view of knowledge?

The activity of art is not in itself an activity of knowledge, but of creation; what it aims at is to *make an object* according to the internal exigencies and the proper good of that object.

It presupposes, it is true, it utilizes a *previous* knowledge: being an intellectual or spiritual productivity, it cannot in fact be content with the object itself, toward which it tends as a simply productive activity, an object which is enclosed in a genus. As *intellectual* activity it tends in a certain fashion, even in its act of creating, toward being, which transcends all genera. It will be necessary then that this object which it forms, whether a vase of clay or a fishing boat, be *significant* of something else than itself, be a sign at the same time as an object; it will be necessary that some sense animate it and make it say more than it is. From which it follows that art, while it is productive in its essence, always supposes a moment of contemplation, and the work of art a melody, that is to say, a sense animating a form.[3] It is upon this fact that Aristotle based his declaration that imitation is inherent to art; and this, as the word imitation clearly indicates, relates primarily and on the most apparent visible level (but not the most profound)[4] to a (speculative) knowledge previous to the activity of art and *pre-supposed* by it, but extrinsic to it;

to knowledge, to all the ordinary human knowledge which the artist procures for himself in opening his eyes and his intelligence upon the things of the world and upon culture. The activity of art begins *after* that, because it is a creative activity and because, in itself, it does not ask that the mind *be formed* by an object to be known, but that it *form* an object to proffer into being.

With these considerations, however, we have reached only the exterior of the mystery. Let us try to go further.

What is it that an act of thought which in its essence is creative, which forms something in the realm of being instead of being formed by things, expresses and manifests in producing its work, if not the very being and substance of him who creates? But the substance of a man is obscure to himself; it is in receiving and suffering things, in awaking to the world, that it awakes to itself. The poet, we have said elsewhere, cannot express his own substance in a work except on the condition that things resound in him, and that within him, in a single awakening, those things and his own substance rise together out of sleep. It is thus as if all that he discerns and divines in things he discerns and divines as inseparable from himself and his emotion, indeed as himself, and so he grasps obscurely his own being, with a knowledge which will only come to fruition in being creative.[5] That is why he shows the Grail to others and does not see it himself.[6] His intuition, the creative intuition or emotion, is an obscure grasping of the self and things together in a knowledge by union or by connaturality which is not completed, does not fructify, does not achieve its word, except in the work and which with all its vital enery moves toward making and producing. Here is a knowledge that is different enough from what we commonly call knowledge, a knowledge which is not expressible in ideas and in judgments, but which is rather experience than knowledge, and creative experience, for it wants to be expressed, and is expressible only in a work. This knowledge is neither previous to nor presupposed by the creative activity, but inviscerated in it, consubstantial with the movement toward the work, and this is, properly speaking, what I call *poetic knowledge*, understanding that the word knowledge is an analogical term, which designates here a knowledge in which the mind does not tend, as toward its repose, toward "having become the things" it knows, but toward "having produced a thing in being." *Poetic knowledge* is thus the secret, vital virtue of that spiritual germ that the ancients called the idea of the work, the working idea, or the idea of the artisan.

It has become conscious of itself at the same time as poetry has; or rather, that divining plunge *is* poetry itself, it is the spirit which, in the sensible and through the sensible, in passion and through passion, in and through the density of experience, seizes the secret *meaning* of things and of itself in order to embody them in matter; the same meaning constituting at the same time the meaning thus perceived in being and the meaning which animates the work produced, or what I called a moment ago the melody of every authentic work of art, so that in this meaning or melody the work and the depth of existence and of the poet, the signifying and the signified, communicate, exist as two in a single song and in a single intentionality.

Ancient and modern philosophers have speculated a great deal about poetry; but, necessarily, from without. We admit —I tried to say why a moment ago—that it is in the nineteenth century, with the preparations made by the romantics, and above all with Baudelaire and Rimbaud, that poetry began *among the poets* to become deliberately and systematically conscious of itself. Every new consciousness is accompanied by a risk of perversion. The risk here was that poetry would want to escape from the line of the work-to-be-made in order to turn back upon the soul itself, thinking to fill the soul with pure knowledge and become its absolute.

Now it is quite true that one may be a poet without producing—without having yet produced—any work of art, but if one is a poet one is virtually turned towards operation. It is of the essence of poetry to be in the operative line, as a tree is in the line of producing fruit. But in becoming conscious of itself, poetry in some measure frees itself from the work-to-be-made, in the measure in which to know oneself is to turn back upon oneself.

At the same time poetry disengages its active principle in a pure state, I mean poetic knowledge itself, that indescribable and fecund experience which Plato called enthusiasm, and which the brief indications given above tried to characterize. And at that instant there awakens in poetry a desire hidden in its transcendental character and in its very spirituality, a metaphysical aspiration, to pass beyond, to transgress the limits which enclose it in a nature, at a certain degree on the scale of beings. At once poetry enters into conflict with art, with that art in whose way its nature condemns it to go: when art demands to form intellectively, according to a creative idea, poetry demands to suffer, to listen, to descend to the roots of being, to an unknown that no idea can circumscribe. "For *I* is an other," said Rimbaud,[7] and could one better define that engulfment in the *inhabited* subject which is poetic knowledge? An instant of vertigo is enough then. If poetry loses its footing, there it is, detached from its operative ends. It becomes a means of knowing; it no longer wants to create, but to know. When art demands to make, poetry, loosed from its natural ties, demands to know.

But knowledge—what a temptation, what an absolute! And such a knowledge, which engages the whole of man! And which gives the world to man in causing him to suffer the world! If, freed (or believing itself freed) from the relativities of art, poetry finds a soul which nothing else occupies, nothing confronting it, it is going to develop an appalling appetite to know, which will vampirize all that is metaphysical in man, and all that is carnal as well.

The experience of Rimbaud is decisive here. Whereas later, while appealing to Rimbaud, the surrealists were to try to use poetry as an instrument for their quasi-"scientific" curiosity, Rimbaud himself obeyed, he consciously and voluntarily obeyed the ultimate tyrannical exigencies of poetic knowledge let loose in its full state of savagery—it is that which made him search for all the treasures of the spirit in the forbidden byways of a heroic and "debauched" banditry.

A moment ago I quoted from the *Lettre du voyant*, in which, precisely, while explaining that he is giving himself to knowledge, he declares in the same breath that he is "debauching" himself.[8] Let us limit ourselves to this capital text, and to the evidence it offers us, the significance of which one's commentary would never exhaust.

"The first study of a man who wants to be a poet"—who *wants* to be a poet, says Rimbaud: taking consciousness, a deliberate undertaking, and there already the trap is hidden—

is knowledge of himself, complete. He seeks his soul, he inspects it, he tries it, learns it. As soon as he knows it, he must cultivate it: that seems simple: in every brain a natural development is accomplished; so many *egotists* proclaim themselves authors; there are many more of them who attribute to themselves their intellectual progress! But it is a matter of making the soul monstrous: in the manner of the comprachicos, what! Imagine a man planting and cultivating warts on his face. I say it is necessary to *be a seer,* to make oneself a *seer.*

The poet makes himself a *seer* by a long, immense, and reasoned *derangement* of *all the senses.* All the forms of love, of suffering, of madness; he searches in himself, he drains from himself all the poisons, that he may keep only their quintessences. Ineffable torture, in which he needs all the faith, all the superhuman force, in which he becomes, among all, the critical case, the great criminal, the great outcast—and the supreme Savant!—For he arrives at the *unknown*—since he cultivates his soul, already richer than any! He arrives at the *unknown;* and when, frantic, he would finish by losing the understanding of his visions, he has seen them! Let him croak in the bouncing about by unheard-of and unnamable things; there will come other horrible laborers: they will begin at the horizons where the other gave way! [9]

The conclusion, enunciated with an astonishing lucidity in *A Season in Hell,* was inevitable. Poetry aiming, in order to realize itself in full plenitude, to deliver itself from every condition of existence, poetic knowledge exalting itself to the point of claiming *absolute* life, engages itself in a dialectic which kills it. It wants to be everything and give everything, the act, sanctity, transubstantiation, the miracle; it has charge of humanity. And whatever it does, it is limited by nature, in reality, to one line only, to a particular and very humble one indeed, to the line of art and of the work-to-be-made. In the end there is nothing left but to lapse into silence, to renounce the work and poetry at the same time. Rimbaud not only stopped writing, he avenged himself on poetry, applied himself to casting it from him as a monster.

The preceding considerations suggest to us the idea that poetry does not *of itself* accord with anything other than itself, not with faith, nor with metaphysics, nor with sanctity; just as in general nothing which reaches toward the infinite accords of itself with anything else. It is folly, as we have just seen, to want it *alone* in the soul. But *with the rest*—with all the other virtues and energies of the spirit, how should it get along? The fact is that all these energies, insofar as they pertain to the transcendental universe, aspire like poetry to surpass their nature and to infinitize themselves. They compose the one for the other a condition of existence, they help one another exist, but all the while hating one another (in a sense, for they love one another too), imposing limits on one another, seeking to reduce one another to impotence. It is only in this conflict that they can exist and grow. Art, poetry, metaphysics, prayer, contemplation, each one is wounded, struck traitorously in the best of itself, and that is the very condition of its living. *Man* unites them by force, weeping all his tears, dying every day, and thus he wins his peace and their peace.

3

The experience of Rimbaud was too complete and too hard for the lesson to be learned from it. In spite of Rimbaud, in spite of *A Season in Hell,* still attempting to enter by main force further into the consciousness of poetry, still persisting in this travail, and, what is more, making a glory of it, poets had to commit the same error of misdirection. But this time pretending to continue the trip up this blind alley, to go to the end of the world and beyond the world in a motionless vehicle: and can this not be accomplished by way of illusion, and thanks to a certain magic?

It is in its attempt to use poetry to fulfill the desires of man and his thirst for knowledge, and his need to see the face of the absolute, that surrealism has for us an exceptional historical interest.

According to the remark of M. Marcel Raymond, "to attest that the game is not yet up, that all can perhaps be saved—that was the essential of the surrealist message." In short, the surrealists also have been victims of poetic knowledge. In the beginning for them, it was a matter above all of rediscovering, as Raïssa Maritain writes, "that river of the spirit which flows under all our customary activity, that profound, authentic reality, foreign to all formulae, perceived in those 'minutes of abandonment to hidden forces' which vivify." [10] The fact was, I doubt not, that they had actually known those privileged instants of natural ecstasy in which the soul "re-immerses itself so to speak in its source, and from which it issues renewed and fortified" by the poetic experience. That experience they had, let that fortune not be denied them! It is what makes for the value and the tragedy of their adventure. They had it while turning away, by reflexion, from the poetic work and from song, to engage themselves desperately in the circumvolutions of the consciousness. But they were caught in the trap. Wresting poetry almost completely from its natural finalities, they wanted to make of it a means of speculative knowledge, an instrument of science, a method of metaphysical discovery.

And they not only confounded poetry with metaphysics; they confounded it with morality, and they confounded it with sanctity. They charged it thus with a burden it could not bear. What end, then, could its power of seduction serve, if not to astonish us with tricks, to open up to us a world of mere appearances and of tinsel?

Finally, because they confounded the passivity of the poetic experience with that of psychic automatism, the surrealists believed that the means par excellence, or rather the unique source, of poetry was the delivering of images, the liberating of charges of emotion and dream accumulated in our animal subconscious filled with desires and signs. What then developed among the poets of that generation was a remarkable sharpness of instinct to confuse the traces and to disconcert the mind by means of surprise and the stimulative wounding of the imagination; and of how much more value is this allusive rapidity than the classic *discursus!* But in itself, if one remains at that point, it is only another technique, a feat of taste and of talent.

From all this, and from the history and the disappointment of the surrealist attempt, I conclude that errors can occur in the coming to consciousness of poetry, as in every human achievement of consciousness; that is one of the inevitable dangers, as we noted at the beginning of this essay, that the life and progress of the spirit carries with it in man.

To imagine, however, that coming to consciousness in itself, or progress in reflexivity, is a bad thing, a thing which by its nature tends to deform, would be to fall into a sort of Manichaean pessimism, which is, moreover, as false as possible, if it is true that reflexivity is, as I have said, a typical property of the spirit. In the very errors of coming to consciousness there are always coexistent discoveries.

Not to know what one is doing—it is thus, especially when it is a matter of self-forgetfulness due to a superior motion, that one makes the most beautiful things and performs the most generous acts. But not to know what one is doing—it is thus also that one commits the greatest crimes (and has the best chance also of being pardoned for them). All in all, other things being equal, it is better, however dangerous it be, and to whatever sanctions one expose oneself, to *know what one is doing*.

In any case, for that matter, we do not have the choice. When the naive ages are past, they are *quite* past. The only resource left to us is a better and purer self-consciousness.

May I point out here the danger, which does not seem to me totally imaginary, of another possible error in the opposite direction? Among the normal reactions which take place against the experiences of these last years, it could happen—if we had to do with a simple phenomenon, as if of a pendulum, of action and reaction—that after having wished to give all to the subterranean powers of the world of images, one would turn, again in too *exclusive* a manner, and as if they alone counted, toward the powers, sometimes not less obscure, and the fecundity proper to the world of intelligence and discourse. And God preserve me from speaking ill of the intelligence! But it must not be mediocre, and in poetry it is far from being everything: error, said Pascal, comes from exclusion—that is the point I wish to make.

I add that in fact, when one invokes the primacy of the intelligence, not in order to seek out the internal hierarchies of the soul but in order to give passwords and collective instructions, it is not the intelligence as seeker of wisdom, the true intelligence (which is rarely met with), that profits from the operation; it is the facile and social intelligence, anti-metaphysical, empirical, and rationalizing, and which is found everywhere. And for this latter kind of intelligence poetry can very well on occasion express philosophical ideas, and sing *de natura rerum*—the foundation of the authority of such intelligence is neither metaphysical nor mystical, but only psychological, or even sociological.

If then things should take the course I have just indicated, by way of a simple reaction on the surface, we should run the risk of forgetting that though poetry cannot be confounded with metaphysics, it yet responds to a metaphysical need of the spirit of man, and is metaphysically justified. And though it cannot be confounded with sanctity, nor charged with the duties of sanctity, yet in its own line, which is not that of the good of man but rather of the good of the work, it involves a *kind* of sanctity, demands purifications and woes which are in a certain way symbolic of those of souls on the way toward the perfection of love. And we should run the risk of forgetting that the source of poetry is not the intelligence alone, from whatever depths it may surge up in certain men.

In brief, it could happen, on the pretext of Latinity, and of the primacy of the reason (of a reason more or less rationalist), and in the name, if one may speak thus, of a Mediterranean catholicity, that a neoclassical reaction would ask poetry to *exhibit ideas and sentiments*, to charge itself with the rubbish of human notions in their verbosity and their natural meanness, and to fabricate *versified discourses* for the delectation of the formal intelligence. We should then see born a poetics "of abundance," of verbal abundance and of intellectual reduplication. And the word would again become master, the glory of the word, the endless and buzzing heroism of language—and all the stupidity of man.

Poetry is ontology, certainly, and even, according to the great saying of Boccaccio, poetry is theology. But in the sense that it finds its birth in the soul in the mysterious sources of being, and reveals them in some way by its own creative movement. Though the unconscious from which it proceeds is not, unless secondarily, the Freudian unconscious of instincts and images, it is, however, an unconscious more vital and deeper, the unconscious of the spirit *at its source*—hidden from the reasoning intelligence in that density of the soul where all the soul's powers have their common origin.

In short, it is toward the totality of his being that the poet is led back, if he is docile to the gift he has received, and consents to enter into the depths and let himself be laid bare. We think that this poetics of integrality, or rather of integration, not by an effort of voluntary concentration, but by the quietude of creative retreat and of poetic knowledge left to its own nature, is that which the present situation of poetry allows us to hope for—because it answers to the best and purest achievement of self-consciousness that one can expect from poetry today.

Let us transcribe here the witness of the poet Raïssa Maritain:

> Born in a vital experience, life itself, poetry asks to be expressed by life-bearing signs, signs which conduct the one who receives them back to the ineffability of the original experience. Since in this contact all the sources of our faculties have been touched, the echo of it ought itself to be total. . . .
>
> Song, poetry in all its forms, seeks to liberate a substantial experience. . . . The brooding repose which is provided by such an experience acts as a refreshing bath, a rejuvenation and purification of the spirit. . . . We cannot esteem too highly the profundity of the quiet which all our faculties then enjoy. It is a concentration of all the energies of the soul, but a peaceful, tranquil concentration, which involves no tension; the soul enters into its repose, in this place of refreshment and of peace superior to any feeling. It dies . . . but only to revive in exaltation and enthusiasm, in that state which is wrongly called "inspiration," because inspiration was nothing other, indeed, than this very repose itself, in which it escaped from sight. Now the mind, reinvigorated and enlivened, enters into a happy activity, so easy that everything seems to be given to it at once and, as it were, from outside. In reality, everything was there, in the shadow, hidden in the spirit and in the blood; everything that is going to be manifested in operation was there, but we knew it not. We knew neither how to discover it nor how to make use of it before having re-immersed ourselves in those tranquil depths.[11]

It is in no sense a matter of diminishing the role of the intelligence, nor the importance of intelligibility, of human experience, of conscious metaphysics involved in the poetic work, especially when that work is a tragedy for example, or a drama or epic. I say only that the fire of creative intuition must be hot enough to consume these materials, and not to be extinguished by them. Discursive lucidity is itself an integral part of the poetry of a Shakespeare, but the lucidity and all the logic, all the rationality and all the acquired knowledge, have been brought back to the secret source of refreshment and of peace of which we spoke a moment ago, in order to be transfigured and vivified there, and brought, if I may so express it, to the *creative state*, because they have all become poetic knowledge there. In that interior source the words of the tribe and the human notions lose that verbosity and that natural meanness which we referred to a few moments ago, because they undergo there, if I may so express it, a second birth.

Then, then alone, the poet has neither to escape from language nor submit himself to it, because the language is newly born in him and of him, as on the first morning of the terrestrial paradise.

All of these considerations suggest to us the conclusion that "in order that the life of the creative spirit grow without ceasing, conformably to its law, it is necessary that it deepen without ceasing the center of subjectivity where, in suffering the things of the world and those of the soul, it awakens to itself. . . . Creation takes place at different levels in the substance of the soul—thereby each person shows what he is— and the more the poet grows, the more the level of the creative intuition descends into the density of his soul." [12] The more the poet at the same time simplifies himself, so much the more he rejects masks, consents to say what he is, feels the worth of human communion. The whole question for him is to have—along with a strong enough art (which can be learned)—a deep enough soul, which cannot be learned. Woe itself is not sufficient.

In an important study on melody, Arthur Lourié wrote a few years ago: "Modern music has lost the melodic element to the same degree that poetry has lost the lyric element." And what Lourié called melody here is an element of an order quite apart, which is developed in time but is not of time, and which is born of a breaking of the connections of time. "Melody, by itself," he writes further, "is not connected with any action, and does not lead to any action. It is like an end in itself. The *motif* serves to justify the action; the *theme* is a means of developing a thought. The *melody,* itself, serves no end. It gives liberation." [13] That is to say that the melody is the very spirit of the music and the revelation of the intimate being of the musician. There is in poetry an element of the same nature, which is the spirit of poetry, and that revelation in act of the intimate person of the poet which is the same thing as poetic knowledge. I do not believe it to be true that modern poetry has lost that element. It has dissimulated it more or less, has been ashamed to avow it too loudly. But it is that element above all that it is trying to grasp in becoming conscious of itself.

There is at this moment in France a singular increase in

poetry. I know some young poets who inspire me with a great confidence. I believe that their task will be to liberate the element of which we are speaking, that spring of living water born in the spiritual depths of the person, revealing, like melody, "the undisfigured essence of what is," and not "the lie imagined by its author."

The condition imposed—and it is dangerous enough to wound or to kill the seekers—is that the waters of that source be *true* enough, and well up from sufficient depth, to be able to carry away and transfigure the astonishing vegetation of images whose secret rites poetry has been learning for twenty years, but which by themselves are still only matter. If modern poetry must become more ontological, get into closer contact with being, with human and terrestrial reality (and perhaps also with divine reality), it is not by cares foreign to its nature and a well-intentioned zeal that it will accomplish this, but only through that lyric element which is almost as hidden as grace, hidden in the deepest of creative sources.

THREE PHILOSOPHICAL CONCLUSIONS

After this metaphysical description, we should like to propose briefly three more systematic conclusions.

In the first place: poetic knowledge is a knowledge *by affective connaturality* of the *operative* type, or tending to express itself in a work. It is not a knowledge "by mode of knowledge," it is a knowledge by mode of instinct or inclination, by mode of resonance in the subject, and which proceeds toward creating a work.

In such a knowledge it is the created object, the *work made*, the poem, the picture, the symphony, which plays the role of the mental word and of the *judgment* in speculative knowledge.[14]

It follows from this that poetic knowledge is not fully conscious except in the work made; it does not completely attain consciousness except in the work—in the work which in other ways materializes it and disperses it in some way in order to bring it back into a new unity, that of the thing posed in being.

Precisely as knowledge or experience (and more experience than knowledge), and taken separately from the production of the work, poetic knowledge is, in its essential character, unconscious—barely signaled to the consciousness by a shock which is at the same time emotional and intellectual, or by a spurt of song, which gives notice of its presence but does not at all express it.

We are here confronted by an unconscious of a special type. As we noted above, it is the unconscious of the spirit *at its source,* quite a different thing from the Freudian unconscious of images and instincts.

If on the other hand, it is remarked that the idea as such (insofar as it is distinguished from the judgment) is not necessarily conscious, one understands that it is with good reason that the ancients designated the intentional form of poetic knowledge not as a judgment but as an *idea,* as a factive or formative idea—which, inasmuch as it is nourished by poetic knowledge and vivified by the grace of poetry, is at the same time intuition and emotion.[15]

Our second conclusion concerns the relation of poetic knowledge to other kinds of knowledge by connaturality.

Leaving aside the knowledge by tendential or affective connaturality with the ends of human action, which is at the heart of *prudential* knowledge, we will distinguish three other kinds of knowledge by connaturality:

(1) A knowledge by intellectual connaturality with reality as *conceptualizable* and rendered proportionate in act to the human intellect. It goes along with the development of the *habitus* of the intelligence; and it is from this knowledge that comes the *intuition*—intellectual and expressible in a mental work—of the philosopher, the scientist, of him who knows by mode of knowledge.

(2) A knowledge by either intellectual or affective connaturality with reality as *non-conceptualizable* and at the same time *contemplated,* in other words as non-objectifiable in notions and yet as a terminus of objective union. This is the knowledge of *contemplation:* whether it is a matter of a natural contemplation attaining, if that be possible, a transcendant reality inexpressible in itself in a human mental word, by means of a supra- or para-conceptual intellection; or of a supernatural contemplation attaining as object the divine reality inexpressible in itself in any created word, by means of the union of love (*amor transit in conditionem objecti*) and by a resonance in the subject, becomes a means of knowing.

(3) A knowledge by *affective* connaturality with reality as *non-conceptualizable* because *awakening to themselves the creative depths of the subject*—I mean by connaturality with reality according as reality comes to be buried in subjectivity itself in its quality of intellectually productive existence, and according as it is attained in its concrete and existential consonance with the subject *as subject.* This is *poetic* knowledge: radically factive or operative, since, being inseparable from the productivity of the spirit (owing to the fact that the connaturality which awakens it actuates the subject as subject,

or as center of productive vitality and spiritual emanation), and being unable nevertheless to issue in a concept *ad intra,* it can only issue in a work *ad extra.*[16]

It seems likely that in the case of all those who have great intuitive gifts there is an element of poetic knowledge, in the sense that it underlies philosophic and scientific intuition and works together with it, and that by a kind of inevitable psychological resonance it also accompanies, be it only virtually, the natural and supernatural contemplation of which it is an analogue. But it is essentially distinct from the one and the other.

Being a knowledge by affective connaturality, the knowledge of supernatural contemplation itself awakens in the soul the poetic instinct, though it be an entirely rudimentary and virtual manner. That is why it is natural to the mystical experience to be expressed lyrically. But insofar as it is expressed, and wells up in song, it is that the mystical experience itself—when the contemplative is also a poet—has provoked in the depths of the subjectivity a present poetic knowledge of the realities mystically experienced; or it may be also that by virtue of the superabundance of a perfect actuation it pours out gratuitously, without the least operative tension, in words which can be richer in poetry than the work of a poet, and which all the same, in the case in question, come not from a poetic knowledge, but from the excess of a higher experience.

It is also to be remarked that poetic knowledge, like the knowledge of contemplation (when it expresses itself), employs similitudes and symbols—in order to *seduce the reason,* as St. Thomas says; [17] precisely because both of these kinds of knowledge have to do, in different ways, with the nonconceptualizable.

But what we should like above all to remember is that being in itself radically operative, oriented toward the creation of a work, poetic knowledge does not liberate itself *in the mode of knowledge* except in turning back upon itself in a reflexive consciousness in which it is detached in a way (in a purely virtual way when everything remains normal) from its natural finalities. It does not reveal itself thus to itself as knowledge and as appetite for knowledge without running the risk in some measure of "perversion," or misdirection, of which we have spoken. And if this misdirection occurs, if this separation from its natural ends takes place really and effectively, poetic knowledge engenders an endless voracity to know—endless because resulting from turning aside from the natural ends.

And being unable to end either in a *work* (which it renounces and from which it turns away), or in a *speculative conceptualization* (which is repugnant to it and for which it has not the means), it involves the spirit in a tragedy, strangely instructive and fecund in discoveries, but, in itself, monstrous.

In short, poetry *is* knowledge, incomparably: knowledge-experience and knowledge-emotion, existential knowledge, knowledge which is the germ of a work (and which does not know itself, and which is not *for* knowing). To make of it a *means of knowledge*, an instrument of knowledge, to take it out of its proper mode of being in order to procure that which it is, is to pervert it. In this sense it is a sin for the poet to eat of the fruit of the tree of knowledge. Let us add concerning the poets who have suffered most from this evil that their work, insofar as they have created works, is a victory over it, and all the more precious.

The third and last conclusion concerns the law of *transgression* of which we spoke a moment ago, and according to which all energies of a transcendental order aspire, inefficaciously, to go beyond the nature enclosed in a genus which they have in man, in order to follow the inclination of their transcendentality, and ultimately, tend toward pure act and infinitization.

Taken as transcendental and in its analogical polyvalence, a perfection of the transcendental order is not an essence, a specific nature; it is found in an essentially varied manner in a series of distinct specific essences. If here or there it follows the aspiration of its transcendentality taken as such, it aspires to go beyond these natures, it aspires in an inefficacious manner to pass beyond, to become in a certain way what it is in the pure Act.[18]

An energy of transcendental order like that of metaphysics aspires in this way to the vision of God; an energy like that of mystical contemplation aspires to the divine liberty. It is only at the moment of becoming conscious of itself, when it discovers itself reflexively, that poetry also discovers such an aspiration within itself. This may tend toward pure creation (to create as God creates, that is the torment of certain great artists, who in the end, by force of wishing to be purely creators, and to owe nothing to the vision of the beings which God has had the indiscretion to make in front of them, have no other resource than that of artistically forcing and ravaging their art); or, on the contrary, if poetry detaches itself from its operative ends in the way we indicated a moment ago, if in becoming conscious of itself it takes a wrong direction, this aspiration will tend toward a kind of divine intuition or divine experience of the world and the soul, known as God knows them, from within, and within the essence of their

Poet. And this will be the more violent in proportion as the poetic experience has been truly and really detached from its natural finalities.

NOTES

1. *Frontières de la poésie,* 3rd ed., p. 28 (*Art and Poetry* [New York: Philosophical Library]).
2. There are some *speculative* arts, like logic. As such, they remain purely intellectual, and the will has nothing to do with them, unless with the exercising of them. This is a limiting case in which the notion of art is retained, and even carried to an extreme of purity, because there is a *factibile* here, but one which remains purely intellectual and interior to the spirit. Note that one can speak of the poetry of logic as of that of mathematics, insofar as logic is an object that one contemplates; but at the heart of logic itself poetry and poetic knowledge have no place. If logic is an example of the purest art, it is seen how poetry in its pure state, which will be treated below, and art in its pure state can find themselves in diametrical opposition.
3. Cf. Arthur Lourié, *"De la Mélodie," La Vie Intellectuelle,* December 25, 1936.
4. On the profoundest, most hidden level, it is to poetic knowledge itself that the Aristotelian notion of imitation must be related. Cf. below, pp. 246–7.
5. Cf. *Frontières de la poésie,* p. 197.
6. Jean Cocteau, *Les Chevaliers de la table ronde.*
7. Letter to Paul Demeny (*"Lettre du voyant"*), May 15, 1871, first published by Paterne Berrichon in *La Nouvelle Revue Française,* October 1912.
8. Cf. Benjamin Fondane, *Rimbaud le voyou.*
9. Letter to Paul Demeny (*"Lettre du voyant"*), cited above.
10. Raïssa Maritain, "Sense and Non-Sense in Poetry," *The Situation of Poetry,* p. 11.
11. Ibid., pp. 9, 26.
12. *Frontières de la poésie,* pp. 199–200.
13. Arthur Lourié, op. cit.
14. To eliminate all confusion, let it be noted that it is of *poetic knowledge* precisely understood, not of the *artistic habitus* that we are speaking here. The habitus of art produces its fruit in the practical *judgment* on the work to be made; poetic knowledge, in the *work done.*
15. If in their theory of the artistic idea the old schoolmen seem

to have neglected this character—essential to the human creative intuition—of enveloping a knowledge by emotion and by affective connaturality, it is that they considered art and the creative activity above all as theologians, and concerned themselves with the analogical values according to which the activity of art is proper to God as well as to the human creature.

16. The distinction of these two different modes (nos. 2 and 3) of transcending conceptualization can be regarded as a free gloss of the following texts of Saint Thomas. "*Poetica scientia est de his quae propter defectum veritatis non possunt a ratione capi; unde oportet quod quasi quibusdam similitudinibus ratio seducatur; theologia autem est de his quae sunt supra rationem; et ideo modus symbolicus utrique communis est, cum neutra rationi proportionetur.*" (I Sent., prol., q. 1, a. 5, ad 3.) "*Sicut poetica non capiuntur in ratione humana, propter defectum veritatis quae est in eis; ita etiam ratio humana perfecte capere non potest divina, propter excedentem ipsorum veritatem. Ed ideo utrobique opus est repraesentatione per sensibiles figuras.*" (Sum. Theol., I–II, 101, 2, ad 2.)

17. See I *Sent.*, prol., q. 1, a. 5, ad 3 (text cited in the previous note); and *In Johan.*, cap. 7, lect. 2.

18. St. Thomas (*Sum. Theol.*, I, 63, 3) explains that a thing constituted with a given nature (with a given nature enclosed in a species and a genus) cannot aspire to a superior specific nature, "*sicut asinus non appetit esse equus: quia, si transferretur in gradum superioris naturae, jam ipsum non esset.*" But precisely the perfections of the transcendental order, not being enclosed in a species and a genus, do not lose their being when they pass from what they are in an inferior species to what they are in a superior species; on the contrary, they approach their "maximum" of being. That is why it is possible that in a given nature an energy of the transcendental order aspires in an inefficacious manner to pass in some way into what it is in a superior nature, and especially in the *Ipsum esse subsistens*.

SOME NOTES CONCERNING THE AESTHETIC AND THE COGNITIVE *

Henry David Aiken

There are, I suppose, times when all of us are so afflicted with what Mr. Passmore has called "the dreariness of aesthetics" that we yearn to pull down the disgusting old house on Queer Street by main force and start over again, cleanly and freely, to construct a scheme sufficiently commodious to accommodate our talk about the arts. To be forever faced with the foolish little paradoxes and the imponderable little questions which traditional aesthetics has foisted upon us is a dispiriting prospect, and no one could reasonably be charged with impiety if, in desperation, he simply consigned the categories of aesthetics to limbo. Yet, at bottom, dreariness is always due to some form of poverty. It is worth asking, therefore, whether our troubles are due so much to the concepts of aesthetics themselves as to our inability, or unwillingness, to relate them directly to our actual encounters with works of art rather than to the a priori categories of some misbegotten theory of knowledge or meaning. My impression is that if we do not lay upon them too heavy a burden of philosophical preconception, the concepts of aesthetics may be rendered sufficiently serviceable for our purposes.

It was in this spirit that I made some suggestions, a few years ago, concerning the aesthetic relevance of belief.[1] I was aware that some would think my use of the term "aesthetic" unduly broad, and that some would also cavil at my attempt to formulate a generic idea underlying the term "belief" which would apply not only to beliefs that are expressed in words but also to pre-linguistic forms of expectation, anticipation, and commitment. My justification was that the ordinary use of the word "aesthetic" already permits the range of application I proposed for it, and that although the ordinary use of the word "belief" may not be so broad as my interpretation would suggest, the analogy between verbally expressed beliefs and non-verbal anticipatory sets is so close and so illuminating that no great harm would be done by my extension of its range of application. At all events, my aim was to direct attention as forcibly as I could

* [From *The Journal of Aesthetics and Art Criticism*, Vol. XIII, No. 3 (March 1955). Reprinted by permission of the author and *The Journal of Aesthetics and Art Criticism*.]

to levels of intrinsic significance in the arts which, as I thought, had been unduly neglected by most of my contemporaries. If I could do this, then it didn't much matter whether I had slightly stretched the use of a pair of terms whose normal ranges of application are wide and flexible enough to suggest and perhaps even to encourage what might be the still wider use I had for them.

I am still prepared to defend, whether in these or in other terms, the essential theses of my earlier essay. If nothing more, they provide a wholesome antidote to the unduly heavy doses of sensationalism, emotivism, and misapplied semantics that we have recently been asked to swallow. Yet one's perspectives change, and I now find it more convenient to state my case in a somewhat different way which does not expose me to the charge of manhandling the term "belief." I now see, moreover, the desirability of placing the problem in a somewhat wider context which includes the whole issue of the aesthetic relevance of the cognitive in a sense of the latter term which encompasses but is not restricted to belief. The relevance of belief, in any important sense, cannot be successfully defended unless the distinctively cognitive meanings of symbols have already been granted aesthetic relevance. For if the more general thesis is disallowed from the outset, then the more limited one becomes automatically untenable.

My earlier essay was mainly positive in its intent; it contained only a very schematic and limited rebuttal of my opponents' views. Strategically this left me somewhat vulnerable to the inevitable charge of question-begging—not that this bothered me too much, since every discourse must beg some question or it can never make a beginnning. Yet something more can be done to discomfit the opposition. On this occasion, therefore, it will be desirable to consider in some detail several important types of argument which have been proposed against the aesthetic relevance of cognitive meanings and beliefs. My more positive ideas will here be allowed to emerge contextually.

2

The first case against the aesthetic relevance of cognition derives from a doctrine which I shall call "aesthetic sensationalism." Its vogue, although still considerable, has perhaps passed its zenith. We will find, however, that in one form or another it underlies other positions that initially appear to approach the topic with different models in view.

It is the contention of aesthetic sensationalism that the aesthetic irrelevance of the cognitive follows analytically from the very meanings of the terms involved. The "aesthetic," so it is said, refers exclusively to sensuous presentations immediately "given" in experience and to the mode of awareness required for the apprehension of such presentations. Cognition, on the other hand, is taken to involve by definition the mediation of symbols. It is not a form of immediate awareness, but rather a mediated "taking-account" involving a symbolic discursus in which attention is directed away from the sensuous surface of the sign design to some ulterior "object" signified by the latter.

There is little or no justification for so narrow an interpretation of the aesthetic. The etymology of the term, which proves nothing in any case, suggests perceiving as well as sensing. But since the beginning of its modern use, even this more extended sense of the term has never been consistently adhered to. It was construed by the father of our sorrows, Baumgarten, to refer to something called "sensuous knowledge" and not to sensing merely as such. It was also closely associated by him and his successors with the concepts of the beautiful and the artistic. Even Kant, who in the first *Critique* used it to refer to sense perception, employed it later in the third *Critique* to refer to judgments of the beautiful in art and in nature. Hegel used it somewhat more narrowly than Kant to refer to the beautiful in art alone, and for better or worse, his usage has frequently prevailed in subsequent discourses on art. Gradually the term has come into more general use, and if Webster is to be trusted, it is now normally taken to refer primarily to any appreciation of the beautiful in nature or in art, with no qualification that this must be restricted to sensuous presentations.

It is not hard to see why the general usage of the term should have taken this course. As a synonym for "sensation" or "perception" the word would be redundant. As such its currency would be difficult to explain, since if what we wish to talk about is sensation, perception, pleasure, or attention (the words which analysts most commonly identify with the aesthetic), other simpler and clearer expressions are already at our disposal. What *was* wanted is a term that could be used in a general way to refer to appreciations of beauty of all types and on all levels of experience.

In this connection it is worth noting that through its associations with the beautiful and the artistic the word "aesthetic" has acquired, in certain contexts, a somewhat laudatory or honorific meaning which could not easily be accounted for had its etymological sense remained dominant. It stands, indeed, to the admired and to the enjoyed in a relation not unlike that in which the desirable stands to the desired and the preferable to the preferred. Hence the effect of laying down "definitions" equating it with "sensuous surface" or with what C. I. Lewis so masterfully calls "the primordial empirical given" is not so much to stake out an area for investigation as to redirect our attitudes of admiration and our judgments of artistic praise and blame to the sensuous features of works of art. Such a definition does not so much provide a clue to the meaning of "the aesthetic" as it tacitly lays down a critical standard of artistic relevance which undermines our interest in and admiration for the representational and intellectual features of works of art. The more widely it is accepted, the more paradoxical become such phrases as "intellectual beauty" and "moral beauty," and the more questionable become those persistent and apparently inescapable forms of artistic commendation which praise works of art, on occasion, in terms of their "credibility" or "sense of reality."

These paradoxes and questions are morally and critically important precisely because they lay open to the charge of vulgarity, philistinism, and confusion of values anyone whose praise of a work of art is in any way justified by reference to its conceptual or representational meanings or to the beliefs, implicit or explicit, to which it exposes us. Theoretically, however, the doctrine is interesting only as a piece of persuasive definition. It does not begin to provide a unifying concept in terms of which we may adequately characterize the full range of what we admire in contemplating works of art. On the contrary, it violates a sound and serviceable usage, while at the same time leaving isolated those intrinsic values of art whose expression and appreciation involve the conceptual powers that are the product of the learning process. It creates, in short, a tension between criticism and appreciation which is as harmful to the authority of the one as it is to the satisfactions of the other.

3

The second case against the aesthetic relevance of the cognitive derives from a doctrine which I shall call "aesthetic perceptualism." According to it, the aesthetic is to be conceived as the "self-motivated and self-gratifying exercise of perception." Now since perception, in the ordinary sense, is obviously a form of cognition entailing, through the mediation of natural signs, the apprehension of things not "given" in sensation, it might be thought that perceptualism automatically allows for the aesthetic relevance of cognition on at least one level. Moreover, since, as Russell and others have frequently remarked, perceptions normally embody pre-verbal beliefs or acceptances, it might be supposed that perceptualism also grants the aesthetic relevance of belief. And so indeed it would be if perceptualisms always meant what they say. Unfortunately the doctrine has been afflicted with tenacious ambiguities in its usual formulations which have appeared to entail precisely the opposite conclusion. It is these ambiguities which I wish to expose in this portion of the paper.

As commonly stated the perceptualist theory runs something like this: Only that which is immediately perceived may be granted aesthetic relevance; but the "objects" apprehended in cognition are not so perceived; by definition cognition involves a conceptual discursus which directs attention away from the symbol which is immediately apprehended to an object which is not; hence cognition, and the sign processes involved in cognition, are aesthetically irrelevant. Here is a tissue of confusions and equivocations. Some of them I will reserve for comment in later portions of the paper; for the present I wish to direct attention to the slippery phrases "immediately perceive," "immediately apprehend," and "given."

Now it is plain that perceptualism has been formulated with a certain critical animus in view. It is a good animus which is widely shared by critics and lovers of the arts who neither know nor care about aesthetics. Speaking for this group, the perceptualist insists upon the irrelevance of every idea, every belief, every association, and every feeling which distract us from the work of art itself or which reduce our sensitivity to its inherent values. Everyone has been bemused by sentimental associations when listening to music. Such associations, however agreeable in themselves, divert our attention from the music and thereby jeopardize our enjoyment and appreciation of *it*. They are, therefore, aesthetically irrelevant to the quality and to the value of the music. Everyone has also been victimized by the pride of learning which interferes with the authority of the lines of a poem as we read them. Since man is the curious animal, contextual information has an interest, quite apart from any power it may have to illuminate the beauty of a poem. But unless it can be funded back by the re-creative imagination into our awareness of the poem itself, it is, at the least, aesthetically irrelevant to its artistic quality and value. Every lover of truth has at times been the victim of what fallacy-mongers might call "the fallacy of misplaced veracity." On such occasions we are so busy asserting ourselves and so diligent in the raising of wrongheaded questions that we never give the winged horse a chance to get off the ground. Who really cares whether there is or could be such an incredible creature as Little Aggie or Prince Mishkin? The fiction's the thing; and to this questions of truth-value are irrelevant.

All this the perceptualist recognizes; and he seeks to express his profoundly important insight by the dark saying that anything aesthetic must be immediately perceived, and that what is not so perceived is aesthetically irrelevant to our experience of any object. But unhappily the saying misleads him. For consider: the only significant thing which the qualifying adjective "immediate" adds to the noun "perception," in its aesthetic employment, is the condition that in relation to any aesthetic object, relevant perception must remain close to its primary structure and texture, and this for the reason that when we depart from them the power of the object to move and to please eludes us. Here, in short, the qualifying adjective "immediate" has simply the force of "close." This is certainly a decent and permissible use of the term which, as Webster tells us, means, in its primary sense, "near rather than far; not distant or separated in time or space." Unfortunately it has been frequently confused with another and very different sense of "immediate" which, whatever its importance for the theory of knowledge, is simply obfuscating when transferred to aesthetics. In this sense "immediate" means "not mediated." In this sense, of course, no ordinary perceptions are immediate; in this sense no response involving the mediation of signs, whether natural or conventional, could be regarded as immediate. A perception that involved no element of learning and hence no element of symbolic mediation would be, at best, only a form of sensation. Such perceptions we call "sense perceptions"; we do not call them "immediate perceptions." When we perceive any object or any likeness of any object whatever, however immediate to our aesthetic concerns such a perception may be, what we are aware of or taking account of in the perceptual act is never just an unmediated sense-datum, sense-impression, or image. What it is can at best only be made out in terms of the mediating references of the sense-impressions involved. In this second sense of the term, therefore, the thesis that nothing is aesthetically relevant save what is "immediately perceived" reduces at once to the doctrine of aesthetic sensationalism which we already have considered.

The fundamental source of the equivocation which I have tried to expose is to be found in those theories of knowledge and meaning which, in their search for something which, as they say, is incorrigibly, unassailably "given," i.e., something that may function as unimpugnable evidence for the truth or probability of factual statements, have unwittingly vacillated between the two senses in which any "perceivable" might be said to be immediate. Such theories of knowledge, wishing to apply the ritual of Cartesian doubt to all beliefs for which the evidence is indirect, have taken this to mean that no act of awareness involving "interpretation" or the "mediation of signs" could possibly count as direct or immediate evidence in any sense. Certainly this is mistaken. All compact with this error is the corresponding failure to distinguish between something which may be said to be "given" in experience in the sense of "unquestionable" or "indubitable" and that which is "given" in the sense of "assumed" or "taken for granted." But plainly many things that are "given" in the second sense are not given in the first, and vice versa.

Transferred to the domain of aesthetics, these confusions and equivocations have played havoc. It is often maintained, and I do not wish at this point to place it in question, that the aesthetic interest, as distinct from the interest in knowledge or truth, is an unquestioning attitude which takes for granted, in contemplative fashion, much that the scientist or the philosopher would find problematic or doubtful. In the contemplative mood, all questions are, for the nonce, put aside; probabilities are no longer weighed, nor truths defended and errors exposed. In the scientific or philosophic frame of mind, on the other hand, the reverse is true. But what does this imply to our present purpose? Does it matter that the "givens" which concern us aesthetically must have run the gamut of Cartesian doubt, or, to vary the figure, be run through the wringer of disinterpretation? Not at all. We need not thus demean what we perceive (or understand) in contemplating a work of art in order to exclude the questionable irrelevances which, if allowed their head, would destroy our contemplative poise.

I take it, then, that there is no reason of much deeper significance than the possibility of punning on the word "immediate" to inhibit the perceptualist from acknowledging, at the perceptual level, the aesthetic relevance of the non-immediacies of cognition or even of belief. The importance, for critical theory, of acknowledging a dividing line between those aesthetic immediacies which are relevant to appreciation of a work of art and the vagrant associations of idea and feeling which are not can be made out without forcing us back upon the self-denying ordinances of the sensuous-surface theory. The fact that the "objects" contemplated in works of art are not, nor are ever regarded as, the appearances of material objects is nothing to the point. So far as my present point is concerned, it is enough that the representational forms of painting are perceived to be such that they are apprehended directly and intuitively as discernible object-likenesses and not merely as the sensuous surfaces of material entities in the external world.

Perceptualistic aesthetics can have no serious quarrel with the thesis concerning the aesthetic relevance of the cognitive so long as this is not misunderstood. Even so, it is inadequate to its theme. For as we direct attention toward levels of significance which lie beneath the surface of perception, we move away from the sorts of experience that can be adequately discussed in the terms we employ in speaking of perceiving objects. Perceptualism fails most miserably when it tries to accommodate itself to works of art whose primary medium is the conventional symbolism of language. It compels us to misconceive the aesthetic roles of linguistic signs by forcing us to regard their meanings as perceptual images, which they are not. If we accept perceptualism we are then impelled to treat every metaphor as a virtual image and every poetic description as nothing but a stimulus to a series of imaginal likenesses of ordinary perceptual objects. It is, however, as clear as can be that our interest in poetry, even of the metaphorical, figurative, and descriptive sorts is not directed to the perceptual images we may happen to form as we read. Nor do our appreciations of such poetry depend upon our power to form such images. What *is* required for just appreciation is that we *understand* the metaphor or the description, that, in short, its conceptual meaning be not entirely opaque to us. Granted such understanding and the powers of conception which it presupposes, we can fully enjoy a descriptive poem though not a single perceptual image has crossed our minds. In many instances, indeed, the power of a great metaphor or a great descriptive passage is actually broken when we try to form images of what is meant. What some writers call pictorial meaning is largely irrelevant to the poetic imagination.

It must be acknowledged, then, that a perceptualistic aesthetics, even at its best, is incapable of adequately dealing with all of the levels of significance in art which are of intrinsic value to us. At its worst it is fraught with serious ambiguities and equivocations. In this form it is hardly distinguishable from the sensuous-surface theory. But no matter how we regard it, it provides a model for the interpretation of aesthetically relevant meanings in art which often results in an egregious misunderstanding of their more serious artistic uses. The ordinary meanings of words are the foundations of any appreciation of their aesthetic employment. Understanding of them is not all that is required for the appreciation of poetry; but it is its *sine qua non*.

4

Throughout the preceding discussion, there has been lurking, barely beneath the surface, another conception of the aesthetic which seems to challenge the aesthetic relevance of the cognitive dimensions of art. When we look closely we usually find that behind theories of the sort hitherto considered lies a preconception concerning a certain kind of attitude which is supposedly involved in aesthetic appreciation.

The sensationalist, for example, usually can be made to admit that the aesthetic is identical, not with the sensuous as such, but rather with the sensuous conceived as an object of intrinsic interest. This assumption that the aesthetic is, or involves, a form of interest is even more apparent in the case of perceptualism. For present purposes, however, it is necessary to disengage the notion of the "aesthetic attitude" from any prior commitments concerning the nature of its "object." Let us, rather, consider what this notion commits us to when regarded simply as that disposition or complex of dispositions which are involved in our appreciations of beauty in art and in nature. We may then inquire whether such an attitude can accommodate itself to the cognitive features of art or whether, as some contend, it can only be directed to the sensuous or perceptual features of the things we call beautiful.

Now the usual descriptions of the "aesthetic attitude" characterize it as a mode of response which is, above all, contemplative. It is thought to be indifferent to the ulterior practical import of experience or to *questions* concerning the ontological status of the aesthetic object, its correspondence to external reality, or, in case the object is symbolic, its truth. In this way it is contrasted with practical or problem-solving attitudes of all sorts and hence with so-called cognitive attitudes so far as these are practical.

Approaching cognition from a primarily pragmatic standpoint, most proponents of this view conceive the cognitive attitude to be characteristically one of "inquiry" in which items of experience are taken as "problems" for solution. When we are possessed by this attitude, our energies are said to be drawn away from the ongoing course of experience toward its eventual issue or "meaning." In the case of symbolic activity, our attention is diverted away from the symbol, as something seen or heard, to its ulterior "object."

The aesthetic attitude is thus held to be concerned, not with the intelligible meanings of signs, which lies ahead in the future, but only with their immediate qualities and effects as items of experience. The implication usually drawn from this is that the only "meanings" which are aesthetically available are of the immediately experienced pictorial and emotive sort. On the other hand, the cognitive attitude is held to have no interest in these meanings at all; it is concerned exclusively with the referential meanings of signs, and with the truth or falsity of those concatenations of signs which we call statements. In a word the aesthetic attitude is thought to be threatened by precisely those meanings and uses of signs which alone interest those who are governed by a cognitive attitude, whereas the cognitive attitude in its turn is threatened the moment we attend to the aesthetically interesting images and feelings which are thrown off in the wake of references, predictions, and verifications.

This contrast between the "aesthetic attitude" and the "cognitive attitude" has been accompanied by parallel, or supposedly parallel, distinctions between the "aesthetic functions of signs" and the "cognitive functions of signs" and between "aesthetic meanings" and "cognitive meanings."

Here, it must be confessed, is a whole nest of problems which would have to be disentangled before we could adequately appraise the view that the aesthetic and cognitive occupy opposite poles of human experience. In any full treatment, we would have to ask whether the phrase "cognitive attitude" is best taken as referring to one sort of attitude or, rather, as I believe, a family of related attitudes, whether the cognitive process must be thought of as directed to the as yet unfulfilled solution of a problem, and whether aesthetic standards are never relevant to the criteria of adequacy which it proposes for the solution of its own problems. We would have to ask, also, whether aesthetic attitudes are best conceived in contrast to attitudes of the problem-solving sort, or whether in certain cases, and approached in a certain way, even a problem might be thought to have for us its own distinctive aesthetic use or aspect. Indeed, we would have to ask whether the aesthetic dimension is well conceived as an attitude at all, or whether it might be preferable to approach it in another way that regards it, not as a special form of interest, like the interest in apples, politics, or knowledge, but as a phase into which any interest may enter under certain conditions or when it reaches a certain point of equilibrium and assurance. Finally, and with particular relevance to our present theme, we would have to ask whether the distinctions which have been drawn between the "aesthetic use of signs" and the "cognitive use of signs" and between "aesthetic meaning" and "cognitive meaning" have been well drawn, or whether they may have been subject to certain fundamental confusions which make their employment at once questionable in itself and obfuscating with respect to the question of the aesthetic relevance of the cognitive. It will be impossible here, of course, to discuss all of these issues adequately. The most that I can hope to accomplish will be to indicate what seems to me the more reasonable view toward a few of them.

Let me first explain why I find the contrast between the so-called aesthetic attitude and the cognitive or moral attitude unilluminating and misleading. Much of the trouble lies in the word "contemplation" which is nearly always associated directly with notion of the "aesthetic attitude." Now in its primary sense "contemplation" connotes an act of continuous attention. In this sense, it is quite compatible with, and on occasion even suggests, expectancy. What it does not, in this sense, entail is the notion of passivity, mere receptivity, or indifference to eventualities. Only in a secondary sense, which tends to be confused with the other, does it convey a condition of ruminative, meditative, bemused inward withdrawal from action or practical involvement. In its primary sense the notion of contemplation fairly characterizes a distinctive aspect of the aesthetic experience. Indeed, one of the main hallmarks of the aesthetic is absorbed and continuous attention to the object. But in its secondary sense the notion of contemplation does not convey what is intended when we speak of aesthetic appreciation. Quite the contrary. It is through an equivocation between these senses of the term, that we are mistakenly led to suppose that because aesthetic appreciation involves attention to the aesthetic object it also therefore involves a passive indifference to its significance or meaning.

Consider certain other characterizations of the aesthetic which, although certainly inadequate if taken as definitive, nevertheless do truly describe some of its aspects. Many writers have stressed the empathic and projective character of our responses to works of art, and although I should not wish to maintain that all aesthetic responses are empathic and projective, at least some of them plainly are so. But to the extent that this is so, it follows that the aesthetic is a form of internal activity, and not a passive, unengaged rumination or meditation. Many aestheticians and critics have also emphasized the important role of the imagination in our responses to works of art. In so doing, they are evidently calling attention to the genuinely constructive and interpretive character of our responses to works of art.

Now I am not in the least suggesting here that works of art are wholly to be understood as symbolic forms. Such a view neglects the genuine relevance to our appreciation of the sensuous textures of art. Yet when such a writer as Kenneth Burke speaks of a poem as a "symbolic action" he is, I think, forcibly calling attention to something which is fundamental to it. And any aesthetics which defines the "aesthetic attitude" in such a way as to render this fact otiose is so far simply mistaken.

All this being so, it is evident why it is so misleading to distinguish between the aesthetic and the cognitive attitudes on the ground that the one is "contemplative" whereas the other is "active" or on the ground that the one merely acquiesces in experience whereas the other is urgent and problematic. Not all aesthetic experience is active or urgent. The real, if fugitive, satisfaction one may take in the smell of perfume is an elementary form of aesthetic appreciation. Yet the response to great art is very different from this. Nothing is more gravid with anticipation and foreboding than the rising action of *Oedipus Rex;* nothing is more sickeningly problematic than the opening pages of *Crime and Punishment.* If, from a misguided desire to maintain our contemplative poise, we insist on remaining unimplicated in or detached from Raskolnikov's hideous predicament, we will simply miss the point of the symbolic action which transpires before us. Not every work of art demands such an involvement. Some so much as ask us to keep our distance. But if we approach Dostoyevsky or Kafka or Henry James in a merely "contemplative mood," on the mistaken assumption that such a mood is required for aesthetic appreciation and enjoyment, we will not find what is there; indeed the whole business will then appear to us, as for some unlucky persons it always does, faintly ridiculous.

The aesthetic, like so many other things, is best known by its enemies. These are not conception and concern, but boredom, indifference, worry, confusion, and, past a certain point, pain. The concept of the aesthetic attitude, if it is to be usefully employed, must not be regarded as occupying an opposite pole from the cognitive or from the moral. In certain circumstances, any human faculty may be engaged in an aesthetic response, just as, under other conditions, any faculty whose exercise is pressed beyond a certain point may threaten it. In my view, the best model for conceiving the aesthetic response is not that of a mood at all, but rather the psychological concept of the consummatory response pattern. So conceived, the whole series of contrasts between the aesthetic and the cognitive or between the aesthetic and the moral become gratuitous. On the contrary, they merely stand in the way of our theoretical grasp of the variability and complexity of which art appreciation and *therefore* the aesthetic experience is capable.

5

We may now consider the alleged incompatibility between so-called "cognitive meaning" and "aesthetic meaning." These phrases have no clear or well-established uses in ordinary discourse; they belong at best to the semitechnical jargon of contemporary analytical philosophy and aesthetic theory. Their respective ranges of application are thus somewhat indeterminate and may be expected to vary from author to author and from school to school.

In the case of cognitive meaning one thing at least seems sufficiently evident: whatever it may otherwise exclude as "non-cognitive," its scope cannot be restricted to words that name or to statements that actually describe or predict matters of fact. False statements are still cognitive, and suppositions contrary to fact are still intelligible. A term does not lose caste as a cognitive sign simply because, as it turns out, there is nothing to which it may refer; nor does a statement lose cognitive status because what it purports to describe or predict happens not to be the case. There is no good reason why we should assume, therefore, that in responding to the cognitive meaning of a sign complex we are thereby necessarily attending to some ulterior state of affairs or object which, because it is not now present to the senses, destroys the immediacy essential to aesthetic contemplation. Nor does the lifting of attention beyond the qualitative character of a sign-design that is involved in any act of conceptualization necessitate the conclusion that we are thereby rendered indifferent to what is going on in experience or that we are distracted by a preoccupation with what is transpiring in the "real world." The presence of cognitive meaning does not cause us to ignore our ongoing experience, but, rather to view it in another way, to add to it another dimension of interest and significance. Cognitive meaning requires understanding or thought; but it does not require the postulation of an "object of thought," attention to which diverts us away from the aesthetic immediacies of the art object. If the scientist may be reasonably supposed to mean something and to understand what he means even when his theories turn out to be false, the lover of art may gratefully avail himself of the same intellectual apparatus without being supposed to be elsewhere occupied. He is not called upon to renounce certain "objects," in the interest of aesthetic immediacy, which not the veriest tyro of science could make his own. The difference between the lover of art and the scientist in this respect is patently a difference in range of interest and not necessarily a difference in the ways in which they take a given form of words to mean. The scientist loses interest in a statement, as a rule, when he cannot confirm it; confirmation is not the concern of the lover of art, and his interest is not immediately affected by questions concerning the confirmability of statements. But this difference in interest does not necessarily affect the meanings which they respectively attach to a certain form of words. True, the reader of poetry is concerned not merely with the core cognitive content of a statement but also with its associations and emotional significance. This implies, however, that his interest encompasses a wider range of meanings than that of the scientist, and not a completely different range of meaning. He does not ignore what the scientist understands or apprehends; he regards it, rather, in a different light, with respect to which different criteria of relevance and adequacy obtain. There is no reason to suppose that reading with understanding entails preoccupation with *problems* of verification or validation; such admissions as are called for in this direction require only that when we read a poem we may be supposed, not irrelevantly, to read it as intelligently as the occasion requires, or that when we look at a picture we may, without fatuity, be thought to acknowledge the presence of whatever representational forms it may contain.

Troubles begin to afflict us when we pass unwittingly back and forth between "cognitive meaning" or "descriptive meaning" and something else referred to by such locutions as the "cognitive attitude" and the "cognitive use" of signs, without fully realizing that we are pairing or identifying concepts of very different sorts. "Cognitive attitudes," I take it, are primarily interests of the problem-solving variety; under their suasion we ask questions, pose problems, raise issues, perform experiments, and verify hypotheses. They are the attitudes that may be supposed most characteristically to govern the scientist in his laboratory or the mathematician at his blackboard. In their initial phases, at least, such attitudes connote perplexity, puzzlement, and effort. But in whatever terms we may choose to describe them, there is no justification for identifying or pairing them exclusively with a certain mode of meaning which could conceivably mediate no other type of interest. The meanings of signs, as such, are normally fixed by usages which are usually well ingrained in us before we consider the possibility of their variable uses, before, indeed, we become aware of their suitability to the uses which they are characteristically made to serve. It is true, of course, that persistent or conventional uses do normally attend a prevailing usage so that when a symbol is made to serve purposes that conflict with its more normal use, it may be said on occasion to be misused. It is equally true, however, that we also learn by degrees to divert symbols to other characteristic uses without thereby altering the usage which determines what they mean.

The characteristic uses of signs are to be understood as functions of the goals or purposes with respect to which they are instituted. They are not and need not be thought to be mutually exclusive; rather do they demarcate frequently overlapping spheres of interest which the same sign complex may happen to serve. It is simply a mistake to suppose that the uses of signs, any more than the purposes which govern them, must always march in single file. A sign that is used successfully for the sake of contemplation may also serve to convey information of some importance to the conduct of life; and if it does happen to do so there is no reason for supposing that its integrity as an artistic phenomenon is thereby violated.

There are innumerable reasons for enforcing a distinction

between the personal uses and the conventional meanings of signs. One such reason may be discerned in the fact that although their interests are different, the same system of usages governs the discourse of artists, scientists, politicians, and ordinary men of affairs. If the meanings of signs were wedded indissolubly to their uses, each different use of language would require, in effect, a different language, or at any rate a different system of usages. Some such idea, in fact, seems to underlie the once widely held view that within ordinary language there are actually a number of distinctive and independent vocabularies and idioms, including a factual or scientific vocabulary, a literary or poetic vocabulary, and an ethico-religious vocabulary. This arthritic doctrine, I take it, has fortunately been abandoned even though some of its pernicious aftereffects are still in evidence. No one any longer seriously pretends that certain words, as such, are characteristically poetic, and others not. There is no such thing as an intrinsically poetic word any more than there is an intrinsically poetic subject-matter. Any word and any sentence may function poetically in the proper context, and any word, however overworked by literary men, may still retain a modicum of sense. There is no list of poetic words or usages, and none of scientific or of ethical terms. There is, rather, a common vocabulary and a common fund of usages upon which the poet, the scientist, or the man of affairs may draw at will to serve his own distinctive interests.

Another consideration which supports our distinction is the fact that signs may have meanings for us, on occasion, in the absence of any deliberate use at all. It happens, not infrequently, that like Robinson Crusoe, we simply stumble upon a form of words and find ourselves construing it willy-nilly with no thought to the use intended by its producer or to the use it might subsequently have for ourselves. In the same way, also, we sometimes find ourselves strangely affected by something we read without having decided to use it contemplatively. The response we make to signs is not entirely and never immediately within our control; only the approach to the response we may hope to make is at our disposal. No one, I suppose, intended that Gibbon's *History* should come to be a great work of literary art; it simply *happened* that after its original informative and instructive purposes had been superseded or forgotten, it was found to remain as a source of contemplative delight for cultivated men. We now habitually use the *History* for the sake of aesthetic pleasure, but the wisdom of our purpose comes after the fact.

Confusion of the uses and the meaning of expressions is largely responsible for what Messrs. Wimsatt and Beardsley have called the "intentionalist fallacy." [2] At bottom this pernicious source of critical error and irrelevance consists in the supposition that the meaning of a poem is for all time fixed by the intention of its creator, and that it can have no meaning save that supposedly invested in it by him. Such a doctrine is at once misleading and mistaken. For the most part, even when he knows what he is doing, the poet does not and cannot literally give meaning to the words he employs; he can only avail himself of the meanings they already have in order to produce a certain vital effect. Freedom in the choice and arrangement of the words that constitute a poem is open to the poet, and by his choice and arrangement he can cause to be released the meanings that are relevant to the effect he desires; but the fact that together they produce a particular unified impact is a function also of the antecedent usages of the words selected and, to that extent, of involuntary linguistic dispositions in his readers. If the poet's vaulting aspiration should cause him to ignore these antecedent meanings, as sometimes happens, for example, in the poetry of Hart Crane or D. H. Lawrence, his private intent, however ravishing to himself, will simply not exist as a literary work of art. It is because of this autonomy of usage also that literary works inevitably achieve their post-umbilical independence of meaning and of use. For the same reason, it so often happens that artists are such poor interpreters of their own works. Confusing meaning with intention, they tell us what they wanted to say, not what they did say. It is only rarely, as in the case of Henry James's prefaces, that the artist is able to function autonomously as an observer and as a critic; but when he does so, he, like anyone else, must approach his work as an independent fact, to whose meaning his original intention is a dimly remembered irrelevance.

In the preceding remarks I have sought to show the logical independence of the meaning and the uses of signs, and to indicate some reasons for supposing that the cognitive meanings of signs need not inevitably be tied to a cognitive interest. I now wish to show that in many instances, particularly in the case of literary art, the presence of cognitive meanings is not only not inimical to the contemplative interest but actually its primary support. From this I will infer, I think justifiably, that just as no mode of meaning necessarily conflicts with or impairs the aesthetic quality of a work of art, so also no mode of meaning can be regarded as exclusively or pre-eminently aesthetic. "Aesthetic meaning," I shall maintain, is a meaningless phrase which designates no distinctive aspect of the symbolic process.

It is agreed on all sides that the aesthetic value of a work of art is in some measure a function of its emotionally evocative or expressive power. I do not in the least wish to identify the aesthetic merit or the aesthetic quality of art with that power, and I have elsewhere severely criticized expressionist and emotionalist theories which make such an identification. It is nevertheless undeniable that the quality and value of works of art is in part determined by the richness and depth of their emotional expressiveness. But it is also a commonplace, both of the psychology of art and of art criticism, that just as in ordinary circumstances an emotional response is the product of a perceived situation which is apprehended by the individual as promising or threatening, so the expressiveness of an imaginative work arises, at least in part, from the fact that it provides a dramatic representation of an action of which the evoked emotion is the expressive counterpart. And such a representation must be understood as such if the expressive values of the work are to become actual; without it such emotion as the observer might experience would have no ground, and if, by a miracle, it could be sustained, it would still remain the private, dumb, inexpressive importation of the observer himself. As such it would be nothing more than an accidental, adventitious subjective coloring which, having no artistic basis in the thing perceived, would be devoid of aesthetic relevance to it. Aesthetically relevant emotion in art is something which is expressed to us by the action or gesture of the work itself; it is something aroused and sustained by the work as an object for contemplation, and it is found there as a projected quality of the action. In the case of music, it is perhaps plausible to suppose that the "power of sound," as Gurney calls it, is inherently expressive, independently of any meanings or associations that may accrue to it. But in the case of literary art, whose medium is the conventional symbolism of language, the inherent expressiveness of the sensuous forms of that medium is relatively slight. The predominant power of words to arouse, sustain, and project emotion is a function, not of their quality as sounds, but of their meaning—and in this case, their cognitive meaning. Poetry which relies heavily upon words whose meaning is primarily emotive is almost always poetry of the second order. In the case of the greatest poetry, and this includes also the greatest lyric poetry, it is our awareness of the cognitive meanings of words, as they are deployed directly or in metaphor and simile, upon which depends the sustained emotional effect.

No doubt most theorists would allow that cognitive meanings have *some* relation to the total aesthetic impact of a work of art, but many of them would tend to relegate such meanings to the status of external contextual conditions. Such a concession to relevance of cognitive factors to the aesthetic experience of art will not suffice, and in any case my present claim goes much further. It is my contention that such factors have not merely external contextual relevance, but internal aesthetic relevance as ingredients which at once belong integrally to the aesthetic object itself and sustain its other aspects. Whatever may be true in the case of moral or religious discourse, the relation of cognition to emotion in art is not that of mere cause to effect. For in art, the emotion itself is experienced only as a quality of the work itself. The relation here is, aesthetically, that of aspect to aspect, of part to part, and of part or aspect to the aesthetic whole. A work of art does not exist, contemplatively, as an emotional afterbirth, as some extreme or ill-guarded expressionist theories seem to suggest. Nor is the symbol which carries the feeling an external husk which may be put in its place as a merely contextual "condition," once the emotional heart of the matter has been reached. Such a view would leave the artistic expression of emotion indistinguishable from the emotional reaction induced by drugs or by any random prod. What invariably distinguishes aesthetic emotion is the fact that it is experienced as a quality or dimension of the work of art as it is read, looked at, or heard. It is therefore both a theoretical and a critical error to speak of the cognitive meanings ingredient in a work of art as though they were no more than external causal conditions. As intelligible aspects of the work which we as naturally and immediately apprehend as its sensuous surface, they belong as integrally to it as any sensuous, perceptual, or expressive feature which the work may embody.

Perhaps the fundamental error which has been responsible for the prevailing doubt concerning the aesthetic relevance of cognitive meanings is the tendency to take the verb which appropriately describes the activity involved in comprehending works of art in one medium as paradigmatic for the rest. Thus, although it would be inappropriate to speak of "looking at a poem" or of "reading a piece of music" when referring to what we do in the act of appreciating poetry or music, what is involved in "looking" at a picture or in "listening" to a piece of music is stretched to cover what is understood when we are said to "read" a poem, without noticing that such a stretching of the verbs "to look" and "to listen" will inevitably tend to be misleading when made to apply also to the activity of reading. Even the term "contemplation" has had its share in creating misapprehension as to what is involved in the appreciation of literary art.[3] It is quite natural and appropriate to speak of "contemplating" a picture or a statue, but we are at once made uneasy when someone speaks of "contemplating" a novel or an epic. In using "contemplation" as the generic term in referring to the aesthetic response to works of art of all sorts, therefore, we are stretching this term also, and the result will be both confusing and theoretically stultifying unless we constantly bear in mind that we *are* stretching "contemplation" to cover "reading" and not reducing the latter to what is more literally intended by the former term. Any adequate account of literary works as aesthetic objects must begin with the salient and essential fact that they are read, and not looked at. If this is borne in mind, there will be no temptation to deny the relevance of the cognitive meanings inherent in poetry or in fiction; but perhaps more to the point, there will be no tendency to view the aesthetic relevance of meanings as a "problem." There is no problem; difficulties arise solely from the failure of aestheticians to attend carefully to the meanings of the key terms of their analyses.

It should require no extended commentary, at this point, to convince the reader that no useful theoretical or critical purpose would be served by trying to give meaning to such an expression as "aesthetic meaning." Different types of art normally employ the symbolic forms that are natural and appropriate to the media in which they are conceived. Those appropriate to the plastic arts will tend to be unnatural to music or to literature; those natural to literature will tend to be inappropriately "literary" when attached to music or to painting. If there is a generic form of response which answers to the name "aesthetic," it must be assumed to be capable of availing itself, without prejudice to its integral character, of all types of symbolic form in any mode of meaning. The notion of the "aesthetic use" of symbols is another matter; but this concept cuts clean across any classification of signs that distinguishes them in terms of their modes of meaning.

But even the notion of an aesthetic use of symbols becomes theoretically vicious as well as detrimental to the interests of appreciation and criticism when it is conceived too narrowly, without a constant view to the revealed character of works of art as we find them in experience. Only by constantly attending to what we are naturally impelled to say either in praise or in critical commentary of such different works as *Hamlet* and the "Landscape of Toledo" can we hope to acquire an adequate conception of the full range of artistic symbolism. When we do so, the fact will be inescapable that there is no dimension of meaning which is beyond the pale of aesthetic relevance.

Elsewhere I have adumbrated a theory as to the nature of aesthetic experience that suggests why we should find this to be so. Aesthetic experience, as I conceive it, is perhaps best understood on the model of those consummatory response patterns which pass above the threshold of consciousness. Now any interest has its own characteristic forms of consummation and satisfaction; but whether it be appetitive or perceptual, sensory or intellectual, constitutional or derived, substantive or substitutive, it is usually possible for any interest to enter upon a postpreparatory phase in which the urgency of personal anxiety and need are relaxed and appreciation becomes in some degree possible. When this happens we find the *Ur*-form of the aesthetic experience. Apart from intolerable pain or anxiety, there is no form of human experience or activity that may not provide some measure of aesthetic satisfaction. Any interest, as it approaches maturity, tends to become aesthetic; any activity which is not too hard pressed may reveal an aesthetic side. This being so, any sort of interest may be engaged in aesthetic contemplation; and in the many-leveled satisfactions engendered by great art, many interests, sensory, appetitive, and intellectual, may find either substantive or substitutive fulfillment. It is certainly true that the aesthetic response is not a limited or partial version of some other sort of human concern. Nor is it in any sense a critical limitation of the aesthetic response that it is not preoccupied or urgent in the way that practical moral or intellectual perplexities are so. In practice, no one seriously doubts this. But whatever limitations its own integral character imposes upon aesthetic experience, its domain is sufficiently commodious to include not merely the sensuous surfaces and emotive meanings of signs, but also the full range of what, all too obscurely, we lump together under the rubric of cognitive meaning. The aesthetic thus cannot be understood, as Morris suggests, as a type of discourse, or in terms of a distinctive type of symbol in the way intimated by Mrs. Langer. It is not sensation or the interest therein; it is not perception or the enjoyment thereof. Neither is it a species of emotive meaning, nor of pictorial meaning, nor of mythic symbol. All of these things may be found in some form of aesthetic experience; none can be identified with it.

Underlying these remarks I am aware of no concealed intellectualistic or philosophical ax-grinding. I am well content to leave to the artistic life the values which it alone can adequately embody; my aim is rather to protect, theoretically and critically, the fullness of that life. I aspire only to a theory of the aesthetic use of symbolic forms that is hospitable to any and all modes of symbolization which may enhance the satisfactions we derive from art. My criticism, by implication, is directed entirely to those theories which, for unavowed normative reasons, would deprive us of the full aesthetic use of everything which pleases when—in the metaphorical as well as in the literal sense—"seen." There is no way of telling, in advance of experience, what sensory, emotional, and cognitive powers a work of art may relevantly call into play in appreciation. Nor can we be sure, in the absence of sensibilities that we do not possess or have not acquired, how far our inability to understand or to believe impairs the total response which a great work of art calls upon us to make. Those who do not share or are unable vicariously to acquiesce in Dante's religious world-view are scarcely in a position to deny the depth of its relevance for those who are not so limited. We make what we can of works of art with the spiritual resources available to us; but what a work of art can be or mean should not be defined in terms of our own parochial inhibitions. Understanding, like belief, is always a matter of degree; what matters is that the degrees of understanding and belief which we must give for contemplation's sake not be gratuitously disavowed. When, at the instigation of a foolishly penitent aesthetic, we deny ourselves the use of all real toads that may inhabit our imaginary gardens, the loss is our own. The pity of it is that there is no compensating gain.

NOTES

1. Cf. my "The Aesthetic Relevance of Belief," *JAAC*, Vol. IX, No. 4 (June 1951), pp. 301–15.
2. I have since had second thoughts on this point. Cf. my "The Aesthetic Relevance of Artists' Intentions," *The Journal of Philosophy*, Vol. LII, No. 24, pp. 742–53. (H. D. A., 1960.)
3. This point was called to my attention by my colleague, Professor Paul Ziff.

PSYCHOLOGY AND AESTHETICS
INTRODUCTION

The psychology of art—of its creation and of its appreciation —has been, during the past half century, the enterprise of the most intense fascination for aesthetics. As an instance of social or natural scientists throwing a bridge across into the humanities and making a foray to bring back trophies to their liking, psychoanalysts are leagues ahead of other psychologists—to say nothing of sociologists and anthropologists. Unfortunately, there has been little cross-cultivation of thought. In most cases (certainly in the "great cases," namely of Freud and Jung) the analysts simply do not know enough about the arts into which they make their commando attacks. Their speculative remarks about art are stimulating, but are not sufficiently well founded to bear the weights that have come to roost on them. In the end their principal supporters have had to defend them against themselves. By the same token, most critics and art historians, even those sympathetic to analytic thought, are not sufficiently experienced to use its principles and axioms for other than superficial purposes. The result has been some twenty-five years' worth of pseudoscientific criticism and equally misleading pseudoaesthetic writings by analysts.

For the history of serious efforts concerning the investigations into the psychology of art, Douglas N. Morgan's 1950 article is still the best single summary and guide. It is a bibliographical gold mine and a helpful schematic organization of the fragmented field. Morgan presents the three groups—the psychoanalysts, the Gestalt psychologists, and the experimentalists—in respect to their primary assumptions or principles; he asks significant questions of their methods and goals; and indicates their actual and possible achievements. It should be perfectly obvious that none of the psychological schools contributes anything toward solving the "normative problem," i.e., the question of means for determining what is good or bad in the arts. Even if lip service is paid to it, formal values are ignored. They either search for explanations of preferences in, and effective powers over, the audience, or try to disclose the creative motivation and driving power within the artist's psyche. Both approaches are causally reductive and tend to "explain away" the work of art. Freud and Jung, for example, are particularly interested in what they call the "meaning" of an art work, and such single significance as they countenance, it is not surprising to discover, has the structure of a case-history interpretation of one of their neurotic clients. It remains more than a little questionable whether a work of art is amenable to precisely the same kind of analysis as would be most significant for one of their patients.

Psychology is not a unified science, however, and its intermural fights tend to make the spectator more than a little sceptical of its virtues. It is for this reason that no selection from any certified public psychoanalyst is included here. We have, rather, after the Morgan "outline," the essays of Burke, Read, and Whyte.

Kenneth Burke accepts Freud's "suggestions" but asks for extensions. In the course of considering the bearing of Freud's theories on literary criticism, Burke offers some extensions and criticisms of his own. Crucial among these are the over-all methodological criticism of "essentializing," and his suggestion that beyond the structural analogy between certain works of art and *dreams*, there are analogies with *prayers* and with *charts*. Since Burke's focus is aesthetic rather than psychological he makes the necessary revision in thought, for the purposes of criticism, from the primary category of *wish* to that of *communication*. Lastly, Burke points out that while Freudian psychology is a reductive and therapeutic pursuit of a negative kind (a process of getting-rid-of) it offers no positive directives for the means of discovering purposes that should replace neurotic ones.

It is one of the differences between Freudian theory and Jung's analytical psychology that the latter purports to include just such directive concepts within its framework. The Jungian position is that "guidelines" for future positive development are to be found within the particular individual analysis through the proper interpretation of symbols. Here again is a crucial division between the two schools. Jung distinguishes between signs and symbols by reference to their source and their significance. Neurotic manifestations are *signs*, giving expression to malfunctions in the natural (biological) system of the individual patient and serving as hints or clues to their causes. Reductive analysis of such symptoms is meant to free the patient for future effective work. On the other hand, *symbols* have an entirely different etiology, reflecting not blockages in the natural system but archetypes of the collective unconscious which indicate "lines" for the future healthful development of the patient. A symbol functions in a compensatory way to the conscious conflict so that the resolution can be achieved by a synthesis of the two rather than a victory either for the conscious mind over the unconscious (personal or collective) or vice versa.

Jung sees the nature of art as analogous to the signal and

symbolic functions in individual psychology. He distinguishes between two modes of art: Psychological and Visionary. The former he considers comparable to neurotic signs insofar as it can be understood completely in the terms of present psychological knowledge; whereas, the latter "outstrips" present psychological theory both by its subject matter and methods.

Jung is particularly concerned with defending the sphere of Visionary art against what he considers the destructive analysis of Freudian aesthetics. It is the work of art itself which must be taken seriously, he argues, and that means it should not be "interpreted" by reduction to the (supposed) psychology of the artist; rather, it must be examined to discover what it has to say "in itself." This turns out to be some reference to an archetype of the collective unconscious rather than anything essentially "personal" to the particular artist who created it.

Jung holds that this is not a reductive analysis of the sort he finds in Freud's theory of art, since the nature of the archetypes is not "better known." But this line of thought appears to be circular, since Jung certainly writes *as if* the archetypes *are* "better known," i.e., more readily comprehensible than any work of art in the Visionary mode, and *as if*, by reference to them, what an art work says "in itself" is made more amenable to rational comprehension.

Herbert Read is perhaps more intimately familiar with Jung's thought than Kenneth Burke is with Freud's; but he is less critical than Burke. Read assumes the validity of the distinction between the personal and impersonal orientation for the explication of works of art, he assumes the multifarious functions of the assumed archetypes of the assumed collective unconscious, etc. While it is true that in any number of essays and books, Read has pointed out some of the inadequacies of Jung's theories for aesthetics, in respect to completeness, consistency, and coherence, in the essay on creative dynamics, he presents the Jungian position without critical perspective, and this does have the great advantage for the general reader of offering most compactly and with immediately appreciable examples a considerable amount of complex material within a small space and with an admirable degree of cogency.

There is no question of the vast influence that both Freud and Jung exert over artists and critics alike. Nor is there much doubt of the imperfections in their "systematic" thoughts concerning art. Whether their respective followers will be able to improve upon their theories remains to be seen. The inadequacies are already well seen. Nevertheless, they should be taken for what they truly are: flaws in mountains, not in molehills.

Lancelot Law Whyte's essay begins as an examination of

what science has to tell us about the human creative faculty and its place in nature. Since there is no biology of thought, since no theory has even relative general support as an explanation of the creative process or of productive thinking, Whyte's speculations are as suggestive and reasonable as may that creative thought becomes an integral part of the picture be found anywhere. His argument has such a broad scope of nature, sacrificing nothing of the complexity of relations between consciousness and the functions of the unconscious, science and religious or aesthetic imagination, or the relations between atomistic theories and process theories. Whyte's essay pursues the question of how we are to understand the shared formative character (the root) of both problem-solving thought and imaginative fantasy. In the future, *the biology of thought* will surely be indispensable to whatever further understanding the psychology of art will hope to offer us.

PSYCHOLOGY AND ART [1950]: A SUMMARY AND CRITIQUE [*][1]

Douglas N. Morgan

For some 75 years, investigations into the psychology of art have been developing under that name, and for some 2,300 years before that time some somewhat similar work was being done under the name of philosophy. I offer here no pseudo-comprehensive synopsis of this vast, rich range of material, but merely a brief summary and methodological criticism of some of the work being done today within the field. After a quick glance at certain psychological insights no longer being avidly pursued,[2] I shall try to classify in three broad groups the work being done now, offering examples of each approach in its application to various works of various arts. In the second part of my paper, I shall venture certain comments and criticisms—some new and some old—on ways and means by which, perhaps, somewhat more ground may be gained in our understanding of the psychology of the arts.

Following Fechner, who published his *Vorschule der Aesthetik* in 1876, and thereby founded experimental aesthetics, three major directions developed around three central and fertile ideas. The first of these, called "empathy," had grown from Aristotle[3] through Robert Vischer[4] to Lipps[5] and Lee.[6] Its central idea was an interpretation of the appreciative act in art as a kind of identification: a feeling-into or personification of the object by the spectator. The second central idea gave rise to a theory which stresses certain similarities found between the phenomenon of play and the act of creating or appreciating works of art. It descended from Schiller[7] through Herbert Spencer[8] to Karl Groos[9] and Konrad Lange.[10] The third of these ideas emerges from a concept of an aesthetically necessary "psychical distance" between spectator and aesthetic object, and finds its fullest statement in the work of Edward Bullough.[11] All three of these ideas—empathy, play, and psychical distance—have materially conditioned our present interpretations of art, but none of them seems to be receiving active attention from a significant number of psychologists now at work, at least in this country and in this language. The ideas appear to have

[*] [From *The Journal of Aesthetics and Art Criticism*, Vol. IX, No. 2 (December 1950). Reprinted by permission of the author and *The Journal of Aesthetics and Art Criticism*.]

performed their service and been set aside, at least for the time being; they are not in the main stream of the three approaches now being vigorously explored, especially in America, England, and Italy. I am labeling these approaches respectively *psychoanalytic, Gestalt,* and *experimental,* for want of better terms. I now propose to characterize each of these approaches independently, in terms of what we may call its "core idea," to state its specifically aesthetic questions, and to offer examples of its research.[12]

2

No extended or properly qualified epitomization of the core idea of psychoanalysis will be necessary or desirable before this audience; besides, I do not see that a philosopher need rush in where psychologists themselves fear to tread. In broad terms, let it simply be said that the psychoanalytic approach germinates out of the fundamental notion that man's behavior can be explained in terms of the working out of a complex of conscious and unconscious personality needs and drives, at least some of which are erotic, and all of which strive toward and often find symbolic expression, as in dreams and in the fine arts.

The most characteristic aesthetic question asked by the psychoanalysts is an inquiry into the personality factors which condition the creation and/or appreciation of works of art. It has developed from the "divine frenzy" of Plato's poet [13] who creates because of an irrational love-force; through the idea-dream-reality identification of Schopenhauer,[14] and the "Dionysiac" voluntarism of Nietzsche; [15] to the comprehensive contributions of Freud and his followers.[16] Today Edmund Bergler [17] has challenged the conventional psychoanalytic theory that the artist expresses through his work his unconscious wishes anl fantasies in sublimated, symbolic form; Bergler urges instead that the artist is unconsciously *defending himself against* his own unconscious wishes and fantasies.

The general theoretical development of this core idea may be exemplified in the work of Charles Baudouin [18] and of Harry B. Lee.[19] Baudouin stresses psychoanalytic factors in appreciation, offering an extended example in the analysis of the poetry of Verhaeren; Lee attempts, within a psychoanalytic framework, to describe factors leading up to artistic creation and explaining differential aesthetic responses. He makes frequent and interesting references to his own clinical experience.

Far more work is being done in the direction of detailed, applied interpretations of particular works of art. The attempt seems to be to read the work, in whatever field, symbolically, and to correlate these readings with whatever biographical data may be available, to the end that we understand more fully the personality of the creating artist, and that through this understanding, light may be thrown upon the "mystery" of creation in the arts.

In literature, an enormous amount of analysis is being done; we take only a few, fairly random samples as typical. Hamlet has been a favorite subject for psychoanalysis; [20] King Lear was a narcissist; [21] Baudelaire and Poe are said to displace the death-bringing attributes of their fathers onto their mothers, as a result of infantile menstruation traumas.[22] The body images in the limericks of Edward Lear have been used as psychoanalytic data.[23] Charles Kingsley, author of *The Water Babies*, appears to have suffered from a respiratory neurosis, stammering asthma.[24] Lewis Carroll is said [25] to be the romantic, erotic, wish-fulfilling, schizic *alter ego* of the dignified mathematics professor Charles Dodgson. His heroine Alice is a phallus, and her adventures in Wonderland represent a trip back into the mother's womb.[26]

In music too this fertile idea has been generously applied. Perrotti [27] has exhumed Schopenhauer, suggesting that the mysteries of music may be explained in terms of the unconscious. The language of music is held to be a universal language in that the language of the unconscious is equally universal. Max Graf [28] has set boldly about the historical explanation of composition in terms of erotic powers and other impeti to creation; his ultimate conclusion is, unfortunately, somewhat mystical.

Freud himself presents the most extended analysis in painting, in his admittedly speculative, but stimulating, *Leonardo da Vinci*. Leonardo's childhood phoenix dream, the loss of his father and consequent intimacy with his mother, the details of his account book and manners with his assistants in the studio: all these and more are brought to bear upon the perennial question of why the Mona Lisa smiles. More recently, an Italian student [29] has done some interesting work in interpreting contemporary painting. He suggests, for example, that surrealism exhibits on a social plane what had hitherto been observed only clinically: a general tendency of the libido to regress from adult genitality to a pregenital phase of undifferentiated cell-activity; there is a consequent increase in forgetting and liberation of aggression tendencies. While psychoanalysts seek to *integrate* the self, surrealists seek its *disintegration*. Whether this hypothesis will prove ultimately satisfactory, I cannot say; but at least it seems to me more enlightening than the mountains of incoherent words which the surrealists themselves have had to utter in their own defense. Wight [30] interprets some of Goya's etchings. Bergler [31] suggests a highly stimulating psychoanalytic interpretation of one of Millais's paintings, in terms of the painter's loving sympathy for the frustrated wife of impotent John Ruskin, and argues for his interpretation in terms of material external evidence.

Even sculpture is coming within the purview of the psychoanalysts. If I may, however, I should like to defer my example for a few minutes, when we shall be able to compare the psychoanalytic with the *Gestalt* interpretations of a given series of works.

3

The hesitancy expressed earlier about the "core idea" of psychoanalysis holds also in connection with the Gestalt approach. Suppose that we characterize it, quite simply, as the belief that perception (and perhaps other psychological phenomena as well) can be explained in terms of neural factors tending to produce organized, though dynamically changing patterns or segregated groups of units, or "wholes." The application of these "functional concepts" to aesthetics follows quite clearly. Thinkers in this tradition ask, What perceptual organizing factors condition the experience of seeing or hearing a work of art?

We think, of course, of the work of Wertheimer,[32] Köhler,[33] and Koffka [34] in their general elaboration of the Gestalt thesis. The most recent full-scale development in aesthetics seems to be Schaefer-Simmern's study of art education.[35] Gestalt studies of aesthetic perception [36] also appear from time to time.

As has been the case with psychoanalysis, we find here also some extended attempts to apply the psychological categories to particular works of art, and to our experiences of them. Stephen Pepper [37] has given us many interesting working examples of figure-ground, positive-negative space relationships, and of the operation of sensory fusion, closure, and sequence principles in actual paintings and works of sculpture. Hans Ruin [38] discusses the works of Monet, Cézanne, Gauguin, Munch, Van Gogh, and Matisse, suggesting that painters have, in their treatments of color, figure, and structure, often anticipated theoretical Gestalt psychologists.

In music, Reymes-King [39] is studying the perceptual relationships of verbal and tonal stimuli as they are simultaneously presented in song. He asks whether any phenomenon analogous to sensory fusion may be found when stimuli come through different sense organs. Tentatively, he suggests that this is doubtful, but that a distinction among levels of perception may help to explain the differences between our responses to instrumental music and to song.

Even the movies are being studied by the Gestaltists.

Rudolf Arnheim [40] examines the relationships between visual and auditory stimuli in the act of perception, suggesting that one weakness in some sound movies (and, by extension, presumably also in television) may be a perceptual competition, and hence distraction, division, and loss of attention.

In summary of the discussion thus far, I should like to present two interpretations of what is essentially the same subject matter: the sculpture of Henry Moore. I choose first the recent analysis of a psychoanalytical critic, Frederick Wight. [41] For brevity I paraphrase.

Moore's figures have no soft parts or textures; he eviscerates his figures, eliminating hollow parts of the body, leaving only the bony structure. His father was a miner. Moore mines into the hollow of the breast, which is the feeding ground of the child. Subconsciously an infant cannibal, he eats away the flesh, feels himself inside his mother in image, regressing to the womb. But this is only the least profound of his subconscious interests. More subtly, he builds his sculpture for eternity. His drawings and his writings exemplify this need to transcend death. Everything temporal, soft, is wasted away. Nearly all figures are female. Is not the mine the grave? And is Moore not consigning his father to the mine forever, feeling his way *permanently* inside his mother? But death, as Moore presents it, is not revolting; it is almost dignified, after the British manner. The British national church is floored with graves; it is built on the serene acceptance of the dead underfoot; "for the Englishman the easy unrepugnant moldering of the dead exhales a rich philosophic savor." Not a Christian, Moore wants quite simply a particular image, a material and perhaps a national image, to survive.

We now turn to a Gestalt interpretation of the same material, selecting that of Arnheim, [42] and again paraphrasing. The problem of composing the human form has plagued sculptors for centuries; the solid trunk contrasts with the flying appendages. Moore transforms the trunk into a series of ribbons, and thus finds a common denominator for the whole. Plastic forms are dynamic: conic, pyramidal, ovoidal, rather than static cubes and cylinders. Brain-carrying heads are diminished in size; faces are placid; physical-subrational abdomens are emphasized in the characteristic reclining position. The holes, as perceived, are not merely dead and empty intervals but peculiarly substantial, as though they were filled out with denser air, puddles of semisolid air hollowed out, scooped out by mostly concave surfaces. Principles of three-dimensional figure-ground relationships (concavity making for ground, convexity for figure; enclosed areas tending to be figure, enclosing areas tending to be ground, etc.) apply here also. Instead of pushing shapes out into space, Moore invites space inside his figures, adds to their substance with space. The resulting deliberate figure-ground ambivalence results in a dynamic interplay between two figures in the same work, a lessening of importance of sharp boundaries, and a strong feeling for movement within the work.

Now it is apparent that these two criticisms do not contradict each other; they ask different questions about the aesthetic object, and arrive at different answers. I find both suggestive and interesting, and feel that they may well contribute side by side to our understanding of Moore's work, and of our responses to it.

4

Finally, we come to our third principal approach to the problems of psychology of art: the approach which is usually labeled "experimental." An apology for the term is in order, since Gestaltists certainly also perform experiments. What I mean to indicate is the group of investigators sometimes loosely known as "behaviorists." Because I do not wish to limit the discussion to literal Watsonians, if there are any still around, or to "physicalists," I shall define this group as comprising those who distrust as "unscientific" or "merely philosophical" any investigations (including most of those already discussed) which make inferences on any basis other than precise mathematical measurements of behavior, and which make predictions to any other conclusions than those measurable in such precise terms.[43] The most recent experimental attempts at any kind of comprehensiveness in aesthetics seem to be those of Norman C. Meier,[44] who has outlined an elementary general interpretation of aesthetics and suggested an "interlinkage" theory of artistic creation, and of Albert Chandler.[45] The specific applications of experimentalism to aesthetics are too various to classify under one simple heading; let us rather discover the directions of work from particular examples, which I have very roughly classified as aptitude tests, physiological correlations (Wundt's "expression" category), and preference tests (Wundt's "impression"). A few investigations do not fit conveniently under any of these headings, and must be reserved for brief notation later.[46] Our examples, again, are fairly random samples from the vast contemporary literature, and represent only a fraction of the work being done. They are intended as typical, rather than as definitive.

Aptitude testing is fairly well advanced in music and in painting. The famous Seashore tests of pitch and tonal memory are, I understand, in use in schools today. The Tilson-Gretsch test, and others, have since been developed to measure tonal, harmonic, and rhythmic discrimination. In painting and the plastic arts we have the McAdory Art Test, the Meier Art Judgment Test, the Knauber Test of Art Ability, and the Lewerenz tests in fundamental abilities of the visual arts. Color discrimination tests, line-drawing aptitude tests, and the like, have multiplied profusely. Perhaps the most difficult theoretical question in this field is whether the testers are testing aptitude or achievement: it is sometimes not easy to distinguish the two on experimental grounds. In either case, the practical value of the work is apparent; if we develop tests to the point where we can examine a youngster young enough, and decide what his prospects for a musical career might be, we ought to be able to make significant recommendations about his education, at least in a negative direction. Theoretical advantages of this work are perhaps not so immediately apparent.

Physiological testing is being done, primarily on subjects exposed to works of art, mainly works of music. Dreher [47] has observed that 33 college students trained in music sweat more when listening to certain pieces of piano music than do 33 students who are not so trained. There is some experimental correlation between physical characteristics of music and moods or feelings reported by listeners: music called "dignified" tends to be slow, low-pitched, and of limited orchestral range; music called "animated" tends to be fast, etc. [48]

Preference tests represent the major part of the work being done by experimental psychologists in aesthetics. Most of the work follows the by now well worn footsteps of Fechner. We take only a few samples from the wide range of literature.

In music, Olson [49] has concluded (by asking 1,000 people whether they prefer "this" to "that") that people prefer full frequency sound ranges over limited frequency ones. Pepinsky [50] modestly suggests that the emotion aroused by instrumental music depends partly on how the instrument is played, and not altogether on the physical characteristics of the tone or instrument.

In the field of painting, C. W. Valentine [51] has identified four distinct "types" of appreciators. From other workers [52] we learn that little boys prefer seascapes to landscapes, while little girls prefer pictures of people. Little children of both sexes like bright pictures. Children like bigger cardboard rectangles than adults do; preferred shapes approach the golden mean. [53] One of Great Britain's leading psychologists of art, R. W. Pickford, selected 45 pictures to include 10 aesthetic qualities. Eighteen judges who were interested in the psychology of art rated the pictures. Intercorrelations between the responses were factorized. The general conclusion was drawn that design, feeling, and rhythm were the "essence of art." [54] One of the most careful of recent experiments was performed by Sister Agnes Raley at Nazarene College.[55] Dissatisfied with speculative theories of humor, she set about psychometrics in this field. Twenty-eight cartoons were grouped into seven rows of four. A Thurston scale was developed, and a rank order preference technique explained to her students. Test-retest correlation on the experiment ran .98. Probable error was computed at + .007 . . . a very high reliability. Sister Agnes suggests, on the basis of this experiment, that girls below the age of fifteen like different cartoons than do girls of sixteen, seventeen, and eighteen.

Rather less "preference" work has been done with literary or quasi-literary situations. I report only three experimental results. First: people of different ages aesthetically prefer familiar first names (Robert, Jean) over bizarre first names (Hulsey, Minna); children resent outlandish first names.[56] Second: a reader of poetry and prose is better understood if he speaks in a normal voice than he is if he talks through his nose.[57] Third: literary authors' punctuation habits differ; in poetry, fiction, and drama, the use of the colon (counted per thousand marks of punctuation) is declining; punctuation profiles can be constructed, but are probably unreliable indices to total personality.[58]

Three last examples, which do not fit tidily under the headings listed above, will complete our "experimental" list. The first is quite an interesting experiment performed on a group of 100 college students to test the influence of prestige factors in directing affective response.[59] There does seem to be some such influence. Another investigator has shown that some music sounds funny, even without any program or title.[60] And finally, Paul Farnsworth, former president of the Esthetics Division of the A.P.A., among many other contributons to the psychology of music, has demonstrated [61] that there is some correlation among the following factors: the amount of attention certain eminent musicians receive in certain encyclopedias and histories of music (presumably measured in number of lines of type, so as to remain objective); the number of phonograph records of their music; the frequencies with which their names appear on the programs of certain symphony orchestras; and how well grade school, high school and college students say that they like the musicians' music. These materials are in turn correlated with the musicians' birthdays.

5

Broadly, what contributions may each of these various approaches claim to have made to our understanding of the arts? What do its limitations seem at present to be?

We might first note, in an overview of all three positions,

that none of them by any means definitely solves the *normative* problem—if there is any such problem—which has worried so many philosophers of art. Some, but not all, psychoanalysts frankly disavow any such interest, admitting that "bad" poems are equally revealing psychoanalytically as "good" ones.[62] The Gestaltists worry about the problem,[63] but I am not yet satisfied that their suggestions will prove ultimately satisfactory. The experimentalists, quite obviously, beg the normative question. This general scientific disinterest in aesthetic norms is, I believe, a healthy sign. A degree of philosophical naïveté is excusable and perhaps even desirable in a scientist; the converse, however, is not true. This whole question of the methodology of value-psychology needs consideration, but is much too extended to discuss here.

It seems, generally, that we owe to the psychoanalysts a broad set of categories, of hypothetical constants, of (charitably) "as if" personality factors analogous to the "as if" constituents of the atom, which seem in some cases to help us partially account for what hitherto had appeared to be the "miracle" of creation. We have been provided with a very schematic picture of a "hidden mechanism" whose workings we are only beginning to understand. Miscellaneous groups of data, hitherto disorganized in our understanding, are brought under these categories and seen to have some kind of a common explanation, however broad. Some sort of "intellectual at-homeness" may be brought about in this way . . . although it may not be exactly the kind of a home of which we may be very proud.

In terms of these categories, certain very general generalizations do seem to be allowable, on an admittedly semispeculative basis, as, for example, that erotic desires repressed by the censorial superego tend toward external vicarious or sublimated expression by means of art-symbols, analogous to dream-symbols. We find at least a serious attempt to give one kind of explanation of the symbols in art, and to bring together observed facts from various fields into a coherent explanation. There seems to be no reason why such explanations, when developed, may not warrant prediction; and their clinical efficacy seems fairly well established.

Among the many criticisms which have been leveled at the psychoanalytical approach to works of art I shall mention only a few. There are two naive and equally dogmatic rejections of the entire Freudian-Voluntaristic approach. The first of these is the lay rejection of the man in the street: "The whole business sounds cockeyed. It must be crazy." To be sure, some of the speculative analyses do sound cockeyed to the layman, but that is neither here nor there. Einstein's hypotheses, watered down to the lay level, sound cockeyed too. It is a dogmatic and quite clearly extraempirical demand that every scientific explanation make clear good sense to the man in the street. The question at issue is not whether Freudian interpretations sound farfetched, but whether they are true, interesting, and useful.

A second general criticism, less obviously naive but still, I think, dogmatic, amounts to little more than a blanket categorical refusal to grant the honorific title "science" to such enterprises, on grounds that they are not both experimental in a literal sense and quantitative in their data. This is the criticism we used to hear from the extreme behaviorists. Insofar as the dispute is a rather petty quibble over who has a right to the precious word "science," I do not find it enlightening. It is worth pointing out that many disciplines which we do ordinarily call by that name—astronomy, for example—do not feature literal experimentation. Similarly observational rather than literally experimental are all the so-called historical sciences of man, such as anthropology . . . sciences which (like psychoanalysis) take ranges of data and attempt generalizations on the basis of them. Nor is it the case that all of what we commonly call "sciences" constantly engage in statistical correlations: botany furnishes a familiar example.

There are, however, certain other criticisms which may be raised with perhaps somewhat more force. They are not intended as a priori categorical denunciations of a whole field of endeavor, but rather simply as requests. What Baudouin said in the twenties [64] remains true today: "The new doctrine requires criticism; but it is absurd, at this date, to regard psychoanalysis as null and void."

First, it would be helpful if it were possible for the psychoanalysts to clarify in empirical terms the grounding definitions of their categories: id, ego, superego, etc. Presumably we should be able to specify (or at least we should like to be able to specify) some sort of operational definitions for them, yet it seems to be exceedingly difficult to do so. We would like to be able to say, "If the painting contains this symbol, we see the artist's ego at work; if it contains that symbol, we see his superego." This demand may now be altogether impossible of fulfillment, because of the rich complexity of the subject matter with which the psychoanalyst is dealing. He himself assures us that all of the different factors are represented in our every action. Just exactly how, then (we would like to know), can we recognize the activity of the various personality factors when we meet them? How shall we even work *toward* precise measurement, granting that precision is impossible at the present time?

Furthermore, we are somewhat worried, on reviewing psychoanalytic-aesthetic literature, about an apparent tendency to reify categories, to make theoretical entities into "things out there." We are anxious to keep clearly before us in our analyses that the unconscious is a hypothetical construct, rather than a metaphysical entity; it is to be justified in use, rather than to be intuited as a self-evident criterion and set up as an independent court of authority. We must be careful to use our categories as instruments of generalization *from* facts, rather than as prejudicial definitions of what kind of evidence will be admitted as factual.

And finally, we would like with psychoanalytic-aesthetic hypotheses, as with any other, some suggested pattern of verification. This will entail the presentation of specific predictions about human behavior, and it may be that we do not yet have adequate generalizations on which to base any far-reaching predictions. But at least some of us will be happier when we see the way clear to a confirmation or disconfirmation of the hypotheses in terms of predictions fulfilled or frustrated. It seems fair to charge the proponents of any scientific theory with showing us at least in principle what kind of evidence will be accepted (when and if we can get it) as confirmatory, and what kind as disconfirmatory.

An estimate of the contributions of Gestalt psychology to our understanding of the arts would have to include our debt for several sensitive and enlightening criticisms of particular works of art, and for a set of principles, only now in process of fuller formulation, which seem to have widening application. Many of our actual experiences of familiar works can be enriched by looking for and finding these principles at work in our own perception. And again, we are always grateful for any fertile ideas which help us to organize into intelligible patterns miscellaneous ranges of data, to "make sense out of experience."

The naive criticisms of psychoanalysis in art have also been leveled against Gestaltism. Let our earlier comments apply here too.

A warning may, I think, be reasonably issued to the Gestaltists, analogous to one which is sometimes issued to the pschoanalysts, namely the stark and real possibility that the hypotheses may become so thin, in order to accommodate many various data, that they no longer say very much. It seems that some changes in this direction have taken place during the past twenty years . . . qualifications and refinements which rather dangerously broaden the scope. Any broad scientific or philosophical hypothesis runs this risk, of course; in striving for breadth, it becomes thin, just as, in striving for specificity, it becomes narrow.

Hardly anyone today doubts that the *Gestalt* is a good idea, but it has been suggested that at least some of its principles may already have done their work, have run their courses in art. We find in the arts magnificent textbook examples of fusion, closure, sequence, figure-ground principles, especially so long as we confine our attention to classical architecture and to sculpture. But, as Ehrenzweig points out,[65] the most persuasive Gestalt interpretations hinge quite naturally around those perceptual surfaces and depths in which the eye and the attention are expressly confined. But in much of contemporary painting and poetry, the eye and attention are invited to wander. There seem to be simply no well-defined wholes in perception. Figure and ground blend indistinguishably. The presented surface may as well be seen as all figure, or all ground, or neither, like wallpaper. The Gestaltist can, of course, answer this criticism, but only by digging rather deep for evidence of the principles which he brings to the work of art. In no very clear sense does he find them "there" so to speak in the evidential work of art presented to him. To justify such "digging," overwhelming prior evidence, of a more direct sort, must warrant the hypothesis as highly probable. There is a suspiciously *ad hoc* feeling about any such extreme hypothetical extension; quite justifiably, I feel, it weakens our original, fresh faith in the hypothesis.

We come finally to an estimate of the contributions of what we have called the "experimental" approach to aesthetics. Here, I think, we may be most grateful for the aptitude tests, which are doing practical work every day. As for theoretical contributions to our understanding of the fine arts, however, I find myself (with few exceptions)[66] at a loss. Frankly, I don't think we have yet learned very much about art by the kind of experimentation and measurement which has been going on. If pressed, I will admit that I do not expect—unless we alter our approach somewhat—that we will learn a great deal more in this direction, at least within the next three thousand years. Beyond that I do not care to predict. Indirectly, of course, we in aesthetics have benefited materially from experimental psychology. Experiments in perception, learning, and emotions have made some important contributions . . . but these investigations have, for the most part, been carried on outside the field of psychology of art.[67] Within that field, as practiced by the experimentalists, we have found some models of experimental technique, complete with control groups and probable error computations. We have found examples of highly refined statistical procedures and high-powered correlations; even factor analysis has found its way into this field.[68] And we have come out with fairly suggestive evidence quite strongly indicating that several things which we believed all along to be true are really true.

This latter-day sophisticated behaviorism in aesthetics

seems to many of us to be frankly thin, to present results disappointing and even insignificant in proportion to the enormous labors which have been put into it. Why is this?

The naive answer to this question is one which perennially arises in cases of this sort: just because we find our scientific row difficult to hoe, some people deny the possibility of ever hoeing it, and illogically infer that the field is somehow forever "autonomous," "beyond science" in some mysterious sense in which the field of physics is not. "Art," it is argued, "is too pure, too unique, too otherwordly and intuitive to be a subject-matter for such 'atomistic' science." [69] I suppose that psychologists still have to listen to this sort of complaint from time to time, just as philosophers do. But I submit that it is vestigial nineteenth-century romanticism and not worth taking seriously within the framework of our present-day lives and works. We cannot prove it false, because of the very nature of the position: it doesn't say anything explicit enough to be proved true or false. But in attempting a science of art, as in attempting a science of anything else, we must assume it to be false. Since this assumption seems (although admittedly extra-empirical) to be a condition of any knowledge about anything, I am willing to make it cheerfully, and I suggest that we all do so. I do not know of any evidence which could possibly prove our assumption to be mistaken, since it is at least primarily procedural rather than descriptive. The *analysis* of this assumption, by the way, I take to be one of the primary tasks of philosophy.

Three other answers however suggest themselves as possible explanations for our dissatisfaction with the results of experimental-quantitative aesthetics. The first of these points to the empirical fact that our experiences of works of art in appreciation, and artists' experience in creation, are admitted by all hands to be highly complex. A positively enormous number of variables enter into the perceptual situation; many, but not all, of these have been pointed out in philosophical analyses of art. The entire physical and psychological history of the percipient seems to condition his response, often in apparently irrelevant and certainly unexpected ways. A large number of the qualities of the work itself are clearly relevant. The physical and social environment of appreciation obviously plays an important part. The whole "as if" representational world of the visual and literary arts presents special psychological complexities. And all of these variable factors seem to fuse in extraordinarily complicated fashions. It is not at all evident, or perhaps it is even unlikely, that discrete observations gleaned in the sterile atmosphere of the usual psychological laboratory are now legitimate warrant for *any* very interesting or useful generalizations about the aesthetic experience. Responding to an El Greco on a museum wall simply isn't much like comparing cardboard rectangles in a classroom, and it is difficult to see from here how any number of such cardboard comparisons will ever pile up, one on top of another, to give a description of the aesthetic response. In order to get the problem into the laboratory, it has quite naturally been necessary to control the number of variables. It may be that this control has resulted in a fatal oversimplification of the problem.

Note that this is emphatically *not* a retreat into mysticism. I do not believe that these problems of aesthetics—or, for that matter, any real problems of description of any phenomena at all—are forever inevitably beyond the scientist. But I am not encouraged that they are now within the grasp of the quantitative experimentalist in anything closely approximating the rather cavalier attack we find in the books and journals of the nineteen-forties. The counsel is one of caution rather than of surrender. Let us beware of the subtleties and complexities, lest we distort the problems into oversimplified caricatures in the name of empirical science.

As a second general observation, I suggest that at least in some cases in which aesthetic behavior patterns have been studied by experimentalists, the experimenters have apparently failed to ask significant and crucial questions *in advance of* experiment. Charles Darwin once remarked that he never heard of anything sillier than a man setting up an experiment without trying to prove or disprove something, just going into the laboratory to perform an experiment for the sake of the experiment. It does look sometimes as if some of these investigators into aesthetics have been willing to settle for just any old correlation between any old sets of behavioral data at all, so long as they are "objective." Small wonder that correlations are found: it is a tautology to say that *any* sets of data will correlate somewhere between -1.0 and $+1.0$. There are indeed behavioral correlations to be found; the trouble is that there are too many of them. In the psychology of art we must imaginatively select in advance of experiment *which* factors, when correlated, will give us interesting and important results. This requires some hard thinking, some imagination, some kind of a *theory,* however tentative, some "exploratory hypothesis" guessed at from earlier work, or from common-sense observation, or wherever. *Mere* laboratory observations, however accurately made and acutely correlated, will never give us anything remotely resembling a scientific description of the aesthetic experience. Statistical calisthenics may be a fine exercise for a student of psychology; I expect it is; the études of Czerny are fine exercises for

students of piano. But (to borrow a figure) we do not expect
to hear Czerny études from the concert platform.

It may be that physics is indeed the proper model for
psychology to emulate. But the emulation should be *methodological* rather than *material*. Psychologists of art may of
course, but need not, make the rather extravagent assumption
that every aesthetically relevant consideration is a space-
time event measurable in physiological terms. And, as Köhler
pointed out, if we are to take physics as our model, we might
well remember that physics went through centuries of qualitative refinement before its quantitative methods became
applicable. It is at least possible that our understanding of
the psychology of art is still in a stone age, a period of pre-
scientific or better "pre-quantitative" discrimination.[70] After
all, even physics has occasionally had difficulty with its quanti-
fication techniques. I know of no one who would want to
maintain seriously that the problems of psychology of art
are simpler than those of physics . . . except where they
have been made simpler by radical surgical excisions of important and relevant complexities. Frank recognition of these
complexities is surely a prime duty of the empirical scientist.

This paper has included a summary, classification, and tentative criticism of psychology at work today among the arts.
No moral need be drawn, but if one is requested, let it be
simply this: we need hardheaded, cautious, clear scientific
thinking about the arts; perhaps right now we need it most on
the level of fundamental theory developed by trained psychologists who have a love for the arts and a healthy curiosity about what makes them tick.

NOTES

1. This paper was read to the Psychology Colloquium of Northwestern University on January 30, 1950. It is intended as one
contribution in partial fulfillment of Thomas Munro's reasonable request ("Methods in the Psychology of Art," *Journal of
Aesthetics and Art Criticism,* March 1948, p. 226) for "more
discussion of aims and methods." In this valuable article,
Mr. Munro brings to the attention of American students the
important work of Müller-Freienfels (*Psychologie der Kunst,*
3 vols. [Leipzig: 1923]), Sterzinger (*Grundlinien der Kunstpsychologie* [Graz: 1938]), and Plaut (*Prinzipien und Metho-
den der Kunstpsychologie* [Berlin: 1935]). The reader is

referred to these books, and to Munro's article, for a survey of psychological approaches in Germany and Austria to 1935. Chandler's fine book, *Beauty and Human Nature* (New York and London: 1934) still contains interesting material; its approach is, however, almost wholly restricted to that called "experimental" in this paper. It goes without saying that interested readers will refer to one of the masterpieces in the field by one of its masterworkers, the late Max Dessoir: *Aesthetik und allgemeine Kunstwissenschaft* (Stuttgart: 1923).

2. Except perhaps in France, and there only in an attenuated form. See the June 1949 issue of *Journal of Aesthetics and Art Criticism*. R. Bayer's article, "Method in Aesthetics," in this issue, contains a quasi-critical and quasi-poetic discussion of psychological methodology in aesthetics.

3. 1411b, *34; Rhetoric* III, 2.

4. *Das optische Formgefühl* (Tübingen: 1873).

5. *Aesthetik* (Hamburg and Leipzig: 1903–1906).

6. With C. Anstruther-Thompson, "Beauty and Ugliness," *Contemporary Review*, 1897, pp. 72, 544–69; 669–88.

7. *Letters upon the Aesthetical Education of Man*, 1793–1794. More convenient is the 1905 London edition *Essays, Aesthetical and Philosophical*, etc.

8. *The Principles of Psychology* (London: 1870–1872).

9. *The Play of Animals* (New York: 1898), *The Play of Man* (New York: 1901).

10. *Das Wesen der Kunst* (Berlin: 1901).

11. Miscellaneous articles in *British Journal of Psychology, c.* 1913.

12. It should be noted that serious attempts have been made, and are still being made, to organize these various approaches into a unified program which will incorporate also discoveries contributed by anthropological, historical, and sociological disciplines. See Munro, op. cit., p. 233.

13. *Phaedrus*, 245.

14. See Baudouin, *Psychoanalysis and Aesthetics*, trans., Paul (New York: 1924), p. 29.

15. *Das Geburt der Tragödie* (Leipzig: 1872), available in translation, *The Will to Power*, 1878 (New York: 1924).

16. Freud's own chief contributions to aesthetics include *Leonardo da Vinci* (New York: 1916), *Wit and Its Relation to the Unconscious* (New York: 1916), *Dream and Delusion* (New York: 1917), *Totem and Taboo* (New York: 1918). The Jungian approach may be found in "Psychology and Literature," pp. 175–99 in *Modern Man in Search of a Soul*, trans., Dell and Baynes (New York: 1934), and in *Contributions to Analytical Psychology* (London and New York: 1928), pp. 225–49.

17. *American Imago*, 1948, p. 200, and elsewhere. *The Writer and Psychoanalysis* (New York: 1950).

18. Op. cit. We might almost take as a text Baudouin's quotation (p. 25) from Wagner's *Meistersinger:* "Poetry is nothing but the interpretation of dreams."

19. "On the Esthetic State of Mind," *Psychiatry,* 1947, pp. 281–306, and elsewhere.

20. See, for only one example, Ernest Jones, *Hamlet* (London: 1947), pp. 7–42.

21. Abenheimer, "On Narcissism, etc.," *British Journal of Medical Psychology,* 1945, 20, pp. 322–9.

22. Daly, "The Mother Complex in Literature," *Samiksa* 1947, 1, pp. 157–90. I am grateful to Dr. Edward Weiss of Chicago for his kindness in sharing his personal copy of this journal, and of those cited in notes 27 and 29 below.

23. Reitman, "Lear's Nonsense," *Journal of Clinical Psychopathology and Psychotherapy,* 1946, 7, pp. 64–102.

24. Deutsch, "Artistic Expression and Neurotic Illness," *American Imago,* 1947, pp. 64–102.

25. Skinner, "Lewis Carroll's *Adventures in Wonderland,*" *American Imago,* 1947, pp. 3–31. The earliest article on this subject seems to be that of Schilder, "Psychoanalytic Remarks on *Alice in Wonderland* and Lewis Carroll," *Journal of Nervous and Mental Diseases,* 1938, 87, pp. 159–68.

26. Grotjohn, "About the Symbolization of Alice's Adventures in Wonderland," *American Imago,* 1947, pp. 32–41.

27. *"La Musica, linguaggio dell'inconscio,"* *Psicoanalisi,* 1945, pp. 60–82. He suggests that whereas ordinary verbal language tends to express cold, abstract concepts, music expresses the determinate "charge" (*carica*) of the unconscious.

28. *From Beethoven to Shostakovich: The Psychology of the Composing Process* (New York: 1947).

29. Servadio, "*Il Surrealismo: storia, dottrina, valutazione psicoanalitica,*" *Psicoanalisi,* 1946, p. 77. See also Akin (or Atkin), "Psychological Aspects of Surrealism," *Journal of Clinical Psychopathology and Psychotherapy* 1945, pp. 35–41.

30. "The Revulsions of Goya," *Journal of Aesthetics and Art Criticism,* 1946, 5, pp. 1–28.

31. Loc. cit. Schneider also has done psychoanalyses of paintings: see his work on Picasso (*College Art Journal,* 1946, 6, pp. 81–95) and on Chagall (ibid., pp. 115–24).

32. *Productive Thinking* (New York and London: 1945).

33. *Gestalt Psychology* (New York: 1947).

34. *Principles of Gestalt Psychology* (New York: 1935). I cite only recent editions.

35. *The Unfolding of the Artistic Activity* (Berkeley: 1948).

36. As, for example, that of Koffka, "Problems on the Psychology of Art," *Bryn Mawr Notes and Monographs IX,* (Bryn Mawr: 1940), cited by Heyl, *New Bearings in Esthetics and Art Criticism* (New Haven: 1943), p. 110 n.

37. *Principles of Art Appreciation* (New York: 1949).

38. *"La Psychologie structurale et l'art moderne," Theoria* (Lund: 1949), pp. 253–75. "The holistic way of seeing," says Ruin (p. 259), "is, once and for all, innate in artists."

39. In an interesting but, so far as I can discover, still unpublished paper read at the 1949 meeting of the Society for Aesthetics, in Oberlin, Ohio. It should be noted that my report is from memory; Reymes-King is not to be held responsible for these views.

40. Also from an unpublished paper read at the 1949 meeting (see note 39). Arnheim is not to be held responsible for these views; they are quoted from memory.

41. "Henry Moore: The Reclining Figure," *Journal of Aesthetics and Art Criticism,* 1947, pp. 95–105.

42. "The Holes of Henry Moore," *Journal of Aesthetics and Art Criticism,* 1948, pp. 29–38.

43. Consider, for example, the attitude expressed by Carl Seashore, *Psychology of Music* (New York: 1938), p. 377.

44. *Art in Human Affairs* (New York and London: 1942).

45. Op. cit. See note 1, above.

46. I here deliberately set aside applied psychology experiments on the use of music in psychotherapy, and in increasing production in factories and chicken coops, the visual appearance of advertising layouts, and the like, since such experimenters generally make no claim to be contributing to our understanding of the arts.

47. "The Relationship Between Verbal Reports and Galvanic Skin Responses to Music," abstract, *American Psychologist,* 1948, 3, p. 275.

48. Gundlach, "Factors Determining the Characterization of Musical Phrases," 1935, 47, pp. 624–43.

49. "Frequency Range Preference for Speech and Music," *Journal of Acoustical Society of America,* 1947, p. 549.

50. "Musical Tone Qualities as a Factor in Expressiveness," *Journal of Acoustical Society of America,* 1947, p. 542. Pepinsky cites no actual experimental evidence; his inclusion in this classification is perhaps open to question.

51. *An Introduction to the Experimental Psychology of Beauty* (London and New York: 1913).

52. Dietrich and Hunnicutt, "Art Content Preferred by Primary Grade Children," *Elementary School Journal,* 1948, pp. 557–9.

53. Shipley, Dattman, Steele, "The Influence of Size on Preferences for Rectangular Proportion in Children and Adults," *Journal of Experimental Psychology,* 1947, p. 333.

54. Abstract: "Experiments with Pictures," *Advancement of Science,* 1948, 5, p. 140.

55. Abstract: *American Psychologist,* 1946, 1, p. 205.

56. Finch, Kilgren, Pratt, "The Relation of First Name Preferences

to Age of Judges or to Different Although Overlapping Generations," *Journal of Social Psychology*, 1944, 20, pp. 249–64.

57. Glasgow, "The Effects of Nasality on Oral Communication," *Quarterly Journal of Speech*, 1944, 30, pp. 337–40.

58. E. L. Thorndike, "The Psychology of Punctuation," *American Journal of Psychology*, 1948, 61, pp. 222–8.

59. Rigg, "Favorable Versus Unfavorable Propaganda in the Enjoyment of Music," *Journal of Experimental Psychology*, 1948, pp. 78–81.

60. Mull, "A Study of Humor in Music," *American Journal of Psychology*, 62, October 1949, pp. 560–6.

61. Abstract: "Musical Eminence," *American Psychologist*, 1946, 1, p. 205.

62. Stekel, *Die Träume der Dichter* (Wiesbaden: 1932), p. 32; quoted by Langer, *Philosophy in a New Key* (Pelican ed., 1948), p. 168.

63. See Köhler's *The Place of Value in the World of Facts* (New York: 1938).

64. Op. cit., p. 20. Baudouin claims (pp. 33–4) that psychoanalysts "have laid the foundations for the psychology of art, of a science of aesthetics which shall be genuinely scientific without thinking itself bound for that reason to approach art as a psychological 'case' or as a 'subject' to be catalogued, without succumbing to the danger of manifesting a sterile erudition, without losing contact with life, and without forfeiting the sense of beauty." Or again (p. 294): "Psychology is no longer [c. 1922] content to make use of the methods proper to the physical sciences; it has sought out, and to a large extent has already found, methods proper to itself."

65. "Unconscious Form-Creation in Art," *British Journal of Medical Psychology*, 1948, pp. 185–214. Ehrenzweig attributes the basic idea to Herbert Read (*Art in Industry* [London: 1934]), and points out that education both in creation and in appreciation often seems to contradict Gestalt principles: we learn, for example, to see ground, or negative space, as *figure*, as shaped.

66. As sample exceptions, the investigations of Gundlach, Mull, and Rigg, cited above.

67. Buswell, for example (*How People Look at Pictures* [Chicago: 1935]), presents relevant and important data on perception in art. He trained cameras on corneas and mapped out eye movement diagrams, timing fixations. Alschuler and Weiss (*Painting and Personality: A Study of Young Children* [Chicago: 1947]), present an intensive and fairly extensive study of the relations between creative expression and personality in children between the ages of two and five.

68. Guilford and Holley, "A Factorial Approach to the Analysis of Variations in Aesthetic Judgments," *Journal of Experimental*

Psychology, 1949, 39, pp. 208–18, an ingenious methodology applied to choices of designs of playing cards.

69. See Jung, *Modern Man in Search of a Soul* (New York: 1934), p. 177: "Any reaction to stimulus may be causally explained; but the creative act, which is the absolute antithesis of mere reaction will forever elude the human understanding."

70. For examples of psychologists' critiques of psychological experimentations in aesthetics, see Max Dessoir, op cit., pp. 17 ff. R. M. Ogden, *The Psychology of Art* (New York: 1938), p. 22, says: "A work of art eludes all efforts to quantify it in terms of a precise formula. 'Aesthetic measure' is a contradiction in terms." He refers, of course, to Birkhoff's *Aesthetic Measure* (Cambridge: 1933). A more moderate, and I suspect, more nearly correct, view is that of Thomas Munro (*Scientific Method in Aesthetics* [New York: 1928], pp. 15–17): "quantitative measurements . . . when erected into a fetish, as they have been by 'experimental aesthetics' . . . usually lead to premature inferences that have a specious air of certainty, and the neglecting of more fruitful methods of inquiry. . . . Too rigorous an insistence on absolute reliability and 'objectivity' of data, too impatient a zeal for universally valid generalizations, may be an obstacle in a field where these cannot be attained at once, if ever." See also Jung, *Modern Man*, p. 176.

FREUD—AND THE ANALYSIS OF POETRY *

Kenneth Burke

The reading of Freud I find suggestive almost to the point of bewilderment. Accordingly, what I should like most to do would be simply to take representative excerpts from his work, copy them out, and write glosses upon them. Very often these glosses would be straight extensions of his own thinking. At other times they would be attempts to characterize his strategy of presentation with reference to interpretative method in general. And, finally, the Freudian perspective was developed primarily to chart a psychiatric field rather than an aesthetic one; but since we are here considering the analogous features of these two fields rather than their important differences, there would be glosses attempting to suggest how far the literary critic should go along with Freud and what extra-Freudian material he would have to add. Such a desire to write an article on Freud in the margin of his books must for practical reasons here remain a frustrated desire. An article such as this must condense by generalization, which requires me to slight the most stimulating factor of all—the detailed articulacy in which he embodies his extraordinary frankness.

Freud's frankness is no less remarkable by reason of the fact that he had perfected a method for being frank. He could say humble, even humiliating, things about himself and us because he had changed the rules somewhat and could make capital of observations that others, with vested interests of a different sort, would feel called upon to suppress by dictatorial decree. Or we might say that what for him could fall within the benign category of observation could for them fall only within its malign counterpart, spying.

Yet though honesty is, in Freud, methodologically made easier, it is by no means honesty made easy. And Freud's own accounts of his own dreams show how poignantly he felt at times the "disgrace" of his occupation. There are doubtless many thinkers whose strange device might be *ecclesia super cloacam*. What more fitting place to erect one's church than above a sewer! One might even say that sewers are what churches are for. But usually this is done by laying all the stress upon the ecclesia and its beauty. So that, even

* [From *The Philosophy of Literary Form,* originally published by Louisiana State University Press, 1941. Reprinted by permission of the author.]

when the man's work fails to be completed for him as a social act, by the approval of his group, he has the conviction of its intrinsic beauty to give him courage and solace.

But to think of Freud, during the formative years of his doctrine, confronting something like repugnance among his colleagues, and even, as his dreams show, in his own eyes, is to think of such heroism as Unamuno found in Don Quixote; and if Don Quixote risked the social judgment of ridicule, he still had the consolatory thought that his imaginings were beautiful, stressing the ecclesia aspect, whereas Freud's theories bound him to a more drastic self-ostracizing act—the charting of the relations between ecclesia and cloaca that forced him to analyze the cloaca itself. Hence, his work was with the confessional as cathartic, purgative; this haruspicy required an inspection of the entrails; it was, bluntly, an interpretative sculpting of excrement, with beauty replaced by a science of the grotesque.

Confronting this, Freud does nonetheless advance to erect a structure which, if it lacks beauty, has astounding ingeniousness and fancy. It is full of paradoxes, of leaps across gaps, of vistas—much more so than the work of many a modern poet who sought for nothing else but these and had no search for accuracy to motivate his work. These qualities alone would make it unlikely that readers literarily inclined could fail to be attracted, even while repelled. Nor can one miss in it the profound charitableness that is missing in so many modern writers who, likewise concerned with the cloaca, become efficiently concerned with nothing else, and make of their work pure indictment, pure oath, pure striking-down, pure spitting-upon, pure kill.

True, this man, who taught us so much about father-rejection and who ironically himself became so frequently the rejected father in the works of his schismatic disciples, does finally descend to quarrelsomeness, despite himself, when recounting the history of the psychoanalytic movement. But, over the great course of his work, it is the matter of human rescue that he is concerned with—not the matter of vengeance. On a few occasions, let us say, he is surprised into vengefulness. But the very essence of his studies, even at their most forbidding moments (in fact, precisely at those moments), is charitableness, a concern with salvation. To borrow an excellent meaningful pun from Trigant Burrow, this salvation is approached not in terms of religious hospitality but rather in terms of secular hospitalization. Yet it is the spirit of Freud; it is what Freud's courage is for.

Perhaps, therefore, the most fitting thing for a writer to do, particularly in view of the fact that Freud is now among the highly honored class—the exiles from Nazi Germany (how accurate those fellows are! how they seem, with almost 100 per cent efficiency, to have weeded out their greatest citizens!) —perhaps the most fitting thing to do would be simply to attempt an article of the "homage to Freud" sort and call it a day.

However, my job here cannot be confined to that. I have been commissioned to consider the bearing of Freud's theories upon literary criticism. And these theories were not designed primarily for literary criticism at all but were rather a perspective that, developed for the charting of a nonaesthetic field, was able (by reason of its scope) to migrate into the aesthetic field. The margin of overlap was this: The acts of the neurotic are symbolic acts. Hence insofar as both the neurotic act and the poetic act share this property in common, they may share a terminological chart in common. But insofar as they deviate, terminology likewise must deviate. And this deviation is a fact that literary criticism must explicitly consider.

As for the glosses on the interpretative strategy in general, they would be of this sort: For one thing, they would concern a distinction between what I should call an essentializing mode of interpretation and a mode that stresses proportion of ingredients. The tendency in Freud is toward the first of these. That is, if one found a complex of, let us say, seven ingredients in a man's motivation, the Freudian tendency would be to take one of these as the essence of the motivation and to consider the other six as sublimated variants. We could imagine, for instance, manifestations of sexual impotence accompanying a conflict in one's relations with his familiars and one's relations at the office. The proportional strategy would involve the study of these three as a cluster. The motivation would be synonymous with the interrelationships among them. But the essentializing strategy would, in Freud's case, place the emphasis upon the sexual manifestation, as causal ancestor of the other two.

This essentializing strategy is linked with a normal ideal of science: to "explain the complex in terms of the simple." This ideal almost vows one to select one or another motive from a cluster and interpret the others in terms of it. The naive proponent of economic determinism, for instance, would select the quarrel at the office as the essential motive, and would treat the quarrel with familiars and the sexual impotence as mere results of this. Now, I don't see how you can possibly explain the complex in terms of the simple without having your very success used as a charge against you. When you get through, all that your opponent need say is: "But you have explained the complex in terms of the simple—and the simple is precisely what the complex is not."

Perhaps the faith philosophers, as against the reason philosophers, did not have to encounter a paradox at this point. Not that they avoided paradoxes, for I think they must always cheat when trying to explain how evil can exist in a world created by an all-powerful and wholly good Creator. But at least they did not have to confront the complexity-simplicity difficulty, since their theological reductions referred to a ground in God, who was simultaneously the ultimately complex and the ultimately simple. Naturalistic strategies lack this convenient "out"—hence their explanations are simplifications, and every simplification is an oversimplification.[1]

It is possible that the literary critic, taking communication as his basic category, may avoid this particular paradox (communication thereby being a kind of attenuated God term). You can reduce everything to communication—yet communication is extremely complex. But, in any case, communication is by no means the basic category of Freud. The sexual wish, or libido, is the basic category; and the complex forms of communication that we see in a highly alembicated philosophy would be mere sublimations of this.

A writer deprived of Freud's clinical experience would be a fool to question the value of his category as a way of analyzing the motives of the class of neurotics Freud encountered. There is a pronouncedly individualistic element in any technique of salvation (my toothache being alas! my private property), and even those beset by a pandemic of sin or microbes will enter heaven or get discharged from the hospital one by one; and the especially elaborate process of diagnosis involved in Freudian analysis even to this day makes it more available to those suffering from the ills of preoccupation and leisure than to those suffering from the ills of occupation and unemployment (with people generally tending to be only as mentally sick as they can afford to be). This state of affairs makes it all the more likely that the typical psychoanalytic patient would have primarily private sexual motivations behind his difficulties. (Did not Henry James say that sex is something about which we think a great deal when we are not thinking about anything else?)[2] Furthermore, I believe that studies of artistic imagery, outside the strict pale of psychoanalytic emphasis, will bear out Freud's brilliant speculations as to the sexual puns, the *double-entendres*, lurking behind the most unlikely façades. If a man acquires a method of thinking about everything else, for instance, during the sexual deprivations and rigors of adolescence, this cure may well take on the qualities of the disease; and insofar as he continues with this same method in adult years, though his life has since become sexually less exacting, such modes as incipient homosexuality or masturbation may very well be informatively interwoven in the strands of his thought and be discoverable by inspection of the underlying imagery or patterns in this thought.

Indeed, there are only a few fundamental bodily idioms—and why should it not be likely that an attitude, no matter how complex its ideational expression, could only be completed by a channelization within its corresponding gestures? That is, the details of experience behind A's dejection may be vastly different from the details of experience behind B's dejection, yet both A and B may fall into the same bodily posture in expressing their dejection. And in an era like ours, coming at the end of a long individualistic emphasis, where we frequently find expressed an attitude of complete independence, of total, uncompromising self-reliance, this expression would not reach its fulfillment in choreography except in the act of "practical narcissism" (that is, the only wholly independent person would be the one who practiced self-abuse and really meant it).

But it may be noticed that we have here tended to consider mind-body relations from an interactive point of view rather than a materialistic one (which would take the body as the essence of the act and the mentation as the sublimation).

Freud himself, interestingly enough, was originally nearer to this view (necessary, as I hope to show later, for specifically literary purposes) than he later became. Freud explicitly resisted the study of motivation by way of symbols. He distinguished his own mode of analysis from the symbolic by laying the stress upon free association. That is, he would begin the analysis of a neurosis without any preconceived notion as to the absolute meaning of any image that the patient might reveal in the account of a dream. His procedure involved the breaking down of the dream into a set of fragments, with the analyst then inducing the patient to improvise associations on each of these fragments in turn. And afterward, by charting recurrent themes, he would arrive at the crux of the patient's conflict.

Others (particularly Stekel), however, proposed a great short cut here. They offered an absolute content for various items of imagery. For instance, in Stekel's dictionary of symbols, which has the absoluteness of an old-fashioned dreambook, the right-hand path equals the road to righteousness, the left-hand path equals the road to crime, in anybody's dreams (in Lenin's presumably, as well as the Pope's). Sisters are breasts and brothers are buttocks. "The luggage of a traveller is the burden of sin by which one is oppressed," etc. Freud criticizes these on the basis of his own clinical experiences—and whereas he had reservations against specific equations, and rightly treats the method as antithetical to his own contribution, he decides that a high percentage of Stekel's purely intuitive hunches were corroborated. And after warning that such a gift as Stekel's is often evidence of paranoia, he decides that normal persons may also occasionally be capable of it.

Its lure as efficiency is understandable. And, indeed, if we revert to the matter of luggage, for instance, does it not immediately give us insight into a remark of André Gide, who is a specialist in the portrayal of scrupulous criminals, who has developed a stylistic trick for calling to seduction in the accents of evangelism, and who advises that one should learn to "travel light"?

But the trouble with short cuts is that they deny us a chance to take longer routes. With them, the essentializing strategy takes a momentous step forward. You have next but to essentialize your short cuts in turn (a short cut atop a short cut), and you get the sexual emphasis of Freud, the all-embracing ego compensation of Adler, or Rank's master-emphasis upon the birth trauma, etc.

Freud himself fluctuates in his search for essence. At some places you find him proclaiming the all-importance of the sexual, at other places you find him indignantly denying that his psychology is a pansexual one at all, and at still other places you get something halfway between the two, via the concept of the libido, which embraces a spectrum from phallus to philanthropy.

The important matter for our purposes is to suggest that the examination of a poetic work's internal organization would bring us nearer to a variant of the typically Freudian free-association method than to the purely symbolic method toward which he subsequently gravitated.[3]

The critic should adopt a variant of the free-association method. One obviously cannot invite an author, especially a dead author, to oblige him by telling what the author thinks of when the critic isolates some detail or other for improvisation. But the critic can note the context of imagery and ideas in which an image takes its place. He can also note, by such analysis, the kinds of evaluations surrounding the image of a crossing; for instance, is it an escape from or a return to an evil or a good, etc.? Thus finally, by noting the ways in which this crossing behaves, what subsidiary imagery accompanies it, what kind of event it grows out of, what kind of event grows out of it, what altered rhythmic and tonal effects characterize it, etc., one grasps its significance as motivation. And there is no essential motive offered here. The motive of the work is equated with the structure of interrelationships within the work itself.

"But there is more to a work of art than that." I hear this objection being raised. And I agree with it. And I wonder whether we could properly consider the matter in this wise:

For convenience using the word "poem" to cover any complete, made artistic product, let us divide this artifact (the invention, creation, formation, poetic construct) in accordance with three modes of analysis: dream, prayer, chart.

The psychoanalysis of Freud and of the schools stemming from Freud has brought forward an astoundingly fertile range of observations that give us insight into the poem as dream. There is opened up before us a sometimes almost terrifying glimpse into the ways in which we may, while overtly doing one thing, be covertly doing another. Yet, there is nothing mystical or even unusual about this. I may, for instance, consciously place my elbow upon the table. Yet at the same time I am clearly unconscious of the exact distance between my elbow and my nose. Or, if that analogy seems like cheating, let us try another: I may be unconscious of the way in which a painter friend, observant of my postures, would find the particular position of my arm characteristic of me.

Or let us similarly try to take the terror out of infantile regression. Insofar as I speak the same language that I learned as a child, every time I speak there is, within my speech, an ingredient of regression to the infantile level. Regression, we might say, is a function of progression. Where the progression has been a development by evolution or continuity of growth (as were one to have learned to speak and think in English as a child, and still spoke and thought in English) rather than by revolution or discontinuity of growth (as were one to have learned German in childhood, to have moved elsewhere at an early age, and since become so at home in English that he could not even understand a mature conversation in the language of his childhood), the archaic and the now would be identical. You could say, indifferently, either that the speech is regression or that it is not regression. But were the man who had forgot the language of his childhood, to begin speaking nothing but this early language (under a sudden agitation or as the result of some steady pressure), we should have the kind of regression that goes formally by this name in psychoanalytic nomenclature.

The ideal growth, I suppose—the growth without elements of alienation, discontinuity, homelessness—is that wherein regression is natural. We might sloganize it as "the adult a child matured." Growth has here been simply a successive adding of cells—the growth of the chambered nautilus. But there is also the growth of the adult who, "when he became a man, put away childish things." This is the growth of the crab, that grows by abandoning one room and taking on another. It produces moments of crisis. It makes for philosophies of emancipation and enlightenment, where one gets a jolt and is "awakened from the sleep of dogma" (and alas! in leaving his profound "Asiatic slumber," he risks getting in exchange more than mere wakefulness, more than the eternal vigilance that is the price of liberty—he may get wakefulness plus, i.e., insomnia).

There are, in short, critical points (or, in the Hegel-Marx vocabulary, changes of quantity leading to changes of quality) where the process of growth or change converts a previous circle of protection into a circle of confinement. The first such revolution may well be, for the human individual, a purely biological one—the change at birth when the fetus, heretofore enjoying a larval existence in the womb, being fed on manna from the placenta, so outgrows this circle of protection that the benign protection becomes a malign circle of confinement, whereat it must burst forth into a different kind of world—a world of locomotion, aggression, competition, hunt. The mother, it is true, may have already been living in such a world; but the fetus was in a world within this world—in a monastery—a world such as is lived in by "coupon clippers," who get their dividends as the result of sharp economic combat but who may, so long as the payments are regular, devote themselves to thoughts and diseases far "beyond" these harsh material operations.

In the private life of the individual there may be many subsequent jolts of a less purely biological nature, as with the death of some one person who had become pivotal to this individual's mental economy. But whatever these unique variants may be, there is again a universal variant at adolescence, when radical changes in the glandular structure of the body make this body a correspondingly altered environment for the mind, requiring a corresponding change in our perspective, our structure of interpretations, meanings, values, purposes, and inhibitions, if we are to take it properly into account.

In the informative period of childhood our experiences are strongly personalized. Our attitudes take shape with respect to distinct people who have roles, even animals and objects being vessels of character. Increasingly, however, we begin to glimpse a world of abstract relationships, of functions understood solely through the medium of symbols in books. Even such real things as Tibet and Eskimos and Napoleon are for us, who have not been to Tibet, or lived with Eskimos, or fought under Napoleon, but a structure of signs. In a sense, it could be said that we learn these signs flat. We must start from scratch. There is no tradition in them; they are pure present. For though they have been handed down by tradition, we can read meaning into them only insofar as we can project or extend them out of our own experience. We may, through being burned a little, understand the signs for being burned a lot—it is in this sense that the coaching of interpretation could be called traditional. But we cannot understand the signs for being burned a lot until we have in our own flat experience, here and now, been burned a little.

Out of what can these extensions possibly be drawn? Only out of the informative years of childhood. Psychoanalysis talks of purposive forgetting. Yet purposive forgetting is the only way of remembering. One learns the meaning of "table," "book," "father," "mother," "mustn't," by forgetting the contexts in which these words were used. The Darwinian ancestry (locating the individual in his feudal line of descent from the ape) is matched in Freud by a still more striking causal ancestry that we might sloganize as "the child is father to the man." [4]

As we grow up, new meanings must either be engrafted upon old meanings (being to that extent *double-entendres*) or they must be new starts (hence, involving problems of dissociation).

In the study of the poem as dream we find revealed the ways in which the poetic organization takes shape under these necessities. Revise Freud's terms, if you will. But nothing is done by simply trying to refute them or to tie them into knots. One may complain at this procedure, for instance: Freud characterizes the dream as the fulfillment of a wish; an opponent shows him a dream of frustration, and he answers: "But the dreamer wishes to be frustrated." You may demur at that, pointing out that Freud has developed a "heads I win, tails you lose" mode of discourse here. But I maintain that, in doing so, you have contributed nothing. For there are people whose values are askew, for whom frustration itself is a kind of grotesque ambition. If you would, accordingly, propose to chart this field by offering better terms, by all means do so. But better terms are the only kind of refutation here that is worth the trouble. Similarly, one may be unhappy with the concept of ambivalence, which allows pretty much of an open season on explanations (though the specific filling-out may provide a better case for the explanation than appears in this key term itself). But, again, nothing but an alternative explanation is worth the effort of discussion here. Freud's terminology is a dictionary, a lexicon for charting a vastly complex and hitherto largely uncharted field. You can't refute a dictionary. The only profitable answer to a dictionary is another one.

A profitable answer to Freud's treatment of the Oedipus complex, for instance, was Malinowski's study of its variants in a matriarchal society.[5] Here we get at once a corroboration and a refutation of the Freudian doctrine. It is corroborated in that the same general patterns of enmity are revealed; it is refuted in that these patterns are shown not to be innate but to take shape with relation to the difference in family structure itself, with corresponding difference in roles.

Freud's overemphasis upon the patriarchal pattern (an assumption of its absoluteness that is responsible for the Freudian tendency to underrate greatly the economic factors influencing the relationships of persons or roles) is a prejudicial factor that must be discounted, even when treating the poem as dream. Though totemistic religion, for instance, flourished with matriarchal patterns, Freud treats even this in patriarchal terms. And I submit that this emphasis will conceal from us, to a large degree, what is going on in art. (We are still confining ourselves to the dream level—the level at which Freudian co-ordinates come closest to the charting of the logic of poetic structure.)

In the literature of transitional eras, for instance, we find an especial profusion of rebirth rituals, where the poet is making the symbolic passes that will endow him with a new identity. Now, imagine him trying to do a very thorough job of this reidentification. To be completely reborn, he would have to change his very lineage itself. He would have to revise not only his present but also his past. (Ancestry and cause are forever becoming intermingled—the thing is that from which it came—cause is *Ur-sache*, etc.) And could a personalized past be properly confined to a descent through the father, when it is the *mater* that is *semper certa?* Totemism, when not interpreted with Freud's patriarchal bias, may possibly provide us with the necessary cue here. Totemism, as Freud himself reminds us, was a magical device whereby the members of a group were identified with one another by the sharing of the same substance (a process often completed by the ritualistic eating of this substance, though it might, for this very reason, be prohibited on less festive occasions). And it is to the mother that the basic informative experiences of eating are related.

So, all told, even in strongly patriarchal societies (and much more so in a society like ours, where theories of sexual equality, with a corresponding confusion in sexual differentiation along occupational lines, have radically broken the symmetry of pure patriarchalism), would there not be a tendency for rebirth rituals to be completed by symbolizations of matricide and without derivation from competitive, monopolistic ingredients at all? [6]

To consider explicitly a bit of political dreaming, is not Hitler's doctrine of Aryanism something analogous to the adopton of an new totemic line? Has he not voted himself a new identity and, in keeping with a bastardized variant of the strategy of materialistic science, rounded this out by laying claim to a distinct blood stream? What the Pope is saying, benignly, in proclaiming the Hebrew prophets as the spiritual ancestors of Catholicism, Hitler is saying malignly in proclaiming for himself a lineage totally distinct.

Freud, working within the patriarchal perspective, has explained how such thinking becomes tied up with persecution. The paranoid, he says, assigns his imagined persecutor the role of rejected father. This persecutor is all-powerful, as the father seems to the child. He is responsible for every imagined machination (as the Jews, in Hitler's scheme, become the universal devil-function, the leading brains behind every "plot"). Advancing from this brilliant insight, it is not hard to understand why, once Hitler's fantasies are implemented by the vast resources of a nation, the "persecutor" becomes the persecuted.

The point I am trying to bring out is that this assigning of a new lineage to one's self (as would be necessary, in assigning one's self a new identity) could not be complete were it confined to symbolic patricide. There must also be ingredients of symbolic matricide intermingled here (with the phenomena of totemism giving cause to believe that the ritualistic slaying of the maternal relationship may draw upon an even deeper level than the ritualistic slaying of the paternal relationship). Lineage itself is charted after the metaphor of the family tree, which is, to be sure, patriarchalized in Western heraldry, though we get a different quality in the tree of life. MacLeish, in his period of aesthetic negativism, likens the sound of good verse to the ring of the ax in the tree, and if I may mention an early story of my own, "In Quest of Olympus," a rebirth fantasy, it begins by the felling of a tree, followed by the quick change from child to adult, or, within the conventions of the fiction, the change from tiny "Treep" to gigantic "Arjk"; and though, for a long time, under the influence of the Freudian patriarchal emphasis, I tended to consider such trees as fathers, I later felt compelled to make them ambiguously parents. The symbolic structure of Peter Blume's painting, "The Eternal City," almost forces me to assign the tree, in that instance, to a purely maternal category, since the rejected father is pictured in the repellent phalluslike figure of Mussolini, leaving only the feminine role for the luxuriant tree that, by my interpretation of the picture, rounds out the lineage (with the dishonored Christ and the beggarwoman as vessels of the past lineage, and the lewd Mussolini and the impersonal tree as vessels of the new lineage, which I should interpret on the nonpolitical level as saying that sexuality is welcomed, but as a problem, while home is relegated to the world of the impersonal, abstract, observed).

From another point of view we may consider the sacrifice of gods, or of kings, as stylistic modes for dignifying human concerns (a kind of neo-euhemerism). In his stimulating study of the ritual drama, *The Hero*, Lord Raglan overstresses, it seems to me, the notion that these dramas appealed purely as spectacles. Would it not be more likely that the fate of the sacrificial king was also the fate of the audience, in stylized form, dignified, "writ large"? Thus, their engrossment in the drama would not be merely that of watching a parade, or of utilitarian belief that the ritual would insure rainfall, crops, fertility, a good year, etc.; but, also, the stages of the hero's journey would chart the stages of their journey (as an Elizabethan play about royalty was not merely an opportunity for the pit to get a glimpse of high life, a living newspaper on the doings of society, but a dignification or memorializing of their own concerns, translated into the idiom then currently accepted as the proper language of magnification).[7]

But though we may want to introduce minor revisions in the Freudian perspective here, I submit that we should take Freud's key terms, "condensation" and "displacement," as the over-all categories for the analysis of the poem as dream. The terms are really two different approaches to the same phenomenon. Condensation, we might say, deals with the respects in which house in a dream may be more than house, or house plus. And displacement deals with the way in which house may be other than house, or house minus. (Perhaps we should say, more accurately, minus house.)

One can understand the resistance to both of these emphases. They leave no opportunity for a house to be purely and simply a house—and whatever we may feel about it as regards dreams, it is a very disturbing state of affairs when transferred to the realm of art. We must acknowledge, however, that the house in a poem is, when judged purely and simply as a house, a very flimsy structure for protection against wind and rain. So there seems to be some justice in retaining the Freudian terms when trying to decide what is going on in poetry. As Freud fills them out, the justification becomes stronger. The ways in which grammatical rules are violated, for instance; the dream's ways of enacting conjunctions, of solving arguments by club offers of mutually contradictory assertions; the importance of both concomitances and discontinuities for interpretative purposes (the phenomena of either association or dissociation, as you prefer, revealed with greatest clarity in the *lapsus linguae*); the conversion of an expression into its corresponding act (as were one, at a time when "over the fence is out" was an expression in vogue, to apply this comment upon some act by following the dream of this act by a dreamed incident of a ball going over a fence); and, above all, the notion that the optative is in dreams, as often in poetry and essay, presented in the indicative (a Freudian observation fertile to the neopositivists' critique of language)—the pliancy and ingenuity of Freud's researches here make entrancing reading, and continually provide insights that can be carried over, *mutatis mutandis*, to the operations of poetry. Perhaps we might sloganize the point thus: Insofar as art contains a surrealist ingredient (and all art contains some of this ingredient), psychoanalytic co-ordinates are required to explain the logic of its structure.

Perhaps we might take some of the pain from the notions of condensation and displacement (with the tendency of one event to become the synecdochic representative of some other event in the same cluster) by imagining a hypothetical case of authorship. A novelist, let us say, is trying to build up for us a sense of secrecy. He is picturing a conspiracy, yet he was never himself quite this kind of conspirator. Might not this novelist draw upon whatever kinds of conspiracy he himself had experientially known (as for instance were he to draft for this purpose memories of his participation in some childhood bund)? If this were so, an objective breakdown of the imagery with which he surrounded the conspiratorial events in his novel would reveal this contributory ingredient. You would not have to read your interpretation into it. It would be objectively, structurally, there, and could be pointed to by scissorwork. For instance, the novelist might explicitly state that, when joining the conspiracy, the hero recalled some incident of his childhood. Or the adult conspirators would, at strategic points, be explicitly likened by the novelist to children, etc. A statement about the ingredients of the work's motivation would thus be identical with a statement about the work's structure—a statement as to what goes with what in the work itself. Thus, in Coleridge's "The Eolian Harp," you do not have to interpret the poet's communion with the universe as an affront to his wife; the poet himself explicitly apologizes to her for it. Also, it is an objectively citable fact that imagery of noon goes with this apology. If, then, we look at other poems by Coleridge, noting the part played by the Sun at noon in the punishments of the guilt-laden Ancient Mariner, along with the fact that the situation of the narrator's confession involves the detention of a wedding guest from the marriage feast, plus the fact that a preference for church as against marriage is explicitly stated at the end of the poem, we begin to see a motivational cluster emerging. It is obvious that such structural interrelationships cannot be wholly conscious, since they are generalizations about acts that can only be made inductively and statistically after the acts have been accumulated. (This applies as much to the acts of a single poem as to the acts of many poems. We may find a theme emerging in one work that attains fruition in that same work —the ambiguities of its implications where it first emerges attaining explication in the same integer. Or its full character may not be developed until a later work. In its ambiguous emergent form it is a synecdochic representative of the form it later assumes when it comes to fruition in either the same work or in another one.)

However, though the synecdochic process (whereby something does service for the other members of its same cluster or as the foreshadowing of itself in a later development) cannot be wholly conscious, the dream is not all dream. We might say, in fact, that the Freudian analysis of art was handicapped by the aesthetic of the period—an aesthetic shared even by those who would have considered themselves greatly at odds with Freud and who were, in contrast with his delving into the unbeautiful, concerned with beauty only. This was the aesthetic that placed the emphasis wholly upon the function of self-expression. The artist had a number—some unique character or identity—and his art was the externalizing of this inwardness. The general Schopenhauerian trend contributed to this. Von Hartmann's *Philosophy of the Unconscious* has reinforced the same pattern. This version of voluntaristic processes, as connected with current theories of emancipation, resulted in a picture of the dark, unconscious drive calling for the artist to "out with it." The necessary function of the Freudian secular confessional, as a preparatory step to redemption, gave further strength to the same picture. Add the "complex in terms of the simple" strategy (with its variants—higher in terms of lower, normal as a mere attenuation of the abnormal, civilized as the primitive sublimated); add the war of the generations (which was considered as a kind of absolute rather than as a by-product of other factors, for those who hated the idea of class war took in its stead either the war of the generations or the war of the sexes) —and you get a picture that almost automatically places the emphasis upon art as utterance, as the naming of one's number, as a blurting-out, as catharsis by secretion.

I suggested two other broad categories for the analysis of poetic organization: prayer and chart.

Prayer would enter the Freudian picture insofar as it concerns the optative. But prayer does not stop at that. Prayer is also an act of communion. Hence, the concept of prayer, as extended to cover also secular forms of petition, moves us into the corresponding area of communication in general. We might say that, whereas the expressionistic emphasis reveals the ways in which the poet with an attitude embodies it in appropriate gesture, communication deals with the choice of gesture for the inducement of corresponding attitudes. Sensory imagery has this same communicative function, inviting the reader, within the limits of the fiction at least, to make himself over in the image of the imagery.

Considering the poem from this point of view, we begin with the incantatory elements in art, the ways of leading in or leading on the hypothetical audience X to which the poem, as a medium, is addressed (though this hypothetical audience X be nothing more concrete, as regards social relations, than a critical aspect of the poet's own personality). Even Freud's dream had a censor; but the poet's censor is still more exacting, as his shapings and revisions are made for the purpose of forestalling resistances (be those an essay reader's resistances to arguments and evidence or the novel reader's resistance to developments of narrative or character). We move here into the sphere of rhetoric (reader-writer relationships, an aspect of art that Freud explicitly impinges upon only to a degree in his analysis of wit), with the notion of address being most evident in oration and letter, less so in drama, and least in the lyric. Roughly, I should say that the slightest presence of revision is per se indication of a poet's feeling that his work is addressed (if only, as Mead might say, the address of an "I" to its "me").

Here would enter consideration of formal devices, ways of pointing up and fulfilling expectations, of living up to a contract with the reader (as Wordsworth and Coleridge might put it), of easing by transition or sharpening by ellipsis; in short, all that falls within the sphere of incantation, imprecation, exhortation, inducement, weaving and releasing of spells; matters of style and form, of meter and rhythm, as contributing to these results; and thence to the conventions and social values that the poet draws upon in forming the appropriate recipes for the roles of protagonist and antagonist, into which the total agon is analytically broken down, with subsidiary roles polarized about one or the other of the two agonists tapering off to form a region of overlap between the two principles—the ground of the agon. Here, as the reverse of prayer, would come also invective, indictment, oath. And the gestures might well be tracked down eventually to choices far closer to bodily pantomime than is revealed on the level of social evaluation alone (as were a poet, seeking the gestures appropriate for the conveying of a social negativeness, to draw finally upon imagery of disgust, and perhaps even, at felicitous moments, to select his speech by playing up the very consonants that come nearest to the enacting of repulsion).

As to the poem as chart: the Freudian emphasis upon the pun brings it about that something can be only insofar as it is something else. But, aside from these ambiguities, there is also a statement's value as being exactly what it is. Perhaps we could best indicate what we mean by speaking of the poem as chart if we called it the poet's contribution to an informal dictionary. As with proverbs, he finds some experience or relationship typical, or recurrent, or significant enough for him to need a word for it. Except that his way of defining the word is not to use purely conceptual terms, as in a formal dictionary, but to show how his vision behaves, with appropriate attitudes. In this, again, it is like the proverb that does not merely name but names vindictively, or plaintively, or promisingly, or consolingly, etc. His namings need not be new ones. Often they are but memorializings of an experience long recognized.

But, essentially, they are enactments, with every form of expression being capable of treatment as the efficient extension of one aspect or another of ritual drama (so that even the scientific essay would have its measure of choreography, its pedestrian pace itself being analyzed as gesture or incantation, its polysyllables being as style the mimetics of a distinct monasticism, etc.). And this observation, whereby we have willy-nilly slipped back into the former subject, the symbolic act as prayer, leads us to observe that the three aspects of the poem, here proposed, are not elements that can be isolated in the poem itself, with one line revealing the "dream," another the "prayer," and a third the "chart." They merely suggest three convenient modes in which to approach the task of analysis.[8]

The primary category, for the explicit purposes of literary criticism, would thus seem to me to be that of communication rather than that of wish, with its disguises, frustrations, and fulfillments. Wishes themselves, in fact, become from this point of view analyzable as purposes that get their shape from the poet's perspective in general (while this perspective is in turn shaped by the collective medium of communication). The choice of communication also has the advantage, from the sociological point of view, that it resists the Freudian tendency to overplay the psychological factor (as the total medium of communication is not merely that of words, colors, forms, etc., or of the values and conventions with which these are endowed, but also the productive materials, co-operative resources, property rights, authorities, and their various bottle-necks, which figure in the total act of human conversation).[9]

To sum up: I should say that, for the explicit purposes of literary criticism, we should require more emphasis than the Freudian structure gives, (1) to the proportional strategy as against the essentializing one, (2) to matriarchal symboliza-tions as against the Freudian patriarchal bias, (3) to poem as prayer and chart, as against simply the poem as dream.

But I fully recognize that, once the ingenious and complex structure has been erected, nearly anyone can turn up with proposals that it be given a little more of this, a little less of that, a pinch of so-and-so, etc. And I recognize that, above all, we owe an enormous debt of gratitude to the man who, by his insight, his energy, and his remarkably keen powers of articulation, made such tinkering possible. It is almost fabu-lous to think that, after so many centuries of the family, it is only now that this central factor in our social organization has attained its counterpart in an organized critique of the family and of the ways in which the informative experience with familiar roles may be carried over, or "metaphored," into the experience with extra-familiar roles, giving these latter, insofar as they are, or are felt to be, analogous with the former, a structure of interpretations and attitudes borrowed from the former. And insofar as poets, like everyone else, are regularly involved in such informative familiar relationships, long before any but a few rudimentary bodily gestures are available for communicative use (with their first use unques-tionably being the purely self-expressive one), the child is indeed the adult poet's father, as he is the father of us all (if not so in essence, then at least as regards an important predisposing factor "to look out for"). And thence we get to Freud's brilliant documentation of this ancestry, as it affects the maintenance of a continuity in the growing personality.

Only if we eliminate biography entirely as a relevant fact about poetic organization can we eliminate the importance of the psychoanalyst's search for universal patterns of biography (as revealed in the search for basic myths which recur in new guises as a theme with variations); and we can eliminate biography as a relevant fact about poetic organization only if we consider the work of art as if it were written neither by people nor for people, involving neither inducements nor resistances.[10] Such can be done, but the cost is tremendous insofar as the critic considers it his task to disclose the poem's eventfulness.

However, this is decidedly not the same thing as saying that "we cannot appreciate the poem without knowing about its relation to the poet's life as an individual." Rather, it is equivalent to saying: "We cannot understand a poem's structure without understanding the function of that structure. And to understand its function we must understand its purpose." To be sure, there are respects in which the poem, as purpose, is doing things for the poet that it is doing for no one else. For instance, I think it can be shown by analysis of the imagery in Coleridge's "Mystery Poems" that one of the battles being fought there is an attempt to get self-redemption by the poet's striving for the vicarious or ritualistic redemption of his drug. It is obvious that this aspect of the equational structure is private and would best merit discussion when one is discussing the strategy of one man in its particularities. Readers in general will respond only to the sense of guilt, which was sharpened for Coleridge by his particular burden of addiction, but which may be sharpened for each reader by totally different particularities of experience. But if you do not discuss the poem's structure as a function of symbolic redemption at all (as a kind of private-enterprise Mass, with important ingredients of a black Mass), the observations you make about its structure are much more likely to be gratuitous and arbitrary (quite as only the most felicitous of observers could relevantly describe the distribution of men and postures in a football game if he had no knowledge of the game's purpose and did not discuss its formations as oppositional tactics for the carrying-out of this purpose, but treated the spectacle simply as the manifestation of a desire to instruct and amuse).

Thus, in the case of "The Ancient Mariner," knowledge of Coleridge's personal problems may enlighten us as to the particular burdens that the Pilot's boy ("who now doth crazy go") took upon himself as scapegoat for the poet alone. But his appearance in the poem cannot be understood at all, except in superficial terms of the interesting or the picturesque, if we do not grasp his function as a scapegoat of some sort—a victimized vessel for drawing off the most malign aspects of the curse that afflicts the "greybeard loon" whose cure had been effected under the dubious aegis of moonlight. And I believe that such a functional approach is the only one that can lead into a profitable analysis of a poem's structure even on the purely technical level.

I remember how, for instance, I had pondered for years the reference to the "silly buckets" filled with curative rain. I noted the epithet as surprising, picturesque, and interesting. I knew that it was doing something, but I wasn't quite sure what. But as soon as I looked upon the Pilot's boy as a scapegoat, I saw that the word *silly* was a technical foreshadowing of the fate that befell this figure in the poem. The structure itself became more apparent: the "loon"-atic Mariner begins his cure from drought under the aegis of a moon that causes a silly rain, thence by synecdoche to silly buckets, and the most malignant features of this problematic cure are transferred to the Pilot's boy who now doth crazy go. Now, if you want to confine your observations to the one poem, you have a structural-functional-technical analysis of some important relationships within the poem itself. If you wish to trail the matter farther afield, into the equational structure of other work by Coleridge, you can back your interpretation of the moon by such reference as that to "moon-blasted madness," which gives you increased authority to discern lunatic ingredients in the lunar. His letters, where he talks of his addiction in imagery like that of the "Mystery Poems" and contemplates entering an insane asylum for a cure, entitle you to begin looking for traces of the drug as an ingredient in the redemptive problem. His letters also explicitly place the drug in the same cluster with the serpent; hence, we begin to discern what is going on when the Mariner transubstantiates the water snakes, in removing them from the category of the loathsome and accursed to the category of the blessed and beautiful. So much should be enough for the moment. Since the poem is constructed about an opposition between punishments under the aegis of the sun and cure under the aegis of the moon, one could proceed in other works to disclose the two sets of equations clustered about these two principles. Indeed, even in "The Ancient Mariner" itself we get a momentous cue, as the sun is explicitly said to be "like God's own head." [11] But, for the moment, all I would maintain is that, if we had but this one poem by Coleridge, and knew not one other thing about him, we could not get an insight into its structure until we began with an awareness of its function as a symbolic redemptive process.

I can imagine a time when the psychological picture will be so well-known and taken into account—when we shall have gone so far beyond Freud's initial concerns—that a reference to the polymorphous perverse of the infantile, for instance, will seem far too general—a mere first approximation. Everyone provides an instance of the polymorphous perverse, in attenuated form, at a moment of hesitancy; caught in the trackless maze of an unresolved, and even undefined, conflict, he regresses along this channel and that, in a formless experimentation that "tries anything and everything, somewhat." And insofar as his puzzle is resolved into pace, and steady rhythms of a progressive way out are established, there is always the likelihood that this solution will maintain continuity with the past of the poet's personality by a covert draw-

ing upon analogies with this past. Hence the poet or specu-
lator, no matter how new the characters with which he is now
concerned, will give them somewhat the roles of past characters; whereat I see nothing unusual about the thought that
a mature and highly complex philosophy might be so organized as to be surrogate for, let us say, a kind of adult breast-
feeding—or, in those more concerned with alienation, a kind
of adult weaning. Such categories do not by any means encompass the totality of a communicative structure; but they
are part of it, and the imagery and transitions of the poem
itself cannot disclose their full logic until such factors are
taken into account.

However, I have spoken of pace. And perhaps I might
conclude with some words on the bearing that the Freudian
technique has upon the matter of pace. The Freudian procedure is primarily designed to break down a rhythm grown
obsessive, to confront the systematic pieties of the patient's
misery with systematic impieties of the clinic.[12] But the emphasis here is more upon the breaking of a malign rhythm
than upon the upbuilding of a benign one. There is no place
in this technique for examining the available resources
whereby the adoption of total dramatic enactment may lead
to correspondingly proper attitude. There is no talk of games,
of dance, of manual and physical actions, of historical role,
as a "way in" to this new upbuilding. The sedentary patient
is given a sedentary cure. The theory of rhythms—work
rhythms, dance rhythms, march rhythms—is no explicit part
of this scheme, which is primarily designed to break old
rhythms rather than to establish new ones.

The establishing of a new pace, beyond the smashing of
the old puzzle, would involve a rounded philosophy of the
drama. Freud, since his subject is conflict, hovers continually
about the edges of such a philosophy; yet it is not dialectical
enough. For this reason Marxists properly resent his theories,
even though one could, by culling incidental sentences from
his works, fit him comfortably into the Marxist perspective.
But the Marxists are wrong, I think, in resenting him as an
irrationalist, for there is nothing more rational than the systematic recognition of irrational and nonrational factors. And I
should say that both Freudians and Marxists are wrong insofar
as they cannot put their theories together, by an over-all
theory of drama itself (as they should be able to do, since
Freud gives us the material of the closet drama, and Marx
the material of the problem play, the one treated in terms
of personal conflicts, the other in terms of public conflicts).

The approach would require explicitly the analysis of role:
salvation via change or purification of identity (purification in

either the moral or chemical sense); different typical relationships between individual and group (as charted attitudinally
in proverbs, and in complex works treated as sophisticated
variants); modes of acceptance, rejection, self-acceptance,
rejection of rejection [13] ("the enemies of my enemies are my
friends"); transitional disembodiment as intermediate step
between old self and new self (the spirituality of Shelley and
of the Freudian cure itself); monasticism in the development
of methods that fix a transitional or otherworldly stage, thereby making the evanescent itself into a kind of permanency
—with all these modes of enactment finally employing, as part
of the gesture idiom, the responses of the body itself as actor.
(If one sought to employ Freud, as is, for the analysis of the
poem, one would find almost nothing on poetic posture or
pantomime, tonality, the significance of different styles and
rhythmic patterns, nothing of this behaviorism.) Such, it
seems to me, would be necessary, and much more in that
direction, before we could so extend Freud's perspective that
it revealed the major events going on in art.

But such revisions would by no means be anti-Freudian.
They would be the kind of extensions required by reason of
the fact that the symbolic act of art, whatever its analogies
with the symbolic act of neurosis, also has important diver-
gencies from the symbolic act of neurosis. They would be
extensions designed to take into account the full play of
communicative and realistic ingredients that comprise so
large an aspect of poetic structure.

NOTES

1. The essentializing strategy has its function when dealing with
   classes of items; the proportional one is for dealing with an
   item in its uniqueness. By isolating the matter of voluntarism,
   we put Freud in a line or class with Augustine. By isolating
   the matter of his concern with a distinction between unconscious and conscious, we may put him in a line with Leibnitz's
   distinction between perception and apperception. Or we could
   link him with the Spinozistic *conatus* and the Schopenhauerian
   will. Or, as a rationalist, he falls into the bin with Aquinas
   (who is himself most conveniently isolated as a rationalist if
   you employ the essentializing as against the proportional strategy, stressing what he added rather than what he retained).
   Many arguments seem to hinge about the fact that there is
   an unverbalized disagreement as to the choice between these

strategies. The same man, for instance, who might employ the essentializing strategy in proclaiming Aquinas as a rationalist, taking as the significant factor in Aquinas's philosophy his additions to rationalism rather than considering this as an ingredient in a faith philosophy, might object to the bracketing of Aquinas and Freud (here shifting to the proportional strategy, as he pointed out the totally different materials with which Aquinas surrounded his rational principle).

2. We may distinguish between public and universal motives. Insofar as one acts in a certain way because of his connection with a business or party, he would act from a public motive. His need of response to a new glandular stimulation at adolescence, on the other hand, would arise regardless of social values, and in that sense would be at once private and universal. The particular forms in which he expressed this need would, of course, be channelized in accordance with public or social factors.

3. Perhaps, to avoid confusion, I should call attention to the fact that symbolic in this context is being used differently by me from its use in the expression "symbolic action." If a man crosses a street, it is a practical act. If he writes a book about crossings—crossing streets, bridges, oceans, etc.—that is a symbolic act. Symbolic, as used in the restricted sense (in contrast with free association), would refer to the imputation of an absolute meaning to a crossing, a meaning that I might impute even before reading the book in question. Against this, I should maintain: One can never know what a crossing means, in a specific book, until he has studied its tie-up with other imagery in that particular book.

4. Maybe the kind of forgetting that is revealed by psychoanalysis could, within this frame, be better characterized as an incomplete forgetting. That is, whereas table, for instance, acquires an absolute and emotionally neutral meaning as a name merely for a class of objects, by a merging of all the contexts involving the presence of a table a table becomes symbolic, or a *double-entendre,* or more than table, when some particular informative context is more important than the others. That is, when table, as used by the poet, has overtones of, let us say, *one* table at which his mother worked when he was a child. In this way the table, its food, and the cloth may become surrogates for the mother, her breasts, and her apron. And incest awe may become merged with "mustn't touch" injunctions, stemming from attempts to keep the child from meddling with the objects on the table. In a dream play by Edmund Wilson, *The Crime in the Whistler Room,* there are two worlds of plot, with the characters belonging in the one world looking upon those in the other as dead, and the hero of this living world taking a dream shape as werewolf. The

worlds switch back and forth, depending upon the presence or removal of a gate-leg table. In this instance I think we should not be far wrong in attributing some such content as the above to the table when considering it as a fulcrum upon which the structure of the plot is swung.

5. It is wrong, I think, to consider Freud's general picture as that of an individual psychology. Adler's start from the concept of ego compensation fits this description par excellence. But Freud's is a family psychology. He has offered a critique of the family, though it is the family of a neopatriarch. It is interesting to watch Freud, in his *Group Psychology and the Analysis of the Ego,* frankly shifting between the primacy of group psychology and the primacy of individual psychology, changing his mind as he debates with himself in public and leaves in his pages the record of his fluctuations, frankly stated as such. Finally, he compromises by leaving both, drawing individual psychology from the role of the monopolistic father, and group psychology from the roles of the sons, deprived of sexual gratification by the monopolistic father, and banded together for their mutual benefit. But note that the whole picture is that of a family, albeit of a family in which the woman is a mere passive object of male wealth.

6. Or you might put it this way: Rebirth would require a killing of the old self. Such symbolic suicide, to be complete, would require a snapping of the total ancestral line (as being an integral aspect of one's identity). Hence, a tendency for the emancipatory crime to become sexually ambivalent. Freud's patriarchal emphasis leads to an overstress upon father-rejection as a basic cause rather than as a by-product of conversion (the Kierkegaard earthquake, that was accompanied by a changed attitude toward his father). Suicide, to be thorough, would have to go farther, and the phenomena of identity revealed in totemism might require the introduction of matricidal ingredients also. Freud himself, toward the end of *Totem and Taboo,* gives us an opening wedge by stating frankly, "In this evolution I am at a loss to indicate the place of the great maternal deities who perhaps everywhere preceded the paternal deities." This same patriarchal emphasis also reinforces the Freudian tendency to treat social love as a mere sublimation of balked male sexual appetite, whereas a more matriarchal concern, with the Madonna and Child relationship, would suggest a place for affection as a primary biological motivation. Not even a naturalistic account of motivation would necessarily require reinforcement from the debunking strategy (in accordance with which the real motives would be incipient perversions, and social motives as we know them would be but their appearances, or censored disguise).

7. Might not the sacrificial figure (as parent, king, or god) also

at times derive from no resistance or vindictiveness whatsoever, but be the recipient of the burden simply through "having stronger shoulders, better able to bear it"? And might the choice of guilty scapegoats (such as a bad father) be but a secondary development for accommodating this socialization of a loss to the patterns of legality?

8. Dream has its opposite, nightmare; prayer has its opposite, oath. Charts merely vary—in scope and relevance. In "Kubla Khan," automatically composed during an opium dream, the dream ingredient is uppermost. In "The Ancient Mariner," the prayer ingredient is uppermost. In "Dejection" and "The Pains of Sleep," the chart ingredient is uppermost: here Coleridge is explicitly discussing his situation.

9. I have since come to realize that "communication" is itself but a technical species of "love," hence always lurks about the edges of the Freudian "Libido."

10. Those who stress form of this sort, as against content, usually feel that they are concerned with judgments of excellence as against judgments of the merely representative. Yet, just as a content category such as the Oedipus complex is neutral, i.e., includes both good and bad examples of its kind, so does a form category, such as sonnet or iambic pentameter, include both good and bad examples of its kind. In fact, though categories or classifications may be employed for evaluative purposes, they should be of themselves nonevaluative. Apples is a neutral, nonevaluative class, including firm apples and rotten ones. Categories that are in themselves evaluative are merely circular arguments—disguised ways of saying "this is good because it is good." The orthodox strategy of disguise is to break the statement into two parts, such as: "This is good because it has form; and form is good." The lure behind the feeling that the miracle of evaluation can be replaced by a codified scientific routine of evaluation seems to get its backing from the hope that concept of quality can be matched by a number. The terms missing may be revealed by a diagram, thus:

Quantity	Number
Weight	Pound
Length	Foot
Duration	Hour
Quality	( )
Excellence	( )
Inferiority	( )

Often the strategy of concealment is accomplished by an ambiguity, as the critic sometimes uses the term "poetry" to designate good poetry, and sometimes uses it to designate "poetry, any poetry, good, bad, or indifferent." I do, however, strongly sympathize with the formalists, as against the sociologists, when the sociologist treats poetry simply as a kind of haphazard sociological survey—a report about world conditions that often shows commendable intuitive insight but is handicapped by a poor methodology of research and controls.

11. That's not the whole story. A few lines later the sun becomes "No bigger than the Moon." And earlier, the Mariner's disclosure that he killed the Albatross had emerged from a description of "Moon-shine." Thus not only the cure, but also the offense and the avenger, have moony ingredients.

12. There are styles of cure, shifting from age to age, because each novelty becomes a commonplace, so that the patient integrates his conflict with the ingredients of the old cure itself, thus making them part of his obsession. Hence, the need for a new method of jolting. Thus, I should imagine that a patient who had got into difficulties after mastering the Freudian technique would present the most obstinate problems for a Freudian cure. He would require some step beyond Freud. The same observation would apply to shifting styles in poetry and philosophy, when considered as cures, as the filling of a need.

13. I am indebted to Norbert Gutermann for the term "self-acceptance" and to William S. Knickerbocker for the term "rejection of rejection."

THE DYNAMICS OF ART *

Herbert Read

Any discussion of the psychology of art must begin with an affirmation that is not always acceptable to the psychologist; or, if acceptable, is often conveniently forgotten. This is the fact that the work of art exists as such, not in virtue of any "meaning" it expresses, but only in virtue of a particular organization of its constituent material elements. We say that this organization is *formal,* but we are soon aware that any metrical analysis of form, any morphology of art, does not yield up art's secret. Form refers back to measures of area, volume, time intervals, tones; the appeal of these measures, which is called aesthetic because it operates through perception and sensation, is accepted pragmatically, as an evident fact. There have been various attempts to explain this appeal, beginning with the early Greek philosophers, and they have generally been attempts to relate the measurements of art to the measurements of nature, and to see in the proportions of the crystal, of vegetation, of man himself, the prototypes of the proportions discovered in the work of art. I say *discovered* in the work of art because though the Greek architects and sculptors, like Le Corbusier and others today, began to make conscious use of natural proportions, the significant fact is that these proportions appear without conscious intervention in all works of art. That, perhaps, is no more than a hypothesis which has yet to be proved, and certainly a few traditional concepts of natural proportion, such as the Golden Section, do not suffice to explain all the phenomena of art. Form, that is to say, is not necessarily so obvious that it can be expressed in a single formula such as the Golden Section; and we must beware of limiting our notions of form to the canons of a particular tradition or culture. Most of you will remember a book that was published in Berlin in the 1920's—Professor Karl Blossfeldt's *Urformen der Kunst.*[1] It was a book that at the time was a revelation of the beauty inherent in plant forms, but Professor Blossfeldt had looked on nature with classical eyes, and found everywhere the motifs of Greek or

* [From *Eranos-Jahrbuch 1952* (Zurich: Rhein-Verlag, 1953). Reprinted by permission of the author and the Bollingen Foundation, Inc. The essay is also published by Horizon Press, in *The Forms of Things Unknown,* by Herbert Read (New York: 1960). The illustrations originally accompanying this essay are here deleted.]

Gothic architecture and decorative art. About the same time the *surréalistes* in Paris, inspired by Rimbaud, Lautréamont, and Freud, began to find beauty in phenomena of a different kind which, in spite of their strangeness, are equally natural —it might be an octopus, a fungus, or the proliferations of disease or decay. Basically no doubt all these forms are the same, or relate to one universal system of formal articulation. What is significant is the selection and combination of forms made by the artist. The forms selected by Karl Blossfeldt tell us something about Karl Blossfeldt, just as the forms selected by a surrealist painter like Max Ernst tell us something about Max Ernst.[2] There is "no hierarchy in the cycle of natural forms," remarks, very truly, another painter of this school, André Masson: "The royal structure of the human body is no more *beautiful* than the radiolaria, an oceanic star with solid rays."[3] The artist, we might say, expresses himself with "forms already plastic," forms discovered in nature, the signs which, according to Novalis, occur everywhere, and which, in the activity of art, we merely disinter, isolate, and re-combine.

With what purpose? Here, at the opening of our discussion, it must be recognized that the purpose of a work of art is not necessarily definable in the terms of rational discourse. Art is a form of symbolic discourse, and its elements are not linguistic but, as Conrad Fiedler recognized seventy years ago, perceptual. We are not in a realm of abstract thought at all, but in one of "visual cognition." The work of art remains in what André Masson has called "the secret world of analogy." Masson draws attention to some remarks made by Goethe in a conversation reported by J. Daniel Falk which go immediately to the heart of our problem:

We talk too much, we should talk less and draw more. As for me, I should like to renounce the word and, like plastic nature, speak only in drawings. This fig tree, this little serpent, this cocoon lying there under the window and quietly awaiting its future, all these are profound seals; and he who can decipher their true sense, can in the future do without spoken or written language! . . . Look, he added, pointing to a multitude of plants and fantastic figures which he had just traced on the paper while talking—here are really bizarre images, really mad, yet they could be twenty times more mad and fantastic and still there the question would arise—if their type did not exist somewhere in nature. In drawing, the soul recounts a part of its essential being and it is precisely the deepest secrets of creation, those which rest basically on drawing and sculpture, that the soul reveals in this way.[4]

One might find other expressions of the same idea in Goethe's writings, and he indeed was the first to realise that there are two distinct and uninterchangeable nonlinguistic modes of communication, one elaborated by man and of limited scope, the other elaborated by nature, of unlimited scope, both of which man may use in that expressive process which we call art.

Nature, we might say, is a world of plastic forms, evolved or in the process of evolution, and man perceives these forms or carries in his memory images of these forms. Images, totally distinct from words or any signs used in discursive reasoning, assume an autonomous activity, combine by way of analogy or metaphor, and produce an effect in us which may be merely personal or sensational and which, when pleasurable, is called beautiful; or may be supra-personal and will then convey what Goethe calls "the deepest secrets of creation"; or what Dr. Erich Neumann, in his contribution to the *Eranos-Tagung* last year,[5] called *"die Gefühlsqualität des Numinosen."* I favor this emphasis on the quality of feeling, for it must never be forgotten that in art the way from the personal to the supra-personal lies along the path of sensation. There are no mental aids in art; without sensibility there is no revelation.

Obviously there is, as Dr. Jung has recognized, a creative process at work here which involves the artist as a medium, or as a field of operations. The artist is responsible only as the possessor and activator of a releasing mechanism. It therefore becomes very difficult to apply to this process the ordinary laws of causality. I am not referring to the biological difficulty of explaining the sudden emergence of a genius like Michelangelo or Mozart: the science of genetics can juggle with its genes and chromosomes to some purpose in that direction. But given the genius, how explain the Sistine Chapel or *Figaros Hochzeit*? It is not the fact but the quality of genius that calls for explanation, and of this quality genius itself, in its operations, may be in some sense unaware.

Dr. Jung has expressed such a view:

> Personal causality has as much and as little to do with the work of art, as the soil with the plant that springs from it. Doubtless we may learn to understand some peculiarities of the plant by becoming familiar with the character of its habitat. And for the botanist this is, of course, an important component of his knowledge. But nobody will maintain that he has thereby recognized all the essentials relating to the plant itself. The personal orientation that is demanded by the problem of personal causality is out of place in the presence of the work of art, just because the work of art is not a human being, but supra-personal. It is a thing and not a personality; hence the personal is no criterion for it.[6]

Dr. Jung has also said, at the beginning of this same essay on "Poetic Art," that that which constitutes the essential nature of art must always lie outside the province of psychology—"the problem what is art in itself, can never be the object of a psychological, but only of an aesthetic-artistic method of approach." I am myself an aesthetician, and with this warning in mind I shall disclaim any intention of providing a psychological explanation for phenomena which have been so magisterially excluded from the province of psychology. At the same time it must be observed that it is very difficult to talk about the creative process in art without at the same time giving some information about the thing created, and Jung himself was the first to break his rule—he has made some very important observations about the specific qualities of works of art. He has said, as we have just heard, that art is suprapersonal. He goes on to make a distinction between works of art that are deliberate, created by the artist's conscious will and judgment; and works of art that are spontaneous, fully formed before delivered, for which the artist merely acts as a channel. He says of such a work of art that it is "a force of nature that effects its purpose, either with tyrannical might, or with that subtle cunning which nature brings to the achievement of her end, quite regardless of the weal or woe of the man who is the vehicle of the creative force." He distinguishes between symbolic works of art which rarely permit of aesthetic enjoyment and non-symbolic works of art which invite such enjoyment and offer us "an harmonious vision of fulfilment." And finally, and this is the point of departure for our present deliberations, he suggests that the creative process is an autonomous complex, a living independent organism implanted, as it were, in the souls of man—"a detached portion of the psyche that leads an independent psychic life withdrawn from the hierarchy of consciousness, and in proportion to its energic value or force, may appear as a mere disturbance of the voluntarily directed process of consciousness, or as a superordinated authority which may take the ego bodily into its service." [7]

The notion of a detached portion of the psyche, capable of independent activity, is difficult to accept, since we are so prejudiced in favor of the unity or integrity of the personality. And yet such an autonomous force is one of the oldest and most persistent ideas in human history. It is the Ancient Greek notion of a *daemon*, which goes back at least as far as Heraclitus, and which was used by Plato specifically to explain the phenomenon of poetic inspiration. Daemons were not always good: they shared, and might even be responsible for, the perversity of mankind. In the Middle Ages they were divided into guardian angels and devils, and the autonomous complexes of modern psychology are equally ambiguous. They may even remain ambiguous, from an ethical point of view, when they emerge into consciousness as works of art. But ethical ambiguity does not affect aesthetic harmony, and it is the source and significance of that harmony which is our present concern.

At the source of all autonomous psychic activities Jung finds a phenomenon which has enjoyed several names and undergone certain transformations as the evidence accumulated. The name which Jung has given to this phenomenon is the *archetype*, a somewhat theological term which may hide, from the uncautious, the essentially materialistic basis of the whole conception, as it took shape in Jung's mind. I think I am right in saying that the term "archetype" was preceded by the equivalent term "primordial image," which was more concrete and more directly related to the current terminology of psychology. Indeed, while for the historical description of the archetypes we may have to range over wide fields of myth and fable, as phenomena they are nevertheless firmly rooted in the physiological structure of the brain. Their functions cannot be revealed by anatomical dissection, any more than the "engrams" and other hypothetical entities of the modern physiologist. But the brain has evolved—has grown in size and complexity through vast stretches of time—and its structure is related to the experiences of countless generations of the human species. It is Jung's reasonable assumption that the profoundest social experiences of mankind must have left some physiological trace in the structure of the brain; and in particular that some of the earliest experiences of the species, long forgotten in the comparative security of historical times, left the deepest traces.

Archetypes, therefore, must be conceived, as the engrams of the physiologist are conceived, as "inherited with the structure of the brain"; indeed, they *are* engrams, the lowest layer of these physical impresses, and because they are so primordial, Jung described them as "the chthonic portion of the mind . . . that portion through which the mind is linked to nature, or in which, at least, its relatedness to the earth and the universe seems most comprehensible." Jung says specifically, and it is a saying to which I shall return, that the primordial images which proceed from this chthonic level of the brain show most clearly "the influence of the earth and its laws upon the mind." [8]

The archetypes, therefore, are a function of the brain, but we are not normally aware of their existence. They are not so much unconscious as *unactivated*, dynamos that do not go into action until charged with some psychic current. When they do go into action, they act in a predetermined way—in the way predetermined by their physical constitution and mechanism. They connect up with mnemonic images, deeply buried memories of racial experience, and as these images emerge into individual consciousness, perhaps transformed on the way, they inevitably revive and re-present "countless typical experiences of our ancestors." [9]

But there is nothing inevitably aesthetic about such revived images, even if we regard them, not so much as concrete symbols, but rather, as Jung himself has suggested, as "typical forms of apprehension," as "regularly recurring ways of apprehension." [10] Ways and forms of apprehension imply a structural organization of the symbolic content, and what is structural *may* be aesthetic. "A factor determining the uniformity and regularity of our apprehension"—that is another of Jung's definitions of the archetypes, and it comes very near to the Gestalt definition of the aesthetic factor in perception as "a disposition to feel the completeness of an experienced event as being right and fit." [11] The farther modern psychology has probed into the distinctive quality of the work of art, the more it has tended to recognize the presence of autonomous processes of organization within the nervous system, and to attribute to these processes the formal characteristics that constitute the aesthetic appeal of the work of art. I refer in particular to the approach of a Gestalt psychologist like K. Koffka to the problems of art. [12]

There is an inherent biological necessity in such aesthetic organization of the data of perception. As Susanne Langer has said:

> Our merest sense-experience is a process of *formulation.* The world that actually meets our senses is not a world of "things," about which we are invited to discover facts as soon as we have codified the necessary logical language to do so: the world of pure sensation is so complex, so fluid and full, that sheer sensitivity to stimuli would only encounter what William James has called (in a characteristic phrase) "a blooming, buzzing, confusion." Out of this bedlam our sense organs must select certain predominant forms, if they are to make report of *things* and not of mere dissolving sense. The eye and the ear must have their logic. . . . An object is not a datum, but a form construed by the sensitive and intelligent organ, a form which is at once an experimental individual thing and a symbol for the concept of it, for *this sort of thing.*[13]

I must quote further from Mrs. Langer's book, because apparently without any awareness of Jung's psychology, approaching our problem as a logician and philosopher, she arrives at identical conclusions:

A tendency to organize the sensory field into groups and patterns of sense data, to perceive forms rather than a flux of light-impressions, seems to be inherent in our receptor apparatus just as much as in the higher nervous centres with which we do arithmetic and logic. But this unconscious appreciation of forms is the primitive root of all abstraction, which in turn is the keynote of rationality; so it appears that the conditions for rationality lie deep in our pure animal experience—in our power of perceiving, in the elementary functions of our eyes and ears and fingers. Mental life begins with our mere physiological constitution. A little reflection shows us that, since no experience occurs more than once, so-called "repeated" experiences are really *analogous* occurrences, all fitting a form that was abstracted on the first occasion. *Familiarity* is nothing but the quality of fitting very neatly into a form of previous experience. . . .

No matter what heights the human mind may attain, it can work only with the organs it has and the functions peculiar to them. Eyes that did not see forms could never furnish it with *images;* ears that did not hear articulated sounds could never open it to *words.* Sense-data, in brief, would be useless to a mind whose activity is "through and through a symbolic process," were they not *par excellence* receptacles of meaning. But meaning . . . accrues essentially to forms. Unless the *Gestalt* psychologists are right in their belief that *Gestaltung* is of the very nature of perception, I do not know how the hiatus between perception and conception, sense-organ and mind-organ, chaotic stimulus and logical response, is ever to be closed and welded. A mind that works primarily with meanings must have organs that supply it primarily with forms.[14]

That is the point: form exists and then a meaning "creeps into it." [15] But where do these forms come from—what forms the forms? A form, Susanne Langer says, was abstracted on the first occasion; a separate pattern was segregated from the sensory field, and once imprinted on the cortex, was gradually "developed" by analogous or identical experiences until it acquired what we call meaning. The form became detachable, as a sign or symbol. According to Jung, as we have seen, by reason of their intensity or their frequent recurrence, certain experiences have left formal imprints on the cellular structure of the brain: they are engrams, and as such heritable.

From the aesthetic point of view there are two possibilities here: (1) that a pattern or form can be organized from sense data in virtue of an inner coherence—that we only see a pattern because it has certain physical characteristics, such as symmetry, balance, and rhythm; or (2) that among the forms segregated by this organization of the sensory world, some are merely utilitarian, others aesthetic—a view which implies ideal categories of beauty independent of experience. Personally I do not see how the conception of such ideal categories could arise except on the basis of experience—they are meanings read into forms which have been determined by the physical necessities of animal evolution. What is certain is that the forms into which sensory experience is organized were gradually differentiated into two distinct types: signs or symbols whose meaning remained magical, sensory, unexplained; and signs or symbols whose meaning became conventional, conceptual, and discursive. We now reserve the word "signs," or better still, "signals," [16] for the latter type of communication, and the whole structure of discursive reasoning and nonaesthetic communication is based on such signals, most generally and effectively in the form of word-syllabic systems.

We are to be concerned only with the first method of communication: nondiscursive symbols; and only with symbols insofar as they exhibit those characteristics, or convey those sensations, which we call aesthetic. We must first ask why some such symbols have aesthetic characteristics, others not.

It would seem that those nondiscursive symbols which are devoid of aesthetic appeal must have lost such appeal, for as we have seen, they only became differentiated from the buzzing confusion of sense impressions in virtue of their attractive form, the "goodness" of their *Gestalt*.

Jung's theory, if I understand it rightly, is that the symbol loses its original force (and I think the implication is that this original force is aesthetic—a point I shall discuss presently) when it becomes too explicit—when the libido, instead of being retained in the image, is squandered in sexuality or any other physical dispersion of the retained energy. In discussing the relativity of the symbol with special reference to *The Shepherd of Hermas,* and also with reference to the symbolism of the Grail, he makes it "abundantly clear" that it is the repressed libido which evokes a powerful transformation in the unconscious, and endows the symbol with its mysterious efficacy. He even suggests,[17] that an aesthetic form is an essential component of the symbol's efficacy.

I think the necessity of an aesthetic factor is explained by the psychological facts already considered: the symbol only becomes perceptually definite and sensationally effective if it has a good form. Its potency will depend on the relative degree of goodness in the form: the degree of aesthetic appeal depends on the organization of parts into a whole, and on the direct, undifferentiated appeal of the unity achieved by aesthetic organization. In short, we return to the problem of form.

This is not, of course, a problem peculiar to aesthetics. It has been more and more the tendency, during recent years, to reduce science in general to a problem of form, and the contributions to this problem, particularly from physicists and biologists, are of the greatest significance for our study of the aesthetic aspects of symbolic form.[18] Mr. Lancelot Law Whyte dealt with some of the general problems of form in his contribution to the *Tagung* last year (1951),[19] and I have no intention of going over once again the ground he so adequately surveyed. Admittedly, as we have already noted, there are many analogies between natural forms and aesthetic forms, and perhaps there are no forms conceivable that are not echoes or correspondences of one another. But it would be a poor end to our speculations if all we could prove is that the aesthetic significance of symbolic form lies in its more or less conscious reduplication of natural forms! I am not forgetting that a distinction must be made between natural forms in the widest cosmical sense, and organic forms in the limited biological sense. We know that there have been whole epochs in the history of art that have renounced organic forms, that have taken refuge in geometrical abstractions; there is even a tendency to such abstraction in our own epoch! But it would seem that the more the human psyche tries to escape from organic forms, the more it finds itself involved in the universal matrix from which these forms emerge.

At this point we might consider a little more closely the distinction between organic forms, such as we find in a shell, a leaf, a flower, or the human body itself, and those proportions, inherent in these forms, but typical also of a range of phenomena far wider than the phenomena of organic life. Not only is form typical of inorganic as well as organic phenomena, as in the geometrical proportions of a crystal, but proportions can be discerned in the operations of the universe itself, the so-called "harmony of the spheres"; and there is a similar order discernible in the microscopic world of atoms and molecules. The whole universe is "patterned," and there can be little wonder, therefore, in the fact that the psychic element in life conforms to the all-environing physical mold. Dr. Jung has compared the archetype to the ancient bed of a river to which the stream of life may return after some indefinitely long period. As an image it is perhaps too irregular: the stream actually flows in channels that are of regular proportions, into basins and cascades of an order that we agree to call beautiful. The freedom, which we inevitably associate with the creative activity, can perhaps be explained as an apparently infinite series of variations on a relatively few fixed forms. There is no need to shrink from such an explanation as from an intolerable restriction of the possibilities of art, for what has the art of music, to a naive apprehension the freest of all forms of art, ever been but such a play with a determinate number of fixed forms?

A philosopher might complain at this point that we are making metaphysical assumptions. How do we "cognize" form: by what faculty of the mind do we determine its regularity? Are we not involved in a Kantian system of categories? Perhaps: but personally I believe that our argument can proceed on a purely pragmatic level. The forms of beauty relate to the forms of life, to biological forms; and these are determined by the organic process itself—by efficiency, by natural selection, by environment. Form is determined by physical causes, and "forms mathematically akin may belong to organisms biologically remote." [20] But forms, in the sense of regular figures, have a limited range of variation—Plato, in the *Timaeus,* argued that in three-dimensional space there are only five absolutely regular solids. "These solids interpenetrate; according to Plato, they intersect in such a way that out of their perfect harmonies in themselves, they produce all the various discords and resolutions which we find in space within the universe." [21] The main purport of D'Arcy Thompson's great book *On Growth and Form* is to show how the varieties of form in nature can be explained by a few physical causes.

In the same way a limited number of mathematical figures account for the symbolic significance of the forms of art. A modern physicist has recently remarked that:

> Numbers and figures, as the emptiest and most primary forms of thought, are the simplest and perhaps the purest vessel into which inexpressible experiences can still be poured. To be sure, mathematical symbols are not the truth, but they exhibit as much of it as can be exhibited and hide the rest. The formal laws of art are the residues of this experience [which are] still present in the consciousness of the present age. All laws of artistic form have a core of the simplest mathematics. Let us but recall the ratios of musical harmony, the meaning of symmetry and regular sequence in all the arts, the pictorial beauty of mathematically simple figures. And it is the very secret of art that the strictest law of form which has apparently nothing to do with content permits it to express things which escape unrestricted speech. [22]

The causes that determine the varieties of form in art are likewise few—indeed, insofar as we are concerned with composition, i.e., the disposition of forms within three-dimensional space, the physical limitations are the same in art and nature: a fact which was probably known to Greek artists of the classical period, and certainly to Renaissance artists like Leonardo and Piero della Francesca. We are reduced to the conclusion, therefore, that the forms of art, insofar as they are symmetrical, rhythmical, and proportionate, have no psychological significance at all—at least, they are not determined physically, and any psychological or symbolical or analogical significance they have for human consciousness arises in the act of choice and combination. We may, to adopt the terminology of Wölfflin, choose an open rather than a closed form; we may stand a pyramid on its base or on its apex; but always we find ourselves manipulating a few simple forms, which are the predetermined forms of visual order, of visual significance. The psychic content of art has to fit into these predetermined forms, like jelly into a mold. What remains of psychological significance, therefore, is the manipulation and variation of typical forms, and the energy displayed in their manipulation, together with such subjective attributes as color, texture, and that visual mark of nervous sensibility known as "facture" or "handwriting." All these secondary features in the work of art are in themselves also formal and can be referred to the artist's physical constitution or disposition, and though such features may indicate the psychological type to which the artist belongs, they are of no wider significance. Collectively they constitute the talents of the artist: they do not explain genius.

The nearer we get to that central mystery of art the more obvious it becomes, as Jung has often remarked, that there is nothing personal about it. The artist is merely a medium, a channel, for forces which are impersonal, and though there can be no great art without enabling instruments of sensibility and talent, it is the power and purpose with which those instruments are used that make the difference between the major work of art and those trivial but charming expressions of sentiment which are not merely minor in degree, but also essentially different in kind. The fact that the very gifts which enable major works of art to be created are often used by the same artist for minor effects, or as aesthetic exercises, should not blind us to the radical difference which nevertheless exists between the songs and lyrics of Shakespeare or Goethe, and works like *Lear* and *Faust*. The same difference may exist between a painter's sketches and his finished compositions —between a melody and a symphony. What intervenes, to convert the personal into the supra-personal, to give unity to a diversity of effects, is always in the nature of a myth; and because the word myth has associations which are historical or literary we must speak in our present context of the archetype. The archetype is thus clearly differentiated as the principle which gives significant unity to a diversity of aesthetic perceptions. In itself, as Dr. Neumann said, it may be *"bildnislos, namenlos, gestaltlos,"* but it takes our images and forms, the fine phenomena of our aesthetic perception, and organizes them to some unconscious purpose, gives them a supra-personal significance.

Myth and archetype must therefore be conceived as unifying forces in art, and not as projections from the artist's own unconscious—much less as constructions of his intellect. One can conceive them as magnetic forces that, to use Dr. Neumann's metaphor,[23] induce a pattern into a field of scattered perceptions, impressions, intuitions, feelings: and in my opinion we must assume that the force is induced, or brought into play, by a certain ripeness or maturity in the artist. Only artists with a richness of perception and a readiness of expression realize the formal significance of a particular "constellation" of events in the phenomenal field. The great intuitions come to minds rendered abnormally alert by constant exercise of their talents—a fact which perhaps explains the psychological similarities that exist between artists and mystics.

In comparing form to a mold into which the artist pours a certain content I have ignored the important fact that it is the artist who discovers the form—that is to say, the artist's peculiarity is that he possesses what Schiller called the *formative instinct (Formtrieb)*, and there is an intimate relationship between the pregnancy of the artist's inspiration and the ability to give that inspiration its appropriate form. The form is found by instinct ready at hand like a glove already shaped by personal use—or, as Goethe expressed it, the form evolves organically—

geprägte Form, die lebend sich entwickelt.

A failure to realize that fact has been responsible for all the lifeless academicism of the schools. Focillon, in *The Life of Forms in Art,* has expressed the same truth with admirable clarity:

The idea of the artist is form. His emotional life turns likewise to form: tenderness, nostalgia, desire, anger are in him, and so are many other impulses, more fluid, more secret, oftentimes more rich, colorful, and subtle than those of other men, but not necessarily so. He is immersed in the whole of life; he steeps himself in it. He is human, he is not a machine. Because he is a man, I grant him everything. But his special privilege is to imagine, to recollect, to think, and to feel in *forms.* This conception must be extended to its uttermost limit, and it must be extended in two directions. I do not say that form is the allegory or symbol of feeling, but, rather, its innermost activity. Form activates feeling.

Let us say, if you like, that art not only clothes sensibility with a form, but that art also awakens form in sensibility. And yet no matter what position we take, it is eventually to form that we must always come. If I were to undertake . . . the establishment of a psychology for the artist, I should have to analyse formal imagination and memory, formal sensibility and intellect; I should have to define all the processes whereby the life of forms in the mind propagates a prodigious animism that, taking natural objects as the point of departure, makes them matters of imagination and memory, of sensibility and intellect—and it would then be seen that these processes are touches, accents, tones, and values. . . . Between nature and man form intervenes. The man in question, the artist, that is, forms this nature; before taking possession of it, he thinks it, sees it, and feels it as form.[24]

What Focillon means by nature is the life-process itself, the underlying dynamics of existence. The whole of our theory of art may therefore be conceived as one which allows for the spontaneous emergence of a psychic energy which, passing through the brain, gives unity to a variety of forms, which forms are in no sense nondescript or arbitrary, but are the typal forms of reality, the forms in which the universe exists and becomes discretely comprehensible to mind. Art might therefore be described as a crystallization of instincts—as the unifying of all feelings and desires; as a marriage of Heaven and Hell, which was Blake's profound intuition of the process. That psychic energy which is given form by the archetype, Blake defined as Eternal Delight.

It is a process of crystallization which takes place through the senses; we never celebrate the marriage of Heaven and Hell unless we celebrate it in the flesh, in *Schaudern*, in ecstasy, in a piercing vibration of the nerves, in the *felix transitus* of consummation. In the second part of this lecture, I shall try to come a little nearer to the reality of the process in the analysis of certain specific works of art.

2

We must now try to demonstrate our theory in the evolution of art itself, more particularly in the development of typical artists. I shall confine myself mainly to contemporary art, not only because it is the phase of art best known to me, but also because it offers some opportunity of confirming our theories by the cross-examination of the artists themselves.

But there is another and more important reason for confining ourselves to modern art. Excluding the past fifty years, there has prevailed for centuries a conception of art which

identified *reality* with *appearance,* and the whole energy of
the artist was devoted to the task of giving the reality of his
feelings the illusory mask of appearances. This disparity was
already obvious to Schiller, and the XXVIth *Aesthetischer Brief*
is devoted to an examination of the paradox. Schiller pointed
out that although a devotion to semblance (*Schein*) is
required of man for the purposes of social intercourse and the
mastery of the objective world, when this need is stilled, an
inner freedom develops its limitless possibilities, and we
become aware of an energy which is independent of outer
things. Then we see that a distinction exists between the
reality of things and the semblance of things, and that the
latter is the work of man. Feeling, Schiller then notes, that
feeds on appearances, no longer takes delight in what it experiences, but on what it does; it evades reality and plays with
form, with independent energy and freedom of heart. In
Schiller's view the separation of form from essence, of reality
from appearance, was wholly to the good because it left
reality at the mercy of the understanding; it left art in ideal
freedom, and gave to man the possibility of enjoying pure
beauty. The modern artist cannot accept this divorce from
reality; rather, he insists on leaving appearance to the philosopher, or the psychologist, or the photographer, and on being
himself the exponent of the inner reality. He has forever finished with an idealism that is based on illusion, and would
now master the essence of reality. This means, in our terminology, that he has taken on the job of mastering the unconscious
—or, if that seems too ambitious a project, at any rate he will
attempt to find some degree of correspondence between the
concrete symbols of his art and the subjective reality of his
imagination.

I will not stop to discuss whether modern art is unique in
this respect—I suspect not, but an investigation of the subject
would require a discussion of the precise relation between
symbol and sign at different stages of human evolution—for
example, Was the bison (*Wisent*) a symbolic image for prehistoric man, as Dr. Neumann assumed (he called it "*ein
geistig-psychisches Symbolbild*"), or was it an eidetic image,
a *Scheinbild,* with purely utilitarian connotations?—an open
question. But when a modern artist like Picasso paints a bull,
there is no longer any question: he is using this animal as a
symbol, and as a symbol whose significance can be determined.

Whatever the theoretical justification for the use of such
symbols, their predominance in the history of art is inescapable, and Picasso is merely reverting, in this respect, to a
predilection which was evident enough in Mycenaean and
Minoan art, and is recurrent in the plastic arts, in myth and

poetry, throughout the history of Western civilization. The bull as a symbol, and the equally archaic symbol of the horse, were embodied in the ritual of the *tauromachia* or bullfight, a pagan ritual that has maintained, in the hearts of the Spanish people, a hold as strong as the Christian ritual. The art of Picasso, in the course of his development, builds up to the most complete revelation of the unconscious sources and symbolic significance of this same rite. I am referring to his painting called "Guernica," regarded by some critics of art as Picasso's greatest achievement: it is certainly, in scale and execution, his most monumental work.

Let me recall the origins of this painting. On April 28, 1937, the world was shocked to hear that the Basque town of Guernica had been destroyed by bombs dropped by German aeroplanes in the service of General Franco. Picasso began to paint his picture two days later, on May 1, and worked on it with maniacal intensity until it was finished some weeks later. During the course of the work he declared: "In the panel on which I am working which I shall call Guernica, and in all my recent works of art, I clearly express my abhorrence of the military caste which has sunk Spain in an ocean of pain and death."

The motive of the painting is therefore not in doubt. How is that abhorrence expressed?

By symbols—by the traditional symbols of the bull and the horse, with a number of minor symbols in association with them. Before commenting on the use of these symbols in "Guernica," let us note that two years before the town of Guernica was bombed, before there was any question of expressing abhorrence for a particular deed, Picasso had used virtually all the same symbols in a large etching which he called "Minotauromachy."

There is a significant omission in the later picture—the figure of the bearded man who, in "Minotauromachy," is climbing up a ladder on the left edge of the picture, as if to escape from the scene. It is the archetypal image of the wise man—"the savior or redeemer" who, as Jung says, "lies buried and dormant in man's unconscious since the dawn of culture," and who is "awakened whenever the times are out of joint and a human society committed to a serious error." [25]

The scene that Wise Man abandons shows the Minotaur advancing with uplifted arms toward a child who, with a light uplifted in one hand and a bunch of flowers in the other, surveys a horse uprearing, under the threat of the Minotaur, with a woman, apparently dead, stretched on its back. From an opening in the towerlike building in the background, which may be intended as the labyrinth of the Minotaur, two figures in loving embrace, and associated with doves, look down on the scene.

It is a picture so rich in symbolic significance, that one is almost persuaded that Picasso has at some time made a study of Jung and Kerényi! In addition to the figure of the Wise Man, already mentioned, we have the Minotaur, representing the dark powers of the labyrinthine unconscious; the sacrificial horse, bearing on its back the overpowered libido; and confronting them the divine child, the culture bearer, the bringer of light, the child-hero who fearlessly confronts the powers of darkness, the bearer of higher consciousness.[26] How easily a Jungian interpretation can be given to this picture may be judged from the following passage from Jung's contribution to an *Introduction to a Science of Mythology:*

> It is a striking paradox in all child-myths that the "child" is on the one hand delivered helpless into the power of terrible enemies and in continual danger of extinction, while on the other he possesses powers far exceeding those of ordinary humanity. This is closely related to the psychological fact that though the child may be "insignificant," unknown, "a mere child," he is also divine. From the point of view of the conscious mind we seem to be dealing with an insignificant content that is gifted with no liberating let alone redeeming character. The conscious mind is caught in its conflict-situation, and the combatant forces seem so overwhelming that the "child," emerging in isolation, appears not to be proportionate to the conscious factors. It is therefore easily overlooked and falls back into the unconscious. At least, this is what we should have to fear if things turned out according to our conscious expectations. Myth, however, emphasizes that it is not so, but that the "child" is endowed with exceeding powers, and despite all dangers, will unexpectedly pull through. The "child" is born out of the womb of the unconscious, begotten out of the depths of human nature, or rather out of living Nature herself. It is a personification of vital forces quite outside the limited range of our conscious mind; of possible ways and means of which our one-sided conscious mind knows nothing; a wholeness which embraces the very depths of Nature. It represents the strongest, the most ineluctable urge in every being, namely the urge to realize itself.[27]

The "Minotauromachy" may therefore be regarded as Picasso's affirmation of the grandeur and invincibility of the "child," a child holding the light of revelation and not at all terrified by the powers of darkness confronting it. An obvious allegory, it might be said, of no great interest because it "nowhere oversteps the bounds of conscious comprehension";[28] but then this dominant theme by no means exhausts the symbolical significance of the picture. If the dead or unconscious woman represents the libido, why does she carry a sword in her right hand? And what is the significance of the maidens and doves who lovingly look down on the strange scene? All these symbols, no doubt, would yield to rationalistic explanation, but I must be forgiven if I do not dwell on them because what matters, in my present context, is not the interpretation of meaning, but the fact that the artist has employed universal symbols of this kind.[29] Before making any general comment on this process of symbolization I would like to return to "Guernica."

We are lucky to possess photographs which show the evolution of this painting in Picasso's studio[30]—not only the various stages in the composition of the canvas itself, but also a considerable number of preliminary sketches of details. This preliminary material shows that the constituent symbols of the painting—the bull, the horse, the woman with dead child, the light-bearer, the figure representing the sacrificed republic— were present in Picasso's mind from the beginning as discrete phenomena. He began with these symbols—the bull, the horse, and the woman bearing a light. In some of the composition studies, pencil sketches on gesso made on May 1 and 2, 1937, a Pegasus is introduced, at first perching on the bull's back, but next day emerging from a wound in the horse's flank. But this symbol was quickly discarded, and others were introduced, notably the one of the victim, at first the traditional republican figure with helm and spear. These traditional accessories are gradually discarded, and in general there is a tendency to get away from literary or historical associations and to let the symbols tell by their inner expressive power. The artist is seen, in these preliminary sketches, exploring the expressive tensions of distortion and exaggeration, until he has substituted his own symbols of power, sacrifice, terror, death, and resurrection.

As in the "Minotauromachy," the horse is the sacrificial animal of the Upanishads, where it signifies a renunciation of the universe. "When the horse is sacrificed," comments Jung, "then the world is sacrificed and destroyed, as it were. . . . The horse signifies the libido, which has passed into the world. We previously saw that the 'mother libido' must be sacrificed in order to produce the world; here the world is destroyed by the repeated sacrifice of the same libido, which once belonged to the mother. The horse can, therefore, be substituted as a symbol for this libido, because, as we saw, it had manifold connections with the mother. The sacrifice of the horse can only produce another state of introversion, which is similar to that before the creation of the world." [31]

This is only a casual comparison, but Picasso's use of these symbols is unerringly orthodox, and the question is whether he is orthodox because he is learned in the history of symbolism, or because he allows his symbols to emerge freely from his unconscious. They not only emerge as orthodox symbols, but in significant association: the sacrificial horse with the figure representing the sacrificed republic, the bull with the horse, the light-bearer with the bull, minor symbols like the flower that grows by the side of the broken sword, and the dove of peace that flies above the carnage.

The question could only be settled by a direct approach to the artist, and this I feel too diffident to make—it would be to invite a confession which in the estimation of psychologists like yourselves, would be damaging to the dynamic force of the work of art. It is generally known, however, that Picasso is not a naive artist: he is a man of culture, who reads voraciously. It is not inconceivable, therefore, that the traditional symbols he uses are used with deliberate intention. Such symbols are activated by surface emotions, and not by the unconscious. But as Jung has said,[32] "a symbol loses its magical power . . . as soon as its dissolubility is recognized. An effective symbol, therefore, must have a nature that is unimpeachable . . . its form must be sufficiently remote from comprehension as to frustrate every attempt of the critical intellect to give any satisfactory account of it; and, finally, its aesthetic appearance must have such a convincing appeal that no sort of argument can be raised against it on that score."

In the past I have praised "Guernica" as a work of art, and even now I am not going to suggest that it can be dismissed as a work of art merely because its symbols are traditional—the criterion would exclude the best part of all the visual arts ever created by man. But I would maintain that there is a stage in the evolution of symbolism at which the symbols become clichés, and clichés can never be used in a work of art. A dead or exhausted symbol is just as much a cliché as a stale epithet or hackneyed metaphor. The situation obviously is not improved by beginning with the clichés and then deliberately disguising them. Artistic creation, to the same degree and in the same manner as effective symbolism, implies spontaneity: the artistically valid symbols are those which rise, fully armed by the libido, from the depths of the unconscious.

What redeems this picture, to a degree I would not now venture to determine, is what saves any painting of the past that makes a conscious use of traditional symbolism—any painting making use of the symbols of the Christian faith, or a painting by Poussin making use of the symbols of classical mythology: I mean the fact that every line, every form, every color, is dominated by the aesthetic sensibility of the artist. What the symbols import into this aesthetic organization is a certain element of collective or traditional significance. A painting of the Madonna may be merely the direct portrait, full of sensuous charm, of a contemporary woman; aesthetically it is never anything else, but the fact that the woman represents the Mother of God imparts into the aesthetic experience a feeling of devotion which is actually a trancelike opening-up of the way to the unconscious, and the woman the artist painted then becomes, not only immediately the Mother of God, but more remotely the representative of still deeper complexes. One way of putting it (it is Jung's way) is that "humanity came to its gods through accepting the reality of the symbol"; but equally one might say that it was only possible to accept the reality of the symbol because the artist had succeeded in giving it *living form*.

The complex but deliberate symbolism of works like "Minotauromachy" and "Guernica" has simplified our task, which is to show the interrelations between the forms of art and the energies of the psyche. I have admitted that to the extent the symbols used by Picasso in these two pictures are deliberate and allegorical, to that extent we may suspect that they have been fished from waters that are relatively shallow; but "Minotauromachy" and "Guernica" occupy a small place in the copious repertory of images created by Picasso throughout his career, most of which resist any attempt at rationalistic explanation. Other images are vital, and their vitality comes, not from any identity with the outward world of visual appearances, but from a fidelity to an inner world where vision is archetypal.

I would like now to turn to the work of another contemporary artist, and one well-known to me personally for many years, the sculptor Henry Moore. By comparison with Picasso his work presents a certain unity and consistency of development, together with a drastic limitation of theme. Apart from a few abstract works, in themselves nearly always suggested by natural forms, the work of this sculptor consists almost entirely of representations of the female figure, representations that depart considerably from the phenomenal appearances of that object.

A preference for the human form as a motif for sculpture is characteristic of the art from its prehistoric origins, and although there have been periods, in Greece in the fifth century and in Renaissance Italy, when an integrated humanism found expressions indifferently in the form of either sex, in general the male sculptor has devoted his talent to the female form. We do not know whether the first prehistoric carvings of female figures, evidently fertility charms, were the work of men or women; but it is not important, for surely it does not need any profound theory to account for a male preoccupation with the female form. Apart from normal sexuality, it is quite usual for a man to have a mother-fixation, and there is evidence to suggest that an unusual proportion of artists, poets as well as plastic artists, have this psychic bias. But such psychological tendencies merely explain a preference for a particular subject matter: the aesthetic interest only begins with the transformation which the mother-symbol undergoes in the process of artistic creation.

In the case of Henry Moore, we can simplify our analysis by confining ourselves to a single pose—the reclining figure. His treatment of this theme begins about 1930 in a traditional manner, though it is the tradition of Mayan (Mexican) sculpture rather than of classical Renaissance sculpture. Moore then felt the need to expel all traditional concepts from his psyche, and to proceed to a complete disintegration of the human form (43a: 1934),[33] and then to an abstract reconstruction (51: 1937). From this geometrical basis, he reanimates the form, gives it recognizably organic shape; and then follows a whole series, continuing to the present day, in which the basic elements of the female figure are the theme for an almost countless series of variations, in various materials. These variations can be studied in greater detail in the numerous sketches in which the sculptor makes a preliminary exploration of his form (139a, b; 150a; 237).

It would be possible to interpret this development in a purely formal sense. Here is a mass of stone or wood, isolated in space, in dialectical opposition to the space which is its environment, forms weaving and undulating with a life of their own. The aesthetic experience begins with an empathetic response to such a closed world of form—we enter it and fill it and are moved round within it, with sensational reactions which we do not stop to analyze, but which are harmonic and pleasant. But the sculptor himself has told us that "the humanist organic element will always be for me of fundamental importance in sculpture, giving sculpture its vitality. Each particular carving I make takes on in my mind a human, or occasionally animal, character and personality, and this personality controls its design and formal qualities, and makes me satisfied or dissatisfied with the work as it develops." [34]

His design, Moore tells us in this passage, is not an intellectual invention: it is not even a direct intuition of form—it is dictated by an inner life, a personality, a daemon, which has entered the block of stone or wood, and imperiously demands a living form.

Moore is here confessing that the creation of a work of art is a genuine, primordial experience—that it is "the expression of something existent in its own right, but imperfectly known," to repeat Jung's phrase.[35] Moore does not claim to have invented the life of his artistic forms—on the contrary, he asserts that the work of art takes on its own personality, and that this personality controls the design and formal qualities. In other words, Moore confirms Jung's view that "personal causality has as much and as little to do with the work of art, as the soil with the plant that springs from it. . . . The personal orientation that is demanded by the problem of personal causality is out of place in the presence of the work of art, just because the work of art is not a human being, but essentially supra-personal." [36]

Jung's further perception, in this essay on "Poetic Art," that "the work of art is not merely transmitted or derived—it is a creative reorganization of those very determinants to which a causalistic psychology must always reduce it"; that it is like a plant which is "not a mere product of the soil; but a living creative process centred in itself, the essence of which has nothing to do with the character of the soil"; that, in short, the work of art "must be regarded a creative formation, freely making use of every pre-condition" [37]—all this is fully and precisely illustrated in Moore's sculpture, and confirmed in his personal statements. The artist in him is "simply identical with the creative process," [38] and to watch Moore work is to confirm Jung's description of the poet as one "who is not identical with the process of creative formation"; who is "himself conscious of the fact that he stands as it were underneath his work, or at all events beside it, as though he were another person who had fallen within the magic circle of an alien will." [39]

That being so, it is still permissible to speculate on the significance of the forms proliferated by this dynamic force, using the artist as its channel. In Picasso's two pictures the symbolic figures stand outside the labyrinth itself; and this labyrinth is the archetypal womb, the hollow earth from which all life has emerged.

I might mention, in passing, and without attaching any particular significance to the fact, that Moore's early childhood was dominated by an actual labyrinth, that of the coal mine. Moore's father was a miner, descending daily into the earth to bring to the surface the substance of fire, which was also the substance of the family's livelihood. It was an enterprise involving danger, and anxiety in the mind of the beloved mother. There are possibilities here of an unconscious association of the labyrinth and the womb. During the war Moore himself descended into the labyrinth, the "Underground" of the Tube stations, used as bomb shelters, and made a series of drawings which, apart from their immediate interest as records of war, re-emphasize his obsession with the labyrinth. In some of his drawings the figures are seen standing outside a cave or labyrinth, and in many others the figures seem to be embedded in rock.

Moore's reclining figures are not substantial solids, as are the sculptures of the classical tradition, but arched and winding caverns. The female body, its superficial protuberances reduced to insignificance, becomes an exposed womb, an excavated mine, and where one might expect emptiness, there is life—the life of shapes and forms which by their convolutions and transformation of masses and volumes, have created an artistic form. We might say that there is a fetus in this womb, but it is the space of the womb itself, the form defined by its rhythmic outlines. In some of his later figures Moore has actually filled these caverns with separate, fetuslike forms, but they were not necessary to express the significance of his symbols.

The Mayan reclining figure which was the point of departure for Moore's series of reclining figures was a god or goddess of fertility, Chac Mool, whose particular function was to ensure an adequate rainfall. Round the head are bands of threaded grain, and across the breast an ornament in the form of a butterfly, emblem of regeneration. The hands meet above the womb or belly, and form a hollow depression, basinlike, destined to contain the human hearts demanded as a sacrifice by this cruel deity.

Such symbolism, elaborated no doubt by priests, in the service of a cult, is precise and interpretable. Moore's symbolism is completely unconscious, and is not dictated by any priesthood, or dedicated to any ritual. Nevertheless, it is not entirely unconnected with the same archetypal pattern as the Chac Mool of Mayan religion. Moore assures me that when he first became familiar with the Mexican reclining figure, he had no knowledge of its ritualistic or archetypal significance—to him it was just a piece of sculpture which attracted him by its formal qualities as a work of art. If we interpret Moore's figures as archetypal images of creation, we are then free to relate them to the same archetypal pattern that prevailed in Yucatan more than three thousand years ago, not as conscious formal imitations, but as identical expressions of the same archetype. The Mayan sculptor proceeded from image to form —his symbols were predetermined by his cult. The modern sculptor proceeds from form to image—he discovers (or we discover for him) the significance of his forms *after* he has created them. What we must admire, in the modern artist, is the confidence with which he accepts as a gift from the unconscious forms of whose significance he is not, at the creative moment, precisely aware.

He has that confidence—and this is really the main consideration which I want to put before you—because he knows instinctively that there is an intimate connection between the vitality of art and the deeper significance of form. Form is not merely a play with abstractions, a communication of pleasure by the skillful manipulation of proportions and intervals and other geometrical elements. In that way our nerves, our sensibility, may be stimulated—the tone of our physical existence may be enhanced. But it has always been obvious that there was more in artistic creation than could be accounted for by such a direct chain of causality. The forms of art must refer to something hidden, to something not contained in the circuit of nervous reflexes. The aestheticians of former ages—with a few exceptions like Schiller and Fiedler—have been satisfied with an idealistic explanation: art was significant, not in itself, but because it embodied transcendental *ideas*. That fallacy, which even on a basis of the art of the past, should never have been entertained, has forever been exploded by the creative achievements of modern art, achievements which are neither conceptual nor—in the metaphysical sense—transcendental, but which are nevertheless super-real. Modern art—art such as Picasso's and Moore's—is significant, but not significant of any expressible ideas. It gives concrete existence to what is numinous, what is beyond the limits of rational discourse: it brings the dynamics of subjective experience to a point of rest in the concrete object. But it only does this in virtue of a certain imaginative play—*eine psychische Spielerei*. The forms of art are only significant insofar as they are archetypal, and in that sense predetermined; and only vital insofar as they are *trans*-formed by the sensibility of the artist and in that sense free. The artist releases these dynamic energies within his own psyche, and his peculiarity, his *virtue*, is that he can direct such forces into matter: can "realize" them as forms of stone or metal, dimensions of space, measured intervals of time. In this sense the artist has become the alchemist, transmuting the *materia prima* of the unconscious into those "wondrous stones," the crystal forms of art.

NOTES

1. *Verlag Ernst Wasmuth,* second edition (1929).
2. Cf. Max Ernst, *Histoire naturelle* (Paris: Jeanne Bucher, 1926).
3. André Masson, *Anatomy of My Universe* (New York: Curt Valentin, 1943).
4. *Goethes Gespräche,* J. D. Falk, June 14, 1809.
5. *"Kunst und Zeit," Eranos-Jahrbuch 1951* (Vol. XX, *Mensch und Zeit* [Zurich: 1952]).
6. "On the Relation of Analytical Psychology to Poetic Art" (1922), *Contributions to Analytical Psychology* (London: Kegan Paul, 1928), pp. 233–4.
7. Op. cit., p. 238.
8. *Contributions to Analytical Psychology,* pp. 118 ff.
9. Ibid., p. 246.
10. Ibid., p. 281.
11. R. M. Ogden, *Psychology and Education* (New York: 1926), p. 133.
12. Cf. "Problems in the Psychology of Art," *Art: A Bryn Mawr Symposium* (Bryn Mawr: 1940).
13. *Philosophy in a New Key* (Harvard University Press, 1942), p. 89.
14. Ibid., pp. 89–90.
15. Cf. Wolfgang Köhler, *Gestalt Psychology* (1929), p. 208.
16. Cf. Charles Morris, *Signs, Language, and Behavior* (New York: Prentice-Hall, 1946), pp. 23–7.
17. Cf. *Psychological Types* (London: Kegan Paul, 1938), p. 291.
18. For a general discussion of the subject see the symposium edited by L. L. Whyte, *Aspects of Form* (London: 1951).
19. "Time and the Mind-Body Problem: A Changed Scientific Conception of Process," *Eranos-Jahrbuch 1951* (Vol. XX, *Mensch und Zeit*), pp. 253–70.
20. D'Arcy W. Thompson, *On Growth and Form* (1942), pp. 693–4.
21. Edgar Wind, "Mathematics and Sensibility," *The Listener,* XLVII (1952), p. 705. Cf. the "Notice" by Albert Rivaud to his translation of the *Timaeus,* Budé edition (Paris: 1925); also, F. M. Cornford, *Plato's Cosmology: The Timaeus of Plato* (London: 1937).
22. *The World View of Physics,* by C. F. von Weisäcker, trans., Marjorie Grene (London: Routledge and Kegan Paul, 1952), p. 151.
23. *Eranos-Jahrbuch 1949.*
24. Henri Focillon, *The Life of Forms in Art,* trans., Hogan and Kubler (New York: Wittenborn, Schultz, second edition, 1948), p. 47.

25. *Modern Man in Search of a Soul* (London: Kegan Paul, 1936), p. 197.
26. These are Jung's epithets for the divine child. Cf. *Introduction to a Science of Mythology*, C. G. Jung and C. Kerényi (London: Routledge and Kegan Paul, 1951), p. 122.
27. Op. cit., pp. 123–4.
28. Op. cit., p. 127.
29. In a drawing made two years later (see Barr, p. 211), entitled "The End of a Monster," Picasso shows a sea goddess emerging from the sea to hold up a mirror to the Minotaur, who lies on the beach transfixed by an arrow.
30. They are reproduced in *Guernica,* a volume of illustrations accompanied by a text by Juan Larrea, published by Curt Valentin (New York: 1947).
31. *Psychology of the Unconscious,* pp. 466–7.
32. *Psychological Types,* p. 291.
33. I give references to the illustrations in *Henry Moore: Sculptures and Drawings* (London: Lund Humphries, second edition, 1949).
34. Op. cit., p. xlii.
35. *Modern Man,* pp. 186–7.
36. *Contributions to Analytical Psychology,* p. 233.
37. Ibid., p. 234.
38. Ibid., p. 235.
39. Ibid., p. 236.

A SCIENTIFIC VIEW OF THE
"CREATIVE ENERGY" OF MAN *

Lancelot Law Whyte

The main concern of *Eranos* is the study of Man and his place in the Universe, and our present theme: the human creative faculty and its place in the universe of science, comes near to the heart of the matter. For the creative imagination of the individual is the factor which most sharply distinguishes man from the rest of organic nature, and it is inevitable that sooner or later we should ask what science can tell us about it. We know very little about man's place in the universe until science can give us some understanding of the creative process.

But this process presents a difficult problem for science. Creation implies that something new comes into existence, while scientific method must assume a continuity in every process. Moreover the unconscious phases of the creative process seem to lie beyond the reach of our ordinary time measures, for they bear no apparent relation to other human processes or to events in the environment. Then the creative imagination displays a strange power of anticipation or prophecy, for the full significance of a new idea or work of art may only become evident a generation later. And the creator often seems to be the instrument of a process of universal import, far transcending his own personality and experience. Finally the process does not serve any immediate biological purpose, but carries organic forms beyond themselves, expressing a surplus vitality which explores the unknown and realizes latent potentialities. All these characteristics of the creative process seem at first sight to lie beyond the scope of traditional scientific method.

So it is scarcely surprising that science can as yet say very little about it. There is no recognized biology of thought, no scientific theory of the creative process or of productive thinking. Thus the most one can offer is a hypothesis, a view of the relation of productive thought to other natural processes which may be proved wrong in the future, but can serve as a working assumption in the meantime.

This is a perilous task, like all which must rely on intuition prior to careful testing, but there are reasons for undertaking

---

* [From *Eranos-Jahrbuch 1952* (Zurich: Rhein-Verlag, 1953). Reprinted by permission of the author.]

it. There is no more challenging problem in the realm of science, and it is now becoming ripe for solution. Whether right or wrong, the suggestions which I shall offer are not far ahead of the advancing front line of scientific knowledge.

Moreover it is not merely a question of satisfying our curiosity. The matter is one of social importance. For since 1600 scientific method on the one hand, and the creative powers of the individual on the other, have been the sources of the rapid transformation of the Western world. Together they have created the contemporary scene—but they have not acted together. In the Western mind science and the creative imagination stand apart, like two great antagonists, inevitably drawn together and yet afraid to come to grips. It is possible that a fresh vitality and productivity may come to us, or to our descendants, when the creative processes of the human mind are understood as part of the universe of natural process, for then only will man truly understand himself as part of nature. This source of strength is potentially open to us, and yet many fear and resist the recognition that the operation of this supreme human faculty is as natural a process as any other.

There are grounds for this fear. Science rests on the use of deliberate systematic methods, and there is no method, no general technique, for forcing the imagination. Thus the scientist cannot regard the operation of his own imagination as part of scientific method, and his attitude toward the imaginative element in science, such as the emergence of new ideas, has often been coy and embarrassed, like an adolescent who prefers that one should not refer to matters which he or she does not yet understand. The parallel is close: exact science is still immature, for it does not understand the process by which it was itself created. Prior to mathematics and experiment there must be an idea, but how does this idea come into being? The sciences of physiology and psychology do not yet know the answer.

On the other hand the poet or artist tends to resent the approach of science to his own sensitive processes. He does not trust the standardizing scientist to recognize the importance of the peculiar, highly individual working of his mind, whether conscious or unconscious. Thus the attitudes of both the scientist and the artist have tended to prevent any close examination of their imaginative powers.

This divorce of scientific method and the creative imagination is as natural as its result has been disastrous: the dyarchy in the Western mind. Scientific method enjoys authority in the realm of the analytical intellect and its technical applications, and the creative principle in the realm of religious and aesthetic value. But this situation is intolerable, for in the present historical phase human personality cannot be stable without a harmonizing principle, consciously accepted, serving to hold all aspects of life in balance. And what we cannot tolerate, we must transform. One of the most urgent tasks for human welfare—I recommend it to the Ford Foundation—is the development of a view of man which reconciles scientific method and the creative imagination.

The ground has been well prepared during the first half of this century, as though some necessity in the development of the human community were guiding men's minds toward this issue. I shall give only two examples. C. G. Jung has sought to combine a primary concern for the creative aspects of human personality with respect for the achievements of science. And Herbert Read, as an interpreter of the visual arts, has emphasized the influence of science on the mind of the contemporary artist. These are signs of a widespread preoccupation. The time has arrived for a deeper understanding of the relation of science to the imagination.

So what we are attempting here is to make a reconnaissance beyond the ground already won by science, seeking to discover how far the characteristics of the creative process are shared by other natural phenomena. If such a link exists to neglect it is to rob man of his deepest root in nature, and nature of its most human aspect. No philosophical anthropology or scientific view of man can be valid without it.

In order to rid our minds of certain irrelevant associations of the term "creative," we shall use "formative" to describe any process, whether expressed in physical or mental language, in which some kind of form, order, or unity is developed. These words, "form," "order," and "unity," are rather subtle. We feel we know roughly what they mean, but they are not easy to define. For our present purposes it is sufficient to say that we shall use "form" for anything which is simple, i.e., simple relatively to its more complex and arbitrary variants. It may be a simple shape in space, or a simple idea in the mind. Form is what can be adequately represented by a few internal relations, and it is thus a matter of degree. Form is heightened in every formative process. This recalls the *nisus formativus* and the principle of pregnance of the Gestalt psychologists: *the organization tends to become as simple as conditions permit.* But even they have so far failed to pay adequate attention to the development history of their Gestalts.

You will notice that in suggesting that "formative" can be substituted for "creative" I am really begging the question of the essential character of the creative process. For it is implied that the characteristic feature of this process is the bringing together into one relatively simple form of elements which were previously separate, disparate, or disordered. The precise meaning of a "relatively simple form" in relation to a complex work of art is far from clear at this stage. But a reasonable first assumption regarding the creative process is that it always brings separate elements together into a unified scheme. Creation is the development of a new unity, which may be highly complex, but always displays simplifying relationships. This unity is characteristic of every authentic product of the creative process. The creative imagination operates in single coherent endeavors, each of which culminates (if at all) in a single result. Creative activity never leads to a litter of simultaneous unrelated productions. Its essence lies in an integrating tendency, and it is with this aspect only of the creative process that we shall be concerned.

The term "formative" is used to identify this ordering, simplifying, shaping, tendency in a wider field than that to which "creative" is normally applied. As examples of formative processes we can take the shaping of the spiral nebulae out of the primitive chaos (if that view of their origin is correct); the growth of crystals and the formation of molecules; the assimilation of foodstuffs within a growing organism; the development of the human embryo and child, and in particular the development and working of the brain or mind. These are formative processes, since they display the emergence, either of new spatial forms and structures, or of some other kind of ordered unity such as an idea in the mind. The processes described as the "constructive synthesis of perceptions," "synthetic apprehension," "creative synthesis," "inductive synthesis," and so on, in which contrasted elements are assimilated, and perhaps modified, to form a new ordered unity—these are all examples of formative processes. The choice of this term "formative" is the first step toward the identification of a common principle underlying the creative imagination and other natural processes. The words "creative" and "synthesis" have too many vague overtones.

The term "formative" helps us to recognize that, in addition to those processes in which new forms are developed, we must allow for those in which existing forms are distorted or dispersed. Growth is sooner or later balanced by decay; the growth of one organism may damage that of another; formative processes may come into conflict; in the organic and mental realms there is deformation and disintegration. The creative imagination is subject to disease; there is no guarantee against distorted forms of the creative process. There is a pathology of the creative imagination, though we have only recently begun to understand it, for example in the artistic productions of the abnormal.

I have mentioned this, not in order to throw any light on it, but to lessen the risk of a sentimental valuation of all creativity. *"Im Schaffen ist aber das Zerstören eingerechnet"* (Nietzsche). Moreover we misunderstand the nature of creative activity if we assume that even in its purest forms it is well-disposed towards comfortable, satisfying, personal life and relationships. The genuinely creative is rebellious; by its nature it is the enemy of the utilitarian values of every existing mode of life. It often involves the painful assertion of the priority of what is not yet over what is and has been, and in such a struggle there is little mercy.

A moment ago I gave a provisional explanation of the term "formative" in order to let us make a start. If we already knew the most appropriate precise meaning to give to it we should be in possession of a satisfactory theory of formative process, and that is not the case. We merely use the word "formative" to indicate a broad realm of phenomena which we propose to investigate, to announce a strategy, not a success. The term represents the indefinite (and possibly mistaken) intuition which, in scientific research as in artistic production, must precede the final, precise, and adequate expression. This passage from vague and less adequate ideas to more precise and adequate ones, is itself one of the formative processes which we are considering.

We can start by asking what contemporary philosophy and science can tell us about formative processes in general. The answer is the opposite of what one might expect. The importance of form (in various senses) has been realized since the time of Plato and Aristotle, and the West has now for ten generations—roughly since Vico—been increasingly concerned with the historical, dynamic, or process aspect of phenomena. But there is as yet no general doctrine explaining how regular spatial forms, or other ordered unities, come into existence. Certain static and relatively stationary spatial forms, such as atoms, molecules, crystals, and adult organisms, have been thoroughly classified, but *there is no recognized philosophy of formative process, no scientific theory of the conditions under which specific forms develop, and no mathematical calculus appropriate to this task.*

You may question such a radical assertion, but let me give one example. It is commonly held that entities called *genes,* possibly identifiable as minute units of protein of characteristic structure, constitute the carriers of heredity and, in interplay with the environment, determine the form and properties of the adult organism. But as yet no one has even suggested how this may come about in any particular case. There is no biochemical or other hypothesis which describes how the presence of a particular gene, or set of genes, leads in a given environment to the development of a particular adult character, or set of characters. And there cannot yet be, for the intellectual armory of quantitative science lacks any general principles indicating how particular forms develop and multiply, for example how certain kinds of protein unit (genes, enzymes, etc.) are capable of reproducing themselves within the living cell. Without such a principle it is impossible to construct a detailed theory showing how adult organic forms come into existence, and there certainly is no such theory today. The sciences of embryology, heredity, and evolution still lack a structural foundation.

This neglect of the developmental aspect of structure and form is startling, but it becomes easier to understand when we realize that the Western intellect has so far kept separate the static aspect of $\dot{\epsilon}\iota\delta o\varsigma$ and $\chi\rho\acute{o}\nu o\varsigma$, or static *form* and *time*, and has made no serious attempt to combine them in one principle. Since Descartes confirmed the Western mind in its search for clear static ideas, this has been the blind spot of philosophy, science, and mathematics. The developmental aspect of form, the Aristotelian $\dot{\epsilon}\iota\delta o\varsigma$ or formative tendency including the time aspect, has been neglected by mathematicians and logicians, misconceived by the vitalists, and underestimated by the leading philosophers. There is a simple explanation of this blindness: the advance toward a developmental view requires a shift from pure *atomism*, whether physical or logical, toward a "wholistic" or *system* view, and that implies a profound revolution in scientific habits. Yet the scandal calls for clear speech. Neither Bergson, nor Whitehead, nor Russell, nor any of the Gestalt psychologists—to mention some of those whose equipment might have fitted them for the task—has formulated the problem as it must be, if it is to receive a solution. Here is the crucial question stated without prejudice in all its simplicity and difficulty:

In an atomistic world how can forms develop? Or alternatively: *If this is a universe of process, and if process is essentially formative, how has the doctrine of atomism been so successful?*

This is surely a constructive question, capable of being answered. Indeed I believe it is already clear how the answer will be found. Hitherto all logic, whether Aristotelian-verbal or twentieth-century-symbolic, has been atomistic and reversible, in the sense that it applies to ultimate units and uses elementary operations which can be performed equally backwards or forwards. There is nothing in any existing system of logic which gives preference to any logical operation as against the opposite or reverse operation. This reversible logic is very powerful, but not all-powerful, for it cannot represent the structure of processes which go one way, such as the irreversible development of complex systems, the history of the universe or of an organism. Thus a new kind of formal logic (and mathematics) is required which can discriminate between the direction or temporal tendency of irreversible processes, and the reverse processes which we can imagine though they never happen. The new logic must apply not to ultimate units or entities, but to complex systems of relationships, and its operations must possess a privileged sense or direction corresponding to the one-way temporal tendencies of natural systems. What is required is a mathematical logic of the one-way transformation of complex systems. This suggestion cannot be further developed here, but it implies that the answer to our crucial question will only be found when a logical procedure or mathematical notation has been developed which is appropriate to the one-way character of formative processes.

The discovery of the answer cannot fail to have dramatic consequences. For it must tell us whether the general laws of this universe, as far as they are recognizable by twentieth-century man, are atomistic, or morphological, or somehow combine these two aspects. The scientist rightly seeks to avoid sudden fundamental challenges, preferring to advance cautiously by gradual stages. But here there seems to be no choice. I believe that the problem cannot be postponed much longer and that its resolution will provide a new intellectual vista running across the three realms: inanimate, animate, and mental.

For if we translate the question into the language of these realms it becomes—in the *inorganic* realm: How do fundamental physical particles cohere to form regular figures, such as atoms, molecules, and crystals? In the *organic:* How do the biochemical constituents of the organism interact so as to sustain and develop the working unity of the system? And in the *mental:* How do the units of experience, the single perceptions, memories, and mental habits of the individual, fuse into new unities within the processes of the creative mind?

Thus the problem of the development of form, and the avenue of thought which will be opened up by its solution, runs through all three realms. But here we must confine ourselves to one process: the story of the development of the human individual and, within this, of the working of his creative imagination. This is a continuity within a greater continuity, and we isolate it only for convenience. We have to ask whether all the formative processes revealed in the history of a single human individual cannot be interpreted as expressions of one underlying principle. In other words, may there not in some degree be an identity of structure between the *organic* processes, which maintain the physiological unity of the organism, and the *mental* processes, which maintain the unity of the thought and behavior of the person? May not biological organization and mental activity be names for processes of closely similar, or even identical character, operating in different situations?

The idea of a similarity or identity between organic and mental processes is very old. Plato drew an analogy between poetic creation and the development of organic forms, and countless others have followed him. "Let us open our leaves like a flower and be passive and receptive—budding patiently under the eye of Apollo"; that is Keats.

This poetic analogy has reappeared as a scientific problem. Thus many biologists have asked what is the relation of mind to organism, or of mental processes to biological organization. Recently an American geneticist, E. W. Sinnott, has suggested that biological organization and mental processes are essentially identical, and a Belgian embryologist, A. M. Dalcq, has stressed the developmental continuity of the differentiating and organizing processes which lead through from the unfolding embryo to the thinking adult. At some point in this continuity the science of embryology must hand on the study of the morphogenetic processes to the science of developmental psychology, as Piaget has pointed out. "*Die Denkgesetze als Resultate der organischen Entwicklung; eine fingierende setzende Kraft muss angeonommen werden*"; that is Nietzsche, and my task today is to try to say something about that "*fingierende setzende Kraft.*"

I shall not attempt to sketch the extraordinary succession of formative processes evident during the development of the human embryo, infant, and adult. To the theoretical scientist this is a structural drama of the first order, presenting many fascinating intellectual problems. The sequence opens with the explosion of formative processes released by the act of fertilization. The potential or intensity of the process appears then to be at its height, and to decline steadily, in our ordinary time measure, through childhood, adolescence, maturity, and old age. On the other hand, the subtlety and complexity of the phenomenon rises steadily until the imagination attains its full power, usually sometime between 20 and 50 years of age. How does this complex process come about? What continuity links all this variety?

At the present time we are compelled to describe this sequence by using a confusion of words and assumptions, inherited from several alien sources. Nevertheless I believe we can, as it were, look through our clumsy words, such as "brain" and "mind," to the true character of the single phenomenon as a steadily unfolding, irreversible process, with a rhythm of transformations imposed on an underlying continuity.[1] Thus we should not ask whether the process itself is continuous or discontinuous, for it is both. On the one hand certain general characteristics persist right through, and on the other, more specific properties change rather suddenly.

In the present state of knowledge no purpose is served by asking when precisely some new faculty, such as "mind," first appears. But it is clear that any new faculty which emerges in an organism must be in full conformity, as regards its general structure and characteristics, with the earlier stages of the system. Whatever definition we give to "mind," it cannot be regarded as a principle or function alien to the organic system within which it develops. There must be an essential conformity of the properties of mind with those of organism. Mind is not a rebellion or cancer in the human organism, but its flower and fruit.

A sound methodological principle underlies this assumption. It has long been clear that entities should not be multiplied without good reason, and the same rule of intellectual economy applies to principles. If possible we must treat the properties of organism and of mind as the consequences of one principle operating in two different situations, that is as two expressions of one underlying form of process. Thus the physiological processes of the human organism and the mental processes of the person may be expressions of one set of organic principles operating under different conditions. The image of Plato and Keats anticipates this scientific hypothesis.

But science requires that the search for unity be disciplined by the recognition of differences. We cannot rest satisfied with the intuitive vision of a pervasive unity between organism and mind: we have also to identify what distinguishes them. If a formative process is at work in both realms, we may expect that the difference lies in the character of the units on which it operates in the two cases.

This supposition is correct. Using the language of the physical sciences we can say that the main difference between most physiological processes and mental processes lies in the fact that in the former the units on which the process operates are *relatively stable biochemical structures of universal type,* whereas in mental processes the units are the memory traces of past experience, i.e., *relatively plastic records of varied processes* in the structure of the cerebral cortex. The formative process is identical in character in the two cases, but in the first it operates on units of standard biochemical structure, and in the second on brain traces or records which are not of absolutely standardized pattern, but reflect the immense variety of particular situations in which the individual has been placed.

The physical organism is a formative system of stereotyped parts, characteristic of its heredity, diet, and so on; while the brain-mind is a formative system of patterns, each recording a specified feature of the experience of the individual. Just as the tissues of the organism synthesize their own fabric, so the brain-mind synthesizes unified activity patterns in the fabric of the brain. While the organism is a plastic result of a fairly standardized heredity operating in a rather stable environment, the brain-mind is a plastic record of highly variable individual processes. And "plastic" here means *self-molding,* spontaneously developing its own appropriate form of order.

This brings us to the threshold of the creative process. For we shall assume that the supreme faculty of genius is the expression, in special individuals, of a process that operates in all human minds nearly all the time. "*In jeder Handlung eines Menschen wird die ganze Entwicklung des psychischen Lebens durchgemacht*" (Nietzsche). The formative property of the mind-brain must be assumed to be at work in everyone, through all waking hours. For it is the essence of mentality, common to all its expressions, and the operations of relatively specialized faculties, such as the visual imagination or the logical intellect, must be interpreted as differentiated expressions of this underlying activity. Though we cannot yet describe it in scientific language, there is an inner consistency and continuity, a living logic of its own, in the workings of the creative imagination, just as there is a formative or intuitive element in the most abstract logical reasoning.

Only the assumption of a formative character in every thought process can make possible a general theory of the mind covering all its differentiated faculties. Thought, in the most general sense, is neither mere *problem solving* nor the play of an *arbitrary fancy,* but something which contains both of these and more. There can be no theory of logical mental operations, of cognition of the external world, of imagination, invention, or creation, which does not look beneath these special modes to find their common root in a formative process itself rooted in organism, just as organism is in turn rooted in universal nature. "Rooted in" means: sharing their formative character.

It is probable that within a few decades the precise space-time structure of this formative process in the brain-mind will be identified by the techniques of the emerging science of neuropsychology. The convergence of research on the problem of thought, on the working of the brain-mind, is striking. Psychoanalysis is advancing on it through the introspective study of the mind and its symbolic substitutes for experience; experimental psychology through the study of behavior, perception, learning, insight, and so on; many overlapping schools through the study of the symbol in the origins of human culture, in art, religion, language, and mathematics; physics through the comparison of calculating machines with the human brain; medicine and neurology through their own methods, including research on the electrical aspects of brain processes. Thus many distinct techniques are now being used to investigate the operations of the animal and human brain-mind, and their common aim is a theory of mental processes, of thought in the widest sense.

Advance toward this common objective might be more rapid if it were not for two major barriers which stand in the way: First, the sciences have no single system of ideas which can overcome the dualism of the matter-body-brain language and the consciousness-mind language. This difficulty is well-known, and needs no emphasis. Secondly, in neither language is there a clear conception of the manner in which novelty comes into existence or new forms merge. As I have already explained, neither in the language of physics nor in that of subjective psychology is there a theory showing how new forms come into being. The formative aspect has been neglected in both. This difficulty is less clearly recognized.

It is often a wise policy to meet problems one by one, to divide in order to conquer. But this procedure is ineffective if the various difficulties express one underlying problem which has not yet been clearly identified, and that may be so here. What seem to be two barriers may in fact be one. *The failure to develop a single language may be due to the neglect of the formative aspect of process.* It may be that only by explicit recognition of the formative character of natural processes can we come to see that there is in fact only one realm, and discover the language appropriate to it. So it may be helpful to offer a view of the processes of productive thought which seeks to transcend the dualism.

I shall therefore attempt to define the formal character of all productive thought, under which term I include the entire range of mental processes, from the creative activity of genius, through the ordinary procedures of constructive reasoning, to the basic synthesis of sense perceptions. This will represent my own preferred guess, but it makes no claim to originality, for it rests on a long tradition of philosophical enquiry and uses recent scientific ideas, such as those of Wertheimer, Blanchard, Piaget, Hebb, and Hearnshaw, among others.

In current psychological discussions different aspects of mental processes are described by terms such as: learning, generalization, symbolization, intelligence, intellect, insight, attention, interest, expectancy, and so on. But no one of these points unmistakably to the essential character of all thinking. One factor in all productive thought is the emergence of new relationships, so that thought and behavior acquire a fresh direction. Many philosophers have held that thinking is relationing. However this does not sufficiently stress the crucial feature: the inherent tendency toward *comprehensive unification* or *improved single ordering*. Thus the characteristic property of all brain-mind processes is an *inherent self-ordering tendency* whereby partial, incomplete, or imperfect forms are extended, completed, or perfected—as far as possible under the given conditions. These forms or wholes are not merely *logical*, or *geometrical*, but more generally, as I shall suggest, *aesthetic*. But since the brain-mind is modified by processes occurring in it and thus becomes a record of those processes, we can go further and interpret the brain-mind as a *plastic self-ordering system of records*, just as the organism as a whole is a plastic self-ordering system of persisting biochemical or physical entities. In its plastic forms and images the brain-mind orders the chaos of appearances, in accordance with its own ordering tendency, aesthetic and symbolic.

This conception of a plastic, self-formative record takes us about as far as we can safely go at this stage. The word "record" reminds us that we are dealing with the reorganization of the traces of processes which have occurred in one individual, though we must note that each record is itself a simplification of the process which it records; "self-formative" recalls the spontaneous productive aspect; and "plastic" emphasizes that the process usually involves the remolding of earlier clarified forms as a new dominant form emerges. The creative process is neither addition nor selection, but *elimination and remolding in the process of unification*.

On this view thought consists in the emergence of new single forms within a self-developing system of records. The system continually receives new elements from the environment, and perpetually seeks to assimilate them to itself, if necessary by a fargoing readjustment of its own structure.

This continuous self-adjustment, perpetually producing novelty, is not outside natural law. On the contrary it is itself a direct expression of a very general law: the tendency toward the development of form. Thus the formative or creative property of the human mind can be included within the order of nature if, and only if, we recognize that the natural order is itself formative.

This self-formative process in the brain-mind has two inseparable but distinguishable aspects: the temporal tendency, and the specific spatial form or structure which it produces. The first, the temporal aspect, corresponds to the emotional, energetic, conative side; the second, the spatial aspect, to the structural or cognitive. But these two are aspects of one process.

Moreover in the brain-mind we see one part of nature in process of becoming a symbol or representation of the rest of nature. The formative pulsations of the brain-mind are processes which mimic the corresponding formative processes in the rest of nature. We should not say: "the mind symbolizes nature," but rather: "the processes of the brain-mind perpetually shape themselves into more adequate representations of other processes." And the brain-mind processes are often anticipatory; they predict what has not yet happened. This is because "in the processes of thought certain components of the processes of nature work out their own development at lightning speed, far more swiftly than the corresponding, but more complex processes in the rest of nature." [2]

If all this be granted as a working hypothesis, then we may ask: What processes in the operation of the plastic self-ordering record are conscious, and what unconscious? Here we are on difficult ground because the only language available fails to reflect the wide variety of the characteristics of the various modes of awareness. But it seems probable that those formative processes which involve the remolding of pre-existing elements, and not merely their rearrangement, must take place outside the field of fully focused attention, and that only when this plastic reshaping is nearly complete and the resulting integral pattern already clearly defined, does the result of the process become the object of conscious attention as a new intuition. It is as though the full reflective consciousness could reversibly rearrange constant elements, but achieve no basic irreversible reshaping of the individual components. A form in the brain-mind cannot be remolded and clarified while it is the subject of concentrated attention; what is fully conscious must remain constant, as it were; the emergence of a new pattern, which depends on the modification of the old parts, must proceed unconsciously. True creation is always unconscious, as has been long realized.

But we must remember that these intuitions from the unconscious are often misleading. When they appear most reliable they may be subtly treacherous. Only time and conscious work can establish the objective value of an intuition.

The conscious mind has not only to check the work of the unconscious, it must also set the unconscious its homework. All the material must be gathered together, thought over, and worked over. And this work must be carried out under the pressure of an enthusiastic longing, itself the expression of a dominant purpose. The conscious mind must have felt a passionate interest in a particular theme and have grown to the conviction that in a special direction a satisfying result can be reached. In the language of psychology the mind must be fascinated by an anticipatory schema, a dynamic schema as Bergson called it.

Without this intense interest and conviction experienced repeatedly and stabilized during sustained periods of conscious work, the unconscious mind lacks both the material and the direction which are normally indispensable for its most fertile working. But given these conditions and a sufficient plasticity of mind, or readiness to discard the ruts of habit and to venture into new realms, then the unconscious processes will get to work. The secret lies in *controlled formative plasticity*. The conscious mind supplies the specific material and stabilizes the direction of advance; the plasticity is presumably a matter of fortunate heredity or parental example; and the formative power comes from nature, that is from the inherent properties of the organ which we call the brain-mind. When we say that we do not fundamentally explain the creative process, still less explain it away. But it becomes no more and no less mysterious than is the whole of existence, because it is on the way to becoming an integral part of our picture of the whole.

On this view all mental processes are in some degree formative; that is the essential property common to all types of mental operation. At every moment when the brain-mind is functioning fully the plastic record is ordering itself, a new ordered unity is in course of development. When the fringes of this formative process enter the field of our attention, we become aware of the operation of the aesthetic intuition or recognition of order. Thus the aesthetic intuition can be regarded as the first aspect of the complete brain-mind process to enter awareness. The aesthetic sense, in the most general meaning of the term, as the sense of order, is then the awareness of the culminating phase of an internal mental process tending one way, toward order and unity. Our preference for order, for harmony, and for the complex forms of organization and tension possessing "beauty," is the expression of this tendency or search continually proceeding in the brain-mind. If we could look deep enough we would recognize that without this aesthetic faculty, which is the ultimate source of all mental material, no more highly differentiated function could operate.

The other extreme is represented in the operations of that abstraction: the strictly logical intellect. In processes which seem to be purely logical the brain-mind operates with the minimum of dependence on the unconscious formative process and its conscious fringe, the aesthetic sense. For logic, as currently understood, can only operate with elements that are already clear and constant, and all it can do is to arrange and reversibly rearrange these elements as, for example, in a mathematical system whose symbols, axioms, and reversible procedures are explicitly laid down at the start. But even here we note that the elements of the mathematical system must come from somewhere, logic can only begin when these have already been posited, and it is the aesthetic function —in the sense used here—which has formed them out of the confused data of experience. Moreover, in the daily practical working of the human mind what we call logic would be impotent unless it were kept on the rails by countless unconscious or scarcely conscious acts of selection and judgment, all of which depend on the underlying formative-aesthetic process.

This is an important point, not yet adequately appreciated. Let me illustrate it. Since the development of modern logic much has been written about the role of logical inference in scientific theory, and mathematical physics is supposed by some to provide the example par excellence of explicit logical inference about the external world: a symbolism which permits only correct deductions, provided that the correct rules of manipulation are followed. But if we apply this standard to Newtonian mechanics, the prototype of physical theories, we discover something very curious. Though there is no dispute about the observational implications of Newton's theory, and these are amply justified by observation (subject only to Einstein's adjustments), no one has yet given strict symbolic expression to the complete system of axioms on which this theory is based and developed the theory from such symbolic axioms!

In fact the intellectual structure of Newtonian theory rests, not on fully explicit mathematical postulates expressed in algebra, but on subtle, intuitive, and complex notions such as "space," "time," "quantitative measurement," etc., the empirical and mathematical implications of which have not yet been axiomatized and expressed in algebraic form. To the extreme logical positivists of some time back, who held that only what was logically explicit could have a scientific meaning, the success of the Newtonian theory should have appeared incomprehensible, for (like all other scientific theories) it is a superstructure of logic and mathematics resting on nothing more definite than certain intuitions which have been well tested and widely accepted, but are still logically obscure. Yet there is nothing strange or unusual in this. For all human thought is the gradual development toward logical clarity of ideas which were originally vague and formless, but none the less valuable, for they were in course of being shaped by the formative process in a succession of minds.

Let us turn to another kind of mental activity. When we "think something over," "weigh up the factors in a situation," or "exercise our judgment," the self-ordering process in the plastic brain-mind is occupied in grading various factors in relation to a particular conscious aim characterized by some latent order or unity. Purposive thought is the relative ranking of factors in relation to a formative process directed toward a consciously conceived end, but the actual process of weighing up the situation, the process which precedes and determines the act of judgment, is itself formative and unconscious. This is true whether the judgment is aesthetic, practical, moral, or logical; all "weighing up" is a process of ranking in relation to a specific process in the brain-mind, and the actual weighing up cannot be fully explained or logically justified without residual. We are making use of the intuition: "I don't know why, but I feel A matters more than B."

This view of the creative process in the human brain-mind is in conformity with many recent psychological investigations. Moreover most of its features have already been clearly formulated by a long line of thinkers. For example, if we consider the German language alone one can find most of these ideas, though sometimes in a different context, in the works of Schelling, Schopenhauer, Carus, Von Hartmann, and Wundt, as well as other later writers. But in order to indicate how diverse are the avenues toward the truth I will cite some further passages [3] from Nietzsche, perhaps the most highly intuitive and the least systematic or scientific of all great psychologists.

> *Unsere Lust an Einfachheit, Uebersichtlichkeit, Regelmässigkeit, Helligkeit . . . davon gestehe ich einen starken Instinkt als vorhanden zu. Er ist so stark, dass er in allen unseren Sinnesthätigkeiten waltet und uns die Fülle wirklicher Wahrnehmungen (der unbewussten) reducirt, regulirt, assimilirt u. s. w. und sie erst in dieser zurechtgemachten Gestalt unserem Bewusstsein vorführt. Dies "Logische" und "Künstlerische" ist unsre fortwährende Thätigkeit. Was hat diese Kraft so souverän gemacht? Offenbar, dass ohne sie, vor Wirrwarr der Eindrücke, kein lebendes Wesen lebte.*

> *Es giebt keine unmittelbaren Thatsachen! Es steht mit Gefühlen und Gedanken ebenso: indem ich mich ihrer bewusst werde, mache ich einen Auszug, eine Vereinfachung, einen Versuch der Gestaltung: das eben ist bewusst-werden: ein ganz actives Zurechtmachen.*

> *Damit in einer mechanischen Weltordnung Etwas gewusst werden kann, muss ein Perspectiv-Apparat da sein, der a) ein gewisses Stillstehn, b) ein Vereinfachen, c) ein Auswählen und Weglessen möglich macht. . . . Die innere Welt muss in Schein verwandelt werden, um bewusst zu werden: viele Erregungen als Einheit empfunden.*

Unsere fortwährende Einübung von Formen, *erfindend, vermehrend, wiederholend:* Formen *des sehens, Hörens und Tastens.*

Alles Organische, das "urtheilt," handelt wie der Künstler: es schafft aus einzelnen Anregungen und Reizen ein Ganzes, es lässt vieles Einzelne bei Seite und schafft eine Simplification, es setzt gleich und bejaht sein Geschöpf als seiend. . . . Das schöpferische (aneignende auswählende, umbildende) Element, das selbstregulirende, das ausscheidende Element.

So far we have mainly been using either mental terms or the language of subjective psychology to describe the creative process, and the question arises of the relation of this description to the physiological or physical picture of brain processes. There are some to whom any attempt to link the creative imagination with the physiology of the brain is repugnant and seems to involve an insult to human dignity, and there is a school of psychology which holds that mental processes can never be reduced without residual to physical processes. Both these attitudes appear to be based on a serious misunderstanding, the result of deep-lying prejudices.

As scientists, philosophers, and human beings we are engaged on a continuing search for understanding, an attempt to discover the relatedness of things. In this search we have attained some comprehension of certain kinds of phenomena, loosely called mental and physical. But we do not yet know any unquestionably fundamental and permanent physical laws, and we have only recently begun to gain some light on mental phenomena. Thus it is premature to adopt an absolute attitude toward either method of description. Moreover a clarification of the relationships between phenomena cannot result in prejudice to human values, unless these values were based on misconceptions. Even philosophical dualists who recognize two distinct realms of existence must allow the scientist to continue his task of identifying the apparent connections between those realms.

Now when we consider the relation of this conception of the brain-mind to the structural facts of anatomy and physiology, we at once notice an important fact. The neurologists have studied in considerable detail the anatomical distribution of the fibers in the nervous system, and the pulses of excitation, or waves of electrical depolarization and repolarization, which travel along the cylindrical surface of the individual fibers or axons. But they can say very little about what occurs when the single fibers and the pulses along them enter the cerebral cortex. Neurophysiology has so far provided no picture of what happens *after* the arrival of a pulse of excitation at a sensory area of the cortex and *before* an outgoing pulse leaves the motor area. The cortical processes which reorganize the data of the senses, the constructive processes of thought, have not yet been studied by neurological methods. This is partly due to experimental difficulties, and partly to the fact that the methods of exact science have mainly been designed for simple systems, while the operations of the cortex involve a highly complex system of relationships and it is therefore difficult to know how to begin.

Fresh ideas and methods are probably required if the cortical processes are to be effectively studied. Before suitable experiments can be planned it may be necessary to make a constructive guess concerning the mode of operation of the cortex. Hence the following suggestion [4] regarding the character of the cortical processes may possess heuristic value.

What are the principal characteristics of brain-mind processes which must be accounted for by any theory? They display three main aspects which can be called *unification, modification,* and *facilitation.* "Unification" refers to the formative property that has already been described, the tendency toward improved ordering or simple form; "modification" to the fact that the structure of nervous material is changed by the processes occurring in it so that it retains a record (trace or engram) of past events; and "facilitation" to the property which these modifications possess (in certain circumstances) of making the repetition of the original process easier or more probable, so that what we call "learning" occurs.

These three properties are fundamental to the understanding of all brain-mind processes. Neural modifications of some kind must underlie all memory in animals possessing a central nervous system, and these modifications must act by facilitating the repetition of the processes which produced them, or of similar processes, though often in a more unified form. And these properties apply to units or unified patterns of activity, resulting from the ordering, integration, or simplification of separate or disparate elements. This underlying process of unification is responsible for the organized character of neural responses, including in particular the process called "generalization," by which a single modification and response is established corresponding to a constant feature in a series of similar but not identical situations.

But these properties do not appear separately; they are aspects of a single phenomenon. So we can say that the main task of a theory of cortical processes is to account for unified modifications of neural material which ease the repetition, often in a more unified form, of the processes which produced them. The question is: How do the electrical pulsations of cortical nerve cells result in a unified modification of the neural material which facilitates the repetition of a unified pattern of pulsation latent in the original pulsations? A relatively disordered or incomplete pattern of pulsations tends to leave a residual modification which eases the repetition of the original complex process, but in a more unified form. How does this come about?

This result can be produced if the pulsating protein fabric of the cortex, or of certain parts of it, has a self-molding property, so that as it pulsates it tends to eliminate any arbitrary structural discrepancies, to straighten out its own structure, to work its parts into position—this structural "improvement" being in relation to the dominant pattern latent in the original set of stimuli—with the result that the fabric repeats this simplified pulsation more readily the next time the same set of stimuli, or an adequate part of it, is received. To account for the required unified facilitating modifications one need only assume that electrical pulsations in cortical protein leave a residual structural adjustment of a unified character so that this unified pulsation occurs again more easily.

This hypothesis of a self-molding property in the protein structure of nervous tissue is reasonable. Protein consists of molecular chains which can be moved to and fro, and worked into new stable positions, as electrical pulses pass through them. There are physical arguments which suggest that mobile parts of the protein chains would gradually be worked into those positions and orientations where they can best respond to the pulsation to which they are most frequently exposed. If you fold a sheet of paper, it folds more easily next time along the line of the fold. The carbohydrate structure has been modified so that it facilitates the repetition of the folding. Some molecular chains have been broken, and others rearranged, so that the fabric works to and fro more easily along the same line.

But the behavior of the protein is more subtle. The protein structure spontaneously selects the latent simple "fold" or pattern underlying a set of pulses, because unified modifications are most stable. As the cortex pulsates in any given manner those components which cannot be assimilated into one overriding pattern are damped down, while those components which contribute to this pattern are reinforced, so that the emergent pattern is strengthened and clarified.

On this view cortical protein spontaneously works up, accumulates, and stabilizes, the unified form latent in any set of relatively disordered pulsations. It does this because every pulsation tends to leave a slight residual modification in the structure of the protein, a modification which corresponds to the pulsation and renders it easier, and because modifications which represent a unified pulsation are more stable than those which do not.

This unified structural adjustment, facilitating the repetition, usually in a more unified form, of the processes which produced it, is, I believe, the long-sought modification or engram, the mental recording process, the structural foundation of memory and learning. The three properties of brain-mind processes: unification, modification, and facilitation, are three aspects of this single structural adjustment. If systems of protein molecules somewhere in the cortex tend to pulsate together, and thereby to remold their structure so as to form a stabilized unit which repeats this pulsation more easily, then the central factor in animal intelligence and human creative imagination is accounted for. The structural basis of the creative faculty may lie in this self-molding property of the electrically pulsating protein of the cortex. What we call "creative novelty" is the gradual emergence into explicit dominance of a single form latent in a relatively disordered set of elements.

Where, then, is the "creative energy" of man? We must distinguish two scientific usages of the term "energy." First there is the *total energy*, the quantity which is conserved in every isolated physical system. Then there is the available or *free energy*, that part of the total energy which can be used to initiate and carry through some transformation. It is this free energy which is the effective factor in causing transformations to occur, and it corresponds closely to the original meaning of energy as the active principle which does work. So we can say that the "creative energy" of the brain-mind is the free energy underlying the formative process. More precisely, since the free energy disappears in the course of the processes which it initiates, the free energy corresponds to the arbitrary differences which are eliminated by the formative tendency in heightening the degree of order in the records of the brain-mind. In fact the initiating factor or free energy of *any* organic process is always some difference or contrast, and the creative energy of the brain-mind derives from some element of apparent disorder in phenomena, which the formative process seeks to overcome.

While this ordering process, or self-adjustment of the records, is still proceeding the successive formative pulses die out and the process remains unconscious. But when the new modification is sufficiently complete and the pulses derived from sensory stimuli can pass through it into motor channels, it can become the object of conscious attention, sometimes suddenly in the form of a new intuition.

When the pattern of activity is relatively simple the unconscious formative process may be completed and the result brought to the attention of the conscious mind within a fraction of a second, and without the individual noticing that for a moment his attention had been relaxed to permit the shaping process to do its work. In more complex situations it may be necessary for the brain to be set free from the tension of conscious preoccupation with the problem for a short time, until the remolding is complete and the solution can be brought to the attention of the conscious mind.

As I have said, next to nothing is known about the actual course, the detailed space-time structure, of this unconscious brain process. But in cases where the material is complex and the solution is not directly suggested by any analogy, the material may have to be worked over countless times and the brain given long periods of rest to coax it to do its job. There are cases in the history of mathematical physics where a clearly conceived problem was solved by a new idea which came after five, ten, or even twenty years of alternating concentration and relaxation. In other recorded examples the solution to a mathematical problem has been found rather quickly, perhaps in an hour, but without the conscious mind being able to prove that the solution was correct or knowing how it was obtained. Thus the unconscious mind of Isaac Newton brought to his attention a particular mathematical theorem which was correct, though no proof of its correctness was given until two hundred years had passed.

It has sometimes been thought that the unconscious formative processes lie beyond the scope of scientific investigation and that it is necessarily impossible to determine the precise period of time during which the unconscious process is at work. This view is mistaken, as the following example shows.

Recent studies of children who have been blind, say from the age of two to three years, supplemented by observations of chimpanzees brought up in darkness, have shown that in the normal child the result of visual stimuli during certain crucial stages of its development is to initiate formative processes in the brain which help to bring about the maturation of the brain, though the results of these processes do not become evident until several years later. The observations suggest that if the child is deprived of the appropriate visual stimuli during this early period the necessary maturing processes never take place and certain mental faculties never fully develop. These experiments give definite evidence of the presence in children from two to three years of age of an unconscious developmental process in the brain which has no immediate influence on behavior and whose consequences are only evident some years later when the developmental process is complete. There is no doubt that a long process of

cortical maturation, dependent on a sustained series of unconscious formative pulses, the vast majority of which end without motor results, fills the background of the years of infancy,
just as long periods of apparently fruitless incubation often
precede the phases of overt activity in the creative adult.

The suggestion I am making here is that the unconscious
processes which constitute the background of the developing
mental life of the child are closely similar to the unconscious
processes which precede phases of creative activity in the
adult. Moreover, these unconscious mental processes in
the child are themselves the extension and completion of the
earlier processes, also unconscious, of the embryological development of the brain.

In order to clarify this view of the physiology of the creative
process, and of formative thought in general, it may be convenient to present in a more systematic manner some of the
interpretations to which it leads:

Brain-mind
An organ which, in the course of its pulsation, adjusts its
molecular structure so as to unify, record, and facilitate the
repetition, in more unified form, of the processes occurring
in it.

Thought
(including unconscious processes)
The pulsation of an extended cortical structure, unifying
separate incoming pulses and leaving the structure modified so
that it facilitates the repetition of the unified pulsation.

Formative Thought
(the unconscious development of a synthesis)
A sequence of nearly cyclic pulsations, derived ultimately
from sensory sources, each fading out without functional consequences, but all contributing to the progressive development of a unified modification (suited for functional application). Each of these pulses eases the way for the next until
the appropriate unified modification (synthesis) is established,
permitting a fully unified mode of pulsation and its functional
exploitation. This unconscious formative process, shaping a
symbolic synthesis, constitutes a continuation of the sequence
of unconscious processes which develops the brain-mind of
the infant.

Functional Thought
(the conscious use of established modes of thought)
A progressive, continuous, and truly cyclic pulsation which
does not fade out, but links sensory to motor activities. This

pulsation involves modifications which have already been fully developed and stabilized by a succession of pulses of unconscious formative thought. In true functional thought in the adult no further unification occurs.

Modification
(the basis of memory and learning)

The unified structural adjustment produced by a system of pulsations, constituting a record of it, and facilitating its repetition, usually in a more unified form. This adjustment consists in a relatively stable improved ordering of the protein molecular chains—improved in relation to particular paths of propagation of the pulsation—so that the unified pulsation is subsequently excited and transmitted by a smaller or a partial stimulus. There is as yet insufficient information regarding the precise molecular structure of protein in a functional condition inside or between nerve cells to permit a theory of the exact character of the structural adjustment which constitutes a modification, or of its distribution or localization within the cortex.

Intuition

The direction of attention to a new unified modification, already sufficiently clarified by unconscious formative thought processes. The first excitation of a new unified modification as a component in a continuous cyclic pulsation of functional thought. Thus in addition to the exteroceptor channels which bring sensory stimuli from external sensory organs, and the ordinary proprioceptor channels which bring them from internal organs, there may also be a special proprioceptor channel which brings to the part of the cortex concerned with conscious attention the products of the unconscious formative brain processes occurring elsewhere. Intuition would then be the operation of this channel.

This view of the processes of the creative imagination opens up a world of problems. One of the most interesting of these concerns the relation of intellect and intuition. Let me recall to you a well-known passage from a letter written by Chekhov, himself a doctor of medicine:

> I thought . . . that an artist's instinct may sometimes be worth the brain of a scientist, that both have the same purpose and the same nature, and that perhaps in time as their methods become perfect they are destined to become one vast prodigious force which it is now difficult to imagine.

This is taken from a page about dreams, and in the next paragraph he speaks of "the power of the artist to run ahead of the men of science."

It is easy to be misled by Chekhov's idea and to share his excitement at the vision of the artist's instinct and the scientist's brain power fusing into one vast human force at some period in the future. He seems to be suggesting that a time may come when the genius of Leonardo or Goethe, for example, blending scientific curiosity and the creative imagination, may in some degree become the collective possession of ordinary men and women. I think that would be a misunderstanding. Chekhov's thought should not be understood as a prophecy of the future, but like the early Hebraic prophecies as a glimpse into the nature of man, as he has been and will remain as long as he is man. For the united force which Chekhov sees in the future is already at work. It is nothing other than the formative property of all thought, the prodigious fact which, all unnoticed, sustains, organizes, and develops all human activity, the instinct of the artist as well as the brain of the scientist. Everyone of us in our ordinary practical life is continually making use of this primary faculty which, when highly developed, differentiates into the intuition of the artist and the intellect of the scientist. These do not require to be combined, for they are themselves specialized expressions of one principle.

So we come to the role of the imagination in the development of the human species and its cultural tradition. The unique feature in man, as against all other organic species, is that man requires appropriate guiding symbols, in the form of ideas and convictions, in order to live a life in accordance with his potentialities. Moreover the symbols which would permit a stable adapted life suited to human capacities have not yet been found, and if ever they are to be, this can only be achieved by developing existing symbols to correspond more closely to the objective structure of nature including man himself. Thus man cannot evade his unique fate: to have to search, perhaps endlessly, for the symbols appropriate to nature and to his own nature. And the creative imagination, expressing the formative character of natural process within the subtle structure of cortical protein, is the power which he must use, or better which uses him, in this extraordinary adventure.

The ants, the bees, and the birds have established their appropriate symbolisms of scent, and dance, and song. Most of their species are well-adapted, and have remained stable for countless generations. But man has not yet found any condition in which he can rest for more than, say, the hundred generations of the most stable civilization of the past. As far as we are in a position to judge our own situation, we must conclude that for all imaginable time man must continue to discover and develop richer and more powerful symbolisms. The brain-mind of Homo sapiens is apparently the unique reservoir of the unexhausted formative processes of nature. Inorganic nature provides the background, the organic realm provides the living matrix, the process of embryonic development establishes the uniquely structured organ, the unconscious receptivity of the infant and the care of the mother molds the organ toward its mature functional condition, and then within this unique instrument the formative processes continue, and in doing so have created and are still creating the cultural tradition of mankind.

Thus, developing within the context of his prehuman ancestors, man grew to be man, each generation handing on to the next some of the fruits of its own formative activities in new symbolisms of all kinds expressed in ritual or practical behavior. It is not necessary to assume any transcendental divinity or entelechy guiding this process, provided that the formative character of all natural processes is recognized. The development of human culture, miraculous as it is, can, I believe, be accounted for by one major assumption: that there is in the neural material of the cortex a tendency to develop unified modifications which facilitate the repetition, in a more unified form, of the processes which produced them. If this self-organizing, recording, and facilitating property is present in cortical protein, then the human story ceases to be a hopeless mystery. For such unified facilitating modifications are the essence of what we call "creativity."

The story of the development of man can be seen in stages, in accordance with his conscious relationship to this formative-creative process. In the first stage man creates largely unconsciously, without reflective consideration of what he is doing. In the second, from the birth of the earliest civilizations onwards, he studies his own creations; admiring, repeating, and modifying them. In the third, roughly from 1800 A.D., man comes to regard his own creations as symbols or substitutes for something else, and so to place the emphasis on the role of symbolisms in human culture. But this attitude is not final, for in the next stage, now opening, man studies the processes by which he forms symbols. The emphasis is now on the creative process itself, not on its results, the created symbols, and the aim is to see this process in man as one example of more general formative processes in nature. Only in this fourth stage can man truly see himself as part of nature. Indeed only when art, religion, the rational intellect, and practical activities are all viewed as differentiated expressions of one underlying formative faculty can an attitude be established which may allow the disintegration of contemporary culture to be overcome.

If this perspective is accepted, we need no longer be in doubt regarding our role as human beings and our place in history. We are participants in one task: to enrich the tradition and to hand it on to the next generation so that this deeper understanding and richer fulfillment may come about.

NOTES

1. The term "brain-mind" will be used as a neutral label to designate the thinking organ of the human individual, without begging any questions regarding the ultimate superiority of either the physical or the mental language. In their present forms both languages are inadequate.
2. From the author's *Next Development in Man.*
3. Friedrich Nietzsche, *Gesammelte Werke,* XVI, *Aus dem Nachlass* (1882–1888) (Munich: Musarion-Verlag, 1925).
4. See the author's *Unitary Principle in Physics and Biology* (London: 1949) for a fuller treatment.

VI
AESTHETICS AS A PHILOSOPHIC DISCIPLINE
INTRODUCTION

Philosophy is as much subject to fashion, current events, public movements, and charismatic personalities, as is any other social phenomenon. Were this anthology edited in the 1920's, 1930's, or 1940's, the predominantly fashionable elements for consideration in aesthetics as a philosophic discipline would surely have been Marxian thought, the philosophies of John Dewey, Henri Bergson, and Benedetto Croce. Today, it is the existentialism of Jean-Paul Sartre and the ontology of Martin Heidegger.

There is nothing saddening in this fact. Fashions come and go, for the obvious reason that a new formulation possesses the vast importance of engaging *contemporary* interest. It has what appeals to its immediate audience as assimilating the most recent experiences common to that audience, and offering the most encompassing solutions, or at least formulating questions in the style most appropriate for grasping widespread attention. This is not to say that Bergson or Dewey is no longer of interest to aesthetics, or that enough study of Croce has proved that his position leads up a blind alley. But such studies do not represent "Aesthetics Today" in the sense that they no longer stand as guides to unexplored territory, as Sartre and Heidegger are felt to do today. It is the belief that *they* indicate areas which promise undiscovered treasures of understanding which gives the sense of adventure to current philosophic thought.

"The Literature of Extreme Situations" is Robert Cumming's analysis of an aesthetics possible to the existentialism of Sartre. In effect, it is a brilliant comparison of Kierkegaard and Sartre with respect to the nature and functions of literature and philosophy. Both of these writers have used fiction as well as discursive essays for the exposition of their thought. While they share a common concern with questions of the relationship between reflection and action, the difference in their interpretations is expressed in the different uses they make of imaginative literature. It is the role of literature that is crucial to any future aesthetics compatible with existentialism, and Professor Cumming's analysis is the best general introduction to this subject.

Heidegger's interest is, unquestionably, not so much in

the theological possibility or social reality indispensable to Kierkegaard and Sartre as it is in the idea of an "essence" of "existence," in "authentic Being." Truth and Beauty, as eternal abstractions re-emerge in Heidegger's writings as the names of eternal ontological categories. Professor Hans Jaeger summarizes and represents the material of Heidegger's much discussed essay on the origin of the work of art. For those who find it impossible to read Heidegger directly, this is a godsend of scholarly helpfulness. What the study of Heidegger's thought may lead to in the future remains a puzzle for prophecy. Here, by reading these two essays juxtaposed, the greatest advantage to be gained is awareness of the striking differences between Sartre's and Heidegger's positions.

While the spectacularly appealing fashions may come and go, leaving behind them many useful tools for future work as well as debris after a picnic, the work of more modest and methodical thinkers continues at its own pace. In philosophy as in every other discipline there are the hedgehogs and the foxes.

The late Walter Abell's work represents the best of efforts currently being made in the direction of a general synthesis in aesthetics. It is only fitting that this collection should end with his essay "Toward a Unified Field in Aesthetics." Here is enunciated the hope that in the future there will be scholars capable of dealing with the wealth of materials developing in the social and psychological sciences: of organizing them, with the means of philosophically trained historians and aesthetically sensitive critics, to become more capable as the task becomes more complex. The technique Professor Abell recommends—and employs in his own work entitled *The Collective Dream in Art*—is a co-ordination of depth psychology with what he calls "depth history." It is no chimera to imagine that the future will make possible a philosophic integration of the social sciences, at least for the purposes of aesthetics. As such, it would continue the service philosophers have always tried to perform, whatever their particular subject matter, in making use of discoveries in any field of science. The problems of aesthetics cannot be the direct subject matter of any one of the social sciences; but it is Professor Abell's reasonable assumption that aesthetics cannot be adequate to its proper subject matter without making use of the findings of psychology, sociology, history, and economics. Herein lies one of the best hopes of twentieth-century intellectual life.

THE LITERATURE OF EXTREME SITUATIONS *

Robert Cumming

THE POSTWAR MOOD

A philosophy with a label is usually no longer a philosophy. A philosophy proposes some coherent way of handling problems that cuts across their previous arrangement. But the popular acknowledgment of a label marks the impact of a philosophy on what would have been thought had its influence never been exerted. Its cutting edge is blunted as it encounters older recalcitrant and incompatible ways of thinking, which reclaim or rearrange its problems. The question that should then force itself on our attention, I raise specifically with regard to the philosophy labeled "existentialism": Is it merely what it has largely become—a miscellaneous assortment of aches and pains of the human spirit?

Even to reach this question we have first to get past two popular interpretations of existentialism, the theological and the sociological, which pose problems in ways which are not native to existentialism itself. On the one interpretation, existentialism is coping wth a profoundly novel spiritual problem, What is one to do with his soul, now that God is dead? But this announcement, before it was Nietzsche's, was a Lutheran hymn, and a moment in the Christian revelation (not to mention more ancient faiths), so that it is hardly surprising if existentialist soul-searching seems the sapping of human faith by an "old despair." On the other interpretation, such novelty as existentialism retains can be traced to a different intimation of mortality, which finds expression in a less ambiguous announcement, *"Nous autres, civilisations, nous savons maintenant que nous sommes mortelles."* [1] Existentialism then becomes a relatively new despair; a date can be added to the label, identifying existentialism as a postwar mood. But to accept this identification is to interpret existentialism as a transient emotional reaction which never achieved the sustained cogency and articulation of a philosophy, and which can be explained away by the social circumstances of its vogue—the crumbling of bourgeois society.

Furthermore, the arrangement of problems that this sociological interpretation brings with it is incompatible with the theological interpretation. The social historian is not inclined to accept the depths of a soul as fundamental; what happens there is merely evidence of what is happening to the structure of society. Soul-searching as such he is likely to regard as evidence of social disintegration; in a more integrated society men know, without searching, what to do with their souls; they put them at the disposal of their fellow men.

But where does this sociological disparagement and dismissal of existentialism lead us? Existentialism first attained its popular vogue after World War I in Germany. If we interpret Heidegger's despairing preoccupation with death and nothingness as the preoccupation of the German bourgeoisie, whose sense of their social reality was undermined by war and inflation, which left them with nothing—if we similarly interpret Sartre's existentialism as a moral backwash (like black-marketeering) from the French experience of invasion and resistance during Warld War II—we can then expect existentialism to become the mood of America after World War III, when the mortality of our civilization should be amply evident. In other words, the sociological framework of explanation, which sustains the convictions on which we are relying when we dismiss existentialism as a phenomenon of social disintegration, may not itself survive the cumulative disintegration of the structure of our society. Soul-searching might instead come into popular favor as a method of social research.

There is, however, something more obviously awkward about the social historian's dismissal of existentialism as a postwar mood than any anticipation which might disturb our present confidence, it can't happen here. Even if we overlook God's possible role in the soul-searching of the existentialists, we have to recognize that existentialism was not originally a postwar mood. What happened after World War I in Germany, when Heidegger played upon the terms *Stimmung* and *bestimmen* and found that such moods as anxiety and despair define man's *Sein zum Tode*, was in part the revival of a largely neglected thinker, Kierkegaard, whose thoughts had not originally been conceived under postwar circumstances, or indeed with any reference to social circumstances. When after World War II existentialism re-emerges out of the French resistance, Sartre analyzes this public experience by re-employing terminology which had originally been shaped by Kierkegaard's private experience. Kierkegaard's mood of despair over the Fall of Man, when he analyzed the intricacies of the human soul in *Sickness Unto Death*, becomes despair over the Fall of France in Sartre's *La Mort dans l'âme*. Kierkegaard encountered his despair in his anxious struggle to reach some final verdict on himself—*Guilty/Not-Guilty*. And he describes this struggle metaphorically as a "self-torturing" process of putting himself "on trial." This struggle to reach inner clarity withdrew him, moreover, from any contact with matters of public concern, and he describes his withdrawal with the further metaphor of "self-imprisonment." Thus Kierkegaard was self-tortured, self-tried, self-imprisoned. He was never menaced with an actual trial, with actual torture, with actual imprisonment. It took nearly a century for social history to catch up with Kierkegaard's private moods and to supply his metaphors with the literal public references which we find in Sartre's writings to the tortures, trials, and imprisonments actually instituted by the Gestapo in occupied France, and by the French army in Algeria. What were originally Kierkegaard's metaphorical descriptions of his introspective withdrawal have been pulled inside out by the eventual course history has taken. Life has imitated his art.

But Sartre's transformation of existentialism from self-scrutiny into social commentary is not completely unambiguous. For the public drama of a social struggle to the death in Sartre still derives some of its plot from the private theatricals of Kierkegaard's inner struggle. When Sartre, for example, writes of "Torture in the Twentieth Century," his indignation obtains much of its righteousness from the involutions of introspective moral implication which the original existentialist metaphors still retain, even when they have been partially uncoiled to describe the overt activities of an Algerian prison camp.

It is because existentialism has undergone this transformation from a private mood into a postwar mood, from self-scrutiny into social commentary, that it lends itself to both of the two interpretations with which we began. But neither interpretation adequately draws our attention to the process of transformation itself, which is not only characteristic of the long-range evolution of existentialism from Kierkegaard to Sartre, but also takes place (though in a less pronounced fashion) in the writings of each of these thinkers. Kierkegaard's introspective withdrawal originally took the form of a private journal. In an entry for 1837 Kierkegaard finds the prospect of publishing his thoughts "revolting." But in this journal, he explains to himself, "I can let my thoughts appear with the umbilical cord of their first mood." [2] Nevertheless Kierkegaard's private mood later became his postwar mood.

During the Schleswig-Holstein war, the tremors of the social revolutions of 1848 reached quiet Denmark, and in an entry for 1849 Kierkegaard envisages the prospect that his journal "might be published after my death under the title, *The Book of the Judge*." [3] It will then no longer be a question, as in *Guilty/Not-Guilty*, of an individual who is putting himself on trial. Kierkegaard's private court of appeal—his journal—is to become posthumously the book of a judge issuing verdicts on society, and Kierkegaard in fact adopted this public role in such works as his *Attack on Christendom* and on *The Present Age*.

There was also a prewar Sartre as well as a postwar Sartre. His first novel, *Nausea*, was published before World War II began and ostensibly takes the form of a private journal which (like Kierkegaard's) was never intended for publication. For this journal was kept by someone who was "merely an individual without social significance," and his bouts of nausea, are the moods of revulsion which sweep over him whenever he pretends to significance. But after World War II, Sartre takes to public journalism and wrestles with the socially significant. The private revulsion of a mere individual in *Nausea* becomes a revolutionary protest against bourgeois society; it becomes in *"Les Séquestrés d'Altona"* the bad "taste" our whole epoch leaves in the mouth of the protagonist when he anticipates its trial and the eventual verdict of history.

EXISTENCE AND COMMUNICATION

My selecting Kierkegaard and Sartre to exhibit the transformation of existentialism from self-scrutiny into social commentary has rendered even more embarrassing our initial effort to consider existentialism as a philosophy—as a coherent way of handling some range of problems. For they are the foremost representatives of the two major factions into which existentialism is split. The inability of the prevailing interpretation of existentialism to mend this split is well illustrated by Lowrie's denial of any philosophical relationship between them. Lowrie is incensed that the same label, "existentialist," should have become popularly affixed to both their philosophies. He is convinced that when one has "heard in the very words of Kierkegaard what he understood by *existence*, one must feel bewildered by the claim that Sartre is his legitimate successor." So he suspects "a monstrous hoax," when he concludes that "between these two men there is hardly enough likeness to make it easy to define the difference." [4]

I am not concerned to retrieve the popular label "existentialist." The packaging and labeling of an intellectual product, and its consignment to a destination determined by prevailing intellectual commonplaces, rather than by the writer's very words—this monstrous hoax, I have suggested, is played on almost any philosophy which receives common acknowledgment. But the intellectual complacency of this hoax is hardly consistent with the existentialists themselves finding communication so troublesome a problem.

The trouble begins, of course, when thoughts are cherished so long as they remain entangled with the umbilical cord of their first mood, and indeed could not have been conceived had they been originally intended for publication. But the novelty of existentialism does not reside in this moment of self-scrutiny, which is a romantic version of a venerable theological and philosophical tradition with which Kierkegaard identifies himself as a "Christian Socrates." Nor is it displayed by existentialist social commentaries; after all, Sartre's comments on society are largely Marxist. Nor is the bold attempt to lend self-scrutiny the scope of social commentary itself unique to existentialism. The novelty of existentialism is to be sought rather in the way Kierkegaard and Sartre solve the problem of communication that arises in the course of their making this attempt. The respects in which they are both existentialists can be discovered, I shall argue, if we examine the ways in which they are both forced, by their otherwise quite different philosophies, to adopt literary works as a means of communicating these philosophies.[5]

Of course the fact has often been recognized that the actual intellectual influence exercised by existentialists cannot be accounted for by their philosophical writings without reference to their literary writings, but only by the way the prestige of their employment of the one genre enhances the popular appeal of the other. Yet this fact might only betray the flippancy of intellectual fashion. Thus Lowrie himself concedes that "Sartre shows a certain resemblance to Kierkegaard in the fact that he has sought to popularize his views by creating a novelistic literature." But Lowrie deprives this resemblance of any philosophical significance. It does not seem to him to require explanation in terms of their own views of the problem of communication; he offers instead merely extraneous comment on such philosophically inconsequential characteristics of popular mentality as its romantic readiness in the nineteenth century to be tantalized by the minor raptures of Kierkegaard's "Seducer's Diary" and its whetting its jaded appetite in the twentieth with the virulent obscenities of Sartre's novels. But a hostile interpreter of existentialism, who prefers common sense and thinks of himself as a steadier philosopher than Kierkegaard or Sartre, may entertain unflattering suspicions of their stooping to literature in order to conquer the popular mind. He may suspect that their philosophies are merely literary gestures, indistinguishable in intellectual content from their literary works. Thus De Ruggiero allots no role to Sartre's philosophy besides that of waving "a banner for the diffusion of his dramas."[6] I shall try to get behind such references as Lowrie's and De Ruggiero's to existentialism as a popular literary vogue, in order to demonstrate that Kierkegaard's and Sartre's literary efforts are indispensable to, yet distinguishable from, their philosophies. This demonstration will enable me to deal with the other issues I have been raising regarding existentialism, including the claims of common sense.

REFLECTION AND ACTION

The least which a summary exposition of Kierkegaard's very words should make clear are his puzzling terminology and titles. Each of Kierkegaard's literary works, which he himself refers to as his "aesthetic production," he published under a pseudonym, along with an ethical-religious work in his own name. But the relation of these pseudonymous aesthetic works to the ethical and religious philosophy which he acknowledges as his own, is complicated by his distinguishing, in these aesthetic works themselves, three *Stages on Life's Way.* For he draws a particularly sharp distinction between the first stage, which he identifies as itself "aesthetic," and the two succeeding stages, the "ethical" and the "religious." Thus in his first aesthetic work, *Either/Or,* the points of view of the aesthetic and ethical stages are distinguished in terms of the principle of contradiction which this title dramatizes. But the distinction is not evenly balanced. Although *Either/Or* solicits a choice between these two points of view, the defining trait of the aesthetic point of view is its hospitable reconciliation of all different points of view, and its evasion of this particular choice between the aesthetic and ethical points of view; while uncompromising choice is the defining trait of the ethical point of view, and the decisive ethical choice is the refusal to compromise with the aesthetic point of view. But despite the fact that the distinction between these points of view is thus itself an ethical and not an aesthetic distinction, it comes up for clarification in works which Kierkegaard characterizes as aesthetic.

Such paradoxes have encouraged the presumption that existentialism is too incoherent to be considered a philosophy. But for Kierkegaard the problem of existence itself is its fundamental incoherence—"the doubleness characteristic of existence." He explains, "Life must be understood backward, but . . . it must be lived forward." [7] This paradox has the additional interest for us of having been the first existentialist formula to catch the attention of an Anglo-Saxon philosopher. It is cited by William James, who found it in Höffding.[8] Needless to say, James's commitment to scientific prediction, as a way of understanding forward, enables him to dispose promptly of the paradox. But in Kierkegaard the formula implies that the reflective movement of self-scrutiny is inherently introspective and restrospective, in that it can be continued undisturbed only so long as one is abstracting from the actual "external conditions" of one's life, which are continually changing.[9]

What for Kierkegaard is distinctively *aesthetic* is this movement with which reflection "throws away" these actual "external conditions," in the sense that they dissolve into merely imaginary ideal possibilities as soon as they have been reflected upon.[10] What is distinctive of any individual who remains at the *aesthetic stage of existence* is the "illusion" that while he is reflecting he also actually "exists." So long as he is "dabbling" in imaginary possibilities, he is employing reflection as a means for "keeping existence away." [11] In contrast, the individual who makes a "choice" and acts upon it, is an "existing individual." He is "as bifrontal as existence itself," because he respects its "doubleness" by performing a double movement: the aesthetic movement of reflection and the "contradictory" ethical movement of choice and action, which is his "persistent striving" to "reduplicate" himself—to reach a "historical conclusion" that "reproduces" concretely, in the setting of the actual external conditions of the life he is living forward, an abstract imaginative possibility which his reflection has produced.[12]

Despite the fact that the individual's arrival at the ethical stage of existence thus presupposes his previous imaginative passage through the aesthetic stage, the *Either/Or* of ethical choice that demarcates these two stages is not itself blurred. On the one hand, the regressive movement of reflection is inherently inconclusive: a choice, when reflected upon instead of being acted upon, remains a possible choice, and undergoes, so long as reflection continues, imaginative dissolution into further possibilities. Meantime the forward movement of the individual's life also continues: "The ship is all the while making its usual headway." His life "drifts on" until the possibility of choosing itself finally eludes him, for the drift is his succumbing to social pressure: "If he forgets to take into account the headway, there comes at last a moment when there is no longer any question of an either/or . . . because others have chosen for him, because he has lost his self." [13] On the other hand, the movement of ethical action halts and reverses this regressive movement of reflection. To gain a self, the individual must "choose himself" by turning himself around and "pressing" himself "back" into "the most intimate connection and the most exact coherence" with the actual historical conditions of his life, from which he has been abstracting during the course of his reflection.[14] It is this pressure from within which is his "persistent striving" to reach a "historical conclusion" that will lend coherence to his life. He becomes a self—an "existing individual."

The distinction of these two movements acquires emphatic philosophical implications in Kierkegaard's major philosophical work *Concluding Unscientific Postscript to the Philosophical Fragments,* where he takes "A Glance at a Contemporary Effort in Danish Literature." The effort referred to by this chapter title is that represented by his own pseudonymous aesthetic works. In this chapter he glances at *Either/Or* in order to disparage Hegel's reflective philosophical system as merely "aesthetic." It leaves no place for the distinctively ethical movement of reaching a historical conclusion, since it is ostensibly a philosophy of *history*—the progressive realization by reflection of its ideal possibilities as historical conditions. The ethical principle of contradiction is superseded by the aesthetic principle of synthesis. Along with all other antitheses, the reflective movement of Hegel's philosophy melts the fundamental antithesis, "either" reflection "or" action, into a conciliatory "both" reflection "and" action. But because this reconciliation itself is merely reflective, the coherence of Hegel's philosophical system is merely abstract. In contrast Kierkegaard's philosophy is fragmentary, because the intrusion of the *Either/Or* shatters any reflective philosophical system and substitutes for its abstract coherence the concrete coherence of the life of an existing individual.

Hegel's reflective philosophy displays, from the point of view of Kierkegaard's philosophy of action, all the liabilities of reflection. From this point of view reflection is a regressive and inconclusive movement which cannot move forward with history; Hegel's reflective philosophy therefore "turns back upon itself" and again "turns back," so that when Hegel ostensibly reaches a historical conclusion, he is in fact being "wise only after the event." [15] Furthermore, in order to maintain this retrospective point of view undisturbed, Hegel must construct his reflective system by abstracting from the forward moving history of his own life. He is "like a man who constructs an enormous castle and lives in a shack close by." [16] His system "fails to express the situation of the knowing subject in existence," who must act in order to bring his reflection to some conclusion; it expresses instead the illusory aesthetic status of an "imaginary subject" who has withdrawn from existence "by way of recollection." [17]

The same aesthetic characteristics of reflection which attach to Hegel's philosophy, from Kierkegaard's ethical point of view, also attach to Kierkegaard's own aesthetic works. The characteristic form they assume is that of "recollections." This is the reason that Kierkegaard has to shoulder the existential problem of bringing his "esthetic production" to a conclusion by writing *The Concluding Unscientific Postscript,* not as still another aesthetic work, despite its backward "glance" at his aesthetic works, but as embodying an ethical choice which marks a "turning-point in his authorship." [18] Only a glance is permissible, since he is halting with this work the regressive movement of his reflection and hence his writing of aesthetic works. Moreover, he does not glance back at these aesthetic writings as his own works but as a "Contemporary Effort in Danish Literature," because he is "only imaginatively their author." [19] In writing these works he has abstracted from his own life and has, therefore, presented them pseudonymously, as if each were written by an "imaginary subject."

It is from *The Concluding Unscientific Postscript* that Lowrie cites in order that we may hear "in the very words of Kierkegaard what he understood by existence" and feel "bewildered by the claim that Sartre is his legitimate successor." When Lowrie examines Sartre's philosophy he finds that Kierkegaard's criticism of Hegel's philosophy as "aesthetic" equally applies to Sartre's systematic *L'Etre et le néant*. But unlike Hegel and like Kierkegaard, Sartre writes literary as well as philosophical works. Lowrie's extension to Sartre of Kierkegaard's ethical criticism of the aesthetic neglects the paradox that Kierkegaard initially undertakes this criticism in literary works which he himself characterizes as aesthetic. If Kierkegaard's own aesthetic works are to be shielded from a similar extension of his ethical criticism in these works of the aesthetic evasion of the problem of existence, a second problem must be distinguished—the problem of communication.

REFLECTION AND COMMUNICATION

Despite his criticism of the aesthetic from the ethical point of view of his philosophy, it is from this ethical point of view that Kierkegaard adopts aesthetic works as a means of communicating this philosophy. The situation which poses the problem of communication is more complicated than the contradictory relationship, between reflection moving backward and life moving forward, which poses the problem of existence. Two individuals are now on the move:

> To stop a man on the street and stand still while talking to him is not so difficult as to say something to a passer-by in passing, without *standing still* and without *delaying* the other, without attempting to persuade him *to go the same way*, but giving him instead an *impulse to go his own way*.[20]

The first individual's existential situation has already been delineated. His "standing still" is existentially impossible, for if he respects the forward movement of his life, he is persistently striving toward a conclusion that coheres with its particular limiting conditions. Since this ethical action of persistent striving is self-differentiating, the "existential reality" he acquires by it is "subjective" and "incommunicable." [21] A second individual now enters the range of Kierkegaard's concern. Kierkegaard's not "delaying the other" is the existential tact he must display in communicating his subjective ethical philosophy to another individual whose life is also moving forward. To attempt to communicate "directly" his own "existential reality" would be to attempt to persuade the other individual "to go the same way." For instance, in an ordinary novel, one of the characters may be presented as exemplifying the writer's own particular ethical choice and as "having already realized the possibility" the writer himself is striving toward in his own life. But if the writer attempts to supply social pressure in this way, the reader is relieved of the performance of his own subjective act of self-differentiating choice. Someone else has chosen for him, and he has lost his individuality—the prospect of ethical coherence. In order to give the reader instead "an impulse to go his own way," Kierkegaard in his aesthetic works "places the possibility between the example [the particular character in the novel that exemplifies this possibility] and the observer as something they both [the writer and the observing reader] have in common." This mode of communication is "indirect," inasmuch as it "operates in terms of the ideal, not the differentiated ideal, but the universal ideal." [22] The writer and reader can therefore reflect together upon this ideal possibility, even though they must act separately, each differentiating the ideal possibility by his own subjective choice. An ideal possibility that is merely universal floats in the pressureless vacuum of the imagination. Its "aloofness" from the particular conditions of both their lives leaves it up to the reader to "choose himself" by supplying the pressure of realizing the ideal possibility under the limiting conditions of his own life.

Kierkegaard's literary works are aesthetic in that his characters do in fact exemplify abstractly possible ideal points of view. He has abstracted imaginatively from the particular conclusions which they might reach, in relation to each other, in the course of their lives. No concrete historical limitations restrict the imaginary scope of their possibilities. He explicitly contrasts this procedure in *Either/Or* with the techniques of the ordinary novel:

One sometimes chances upon novels in which certain characters exemplify opposing views of life. Such novels usually end by one of them persuading the other. Instead of allowing these views to speak for themselves, the reader is enriched by being told the historical conclusion. I regard it as fortunate that these papers contain no such information. . . . When the book is read then A and B are forgotten. Only their views confront one another.[23]

Their views confront each other as an "either/or" which awaits the reader's own act of self-differentiating choice of the particular limiting conditions of his own life, instead of theirs.

In adopting an aesthetic means of communication, Kierkegaard is not disavowing his ethical criticism of Hegel's philosophy as aesthetic. Rather he is, in effect, criticizing Hegel for writing a philosophy of history instead of literary works. Like Kierkegaard's literary works, Hegel's *philosophy* is aesthetic in that it is an abstract process of reflection from which universal ideals emerge. But as a philosophy *of history* it leaves no place for an ethics, since it presents this abstract process of reflection as at the same time the concrete historical realization of these universal ideals under particular conditions. Since Hegel is failing to distinguish, in the first place, between the abstract aesthetic movement of reflection and the concrete ethical movement of action, he also is failing to distinguish, in the second place, the abstract aesthetic process of reflective communication from the concrete ethical process of self-differentiation, by which the individual acquires "subjective reality." Hegel thereby is failing to distinguish, in the third place, between the different individuals who are involved in the process of communication. Thus he not only abstracts in his philosophy (as Kierkegaard abstracts in his literary works) from the differentiating conditions of his own life as an individual, but he also "confuses himself with humanity as a whole," [24] including his readers, for he assumes the "objective reality" of the social community as the agent at once of reflection and of historical action. In his literary works Kierkegaard remains a pseudonymous "imaginary subject." Just as his philosophy respects the "doubleness," the incoherence, of existence by distinguishing the movement of reflection from the movement of action, so his merely reflective means of communicating this philosophy respects the distinction of the two different individuals who are on the move by "holding" the writer and the reader "devoutly apart from each other." They are not "permitted to fuse or cohere into objectivity," [25] since they are merely reflecting together. In order to acquire "subjective reality" and achieve the coherence of "an existing individual," each must still act independently of the other and "realize" concretely the imaginative possibility they have reflected upon in common.

LITERATURE AND LIFE

Sartre, like Kierkegaard, faces problems which he is not satisfied to treat either philosophically or by employing ordinary literary techniques:

> The problems which the present age poses . . . can be treated *abstractly by philosophical reflection*, but we whose purpose it is to *live* these problems—i.e., sustain our thinking by those *imaginative* and *concrete* experiences which are novels—have available at the outset only techniques . . . which are radically opposed to our purpose.[26]

Sartre's conception of philosophy as abstract reflection derives from Husserl's procedure of "bracketing" the actual conditions of existence in order to carry out an analysis of the structure of consciousness. But Sartre rejects the "transcendental ego," to which the structure of consciousness is firmly anchored in Husserl's phenomenology, so that the procedure of bracketing becomes in Sartre the dialectical movement of consciousness itself, as analyzed in Hegel's phenomenology.[27] Although Sartre accordingly admits that "the reflective consciousness is Hegelian," he also insists that "this is its greatest illusion."[28] For the prerogatives of the actual conditions of existence, as over against the pretensions of philosophical reflection, are reinforced by Sartre's deriving, from Heidegger's reaction against Husserl, a conception of the historical structure of human existence, and from Marx's reaction against Hegel, a sociological conception of the actual movement of history. As a result of this mixed inheritance, rather than of any noteworthy familiarity with Kierkegaard, Sartre's philosophy betrays the inadequacy of its reflective procedure of bracketing the actual conditions of existence, in much the same way as Kierkegaard's literary works, where reflection "throws away" its "external conditions."

The existential requirement remains to be met of "living the problems" which philosophy merely reflects upon abstractly. This requirement is met in Sartre by the novel, insofar as it is not merely an "imaginative" but a "concrete" experience of "a progressive action." (We shall discover later who it is that is acting and having this experience.) It was Kierkegaard's philosophy, not his literary works, that embodied the experience of an "existing individual" who has not merely reflected but who also acts, as his life moves forward, to bring his reflection to some conclusion. These traits of an existing individual's experience in Kierkegaard's philosophy are, in effect, transferred by Sartre to characterize the experience of the novel. What this curious transference of opposed traits suggests is that while Kierkegaard's philosophy of action is distinctively existential, in contrast with his merely reflective literary works, Sartre's novels of action are distinctively existential, in contrast with his merely reflective philosophy. Kierkegaard's "either/or" opposed to the abstract movement of reflection the movement of action, which reproduces concretely the imaginative product of reflection. When he carried this contradiction over into his criticism of the reflective coherence of Hegel's philosophy, he was criticizing Hegel for failing to acknowledge "the doubleness characteristic of existence." Unlike Hegel, both Kierkegaard and Sartre respect this incoherence of existence by reserving for a different genre their abstract reflective analysis, so that it does not intrude upon their treatment, in the other genre, of the distinctively existential problem of securing by action the coherence reflection cannot lend our lives.

When Lowrie sought to interpret their existentialisms, he found "between these two men hardly enough likeness to make it easy to define the difference," even though he admitted that they alike wrote literary as well as philosophical works. So far I have been making a somewhat schematic attempt to prepare the comparison that he denies is feasible. If my resorting to similarities between Sartre's philosophical works and Kierkegaard's literary works, on the one hand, and between Sartre's literary works and Kierkegaard's philosophical works, on the other hand, seems perverse legerdemain, this may be partly due to our traditional preconceptions as to what philosophy is, what literature is, and what can plausibly happen when the two genres are linked by a writer. Thus we are ready to recognize literary philosophy or philosophical novel. But these genres are merely blends, which can be interpreted on the assumption that reflection and life are perhaps not so very far apart after all. Such interpretations of existentialist writings have flooded the market and encouraged the facile presumption that an existentialism is a philosophy of life, albeit a disturbing philosophy of a distraught life. But one of the more significant influences of existentialism should be its disturbance of our traditional preconceptions of the possible relations between philosophy and literature. Although we are ready to recognize blends, we are not so ready to recognize the maneuver which I am suggesting has taken place during the development of existentialism: philosophy and literature have retained distinct intellectual functions and yet exchanged places, so that the one genre performs within Sartre's intellectual scheme what in significant respects resembles the other's function for Kierkegaard. If my suggestion seems perverse, it is no more perverse than Kierkegaard's and Sartre's own use of literary works to criticize Hegel's philosophy, and I am making this suggestion in the hope of eventually explaining their perversity.

EXTREME SITUATIONS

If my suggestion is correct, we can expect that Sartre's treatment of the problem of existence will be illustrated by the literary techniques he employs in handling the characters in his novels, rather than by his philosophical procedure of abstract reflection. And we can further expect that similarities to Kierkegaard's treatment of this problem can be found by comparing Sartre's characters with the "existing individual" of Kierkegaard's philosophy, rather than with the characters in Kierkegaard's literary works. Let us, however, first give way to common sense, accept for the moment the traditional distinction of genre, and attempt a comparison of their literary techniques.

The traditional literary techniques which Sartre disdains as "radically opposed" to the existential requirement of "living . . . the problems which the present age poses," he attributes to what he calls the "retrospective novel," where the events usually take place in the past, as if they had already happened and were only being recollected by the writer.[29] Sartre concedes that the retrospective novel is able to encompass "average situations," but the more strenuous techniques which he himself employs he justifies as an effort to "create a literature of extreme situations." [30] He finds the appropriateness of this effort in the fact that the present age "has forced us to reach, like itself, the limits." [31] Now it is true that Kierkegaard also draws a contrast between the traditional novelist's handling of his characters and the extreme treatment accorded in his own literary works:

> A little psychology, a little observation of so-called real men, they [the readers of psychological novels] still want to have, but when this science or art follows its own devices, when it looks away from the various expressions of psychological states which reality offers . . . then many people grow weary. As a matter of fact in real life emotions, psychological states, are only carried to a certain point. This too delights the psychologist, but he has a different sort of delight in seeing emotion carried to its abstract limits.[32]

The emotions of Kierkegaard's characters, however, reach different limits than Sartre's, and by a different movement. The "abstract limits," to which Kierkegaard here refers, are not the historical limits which in Sartre's view the present age has forced us to reach. The extreme situation in Kierkegaard can in fact only be reached when the writer has abstracted from what might have been the concrete historical conclusions of his characters' lives, had they really existed. Kierkegaard's crucial example of the movement by which the abstract limits of an extreme situation are reached is "The Psychological Experiment" performed by the "self-torturer," whose unremitting imagining himself *Guilty/Not-Guilty* pushes him along an infinite regress of reflection without his ever confronting this "either/or" in the fashion required for action. He never actually arrives at a verdict that would bring his imagined trial to some conclusion. Such a psychological experiment, inasmuch as it "leaves the reader in a lurch by not allowing him any conclusion," satisfies Kierkegaard's requirement for reflective communication by making the reader "still more completely contemporary [i.e., in the psychological sense of participating in the reflections of the self-torturer] than he would be with a real contemporary event." [33] But we shall find that in Sartre real contemporary events dominate the relations of his readers to his characters. In fact, they will be contemporaneous with each other, as a consequence of the common orientation of their lives by the same events.

For the present we need only notice that while Kierkegaard is always prompt with the mock apology that "nothing ever happens" to his characters themselves in his literary works, Sartre defines his "literature of extreme situations" as a "literature of great events." [34] Instead of abstracting from the historical conclusions of his characters' lives, so that their reflections remain an inconclusive movement toward abstract possibilities, Sartre allows this movement to be brought to a halt within the concrete limits imposed by historical situations. As we noted at the beginning of this essay, the crucial examples of these situations in Sartre are not the imaginary self-imposed trials and tortures of introspection, but the trials and tortures actually instituted by the Gestapo in occupied France. Sartre's claim that a novel is not merely an "imaginative" experience but a "concrete" experience as well thus receives some of its meaning from the experience of his characters themselves. Because his novels "evolve on the eve of great events which transcend predictions, frustrate expectations, upset plans," [35] his characters are eventually viewed, not merely in terms of the imaginative evolution of the possibilities they predict, expect, and plan for, but also (in Kierkegaard's phrase) as "living forward" toward these events. The approach of these events forces them to act and dominates their action. Their reflections interpreting the course of their action in the novel are therefore "in movement—*dragged* along by the action itself that is interpreted." [36] To find an existential situation that is similar in Kierkegaard, we cannot avoid turning from his merely reflective literary works, which evolve as the unimpeded exercise of his characters' imaginations, to the "existing individual" of his philosophical works, who respects the actual forward movement of his life by his action, which halts the abstract and inconclusive movement of his reflection.

Nonetheless there still remains a difference between Kierkegaard and Sartre which cannot be probed while assuming, without qualification, that the term "existential" retains identical implications if applied, in Sartre's case, to the experience of the individual characters in his novels, and reserved, in Kierkegaard's case, for the experience of the "existing individual" of his philosophy. Although the term in both cases serves to distinguish the double movement of imaginative reflection and concrete action from the single abstract movement of imaginative reflection, the two movements are not identically related for the two writers. Kierkegaard's individual halts the regressive movement of his reflection when he no longer lives "drifting" forward until he has succumbed to social pressure but, instead, persistently "strives" forward toward a "historical conclusion." But we have just noted that the reflections of Sartre's characters are "dragged" forward by the action of the novel, since it takes place on the eve of some overwhelming event. In Kierkegaard the movements of reflection and action are both initiated by the individual himself, are simply his movements in opposite directions. The movement of his reflection starts from, but "throws away," the external historical conditions of his life, in the sense that these conditions become merely imaginary in retrospect as soon as reflected upon. This introspective movement is not only halted but also reversed by the movement of his action, which starts from his choice of an imagined self, which has been produced as a possibility by his reflection, and "presses" this self "back" into "the most exact coherence" with the actual conditions of his life. The pressure of the action thus comes from within the individual, is his "persistent striving" toward a historical conclusion. Although the action could also be said to press Sartre's characters back into the most exact coherence with actual historical conditions, its pressure comes no less persistently from the relentless approach of the external event. The two movements are not simply opposed as the contradictory movements of an individual pivoting himself first in one direction and then in the opposite direction. The movement of action is eventually oriented by the approaching external event, independently of the inwardly and regressively oriented movement of the individual's own reflection, and therefore does not simply halt and reverse this reflective movement but overlaps and drags it forward. Because of this overlap and drag on his reflection, each of Sartre's characters is incapable of the choice of an imagined self that is the prerogative of Kierkegaard's individual. Sartre's characters are, in fact, "unable to decide within themselves if the changes in their destiny come from their own strivings, from their own failings, or from the course of external events." [37]

Furthermore, it is "their destiny" and not, as in Kirkegaard, the historical destination of a single individual that is at stake. The reflections of all Sartre's characters are overlapped and dragged forward by the action, for the different relation between reflection and action in Sartre involves a different relation between individuals who are reflecting and acting. Although the individual "exists" for both Kierkegaard and Sartre only insofar as he acts as well as reflects, *action* is for Kierkegaard a means of self-differentiation, but becomes ultimately for Sartre a common action. Kierkegaard's individual, when he acts, escapes from social pressure and differentiates himself from others, so that the "reality" which he acquires by his action is "subjective" and "incommunicable." When each of Sartre's characters acts, he is not acting merely under the pressure of his own choice and striving forward toward a different historical destination from that of the other characters, in the fashion in which Kierkegaard's individual "chooses himself" and destines himself for his own particular historical conclusion. "The pressure of a gas on the walls of the container," Sartre reminds us, "does not depend on the individual history of the molecules which compose the gas." [38] Since the different actions of Sartre's individual characters are all oriented by the same impending historical event, they eventually compose a common destiny.

At the same time, *reflection* ultimately becomes for Kierkegaard a means of communication, but is for Sartre an effort at self-differentiation. Each of Sartre's characters, when he reflects upon himself, is attempting to abstract from the course of external events, which he shares in common with the other characters, in order to differentiate his own point of view from theirs. Nevertheless he then finds himself in the same existential predicament, in relation to them, that he finds himself in when he reflects upon and interprets the action and attempts to maintain the point of view of his interpretation against its forward drag. He cannot disentangle his point of view on himself from theirs any more successfully than he can disentangle his point of view on the common action from its movement, which drags all their points of view forward together toward the impending event. The "reality" of each of Sartre's characters is thus not the merely "subjective reality" which Kierkegaard's individual acquires by his self-differentiating action.

Sartre does not become, however, the Hegelian Lowrie suspects him of being. He remains an existentialist, insofar as each of his characters remains an individual. Even though the impending event is itself objective, the "reality" of his characters does not therefore also become objective in the sense this term had in Kierkegaard's criticism of the "objective reality" of the community which Hegel assumed as the historical agent of his philosophical reflection. If their "reality" were "objective" in this sense, the distinction between the process of reflection and the process of historical action would have been removed, and Sartre would be writing a philosophy of history, like Hegel, instead of historical novels. The "reality" of Sartre's characters, he himself explains, "is the *snarled* and *contradictory* fabric of the interpretations each of them passes on all the others, including himself, and that all pass on each." [39] Although the actions of Sartre's characters receive a common orientation from the objective historical event, their reflective points of view on their actions do not thereby receive a collective reconciliation, do not (in Kierkegaard's phrase criticizing Hegel) "fuse or cohere into objectivity," but remain "contradictory" and only become "snarled together," as a consequence of the dialectical fashion in which the common course of the action in the novel supervenes and drags his own reflections along with theirs towards the same historical event.[40]

ACTION AND COMMUNICATION

Since both Kierkegaard and Sartre employ their literary works as a means of communication, the differences between their handling of the relations of their characters to each other turn out to be more fundamentally differences between their handling of their own relations as writers to their readers. When Kierkegaard writes his aesthetic literary works, he views himself as reflecting. Because the movement of reflection is introspective, he becomes, as he writes, increasingly self-enclosed and remote from the presence of other individuals, whose actual selves his reflection "throws away" along with the rest of the "external conditions" of his own actual self. They therefore become, when they enter his literary works as characters, merely imaginary possibilities of himself as a writer; and their relations to each other become the correspondingly imaginary relations between the successive phases of his own introspective process of self-enclosure. Thus the major characters in *Either/Or* are imaginatively related to each other as one possibility enclosed within the other, until the writer himself is reached regressively as enclosing within himself each of these possibilities, "like the boxes," Kierkegaard points out, "in a Chinese puzzle box." [41] Although when the existential problem of action is posed, B's aesthetic papers in *Either/Or* exemplify a possibility which is opposed as its contradiction to the possibility exemplified by A's ethical papers and must, therefore, have been written by a different individual, both sets of papers can also be "looked at from a new point of view, by considering all of them as the work of one individual . . . who had reflected upon" both possibilities.[42]

This one individual, the writer, not only encloses within himself all the possibilities which his characters exemplify, but in order to do so, he must also have become himself an imaginary possibility—a mere pseudonym who is even more abstractly imaginary, because more inclusive and more remote from the actual conditions of anyone's life, than all these other possibilities.

Sartre, however, challenges the writer who pretends to enjoy an aloof imaginary status. "Where is he himself then—in mid-air?" Sartre asks of the retrospective novelist, who is abstracting from the existential problem of action when he writes a novel where the events take place in the past as if they were his recollections. Such a novel's resulting inconclusiveness for the reader, who in turn must face the problem of action as his life moves forward, is evidence for Sartre that the writer is also failing to face the problem of communication: his novel is "only a hesitant guide who stops halfway and allows the reader to continue his own way alone." [43] But although Sartre's criticisms of the retrospective novel resemble Kierkegaard's criticisms, from the point of view of his existential philosophy of action, of the aesthetic individual's merely imaginary status, Kierkegaard's criticisms did not apply to his own aesthetic literary works as a means of facing the problem of communication. Kierkegaard adopted the retrospective point of view of reflection in these works precisely in order to abstract from the problem of action. By merely reflecting as a writer, Kierkegaard stopped halfway in his own life—i.e., stopped short of the existential problem of action. If this left him in mid-air with the merely imaginary status of a pseudonymous writer, his aloofness allowed the reader to go forward his own way alone and to reach his own conclusion independently. For since the reader exists in movement, he must not be "delayed," in his performance of the concrete action which the particular conditions of his own life require, by having his attention diverted to the "historical conclusion" which some one else is striving to reach under different conditions. What the communication furnishes the writer and the reader in common is merely the abstract possibility they both reflect upon. They do not act in common. "Existential reality is incommunicable"; the community of reflection, established by the communication, is merely transitional and breaks down as soon as the existential problem of action is faced and reflection itself is halted. Therefore when Kierkegaard views himself as an "existing individual," he not only denies that he is the writer of his literary works by substituting their pseudonymous authors, he even insists on the paradox that he is only "a reader" of these works.[44] As the writer he becomes, during the process of communication, the series of imaginary possibilities exemplified by his characters. To become an "existing individual" he must retain, over against the reflective process of communication, what this process has been designed to enable a reader to retain—his existential initiative in action.

I have also already noted that Sartre regards the novel as "progressive action" instead of as abstract reflection, just as he treats its characters as acting instead of merely reflecting. Like Kierkegaard, Sartre models his treatment of his readers on his treatment of the problem of existence and distinguishes in terms of this model his own status as the writer from that of his readers. But since Sartre's problem of existence is woven out of a different relation between reflection and action, a different relationship is also involved between the writer and his reader as well as between his characters. Sartre therefore copes with a different paradox—that "the writer cannot read what he writes," for "he knows the words he is writing before writing them." [45] In this sense, Sartre's writer, like Kierkegaard's writer, merely recollects. Like Kierkegaard's reader, Sartre's readers exist in movement. But they do so, not only in the course of their lives, but also in the course of reading a novel in which they "live" its problems. For they do not know the words they are reading before reading them. They are in suspense—"always ahead of the sentence they are reading." For their reflections, like those of the characters, "can always be frustrated instead of confirmed" by the impending events of the novel.[46] So long as the literary work is merely what it is for Kierkegaard, an imaginary product of the writer's reflection, it is not for Sartre actually a literary work, even though it may have been transferred to paper. The writer's reflection by itself is "only an inconclusive and abstract moment of the production of a literary work; if the writer existed alone, he could write as much as he pleased, the novel would never emerge.... The literary work is a curious kind of top which only exists in movement; for it to emerge a concrete action known as reading is necessary." [47] This action of Sartre's readers, like the action of Kierkegaard's reader independently of his reading, is the concrete realization of a possibility previously imagined by the writer. But for Sartre the possibility realized is the novel itself. Their reading is not merely imaginative reflection but "a concrete action" which carries over into overt political acts, performed by his readers, who come together as members of the community established by the novel as a communication.[48] Thus the abstract movement of Sartre's reflection as a writer does not remain an abstract movement but is overlapped by the reflections of his readers and dragged forward by their common action, in the same way that the reflection of each of his characters does not remain an abstract movement (like that of each of Kierkegaard's aesthetic characters) but is overlapped by the reflections of the other characters and "dragged" forward by the action they share in common.

In other words, the problems of existence and communication, which I have argued must be distinguished in interpreting Kierkegaard, cannot ultimately be distinguished in interpreting Sartre. His existence, as the writer of his novels, is in this way as dependent on the action of his readers, as Kierkegaard's existence, as a reader of his literary works, is independent of their reflective pseudonymous writers. Because they both model the relation between the writer and the reader on the existential relationship between reflection and action, the difference between Kierkegaard, who is only "a reader" of his literary works, and Sartre, who "cannot read what he writes," is the difference between Kierkegaard's "existing individual," who can acquire "subjective reality" only by his own action independently of other individuals, and Sartre's individual character, who cannot acquire "reality" by reflecting on himself independently of the other characters. The difference is no arbitrary literary convention. It is implicit in the different term each uses for the individual. Kierkegaard's characteristic description of the "existing individual" as an "exception" implies the individual's acquisition of "subjective reality" by a self-differentiating action, which slips him outside of the scope of any abstractly universal possibility that he could reflect upon in common with others. Sartre's individual characteristically reflects that he has become "superfluous" (*de trop*). For his sense of his own individual existence is his reflection upon his loss of initiative, which has passed into the hands of others.

ANXIETY AND DESPAIR

The different relationship between reflection and action in Kierkegaard and Sartre is illustrated not only by the different relationship between the individual and others but also by the different way in which the individual's anxiety evolves dialectically into despair. For such existentialist moods are not the miscellaneous assortment we suspected they might be at the beginning of this essay. In Kierkegaard anxiety is merely the self-consciousness that accompanies all reflection. To reflect is not to become conscious of one's actual self, which is limited by "external conditions"; reflection instead produces a possible self, by "throwing away" these "external conditions," in the sense that they become imaginary as soon as they have been reflected upon. Anxiety in Kierkegaard is the recognition that the self has thereby lost its footing in the external world. This feeling of precariousness Kierkegaard compares to the giddiness felt on the edge of an abyss.[49] In Sartre too self-consciousness is the anxious recognition of the precariousness of the self one is conscious of. But the reflection involved in this recognition is reflection upon one's possible performance of an action, to which the actual limitations imposed by external conditions remain relevant. The giddiness felt on the edge of an abyss in Sartre is itself anxiety over the possibility of throwing oneself into the abyss, and the actual presence of a physical abyss and the law of gravity in accordance with which all bodies fall, are indispensable external conditions.[50] But the abyss in Kierkegaard's use of this example of an extreme situation is merely a metaphor for the imagined depths of the reflective self-consciousness—its infinite inwardness. The individual's metaphorical throwing away the external conditions of his actual self, and his metaphorical falling into the abyss between his actual self and a possible self, are one and the same movement of reflection.

In Kierkegaard anxiety ripens into melancholy when this self-enclosing movement of reflection also becomes an effort to imagine some external condition, which—if it could be retrieved—would provide an exit from the process of reflection and a mode of self-disclosure. In Sartre the movement of reflection is instead an effort to withdraw inwardly from the presence and pressure of an external condition which cannot be thrown away. The forms of psychological sickness which correspond in Sartre to Kierkegaard's "melancholy of morbid introversion," are nausea and shame. Something external has invaded the field of consciousness and remains present to self-consciousness—something faintly disgusting which consciousness cannot stomach but can neither digest nor disgorge.[51] If unassimilable by one's own consciousness, it is at the same time one's intimate exposure to the consciousness of others. To become self-conscious for Sartre is to become ashamed of the self that others are conscious of from observing one's physical actions.[52]

We have reached a juncture in the evolution of anxiety where we again realize that the differences between Kierkegaard's and Sartre's analyses of consciousness illustrate not only their different rendering of the relationship between reflection and action but also the implications of this relationship for the individual's relationship to others. Kierkegaard's account of the way the reflecting individual falls into the imaginary abyss between his actual self and some possible self, enables him to explain that the Fall of Man was Adam's dawning self-consciousness and cannot be imputed to the intervention of anyone else—God, Satan, or Eve—stacking the external conditions against Adam.[53] But the revealing moment in Genesis for Sartre is the moment when Adam and Eve "knew that they were naked." [54] Burning shame indicates that "Hell is other people." There are no private hells; the Fall of Man takes place in the presence of his fellow man.

In Kierkegaard melancholy at not finding an exit from reflection and some mode of self-disclosure, finally evolves into despair over the impossibility of finding an exit. This is the predicament of the seducer—not the physical seducer who merely leads others astray—but a "reflective seducer" who has led himself away from himself:

> The lost traveler always has the consolation that the scene is constantly changing before him, and with every change there is born the hope of finding a way out. He who goes astray inwardly has not so great a range. . . . It is in vain that he has many exits from his hole, i.e., imaginary possibilities of exits; at the moment his anxious soul believes that it already sees daylight breaking through it turns out to be a new entrance . . . and he constantly seeks a way out and finds only a way in, through which he goes back to himself.[55]

Such despair, since it is a product of reflection, is not despair over any event external to the self, but is "a sickness in the self."[56] The despairing individual eventually reaches that terminal phase of his inability to find an exit and disclose himself which Kierkegaard describes as "inwardness with a jammed lock."[57] Just as "the troll disappears through a crack which no one can observe," so the despairer "dwells behind an external appearance where it ordinarily would never occur to anyone to look for him." He has "behind reality an enclosure, a world for himself locking all else out."[58]

Kierkegaard's *Sickness Unto Death* identifies this sickness with despair; "the torture of despair is precisely this, not to be able to die."[59] Despair is a "self-consuming gnawing canker; but it is impotent self-consumption."[60] The despairing individual cannot "get rid of himself," because the effort of his reflection to do so is itself the production of still another imaginary self, who has only gotten rid of the previous self. In this ultimate impossibility of psychological suicide, Kierkegaard finds proof of the "indestructibility" of the self, of its immortality.

If the melancholy of Kierkegaard's anxious individual thus evolves into the despairing recognition of the self's psychological indestructibility, the nausea of Sartre's anxious individual evolves into despairing recognition of the physical "fragility" of his exposed self, of its physical "vulnerability," its physical mortality. The affliction of the despairing consciousness in Kierkegaard is a canker gnawing within; in Sartre it is a "hemorrhage." For instead of disappearing through a crack which no one else can observe, Sartre's individual is "pierced by a crack in the middle of his being, through which he is constantly draining out." [61] Instead of having behind reality a private enclosure where no one can look for him—a world for himself locking all else out—Sartre's individual is exiled; his "world flows forth towards the other," as soon as he is "looked at" by another individual, who organizes an alien and antagonistic world out of his own perceptions, oriented by his own body. Instead of being "self-consumed by his own suicidal consciousness of himself," Sartre's individual has his sense of vitality drained off by others' homicidal consciousness of him. The soul's sickness unto death in Sartre is not merely Kierkegaard's sickness inside the self but the exposed self's inability to escape menacing external events. This is the theme of Sartre's *La Mort dans l'âme*. The protagonist reads FRAGILE, stamped on a discarded packing case, into his reflections upon his own superfluousness, which are dominated by his despair over the Fall of France. In Kierkegaard the ostensibly historical details of the account in Genesis of the Fall of Man, merely "represent externally what occurred inwardly," and are therefore to be taken as metaphorical descriptions of what happens when Adam, or any individual, reflects upon himself. But for Sartre the Fall of Man is instanced by the Fall of France, as a historical and public event which Frenchmen reflected upon in the presence of others—the German invaders. "Death" in Sartre's title has the metaphorical psychological significance of Kierkegaard's title. But it also acquires a literal reference. *La Mort dans l'âme* ends with the action of the Germans shooting a French prisoner attempting to escape, and with "the French and the Germans looking at each other across the body." If the end of the phoney war can then be signalized by the concluding realization, *"Enfin, c'était la guerre,"* it is because their struggle has at this moment finally reached the psychological level of their consciousness of each other.

In analyzing the evolution of anxiety, Kierkegaard drew a contrast between the physical changes in the external scene, which give the lost traveler some hope of recovering his sense of direction, and the psychological changes in the "reflective seducer" himself, who has gone astray inwardly and must despair of recovering his sense of direction, because he can no longer refer to the external conditions that his reflection has "thrown away." This metaphorical description itself embodies the reflective procedure of "throwing away" the external conditions. Indeed all of Kierkegaard's descriptions of episodes in the process of reflection—seduction, the abyss, the Fall, torture, trials, death—are metaphors which reflection itself has produced by discarding their literal external reference. Just as Kierkegaard offers mock apologies for the absence of external events in his reflective literary works, so he also offers mock apologies for the lack of scenery: "It is scenery which gives variety, and . . . a reading public needs events, landscapes, and many people." [62] Sartre, however, not only writes novels which are eventful, populous, and dependent for their existence as novels on a reading public, but he also argues that the scenery in a novel should be designed "to plunge things into the action," for "the density of the reality of things is measured by the multiplicity of practical relations they sustain with the characters." [63]

Sartre's use of language to overwhelm us with the consciousness of reality of things provides us with a further illustration of the way the movement of reflection, which in Kierkegaard is a separate movement from that of action, is overlapped in Sartre by the movement of action. According to Kierkegaard, a word can only be understood when its meaning is detached by the individual's reflection, which "throws away," as its external condition, the physical sensation of what is heard or read. But Sartre assumes that language is "a prolongation of our physical senses," that our use of language is a development of our use of our bodies as instruments of action, and that a word, as "a particular moment in the course of action . . . cannot be understood apart from the action." [64] This difference in their conception of language is apparent from the different metaphors each prefers. In Kierkegaard there is no scenery in that reflection substitutes an imaginary scene; visual imagery predominates in his metaphorical descriptions of the reflective consciousness. But Sartre's use of language prolongs other senses besides sight, for in the case of visual perception, reflection has played a preponderant part in abstracting from and interpreting physical sensations. In order to emphasize the way in which the body, as the instrument of human action, grips or even clogs the process of reflection, Sartre disdains visual imagery, which has been the stock in trade of the traditional philosophical analysis of intellectual perception, and employs instead clumsier and murkier metaphors that incorporate those sensations of touch or taste or even visceral sensations—the "nonaesthetic senses," which the philosophical tradition has discounted in epistemology as well as in aesthetics.

This emphasis of Sartre's metaphors, along with the other implications of his treatment of the relation between reflection and action, carries over into his analysis of the way the individual reflects upon his relation to others, where the metaphors still derive from processes of manipulation, seduction, and digestion. Even the seducer's raptures in Kierkegaard are entirely visual as well as entirely metaphorical; even in describing intellectual vision, Sartre resorts to the metaphor of rape.[65] Man in Sartre is no longer the rational animal of the philosophical tradition, but "the only being who can touch other beings." [66] I suspect that the feeling of the body's intrusion within the field of consciousness and the feeling of the resistance of things became for Sartre clues to social relationships, even before the German invasion and the French resistance gave the social historian the opportunity to interpret Sartre's existentialism as a product of World War II. His obscenities are not, as Lowrie assumes, extraneous to his philosophy. The sensory for Sartre is sensual. Sartre's analysis of the way we look at each other, in effect, translates into the indicative mood Valéry's exclamations: *"Que d'enfants si le regard pouvait féconder, que de morts s'il pouvait tuer: Les rues seraient pleines de cadavres et de femmes grosses."* [67]

The considerations now raised by Sartre's use of language were previously raised by his use of literary works, when we found that Sartre's reflective philosophical analysis of the relation between reflection and action was a merely abstract rendering of this relationship, and had to be completed by the concrete rendering provided by his literary works. Now that we have recognized that the use of language itself is for Sartre a development of our use of our bodies as instruments of action, we also recognize that the metaphors of his reflective philosophical analysis undergo a brutal inversion in his realistic novels of action, where they become concrete by acquiring literal physiological implications.[68] Although Sartre extends metaphorically the meaning of nausea, he still insists that his reference to this feeling of something lying heavily on the stomach is "not merely metaphorical." And this theme of the individual's consciousness of his relation to his body is worked out with literal detail in *Nausea*. The metaphor of "hemorrhage" suggests in *L'Etre et le néant* the individual's consciousness that his relationship with others is abortive, and this suggestion is literally carried out by the theme of abortion in *L'Age de raison*.

PHILOSOPHICAL COMMUNICATION

Kierkegaard's and Sartre's different rendering of the relation between reflection and action receives still a further illustration as the difference between the way in which Kierkegaard's philosophy of action is related to his reflective literary works and the way in which Sartre's reflective philosophy is related to his novels of action. In order to render what is for him the blunt opposition of the movement of historical action to the movement of reflection, Kierkegaard adopted the procedure of publishing in his own name a work embodying his concrete ethical and religious philosophy at the same time as he published pseudonymously each of his abstract aesthetic works. Sartre is faithful to his edict that though "the problems which the present age poses can be treated abstractly by philosophical reflection . . . we whose purpose it is to live those problems" must "sustain our thinking by those imaginative and concrete experiences which are novels." Hence his usual procedure is to publish alternatively philosophical and literary works. The abstract movement of his philosophical reflections upon a problem is sustained and indeed dragged forward, when it is followed up in a novel as a literary version of the same problem. Sartre's philosophical reflections thus become concrete when they become the reflections of the readers of his literary works, who then "live" the problems of action which the extreme situations of the present age pose.

We have already recognized that Kierkegaard's and Sartre's resort to philosophy and literature as two distinct genres is a criticism of Hegel for his failure to confront the problem of *existence* which emerges when they distinguish the abstract movement of reflection from the concrete movement of historical action. Their mutual employment of the literary genre, as a means of communicating this criticism of Hegel, is itself a further criticism of Hegel for assuming that a historical community is the agent at once of the movement of reflection and of the movement of action, and of his resulting failure to confront the problem of *communication*. Nonetheless their criticisms differ, because each envisages a different community. Although both their philosophies pose a problem of communication, in Kierkegaard's case this problem is posed by the concrete character of his philosophy, while in Sartre's case, it is posed by the abstract character of his philosophy. In his literary works, Kierkegaard enters with his readers into a community of reflection by abstracting from the historical conditions of their separate lives. But it is because Sartre and his readers are ultimately unable to abstract by reflection from the historical conditions of their lives together that they enter in his novels into a community of action. Since the communities established by the process of communication are different, the publication of each of their literary works, in the sense that it marks the point of entry into these communities, takes on different implications itself, as well as in relation to the timing of the publication of their philosophical works. In Kierkegaard the individual enters the aesthetic stage of existence by initiating a reflective process of self-enclosure. He "throws away" the "external conditions" of his life, which include his actual relations to others. Kierkegaard therefore is not just being tiresomely whimsical when he respects the introspective orientation of his aesthetic works by assigning pseudonyms to their publishers as well as to their writers, by denying that they were actually intended for publication, and by congratulating himself over their poor sales. In Sartre, however, it is impossible for us to maintain an introspective orientation. As soon as we initiate a reflective process of self-enclosure, we are promptly reoriented outwardly and disclosed to others. Instead of our throwing away the conditions external to our reflection, we are ourselves, when we reflect, "thrown onto the highroad in a menacing world under a blinding light." [69] This light is focused on us by others' reflections upon the action which we share in common with them. We are blinded by their reflections, because our exposure to external conditions is "our liberation from the inner life" of our own reflection. In the light of this publicity we recognize that "ultimately everything is external, even ourselves—outside in the world, among others." This recognition is for Sartre the "restoration" of aesthetic experience.[70] Thus the characters in the novels that compose Sartre's tetrology, *Les Chemins de la liberté*, travel the successive stages of liberation from the inner life of reflection which they led in the first novel, *L'Age de raison*. Since the writer's aesthetic experience is his exposure to the pressure of the community into which he is dragged by historical events, it becomes for him a public way in which he "lives" with his readers the menacing "problems which the present age poses." Thus Sartre's novels are journalistic and appropriately read in the context of Sartre's journal, which proclaims itself *Les Temps modernes*. And it is here, in fact, that portions of *Les Chemins de la liberté* were first published.

Kierkegaard might have found himself thrown into Sartre's highroad when the exposures of the Danish journal *Corsair* focused the light of publicity on his own inner life. These exposures gleaned concrete information about the history of his own life from the pseudonymous aesthetic works he imagined he had written by abstracting from his life. But for Kierkegaard, unlike Sartre, aesthetic experience could not be menaced from outside by the pressure of publicity. He had spoken of it as "my castle, which like an eagle's nest is built high upon the mountain peaks among the clouds; nothing can storm it." His introspective entry here had been the liberation of his inner life from its external conditions: "From it [the castle] I fly down to reality to seize my prey, but I do not remain down there; I bring it home, and this prey is a picture I weave into the tapestries of my palace." [71] Kierkegaard's aesthetic experience had been this weaving of his recollections. Since withdrawn from the individuating external conditions of his own life, these recollections could take the form of aesthetic works which were intended to serve as a means of communication with others. Thus Kierkegaard's reaction to the publicity of the *Corsair* was a counterattack on journalism itself and on *The Present Age* as journalistic

—as outwardly oriented, instead of reflective, in its preferred means of communication.

I have regained this essay's starting point—the public impact of existentialism. But I have in the meantime supplied Kierkegaard's and Sartre's different interpretations of what is at stake in its occurrence. Since I have held my comparison close to their "very words," I may perhaps now borrow some of these words in order to describe the existential situation of the contemporary intellectual who has felt this impact and made existentialism fashionable. The problem of action confronts him as an individual either as a problem of self-differentiating action or as a problem of common action; he either feels that he must (in Kierkegaard's words) "strive" to become an "exception," by halting the social "drift" of his life, before others have chosen for him, or he feels that he must (in Sartre's words) discount his individuality as "superfluous" and respond publicly to the "drag" of social history.

In either case the individual remains alienated from the community, and this situation retains its existential significance despite the discrepancy between the vehemently antisocial theological conclusion of Kierkegaard's dialectic and the vehemently atheistic sociological conclusion of Sartre's dialectic. This discrepancy does not serve to distinguish Kierkegaard and Sartre as existentialists: Lutheranism has traditionally been indifferent to social arrangements; communism has traditionally been atheistic. What is existentially significant is that neither the theological conclusion Kierkegaard is "striving" toward nor the sociological conclusion Sartre is "dragged" toward can actually be reached. Theological interpreters of Kierkegaard often display less patience than God Himself, who (according to Kierkegaard) said of Kierkegaard, "as a fisherman says of a fish, 'Let it run awhile, it is not yet the moment to pull it in.'" [72] Kierkegaard reiterates that he is "not a Christian," and explains that "the problem of the religious stage of existence" is "the problem of *becoming* a Christian." Sartre's remonstrances that he is not a Communist can similarly be taken to mean that his existential problem is rather the problem of *becoming* a Communist. For neither the Christian church, in Kierkegaard's case, nor the Communist Party, in Sartre's, is a community that can overcome their alienation as individuals by reconciling the conditions of reflection and action.

In presenting his theological version of the problem of existence, Kierkegaard encounters a version of his problem of communication; his treatment of the problem of becoming a Christian is complicated by the fact that the Christian church is no longer Christian. Thus his attack on *The Present Age* culminates in an *Attack Upon Christendom:* the ostensibly Christian community is actually only the social "drift" of the present age. In presenting his sociological version of the problem of existence, Sartre similarly encounters a version of his problem of communication; the Communist Party is no longer Communist, in the sense that its Marxism has atrophied and is no longer an evolving response to the "drag" of social history. Just as Kierkegaard feels himself debarred from obtaining official status in the Christian community as a clergyman and stresses that he acts as an individual "exception" who is "without authority," so Sartre feels himself debarred from official membership in the Communist Party and denies himself, or any member of the intellectual bourgeoisie (an Albert Camus, for example), the authority to reflect on behalf of the proletariat. For Sartre's dialectic of reflection and action sharpens the reflective individual's sense of alienation from the historical conditions of mass action. If Kierkegaard is only a passer-by, Sartre is only a fellow traveler.

COMMON SENSE

It is not, however, just the individual who finds himself in extreme situations in Kierkegaard and Sartre. Philosophy itself is *in extremis.* At the beginning of my exposition of Kierkegaard, I challenged the frequent supposition that existentialism, because of its orientation toward action, resembles traditional pragmatism. I noted that William James's reliance on scientific prediction enables him to dispose of the paradoxical relationship in which Kierkegaard is caught between the regressive movement of reflection and the progressive movement of action. Now that we have gone on from this relationship to the relationship between the individual and others, we can at last suggest what happens to the philosophical tradition in existentialism. William James defends "the common-sense notion of minds sharing the same objects," explaining, "Our minds meet in a world of objects which they have in common." He labels his assertion, "Two Minds Can Know One Thing," the doctrine of the "co-consciousness," the "co-terminousness" of different minds.[73] The same physical object is an identical point of arrival where two different minds can meet. In this common world, there is no problem of communication. We can identify objects by pointing.

Kierkegaard would concede that there is a common world of physical objects which can be pointed out and located with spatio-temporal co-ordinates. In this common world the moves of the traveler can be mapped, since "he changes his situation without changing himself." He can accordingly give a direct report of his travels to someone else. He can say, "I left Peking and arrived at Canton on the 14th and stayed there." But Kierkegaard adds a metaphorical description of the world of the reflective consciousness, where "the various stages are not like towns on a route of travel." [74] Here a change of situation, as we have already seen in the case with the "reflective seducer," involves a change in the individual himself. Self-identity cannot be achieved in the way physical objects can be identified. The individual's moves cannot be mapped, and he cannot in any simple designative way supply someone else with his own sense of direction.

With this change of scene, we have left behind James's common-sense world where minds can meet and individuals can communicate directly; we have entered a world where individuals must pass each other by and only communicate indirectly. In Sartre too common sense is undermined and communication becomes difficult, inasmuch as the individual cannot rely on his visual perceptions. But in Sartre, in contrast with Kierkegaard, the individual's relation to things, as well as to other men, is complicated by the intrusion of his body within the field of his consciousness. The characteristic human gesture toward things is not pointing but handling, so that the individual cannot even identify physical objects as readily as he can in Kierkegaard.

The modern philosophical tradition has been a working-partnership between philosophy and science. To the extent that this partnership might be said to begin with Descartes's philosophical reconstruction of the science of physics, its commitments can be detected in his *Discourse,* which opens with his assertion that "sense," which Descartes specifies is "the ability to distinguish the true from the false," is "common" to all men, and ends with an appeal for funds to promote collective scientific research. A scientific prediction is not uniquely valid for the individual observer who originally proposes it. In principle its validity can be tested by anyone. It is unencumbered by the umbilical cord of the first observer's first mood. From the point of view of this modern philosophical tradition, existentialism is nonsense, for it is a revolt against common sense—against the assumption that an individual's experience makes sense and can be verified or falsified, only insofar as it can be shared in common with other men. Since "truth is subjective" for Kierkegaard, the ability to distinguish the true from the false is not a common sense but a sense of irony—the ability to retain for oneself and withhold from others the meaning of what one says and does.[75] Sartre reformulates the traditional problem of truth, which was raised by Descartes as a problem of our knowledge of the external world. The problem becomes, in Sartre's analysis of insincerity (*mauvaise foi*), what we colloquially describe as the problem of being true to oneself.

If the existentialist can transform his self-scrutinizing search for truth into social commentary, this is partly due to the philosophical range of his initial revulsion against common sense. The Kierkegaard who in his journal found the prospect of publishing his reflections "revolting," is brandishing the umbilical cord of his first mood, not only on behalf of his private self-consciousness, but also in revolt against the whole development of modern philosophy, beginning with Descartes, as a development in which the self-consciousness of the philosopher has finally become Hegel's *Absolute Mind,* which exposes its process of reflection publicly in the form of the historical development of Western society. It is therefore only a relatively short step from Kierkegaard's initial revulsion against publication to his later denunciation of *The Present Age* for its illusion of fulfilling, as it "drifts," the historical role assigned it by Hegel's dialectic. Similarly Sartre's initial mood of nausea is not just a revulsion the individual privately feels when he becomes conscious of the difficulty of digesting his physiological and social experiences. This sense of revulsion is also a philosophical surrogate for Descartes's process of reflection, and becomes a revolt against the facility with which Hegel's reflective dialectic digests the whole range of human experience, without remainder. It is therefore only a relatively short step from this initially private revulsion to Sartre's later Marxist theory of social revolution, in terms of which he denounces Hegel's universal dialectic for embodying the bourgeois illusion of a homogeneous society from which no social group remains excluded.

Although existentialism may therefore seem dependent for its scope on the philosophical tradition against which it is revolting, it is yet a revolution which subverts the entire fabric of human experience accepted and articulated by this tradition. The individual's relation to things and even the relation between his different sensations of things, the individual's relation to other men and even the relation between his different moods in relation to other men—these relationships, I have shown, all become twisted because they are caught up in the existentialist readjustments of the relation between reflection and action. But any attempt like mine to state what is involved in these readjustments is itself complicated by their effects on the relation between philosophy and science and between philosophy and literature, which are the genres that we use when we attempt to understand all the other relationships and to communicate what we understand to other men. The traditional alliance between philosophy and science has been subverted in favor of an alliance between philosophy and literature. Indeed we have seen that even our language itself, which insofar as it has been shaped by direct communication is the instrument of common sense, does not survive this revolution unscathed.

NOTES

1. Paul Valéry, *Variété* (Paris: 1924), p. 11.
2. *Journals* (London: 1938), p. 48.
3. Ibid., p. 301.
4. Walter Lowrie, "Existence as Understood by Kierkegaard and/or Sartre," *Sewanee Review*, 1950, p. 389.
5. Though I shall restrict my examination to Kierkegaard and Sartre, the role the interpretation of Hölderlin assumes in the exposition of Heidegger's philosophy, of literary classics generally in Jasper's philosophy, of his own dramatic works in Marcel's philosophy, suggests I have located an expedient common to the major existentialists.
6. Guido de Ruggiero, *Existentialism* (London: 1946), p. 1.
7. *Journals*, p. 127.
8. *Essays in Radical Empiricism* (New York: 1912), pp. 238 ff.
9. We shall see that Kierkegaard describes this movement as "recollection." The etymology of the Danish *Erindring* brings out the fact that this is an introspective as well as retrospective movement.
10. *Either/Or* (London: 1946), II, 161.
11. *Concluding Unscientific Postscript* (Princeton: 1944), p. 226.
12. Ibid., p. 83.
13. *Either/Or*, II, 139.
14. Ibid.
15. *Concluding Unscientific Postscript*, p. 34.
16. *Journals*, p. 156.
17. *Concluding Unscientific Postscript*, p. 242.
18. *The Point of View* (London: 1939), p. 97.
19. *Concluding Unscientific Postscript*, p. 552.
20. Ibid., p. 247. Italics throughout the essay are mine.
21. Ibid., p. 320.
22. Ibid., p. 321.
23. *Either/Or*, I, 46. Since *Either/Or*, as an aesthetic work, provides a solution to Kierkegaard's problem of communication, the proponents of the aesthetic and ethical points of view are denominated "A" and "B" in order to suggest their merely

imaginary status as abstract possibilities. But "B" as the proponent of the ethical point of view, must "exist" and be identifiable as a particular individual (Judge William), while "A" as the proponent of the aesthetic point of view has neither name, which would imply personal identity, nor occupation, which would imply particular conditions for his life.

24. *Concluding Unscientific Postscript,* p. 113.
25. Ibid., p. 73.
26. *Situations* (Paris: 1948), II, 251.
27. *"Transcendence de l'ego," Recherches philosophiques,* VI (1936–1937), pp. 85–123.
28. *L'Etre et le néant* (Paris: 1943), p. 201.
29. *Situations,* II, 179.
30. Ibid., p. 250.
31. Ibid., p. 251.
32. *Stages on Life's Way* (London: 1945), p. 184.
33. *Concluding Unscientific Postscript,* p. 257.
34. *Situations,* II, 251.
35. Ibid., 241.
36. *Situations,* I, 46.
37. *Situations,* II, 253.
38. *Situations,* I, 23.
39. *Situations,* II, 253.
40. These relations between reflection and action, and therefore between individuals who are reflecting and acting, are implicit in the prescriptions from Sartre's critical writings that I have been citing. They are also exhibited by Sartre's actual handling of his characters in his projected tetrology, *Les Chemins de la liberté.* In the first volume, as its title *L'Age de raison* suggests, his characters reflect. In the second volume, as its title *Le Sursis* suggests, they are in suspense. Their reflections are halted, for they find themselves (as his critical writings prescribe) "on the eve of a great event [World War II] which will transcend [their] predictions, frustrate [their] expectations, upset [their] plans." The period of halted reflection is Munich Week, during which the characters are "unable to decide within themselves if the changes in their destiny will come from their own strivings, from their own failings, or from the course of external events." The approach of a common destiny is rendered by Sartre's overlapping the episodes in their lives. The shifts from one character to another occur disconcertingly in the middle of a paragraph or even of a sentence. But these episodes do not, in fact, as Edmund Wilson has carelessly suggested, when he has offered misleading comparison with James Joyce, "melt back and forth into each other." Their streams of consciousness are not tributary to each other but remain "contradictory" and are only "snarled" together by the approaching event. In the third volume, *La Mort dans*

l'âme, their reflections are "dragged" forward by the actual events of the war.

41. *Either/Or*, I, 8.
42. Ibid., p. 11. The ethical movement of action excludes, as a movement in the opposite direction, the aesthetic movement of reflection. But the aesthetic point of view includes the ethical point of view of action among the possible points of view that can be reflected upon. In contrast with Sartre, there is therefore no overlapping of these points of view, but instead a relationship "either" of exclusion "or" of inclusion in the Chinese puzzle-box fashion.
43. *Situations*, II, 10, 239.
44. "In the pseudonymous works there is not a single word which is mine. I have no knowledge of their meaning except as a reader." (*Concluding Unscientific Postscript*, p. 551.)
45. *Situations*, II, 92.
46. Ibid.
47. Ibid., pp. 91, 93.
48. Sartre's later phraseology, in *Les Communistes et la paix*, describing the social function of the Communist Party is therefore virtually identical with the phraseology I am citing here describing the social function of the novel.
49. *Le Concept d'angoisse* (Paris: 1935), p. 108.
50. *L'Etre et le néant*, p. 67.
51. Ibid., p. 404.
52. Ibid., pp. 275 ff.
53. *Le Concept d'angoisse*, pp. 91 ff.
54. *L'Etre et le néant*, p. 349.
55. *Either/Or*, I, 255.
56. *Sickness Unto Death*, pp. 26 ff.
57. Ibid., p. 116.
58. Ibid., p. 117.
59. Ibid., p. 28.
60. Ibid., p. 27.
61. *L'Etre et le néant*, p. 319.
62. *Concluding Unscientific Postscript*, p. 255.
63. *Situations*, II, 264.
64. Ibid., pp. 65, 67.
65. *L'Etre et le néant*, p. 666.
66. *Les Temps modernes*, Jan. 1948, p. 1154.
67. Paul Valéry, *Choses tues* (Paris: 1930), p. 187.
68. Sartre's analysis of social relationships derives from Heidegger's analysis of man's relationship to things in the mode of *zuhandenheit*. The implications of this metaphor, Sartre, on the one hand, spells out with tactile imagery, and, on the other hand, expands into a Marxist *technological* analysis.
69. *Situations*, I, 33.
70. Ibid., p. 34.

71. *Either/Or*, I, 34.
72. *The Point of View*, p. 82.
73. *Essays in Radical Empiricism*, pp. 123 ff.
74. *Concluding Unscientific Postscript*, p. 250.
75. *Der Begriff der Ironie mit ständiger Rücksicht auf Sokrates*, trans., W. Rutemeyer (Munich: 1929).

HEIDEGGER AND THE WORK OF ART *

Hans Jaeger

Heidegger is best known for his analysis of human existence in the book *Sein und Zeit* of 1927. Since then he has been called an existentialist or existential philosopher, terms which he rejects for himself on the ground that his main concern is Being. Being, *das Sein,* is not identical with existing reality, *das Seiende,* but clearly to be distinguished from it. The difference between Being and existing reality, *das Sein* and *das Seiende,* is, as a matter of fact, at the basis of all of Heidegger's thinking, if not the source of all his thinking. This "ontological difference," as Heidegger calls it,[1] will therefore play a part also in connection with our present problem, the work of art or, more specifically, the origin of the work of art, *"Der Ursprung des Kunstwerkes."* This is the title of a study by Heidegger which is to be discussed here. It was published in 1950 in *Holzwege* [2] and is based on lectures given in 1935 and 1936.

1

What is the origin of the work of art? Heidegger asks. Origin is to be understood as the source of the essence of the thing in question, in our case the work of art (page 7).

Nothing seems simpler than to determine the origin of a work of art. It originates in the artist. But on second thought, we could just as well say that the work of art is the origin of the artist. Without the project of a work of art and the attempt to realize it, there would be no artist. "Neither is without the other," Heidegger rightly claims. "At the same time," he adds, "neither is solely by means of the other." Their interrelation takes places in the realm of art. Art encompasses both. From art both the artist and the work of art derive their names (7).

Thus the question about the origin of the work of art leads to the question about the essence of art. But without knowing what the essence of art is we cannot determine the essence of the work of art. We are moving in a circle (8). This is by no means surprising. We are always moving in a circle when we deal with human undertakings or human existence as a

* [From *The Journal of Aesthetics and Art Criticism,* Vol. XVII, No. 1 (September 1958). The text has been slightly revised by the author. Reprinted by permission of the author and *The Journal of Aesthetics and Art Criticism.*]

whole, as Heidegger has shown in *Sein und Zeit*. Man projects himself and by realizing this projection he realizes himself, he becomes what he is. There we have the circular structure of human existence. To realize oneself means to jump into that circle of human existence. It is not a vicious circle. It is neither a merry-go-round nor a "worry-go-round" as long as the authentic self is the origin and the goal of human existence.

Origin and goal have just appeared in interrelation. The same holds true for art and the work of art. Art is both the origin and the goal of a work of art. We have to go through with this circle. But we must make a start somewhere. And we can better start with that which is the more concrete of the two, namely the work of art. The work of art is part of art as a whole and must reveal art. Therefore we ask: What is the nature of a work of art? (8).

Is it a thing? In connection with this question, Heidegger could have pointed out that Rilke liked to speak of "art-things," *Kunstdinge*.[3] Not only that, Rilke wanted to make things by means of his art, by means of poetry. If we conceive a thing as something that can be found among other things all unrelated to each other, the concept of a thing does not help us to determine the essence of a work of art or of art itself.

But how can we determine a thing in such a way that it sheds light on the work of art and reveals what makes the work of art a thing? To follow up this question may lead us nowhere. But here is at least a road, Heidegger argues. And even if this road proves to be a detour or even a dead end, we may learn from this fact something that is essential for our undertaking. So Heidegger takes this road, proceeds on it up to its end only to realize that he must turn back and must leave the thing alone. But he gains something that helps him to go on in another direction.

This way of thinking is highly characteristic of Heidegger and just as essential as the final results of his thinking. It reveals the intensity with which Heidegger asks questions and the tenacity with which he pursues them. For his basic belief is that asking questions is the basis of all essential thinking, that every valid question contains in itself at least part of the answer, since the question opens up the realm where the answer might be found. If not, a question may at least open a new vista and point to the direction in which to make a new start.

So for the time being our question is: What is the nature of a thing? What kind of thing should we have in mind when we ask this question? "A deer in the clearing of the forest, a beetle in the grass, a grass blade"? I am deliberately using

Heidegger's own examples. We hesitate to call them things, Heidegger feels. We would rather call a hammer a thing, or a shoe, a hatchet, a clock—tools, implements that we use in daily life. These are "mere" things, as we are inclined to say. Perhaps these mere things are best suited for revealing to us the true nature of a thing (11).

We call these things objects and there are definitions of the nature of such things. One is that the thing is the "bearer of its characteristic traits" (14). But this definition is so wide that it can be applied to all that exists, including the human being. Another definition of a thing is that it is the "unity of a multiplicity of sense perceptions." No doubt, that is right, just as right as the other definition. All the more reason to doubt its truth, Heidegger concludes (15). We see, he makes a distinction between what is right and what is true. Right or correct can be a judgment, a definition. Truth is not fully grasped by the concept of correctness, truth is the revelation of being, i.e., of what existing reality really is. In the above definitions the individual, specific thing, a particular pair of shoes or a particular jug, has vanished in a wide general concept. This abstract rational concept fits everything that exists in this world. The same holds true for a third definition of a thing, namely that it is the "synthesis of matter and form" (16). All three definitions are so general that they block the road to the revelation of what a specific thing really is (20).

Therefore it might be best to abandon all theorizing and simply to describe a particular thing, let us say a pair of peasant shoes. Heidegger does that. And to avoid all generalities, he chooses a very specific pair of peasant shoes, one which Van Gogh painted (22).

If we start our description with the statement that the shoes are made of leather which is given a particular shape, we are still in the realm of our last definition of a thing as the synthesis of matter and form. We have to get away from the desire to make definitions. We come closer to the truth when we ask what the shoes are for. They have a purpose, they are meant to give service. So we must observe them while they fulfill their purpose of being of service. But Van Gogh's painting, Heidegger reminds us, shows only a pair of shoes in an empty space—nothing else. However—and now Heidegger continues his description in the following manner—

The dark opening of the worn inside of the shoes bears the imprint of the toil of heavy footsteps. The rough, heavy solidity of the shoes has gathered up the tenacious steadiness of the slow walk through the wide-stretched and continuously even furrows of the field swept by a rough wind. The leather bears the moisture and satiety of the soil. The soles have slid along the loneliness of the footpath running through the field in the descending night. This pair of shoes reverberates the secret call of the earth; its quiet giving of the ripening grain and its unexplained refusal in the desolate bareness of the wintry field. These shoes are pervaded by the mute worry about the granting of the daily bread, by the silent joy of victory over want, by the anxiety before the hour of childbirth, and by the trembling before the threat of death. These shoes belong to the earth and are well guarded in the world of the peasant woman. [22 f.]

Is this a fair description, or has Heidegger's imagination run away with him? Does not Van Gogh's painting simply show a pair of worn shoes, apparently belonging to a peasant woman? Heidegger foresaw this objection which would not accept anything beyond the fact that those shoes were simply worn by the peasant woman. Heidegger counters the objection with the question whether "this simple wearing is really so simple" (23). All that was said above, Heidegger claims further, the peasant woman has been aware of as often as she has put the shoes away at night after a hard day and has reached for them again in the twilight of the early morning or has passed by them on a holiday (23).

Perhaps we are already doubtful about the validity of our objection. Heidegger did not attempt to describe the pair of shoes as the *object* of a painting but as a *thing* that reveals its true nature in the service it gives. The shoes in the painting have served the peasant woman, they are painted as such, they are not a new impersonal pair of shoes as it comes from the factory. The shoes in the painting belong to those many things the use of which make up the peasant woman's existence. If we are not reminded of the peasant woman's existence when we look at the shoes, we fail to see the shoes as things, i.e., within the whole framework of their usefulness. The shoes and similar things reflect the peasant woman's world by the service which they are giving. This serviceability does not even exhaust their true nature. Such things as a pair of shoes are of service only when they are dependable. It is by force of the dependability of such things as the shoes that the peasant woman feels secure in her world. World and Earth are with her and with those who exist in her way only by means of such "mere" things as a pair of shoes. The fallacy of the "mere" is obvious, Heidegger concludes (23).

Van Gogh's picture has helped Heidegger to discover something about the true nature of things for daily use, a particular type of things (*Zeug*). It is their dependability. But dependability is not limited to such things. Nor have we learned yet what makes a thing a thing, its *Dingheit* (24).

Still less have we discovered what makes the work of art a work of art, *das Werkhafte des Kunstwerks* (28). And yet, we have, just by chance, learned something of importance about the work of art. Van Gogh's painting has revealed to us what the peasant shoes really and truly *are*. Thus the work of art reveals the true being of things, it reveals truth (24). Heidegger conceives truth always in the sense of Greek *aletheia,* unhiddenness, the unhiddenness of existing reality, i.e., its being. So Heidegger can conclude: By revealing the true nature or actual being of things or, generally speaking, of existing reality, art establishes truth by means of a work of art. Truth is conceived here as something that happens, that takes place. Truth is an event in the literal sense of the word (25). Event is derived from *ex-venire,* to come out. Truth conceived as an event means that truth is something that comes out, comes to the fore, rises from the Hidden into the Unhidden. If Heidegger were writing in English, he might very well have used here the etymology of "event," as I have done, to back up his conception of truth semantically and to set it off from the limited concept of correctness appearing in a judgment.

The conception of art as revelation of truth certainly differs from the age-old conception that art is the imitation and representation of reality and that the truth of art consists in the fact that the represented things agree with reality. Nor are we on the right track, Heidegger maintains, if we say that art represents the general essence of things. For where and how is that general essence to which the work of art could correspond? To what essence of what thing should a Greek temple correspond? Or Hölderlin's hymn *"Der Rhein,"* although its title refers to something so concrete as a particular river? (26).

We have made a detour and have come to an impasse. But this detour was not in vain. A particular work of art representing a thing has not helped us in the attempt to determine what makes a thing a thing but has taught us something about the work of art, namely that it brings to the fore the true nature or the being of existing reality, that it discloses truth. Heidegger conceives being and truth as the same. This does not mean that they are identical but that they belong together. His next questions are: What is truth itself so it can realize itself at times in art? And what is the nature of this realization? (28).

2

To find an answer to these questions Heidegger again begins with the description of a specific work of art. This time he chooses a building, a Greek temple. There is a purpose in this choice. A Greek temple does not imitate anything that belongs to external reality. It just stands there in the midst of the raggedness of a rocky valley (30 f.). Here is Heidegger's description:

> The edifice enshrines the statue of the God. Concealing Him in that way it makes Him stand out through the open hall of columns into the sacred grounds. The presence of the God pervades the temple. This presence of the God determines in itself the expanse and the boundaries of the grounds as sacred realm. The temple and its grounds do not fade away into the Indefinite. It is the erection of the temple which creates and, at the same time, gathers around itself the unity of those trends and relations in which birth and death, misfortune and blessing, victory and ignominy, steadfastness and decline attain the character and trend of a humanity in its destiny. The all-determining expanse of this open realm of relations is the world of this historical people. By this world and within this world a people is referred back to its own self for the fulfillment of its destiny.

Let us stop for a moment to consider what Heidegger has said. The temple embodies the world of a people. What does Heidegger mean when he says "world"? To understand this concept we have to combine his short explanation of the world in this study with previous explanations in *Sein und Zeit* and *Vom Wesen des Grundes.*

The world in the sense in which Heidegger uses the word when he calls man's fundamental state of being "being-in-the-world" is not our environment nor the sum total of objects in external reality. The world does not contain objects, it is unobjective. We speak of the American world or of the world of Goethe or of the world of antiquity and mean an individual, unobjective world. The peasant woman has a world. Every human being has his world.

To understand Heidegger's conception of the world one must keep in mind the difference between existing reality, *das Seiende,* and the being of existing reality, *das Sein des Seienden.* Man exists in such a way that he not only transcends himself toward the realization of his possibilities, but he also transcends things that exist around him toward their being so that they reveal to him what they are. Both forms of transcendence are interdependent, one is not without the other, they are the same. For instance, a stone, a rock is in the world of man not merely an object that has such and such dimensions, such and such weight, color, shape, texture, etc. It may reveal itself to me as *being* an appropriate weapon, if I am in danger and have to defend myself. Or it may reveal itself as *being* appropriate building material, or it may appear to *be* beautiful. We are used to saying that it depends on the situation what a stone or a rock *is* for me. This so-called situation is actually part of the realm of my possibilities from which I receive my directives as to their realization. This realm of my possibilities is a unified interrelated realm of *being*, i.e., all things of existing reality that are known to me appear here as what they *are*. A stone can only reveal itself as being a weapon in a unified realm of being which reveals danger. And the revealment of danger is only possible on the basis of the disclosure of a still wider realm of being, and so on until we reach the disclosure of the whole known realm of existing reality as to its being. This realm of being, this unified fabric of relationships is the world and as such it reveals to me my possibilities, it contains my destiny. Without this world I would not be able to react to external reality and to exist as I do. Having a world or being-in-the-world, as Heidegger puts it, means that man exists by transcending existing reality, including himself, towards being which includes the possibility of being his own self. Man's fundamental state of being, his being-in-the-world, is his transcendence.[4] The world is so unique that one cannot characterize its working in any other way than by stating it is at work as a world. Heidegger says "*die Welt weltet.*" And he summarizes the working of the world itself in these words: "The world is the ever-unobjective realm to which we are subjected as long as the courses of birth and death, blessing and curse hold us exposed to being. Wherever and whenever the essential decisions of our history are made, whenever they are accepted by us or forsaken, misjudged, or re-evaluated, the world is at work as the world, *da weltet die Welt*" (33).

With this quotation we are back at our study of the work of art. We can now understand what Heidegger means when he says in his description of the Greek temple that it embodies the world of a historical people. This reveals an important characteristic of the work of art. The work of art erects a world (33). If we take another glance at the description of Van Gogh's picture, we recognize that the same characteristic was implied there too: the shoes reflect the world of the peasant woman. But Heidegger's previous conclusion was more comprehensive. It said: a work of art establishes truth (24 f.). Both statements belong together. A work of art establishes truth by means of erecting a world. The world, however, is a realm that transcends external reality, it is unobjective. A work of art without external reality is unthinkable. Therefore the erection of a world can only be one characteristic of the truth that is established in the work of art. The complementary characteristic will become apparent in the continuation of Heidegger's description of the Greek temple:

Standing there the edifice rests on rock. This resting on the rock makes the rock yield the secret of its unwieldy and yet uncompelled power of holding and sustaining. Standing there the edifice withstands the storm raging above and thus reveals the very nature of the storm in its force. The shining splendor of the stone, apparently so bright only by the grace of the sun, actually makes apparent the light of the day, the vast realm of the sky, the darkness of the night. The firm towering of the temple makes the invisible space of the air visible. The unperturbed calmness of the structure stands out against the mountain waves of the sea and makes their uproar apparent by contrast. The tree and the grass, the eagle and the bull, the snake and the cricket take on their appearance only by means of contrast and thus appear as what they are. The Greeks very early called this rising and appearing in itself and as a whole Φύσις. It elucidates, at the same time, that on which and in which man founds his existence. We call it the earth. [31]

With this description, we have both characteristics of the work of art together. It erects a world but it also is of the earth. The temple stands on rock, is made of stone, and rises into the wide space of the earth. What is the true nature of the earth in the sense in which Heidegger uses this word? His own comment is: "We should neither associate with this word the conception of a mass of matter nor that of a planet" (31). The earth is the complementary opposite of Being as a whole, of the Greek *Physis,* and of the more limited realm of being which Heidegger calls the world. The relation of the earth and the world is that of existing reality and of the being of existing reality. While Being itself and the world are ever-open overtness, the earth is ever enclosed within itself. It guards and hides its secret. It shows no opening no matter how much we penetrate it. We may break the rock and weigh its mass, the rock will remain withdrawn into itself. We may refract the light and measure the waves of colors. The colors will disappear in the scientific analysis. Color is meant to shine and nothing else. "The earth shows itself only as what it is when it remains undisclosed and unexplained" (36). The earth is essentially withdrawn into itself and can become apparent only as such: undisclosable (35 f.).

The earth becomes apparent in itself when it appears in the overtness of Being as a whole or of the world, the more limited realm of being. At the same time, the earth absorbs, shelters, and guards being, the world. Being, *das Sein,* turns to the earth, *das Seiende,* as its shelter and guardian (37).

The description of the temple tried to bring out this interrelation of the world and the earth. In erecting a world the work of art uses the earth, i.e., earthly material, rock, color, tone, words, when we think of the whole realm of art. But in the work of art the material is not used in the same way as in the production of a tool where the material "disappears in its usefulness" (35). The work of art, on the contrary, brings out the true nature of the material. Only now, held in the overtness of the world of the work of art, the rock reveals its sustaining power and massiveness, the color its radiance, the tone its true sound, the word its significance. The work of art erects a world by reinstating the world in the earth. At the same time, by holding the earth in the overtness of the world, the work of art makes the earth apparent as such: withdrawn into itself, i.e., it re-establishes the earth as earth (35).

"Erection of a world and re-establishment of the earth are two essential characteristics which make up the work of art. Both belong together as a unified whole" (36 f.). It is this unity of world and earth which we are looking for in a work of art, when we conceive it as resting within itself, in complete self-composure. And it is this composed unity of world and earth which constitutes the truth of the work of art (37).

The self-composure of the work of art does by no means exclude movement but is the result of strife, a strife between the world and the earth. Its nature is this: The world resting upon the earth strives to lift the earth beyond itself. The earth, however, tends to draw the world into itself, to enclose, to hold, and to guard it. In this strife each of the opponents is striving to assert itself, each of the opponents is lifting the other into the maintenance of its own self, of its essential nature (37 f.). And it is the work of art which, by erecting a world and re-establishing the earth, initiates and accomplishes this strife (38). The strife remains undecided, and its undecisiveness is its decisive characteristic and thus the decisive characteristic of the work of art. By presenting the undecisiveness of the strife between the world and the earth the work of art realizes truth. If we remember that the world is the ever-open, elucidated realm of being while the earth is the ever-closed, concealed realm of existing reality, we can grasp truth more basically: Truth as inherent in the work of art is apparent "as strife between elucidation and concealment in the opposition of world and earth, being and existing reality" (51).

Perhaps this is the proper place to stop for a moment and to ask ourselves whether Heidegger's concept of truth is such that it does not oppose but contains the usual conception of truth as the correctness of a judgment where the statement corresponds to reality. If true, Heidegger's conception of truth must comprise even the nature of such simple truth as, e.g., the statement that this ring consists of gold. The work of art is supposed to present truth in itself, not a truth of a very special nature.

To link up the two conceptions of truth let us start with the question: What must be known to us in order to make such a statement as that this ring is gold? We must already know what gold is. Not only that, the whole realm in which gold appears as being different from other things must be revealed to us. Otherwise we would have no guidance for discovering and stating the truth about a piece of gold. Reality as a unified whole must be revealed to us with regard to what it is, in order that something particular can reveal itself in its being, in order that we can say: that particular thing is this or that. A true statement is only possible on the basis of truth in general (40 f.). And truth in general must be conceived as unhiddenness of existing reality as a whole in its being. Unhiddenness presupposes hiddenness from which the hidden rises into the overt realm of being and is elucidated in regard to what it is. Unhiddenness and hiddenness belong together. Both together constitute truth, paradoxical as it may seem at first glance.[5] We have seen before that truth is not something that is fixed forever. This means that existing reality is not revealed to us all the time and always in the same way. When a given situation reveals itself to me as being dangerous all existing reality is seen in the light of this danger. Only when I and all existing reality are exposed to this elucidating light, something can reveal itself to me as being a means of protection. This is how I interpret Heidegger's words: "In the midst of existing reality as a whole there is an open spot. There is a clearing [*Lichtung*]" (41). Heidegger speaks also of an "elucidating center" (*lichtende Mitte*). We probably must imagine this *Lichtung* as the open realm of being which shines forth in its own light and elucidates existing reality which appears in it. "This open center is not enclosed by existing reality, but the elucidating center itself circles around all that exists [41]. . . . Thanks to this elucidating light existing reality (including ourselves) is in certain and variable degrees unhidden, unconcealed" (42).

Our above example can also clarify the certain and variable degree of unhiddenness. The discovery of danger may lead to the discovery of a means of protection. When this happens it happens at the expense of everything else. In the light of danger the beauty of the surrounding scenery, for instance, remains concealed to us.[6] Unhiddenness and hiddenness, elucidation and concealment belong together. Therefore Heidegger says: "Truth is the primordial strife between elucidation and concealment" (44). Or in a paradoxical formulation: "Truth is in its essence un-truth" (43). Un-truth means, of course, concealment of being, not falsity. There are various ways in which reality is concealed to us, basically two ways. Something is fully concealed to me, if I can say nothing revealing about it except that it *is* (42). Then it is meaningless, a secret, a mystery. This is, e.g., the case when someone to whom the world of bacteria is unknown sees a culture of bacteria through the microscope.[6] It has no meaning for him, he does not know what it is, it is a mystery. But there is also concealment within the realm of the unhidden as we have seen in our previous example. Things of existing reality may appear partially blocked, veiled, distorted. All truth or unhiddenness is linked up with these two basic forms of concealment and determines not only our scientific discoveries, but all our behavior, our decisions (42). The world belongs to the overt realm of unhiddenness of being. The overt constitutes the "light which elucidates the courses of the essential directions [*Weisungen*] which we follow in making our decisions" (43). Also the earth belongs to the overt (43), "it rises in it as the concealing one. . . . The earth penetrates the world, the world founds itself on the earth, whenever truth happens as the primordial strife between elucidation and concealment" (44). Truth happens, e.g., in the standing of the temple and in Van Gogh's painting (44). Truth in the sense of correctness is only one manner in which reality appears unhidden. It is only *a* truth, not truth in itself. A work of art, however, Heidegger insists, does not only reveal something true, but truth itself. We witness "unhiddenness itself in relation to existing reality as a whole" (44). The truth which is "at work" in Van Gogh's painting does not consist in revealing an object as a pair of shoes. The painting represents shoes, to be sure, but it also opens up a whole world and sheds light on a unified whole of existing reality. Therefore Heidegger says that in a work of art all that exists becomes more truly existent, *"alles Seiende [wird] seiender"* (44). In this way something existent reflects being—and being becomes existent. Heidegger says: "Truth establishes itself in some existing reality in such a way that this itself occupies the overtness of truth" (51 f.). In the work of art truth is embodied. The strife between elucidation and concealment in the opposition of world and earth is reinstated in the earth and consolidated. This does not mean that strife is abolished. On the contrary, the very tension and intimate intensity of the strife with which the contenders are at grips and set each other off is tensioned and consolidated by assuming structure (*Gestalt*) in the work of art. This is the essential nature of artistic structure as Heidegger conceives it (51 f.).[7]

3

We have clarified truth as well as we could. We have found that one way in which truth is at work is the work of art.[8] Now we must think of our original question which concerns the origin of the work of art. Obviously its origin is its creator, the artist. Must we now go into the mystery of artistic creation? No. For it is not the artist who interests us, but only the fact that the work of art has been created. The "simple *factum est*" as Heidegger says, is the all-important thing in a work of art (53). Therefore this fact of having been created must be especially apparent in the work of art, so that we are struck by its mere existence, while we take the creation of other things, of a pair of shoes, of a hammer, of a chair, for granted. This is actually the case. The fact that a chair is made by somebody is forgotten. We only ask ourselves whether it properly fulfills its purpose. The fact of creation disappears behind the usefulness and dependability of such a thing as a chair (53).

Quite different in the work of art. It has no other purpose than that of being there, i.e., of having been created. This fact that there *is* such a creation as the work of art is by no means self-understood. On the contrary, it is the extraordinary event. Extraordinary, because every true work of art fills us with wonder about the mere fact that it exists, that it was and could be created. The miracle of creation is inherent in every true work of art and emanates from it, because a true work of art is something hitherto unimagined, unique, extraordinary. "The realm of the extraordinary, of the unfamiliar is thrown open and what has appeared so far as the ordinary, familiar is overthrown" (54). This is the mark of every true work of art, a characteristic which Heidegger stresses particularly. The work of art transports us into a new realm that suddenly opens up and "changes our usual relationship to the world and the earth, so that we arrest all our common doing and rating, knowing and observing, and succumb to lingering in the truth that happens in the work of art [*in der im Werk geschehenden Wahrheit*]" (54). We can illustrate this effect of a work of art resulting from the mere fact of its existence with Rilke, who in the face of an archaic torso of Apollo concludes a poem on this statue with the exclamation: "You have to change your life." [9]

This illustration reveals, at the same time, that a work of art can only be an event in which truth "happens," if the work of art finds those who enter into and linger in the truth revealed by it. In doing so they preserve and guard it. Without its guardians a work of art is just an object among other objects. It needs human response to the unique fact of its existence which consists in "the transformation of the unhiddenness of existing reality and that means of being" (59). If a work of art is to function as a work of art we have to consider both the creative artist who gives structure to truth and the guardians of the work of art who preserve truth in their respective ways. Now we can say what art is. Art (which encompasses both the work of art and the artist) is the "creative preservation of truth in the work of art" (59). In this formulation both the creator and the guardians of the work of art are comprised.

The fundamental revealment of truth occurs in language. The origin of language is poetry. Therefore all art is poetic or, as Heidegger says, "the essence of art is poetry" (62). And "the essence of poetry is the foundation of truth" (62). The word "foundation" (*Stiftung*) is used here in a triple sense: (1) it means giving; (2) it means founding; (3) it means a beginning (62). Art as a foundation of truth gives and founds and begins something for which there is no substitute in existing reality. The establishment of art is something in addition to existing reality, a further abundance, a gift. At the same time, art founds by making the earth the foundation on which our existence rests. In the third place, art is a beginning inasmuch as it opens ever anew the strife of truth, the opposition between the world and the earth (62 f.).

4

In conclusion let us see how well Heidegger's ideas will stand up when they are tested on a particular work of art. I am choosing for this purpose Keats's "Ode on a Grecian Urn." This poem seems to be especially well suited for such a test inasmuch as we have here a work of art which has as its topic a work of art. Keats seems to make it easy for us, since he himself sums up the truth which the poem establishes: "Beauty is truth, truth beauty." Heidegger says the same about the relation of beauty and truth in a work of art. "Beauty is not something that exists besides this truth. . . . [Beauty is] the appearance . . . of truth in the work of art as the work of art" (67).

How does truth appear in Keats's "Ode"? It appears as the beauty of the urn and as the beauty of the whole poem. With the concept of beauty we associate the idea of harmony, balance, repose. And this presupposes two complementary opposites which have come to rest because they are in balance. Fleeting moments of earthly life on the urn in the poem—"mad pursuit," "struggle to escape," the playing of "pipes and timbrels," and "wild ecstasy"—have been lifted into the world of art and have been made eternal. Longing, grief, and happiness, so transitory and problematic on earth now are eternal in the work of art, and thus they truly are. Heidegger's oppositions, the world and earth, appear in the poem as eternity in art and transitoriness on earth. World and earth belong together and have become one. The shape of the urn tells the same story. It outlines the Attic world "O Attic shape!" and the beauty of its shape reflects the attitude of balance and harmony, "Fair attitude!" This line seems to illustrate Heidegger's general contention, that "truth establishes itself in existing reality in such a way that this itself [in the poem the fair-shaped urn] occupies the overtness of truth" (in the poem the attitude or spirit of the Attic world) (51 f.). "O Attic shape! Fair attitude!" This line also sums up the great task of artistic structure, *Gestalt*. Heidegger means the same when he maintains that *Gestalt* constitutes the consolidation of the strife between the world and the earth, elucidation and concealment of being (52). This paradoxical twofoldedness of artistic structure determines the whole structure of Keats's "Ode" and is intoned as its theme at the very beginning when the urn is addressed as the "foster-child of Silence . . . who canst thus express / A flowery tale more sweetly than our rhyme. . . ." This theme that the silence of artistic form speaks runs through the whole poem:

> Heard melodies are sweet, but those unheard
> Are sweeter . . . .

And again in the last stanza:

> Thou, silent form, dost tease us out of thought
> As doth eternity . . . .

> thou say'st

> "Beauty is truth, truth beauty . . ."

But perhaps a poem about a work of art is too specialized to serve as a proper testing ground for Heidegger's conception of art. Therefore let us make one more attempt. I am choosing this time a German poem, the shortest, the simplest, the best known, and perhaps the most perfect lyric in German as it has often been called, *"Wanderers Nachtlied 2,"* by Goethe:

Ueber allen Gipfeln	O'er all the hill-tops
Ist Ruh,	Is quiet now,
In allen Wipfeln	In all the tree-tops
Spürest du	Hearest thou
Kaum einen Hauch;	Hardly a breath;
Die Vögelein schweigen	The birds are asleep in
im Walde.	the trees:
Warte nur, balde	Wait; soon like these
Ruhest du auch.	Thou too shalt rest.[10]

The poem has often been quoted and described for the sake of wresting from it the secret of its beauty. It seems too unassuming to be called the embodiment of truth itself, too simple and natural to represent the primordial strife of the world and the earth, of elucidation and concealment. But this impression may only be the result of the discrepancy of simple poetic diction and ponderous philosophical language. We should keep this in mind in our further discussion. A theoretical analysis will always be on a different level from that of a poem. In our case Goethe's simple verses have to be linked up with Heidegger's difficult formulations. Let us not forget either that truth as the strife of the world and the earth is the same as Being, *das Sein des Seienden,* and that Being is both the simplest and the most mysterious of all the words and concepts, because Being is the very foundation and the very core of all that exists.

It has always been felt that Goethe's *"Nachtlied"* expresses more than the personal, momentary mood of longing for rest. One critic has even pointed out that, in spite of its simplicity, the poem is all-embracing in scope, that it moves in four concentric circles, from the outer circle of mountain peaks *(Gipfel)* over the treetops *(Wipfel)* to the birds in the woods and finally to the innermost circle of the poet's self. They are supposed to represent four different realms: the earth, the flora, the fauna, and the human being. Together they comprise existing reality as a whole. No doubt, there is some truth in this observation. But does not the above characterization load the poem with weighty masses under which its very nature is crushed? The mountain peaks, the treetops, the birds, and the human self do not have the ascribed weight. None of them has a value of its own in the poem, still less that of the respective realm of reality to which each belongs. They are what they are as points of direction toward something beyond them that is fundamentally different. The *Gipfel* do not appear as such, the poem starts: "Ueber *allen Gipfeln.*" and then immediately that other is named: *"Ist Ruh."* This is Goethe's name for Being, the eternal, ever-present, all pervading.

> *Den alles Drängen, alles Ringen*
> *Ist ew'ge Ruh in Gott dem Herrn.*

> For all the striving, all the struggling
> Eternal rest is in God our Lord.

These lines of the old Goethe say the same as the "Night Song": *"Ist Ruh."* This encompasses and pervades the mountain peaks, treetops, birds, and the human being. They do not stand for themselves but are there to bring out this *"Ist Ruh"* by way of contrast. Characteristic for them is the opposite, the constant unrest, the change; for the mountain peaks drifting clouds above them and changing light on them, for the treetops the rustling in the wind, for the birds their singing and flying about, for man his striving and struggling. It is the opposite, into which they are lifted and in which they are held: rest, silence. How can the silence of nature be grasped with any of our five senses? It cannot, it is nonexistent. The nonexistent in existing reality is Being. The poem achieves the miracle that we become aware of the presence of the nonexistent, of Being, of the *Ist Ruh*. The poem achieves it by lifting the mountain peaks, treetops, birds, and the human self into the world of *Ist Ruh* so that they occupy its overtness, as we can say with Heidegger.

The reverberation of the strife between the two realms, rest and change, Being and existing reality, *das Sein* and *das Seiende*, runs through the poem and comes fully to rest at its end. Both realms are one in the "intimacy of their opposition," to paraphrase Heidegger (51). Each of them is elucidated and made apparent only through the other, without the other it would remain concealed. This is the truth which the poem embodies and imparts to us in every detail of its language and structure including its rhythm and rhymes. By that I mean that the two spheres, Being and existing reality, are so interlocked that they are meaningless when separated. The separation is even practically impossible. Nothing is said of the mountain peaks except that they rise into the quiet of the clear sky, nothing is said of the treetops, the birds, and the human self except that they partake of the *Ist Ruh*. As strange as it may have seemed at first, Goethe's poem too confirms Heidegger's conception of the work of art as the strife of truth, the strife between the world and the earth, elucidation and concealment, being and existing reality.

5

We started with the question about the origin of the work of art. We have seen that the work of art—just as well as its creator and guardians—has its origin in art. This is the case, "because art is essentially origin and nothing else: a singular manner in which truth comes into existence and that means, becomes historical. . . . Whenever art happens, i.e., whenever there is a beginning . . . only then history begins or begins anew" (65 and 64).

Heidegger's final question is why we ask the question about the essence of art. We ask it, he answers, because of the historical significance of art, its importance in and for our existence. We ask the question about art in order to be able to ask the further question "whether art in our historical existence is origin or not, whether and under what conditions it can and must be origin" (65). The results of such questioning can perhaps prepare the way for a further development of true art.

Heidegger does not claim to have solved the riddle of art in his study. He regarded as his task something more modest, namely to recognize the presence of the riddle (66). This point of view must be observed in all critical scrutiny of Heidegger's study. But the criticism is better left to those who feel competent in this field. I should like to raise only one question: Whether the origin of the work of art is not the origin of our whole existence as far as it is authentic existence? Whether the truth that is established in the work of art is not the essence of all true, authentic existence? Not only the creative artist but every authentic self is involved in the strife between the world and the earth and engaged in establishing this truth. Or, as Rilke says, even the work of art "appears only as a means . . . of attaining a more intact state in the center of one's own being." [11] The boundaries between the work of a true artist and authentic existence seem to be fluid. Heidegger indicates this himself in his study when at more than one place he refers to the *Werk* in general which in our English translation had to appear in a limited sense, as "work of art," *Kunstwerk*. Furthermore, if poetry is at the basis of all art, is not the realm of the poetic at the basis of all authentic existence? Again Heidegger himself seems to point in this direction in some of his more recent studies, particularly in the study on a poem by Hölderlin which contains this very idea:

> *Voll Verdienst, doch dichterisch, wohnet*
> *Der Mensch auf dieser Erde.*[12]

These considerations are brought forth to point to the real significance of Heidegger's studies on the work of art and on poetry. They show us the place which art occupies in human existence and show human existence in its relation to art.[13]

NOTES

1. *"Vorwort zur dritten Auflage," Vom Wesen des Grundes* (Frankfurt: 1949), p. 5.
2. (Frankfurt: 1950.) Pp. 7–68. Numbers in the text refer to pages of this study.
3. E.g., letter to Lou Andreas-Salomé, August 8, 1903, or letter to Clara Rilke, June 23, 1907.
4. Cf. *Sein und Zeit* (Halle: 1941), pp. 63–88, and *Vom Wesen des Grundes,* pp. 17–39, especially pp. 18 and 34 f. Examples are mine.

5. *Vom Wesen der Wahrheit* (Frankfurt: 1949), pp. 17, 19 ff.

6. Example is mine.

7. At this point (51 f.) Heidegger calls the strife between the world and the earth *"Riss,"* which does not mean "gap," *Kluft,* but the "intimate interdependence of the contenders," *die Innigkeit des Sichzugehörens der Streitenden.* Heidegger continues: *"Der Riss ist das einheitliche Gezüge von Aufriss und Grundriss, Durch- und Umriss." Riss* in this sense, implying the above derivatives, leads easily to the concept of *Gestalt* (structure). This cannot be adequately rendered into English. The whole trend of thoughts could only be paraphrased in English and the term "tension" for *Riss* can only indicate the German implication of the full "outlines" of the strife.

8. For other ways in which truth is at work, see *Holzwege,* p. 50.

9. Ausgewählte Werke, I (Leipzig: 1938), p. 141. Example is mine.

10. Translation by Longfellow. About its quality cf. Walter Silz, "Longfellow's Translation of Goethe's *Ueber allen Gipfeln* . . . ," *Modern Language Notes,* LXXXI (May 1956), pp. 344 f.

11. Letter to Gertrud Oukama Knoop, November 26, 1921, trans., J. B. Greene and M. D. Norton, II (New York: 1948), pp. 266 f.

12. *Vorträge und Aufsätze* (Pfullingen: 1954), pp. 187–204.

13. In his most recent publications, which had not yet appeared when the above article was written and first published, Heidegger has further developed his views on the essence of art, without, however, changing their foundation. His belief that the basis of all art is poetry (cf. above, p. 425) where language appears in "pure" form has led to his ever-increasing interest in the problem of language. It is language which makes man what he is, distinct among all other creatures on earth. In the lecture *"Die Sprache,"* the first of seven studies on language published in 1959 under the title *Unterwegs zur Sprache (UzS),* Heidegger deals with the question of the essence of language. A poem by Trakl serves him as a road of approach, just as the two poems by Keats and Goethe have served us to illustrate and test Heidegger's conception of the essence of art. An important link between Heidegger's essay on the work of art and his lecture *"Die Sprache"* is the study *"Das Ding"* in *Vorträge und Aufsätze,* 1954, pp. 163 ff., where he shows that things, provided they are true things which play a vital part in human existence, reflect the fourfold realm of heaven and earth, of mortal and divine beings, i.e., the world. In the lecture *"Die Sprache"* Heidegger applies this finding to the language of poetry. Here world and things appear distinct from one another and yet as belonging to-

gether, united in the "dimension" that distinguished them (*UzS*, 25), just as two complementary poles form a union of opposites where the very opposition is the mutual bond. The unique difference (*"Unter-Schied"*) between world and thing is of such nature that it brings each of them into its own, establishes the very essence of each of them by means of their union. World and thing pervade one another, *"sie durchgehen einander"* (*UzS*, 24). The intimacy of world and thing, *"die Innigkeit von Welt und Ding,"* which consists in the preservation of their distinctiveness (*UzS*, 24) corresponds to the previous conception of the "intimacy of the opposition" of world and earth (cf. above, p. 428). What seems to be ineffable reveals itself in the language of art which speaks through silence, as Keats has conveyed to us in the above poem. It is also silence, the *Ist Ruh,* which becomes manifest in Goethe's night song. This may help us to understand Heidegger's recent formulation about language whenever it is "pure" as in poetry: "Language speaks as the sound of silence," a key sentence designated as such by italics: *"Die Sprache spricht als das Geläut der Stille"* (*UzS*, 30). As the sound of silence language manifests world and things in the mutual bondage of their distinctive difference: *"Die Sprache west als der sich ereignende Unter-Schied für Welt und Dinge"* (*UzS*, 30).

In the lecture *"Die Sprache"* we can also hear an echo of the above quotation from Hölderlin. His *"dichterisch wohnet der Mensch"* appears now modified to "dwelling in the speaking of language": *"Alles beruht darin, das Wohnen im Sprechen der Sprache zu lernen"* (*UzS*, 33). To grasp the full meaning of this sentence we must remember that, for Heidegger, language is the realm which guards and reveals being, it is "the house of being," *"das Haus des Seins."*

In two other recent studies, *"Das Wesen der Sprache"* and *"Das Wort"* (*UzS*, 157 ff. and 217 ff.), Heidegger uses again a poem, *"Das Wort"* by Stefan George, as the starting point for fathoming the essence of language. "Only the word invests the thing with being" (*UzS*, 164) and the foremost concern of our thinking should be our relation to language (*UzS*, 214). Thus the road of the poet and that of the thinker run parallel and the role of poetry becomes in the eyes of Heidegger ever more significant for man in his search for truth and the realization of truth. (H.J., 1960.)

TOWARD A UNIFIED FIELD IN AESTHETICS *

Walter Abell

The *Journal of Aesthetics* has recently published two articles of special value to those who are seeking to integrate the problems of art and aesthetics with the totality of modern thought. I refer to Douglas N. Morgan's "Psychology and Art Today: A Summary and Critique" (December 1950) and Thomas Munro's "Aesthetics as Science: Its Development in America" (March 1951).

Morgan reviewed recent psychological contributions to the understanding of art in terms of the psychoanalytical, the Gestalt, and the experimental approaches. He found significance in all of them, with the main theoretical gains going to psychoanalytical and Gestalt developments, and more limited practical benefits granted to experimental work in such fields as aptitude testing.

Morgan also pointed out what he considered to be certain limitations of each of the psychological approaches. Among these limitations he included the tendency of the experimentalists to accumulate data without reference to basic principles. "In the psychology of art we must imaginatively select in advance of experiment *which* factors, when correlated, will give us interesting and important results. This requires some hard thinking, some imagination, some kind of a *theory*, however tentative, some 'exploratory hypothesis.'"[1] The article ends on the similar note that what is perhaps most needed in psychological aesthetics at the present time is thinking "on the level of fundamental theory."[2]

Morgan's survey brings the fields of art and psychology, at least as seen from the artistic point of view, into one comprehensive vista. Munro, in the second article mentioned above, directs our attention to even wider horizons. He suggests possibilities of interrelationship, not only between art and psychology, but also between them and other current developments of thought. Among the latter he notes the new universality of outlook made possible by our familiarity with the arts of all ages and of many varieties of culture, and the new instruments for interpretation offered by the social sciences.

Like Morgan, Munro urges, indeed several times reiterates,

* [From *The Journal of Aesthetics and Art Criticism*, Vol. X, No. 3 (March 1952). Reprinted by permission of *The Journal of Aesthetics and Art Criticism*.]

the present need for theoretical unification and synthesis. "In a period of rapid cultural change and mixture, when science is discovering particular facts with unparalleled speed, there is urgent need for the large-scale, organizing phase of philosophic thinking." "The ingredients for scientific aesthetics are present, but more thorough synthesis is needed. The time is overdue for bringing these ingredients together, first of all through a large-scale program of bibliographies, translations, critical summaries, and publications in different languages; second, through more thoroughly integrated, original syntheses." [3]

The present article is a report on one particular attempt to think "on the level of fundamental theory" as urged by Morgan, and to advance toward the kind of correlation, unification, and synthesis advocated by Munro. Like these writers, and no doubt like many more of our contemporaries, I have felt the need for comprehensive studies in the correlation of previously separate fields of thought. My own main efforts of research during the past decade have gone into studies of this kind. The result has been the gradual development of a "psycho-historical" or "psycho-technic" theory of cultural dynamics: a theory which I believe offers a wider basis of synthesis than has been provided by any of its antecedents. I have already had occasion to present certain aspects of the psycho-historical theory in the *Journal of Aesthetics*.[4] What follows is a discussion of some of the problems in correlation that led to the development of the theory and some of the ways in which I hope that psycho-historical thinking can assist us in solving problems of this kind.

Studies in synthesis exert their special lure through the prospect of wider horizons than can be perceived within the limits of any single discipline. I should like to recognize at the outset that they also present their particular discouragements of seemingly endless scope and baffling complexity. I began my personal efforts in this direction in 1942 on the basis of a fusion which had taken place in my thinking between my previous knowledge of art history and psychological insights derived from the writings of Carl Jung. My original intention was to indicate certain correlations within the scope of an article. But in order to clarify what I borrowed from Jung, I found myself involved in a more comprehensive study of his work, and then in an extension of that study to the works of Freud. It eventually became clear that the psychological aspects of my theory would profit by a knowledge of the entire field of depth psychology—a matter requiring years of study, even then only partially attainable by a layman, and perhaps not completely attainable by any single psychoanalyst.

Similarly with other fields of thought. In order to determine what conditions of life had accompanied the development of specific forms of art—let us say those of the Gothic period —I found it necessary to inform myself on the judgments of large numbers of historians and behind their opinions to penetrate back to the original expressions of Gothic mentality itself. Before long I was reading the chronicles of medieval monks like Salimbene and the agricultural treatises of medieval husbandmen like Walter of Henley. Obviously here was another inexhaustible field, to cover which completely and in detail was impossible. And so it went. During the years devoted to these studies, when my friends asked me what I was writing about, I was tempted to reply with ironic despair, "The universe." And indeed the universe is the only limit for studies in synthesis. Precisely because it is a universe, a oneness, everything in it is ultimately related to everything else. The would-be synthesist may as well resign himself to the idea that a bewildering number of its interrelationships will call for his attention. The problem becomes one of finding a system of thought which, at least symbolically, can reflect the universe; yet which can be developed and grasped within the limited time, energy, and capacity vouchsafed to that tiny reflector of the universe, the individual human mind.

If the task is not an easy one, those of us who labor at it may take comfort in two reflections. The personal disqualifications which most of us feel for an undertaking of this kind affect others no less than ourselves. As an art historian and critic, I have often had occasion to regret my imperfect knowledge of psychology, of general history, of sociology, and of other subjects. But I have told myself that a psychologist, a historian, or a sociologist, if he were to undertake the same task, would probably labor under the inverse limitation that he would know less about the history and criticism of art than I do. There is presumably no one living who has an equally thorough knowledge of *all* the fields of thought we are concerned to correlate. If any progress toward synthesis is to be made, it must be made in spite of personal limitations of one kind or another, not in the absence of them. Hence each of us may as well accept his own limitations along with the universe and proceed as best he can. Furthermore—my second comforting reflection—the drive toward correlation and synthesis is a characteristic and widely shared impulse of our time. It has its roots deep in the reservoir of contemporary cultural energy. What the dynamism of an epoch impels in this manner, men will eventually accomplish. Obstacles may impede, but they cannot prevent, the effort, and all who participate in the effort are likely to make some contribution to its eventual success.

2

The synthesis of modern thought that is our goal might be compared to a mountain peak which we must attempt to scale in order to get above the divides between one mental valley and another. Our hope would be to reach an altitude from which we could perceive, in one vast panorama, what was experienced from below as a large number of separate worlds, each hidden from all the others and visible only to itself. Fortunately we do not have to start from the bottom of a valley. We already stand on one of the lower divides of the contemporary intellectual landscape. As Douglas Morgan's article implied, the two spheres of art and of psychology are now in such active communication with each other that we can comprehend them both within the single wider vista of psycho-critical thought. Details of many kinds present themselves for further study, but the basic correlation between the two fields is already an established fact. We can take that correlation for granted and turn our thoughts toward higher altitudes.

When we attempt to scale the ridges surrounding the combined artistic-aesthetic-psychological field of thought, we begin to encounter difficulties. It is true that there have long been traditional links between art and some other subjects, particularly history and philosophy. The field of art is itself a compositive, uniting its own history with its creative and critical aspects. Theoretically, the history of art has always recognized itself as a phase of history in general. It has accepted a twofold objective: first to restore historical order to the forms of art themselves; secondly to study the relationship of those forms to the life and thought of the societies that produced them.

These principles are sound, but the application of them has usually been one-sided. The historical classification of art forms has presented such intricate problems that it has frequently absorbed the entire attention of the art historian, leaving him with only a vague consciousness of the relationships between art and total history. And when he has attacked these broader relationships, attempting to correlate what we may call the two histories, he has usually been handicapped by surface concepts of the nature of history itself. Rarely has the art historian studied, evaluated, and applied the newer historical points of view such as the economic interpretation of history. Rarely, therefore, has he been able to give depth to his correlations.

I shall return to the subject of depth history below. Meanwhile the kind of results obtained by correlating art with surface history can be illustrated by such a work as Henry

Adams's *Mont-Saint-Michel and Chartres.* With the architectural sensitivity of a connoisseur, the historical knowledge of a student of medieval life, and an urbanity and charm that raise his work to a high literary level, Adams envelops medieval architecture in the colorful atmosphere of its historical background. We hear the pilgrims sing and see the people dragging cartloads of stone to the rising pile at Chartres. We learn the folk songs of the day and wrestle with its philosophy as embodied in the works of Abelard and Aquinas. We meet successive generations of French royalty and nobility, listen with William the Conqueror as Taillefer sings the *"Chanson de Rolland,"* feel the military thrusts and counterthrusts of William's invasion of England and the crusades.

All this reanimates the past in much the same way as a good historical novel or motion picture. Its contribution to our thinking, however, goes little beyond the recognition that the various manifestations of medieval culture are all imbued with a common spirit. "The 'Chanson' [de Rolland] is in poetry what the Mount is in architecture." [5] The *Summa Theologica* is the consummation of the Church Intellectual as the Cathedral of Amiens is that of the Church Architectural. In the one as in the other, "Every relation of parts, every disturbance of equilibrium, every detail of construction was treated with infinite labour, as a result of two hundred years of experiment and discussion among thousands of men whose minds and whose instincts were acute, and who discussed little else." The theological and social hierarchies in turn reflect each other. "The Virgin of Chartres was the greatest of all queens, but the most womanly of women . . . and her double character was sustained throughout her palace." "God the Father was the feudal seigneur, who raised Lazarus—his baron or vassal—from the grave, and freed Daniel, as an evidence of his power and loyalty; a seigneur who never lied, or was false to his word."

If one starts from any single pigeonhole of thought, it is an act of correlation thus to realize that medieval architecture, literature, philosophy, religion, and social structure reveal certain common characteristics. But in terms of the universe, it is at best an elementary act, like that of a child raising itself for its first steps. It is descriptive, not analytical. The only principle or procedure which we can derive from it is that of taking the various aspects of any given culture, comparing them one with the other, and pointing out what they have in common. This still leaves us without any basic means of interpreting the culture or correlating it with the totality of human knowledge and experience.

The deeper question is *why* Gothic culture should exhibit

the particular characteristics which all of its manifestations share in common; *why* Gothic art, thought, and life differ in the ways they do from those of other cultural epochs. In more general terms, the question becomes one of trying to discover what laws govern cultural activity and determine the nature of its products. This question writers like Adams do not even raise. When the question *is* raised, it appears that the answer must be sought by correlating the forms of cultural expression with an understanding of mental processes such as we get from psychology, and with an understanding of social processes such as we get from history, sociology, and economics. These larger correlations, for the most part, are still to be made. Hence it seems to me that the links between art and history, though old, are still superficial. We are here faced with a task, not with an adequate working basis, of correlation.

Somewhat the same, I believe, can be said of the links between art and philosophy. Dr. Munro has already provided a comprehensive analysis of this aspect of our subject.[6] I shall content myself with the reminder that while philosophy can help us in the quest for synthesis, if it is willing to share the hardships of the way, it does not provide any ready-made solution to our problems. This is so for several reasons.

If we think of philosophy in the narrower sense as certain inherited systems of thought, then from the correlational standpoint the inheritance is too narrow. Most systems of philosophical aesthetics are not well integrated even as between philosophy and art, for the philosophers in most cases have only a limited knowledge of, or interest in, art. "There has always been, and still is, a great gulf between philosophical aesthetics and the arts themselves. A person may study the former for years in an American philosophy department, without having to examine a single work of art." [7] Obviously this is not a balanced correlation between two fields of thought, but a projection of itself by the one upon what it uncritically assumes to be the other. Furthermore—though here exceptions can be found—the inherited systems are primarily rationalistic, lacking adequate integration with recent knowledge of subrational mental processes, and primarily individualistic, lacking integration with recent advances in the social sciences.

But even assuming, as some readers may wish to maintain, that we possess a philosophical inheritance satisfactory in its relations to art and to other fields, there will still be constant need of revisory correlational activity. Among ideas there is always a class that might be called the *nouveaux vrais*. Like the *nouveaux riches* of society, these upstarts are disturbing to the order within which they evolve, but they are nevertheless destined to play a large part in shaping its future. Philosophy must adapt itself to them in the one case, as must government in the other, or neither can survive. In this adaptive and creative sense, which Whitehead calls the "speculative" as opposed to the "critical" approach to the subject,[8] philosophy may be conceived as a perpetual awareness of changing reality and a perpetual effort to discover principles of unity within the totality of changing knowledge. So conceived, philosophy ceases to be a system and becomes a search for system— precisely that search for correlation and synthesis which now concerns us.

Various philosophers have helped and are helping us along the way. To mention but a few examples, Bergson and Whitehead have both done much to co-ordinate disparate fields of knowledge and to stimulate contemporary correlational thinking. DeWitt Parker indicated some of the links between art and psychoanalysis twenty-five years ago in *The Analysis of Art* (1926) and Susanne Langer has given us an illuminating study of symbolism and "the essentially transformational nature of human understanding" in *Philosophy in a New Key* (1942). But no philosopher or philosophy has given, or can give, us a final and unalterable synthesis because the fields of knowledge and experience are ever changing and widening and the philosophical pursuit of the "active novelty of fundamental ideas"[9] must continue to follow them. Conversely all who labor at problems of synthesis are engaged with philosophy-in-the-making, even though their academic hoods may not happen to be dyed the philosophic hue.

As I see it, then, we have a working correlation between the creative, critical, and historical aspects of the study of art on the one hand, and the study of psychology on the other; we have less adequate links with general history, and a kind of marching companionship with the creative side of philosophy. From there on out the trail toward synthesis is where we can find it.

3

The major barrier confronting us is the sharp division between our traditional individualistic approach to art and an equally possible social or cultural approach. Broadly speaking, the vast preponderance of Western criticism and aesthetics has assumed as axiomatic that the creation, contemplation, and analysis of art are activities to be explained in terms of the impulses, capacities, and responses of individuals. If there has been any recognition of the importance of collective and cultural forces, it has usually been incidental and has remained rudimentary. The point is so important for our discussion that I must elaborate somewhat upon it.

As early as the sixteenth century, Vasari was accepting the

individualistic assumption. Giotto "alone—although born amidst incapable artists, and at a time when all good methods in art had long since been entombed beneath the ruins of war —yet, by favour of Heaven, he, I say, alone succeeded in resuscitating art, and restoring her to a path that may be called the true one. And it is in truth a great marvel, that from so rude and inapt an age, Giotto should have had the strength to elicit so much." [10] In Vasari's eyes the individual Giotto was the prime mover in the whole artistic motivation of the Renaissance—a conception which still echoes down our historical corridors.

Rationalistic criticism and aesthetics, as well as more recent psychological studies, have all tended to perpetuate what is essentially the same point of view. To cite a contemporary connoisseur and critic, Lionello Venturi, "all other categories of the laws of art, of kinds, of types fall to the ground, and the only reality of art is the personality of the artist, as manifested in his works of art." [11] One of our contemporary aestheticians, Louis Flaccus, in contrasting the different effects produced by different artists in treating the theme of the Laocoön, asks why "tragedy and pathos are so arrestingly present" in some of the examples and yet "are all but absent in El Greco's painting. If Michelangelo had painted the picture, they would have been there. The reason must lie in personal preferences and attitudes." [12]

In interpreting the so-called aesthetic types—the sublime, the beautiful, and others—aestheticians have accepted personal perceptive reactions as their primary basis. To quote again from Flaccus's useful summary of the subject, "The sublime, like the tragic, is an imaginative adventure; and, like the tragic, it is often an intensely emotional experience. We are roused, startled, swept off our feet. Intensity of feeling may, however, be lacking; there is none of it in the sublime indecencies of Aristophanes. There is exhilaration in venturing; a sense of expanded life and of stretching to meet its startling possibilities. There is, too, a sense of freedom." [13] The analysis continues to greater length but remains within the sphere of personal reactions. The study of aesthetic types, as it has come down to us, is a dissection of the individual's aesthetic experience, and a classification of its possible varieties and of the stimuli which occasion them.

More recent psychological approaches remain, to all intents and purposes, within the same individualistic frame of reference. This is so whether they involve the experimentalist gathering statistical data on individual responses and testing individual aptitudes, the Gestaltist analyzing the mechanisms of individual perception, or the psychoanalyst probing the depths of the individual consciousness and unconsciousness.

To pause only for an example of the psychoanalytical type, Freud interpreted the work of Leonardo in terms of the artist's illegitimate birth, early absence of a father, resultant mother-fixation, tendency toward homosexuality, and similar effects of personal childhood conditioning.[14] To such conditioning Freud attributes the fact, for instance, that Leonardo painted a "Madonna and Child with St. Anne" rather than the more usual Holy Family group of the child with its mother and father. The child shares the picture with two women: a symbolical reflection of Leonardo's double experience of motherhood. He was brought up first by his true mother, secondly—after adoption into his father's family—by the foster mother who was his father's wife. The omission of the father-image from the picture stems from the absence of a father in Leonardo's infantile experience and his consequent exclusive attachment to his mother. And above all the smile with which the two women, and especially the St. Anne, are regarding the child is the dream-fulfillment of Leonardo's mother-fixation. Left, during his earliest years, "to the tender seduction" of an unmarried mother "whose only consolation he was," the boy was "kissed by her into sexual prematurity." [15] The solicitous smile of his mother remained throughout his life a repressed but haunting and creatively potent fantasy. To it, if we accept Freud's suggestion, we owe the mysterious smiles, not only of the women in the picture mentioned above, but also those of the "Mona Lisa" and of female heads shown in a number of Leonardo drawings.

Certain psychoanalytical writers like Dr. Harry B. Lee have criticized this psycho-biographic, or "psychographic" approach, but their proposals, as I understand them, still deal with art in terms of individual experience. "Contemplative artistic activity is not evoked by an outer stimulus, but by an inner one: an unconscious sense of guilt over hatreds so strong that judgment cannot cure. The values of this experience for the individual are healing and ethical; they derive from its power to convert certain discords within his being into peace. He seeks it in order to liquidate an unconscious sense of guilt over destructiveness." [16]

To repeat in summary what I suggested as a preamble to this part of our discussion, most Western thinking and writing on art, whatever its particular angle of approach, has accepted individuality and personal influence as the foundation alike for creative activity and for aesthetic sensitivity. One may add, of course, that most of these systems of thought, whether critical, aesthetic, psychological or other, involve certain social implications. The distinction between a "legitimate" and an "illegitimate" child, with resultant effects upon the conditioning of particular children, has no inherent existence within the nature of a child himself. It is a distinction determined by social *mores*. It varies widely from culture to culture, and consequently affects individuals only in relation to the particular culture into which they happen to be born. If Leonardo's illegitimate birth played an important part in shaping his creative personality, then in the last analysis the formative influences at work were social, not personal. Similarly behind all the other constituents of individualistic philosophies of art there are social corollaries, but these corollaries have usually remained dormant. Western thought since the Renaissance has not been a soil favorable to their growth.

It is true that we have had some exponents of less personally and more culturally motivated conceptions of art. Winckelmann opened the way for a more social orientation two centuries ago when he ascribed the genius of Greek art less to the traits of individual Greeks than to circumstances of Greek culture and environment. "The superiority which art acquired among the Greeks is to be ascribed partly to the influence of climate, partly to their constitution and government, and the habits of thinking which originated therefrom, and, in equal degree also, to respect of the artist, and the use and appreciation of art." [17] Hippolyte Taine in his *Philosophy of Art* also stressed environmental factors as the dominant ones in conditioning styles of art.

Such socially or culturally oriented thinkers have, nevertheless, been exceptional in our tradition. As a consequence their work has remained relatively elementary as compared to our elaborations of the individualistic axiom. Unless I am mistaken, we have to go back to Thomas Aquinas for any monumental and, in its epoch, commandingly influential analysis of experience which is nonindividualistic in its basic assumptions. In that case the superindividual forces are conceived in theological, rather than in philosophical or scientific terms, and are only incidentally related to art and aesthetics. It might also be observed that our few more recent exponents of the cultural approach, such as Winckelmann and Taine, have tended to stress social factors in comparative isolation from individual ones, rather than to integrate the one with the other.

Now there are a number of considerations, some internal to the study of art, some external to it, which make progress toward universal horizons difficult in direct proportion to the degree in which we ignore or underestimate social factors. On the critical plane, as applied to the study of specific works of art, we discover that many of the analyses based on individualistic premises are limited in their scope. Thus Freud, in his discussion of the Leonardo "Madonna with St. Anne," mentions only three details: the absence of Joseph, the presence of the two women, and the smiles which they are directing toward the child. Important as these details may be, illuminating as is Freud's interpretation of them, they are nevertheless to the totality of the work only as three leaves to the foliage of a full-blown tree.

All three of the elements singled out for discussion are aspects of subject matter. Color, design, medium, technique, and style receive no mention in the analysis, though they play vital parts in the constitution of the work of art. And even within the realm of subject matter Freud ignores more than interprets. He gives no consideration to the distinctive features of the foreground, costumes, and background, to the disposition of the figures, or to the degree of realism with which the figures are represented. In short, Freud examines, not the work of art as a whole, but a few of its details which happen to show through his particular instrument of examination. Yet what matters most for the problems of art criticism and aesthetics is not this or that detail of a work, but its embracing and identity-giving totality.

More recent and artistically better informed exponents of psycho-criticism have overcome this particular limitation in considerable measure. Readers of the *Journal of Aesthetics* will recall Rudolf Arnheim's study of Henry Moore [18] and Frederick Wight's essays on both Moore and Goya.[19] Arnheim approaches art from the angle of the Gestalt psychologist, Wight from the psychographic point of view. Neither author takes any cognizance of social or historical forces, yet both deal with relatively comprehensive aspects of the work they discuss. Individualistic premises, therefore, do not inevitably lead a critic into the first limitation which sometimes results from them: that of diverting his attention from an artistic totality to some of its component details.

More difficult for the individualistic approaches to handle are certain facts that confront us when we consider the work of any artist in its context of historical development. Our Leonardo painting, for example, was one of thousands of representations of the Madonna and Child, with various attendant figures, which were produced in Western Europe from the time of the Dark Ages through the Middle Ages to the Renaissance and then, with diminishing energy, down to the present day. If we observe a comprehensive and consecutive series of such paintings, we recognize that there is a consistent evolution of artistic style permeating the entire sequence. Successive examples do not wander from abstraction to realism and back again in unpredictable fluctuations of individual creative impulse or public taste. On the contrary they reveal a slow cumulative movement toward realism that can easily be followed from the eighth to the seventeenth centuries, a persistent realistic momentum for another century or two and then, in recent times, a reverse trend away from realism toward conventionalization, abstraction, and fantasy.

Long-range historical developments of this kind antedate the birth of individual artists and continue after their death. Obviously the individual Leonardo cannot have determined artistic trends which began centuries before he was born. Obviously also, his individual creative effort, when it came, took its place in the line of development that was under way prior to his birth. He carried one pulsation farther than his predecessors, a movement which had been steadily advancing before he became identified with it, which would have continued its advance whether or not he had become a part of it, and which did continue its advance in the work of hundreds of his contemporaries and successors. The psychic repercussions left by Leonardo's experience in childhood, whatever sense of guilt he may have had, his personal aptitudes for manual, intellectual, and aesthetic activity: these and other aspects of his individuality may well explain the variations which he played upon the inherited traditions of European art, but they cannot explain what is vastly more inclusive and fundamental—the force and direction of those traditions. The same statement could be made of Goya, Picasso, Henry Moore, or any other artist.

In short, the history of art confronts us with realities for which I can find no adequate explanation in terms of any of the approaches based primarily upon the individualistic axiom. Much of what those systems maintain is undoubtedly true. We are not obliged to contradict the aesthetician's analysis of individual reactions, the Gestaltist's analysis of the mechanisms of individual perception, or the psychoanalyst's analysis of childhood conditioning or guilt complexes; but we *are* obliged, if our goal is synthesis, to recognize them as limited departmental or compartmental systems of thought. None of them separately, nor all of them together, can provide the foundation for maximum correlation and synthesis. None nor all of them can solve the more comprehensive, the more truly philosophical, problems of art and of aesthetics. To reach such ends they must be interrelated with each other and, more important and more difficult, they must be interrelated with phases of thought at present entirely foreign, and in some cases seemingly contradictory, to them.

The territory foreign to them—in a sense their antithesis or balancing opposite—is primarily that of the social sciences. It was these sciences which I had in mind in referring above to "external" sources of evidence regarding the limitations of individualistic philosophies of art. While some of us, in the field of art, have been pushed by our own problems to a realization that there must be powerful social factors at work in the creation of art and in the aesthetic reactions which people have to it, large numbers of scholars have been at work studying social phenomena. They have already developed an impressive body of knowledge and they are rapidly extending it. For a thinker today to conjecture on the nature of cultural forces without reference to the information accumulated by sociology, ethnology, anthropology, and related fields, would be as juvenile performance as if he were to conjecture on the nature of mind without consulting any of the branches of psychology.

And when we turn to the social sciences for their contributions to an understanding of art and aesthetics, we find at once that any inclinations we may have had to doubt the completeness of individualistically based philosophies of art is strongly confirmed. Sociologists have concluded that the very cornerstone of the individualistic axiom, the individual personality itself, is less a self-contained individualistic phenomenon than a cultural one. They have called attention to the need for "understanding how the newborn individual is molded into a social being. Without this process of molding, which we call 'socialization' . . . society could not perpetuate itself beyond a single generation and culture could not exist. Nor could the individual become a person; for without the ever-repeated renewal of culture within him there could be no human mentality, no human personality." [20]

These assertions are reinforced by studies of "wolf children" and other individuals who have been deprived of socialization; deprived, in other words, of what we ordinarily conceive under such terms as family care, community influence, and education. Of one such case, "Anna," it is reported that at six years of age she "could not talk, walk, or do anything that showed intelligence. She was completely apathetic, lying in a limp, supine position and remaining immobile, expressionless, and indifferent to everything. She was believed to be deaf and possibly blind. . . . She of course could not feed herself or make any move in her own behalf. Here, then, was a human organism which had missed nearly six years of socialization. Her condition shows how little her purely biological resources, when acting alone, could contribute to making her a complete person." [21]

Such would have been Giotto, Leonardo, Henry Moore, had they been left, or largely left, to what was born within themselves. Such would be we contemporary critics and aestheticians, had we been subjected to the same circumstances. Obviously if what we think of as our individualities is important, it is not self-contained or self-explanatory. It is a gift which society has made to us. The particular form in which any of us has it is in large part a result of the particular society, and the particular strata, institutions, and traditions of society, by which our particular socialization has been affected. It would seem, then, to be a foregone conclusion that this society, those strata, institutions, and traditions, must receive careful study in any comprehensive analysis of our artistic productions, our aesthetic experiences, and our critical and aesthetic theories.

To sum up our present bearings we may say that while students working within the art-aesthetics-psychology area have focused their thought mainly on factors related to individuality, the social sciences have been giving new emphasis and importance to the *collective* aspects of cultural life. It would seem that these new frontiers of social knowledge are as pregnant for an understanding of art and aesthetics as is psychology, that they hold the correctives for the overemphasis on individualism in our recent thinking, and that the chief obstacle to the further unification of thought today is the intellectual great divide between the individualistic and the collective philosophies of life and of culture. Our next problem is to search out ideas or principles that may assist us in scaling this divide.

4

Two aspects of recent thought were particularly suggestive to me in my personal search for unifying principles, though neither one, I believe, quite takes the final step. One is an extension of psychology and thus approaches the center from the side of individualism; the other moves in the opposite direction from the field of social studies. I refer in the first instance to Carl Jung's concept of the "collective unconscious" and in the second to the economic interpretation of history. Let us consider these two ideas in order.

Most psychologists, and indeed most of the contributions of Jung and Freud, give us little help with the ultimate problems of synthesis since, as we have seen, they limit themselves so largely to the psychic phenomena of individual life. In the main, their work constitutes one of the areas to be synthesized rather than a basis of synthesis. But Jung's theory of the collective unconscious brings us—at any rate it was stimulus that brought me—in sight of new and broader psychological horizons.

The very phrase "collective unconscious," with magical inclusiveness, spans the barrier between the two main worlds of thought that we have been considering. Insofar as it involves the unconscious, it has a basis in psychology, and psychology, as we know, is in easy communication with the individualistic aspects of the study of art, aesthetics, and other subjects. Insofar, on the other hand, as the concept involves a *collective* aspect, it suggests possible connections with the social and cultural realities which have been the concern of history and the social sciences. This is certainly leading us in the direction we need to go.

Jung based his concept upon the discovery that the mental imagery studied by psychoanalysts is not an endless propagation of individual fantasies lacking any common bonds of genus and species. On the contrary it reveals recurrent types which "present themselves in the form of mythological themes and images, appearing often in identical form and always with striking similarity among all races; they can also be easily verified in the unconscious material of modern man." [22] These recurrent forms of mental imagery, Jung calls "archetypes" or "primordial images." He attributes them to the activity of psychic dispositions left by the totality of past racial experience. "The unconscious, regarded as the historical background of the psyche, contains in concentrated form the entire succession of engrams [imprints], which from time immemorial have determined the psychic structure as it now exists. These engrams may be regarded as function-traces which typify, on the average, the most frequently and intensely used functions of the human soul." [23] It is these "function-traces" or function-dispositions that reveal themselves in primordial imagery.

The collective unconscious might thus be described as an inherited disposition toward predetermined psychic reactions and preconditioned forms of accompanying mental imagery. A particular archetypal reaction emerges in an individual when he finds himself in circumstances corresponding to those which, on thousands of earlier occasions, left their imprint upon the psychic inheritance transmitted to him by his ancestors. In other words Jung's theory provides a means of interpreting certain psychological experiences and their cultural expressions in terms of a prenatal racial conditioning of the psyche, a conditioning which is presumably more profound and far-reaching in its effects than the restricted childhood conditioning of the individual.

Jung and his followers pursued their studies of the collective unconscious chiefly in terms of the literary material of dream and myth. There is, however, no reason to suppose that the principle cannot be generalized and applied, among other things, to the plastic imagery of visual art. Primitive, archaic, and other types of artistic conception also occur with "striking similarity among all races"; they also can "easily be verified" in the experiences and productions of modern man. It seems reasonable to assume that these recurrent categories of visual conception, like the literary ones of mythological subject matter, may be manifestations of archetypal experiences.

The participation of many individual artists in a common collective unconscious could go far toward explaining such cultural phenomena as the unity of period styles. The realism of the late Middle Ages and the Renaissance, instead of stemming from the personal influence of Giotto or any other individual, might mark the emergence into consciousness and gradual clarification of a primordial mode of vision to which all the artists of the epoch were similarly disposed. One frog peeps first in the spring but the others which subsequently join the chorus do so, not because the first one peeped, but because they are all disposed toward peeping by a common inheritance. No amount of peeping will convince the turtle that it ought to participate in the manifestation.

If Giotto has any influence on most artists today it is an influence *away* from realism, not toward it. Contemporary vision finds its affinities among the conventions which Giotto was discarding rather than the naturalistic goals that he pursued. The work of an individual artist, it would seem, can influence the formation of a period style only to the degree in which it satisfies an emergent cultural necessity. If we ask what force, at any given time and place, determines the nature of the cultural necessity, a possible answer would be the collective unconscious.

Jung's conception certainly provides a suggestive approach to some of the problems of historical criticism that have eluded solution on individualistic grounds. If I follow him adequately, however, even his system of thought stops short of complete synthesis. He proposes an extension of depth psychology from individualistic to collective areas of experience, but when we turn to his more exhaustive works for a close view of the collective factors involved, hoping that they will lead outward to the objective world, they sink back into the inner one. Here is a characteristic passage from one of Jung's most detailed studies of mythological imagery, *Psychology of the Unconscious,* a work which bears two subtitles, *A Study of the Transformations and Symbolisms of the Libido* and *A Contribution to the History of the Evolution of Thought.* The passage deals with certain poetic and mythological material which, Jung asserts, can only be interpreted as expressing an unconscious preoccupation with defecation, excrement, and anal eroticism.

In order to understand this particular material, Jung writes—

we must realize that when we produce from the unconscious the first to be brought forth is the infantile material long lost in memory. One must, therefore, take the point of view of that time in which infantile material was still on the surface. If now a much-honored object is related in the unconscious to the anus, then one must conclude that something of a high valuation was expressed thereby. The question is only whether this corresponds to the psychology of the child. Before we enter upon this question, it must be stated that the anal region is very closely connected with veneration. One thinks of the traditional faeces of the Great Mogul. An Oriental tale has the same to say of Christian knights, who anointed themselves with the excrement of the pope and cardinals in order to make themselves formidable. . . . The association of anal relations by no means excludes high valuation or esteem, as is shown by these examples, and is easily seen in the intimate connection of faeces with gold. Here the most worthless comes into the closest relation with the most valuable. This also happens in religious valuations. I discovered (at the time to my great astonishment) that a young patient, very religiously trained, represented in a dream the Crucified on the bottom of a blue-flowered chamber pot, namely, in the form of excrements. The contrast is so enormous that one must assume that the valuations of childhood must indeed be very different from ours. This is actually the truth. Children bring to the act of defecation and the products of this an esteem and interest which later on is possible only to the hypochondriac. We do not comprehend this interest until we learn that the child very early connects with it a theory of propagation. The libido afflux probably accounts for the enormous interest in this act.[24]

In such passages we follow Jung, culturally speaking, to the end of his analytical trail. Obviously we are not touching hands with the advance guards of history, sociology, and economics, with whom we are trying to establish contact. Instead we are back in the internal world of sexuality, libidinal transformations, and similar psychic figurations. Jung was too exclusively a psychologist to conceive of forces transcending those of psychology as such. His archetypes, as we have seen, correspond to racial dispositions transmitted from the past. The most that historical circumstances can do in Jung's system, as I follow it, is to reactivate the latent potentials of our inheritance. This does indeed imply some activating force or situation which is presumably external, but the possible external factors receive no penetrating attention. Jung found within his psychological world the implications of other worlds beyond; he looked toward the borders of those other worlds, but if he ever crossed over to them it was in surmise and intuition, not in scientific analysis. As a philosopher, we might say, he sensed totality; as a psychoanalyst he could not demonstrate it. Thus while he came close to the summit of the great divide, he never actually stood upon it.

What now of the efforts being made to reach the summit from the opposite side? The most advanced of these efforts, from the point of view of synthesis, appear to me to be those which have resulted in the economic interpretation of history. History may well be considered the mistress of the social sciences. It is social science projected through time along the entire course of human development. The breadth of its commission is implied by the derivation of its name from the Greek ἱστορία, "learning by inquiry."

Each of the contributory social sciences may be conceived as a segment of the historical totality, or as a section cut through it at some particular point and magnified for special study. Those who work with the segment extending from the biological emergence of man to the invention of writing give us anthropology in its more archaeological aspect—which is essentially preliterate history. Those who follow the course of literate civilizations give us history in the more restricted sense of the term. Those who cut sections through the structure of a civilization, exposing the intricacies of its sustaining organism, give us sociology and economics. Those who cut through the structure of primitive societies give us cultural anthropology. History in the broad sense binds all these specialties together within the continuing web of human social evolution. Thus conceived as an inclusive network of social sciences, it offers what is probably our most comprehensive and most accessible approach to the social aspects of the problem of synthesis.

But while this is potentially true, the actual study of history, like that of psychology, was long unbalanced by overemphasis on the factors manifest to surface observation. In the case of history these consisted in the main of political institutions, military conflicts, and commanding personalities. One of the results was the so-called "great-man theory of history" which, in the Emersonian phrase, saw an epoch, a movement, or an institution as "the shadow of one man." Vasari's estimate of the personal influence of Giotto is an example of this attitude as it reverberated through the minds of thinkers concerned with the history of art.

A different and more social philosophy of history dawned when writers like Voltaire and Montesquieu, and later Buckle, Marx, and Engels, perceived that there were significant correlations between certain types of cultural development and certain types of social and economic development. Organic history, depth history, thus emerged to become, in many respects, the social counterpart of depth psychology.

Freud made an interesting observation when he remarked that "psychoanalysis became 'depth-psychology'" at the moment when processes originally studied in their pathological deflections, and for therapeutic purposes, were recognized as extending to normal mental life and as relevant to problems in many other fields beside medicine.[25] So far as concerns the relationship between its more general and its more limited applications, depth history seems to have undergone the inverse evolution. The general conception emerged in the eighteenth century in the work of Voltaire and Montesquieu, Vico, Winckelmann, and other thinkers. The mid-nineteenth century saw both a relatively advanced formulation of the general theory and the beginning of its more specialized application to social problems—in a sense, we might say, to social pathology. The former was achieved by Henry Thomas Buckle, the latter by Karl Marx and Friedrich Engels. Buckle's major work was his projected *History of Civilization in England,* the first and only two volumes of which, comprising an unfinished "General Introduction," appeared in 1857.[26] Neither Marx nor Engels ever produced a major work on their particular theory of economic determinism, that theory being incidental to their social concerns, but in 1859 Marx wrote the "classical" foundation for the Marxist development of the theory: the two-page outline of fifteen propositions contained in the Introduction to his *Criticism of Political Economy.*[27]

The thousand pages of Buckle's *History* reveal a heroic effort to correlate the interpretation of history with the new knowledge that was pouring into the European mind from biology, political economy, psychology, and other scientific sources. The result is not entirely satisfactory today because new knowledge has continued to increase so rapidly during the century since Buckle's death, and because his death occurred before he had crystallized his own conceptions. Yet no single work seems to have replaced Buckle's as a demonstration of the far-reaching complexities of depth history. The extensiveness of his frame of reference may be judged from the fact that he saw history as a process governed by an interplay of material and mental forces; a process in which "from the beginning there has been no discrepancy, no incongruity, no disorder . . . but that all the events that surround us, even to the farthest limits of the material creation, are but different parts of a single scheme which is permeated by one glorious principle of universal and undeviating regularity."[28] In short Buckle saw history as controlled by natural laws and he sought for an understanding of those laws in terms of sociology, economics, and other sciences.

Marx's more categorical statement that the relations inevitably proceed from the material to the mental is given in the second, third, and fourth of his fifteen propositions:

(2) Conditions of production, taken as a whole, constitute the economic structure of society—this is the material basis on which a superstructure of laws and political institutions is raised and to which certain forms of political consciousness correspond. (3) The political and intellectual life of society is determined by the mode of production, as necessitated by the wants of material life. (4) It is not men's consciousness that determines the forms of existence, but, on the contrary, the social forms of life that determine consciousness. [29]

The relative influence exerted by Buckle and Marx illustrates the complexity of the history of thought and at the same time, no doubt, its deep involvement with social and economic forces. Developed purely as learning, Buckle's monumental effort has had comparatively little effect upon learning. A century has passed without major advances in the conception of depth history at which he had arrived, and with relatively little activity in applying that conception to critical ends. Many contemporary historians, like Toynbee, and most contemporary art historians as well, still proceed from narrower foundations than those which Buckle provides. The reason may lie partly in the sheer intellectual difficulty of handling a frame of reference which involves, not one field of knowledge alone, but the interplay of many different fields. But there are probably subconscious reasons as well; our dominantly individualistic philosophy of life has perhaps made us averse to exploring and applying the social implications of depth history.

By way of contrast the formulations of Marx, narrower and more casual than those of Buckle but supported by social movements which encouraged their development, stimulated a wealth of historical and critical literature and became the immediate vehicle for world-wide intellectual controversy involving world-wide awareness of, and reaction to, the more general trend away from surface history toward depth history.

We need not concern ourselves with either the technical or the political disputes between the Marxists and their opponents. In some broad sense that is above dispute, depth history has established itself as one of the important intellectual developments of recent times. An increasing number of historians are now aware that no period can be adequately studied exclusively in terms of its surface phenomena such as military events or leading individuals. They are aware that such phenomena are related to obscure and complex processes of historical metabolism involving the whole range of man's cultural, social, and economic existence. Interdependencies have been recognized that can extend from such physical factors as climate and natural resources, through states of technological development, economic activity, and social organization, to political and military events and to all those cultural phases of life which include art and aesthetics. Again, as in the case of Jung's theory of the collective unconscious—perhaps even more so—we glimpse a spectrum that extends through all the colors of existence from material preconditions to historical conditions and on to their cultural manifestations.

As already suggested, specific applications of the theory to art and aesthetics have chiefly been made by Marxists and have therefore represented the narrower concept of economic determinism rather than the broader one of depth history in general. Undoubtedly they have contributed valuable insights and observations. While I cannot claim to be widely acquainted with this literature, I must recognize a debt to what I take to be one of its cornerstones, Plekhanov's *Art and Society*. Correlating various forms of literature and art with the social conditions under which they arose, Plekhanov arrived at some thought-provoking conclusions. Thus he transposed to a new field of relevance the controversy between the exponents of art for art's sake and the utilitarian view that art should express and subserve social values. Instead of seeking to disprove one of these points of view, Plekhanov suggests that each may be a natural expression of certain relations between artists and the society in which they live. The question then becomes one, not of showing that one view is right and the other wrong, but of finding out what kinds of relations between art and society give rise to each of them. The answer brought forward by Plekhanov on the basis of a number of historical examples is summarized in the two following statements: "The tendency of artists and those concerned with art to adopt an attitude of art for art's sake arises when a hopeless contradiction exists between them and their social environment." "The so-called utilitarian conception of art, that is, the tendency to regard the function of art as a judgment on the phenomena of life and a readiness to participate in social struggles, develops and becomes established when a mutual bond of sympathy exists between a considerable section of society and those more or less actively interested in artistic creation." [30]

Plekhanov published his book nearly half a century ago, in 1905. Subsequent developments have put us in position to modify details, but the basic principles appear to hold and the general approach to be a fertile one. Along with, and in a sense counterbalancing, the writings of the psychoanalysts, this approach has helped to open up new fields for study and new paths of correlation. It was through Plekhanov's discussion that I personally first came to realize that the creative impulse of an individual artist might be, not the bottom of the creative well, but a connecting channel through which a style of art could be motivated by a condition of society.

But if the potentialities of depth history for a fuller understanding of art and aesthetics appear to be great, and its critical contributions already considerable, it still seems to me to be limited in two respects. One may be regarded merely as the immaturity of its youth and in that respect, to paraphrase the French expression, the defect of its value. As yet it has been only spasmodically applied to selected cultural movements. There has, to my knowledge been little comprehensive effort to study the arts and other cultural expressions of given civilizations in close correlation with all the depth changes that went on during long consecutive spans of their history. Instead the tendency has been to select a given artist or movement, or to accept miscellaneously from history various artists or movements that rose to contact with the critic's thought. Plekhanov deals mainly with the French literature and art of the eighteenth and nineteenth centuries, and with Russian equivalents, but he touches on primitive, Byzantine, Renaissance, modern, and other styles. To touch is easy; to establish, difficult. Before depth history can make its maximum contribution to the philosophy of art, the relations between history and culture will have to be followed through in more intensive, comprehensive, and consistent ways. Scholars will have to grapple with the problem of correlating, not a few attractive links between the arts and history, but the whole complex cultural and historical totalities that comprise the life of the societies involved.

I have seen only one work of the kind just mentioned. That is Frederick Antal's *Florentine Painting and Its Social Background*.[31] In 380 pages of text and on the basis of a detailed analysis of several hundred specific works of art, 215 of which are reproduced for the reader's scrutiny, Antal comes to grips at close range with some of the more detailed problems of historical determinism. No one can follow his discussion without receiving a new and more realistic consciousness of the connections between what went on inside Florentine picture frames and what went on inside the city's woolen mills and banking houses. The book seems destined to a permanent place in our literature as one of the pioneering landmarks of a new way. It also, I believe, leaves room for growth in certain respects, to one of which I shall refer below.

While mentioning Antal's study as the only intensive work of its kind which I have seen in print, I may say that my forthcoming *The Collective Dream in Art* * will comprise another effort in this direction. Less exhaustively but more extensively than Antal, I have taken for study the periods of western European history that extend from Neolithic to Gothic times and have attempted to correlate their main cultural and historical developments, extending the inquiry from economic determinism proper to my own more inclusive psycho-historical frame of reference.

These more intensive and, we may assume, more exact studies in historical correlation will no doubt increase in number, thus gradually solidifying the somewhat sketchy treatment of early writers like Plekhanov. But there is a second limitation of economic determinism which, from the theoretical point of view, seems to me more serious and more permanent. That is an inadequate explanation of *how* material preconditions can affect the nature of the cultural expressions which they are believed to determine.

The materialist critic, accepting economic determinism as an axiom, observes particular forms of art and accompanying types of social condition and states that the one is a result of the other. Empirically he appears often to be right; theoretically he can provide no demonstration that he is so. The philosophy of art for art's sake *might* conceivably be an outgrowth of forces as yet undiscovered. The same can be said of the variations of Florentine pictorial style studied by Antal. We cannot accept these cultural developments as proven to be the results of their suggested social causes until we are shown by what means such causes can produce these particular philosophical and artistic results. To the best of my knowledge of their work, the economic determinists have largely evaded this problem.

Stated more generally the problem is this. What are regarded as economic determinants cannot in themselves produce the forms of cultural expression that are attributed to them. Obviously an industrial system or a social condition cannot change itself into a philosophy or a style of painting by a physical metamorphosis like that of a caterpillar turning into a butterfly. All that the economic determinants can be said to do, in reality, is to affect the spirits of the men who create philosophies and works of art. Between the determinants and their expressions lies a transformer that converts the cultural potentials of the one into the cultural actualities of the other. This transformer, immediately centered in the creative impulse of the philosopher or artist, can in its general nature be only one thing, and that is the human psyche with all its flexible

* [Cambridge: Harvard University Press, 1957.]

interplay of perception and thought, impulse, intuition, and emotion.

The branch of knowledge that deals specifically with this psychic transformer is, of course, psychology. It is here, I believe, that the economic determinists have fallen short of an ultimate theoretical basis for synthesis. They have failed to make adequate use of recent psychological developments. They have recognized in a general way the existence of "intermediate links" between material determinants and their expressions, they have even recognized these links as primarily mental in their nature. But they have attempted no intensive study of them. This is the relatively unexplored borderland of their particular intellectual territory.

Now psychic transformation is actually a process of such depth and complexity that scientists have only lately begun to fathom it. It often works by devious ways and in an unconscious manner, producing exactly the *opposite* results from those which surface interpretation might lead us to expect. Only in the light of all that is known about it, only by taking full advantage of the findings of psychology in general and of depth psychology in particular, can we hope to understand so intricate an activity, and only to the degree in which we understand it can we be certain that any given preconditions are actually the cause of their assumed expressions.

In summary we might say that while psychoanalysis, as extended by Jung into a collective sphere, stopped short of our intellectual great divide on one side, the materialist conception of history stopped short of it on the other. It is as if two exploring parties were both within communicating distance of the top, each with scientific data on its own slope and with a vague awareness that there must be an opposite slope, but both unable to reach the top and merge their discoveries in a comprehensive description of the whole two-sided range. Personally I am convinced that both depth psychology and depth history have revealed important aspects of truth, that each is at the same time limited by its lack of what the other possesses, and that the final problem of synthesis—final at least for our present inquiry—is that of integrating the one with the other.

5

If a principle that might serve as a theoretical bridge between depth psychology and depth history has been proposed in the annals of contemporary thought, I have not seen the proposal. But in my search for possible connecting links between the two fields, I did find a theoretical basis which seems to me to imply the necessary principle and to make possible its extraction and development. That basis is provided by Freud's work on the interpretation of dreams.[32]

Briefly, Freud conceived the known or "manifest" form of the dream as a symbolical and often distorted expression of a "latent content" (psychic motivating force, frequently unconscious), and this psychic generator of the dream could owe its nature at least in part to the "historical circumstances" of the dreamer's life. These circumstances could include all the objective conditions of the dreamer's waking intercourse with the world in which he lived. Analytically, the sequence would be followed back in the order just suggested from the manifest dream to the motivating psychic state and then to a discovery of the objective circumstances which engendered the psychic state. Formatively, creatively, the order would proceed in the opposite direction from circumstances to psychic state and to its expression in the imagery of the dream.

To illustrate one point of special importance to us, following the second or formative order, the realities of a dreamer's objective life might include such a material circumstance as an inadequate means of livelihood. This circumstance could induce negative psychic tensions of insecurity, fear, and frustration. Under the mental conditions of sleep (and to a less extent under other mental conditions such as those of waking reverie), the tensions could activate the imagination, generating one of those chains of mental imagery that we call a dream. The dream imagery would be such as to embody, sometimes realistically, sometimes symbolically through fantasy, the nature of the tensions giving rise to it and would therefore reflect, at second range, the nature of the circumstances that gave rise to the tensions.

If the dreamer were a farmer, our suggested circumstance of an inadequate means of livelihood might conceivably be due to the barrenness of the soil he was attempting to cultivate. Or if he were a primitive hunter living in an area with rich soil but poor game resources, it might be due to his lack of a technology suitable for the extraction of resources that were potentially available to him. Or if, at certain times in history, he were a serf working on the estate of a feudal overlord, it might be due to social conventions which allocated the major part of his production to someone other than himself. In these and countless other ways there could thus be an interdependence, an unbroken reality continuum, from material conditions (such as soil and natural resources) through cultural and social conditions (such as states of technological advancement or economic organization) to a psychic experience of life involving various degrees of fulfillment or frustration, and finally to the symbolical expression of that experience in the imagery of a dream.

In emphasizing the fact that material circumstances can thus play a part in helping to initiate the mental activities involved in dream-formation, I suspect that I am leading Freud a little further than he meant to go. Like Jung, he was a psychologist, not a psycho-technologist, and his ultimate basis for dreams remained in the internal psychic world of instinct, impulse, libido, and desire. But if Freud does not analyze the external environment of the psyche with anything like the energy and genius which he devotes to its internal reactions, he certainly recognizes that the psyche operates under the impact of external conditions. As one of the many references that could be cited in support of this statement, we need only recall that Freud describes the ego as "that part of the id which has been modified by proximity to the external world. . . . The ego has taken over the task of representing the external world for the id, and so of saving it; for the id, blindly striving to gratify its instincts in complete disregard of the superior strength of outside forces, could not escape annihilation." [33] The "outside forces" of the "external world" are implicit in Freudian as in all other systems of psychoanalysis, but they present another instance of the unexplored border zones by which any individual discipline is inevitably surrounded.

The relatively passive and unanalytical attitude of the psychoanalysts toward the historical and social circumstances under which the psyche operates has constituted one of the greatest limitations in the extension of depth psychology to cultural problems. It has resulted in forced attempts to solve on subjective and individualistic grounds, problems which in reality are in part objective and social. I gather from a recent conversation with a psychoanalyst [34] that some of the more recent, less orthodox, and I suspect more creative, schools of psychoanalytical thought regard overemphasis on subjectivity as a hindrance even to the practice of psychotherapy itself.

For our present purpose we need extract from the foregoing only this unquestionable minimum: Freud's theory implies, within the dreamer's experience, a continuum that can extend from material facts and social conditions to psychic states and their imaginative expressions. My proposal is that the recognition of such a continuum, and the three-level analytical framework upon which it is based, can be extended from the individual mental processes that produce dreams to the collective ones that produce cultures and that, by means of such an extension, we can span the existing barriers between depth psychology and depth history and so achieve the synthesis we are seeking.

In the terms of the proposed transposition of Freud's theory, cultural manifestations—styles of art and literature, systems of religions and philosophy—present themselves as forms of "manifest imagery"—as it were collective dreams. However solidly and permanently they may be imbedded in the physical structure of paintings or statues, however rigidly they may sometimes crystallize into cultural conventions and institutions, they are in their inception dynamic mental phenomena and can only be fully interpreted in terms of the mental energies and activities that gave rise to them.

The manifest cultural imagery—here we apply the second level of Freud's framework—emerges from and reflects an underlying "latent content" or generating reservoir of psychic energy and impulse. This motivating impulse is experienced in the first instance (more accurately, I should say in the *last* instance) by individuals, but, if exclusively individual in its source and relevance, can give rise only to minor creative expressions and will frequently appear eccentric when viewed culturally.

The culturally important individual, the one whom we regard as the *great* artist, poet, seer, or philosopher, will be one whose psychic faculties include an acute responsiveness to *collective* psychic states. His personal sensitivity will be receptive to latent, or as yet largely unconscious, states of collective intuition; particularly to those charges of collective confidence or apprehension that gather in cultural mentality as a result of the particular state and stage of historical destiny into which the given society is moving. The individual's stature as a cultural leader will depend in part upon the degree of his responsiveness to these collective psychic directives, in part upon his imaginative or intellectual capacity to transmute them into visual, literary, or other symbols.

The motivating psychic states will not be mere mental dispositions inherited from the past in the Jungian sense, though they will certainly be influenced both by the inward psychic and the outward cultural inheritances. Basically—the equivalent of the third level of Freud's dream theory—they will be immediate and dynamic reactions to objective historical circumstances. The instrumental circumstances, like the mental states which they engender, will in our case be primarily collective in their nature. They will be historical not only in the sense in which Freud uses the term, as pertaining to earlier stages of a particular development, but also in the larger sense involving the life cycle of societies. And the influential historical circumstances, conceived in the terms of depth history, will not be envisaged exclusively as wars, systems of government, or outstanding leaders. They will be recognized as including, indeed as in large part depending upon, the states of economic and social energy by means of which the given society is able to fortify itself, expand, and increasingly fulfill its aspirations, or through the failure of which it shrinks, collides with immovable obstacles, and suffers detrition or even, in extreme cases, annihilation.

If we accept such a chain of interrelationships, a work of art, which might come into being at one end of the chain, will embody conditioning influences which include those of individual psychology but which pass through individual psychology into social psychology, through social psychology into history with all its economic and sociological concomitants, and beyond history—if one wishes to press so far back—into the biological, geographical, geological, and other foundations of history.

By way of example let us return to one of those Gothic marvels, such as the Cathedral of Amiens, which Adams discussed in terms of architectural techniques and their contemporary equivalents in Gothic culture. Even had Villard de Honnecourt and the Commune of Amiens stood ready, there could have been no cathedral had there been no available deposits of rock suitable for building stone, had wind velocities in northern France been inimical to great sails of leaded glass, or had there been tropic intensities of solar heat to convert a glass enclosure into a suffocating furnace. Before man even existed, geological and geographical developments were setting a stage which in some parts of the earth included, in others excluded, the potentiality of Gothic architecture.

But even given such embryonic potentials as suitable materials and favorable climate, there could still be no cathedral without the growth of the necessary technological prerequisites. It took three thousand years to develop the building skills of western European man from Stonehenge to Amiens. Even more important, it took the same three thousand years and longer for Western man to evolve his economic and social potentials from the primitive agricultural village to the prosperous city-republic of the thirteenth century. Cathedral building, however ethereal its motives or effects, is a costly enterprise. A community can undertake it only if provided with abundant surplus wealth. In medieval Amiens this wealth was obtained in the main through the cultivation of a plant called *waide,* the industrial conversion of that plant into dye, and the commercial distribution of the dye to various centers of the European textile industry. These activities were possible to Amiens only as a result of earlier developments in the technology of agriculture, the techniques of weaving and dye-making, the establishment of continent-wide and intercontinental channels of commercial exchange, consequent opportunity for industrial specialization, and many other indispensable preconditions. In fact we can say that the whole evolution of Western culture formed another strand that had to wind its course up to a certain juncture before the cathedral-moment could arrive.

Most of these considerations are still in the nature of sub-structures to the artifact. Of the aesthetic qualities of the cathedral only one can be directly and rationally related to the factors thus far mentioned: the technical perfection achieved by Gothic architecture was undoubtedly an aspect of the advanced level of thirteenth-century European technology in general. But what of the other qualities that impress us in the cathedral and that play so large a part in what we might call its unique "dream essence"? How are we to define these qualities and how interpret them in the terms of our proposals?

The all-over aesthetic effect of a cathedral like that of Amiens has most frequently been identified by aestheticians with the category of the "sublime." Linked with the sublimity of the cathedral, indefinably overlapping with it and insep-arable from it, most observers refer to an effect of mystical exaltation. The central impulse of the Gothic epoch has often been described by some such phrase as "religious fervor" and we may accept such fervor as the major psychic directive of Gothic culture.

Religious enthusiasm has usually been accepted as a termi-nal. It has been regarded as in itself a sufficient explanation of Gothic culture; as a premise which it is unnecessary or im-possible to analyze. For us the religious enthusiasm of the Gothic epoch becomes an example of a collective psychic state. It is the second level, the level of latent content, in our analytical framework. And like other states of collective mentality, it presumably owed its existence, at this particular time in this particular part of the world, to the historical circumstances being undergone by the societies that experi-enced it. For an ultimate explanation of the cathedral as a sublime aesthetic and religious phenomenon, we must ac-cordingly descend to our third level and undertake a search-ing study of the depth history of Gothic life.

To make such a historical study in the present context is obviously impossible. I am undertaking to do so in some detail in the book already mentioned. To serve our immediate pur-pose in a few words, I may say that Gothic religious fervor appears to me to be the psychic accompaniment of the arrival of western European peoples at their first experience of a maturing civilization. Thirteenth-century city-states like Amiens, as many historians will testify, saw the emergence of these peoples into a degree of economic security, civic freedom, commercial and military expansiveness, which they had never previously known and which were to them deeply fulfilling experiences.

As a result of thousands of years of earlier uphill evolution, often staggered by the buffets of a nature as yet uncontrollable and by those of more advanced invaders, Gothic man had at last arrived at a collective power-summit on which he had mastered many of the essentials to his own security and fulfillment, and seemed on the way to mastering the world as he knew it. His sense of historical mastery distilled itself psychically into a spirit of collective exaltation. Fulfilled himself, he found the universe divine, and his sense of its divinity, like a rocket bursting into a shower of stars, overflowed in all his cultural creations. We see its mystical expressions in magnificent celebrations of the Mass, its intellectual expression in monumental theological philosophies, its military expression in chivalry and the crusades, its artistic expressions in soaring spires, lofty naves, radiant glass, and a wealth of sacred imagery in sculpture and painting. In addition, it had its musical, its literary, and other expressions.

Thus the cathedral and its most characteristic aesthetic effects, like that of sublimity, become for us manifestations of a state of collective mentality, and that mentality can be attributed to a network of historical circumstances leading back over the horizon of history to protohistorical forces. A small part of the identity of the cathedral as a work of art can be understood in terms of the individuals who commissioned and designed it. The greater part of its artistic identity can be understood only in terms of collective forces within the culture that produced it. Ultimately, philosophically, its determinants do not stop even at the limits of history. In moments of high intuition, when we grasp it as an emergent reality, the cathedral of the Middle Ages (and with it every other form of cultural expression) reveals itself as an outcome of forces within which the whole of existence—all time, all space—converges. Like the granite crests of the mountains, like the snow that may fall or the eagle that may light upon them, it is a product of the living universe, the universe at work.

And as all aspects of reality intermesh in the sequence of forces that gives rise to the work of art, so do all aspects of knowledge in any comprehensive analysis of it. Some characteristics of an artistic totality can be interpreted in terms of the insights afforded to us by individual psychology, but some can be adequately interpreted only through the findings of social psychology, and others only through those of history, sociology, economics, ethnology, or anthropology. To see the work through any one of these intellectual formulations alone is to see it partially. To see it partially is to see it "through a glass darkly," for the full light of knowledge is the white light of its totality, not the colored light of some component band of the intellectual spectrum into which it may be broken.

For practical purposes in interpreting a work of art or analyzing an aesthetic experience, it will never be necessary —indeed it would be impossible—to seek an intellectual understanding of every phase of the creative or aesthetic continuum. But insofar as understanding may be needed to illuminate a particular mystery or solve a particular problem, there is a fund of scientific knowledge available for correlation with every level of the conditioning sequence. And only as we take cognizance of at least the main contrasting masses of thought —only as we confront individualistic with collective considerations, psychic with materialistic ones—can we hope in any study to approach a balanced result.

The point of view which I have attempted to set forth gives an important place to psychological considerations, but it is not exclusively psychological. It gives an important place to historical, technological, and economic considerations, but it is not exclusively historical or materialistic. It assumes that equally serious attention must be given to both psychic *and* material factors, both individualistic *and* collective ones. Hence it seems appropriate to call this approach a "psycho-historical," "psycho-social," or "psycho-technic" one. A student who thinks in these terms is neither a psychologist, a historian, nor an economic determinist as such; he might be called a psycho-historian or psycho-technologist.

I am aware that even in so long an article as the present one, I have not been able to make a detailed, and have therefore perhaps failed to make a convincing, analysis of collective mentality and of the mechanisms through which it achieves cultural expression. I am aware also that I have given only scant illustration of the results to be expected from an application of the psycho-historical point of view. I should like to return to all the types of art and of theory that have been touched on in the course of our discussion—to the work of Giotto and of Leonardo, to that of Goya and Moore, to the question of aesthetic types and other phases of aesthetics. I believe that psycho-historical thinking carries implications for the study of all such subjects. However, it was not the aim of the present article to pursue the applications of the psycho-historical point of view, but rather to indicate the background out of which it evolved, and to offer the general scheme as basis for the synthesis of various branches of contemporary thought. The full unification of our existent and still expanding knowledge can easily absorb lifetimes of further thought and effort, but I hope that the psycho-historical theory will provide at least one of the systems of intercommunication along which such thought and effort can profitably travel.

NOTES

1. D. N. Morgan, "Psychology and Art Today: A Summary and Critique," *Journal of Aesthetics and Art Criticism*, Vol. IX, No. 2 (Dec. 1950). See above, pp. 279–98.
2. Ibid.
3. T. Munro, "Aesthetics as Science: Its Development in America," *JAAC*, Vol. IX, No. 3 (March 1951), pp. 172 and 185.
4. W. Abell, "Myth, Mind, and History," *JAAC*, Vol. IV, No. 2 (Dec. 1945), pp. 77–86.
5. Henry Adams, *Mont-Saint-Michel and Chartres* (Boston: 1913). The sentences which I quote are taken respectively from pp. 12, 380, 73, and 29.
6. T. Munro, op. cit., cf. particularly pp. 161–86.
7. T. Munro, op. cit., p. 171.
8. For Whitehead's discussion of the two approaches, see his lecture, "The Aim of Philosophy," in *Modes of Thought* (New York: 1938), pp. 233–8.
9. Ibid., p. 237.
10. Giorgio Vasari, *Lives of Seventy of the Most Eminent Painters, Sculptors and Architects*, edited and annotated by E. H. and E. W. Blashfield and A. A. Hopkins (New York: 1926), Vol. I, p. 48.
11. L. Venturi, *History of Art Criticism*, translated from the Italian by Charles Marriott (New York: 1936), p. 301.
12. L. Flaccus, *The Spirit and Substance of Art* (New York: 1926), p. 226.
13. Ibid., pp. 260–1.
14. S. Freud, *Leonardo da Vinci: A Study in Psychosexuality* (New York: 1947).
15. Ibid., pp. 113–14.
16. H. B. Lee, M.D., "The Values of Order and Vitality in Art," in *Psychoanalysis and the Social Sciences*, II, Geza Roheim, Managing Ed. (New York: 1950), p. 245.
17. J. Winckelmann, *The History of Ancient Art*, trans., G. Henry Lodge (Boston: 1872), 3 vols., Vol. II, p. 4. Cf. T. Munro, *The Arts and Their Interrelations* (New York: 1949), pp. 337–50, on "Individual and Cultural Factors in Creative Activity."

18. R. Arnheim, "The Holes of Henry Moore: On the Function of Space in Sculpture," *JAAC*, Vol. VII, No. 1 (Sept. 1948), pp. 29–38.

19. F. S. Wight, "The Revulsions of Goya: Subconscious Communications in the Etchings," *JAAC*, Vol. V, No. 1 (Sept. 1946), pp. 1–28, and "Henry Moore: The Reclining Figure," *JAAC*, Vol. VI, No. 2 (Dec. 1947), pp. 95–105.

20. K. Davis, *Human Society* (New York: Macmillan, 1949), p. 195.

21. Ibid., pp. 205–6.

22. C. G. Jung, *Psychological Types, or The Psychology of Individuation*, trans., H. G. Baynes (New York: 1926), p. 211. Passages dealing with the collective unconscious occur in most of Jung's works.

23. Ibid.

24. C. G. Jung, *Psychology of the Unconscious*, authorized translation, with introduction, by B. M. Hinkle (New York: 1949), pp. 210–11.

25. Sigmund Freud, *New Introductory Lectures on Psychoanalysis*, trans., W. J. H. Sprott (New York: 1933), p. 198.

26. For an integral reprint of Buckle's text with valuable recent annotations cf. H. T. Buckle, *Introduction to the History of Civilization in England*, new and revised edition with annotations and an introduction by John M. Robertson (London: n.d.).

27. Marx's propositions, both in the original German and in English translation, are reprinted, among other places, in K. Federn, *The Materialist Conception of History: A Critical Analysis* (London: 1939). Cf. pp. 1–3 and 255–6. Federn takes issue with the Marxist formulation of economic determinism. He brings forward some interesting rebuttals, but makes little positive contribution. More valuable, I believe, for the general student are the following historical and critical summaries: E. R. A. Seligman, *The Economic Interpretation of History* (New York: 2nd ed., revised 1907), H. See, *The Economic Interpretation of History*, translated and introduced by Melvin M. Knight (New York: 1929).

28. H. T. Buckle, op. cit., p. 902.

29. K. Federn, op. cit., p. 1.

30. G. V. Plekhanov, *Art and Society*, translated from the Russian, introduction by Granville Hicks (New York: 1936). Both quotations p. 48.

31. (London: 1947.) The work bears the subtitle: *The Bourgeois Republic Before Cosimo de' Medici's Advent to Power: XIV and Early XV Centuries.*

32. Cf. S. Freud, *The Interpretation of Dreams*, reprinted as Book II in *The Basic Writings of Sigmund Freud*, translated and edited, with an introduction, by Dr. A. A. Brill (New

York: 1938). A summary of the forementioned definitive statement was provided by Freud in Part II of his *General Introduction to Psychoanalysis*. Retrospective comments occur in Ch. i of Freud's *New Introductory Lectures on Psychoanalysis* and in his "Remarks on the Practice of Dream-Interpretation (1923)." The last-named reference appears in *The Yearbook of Psychoanalysis*, Vol. I, 1945. It is particularly important as including a late recognition by Freud of an exception to the wish-fulfillment aspect of his theory of dreams.

33. S. Freud, *New Introductory Lectures on Psychoanalysis*, p. 106.
34. My brother, Dr. Richard G. Abell of New York City.

* NOTES ON CONTRIBUTORS *

WALTER ABELL was for many years professor of art at Michigan State University. Among his writings are articles for encyclopedias and for journals of art and aesthetics, and the book *Representation and Form: A Study of Aesthetic Values in Representational Art* (1946). His major work, *The Collective Dream in Art* (Cambridge: Harvard University Press, 1957), was published posthumously.

HENRY DAVID AIKEN, born in Portland, Oregon, in 1912, was educated at Reed College, Stanford University, and Harvard University. He has taught philosophy at Columbia and at the University of Washington and is now professor of philosophy at Harvard. A frequent contributor to professional and literary journals, he edited *The Age of Ideology* in the Mentor Philosophers Series.

RUDOLF ARNHEIM, who was born in Berlin, Germany, in 1904, has been President of the American Society for Aesthetics. He is a member of the psychology faculty at Sarah Lawrence College and is visiting professor in psychology at the New School for Social Research in New York City. Professor Arnheim has been a Guggenheim Fellow and a Rockefeller Fellow, and during 1959–1960 he was a Fulbright Lecturer in Japan.

JACQUES BARZUN, Provost of the University and Dean of the Faculties of Columbia University, was born in Créteil, France, in 1907. After his early education in Paris, he came to the United States in 1920, when his father was on a diplomatic mission. Throughout his academic career he has been connected with Columbia University, where he is a professor in the Department of History. He has written, translated, and edited numerous books, among which are *Darwin, Marx, Wagner* (1941), *Teacher in America* (1945), *Berlioz and the Romantic Century* (1950), *The Energies of Art* (1956), and *The House of Intellect* (1959).

O. K. BOUWSMA, professor of philosophy at the University of Nebraska, was born in a "one-room white house" in Muskegon, Michigan, in 1898. He went to Calvin College and the University of Michigan; but his sense of humor and various other attitudes and habits of mind prevent him from supplying more of the conventional information for such a section on contributors as this.

KENNETH BURKE, was born in Pittsburgh, Pennsylvania, in 1897, and educated at Ohio State and Columbia Universities. He has published, since the middle twenties, fiction, translations, musical and literary criticism, and analyses of history and art as "symbolic action." Mr. Burke has lectured widely, and taught at the New School for Social Research, Bennington College, the University of Chicago, and elsewhere. He has received a Guggenheim fellowship, and the Dial award for distinguished service to American letters, among many honors. His list of books includes *Counter-Statement* (1931), *Permanence and Change* (1935), *The Philosophy of Literary Form* (1941), *A Grammar of Motives* (1945), and *A Rhetoric of Motives* (1950).

ANANDA K. COOMARASWAMY, late Curator of Indian Art at the Boston Museum of Fine Arts, was one of the great orientalists of recent times. Born in Colombo, Ceylon, in 1877, he was educated in England. He published extensively from 1906 on. Among his books are *Rajput Painting* (1916), *The Dance of the Shiva* (1918), *History of Indian and Indonesian Art* (1927), *Christian and Oriental Philosophy of Art* (1938), and *Hinduism and Buddhism* (1943). *The Transformation of Nature in Art* was first published in 1934, second edition 1935.

ROBERT CUMMING, editor of *The Journal of Philosophy*, was born in Sydney, Nova Scotia, in 1917. He was educated at Harvard, the University of Chicago, and New College, Oxford, where he was a Rhodes Scholar, 1938–1940. A liaison officer between French and American forces during World War II, he was several times decorated by both countries. In 1959 he was a Fulbright Research Fellow in Paris. Professor Cumming became Chairman of the Department of Philosophy at Columbia University in January 1961.

E(RNST) H(ANS) GOMBRICH, who is Professor of the History of the Classical Tradition at London University, and Director of the Warburg Institute, was born in Vienna in 1909. In 1936 he became a research assistant at the Warburg Institute; from 1950 to 1953 he was Slade Professor of Fine Art, at the University of Oxford. Among his numerous publications are *Caricature* (1940), *The Story of Art* (1950), and the distinguished *Art and Illusion: A Study in the Psychology of Pictorial Representation* (1960).

HANS JAEGER is Professor of German at Indiana University, author of *Clemens Brentanos Frühlyrik* (1926) and of articles on Goethe, George, Rilke, and others. For 1960–1961 Professor Jaeger received a Guggenheim grant to pursue his study of Heidegger in Germany.

LOUIS KRONENBERGER, dramatic critic for *Time* magazine since 1938, was born in Cincinnati, Ohio, in 1904. He has been special lecturer at Brandeis University, Harvard University, and the College of the City of New York. His numerous books, of fiction as well as of literary criticism and history, include *The Grand Manner* (1929), *Kings and Desperate Men* (1942), *The Thread of Laughter* (1952), and *Marlborough's Duchess* (1958). Mr. Kronenberger has also edited a number of anthologies.

JACQUES MARITAIN, born in Paris in 1882, was educated there, in Heidelberg, and in Rome. He converted to Catholicism in 1906. Professor Maritain has taught at the Institute Catholique de Paris and has lectured at Louvain, Geneva, Oxford, Chicago, and elsewhere. For 1945–1948 he was French Ambassador to the Holy See; and for 1948–1953, a professor at Princeton University. His long list of books includes *Existence and the Existent* (1948), *Man and the State* (1950), *Creative Intuition in Art and Poetry* (1953). Now professor emeritus, he lives in Princeton, New Jersey.

LEONARD B. MEYER, born in 1918, was educated at Columbia University, where he majored in philosophy (B.A.) and in music (M.A.); he took his Ph.D. at the University of Chicago in the history of culture. He studied composition with Stefan Wolpe, Otto Luening, and Aaron Copland. Since 1946 he has taught at the University of Chicago. During 1960 and 1961 he was a fellow at the Center for Advanced Studies, Wesleyan University. Professor Meyer is the author of *Emotion and Meaning in Music* (1957) and, with Grosvenor W. Cooper, of *The Rhythmic Structure of Music* (1960).

DOUGLAS N. MORGAN, who is now professor of philosophy at the University of Texas, previously taught at Northwestern University. His articles on aesthetics have appeared in various scholarly journals.

JOSE ORTEGA y GASSET, born in Madrid in 1883, died there in 1955. He studied philosophy in his native city and at several German universities. Returning to Madrid in 1910 he became a leading professor of philosophy and an eminent journalist. Having supported the Republic, he left Spain in 1936, residing subsequently in France, and then in Argentina until his return to Europe in 1943. In 1949 he went back to Spain. Among his world-renowned books are *The Revolt of the Masses* (1932) and *The Dehumanization of Art* (1944).

HERBERT READ, born in Yorkshire in 1893, was educated at the University of Leeds. He was Assistant Keeper of the Victoria and Albert Museum, 1922–1931, and lectured on art at such universities as Edinburgh, Liverpool, London, and Harvard. In 1953 he was knighted by Queen Elizabeth II. He is President of the Society for Education in Art, and of the Institute of Contemporary Arts. Sir Herbert is a director of Routledge and Kegan Paul, Ltd., publishers. His long list of books includes the distinguished *Art and Industry* (1934), *Education Through Art* (1943), and *Icon and Idea* (1955).

MEYER SCHAPIRO, born in Lithuania in 1904, was brought to the United States in 1907. He has taught in the Department of Fine Arts and Archaeology at Columbia University since 1928, and has been a full professor since 1952. In both 1939 and 1942 he received Guggenheim fellowships, and in both 1947 and 1957 he was Special Lecturer at the Warburg Institute, London University. He is a Fellow of the American Academy of Arts and Sciences. Highly esteemed as a cultural historian, Professor Schapiro has written extensively on medieval and modern art, and his articles have appeared in learned and popular journals throughout the past thirty-five years. His studies include *Vincent Van Gogh* (1950) and *Paul Cézanne* (1952).

NIKOLAI SHAMOTA, born in 1916 in Poltava, Russia, is a graduate of the Academy of Social Sciences, having specialized in philology. He is the author of a book on aesthetics, *On Artistry* (1954). His critical articles often appear in *Literaturnaya Gazeta* and other Soviet periodicals.

LIONEL TRILLING was born in New York City in 1905. He received his A.B., A.M., and Ph.D. degrees from Columbia University, where he is now professor of English. He has written two critical studies, *Matthew Arnold* (1939) and *E. M. Forster* (1943), and a novel, *The Middle of the Journey* (1947), and he is the author of two widely reprinted stories, "The Other Margaret" and "Of This Time, Of That Place," the editor of *The Portable Matthew Arnold* (1949) and a selection of the *Letters of John Keats* (1950). His two major works of criticism are *The Liberal Imagination*, published in 1950, and *The Opposing Self*, published in 1958.

LANCELOT LAW WHYTE, born in Edinburgh, Scotland, in 1896, studied mathematics and physics at Cambridge University and was subsequently a scholar of Trinity College and a Cambridge research fellow. In 1923 he went into industry. He helped, in 1935, to finance the initial development of jet propulsion, later creating Power Jets, Ltd., and becoming its chairman and managing director. From 1941 to 1945 he was Director of Statistical Inquiries with the Ministry of Supply in London. Since then he has been working privately—doing theoretical research, writing, broadcasting, and lecturing. His major works include *The Next Development in Man* (1944) and *Accent on Form* (1954); he edited *Aspects of Form* (1951). His most recent book is *The Unconscious Before Freud* (1960).

BIBLIOGRAPHY

Constituting a highly selective list of suggested further readings considered to be among the most important current books and articles in the field; by no means "exhaustive"; and with minimal duplication of the innumerable references made through the text of this volume.

Alexander, Sir Samuel, *Artistic Creation and Cosmic Creation* (London: Humphrey Milford, 1927), *Art and Instinct* (Oxford: Clarendon Press, 1927), *Art and the Material* (Manchester: Manchester University Press, 1925), *Beauty and Other Forms of Value* (London: Macmillan, 1933).

Bowman, Herbert E., "Art and Reality in Russian 'Realist' Criticism," *JAAC* (*Journal of Aesthetics and Art Criticism*), Vol. XII, No. 3 (March 1954).

Bradley, A. C., *Oxford Lectures on Poetry* (London: Macmillan, 1909).

Bryson, Finkelstein, MacIver, and McKeon (eds.), *Symbols and Values: An Initial Study* (New York: Conference on Science, Philosophy, and Religion in Their Relation to the Democratic Way of Life, Symposium 13, 1954).

Carritt, Edgar Frederick, *An Introduction to Aesthetics* (London: Hutchinson's University Library, 1949).

Chandler, Albert Richard, *Beauty and Human Nature: Elements of Psychological Aesthetics* (New York: D. Appleton-Century, 1934).

Clark, Sir Kenneth, *The Nude* (New York: Anchor Books, 1959).

Clarke, Henry Leland, "The Basis of Musical Communication," *JAAC*, Vol. X, No. 3 (March 1952).

Collingwood, R. G., *The Principles of Art* (Oxford: Clarendon Press, 1938).

Cowley, Daniel J., "Aesthetic Judgment and Cultural Relativism," *JAAC*, Vol. XVII, No. 2 (December 1958).

Crane, R. S. (ed.), *Critics and Criticism: Old and New* (Chicago: The University of Chicago Press, 1952).

Croce, Benedetto, "Dewey's Aesthetics and Theory of Knowledge," *JAAC*, Vol. XI, No. 1 (September 1952).

Fiedler, Leslie, "Archetype and Signature," *The Sewanee Review*, Vol. LX (1952).

Freud, Sigmund, *On Creativity and the Unconscious* (Benjamin Nelson, ed.) (New York: Harper Torchbooks, 1958).

Gombrich, E. H., *Art and Illusion: A Study in the Psychology of Pictorial Representation* (New York: Pantheon Books,

1960); with Ernst Kris, *Caricature* (London: Penguin Books, 1940).

Goodman, Paul, *Art and Social Nature* (New York: Vinco Publishing Co., 1946).

Hauser, Arnold, *The Social History of Art*, 4 vols. (New York: Vintage Books, 1957), *The Philosophy of Art History* (New York: Alfred A. Knopf, 1959).

Hospers, J., *Meaning and Truth in the Arts* (Chapel Hill: The University of North Carolina Press, 1946).

Huxley, Aldous, *On Art and Artists* (Morris Philipson, ed.) (New York: Meridian Books, 1960).

Hyman, Stanley Edgar, *The Armed Vision* (New York: Vintage Books, 1955), ed., *The Critical Performance: American and British Literary Criticism of Our Century* (New York: Vintage Books, 1956).

Jung, C. G. *Psyche and Symbol* (Violet S. de Laszlo, ed.) (New York: Anchor Books, 1958).

Kaplan, A., "Referential Meaning in the Arts," *JAAC*, Vol. XII, No. 4 (December 1954).

Kepes, Gyorgy, *The Language of Vision* (Chicago: Paul Theobald, 1944).

Langer, Susanne K., *Feeling and Form: A Theory of Art* (New York: Charles Scribner's Sons, 1953), *Problems of Art* (New York: Charles Scribner's Sons, 1957).

Lewis, Wyndham, *The Demon of Progress in the Arts* (London: Methuen, 1954).

Lowenfeld, Viktor, "Psychological-Aesthetics: Implications of the Art of the Blind," *JAAC*, Vol. X, No. 1 (September 1951).

Malraux, André, *The Metamorphosis of the Gods* (New York: Doubleday & Company, 1960), *The Psychology of Art* (New York: Pantheon Books, 1949), *The Voices of Silence* (New York: Doubleday & Company, 1953).

Meyer, Leonard B., *Emotion and Meaning in Music* (Chicago: The University of Chicago Press, 1956).

Morgan, Douglas N., "The Critic Come to Judgment," *Northwestern University Tri-Quarterly*, Vol. I, No. 2 (Winter 1959).

Mundt, Ernest K., "Three Aspects of German Aesthetic Theory," *JAAC*, Vol. XVII, No. 3 (March 1959).

Munro, Thomas, *Toward Science in Aesthetics* (New York: The Liberal Arts Press, 1958).

Panofsky, Erwin, *Gothic Architecture and Scholasticism* (New York: Meridian Books, 1957), *Meaning in the Visual Arts* (New York: Anchor Books, 1955).

Pratt, Carroll Cornelius, *The Meaning of Music: A Study in Psychological Aesthetics* (New York: McGraw-Hill, 1931).

Rank, Otto, *The Myth of the Birth of the Hero, and Other*

Essays (Philip Freund, ed.) (New York: Vintage Books, 1959).

Read, Sir Herbert, *Art and Industry* (New York: Horizon Press, 1954), *Education through Art* (New York: 3rd edition, revised, Pantheon Books, 1958), *The Forms of Things Unknown: Essays Toward an Aesthetic Philosophy* (New York: Horizon Press, 1960), *Icon and Idea: The Function of Art in the Development of Human Consciousness* (Cambridge: Harvard University Press, 1955).

Rodman, Selden, *The Eye of Man: Form and Content in Western Painting* (New York: Devin-Adair, 1955).

Sartre, Jean-Paul, *What is Literature?* (New York: Philosophical Library, 1949).

Schapiro, Meyer, *Paul Cézanne* (New York: Harry N. Abrams, 1952), *Vincent Van Gogh* (New York: Harry N. Abrams, 1950), *The Sculptures of Souillac* (Cambridge: Harvard University Press, 1939), "The Nature of Abstract Art," *The Marxist Quarterly* (January–March 1937), "On the Aesthetic Attitude in Romanesque Art," in *Art and Thought: Essays Issued in Honor of Dr. Ananda K. Coomaraswamy* (London: 1947), "Two Slips of Leonardo and a Slip of Freud," *Psychoanalysis: Journal of Psychoanalytic Psychology*, Vol. IV, No. 2 (Winter 1955–1956), "Leonardo and Freud: An Art-Historical Study," *Journal of the History of Ideas*, Vol. XVII, No. 2 (April 1956).

Shahn, Ben, *The Shape of Content* (New York: Vintage Books, 1960).

Stolnitz, Jerome, "On Objective Relativism in Aesthetics," *Journal of Philosophy*, Vol. LVII, No. 8 (April 14, 1960).

Szathmary, A., "Symbolic and Aesthetic Expression in Painting," *JAAC*, Vol. XIII, No. 1 (September 1954).

Turner, Father Vincent, S.J., "The Desolation of Aesthetics," in *The Arts, Artists and Thinkers* (J. M. Todd, ed.) (London: Longmans, 1958).

Vivante, Leone, *English Poetry and Its Contribution to the Knowledge of a Creative Principle* (preface by T. S. Eliot) (London: Faber & Faber, 1950).

Vivas, Eliseo, "Contextualism Reconsidered," *JAAC*, Vol. XVIII, No. 2 (December 1959).

Wellek, René, and Warren, Austin, *The Theory of Literature* (New York: Harcourt, Brace, 1956).

Wittkower, Rudolf, *Architectural Principles in the Age of Humanism* (London: Warburg Institute, University of London, 1949).

Wölfflin, Heinrich, *Principles of Art History* (New York: Dover, 1950).

MERIDIAN BOOKS

published by The World Publishing Company
2231 West 110 Street, Clevelana 2, Ohio